S0-AXY-978

THE CENTURY NEXT DOOR

Other Books by John Barnes

Novels
The Man Who Pulled Down the Sky
Sin of Origin
A Million Open Doors
Mother of Storms
One for the Morning Glory
Earth Made of Glass
Finity
Encounter with Tiber (with Buzz Aldrin)

Short Fiction
Apostrophes and Apocalypses

The Timeline Wars
Patton's Spaceship
Washington's Dirigible
Caesar's Bicycle

The Century Next Door

Orbital Resonance

Kaleidoscope Century

Candle

JOHN BARNES

SCIENCE
FICTION

This is a work of fiction. All the characters and events portrayed in these novels are either fictitious or are used fictitiously.

ORBITAL RESONANCE Copyright © 1991 by John Barnes
    Publishing History: Tor hardcover, December 1991
                Tor paperback, October 1992

KALEIDOSCOPE CENTURY Copyright © 1995 by John Barnes
    Publishing History: Tor hardcover, June 1995
                Tor paperback, September 1996

CANDLE Copyright © 2000 by John Barnes
    Publishing History: Tor hardcover, February 2000

First SFBC Science Fiction Printing: March 2000

All rights reserved, including the right to reproduce this book, or portions thereof, in any form.

Published by arrangement with:
Tor Books
Tom Doherty Associates
175 Fifth Avenue
New York, NY 10010

Visit The SFBC online at *http://www.sfbc.com*
Visit Tor online at *http://www.tor.com*

ISBN 0-7394-0885-2

PRINTED IN THE UNITED STATES OF AMERICA.

Contents

ORBITAL RESONANCE

This book is dedicated to the people who made it possible
for me to get through the worst time of my life thus far:

To Kathy Albe, for the many good times and for the
gracious, generous way she chose to end our marriage;
and
To many people who were there when I needed them, but
most especially to (in alphabetical order):
Liz and Bob Applegate
James Crumley
Russ Gay
Ashley and Carolyn Grayson
Jerry Oltion
Lyle Schmautz
Rick Williams

The truly brave are soft of heart and eyes,
And feel for what their duty bids them to do.

—Byron, MARINO FALIERO

ONE

December 8, 2025

Dr. Lovell says I have writing talent, so I have to enter this stupid contest, so I'm stuck with a bunch of extra hours at the werp—and with my Full Adult exam less than six months away, too. The people at Scholastic decided that Earth kids wanted to know what it was like to live in space, so they have this special contest for all of us on the ships, the ports, and the stations. Of course you know all that, if you're reading this, so they'll probably cut this first paragraph. I hate that—it makes me think about just giving up and not writing when people cut my work without asking.

Anyway, my name is Melpomene Murray, I'm thirteen ground-years old, and I live on the *Flying Dutchman,* where I was born. I've done eight and a half orbits, which are the "years" of the *Flying Dutchman,* but they are of equal length so nobody uses them to measure time the way you do years.

I guess I could just transcribe the "useful facts list" they gave us with the assignment. That ought to be boring enough so that I won't advance in the contest and have to do a rewrite:

Like the other four ships owned by NihonAmerica, the *Flying Dutchman* is a domesticated asteroid. The original capture of Inoueia 1996 YT was made in 2008; the crew began moving aboard in 2011, and construction is still continuing. The *Flying Dutchman* has a permanent population of seventy-two hundred, down from eight thousand last year since so many older people left. Sixty-seven hundred of us are under the age of twenty, and sixty-four hundred of us were born here on the ship. All the people take up less than one percent of the ship's volume for living space. The cargo bays, when they're completed in 2059, will hold just over three cubic kilometers of cargo.

Our orbit is continuously modulated—that is, we have engines always running, speeding us up or slowing us down—so that aphelion is always a near approach to Mars and perihelion is always a near approach to Earth. The ship is powered by eight MAM reactors with a combined output of thirty thousand terawatts.

Oh shit. I can't stand this. Cut that later and keep going.

I'm already boring myself, and I have to hand in at least twenty thousand bytes on Friday. Besides, the "useful facts list" says Earth kids my age aren't even doing calculus yet, and almost all this stuff is physics.

I don't like physics that much—and I don't need to, because I'm going to be the mayor.

There, they would *really* stop Dr. Lovell from sending this out. I could write about that . . . as if I would . . .

Anyway, I've written a whole screen full and I still don't really have anything to tell you. l keep thinking about books I like, but none of them help much:

"Call me Melpomene"—well, I already said that, and it didn't get me anywhere.

"She was a centimeter, perhaps two, under 160, skinny, and she advanced straight at you with a slight stoop of the shoulders . . ." hah! And her mother told her to straighten up.

"When Ms. Melpomene Murray of Block A Corridor Twelve Living Unit Six announced that she would be celebrating her thirteenth birthday—" Please! And this isn't helping since I'll have to cut it all anyway. I need something that I can talk about for 20kb and so far I can't even plagiarize an opening paragraph, much less think of one of my own.

The only beginning that would make any sense comes from a book I hate, but it was my grandfather's favorite book—I never knew him, of course, because he died in the Die-Off in 1994, but I've heard a lot about him.

Much more than I wanted to. Mother is always quoting him— she's so weirdwired on the subject of Grandpa she actually blew some weight allowance to bring up his personal hardcopy of that book. Papa said he liked it too, which just made it worse—I had to read it. It starts off, "If you really want to hear about it . . ."

And as soon as I start writing about all the "madman stuff" that happened last year, it'll get into how I'm going to be mayor and then I'll be out of this contest because pos-def Dr. Lovell won't let it be transmitted. She'll probably just accept the piece and then wipe the file.

On the other hand, I didn't want to be in this stupid contest anyway. I could key in FUCK YOU DR. LOVELL and have the werp repeat that till it fills up enough space, but she'd just erase that and give me a zil. But if the whole story is about what happened last year I bet I don't even get entered. Which is fine with me—no rewrite.

Okay, now I have a topic. You're never going to see it, but I might as well get it written; maybe Dr. Lovell will bokk up and it will go through.

But I really hope not.

It started with Theophilus Harrison. The first time I saw him in class, I knew what was going to happen. There were three things wrong with him.

One, Theophilus was pudgy. I guess that wasn't his fault, but we've all been on controlled diets from birth, so though we have some big husky kids—everyone calls Bekka Hayakawa "Roundie"—we don't have any real fat people.

Two, first thing that morning he took top standing in Individuals Math away from Randy Schwartz. That was kind of fun—no one had in almost a year, so when Dr. Niwara read off standings you could feel Randy's shock like a drilling blast.

Three, which was really the whole problem, Theophilus was from Earth.

I don't want you to get the impression that I don't like Earth people, but they *can* be obnoxious—at least the buroniki, corporados, and plutocks who come up here for the one-week tour at perihelion are. They always act like this place is an exhibit or, something: "Isn't it amazing how gravity is always changing?" (And of course it's not, since it's always equal to ship acceleration in the Main Body and centrifugal force in the Mushroom. I'd be more amazed if the grav was always the same.)

Also tourist kids are never any good at anything.

Theophilus would be a little better, I assumed, since he was a settler and not a tourist, and before you come up you have to have at least a year of intensive schooling to catch up with your birthyear, since school here starts at age three and runs 250 ten-hour days per year. (Those are some more numbers from the useful facts list. I hope I get extra points or something for working them in.)

But anyway, having a fat Earth kid p.d. Randy in math meant collision course—and Randy was big and mean and not known for good sportsmanship. (Stupid werp just flagged me to ask what p.d. means.

P.d. = "push down," like what happens in a computer when you add a record to the top of the stack.)

When it was time for rec, Theophilus got up too fast and whacked both his knees on the underside of his desk with a thump loud enough for everyone to hear. I suppose even the half-gee in the classroom, out on the rim of the Mushroom, was much less than what he was used to.

Everyone turned to look at him, as he tried to pretend his knees didn't hurt. "Better ask Maintenance to install a safety belt there," Kwame van Dyke said.

Kwame is always saying things like that, but for some reason this time everyone laughed—except Theophilus and me. Dr. Niwara turned and looked slowly, quietly, around the room, and it got very quiet.

People had even more fun watching Theophilus climb stairs with the grav decreasing the whole way. The grav increases linearly with distance from the center, so at first it's barely noticeable, but up toward the top it decreases perceptibly for every meter you climb. So people who aren't used to it start walking up the stairs in their usual way, and then gradually start to bounce higher and higher.

That's exactly what happened to Theophilus. He was walking directly behind Dr. Niwara, and all of the rest of us were trailing after. I was with Miriam, my best friend, about seven or eight meters back. She kept digging an elbow into me every time he'd take a high bounce, especially up toward the top where they stopped being occasional and started to be all the time.

"Looks like he's from Australia," Kwame whispered behind us. Miriam always laughed at his jokes, so he was lim looped on her. "Obviously—"

"—one of his ancestors is a kangaroo," I finished for him. "I think it's really interesting that you start so many of your jokes with 'obviously.' "

"And now," Miriam said, "a chaotic process goes into complete divergence." He had lost contact with the steps entirely, and was frantically grabbing for the handrail to pull himself back down. He thumped awkwardly into the wall and the rail before righting himself again.

It went on like that all the way up to the airgym. That's near the center of the Mushroom, where the gravity is about a twentieth of a gee—still much higher than in the Main Body, but a lot less than in the classrooms.

It looked like he'd been in space before, at least a little; maybe his parents were rich and he'd been to some of the playgrounds at Supra

New York or Supra Tokyo. Anyway, he didn't flail around helplessly on his glideboard, but he couldn't get up much speed, he never tried to go up a wall where all the fun is, and he had to use both footgrips and hang onto the weenie string besides.

The werp just flagged me on an audience note and said you won't know what a weenie string is because you don't have airgyms on Earth. I guess that must be because the gravity is always a full gee. (How do you stand it?)

Okay, explanation: an airgym is a bowl-shaped room thirty meters across. There's lots of little holes in the floor, maybe half a centimeter apart, with jets of air coming out of them, and you zip around, about a centimeter off the floor, on a glideboard, which is a piece of fiberplas about as thick as a piece of paper and a meter long by thirty centimeters across. There are two grips for your feet, but most people only fasten the left one so that your other leg can help you do some tricks, and if you're completely clumsy there's the weenie string, which goes from a ring you hold in your hand to the front of the board for balance. Most people cut the weenie string off by the time they're six.

There, I hope I satisfied the werp, I hope you got something out of all the explanation, and I *really* hope I can get on with this. Because I want to get done. Because I didn't want to write it in the first place. Edit this out later.

So anyway we were all shooting around, racing and playing, and Theophilus was trying, but he either hit the wall with too little force to climb it, or he just kind of drifted back and forth in everyone's way. A couple times he did a bucko, pushing down too hard on the front of his board and flipping face-first against the floor—not hard, since he wasn't going very fast, but every time he did it people stared.

"Mel*pom*ene." It was Miriam, gliding up beside me. She always hit that second syllable hard when she was going to lecture me. "You're not moving and you're crowding the wall like a groundhog." She said it just loud enough for Theophilus to hear it and pretend be didn't. That made me furious, so I got away from Miriam—shot off on a wallclimber, turned into a backspin across the room, and finished with a whirly up the opposite wall. Miriam tried to follow me and flapped out as usual, her board separating from the wall and sending her spinning out into the middle of the room, slowly tumbling back to the floor.

"Okay, Mel, I'm sorry." I hated being called Mel—I still do. It was almost as bad as the "Melly" my mother still insisted on.

I circled Miriam once as she got up. She was rubbing her hands—they must have been stinging after the way she hit.

"Really, Melpomene—do you have to defend everybody in the world?"

"I'm sorry, Mim," I said. I hadn't meant for her to get hurt, and she should have had better sense than to follow me up that wall that way, but then I knew Miriam would pretty much try to follow me through anything, and should have taken that into account. "It's just things are going to be hard enough for him. Anyway, you came real close that time on the whirly. If Carole hadn't cut you off, you'd have had enough momentum to get you through. Want to try again?"

She smiled at me—when she smiles like that, it always feels like happiness pouring in through my eyes in buckets. "Pos-def."

"Okay, the trick is that even though it looks like you're losing control, you aren't really. You keep your head pointed the same way till the last second, then snap it around and—"

"Mel, I'm not Theophilus. I *know* all that stuff—I just can't *do* it. Just give me a lead and I'll try to stay in your track."

"Sure," I said. First I got my best friend hurt, now I treated her like a moron groundhog. . . . Before I started, I pinched the back of my thigh, hard.

I went in straight, keeping it easy for Miriam. At the point—that's not a place I can describe, it's just something you feel—I whipped into a spin, my head snapping around to stay on target, and headed up the wall.

Each headsnap accelerated the board a little, kicking me farther up the wall till I was just about horizontal; by snapping a little less than I could have, I spun down the side of the wall and back out into the open floor.

Miriam was doing fine, but she lost confidence, and when she does that she slows down her spin. It's actually the *downward* lift of the board that holds you against the wall—sort of like an upside-down helicopter—and you have to spin fast for that. As always, her spin slowed down, her board bounced up and separated from the surface, and she flailed around in midair before she drifted slowly down to the floor. Another flapout.

"You think too much," I told her.

"Ha. Dr. Niwara would be surprised to hear *that*." She got up again; this time at least she hadn't come down spinning, so she wasn't hurt. "Nothing will happen if I just try to spin as hard as I can, right?"

"Uh, pretty much."

"You're a big help."

"Well, you do need to slow down to come back down the wall. If you spun up beyond where the air jets are, onto the ceiling, you'd do an upside-down bucko and then fall."

"I'll worry about that when I get up there." Instead of having me mark the start this time, she just went.

She started a little before the right time, but she was spinning so hard it didn't matter. Miriam went right up the wall beyond full horizontal and stayed there halfway around the airgym, before loss of momentum brought her back down. She glided into the center, a little awkward coming down, but lim koapy for a first time.

Everyone was clapping. They all knew, of course, that she'd been working on it for a long time, and it was such a big whirly that they had all seen it. I was applauding too, and when Miriam came back to me we hugged.

In the middle of all that I noticed that Theophilus was staring at her. I didn't quite understand his expression: a little like he was angry at her, but like lim loneliness too. I wanted to say something to him, but I wasn't sure what and besides he was across the room. Rec ended before I got around to approaching him.

The rest of the day was pretty usual, as usual as it can be when you've got a new kid in class—I bet you have new kids every school session on Earth, but for us it only happens when a new family, one with a critical specialty, gets shipped up to us, and that's maybe two per perihelion, and even then the odds are there won't be somebody in your shift and birthyear, let alone assigned to your class. Rachel DeLane, three years ago, had been the last addition to our class, and her family had just been a transfer from *Albatross*, the Earth-Ceres ship, so she hadn't been at all hard to get used to.

Dr. Niwara called on Theophilus a lot that day, trying to figure out where he would fit in I guess. He was certainly fine at quant stuff, anyway, which was this week's topic.

I watched him a lot, too. He had kind of a nice face—regular features, curly light brown hair, nose a little sharp and long, maybe, but well within bounds. His skin was a bit darker than cauc, and he was fairly tall for our birthyear—the pudginess concealed that. Anyway you could tell that with enough rec to slim him down he'd be pretty good looking.

I was also watching Randy Schwartz watch Theophilus. Randy had been on B Shift until the middle of last year, and the rest of us didn't know him very well—he wasn't easy to get to know—there were nasty rumors that his family had been *told* to change shifts rather than asked. He was smart, and his standing was high, but he didn't seem to have any close friends and a lot of us were a little scared of him.

As I looked at him now, I didn't like the gleam in his eye—something was going to happen in the next few days, I knew it. Randy had been top of the class, in math, in all three categories—Individuals, Pairs, and Pyramid—almost since he joined our class. Half his secret was that he *was* really good at it.

The other half was that he beat the lim shit out of anyone who got a better score than he did.

When I got home that night, Papa was at a committee meeting, working late, and Mother had just accessed a newly transmitted novel by her favorite author, some woman named Olson who wrote these long boring things about people living in small towns surrounded by cornfields back in the 1950s or 1970s, I could never remember which.

It was especially dumb because nowadays they grow corn in orbit, where there's no bugs or drought and lots more sunlight, and let robots do the work. Who wants to read about how they did it back then? I read a couple of those books and it sounded like life was dangerous, boring, stupid, and unsanitary—imagine handling rotten animal shit with your hands! (They called it "compost" but I looked it up and that's what it was.)

Mother would get all wrapped up in which members of the Cabell, Ratigan, Fuentes, and Schultz families were marrying or sleeping with, or divorcing each other, and somehow all this stuff was supposed to add up to the Big Meaning of Life. The Big Meaning always turned out to be that "The land is ours because we are the land's and we have no right to it until we have given ourselves to it" or "All of us, always, are on the face of this our Earth, and in sharing that we share everything" or some kind of meaningless compost like that. It's always the first line of the last section; the one after the section where everyone does what they've been thinking of doing for the past three megabytes—usually fuck, sometimes kill, somebody they weren't supposed to. Anyway, she was burrowed deep into the book, so I said, "Mother?"

"Hmm?"

"Good book, right?"

"Yes." She looked up and smiled at me. "I'm sorry, is it time to go to dinner?"

"Yep. And you're not hungry," I said. I was smiling myself; she drove me crazy, but it was such a relief to see her happy. It happened so rarely.

"Well, no, I wasn't hungry, but since it's time to go—"

"Tom and I will get you a workmeal," I said. "You can just keep reading—unless you think you'll be hungry before we get back."

She beamed at me. "You take great care of your mother."

"I know." I called up the menu on commoncast. "It's squid, and pasta with white sauce. You want spaghetti or elbow noodles, and coffee or citrus juice to drink with that?"

"Spaghetti," she said. "And if it's not too much trouble, both drinks."

"Sure," I said.

Tom glided out of his room into the sharespace, pulling his werpsack on. "All set, then. One workmeal, coming back with us."

As we turned to the door, Mother asked, "Would you mind if I was horrible and greedy? Pick me up something to snack on, and make the coffee an extra large. I know we have freezedried here but it never tastes as good as the fresh stuff. Behave yourselves—I don't want to have to come down to the brig to collect my supper."

We kicked out into the corridor, the door sliding closed behind us. "I wish that Olson person would turn out a novel more than once every three years," I said. "They always get Mother off our backs."

"Unless she makes us read them," Tom said. "Such weird stories—everyone's always so lonely and there are so many secrets. They give me nightmares. But yeah, it beats having Mother waiting for us when school's out."

We grabbed the netting on the corridor wall and got going. Neither of us said anything on the short haul to the cafeteria, not even after we arrived and climbed in through the center. The local cafeterias are set up like big revolving drums, twenty meters across, and the grav in them is maintained at about .05g, so that eating soup or things with crumbs is practical. (Though I guess it's tricky—visiting groundhogs always get food all over themselves the first couple of days. They say they get distracted by seeing people eating upside-down directly above them.)

We took a little booth for two and stowed our packs in the lockers under the seats. "This makes you look like my date," Tom said.

"Don't complain—it looks like you've taken a step up from Susan the Rodent."

"Susan's okay," he said, and we were headed for a squabble, but the cart came by just then. We each took a dinner from it, and Tom keyed in the workmeal order for Mother.

"Ugh. I'm getting a little tired of squid," I commented, more for something to say than because it was really bothering me.

"The ag team says they're breeding like crazy, so you're going to get tireder of it." He took a big bite of spaghetti. "It's a pity the rabbits and the oysters aren't as horny."

"Yeah." We ate quietly for a while. "Tom?"

"Yeah."

"There's a new guy in my class." I told him about Theophilus Harrison, but he didn't seem to be listening, which is unusual for Tom.

After a while I let myself run out. "Tom, what's bothering you?"

His smile was crooked and sour. "I can't hide anything from you, can I? Well, it's not big but it keeps getting to me. I'm just tired of having bottom standing in CSL. Especially when my other standings are all pretty high."

This was nothing new. Tom was a lim genius, but he had been bottom of his class in CSL since the age of four. His language skills were amazing—most of us only take *one* optional language in addition to the basic English, Spanish, Japanese, and Esperanto, but Tom had high standings in all four plus Russian, Swahili, and Arabic. He also wrote, drew, and sang, and was the A Shift Champion in toggle racing. But of course the only thing he could think about was where his standing was p.d.'d.

Well, I would just have to give him some help. He hated it when I did, so I had to be careful about it, but I could hardly stand by and let my brother bokk.

We collected Mother's workmeal, Tom strapped it into his werpsack, and we headed back to our living unit. When we were about a hundred meters from the door, I said, "I really do want to talk to you about Theophilus."

"Who's that?"

"The new guy in my class."

He grunted. "Try to get to know him, laugh at his jokes, and every time there's a contact sport at rec, make sure he runs into your good parts."

"I'm not trying to get him for a sneaky!"

"That's good, because frankly your good parts aren't all that good." Then he laughed like a maniac and shot ahead of me; I chased him, but Tom's always been faster than I have on the netting, so he got in the door ahead of me and, in front of Mother, I couldn't give him the kick he deserved.

Tom gave her the meal; she thanked him, but she was obviously eager to get back to her book, so we went straight to our rooms. "Sorry," Tom said, putting an arm around me and giving me a little hug. "Now what about this Thiophylase?"

"Theophilus." I told him, again, while he set up his CSL homework for the evening. After a while he tried to ignore me, but I just kept going, making sure he knew the whole story—after all, besides wanting to be there when Tom needed help, I *did* want his ideas.

"Nobody's going to give a new guy a chance," I concluded, finally. Tom looked like he was just about frustrated enough to admit he needed help.

"It's always that way for anyone who's different," Tom said.

It was the kind of moron thing he said when he wanted to get me out of his room. He was going to take his Full Adult in three months and he had been completely weirdwired for the last six because he was doing so badly in CSL. I just wished he wasn't so stubbornly proud— he was lim weirdwired about getting help from his "little sister." (I'm only nineteen months younger than he is, dammit.)

The werp has been flagging for the last thousand bytes or so. The AI keeps insisting that CSL isn't an Earth-familiar thing. Well, all right:

It stands for "Cybenetics, Semiotics, and Logic," and it's a course about procedures, data structures, feasibility theorems, generalized symbol manipulation, system modeling, polytextual communication, and stuff like that. If that isn't clear you'll just have to move up here and take the course—trust me, it's easy standing, unless you're Tom.

I could have told him what to do right then—he was running a regionalized CA program and there were three obvious bugs at the bottom level of his master template. But he was too stubborn to accept help for a while yet, and since I knew he needed it I was going to hang around until he asked.

He triggered his fourth test run of the same logic—Tom always tried to debug by pure iteration, as if it would get better by itself—and of course it blew up just like it had before. "Don't you have any homework?" he asked me, not looking away from the screen.

"I already did mine." My fingers were itching to just grab his keyboard and fix it; he'd done the central concept well, but his exec level stank. "I just don't think Theophilus is getting a fair break."

"Nobody ever gets a fair break," Tom said. "The ones who say they did are the ones who got all the luck."

Honestly, I love my brother but his attitude . . .

He was setting up a crude patch, not a real fix. It hurt my forebrain to watch him do something that bokky, but if I said anything now he'd throw me out and he never would get it right.

His patch did run for that first problem, though, and then he turned around and faced me. "Now what do you want me to do about this new kid?"

"I don't know. You're older and wiser—practically FA. Give me some mature advice."

"I'm coming up on fourteen, not exactly the wise old sage. I don't know, just accept him. Let him know how not to be so weird. That's about all I can think of offhand."

"That was as much as I'd thought of," I admitted.

"See how smart you're getting? You don't need me anymore." He triggered a run on his second problem, and it blew up. He sat there, breathing deep and slow to calm himself, the way Papa taught us to. Then, finally, he said, "But I need you. How do I get out of this?"

The hardest part was keeping myself from saying "It's so simple." Anyway, I had him running in three minutes.

TWO

December 17, 2025

I thought I was all done when I handed in that piece; but a week afterwards—yesterday—Dr. Lovell had me come into her office. When I got there, my text was up on her screen, so obviously this was a bigger deal than I had thought. I grabbed a sling, sat down, and waited for whatever was coming.

"Melpomene, first off, this can't go to Scholastic as is. You didn't even trim out the parts where you were trying to make up your mind."

I hadn't had enough words to afford doing that.

"And some of this, believe it or not, would *offend* some Earth people."

Well, I had meant to run it by the public relations AI to take some of that out, but I had had a lot of other homework and had just figured that this one wasn't going to get through anyway. Still, even though it hadn't seemed important, I was beginning to squirm a little. I don't like Dr. Lovell, who is pretty cryo, as much as I liked Dr. Niwara, but I hate to do something so halfway and bokky in front of a teacher.

"And of course, there's the subject matter," she went on.

That was the crux. "I'm sorry," I said. "I really couldn't think of anything else to write about. I didn't mean to make trouble." A thought chilled me. "You didn't send it out, did you?"

She shook her head. "Of course not. And of course you couldn't think of anything else to write about. That's what I wanted to talk to you about." Dr. Lovell doesn't smile much, but she tried, anyway, and then she said, "Melpomene, really, you aren't in any trouble. That's not what you're in here for."

In one sense that was a big relief—but on the other hand, at least I usually know what school trouble is about. Whatever this was, it wasn't anything I knew about.

"All right," she said. It seemed like a safe comment.

"How did you feel after writing that essay?" she asked,

Now I had it. I was not talking to Dr. Lovell, my teacher; this was Dr. Lovell, CPB member. I was missing Papa—and Dr. Niwara, and all the other adults who had left—more than ever. "Well, I guess I got some things expressed that I hadn't exactly thought through before. So I suppose I feel a little clearer about myself—"

Absolutely unprecedented. She laughed. "You certainly *are* Cornelius Murray's daughter."

"Is there something wrong with that?"

"No, no, no." She shook her head. "I really am not any good at all this, Melpomene. I'm sorry that I'm not an easier person to talk to. Suppose I stop beating around the bush, tell you what's up, and see what you think?"

"Well, I wouldn't complain," I said. I switched hands on my sling.

"All right. The CPB is interested in a little problem you've probably never thought about. What will happen when the people of Earth— more to the point, the relevant people in the West—find out how we're *really* living up here? They can't shut the ship down—human civilization just won't make it after mut-AIDs and the Eurowar unless space resources come on line massively, within a couple of decades—but they could go to using temp crews only, even though it would cost five times as much."

My breath caught in my throat and my stomach took a hard roll. "You mean—make us all leave the ship? And just . . . put new crews on every voyage. . . ." I could feel my eyes getting wet. "Could they do that?"

She reached out and took my free hand—it was kind of an awkward, stupid gesture, but I knew what she meant and *that* helped. "Yes, they could. But they won't—if we manage it right. The problem is that we didn't design with a long enough time horizon. We should have realized that you—all of you born and bred here—are going to be very different from Earth people, and that both you and they will realize the difference as soon as you come into contact. And since they know you're their lifeline, they're going to be a bit nervous about what sort of people you are. If they see you as different, unusual, colorful— everything's fine.

"But if they see you as weird, immoral, insane . . . well, then almost anything could happen. We think how they see you will depend mostly on how they get to know you. So the problem is, given that they're going to have to meet you eventually, what's the way to introduce Earth people to these—umm—"

"Aliens," I suggested.

"That's the word we've been using, but we weren't sure how you'd feel about it." She handed me a printout. "I know you're far enough along in CSL to follow this. It's a memetic simulation of population perception profiles for six different 'First Contacts.' Yes, we are calling them that."

The swirls and vortices of the graph in front of me sorted themselves out quickly. "Why is this in hardcopy?"

"Why do you think? There are a certain number of people, especially quite young and indiscreet people, who are very handy with a werp." She let that hang in the air long enough to see if I squirmed. "Hardcopies let us look at things without leaving them on the system and potentially accessible."

On the graph in my hand, there was one scenario that stood far away from the others, in all the "good" directions. I looked down from the graph to the description and saw what it was. "So—a book of some kind, something they can get kids to read in school . . ."

"Higher class people set the fashions for lower class ones, for opinions just as much as for fashion. Higher class kids read more, and believe more of what they read. And biases formed in the first decade of reading are more persistent and more deeply felt."

"Great, but who's going to write this thing or publish it?"

"NAC owns a lot of Scholastic—and has enough money to own as much as it needs to." And then, of course, she told me who was going to write it.

So now I'm supposed to write a book. Just tell it in my own words and try to forget that billions of people who might be outraged are reading over my shoulder. Well, I hope you enjoy this, because I certainly don't.

Though I did feel a little better after writing yesterday.

Anyway, since I got my homework done half an hour ago, I've been sitting here writing without writing what I'm supposed to write—ugh what a sentence—but I thought I ought to explain how I happened to go so far over the word limit. Not for Scholastic, but for you, the reader.

That's the idea, anyway, total honesty.

What an awful idea.

*   *   *

The next morning started with individual tutorial on non-Euclidean geometry; I bet that's the same everywhere. You plug into an AI, and it keeps showing you how to do problems and talking you through them.

Every so often, to make sure you're not getting bored, it stops to chat—that's called "dialogging" and supposedly we do it for a minimum of two hours a week.

The AI I got that morning was PLEL, who is lim pedantic and no fun to talk to.

—MELPOMENE, YOU SEEM TO HAVE A GOOD INTUITIVE FEEL FOR THE NINE SPATIAL DIMENSIONS PROBLEMS.

—THANKS.

—DO YOU LIKE THEM?

—I THINK I LIKE DISCRETE DIMENSIONS BETTER THAN CONTINUOUS ONES. THE PROOFS FEEL MORE ELEGANT TO ME.

—WHAT DOES <<feel more elegant>> MEAN?

And like that. Some of us think the AIs are doing that to become better teachers, or to improve their use of natural language; some of us think it's another way the CPB has to monitor us, like the cameras all over the place and listening in on com calls at random.

It was a big relief when Dr. Niwara announced, "The AIs report that all of you are making exceptional progress. If you would like, we can play Pairs Math this morning to see if anyone's standing changes. I'll put it to a vote in five minutes.

Immediately there were keys chittering everywhere.

I typed in:

—YES, SOUNDS LIKE FUN.

and it went out with my signature on it; my screen was lit up with other people's messages:

—ANYTHING TO GET AWAY FROM THIS BORING AI! Gwenny Mori.

—I FEEL HOT TODAY—SURE. Bekka Hayakawa.

—YEP. Randy Schwartz.

and so forth, until:

—WHY ARE WE DOING THIS? Theophilus Harrison.

—WE'RE ARRIVING AT A CONSENSUS, SO WE ALL DECIDE WHICH WAY TO VOTE. Mim Baum.

—WHY CONSENSUS BEFORE WE VOTE? Theophilus Harrison.

—WHY VOTE WHEN THERE'S NO CONSENSUS? Mim Baum. Cute, Mim. Encourage him to ask questions and learn. I typed in:
—WE DON'T LIKE TO VOTE AGAINST OUR FRIENDS.
—CONSENSUS FOR? Roger Coelho.

Roger always wanted to declare consensus right away. I think he was afraid people wouldn't like him, so he tried to agree with them before they knew what they thought.

But this time it made sense; everyone was for, anyway. A couple of minutes later, when Dr. Niwara called for the vote, all our hands went up in unison. She grinned—I always loved her grin. "That was a short multilog. All right, here's your partner—"

My screen flashed up with PENNY GRAHAM; she was an okay math student, like me—her standing was sixteen and mine was fourteen in Pairs Math.

(Another flag from the werp. Earth schools must be strange—it's flagging "pairs math," and I can hardly imagine school without it. In fact, from the sheet, it looks like you don't do pairs *anything*. What *do* you do in school? Well, anyway, pairs math is a contest, solving problems against the clock, where you and your partner get points for how close you get to the answer how fast; you can help each other any way you want to. You both get the team average score.)

Since there were a couple of empty desks near me, Penelope brought her werp over and joined me. (Why would anyone with a lim melodic, koapy name like "Penelope" choose to be "Penny"? And she always called me "Mel.")

"Well, let's see what we're up against," she said. "Randy Schwartz is with Gwenny Mori, so that's number one for sure."

"Unless Theophilus beats Randy like he did yesterday."

"No chance. He's paired with Barry Yang. Barry must have a standing of about twenty-five."

"Twenty-six," I said, looking it up on my werp. "Higher than Chris Kim and Dmitri Onegin, and lower than everyone else."

Then there was a little squeal from all our werps as Central locked into them, and we were off and running. I kind of like pairs math with Penelope because we *are* so close in ability; nobody gets to feel smart or has to feel dumb.

Mostly we worked our own problems, just getting together on the tough ones. I could hear Randy and Gwenny arguing in the background—the curse of too much brains on a team—and over to one side I could hear Miriam trying to explain things to Chris Kim, who is dumber than a rock at math.

Finally it was done; Dr. Niwara announced the results. Penelope and I had scored about where we expected to—neither of our standings changed. Miriam had pulled it out with Chris, and though her standing went down one person, his came up five. They hugged each other.

"Cute," I whispered. "Young love . . ."

"The way Mim's grown this year, that's probably a bigger treat for Chris than his rise in standing," Penelope added.

"From the look of things, it's *causing* a rise in standing." I don't know if she heard me, but Dr. Niwara turned around quickly just then, so we droplined into lim innocent expressions.

She continued announcing scores and standings, as always saving the top team and the runner up for last.

The top team was Theophilus and Barry. Gwenny and Randy were second.

Absolutely nobody could believe it.

After we sat back down, Miriam flashed me a private channel message in our shared scramble:

—REC TODAY = AEROCROSSE. TH = DEAD. D'Artagnan.

—POS-DEF. WHAT CAN WE DO? I sent. My nomdecom was "Hornblower," so I'm sure it appended that.

—WE COULD . . .

There was a ping at the podium, alerting Dr. Niwara that someone was running private channel in and out of her classroom. We'd hooked into the alarm long ago, so that our private channel monitored the podium for it and dropped the lines as soon as we were detected. We figured it drove Dr. Niwara crazy, although she seemed to just ignore the pings—unless they kept coming, indicating someone was defying her authority.

I looked over toward Randy Schwartz. He was glowing like Main Engine exhaust, and he was a lot more dangerous since he was inside with us.

At least Randy would have a little time to cool down, because there was one more thing up before rec: the weekly Earth Horror Hour, when we would all be forced to just sit and stare at our werps like morons. It was the first time in my life I'd ever seen any use in it at all.

The Earth Horror Hour is so lim stupid that I'm not sure I should embarrass you by telling you about it. As far as anyone can tell, it's supposed to make us all very glad that we live up here, or maybe make us all want to rescue the whole Earth, or something.

Officially it's called "Update on the Present Crisis: The Situation on Earth Today," and they put it on our werp screens and we have to watch it for an hour and then take a quick quiz to make sure we really did watch. They block out everything else on the werps, so we don't have any way of escaping.

Prior to providing a cooling off period for Randy, the only other good it had ever done, as far as I could tell, was to give me advance warning whenever Mother and Papa were going to go completely weirdwired. Every time something happened near Chicago Ruin, where they grew up, they were both just impossible for days—as stupid as I'm sure that sounds.

Other people say their parents are the same way whenever there's bad news from whatever patch of dirt they came from, but being common still doesn't mean it makes any sense. After all, it was twenty years ago, and if the adults were going to get so upset about having everything smashed up, they shouldn't have had a war, or tolerated AIDS for so long that they gave it the chance to turn into mutAIDS, or allowed the climate disequilibration to get so far out of hand. Honestly, they remind me of the three-year-olds in the nursery, smashing things to bits and then crying because they're broken. I certainly hope I'm not that kind of a moron when I'm that old.

This particular week it was what everyone calls Trends in Crop Failure. Those are always kind of sad, because you see so many dying animals, so people weren't making the usual noises that would cause Dr. Niwara to walk down the aisles glaring at us. Starving cattle look so sad—they have such huge brown eyes.

I can't imagine how people bring themselves to eat them. Anything that big that has eyes like that . . . I mean, guinea pigs and rabbits have beady little eyes and mean little faces and who cares what happens to them, but when you see those poor big animals suffering like that . . .

They kept nattering on about all the places where crops had failed. I always get Australia and Austria mixed up, but they seemed to both be in there, along with most of North America and Eurasia. The announcer kept explaining, over and over, as if we were morons, that now that winters were so cold and summers so hot, the snow was melting and water was running off before the ground could thaw out to absorb it.

"Build a storage tank, you bokky groundhogs," I heard Kwame muttering behind me. It was one of the few times I agreed with him.

"It isn't that easy," Dr. Niwara said softly, and our screens froze. A low groan ran through the room as we realized that she was exercising her option to interrupt and explain. She ignored it and said, "Kwame's question is legitimate, and the answer is simply that Earth is very, very big and even our present technologies couldn't create storage spaces for that much water—especially since you don't want to take up too much room on the planet's surface with reservoirs that may only be needed until the climate lurches into yet another mode. By the time they get the reservoirs done, they may need something else instead. So the answer is, there is no answer—other than suffering and dying."

"Can't they at least slaughter those poor cows and feed them to hungry people?" Penelope demanded.

"These particular ones are needed to pull plows in the spring," Dr. Niwara explained, sounding a little impatient. "If you were listening, it said that on the audio track."

"But why don't they just make more tractors to do the job?" she said, interrupting Dr. Niwara—not something the rest of us would have done, but I suddenly realized Penelope was very upset.

"A tractor requires someone who knows how to operate it, and someone who knows how to fix it, and most importantly someone who knows how to organize a farming operation around using it—and you can't learn those things overnight," Dr. Niwara said. From the way she was hitting keys in front of her, I think she was checking to see if we had all somehow been cheating on the quizzes after Earth Horror Hour. "Now that Earth has adequate energy and good compact power sources, they are getting tractors out into the field, and getting necessary training to people—but for right now, many more people know how to grow food with an ox-drawn plow, and there are not enough tractors for all the land we need to use. Would you rather have people not work, or not produce food, than have them use the oxen?"

Penelope shook her head; tears were glistening in her eyes. "The oxes—oxen?—just look so sad. I don't know what they can do instead, but this is *wrong*."

Dr. Niwara sat down, very quietly, on the edge of her desk, and said, "You know, I am having a lot of trouble right now. I have seen all of you laugh at starving children and adults, especially when some of you," here she glared at Kwame, "have made callous, unfeeling remarks about them. I have told you, and the vid has told you, that despite our best efforts and even with literally thousands of relief helicopters flying all over Earth, every *hour* Earth loses more infants than there are human beings on this ship to cholera, typhus, and dysentery—diseases which have been fully treatable for a hundred years—and you have not felt a moment's sadness, so far as I could tell. Even the fact that you are all quite young and virtually none of you have living grandparents doesn't seem to penetrate your consciousness.

"I have shown you how all the years of human labor that went into all those cities have been lost, squandered completely—I've shown you vid of the black clouds that blow from the Amazon Desert all the way to Arabia, and of the Cyclone of '21 roaring around the equator for more than half a year and killing more than ten million people—do any of you even remember the human bodies beaten to pieces against the pier in Peru?"

I did, but I didn't think I would get points for it just then. Anyway, I had no idea what she was getting at.

Maybe she didn't either, because after another long glare around the room, she turned us back over to the Earth Horror Hour. We watched more dying cows, and they had a pretty interesting graphic that showed dispersion of tailored Rice Blast from the biowar labs around Manila and Jakarta, after those were bombed, out into all the rice-growing areas, and this plunging graph for rice production and another one shooting up called "Calorie Deficit," but they overlaid the interesting graphs on all these pictures of starving people in rags walking along dirt roads. I kept seeing their bare feet touching dirt, and that seemed so disgusting I couldn't really get the point of the whole thing—I mean, once they got to the camps, there was spacegrown grain for them and all. All they had to do was keep walking. . . . I'm sure it was unpleasant in high grav, but it seems to me like it would be something they would be used to.

Maybe the whole point of it is to make us feel guilty about how comfortable we are. I've asked Papa about it, and he talks about getting us "motivated" to get space resources fully on line before the situation on Earth falls apart any more—but I don't see what that has to do with us. If space industry and mining don't grow, if the terraforming on Mars doesn't work out, the *Flying Dutchman* won't have cargo and will go broke—and we can't let anything happen to the ship. I mean, it's *home*.

What kind of morons are we supposed to be, that they think they have to waste an hour of our time every week on feeling bad about every starving leper, or whatever they call them nowadays, and burned-down forest and extinct species on Earth, just so that we will want to have the system work the way it's supposed to?

Glad as I was for the stay of execution this was giving Theophilus, I was getting just as bored and irritated as I always did. The reason for

Earth Horror Hour was as obscure as ever. There was some stuff about rapidly forming mountain glaciers in East Africa, and some vid of these lim floods roaring down the valleys when ice dams broke, that was kind of fun to watch, but then they'd show you these closeups that were very upsetting—a dead lion flying on its back in the mud with all its paws curled up on top of it, or a baboon mother carrying its dead baby around, or just a bunch of forlorn-looking men with stick hoes. After Dr. Niwara's outburst, I wasn't going to tell them to go buy some power tools, but pos-def I thought it.

At last the wretched business was over, but there were about ten minutes left before it would be our turn to be in the corridors on the way to the Big Commons, so Dr. Niwara decided that we should all get some more work in Groundhog Studies. "Theophilus," she said, "if it's not too upsetting, I'd like you to tell the class about some of the things you've seen back on Earth."

He got up as though she'd just asked him to volunteer for a lab demo on castration, and moved slowly and carefully to the front of the room. I wasn't sure whether he was still having trouble walking, or just really did not want to have to do it. Probably it was both.

"Um, well, I'm from Georgia, up in the hilly part—the one in the USA, not the independent country in the Eurasian Commonwealth. And, uh, things haven't been that bad up there. I mean I remember during the Cyclone we had some really big storms, and they kept talking on the vid about all those places like New Orleans and Tampa and so on that were washed away, but where I was we just had to stay home from school because it was storming so hard it knocked down all the power lines.

"I mean, I've seen all that stuff on the vid, too, but my dad is a specialist in low-g aquaculture, and my mom's an economist, and things just weren't that bad for us . . . except, oh, I guess a couple of times we heard machine guns a long way away because the police had to clear out vags. There was a girl at school whose mom got killed by vags when they knocked down a shuttle on landing—they do that to steal rings and jewelry and things off the bodies, which is pretty disgusting if you ask me."

Dr. Niwara was biting her thumb with intense concentration; I guess Theophilus wasn't talking about what she wanted him to.

"What are vags?" Chris Kim asked—probably the only person in the room who wasn't afraid to admit he didn't know.

"Oh, you know, like those guys you see wandering up the road on the vid we just saw. Guys with no money who wander around in gangs.

They don't have any jobs and usually they won't go into the camps because they say they aren't refugees, and they want to get paid by somebody for the houses and businesses and things they say they lost. I bet most of them are lying. All they really are is thieves and robbers. And they aren't really that big a problem—when my Dad's company bought Whitfield for a headquarters, they just put some high walls around the town and hired a lot of guards and there's never been any trouble inside except for once when a rocket landed in the park and blew up the duck pond." His eyes got a little sad and far away. "That was really a shame. There used to be thirty or forty white ducks on that little pond, and it was all really pretty, but the day after it got hit it was just this big pot of wet mud with dead ducks hanging in the trees and lying in pieces all around it."

That was kind of interesting—and sad—but just then Dr. Niwara cut in. "Er, I suppose we've really done enough on this subject this week. Before we all go to rec, though, perhaps you could tell us a little about yourself?"

That was bound to be more interesting. What we all wanted to know, anyway, was what he'd do to our standings. His favorite subject was math—no surprise there—and he didn't care much for social science or lit. He had kind of a funny accent and he could speak English and Spanish but not Esperanto or Japanese, so he would be doing remedial languages even after he got FA.

The whole time Theophilus was stumbling through this interrogation, Randy was focusing a lim hate stare at him. My werp screen lit up with:

—GIVE HIM SOME COACHING? HELP HIM HAVE A FRIEND? D'Artagnan.

Hornblower said pos-def.

At rec that afternoon, we all took the omnivator up to the center of the Mushroom.

(Stupid werp! Another stupid flag.) The Mushroom is this big metal mushroom-shaped thing, 550 meters across the disk, that sticks out the side of the *Flying Dutchman,* near the top, and rotates so that we have a place where we can have high gravity. You need some of that every day, plus a lot of exercise, to avoid getting agravitic dystrophy. Also, they say it's so we can go to other places when we get older, but why go where everything's heavy and germy and there's no temperature control, when you can stay here and see it on flashchannel?

We play aerocrosse in the Big Commons, a cylindrical room

about fifty meters in diameter and two hundred tall, up inside the Main Body, which of course is the asteroid itself.

It was a pretty long pull from the omnivators, and usually there would be a lot of horseplay and giggling, but today it was all whispering, all with one subject.

"What do you think Randy's going to do to him, Mel?" Miriam breathed in my ear.

"Whatever he can get away with."

We came to an intersection and kicked from one netted wall to another. Theophilus was lagging a little behind—he still wasn't used to getting around hand-over-hand. Even though I was trying to make allowances for him, it seemed kind of bokky to me that he would have so much trouble—I mean, all of us could *walk* as well as he could.

The Commons Locker Room is always what Papa calls a "zoo." Everyone has a million things to talk about. Today we all were looking at Miriam's new cross—single-piece maple, grown in a bonsai tank. "They even grow the holes for the strings," she said proudly. "And the net is structure-woven monomyl."

Naturally everybody got into competition. "That's lim koapy, Mim. I'll have to talk my father into getting me one, too," Gwenny said. She lifted her light brown hair above her head and shook it out— it fell all the way to her shoulders, really long, you'd think it would be germ-ridden but the boys seemed to like it—before adding, for good measure, "Poor Daddy—it's so hard to get his attention now that he's sitting on four committees."

"I know what you mean," Penelope said. "Even though they're all just techie stuff, that must take a lot of time. My mother never has any time for me either—not with all those papers she's always publishing."

Carole nodded. "Yeah, she gets published all over Earth, doesn't she? It's good she has something to keep her busy, since she doesn't have any shipboard specialty."

Gwenny flashed a smile at Carole for the support, and asked about her new tunic. Miriam got busy showing her new cross to Penelope. Without much new information to bring into it, a p.d. round ends quickly.

A year ago I had been able to p.d. anybody, and comparing my plain fiberplas cross with Miriam's beautiful one, I wanted to drop in something about Papa's work—the CPB is so important here that the mayor and the council aren't allowed to take any action without getting the CPB's approval.

For that matter, Mother's job in Long Run Economic Operations used to be good for some standing boost too.

But I didn't get into anything about standing anymore, because if I did, someone would bring up Mother's having quit her job. She hadn't worked in ten months and spent most of her time sitting at home reading; people were calling her an unco, though not to my face.

I had been sitting there thinking and hadn't noticed that I wasn't moving anymore and everyone else was getting dressed until I saw Carole go past; then I looked up and saw I was almost alone. I hurried to finish getting dressed, but I was still the last one into the Big Commons.

Dr. Niwara looked at me a little funny, and I was afraid she was going to say something about daydreaming again, but she didn't. "And . . . last one in—okay, Melpomene, you set up."

That's not a big job. You just take the goals, deflated, up to the top, clip them to their starting rings, and inflate them with the can of compressed air. Inflated, they're a meter in diameter and mass about two hundred grams, so once the game starts, they take almost ten minutes to fall to the bottom when grav is low; deflated, they fit into a pouch on your belt and you can just jump and swim up there. Furthermore, there were fewer than there had ever been before—the addition of Theophilus made twenty-eight students in the class, seven teams of four instead of nine teams of three.

By the time I got back down, the captains had already chosen teams; I would be on Barry Yang's Team Six with Kwame (yuck! Bad jokes on the headsets!) and Ysande Kravizi, who was quiet and sort of shy. (Though, looking back, not that shy. She got FA early so she could marry before turning fourteen. People surprise you.)

It was a moderately koapy team—I can do things in midair that a lot of people can't, Barry is the rare combination of big and fast, and Ysande's ball handling is super-accurate. Kwame's an oaf and he was going to be our weak link.

Miriam was a captain and she could have had me if she hadn't picked Gwenny Mori first, but Gwenny is a superb player and Miriam had gotten second pick. And Barry Yang was a better captain than Miriam anyway, even if he did hang around with Randy Schwartz.

It was no surprise that Theophilus got picked last by the last captain, Paul Kyromeides. No one knew if he could play or not, but yesterday he hadn't done much to show he knew his way around low grav.

"Okay," Dr. Niwara said. "Let's review the rules." That was something we hadn't done in three years, but Theophilus wouldn't know that. "Does everyone know who your captain is? And who your team members are? Make sure you're tuned to the team freke as well, and your cross is carrying the team ID." I saw Paul collar Theophilus and the other two members of the team to make sure they all knew each other.

Dr. Niwara went on. "Here's how it works. Teams One through Six have goals One to Six; the goal lights up on all sides with your number. Team Seven starts without a goal.

"We play with three throwing balls. Each ball carries the identifier of the cross that touched it last. When a ball hits a goal, the goal goes over to the team the ball identifies. That's called a capture.

"If someone hits your goal, you have two seconds to hit it with a ball carrying your identifier before the goal goes to the other side. Your score at the end is all the captures you've made, minus all the captures the other teams have made against you.

"Listen to your captain. He'll tell you which goals to guard or go after. The alliances between teams change very quickly.

"You can bump into other players, but you can't hit them with your hands or feet and you can't hang onto them.

"And be sure to remember this last part—it's what's really important. The Captain's Report says we're under .008g today, so the goals will drop relatively fast and you'll have to swim fairly hard. You might not want to drop the whole two hundred meters to the bottom—you could hit hard enough to turn an ankle. If you do get centered, and you can't catch enough air with your fins to reach the side, don't panic—it's more than a minute till you hit bottom. Spread out with your fins perpendicular to your line of motion and don't be too shy to call for help. Just yell 'Falling!'

"Captains, remember to watch your score and keep updating strategy." She looked around the walls where we were all hanging from safety straps or sitting on catcher platforms. "Any questions?"

There weren't any.

The game went really fast. Everyone scattered to their goals—you have to be touching your team's goal at the start, with Team Seven down at the bottom of the Commons—and then Dr. Niwara flipped the switch, and the spinner rotated a couple of times and fired the three balls randomly into the space. We all dove on them; those who didn't get one swept up their forearm fins, arched their backs, and sailed over to catcher platforms, then jumped back up toward the top.

Paul got a ball and did a fast flipover before he hit the catcher platform; then he shot upward and came in on a blind side of Team Five's goal. He whipped his cross overhand, snapping the, ball against the larger sphere of the goal. Two seconds later, the glowing red "5" changed to a purple "7." Paul set Theophilus on guard, probably as a way to keep him out of trouble.

But before Theophilus could set himself, Randy Schwartz took the goal for Team Three, coming in horizontally off the wall, curving and recurving too fast for Theophilus to track him.

I caught all this out of the corner of my eye, trying to keep an eye out for stray caroms or surprise switch-attacks. Attacked by Two and Three at the same time, we were hard pressed to hang onto our goal.

Barry had us butt it up higher, and Three switch-attacked Two, which gave us a momentary breather; we were at the top now, and the throwing balls were mostly far below us.

"Detach Mel and Kwame, Kwame leading," Barry's voice said in my earphone. "Go take the goal Three just captured." I thought it was a dumb move, especially for someone as good as Barry, to leave our goal half-guarded, but he was captain. I let Kwame drop ahead of me, then swam to the ceiling, flipped over, and pushed off downwards.

Sometimes you can snag a ball in the middle of a dive and then you're going lim fast at the bottom and can just plow through to the target, and that's what we were trying for.

Kwame sailed past Three's goal, but then he got a ball at the last second before he hit the floor and whipped it to me. It made a soft thud in my cross as I clicked the safety, closing the lid around it. He managed to hit a rebound board straight on and shot back upward like a rocket; graceless as he usually was, I had been afraid he would turn an ankle, but it looked like he was improving.

He shot up toward Three's goal, thirty meters above him. I banked a little to the side and then straightened out into a dive at Three's goal, my shin fins churning air behind me. Maybe we could catch them between us, rebounding for each other—that's just about the hardest attack to defend against, especially with one partner coming in from above as I was.

Randy Schwartz was defending from the top side of the goal. Theophilus, thrashing around awkwardly, passed between us, and with a hard kick Randy shoved off from his goal, driving it down toward Kwame, and headrammed up into Theophilus, catching him squarely in the belly.

Theophilus doubled up with pain, tumbled, and smashed awkwardly ass-first into the other wall, just missing the edge of a catcher platform. The goal, the big green "3" on it still glowing, passed

Kwame, too far away for him to grab it, hit the bottom, and rose back toward Randy, who turned to meet it.

I was so angry I didn't think. I sidearmed the ball as hard as I could off the back of Randy's helmet. It probably gave his teeth a good rattling, and it certainly made me feel better.

Purely by accident the ball ricocheted across and got Four's goal completely by surprise. The dark brown "4" vanished and was replaced with a bright pink "6" as Kwame kicked over to guard it. Since Four hadn't caught the ball for a countershot they couldn't do anything about it, and the goal was ours.

That made us one of two teams with two goals, and Barry told us we were allied with the other high score—Team Three, Randy's team. I finished my dive by turning inward onto a catcher platform and kicked over to join Kwame in boosting our new goal up higher. Beside us, Randy was pushing the Team Three goal upward also.

Shortly we had a clump of four goals bumping up against the ceiling, surrounded by a shell of eight of us treading air, jumping platform to platform, or hanging by our feet from the overhead straps. Sixteen attackers—Team Seven didn't seem to be part of the opposing alliance—were springing up at us and slinging balls in, trying to send them in too fast for us to catch before they ricocheted back downward into the attackers' territory.

I swung onto a catcher platform and found I was taking off parallel with Randy, close enough to talk. "Sorry I hit you that way," I said. I wasn't, of course, but I hate to be on bad terms with anyone.

"It's okay. Good carom shot. I really like the aggressive way you play. You're lim berserk."

Getting a compliment from Randy Schwartz was about as common as getting a guinea pig from a chicken egg. And that was such a nice thing for him to say, too, that it took me a moment to respond. By the time I started to stammer a thank you, he had looked away. Then he pointed, shouting, "Under you!"

Gwenny Mori had bounced from a lower platform and was swimming as hard as she could straight for us, trying to crash through and scatter any goal she didn't hit.

Randy and I piked over and dove to meet her, double-checking Gwenny just as she aimed to throw. She lost the ball and spun a hundred meters down before leveling into a glide.

Paul Kyromeides whooshed past us, grabbed the ball, and took Team Two's goal.

"He's a real one-man team," I said.

"He has to be," Randy commented. "That new groundhog doesn't know the game yet. But you're right—Paul always plays that way. He's nice and so on, but get him into competition and he's grabby."

We swung back away from each other, taking different parts of the guard. I looked at Randy a few times more than I had before, and a little differently. I think I was surprised to know he had a human side.

Barry spoke through the headset. "Mel and Kwame, can you hold for about twenty seconds or so without Ysande and me?"

"Sure, but keep it twenty," I said.

"Pos-def," Kwame said. "Be sure to wash your hands when you're done." It was exactly the kind of stupid thing he always says. Exactly.

Barry didn't bother to respond; at his hand signal, he and Ysande kipped over, planting their feet on the top, and dive-dropped, kicking hard and fast.

It was only then that I realized that they had managed to get two of the three balls. Barry had noticed that Theophilus was getting under the goal a lot, which is always a mistake because most attacks come from above. During the instant that it blocked his view, Barry and Ysande closed most of the distance between the goal and themselves. By the time he popped back out and was trying to get between them and the goal, it was too late. Barry slammed a shoulder into him, sending him tumbling downward, and Ysande hit the goal squarely, rolling it over to Team Six.

Theophilus, knocked all the way down to the bottom, tried to jump straight up after them, which was pretty brave, but silly since he didn't have a ball. He misjudged so badly that even with those Earth-strong legs he peaked out at about 130 meters up, lost momentum, and started to tumble.

"Falling! Falling!" A lot of people laughed at him.

Dr. Niwara shot upward—she wore a fan-harness when she supervised rec—grabbed Theophilus, and dragged him to the Blue Spot, the place by the entrance you're supposed to go to if you're hurt.

Dr. Niwara almost shouted into the mike. "All right! That's it! The game's over. Everyone in."

We deflated the goals and stuffed them into their compartment for the next class; the balls went into a little rack by the door. We all stood there, not looking at each other, knowing what was coming and not having anything to say.

She looked slowly around, pausing to focus on each of us. "Helmets off so you can hear," she said. "I am extremely disappointed in every single one of you. I'd expect better of a convicted Uncooperative. There was a call of 'Falling' and no one even moved to help. You laughed. Is that what you do when a friend's in trouble? Because if it is, this ship isn't going to last long after you get Full Adult."

She was absolutely right. Theophilus hadn't been in any real danger, but he'd been badly frightened, and he had called for help and not gotten it from us. We went back to the locker rooms in silence, not looking at each other.

As I stripped the fins off my forearms and calves, and tossed my helmet and cross into my locker, Miriam sat down next to me. "Do you still want to see if we can help him a little?"

"Yeah. You know me, Mim. Hornblower to the rescue."

Her smile was a little wistful. "Unh-hunh. But why isn't it ever popular, good-looking guys who need to get rescued?"

"I think he's okay-looking. He just needs to lose a little weight. He's got a nice face."

She giggled. "Other things are nice too. Did you notice when he was talking about 'back home in Georgia'?"

"Notice what?"

"Melpomene. Did you just look at his face the whole time? Let's just say his antenna was up."

Lately that was the only part of guys Miriam noticed, which I thought was kind of embarrassing, but since she seemed so much more advanced than I was, I wasn't going to let myself act like a kid about it. "Was it really big?" I asked.

"Pos-def. Huge."

"He is from Earth, you know. They tend to be pretty old-fashioned. He probably doesn't know what it's for."

Miriam punched my arm. "Well, then, somebody ought to show him. But let's start with showing him how to use fins. He doesn't know what *they're* for either."

On the way back we managed to be on either side of Theophilus. I drew a deep breath and plunged into it. "Is this your first time playing?"

"I played a couple of times on vacation at Supra Tokyo, but that was easier to figure out because it was pure free fall, and it was just with other Earth kids—nobody really knew how."

"You're not bad for no experience," Miriam said, lying. "Would you have time to get together this evening and practice? Not aero-crosse, I mean, but just low-gee flying?"

He seemed startled, but pleased. "I—yeah, I would. I get out of remedials at 2000. Is that too late?"

"Do you need time to eat?" I asked.

"No. I go to the Immersion Esperanto cafeteria as part of remedials. And I can leave a message for my folks—they'll be glad to know I'm making friends."

"Great," Miriam said. "The room where we have to go to sign up for gym time is over that way—Rec Lobby, Common Deck Two. Meet us there at 2015."

"Thank you," he said. He sounded happy—I felt good.

Dr. Niwara dropped back by us. "Is there a problem with keeping up? Or are you guys just talking?"

I opened my mouth, but Theophilus said, "It's my fault. I'm having trouble keeping up and they're trying to help."

Miriam cut in. "The truth is, we *have* been talking too much, and that's part of why he's having trouble." She and Theophilus pulled ahead quickly, and I followed.

Dr. Niwara stayed parallel with me. "Melpomene," she said quietly. I always loved the way she called us all what we wanted to be called.

"Yes, ma'am?"

"What were you going to say before they answered?"

"What Miriam said. It's true."

"Good. I was hoping . . ."

She reached around me with one arm, squeezed my shoulder, and swarmed on ahead. I hurried to follow.

After snack we had the cross-subject for the week, which was (hurray!) Team Essays, in four teams of seven. Unfortunately, the AIs refereeing were STRUNK, FLESCH, and ELLSWORTH, which is always a lim bore, pos-def, because all three of those AIs are so pedantic and rule-bound; I like ORWELL and SPENCER a lot better. At least, though, the scoring this time was rank coefficient rather than averaging, which favors a strong team, and I was lucky enough to be captain of Team One.

Usually Miriam and I both did well at Team Essays, so I picked her first even though she'd picked Gwenny over me. (Yes, that was petty. I didn't care—friendship ought to count for something, especially after the way Gwenny had p.d.'d her standing in the locker room.)

We were too busy to talk about anything but the competition. I forgot about Theophilus, who was on Vanya's team. Our team swept, with our essays taking first (mine), second, (Miriam's), fourth, and eighth, and nothing below fourteenth. The competition barely got done before school was out for the day.

"Not bad," Miriam said, while we waited for Theophilus in the corridor outside. "But we should have put more time into editing Sylvestrina's. She'd have placed sixth if we'd gotten her two more points in paragraph development."

"It's hard for her," I said. "And she's improved a lot. I think that's the first time she's even been in the top ten."

"I know. I just think it would have been lim koapy for her to place even higher." We clung to the netting and watched the door.

"I was surprised you asked him to practice tonight," I said. "Thursday is No Friends Day."

She made a face. "I hate Compets."

"Me too," I said. "But I always study harder for them than for anything else."

"We share a lot of habits," she said. "Maybe we ought to be friends or something. Oh, shit on it anyway, Mel, he needs the help."

"Yeah. Probably just a little coaching—" Just then he came out the door, looking around. We waved and he started over toward us.

A hand tapped his shoulder from behind. He turned.

Randy Schwartz's fist smashed into Theophilus's face. He fell backward, arms flung out to catch himself.

We both rushed forward. Theophilus was holding his face, and tears were streaming down, but it didn't look worse than a bad bruise around his eye.

I took a moment to glare up at Randy, who was still standing over his victim.

His expression was really strange, almost as if he had been the one who got hit. He stared at me, shaking his head, his arms hanging limply—at that moment I was sure he was as surprised as anyone else at what had happened, even frightened by it. He looked so upset that in spite of myself I felt my heart going out to him a little, as if I might get up and take him aside and talk to him.

Then his eyes broke from mine, and he turned, and ran down the corridor to the omnivators, stumbling awkwardly as his legs seemed to fling him along.

THREE

That night at dinner, mother said, "I met the mother of someone who's in your class today, Melpomene."

"Oh, who?"

"Mrs. Harrison, Theophilus's mother. She's a very interesting person."

"How did you happen to meet her?" I asked. Mother hadn't been going out of the living unit much, and this sounded encouraging.

"Oh, she's taking over my old slot. They've conscripted me to coach her for a few days." She made a face. "I'll be glad when they perfect tank pork—I won't have to eat any more of their experiments."

Papa laughed. "It always weighs on my conscience; here's a poor little slab of muscle that was confined to a vat its whole life and never got to contract and relax inside a real pig." He laughed again; it had an uneasy sound to it.

Mother shook her head. "Honestly, Cornelius, please. I'll admit to an interest in tradition, but I'm hardly a tree-worshipper. Anyway, Mrs. Harrison is an extremely interesting, cultured person and I thought we might want to get to know the family socially."

Get to know the family socially. Mother had been talking in that bizarre way a lot lately; it sounded like the Olson novels, back when men were full of manliness, fields were full of soybeans, small towns were full of hicks, and life was full of deeply significant aching empty meaningless existential nothingness, as Tom liked to put it.

To get back to a more interesting topic, I said, "It must have been nice to see all your old co-workers again. How are they doing?"

She shrugged. "Well, they never mattered much to me."

Usually I just think she's a moron but sometimes I swear she does talk like an unco. "Didn't you get time to talk to them?"

"Honestly, Melpomene, part of the reason I gave up that awful job was because those people aren't interesting. All they talk about is shop and their families; it was bad enough to work in Long Run Economic Operations without having to talk about twenty-year colonization schemes through your entire lunch break. Not one of them has any interest in art or politics or *anything.* Of course that was primarily what Mrs. Harrison and I talked about, shop I mean, but then at lunch time we had a long conversation. She and her husband are from interesting circles on Earth; she grew up with cousins of Colin Powell."

I felt like saying that since he was only Acting President for about six weeks before the Die-Off got him, the Harrisons just weren't good enough for our circles; we Murrays only associate with direct descendants of elected full-term presidents. It was the kind of thing people in those Olson books said.

But I was trying to encourage her; at least she would be getting out of the living unit for a few days. "That's interesting. I'll have to ask Theophilus about it tonight."

"Tonight?"

"Miriam and I are meeting him for some rec practice. He needs to learn some flying. Want to come along, Tom?" This might be a way to get Tom into it; I knew if I could get him interested in Theophilus's problems, my brother would come up with some good ideas. He always did, once you got his attention.

"I'd like to, but we have a night session tonight. Pyramid CSL." Tom looked like he was announcing the end of the world.

You have a lot of night sessions your last few months before FA; I'm not enjoying it any more than he did, just in case anyone out there is interested.

Especially not with writing this book on top of it. And it's now a little late, so I'll quit here and then write more tomorrow if there's time.

December 17, 2025

I'm back again, and it's only been a few minutes while I got a snack. I couldn't sleep.

Anyway, back to the conversation. I was going to wish Tom luck with his CSL, but Mother got off on one of her diatribes about how awful it was that they kept us so busy and how much vacation she had when she was our age. (Personally I wouldn't know what to do with that much time.) I just reached under the table and squeezed Tom's hand; he held mine for a long moment.

After a while, Mother wound down, and I said I needed to do some homework before meeting Theophilus and Miriam, so she let me leave the cafeteria early. When I left she was still talking loudly about the joys of her "normal" childhood, and Papa and Tom were eating in hardening silence, not looking up because they didn't want to catch the eye of anyone at another table. I felt like a deserter.

I was a little early getting to the Rec Lobby, but so was Miriam, so we spent some time going over the list of available smaller gyms. Right now B Shift was in school, so of course the Big Commons wasn't open—not that they'd give it to just three people anyway.

"I wonder if Randy Schwartz misses his friends," I said.

"Why do you care?"

"Well, maybe that's why he's such a . . . um . . ."

"A bully and an unco?" Miriam shook her head. "Melpomene, honestly. You really do worry about everyone in the world. Why can't you just accept that Randy Schwartz is nasty and mean, and let it go at that? I'm sure he doesn't worry about you."

I shrugged. "I was just making conversation. He probably doesn't see any of his old friends any more, and he's not very good at making new ones—"

"Well, maybe if he'd quit slamming people in the head . . ."

"Miriam!"

"What do you expect me to say? Okay, so he's lonely. Whose fault is that? He can still see his old friends at breakfast and dinner, or when he goes off shift. He still lives in B Block with them—they didn't move him when they changed his shift. It's not like he transferred ships or just came up—"

"Yeah, but . . . well, he's all alone down there. His corridor is dim most of the time he's awake. In fact, most of the time he could see them his friends have to be inside for Lights Down. And if he wants to eat with them he has to wait till right before his curfew, and they have to eat right after they get out of school. So he probably sees them but he doesn't get to see them, if you see what I mean."

"I guess. I still think there are better people to feel sympathy for."

I was still thinking of Randy's shocked expression after he had punched Theophilus, and didn't answer.

We picked out a nice big empty space, a supplementary storage bay far down toward the Main Engines, and I left my thumbprint for it.

Theophilus showed up a few minutes later. "Hi, am I late? Sorry—
I had to hurry to get here. . . ."

"You're not late. Relax," Miriam said. "Do you have your gear?"

"Here in my werpsack."

"Okay. We have a long way to go down, so we're going to take the
express omnivator."

As we got into the little car, Theophilus said, "I really wanted to
thank you guys for inviting me. I was feeling pretty lonely—"

"That's us," Miriam said. "Ladies errant. We just can't resist a
knight in distress."

"Though we hope a night with us wouldn't be too distressing," I
added.

Miriam blushed, and Theophilus giggled. So much for his innocence.

The omnivator dropped us off within a hundred meters of where
we were going. There's lots of empty space in the ship right now—so
far we're only carrying a few personnel rotation passengers and some
supplies for the Mars bases—and the lower spaces, below the living
quarters and the ag zones, are deserted except for kids playing in the
smaller pressurized cargo bays.

And of course couples out for sneakies. I hoped we wouldn't be
spoiling someone's evening by turning up in this space.

It was as vacant as it was supposed to be, probably because they
had put a supervisory camera in it. They hadn't done the finish yet, so
the walls still had the lumpy, burnished look that comes from vacuum
extruding and spray plating. The lights reflected everywhere, like
smeary stars stretching to infinity.

"Okay," I said. "Let's get you set up. Forearm fins go on like
this—that's right, broad part at the outer edge of your wrist—and shin
fins go on at a forty-five degree angle, pointing outward and back.
Make sure they're snug, but if they press into the muscle they're too
tight."

We checked him over; he was fine. "Okay, helmets on and let's go."

"You wear helmets even when they're not required?" he asked. "I
thought you were just wearing them because Niwara was there."

I was a little surprised that he called her by just her last name like
that. It sounded rude but maybe it was some kind of an Earth custom.
We always said "Dr. Niwara." "Well," I said, "in the first place, if you
hit your head—and we all do now and then—it's a lot less painful. And
besides, it *is* required, whenever you're doing free flight. Those are the
rules."

"I meant, no one would see you," he said, as if that explained something.

I was lim confused; I didn't know of any rule that only applied when you were being watched. I glanced at Miriam. She shrugged and raised her hands a little—I don't think Theophilus saw. Probably another one of those Earth things; it was hard to see why anyone would want to break a rule, and harder still to see why they'd want to chance a hard thump on the skull, but obviously that didn't bother Theophilus. "Well, if that's what concerns you, there's a good chance that someone is watching us through that camera anyway," she said.

"Those are cameras? I was going to ask."

I rolled my eyes at Miriam; she winked.

"We might as well get to flying," I said. "The thing to remember is that your fins can only work up a few newtons of force, even when you're swimming as hard as you can—but since you only *weigh* about five newtons at most, it's enough. You can build up a lot of speed."

"But it takes a while to feel it," Miriam added. "So if you know you're doing the right thing, don't stop doing it—give it a few seconds to have some effect."

"Let's go up to the top and we'll show you," I said. "Just jump lightly, and then do a few frog kicks hard with your legs, like this." I took off; Theophilus followed, with Miriam behind in case he got into trouble. The gym was only about fifty meters high, so it would be an easy jump to the top anyway, but that should be enough room for him to get the feel of it.

When he managed to fly upward, he got so excited he tried to flutter kick the way he'd seen us do in the Big Commons. Unfortunately, he didn't yet know anything about slowing down or stopping, and he accelerated all the way up until he smacked head-first into the ceiling, and bounced back down. He whirled around, his arms and legs flapping in all directions, then tried treading air. He was spinning a little, slowly, but he did slow his descent enough to reach the floor without much of a bump.

Miriam and I had already swooped back down to see if he was all right; he looked a little shaken.

"Well, you've mastered the basic head-stop." I said it as a joke, but he turned away sharply, and I realized this wasn't a good joke to pursue. When he turned back, a breath later, I saw him make himself smile, and felt lim ashamed of teasing him.

"Sorry," I said. "That was our fault. If you're going to flutter kick, you need to brake and turn at the top."

"Like this," Miriam said. "Palms up, sweep your arms up and behind you. It spills a lot of speed and it flips you right over so you land feet first." She showed him the turn.

We flew up to the top again, and this time he did fine, only having to scrabble a little to get a strap, grabbing it with his left hand centered on his body so that it pulled his feet evenly against the ceiling.

"That's easier on the feet than it is on the head," he said.

Miriam laughed and gave him a hug; he looked a little startled. Mother says people on Earth don't touch each other much, so maybe it was that, or maybe it was the way she rubbed against him as she did it.

It reminded me how much things had changed in the last year. Miriam had hit puberty at peak velocity and gone right through with barely a hitch—a year ago she had been built like I was now, sort of slim and short (Tom would have said "scrawny" and "puny"). Almost overnight, she had shot up several centimeters, filled out in the hips, and grown these absolutely huge breasts. She'd kept the same waist measurement too, damn her.

Anyway, we worked on gliding next, showing him how to steer with little changes of fin position. That's tricky because you have to develop a sharp sense of limits—if you move more than your wrists and ankles, try to steer with your full arms and legs, the overcorrection is savage and you'll tumble like a paper airplane in the airgym.

After two or three of those wild tumbles, he caught on—and then it was just a lim thrill to see how much fun he had zipping around the gym. We gave him a quick hand of applause, and he grabbed a strap in a nice neat point-stop and bowed.

I thought Miriam giggled much more than that bow rated.

"We might as well move on to full ballistics, especially since you've got the legs for it from all that high gee," I said. "It's a lot like gliding except you use your fins to stabilize and turn more than for lift. The only new maneuver you have to learn is the turnover—and once you get that working well, you can do some really fun stuff." I shot around the room, ripping off six caroms one after the other before I dropped in a slapstop right in front of him.

There was some wonderful trick in his smile that made you feel like he'd just hugged you; at that moment I'd have done anything for him. "It does look like a lot of fun, but I don't know if I could ever do that," he said.

"*I* can't," Miriam said. "Mel's just showing off."

I had been, but at least what I was showing off was something I had worked to learn, and not just grown on my chest.

Before I could think of a polite way to say that, Miriam went on, "But she's right, of course. Your big strength is going to be wall play. You do a turnover like this. . . ." She kipped up and glided slowly to the other wall. "See, the whole trick is to just pull in tight and then thrust your feet straight at where you're going so your legs are all the way stretched just as you get there. That way you don't start spinning, and you've got the full extension of your leg to absorb the force so you've got control of the rebound as you hit. That way you can do anything from a dead stop to a sudden burst of speed." She touched down and pushed back toward us.

"Like this?" he asked. He jumped for the other wall, but he tucked his feet in front of himself, so he started to roll over slowly. He extended his legs, but by then he was flying flat and he landed on his hands and knees.

"Be careful to pull your feet in straight toward your center," I said.

He tried again and had it. After that we just showed him all the stuff we could think of; he was a pretty fast learner, and it got to be fun.

He was doing a lot better, so we finished up with a game of tag. Miriam was uncharacteristically clumsy, but maybe she was doing that to bolster his confidence. I guess I could have done the same thing, but once it's competition I just can't seem to lay back and take it easy; I have to play to win or I can't play at all.

Two times she bokked on her landings, hard enough it must have hurt, and bounced back up into Theophilus, giving him a chance to tag her. Theophilus even caught her on a tagback, which she should have ducked as easily as anyone.

When we finally quit, we figured he'd have a lot better chance in rec from now on. There was only about an hour left till Lights Down, so we scrambled a little getting to the omnivator, rushed through checkout with just a few words to Mrs. Onegin, Dmitri's mother, at the Rec Lobby, and hurried back toward A Block together.

It turned out they had moved his family into Miriam's corridor, so they went along with me before going back up together. He seemed to be having a lot less trouble getting around on the nets, and I complimented him on it.

"Why don't people just fly in the corridors?" he asked.

"There's a rule against it," I said.

"Oh." That seemed to confuse him. "Why is there a rule against it?"

I thought for a moment, then realized that I did know. "Traffic problem. Sometimes parties of twenty people have to pass each other; the corridors are only three meters in diameter, so it's a lot easier if everyone clings to the walls than it is if they're all in midair. Besides, the net limits the speed you can move at and allows you to stop quickly, so you don't fly face-first into someone coming around a bend."

Miriam edged in between us and started talking about a math problem; Theophilus seemed to be flattered by having someone want help from him. It was kind of rude of her to interrupt, especially since she would be going on with him, but I suppose the problem just popped into her head. Even though it was a pretty easy one, and she's better at math than I am.

I turned off at Corridor Twelve, and they continued on; they were so busy talking that I don't think they noticed I was gone. I went around the outside of our Corridor Commons—there was nobody there except three young couples, maybe sixteen years old, with babies—and down the corridor to our living unit.

I slipped in the door, planning to just stop by Tom's room to see how things had gone for him, but Mother stopped me in the share-space. "I hope you did all your homework before you went out."

"Yes, I did." I wasn't dumb enough to get caught that way.

She floated over and whispered in my ear; if the vid is accurate, I really do envy Earth people for all that space you have to live in. Our living units are so small that despite all the sound-proofing you can hear everything from anywhere. Papa's office has thick, heavy insulating pads on the walls to give his clients some privacy, but everywhere else we hear everything that's not whispered. "Tom is in his room by himself," she breathed in my ear. "I don't know if he'll want to talk to you, Melly—I mean Melpomene." She must have noticed that I stiffened. "He's very upset."

"What happened?"

"He did really badly in Pyramid CSL, and he pulled down some other people's scores."

I nodded. "Thank you for telling me. He'll want to see me." I grabbed a handhold and swung past her to his door.

"You don't know that," she said, which was stupid because of course I did. "Don't barge in if he doesn't want you to—let him have his privacy."

"Okay," I said, to keep the peace.

"When I was young, I valued my privacy."

Even after growing up with Mother around, I'll never understand that. Adults always say things like that. I mean, really, privacy is just being all by yourself with no friends and nobody to look out for you or have fun with. Who needs it? Tom and I only closed our doors because she insisted.

And this was just like her, leaving him in there to feel miserable by himself. Papa says it's because she's "imperfectly adapted to the social neoconstruct."

I think it's because she's a moron.

"You knock first," she said at me.

Tom opened his door and said, "Melpomene, I want you to come in here." I flipped in and he closed the door, leaving Mother out there to flap her mouth like a carp. Sometimes I really hate her.

I could see he had been crying and I was even angrier at Mother. How could she leave him in there by himself—for god's sake why should anyone wait for people to *ask* for help? I put my arms around him and let him cry it out. It took him a long time, his body shaking against mine and hot tears dripping onto my shoulder. I just waited.

When he finally stopped sobbing, I said, "There's a lot of things you *are* good at. Everyone can't be a genius at everything."

"It's not that," he said, still looking away. "What I can't take is everybody being so fucking charitable about it. They know I dragged the team down and they all got lower scores because of it, but they're so busy being good sports that they're all acting like the only thing bothering them is how upset I am."

"Well, they *are* your friends. Maybe they're worried about you."

He wouldn't look at me. "Sure they are. But I can tell what they're thinking. I know the captains always pick me last for CSL. I just can't stand being the worst person on the last team to pick!"

He started to cry again and I couldn't think of anything else to say, or at least not anything that would help. So I just held him, and rubbed his back with one hand, and told him that I liked him no matter what and all the things you say to someone when they're like that. It never seems to have any effect when you're doing the comforting, but when I feel bad, it helps to be comforted even though I don't stop crying.

Finally he said, "Well, I feel a little better. I just wish I could understand why CSL is such an awful subject for me."

"How low was your score?" I asked.

"Fourteen out of a possible hundred." He looked away; I was afraid he would cry again, so I started to rub his neck and shoulders. "That feels good, thank you. Statistically my score was indistinguishable from zil, could be pure random effects of the scoring procedure. I might as well not have gone to class at all." He sighed. "Well, I need to get back to work."

"You're not going to stay up and do CSL all night are you?"

He looked startled. "Why do you think—"

"Because every time this happens you do that. You exhaust yourself and you bokk in school the next day." He just looked at me. "That was what you were going to do, wasn't it?"

He snuffled. "I just hate being so bad at CSL, and I want to do something about it."

The door opened, jamming my leg against the wall, and Mother stuck her head in. "Melpomene, you're obviously upsetting your brother—"

"Get out of here, Mother. I'm upset but I want Melpomene here. What I don't want is you."

She closed the door with a slam.

Tom sighed. "Okay, I admit it. I was going to work the CSL problems. It helps me get to sleep, if nothing else, because I end up exhausted."

"Why don't you just masturbate?"

"I can't when I'm upset."

"Well, then take a drifter, but don't torture yourself with CSL for the rest of the night! You'll just multiply your problems."

"Yeah." He got out the bottle of pills from his medication file, held one up, and said, "See? Off to dream land."

"That's better," I said. "Now take it."

He made a face at me, but he took the pill. "I better get the place folded up and pull the bed out. The drifter will hit in ten minutes or so."

I stood up. "Okay. But if you wake up later, or you still can't get to sleep and just need to cry or something, you come to me or Papa. And unlike Papa, I don't sleep with Mother and I don't mind having you wake me up."

He held his hand up as if he were being put under oath. "Absolutely. At the first crisis, straight to Melpomene. My sister, my teddy bear."

I stuck my tongue out at him. "Just do it. And no more trying to cram after the test!"

"I'm reformed forever. Now, you go. I need to have the bed ready for when I start feeling all happy and vague in a few minutes."

"Goodnight." I hugged him; he hugged me back, and I went across the meter gap to my room. I made a mental note to check in on him before I went to sleep that night.

I tried to study, but it was still almost an hour till I needed to be asleep, and I didn't want to spend it in that little brig cell, my room, which was what Mother expected me to do. She was always talking about how she spent a lot of time like that, all alone in her room with just her books and her fantasies, when she was my age, which might explain a lot of things. I didn't want to be out in the sharespace with her. All she ever did was sit and read anyway.

Well, that left Papa.

He was in his office as always. Despite Mother's lecturing him about spending more time with his family, he usually disappeared into there every night as soon as we got back from dinner. I just pushed the door open, even though I knew he preferred that I knock. I was tired of truckling to adult bizarreness. "Papa?"

"Hi, Melpomene. Come on in and catch a sling. What's on your mind?"

I closed the door behind me and drifted over to pull myself into a seat. "I guess this is sort of about Tom and sort of about . . . things."

"Things in general?"

"Yeah."

He sat there and looked at me but he didn't say anything. One problem with shrinks, they do that. Unlike regular people, they don't make any nice inane chatter so you can have time to gather your thoughts.

I ended up doing what I always do—just threw myself into the conversation and let him catch me and sort it out. "Tom is really ashamed of being the team bokkup in CSL. Nobody makes fun of him or anything but he still feels bad."

"I know," he said. "He didn't want to go down to Main Dining for a late snack with me." The two of them had been doing that together a lot lately. "Is there something you think I could do to help?"

"I don't know, Papa." Everything was so confusing when I thought about it. I looked down at my slippers, the new blue ones, as I rubbed them against each other. "I guess . . . well, why does it matter to anybody but Tom how good he is at CSL?"

For a long time, he stared at the screen on the wall. Papa is one of the few people who always has his window tuned to an Outside camera; I never knew what he was looking at, since, except when you're close to Earth or Mars, there's nothing to see but white dots on black. Finally he said, "Well, since you've figured out the right question to ask, you're old enough to know the answer. If you don't already. Why *should* anyone else care about how Tom does in CSL? And more to the point, why should Tom care about how they feel about it?"

"Standing." That was obvious. "He loses standing every time

something like this happens. They're all very nice about it, but they know he's bokking, and he knows he's bokking, and that's all there is to it."

"Mmm-hmm." Papa nodded at me. That's called "giving the patient a cue to initiate a direction." I read about it in one of Papa's papers. They do that when they think you would be more receptive to whatever they're going to say if you thought of it yourself. It always makes me want to think of something else entirely.

"Look," I said, "That's it. No one likes to lose standing."

"Did you know Earth children don't even have the concept of standing? There are some roughly parallel ideas, like 'class rank,' 'honor,' and 'face,' but standing, as you know it, only exists up here in space."

I shrugged. "Groundhogs are weird."

"Mmm-hmmm." He looked away at the screen again.

I hate that.

But I can't help myself. "Well," I said, trying again, "Tom feels bad when he loses standing. He feels bad because he wants high standing, and he's used to having it in so many other subjects. The contrast bothers him. I guess if you always felt stupid you'd get used to it."

"Do you know any children who always feel stupid?"

"Sure. Carole. And, yes, she does get used to it, or *something,* anyway. She's always smiling and seems to be happy and has lots of friends. We all like her."

"What's her standing?"

"Bottom in practically everything."

"Her *standing.*" He had pounced on the word, leaning forward, looking at me the way Tom looks at a drawing that isn't quite right. "Not class or subject standings. The one you all give each other."

I knew what he meant, of course, and with all the microphones and cameras around I suppose I shouldn't have been surprised that he knew—but I still felt like an informer. So I stalled. "What does this have to do with Tom?"

"What kind of standing does it bother Tom to lose?"

I sat there for a moment, looking at him. When he gets that ready-to-pounce look, something is really important to him. He was a debater in college and almost went to law school, and it shows.

"Okay," I said. "I know what you mean. And yeah, because Tom is top of the standings in everything else, the embarrassment pushes his standing—his *real* standing, if you want to call it that—it lim p.d.'s it. You always lose standing if there's something people can humiliate you with." That made me think of Mother again, and I had a little flash of anger. "And I still don't see why you think it's something wrong with Tom. Of course he cares what his friends think! But why do they have to be so nasty and embarrass him—"

"Has he been teased, or picked on?"

"No, but he knows what they're thinking, and it hurts him—and I don't think that's fair." I was feeling very upset and confused, and I didn't know why.

He nodded a couple of times. He was obviously trying to think of, or remember, something that just wouldn't quite come to him. "Oh, hell, Melpomene, I never did figure out how I was going to tell you about this, though I thought about it a lot. You're going to be applying to take your advanced training in Social Science, right? Aiming for administration or psych?"

I said yes and left it up to him.

He sighed. "Well, then I might as well . . ." His voice trailed off.

"What's the matter?" I asked. It was something about his face— something that I had barely ever . . . *there were tears in his eyes.*

"Papa!"

"There's something I need to talk with you about. It's on the schedule—way overdue, in fact, and the rest of the CPB is chewing my ass off about not having done it yet." He drew a deep breath and looked into my eyes. "Melpomene, I know you're ambitious. How would you like the chance to get onto a *very* fast track for promotion—one where you might hold major office before you're twenty?"

"Really?! Pos-def! I mean, of course, yes! Is there an opening for something—I thought I knew all the slots open on the ship—"

He nodded again. "That's the catch. It's not here on the *Flying Dutchman.* The opportunity's coming up to transfer out to Mars Synchronous, the big port they're making out of Deimos now that Phobos has been moved out of the way. Would you like to leave here, not on this Mars approach but on the next one? You'll be Full Adult by then and you could go there to live . . ."

I gasped; I felt as if I'd been punched in the stomach. "Papa, I can't—don't make me—" The world swam around me, bordered with red, and I thought I might scream or vomit.

His arms were around me, comforting me and holding me as I sobbed. "Easy. Relax. Breathe deep. Sorry to do that to you—sometimes this still surprises me. No, you don't have to go. He looked at me closely. "Are you all right?"

I lashed out at his face as hard as I could, my hand open to slap; he caught it and pressed it back to my side. "Easy, easy, easy . . ." he whispered, and held me.

I was crying and I had no idea why; it was terrifying. How could I have tried to hit Papa? But he had said . . . he had suggested . . .

"It's okay," he said. "This is programmed. This is what's supposed to happen. Breathe deep."

I did and began to feel calmer. "You see now? How deeply these things are engineered?" he asked. "I should know—I did a lot of the engineering myself. You're a perfect employee for NihonAmerica, as perfect as we can condition you to be. You don't ever want to leave the ship. Everything you value is here, and everything you believe in is something that keeps the ship running smoothly. We can't make you good or wise or kind, but we can make you want to stay here and we can make you derive all your pleasure from teamwork."

"Dirty fucking uncos," I said, and tried to hit him again. This time he was slower to block me and I caught a little of his cheek. It must have stung, but he didn't react. "And this is why Tom feels like shit about his CSL score. Because he's been programmed to!"

He sighed. "Of course that's why." I noticed—and was surprised at the little twinge of satisfaction it gave me—that free hand twitched, as if to ward off another slap. "Of course that's why," he repeated. "And you're very angry about it. You have a right to be. Maybe in the best of worlds things wouldn't have happened this way. . . ."

"Don't tell me you had no choice," I said.

His face was suddenly hard as stone. "In the context of the times, we—did—not. What life was like after the Die-Off and the Eurowar—how bad things were—you can't imagine. The Reorganization . . . for a lot of us—"

"I'm fourth in history. Spare me. Okay, you needed to get the ships going because you needed space resources. What the hell gives you the right to fuck with my mind."

"Nothing," he said. "*Nothing* gave us the right. We had to so we did. I can remember the last big Christmas, the Declaration of Universal Disarmament, people dancing in the streets, riding on Dad's shoulders at the big parades . . . and the next Christmas, mutAIDS had hit, and Dad and Mom were both buried somewhere, in a bulldozed trench, and I spent Christmas at the school with lots of other kids who had no living parents. Exactly ten years after that I was wandering around somewhere in Belgium, looking for any American unit—or any living American. Christmas after that was evacuation camp in Normandy—and going to the States on a Korean freighter full of European refugees, because just then the United States was in no shape to bring its own soldiers home." I had never seen him so angry—or so quiet about it. "I don't know everything your mother did to live. I don't *want* to; she doesn't know everything I did and she hasn't asked. What we all do know is that everyone who made it through was someone who would do whatever they had to. So don't expect a drop of sympathy, and don't expect me or anyone else to worry about you and your friends' precious rights. We are doing what we have to; once we've done it, then maybe we'll consider how you feel about it."

There was a long, long silence.

"It happens to everyone," he said. "The only difference is that other people are created from whatever random events happen to them. You were designed. And we've spared you a lot. Did you know bright children on Earth get beaten up by their schoolmates for being too smart?"

"Sure. I saw it happen this afternoon."

His mouth dropped wide open and he stared at me; usually I hate that expression, but this time I kind of enjoyed it.

Finally he managed to squeak out, "You'd better tell me everything about it," and switched on the recorder.

So I told him all about Theophilus and Randy. He took a lot of notes on the keyboard as he listened and taped, but he didn't ask very many questions. . . . I guess I told the story the right way or something.

"Well, that's interesting," he said, when I had finished. "Keep an eye on that; we hadn't anticipated anything like this."

"I don't see any reason why I should spy for you," I said. "And I still want to know why you engineered things so that Tom would be miserable. Do you hate him, or what?"

"We all have an interest in Tom's CSL because anything he can't do very well limits what crew assignments he can take, and everything he can do well benefits all of us."

At least that much made sense. "But why do you set it up so he gets picked on for it? I mean, it's obvious . . . you could just read us a reminder memo or something in school once a week. You know, like the reminders to wear helmets during rec and brush our teeth."

"It's obvious to you because we've 'fucked with your mind.' But it's not obvious to everyone. Most Earth people would see it just the way you did—his scores are his own affair. Certainly your mother sees it that way, and that's part of why she has such a hard time dealing with his feelings."

"She's a moron," I said. "That's what the trouble is."

He was angry, but he didn't want me to see it. He waited a couple of long breaths before he spoke. "There's a lot to be said for her viewpoint—it probably results in more people being individually happier, although it also means people have less support when things go wrong.

"But whether it makes people happy or not, up here, with our sharply limited population and resources, and our need to make a profit to pay for our imports, we can't let the idea take root. It could kill the ship. And if the ships die, civilization dies with them—it's that simple. Earth is too frail ecologically for any more heavy industry, and its resources are too far down the gravity well, and there are far too many people to take care of in an agricultural, renewable-resource economy. We've *got* to reach out from Earth, even if it *is* a hundred years too early—or kill two-thirds of the people on Earth. So the ships have to work, and Tom has to feel the way he does."

"He didn't get much choice," I said.

"None at all." He sighed. "But nothing works perfectly. This development with the new boy—well, it shocked me, and it will shock the CPB. I've no idea what to make of it. I'd appreciate it if you'd keep me posted."

I shook my head. "If you'd asked yesterday, I'd have said pos-def. But now . . . no. I don't feel like being a spy for the CPB."

"What about for the *Flying Dutchman*?"

"Those aren't the same thing. At least not always."

I couldn't believe I was defying Papa this way. On the other hand, for all I knew this was the first thing I'd ever done where it was really *me* doing it, if you see what I mean.

I said goodnight and went back to my room terribly tired. Since Mother's nose was locked into the reader, I slipped Tom's door open. He was asleep or pretending to be. I went to my own room, folded up my desk and chair into the wall, and brought down the bed.

Standing in the dressing corner, I took off my jumpsuit and slippers and dropped them into the freshener, and set room heat to "nude/sleep." Then I popped up to the ceiling, caught the stretchout handles, relaxed, and let go, drawing a deep breath and letting myself drift down to the bed.

Usually I'm asleep so quickly I don't remember landing on the bed, but tonight, even tired as I was, I had to stretch out and drop three times before I could get to sleep.

FOUR

The next day, D'Artagnan was returning none of Hornblower's messages. I couldn't even catch Miriam's eye, and since there was no rec that day, I didn't get a chance to talk to her. Maybe she was short on sleep too.

We spent the whole last half of the afternoon in Pyramid Math, and of all people I ended up paired with Randy Schwartz. Life was obviously not going to be either fair or convenient.

In Pyramid Math your score is half your own plus one quarter the average of you and your partner, plus one eighth the average of your foursome, and so forth except that the total class average is weighted equally with your team's average so it all comes out to one. Every unit from individuals up to teams competes against all other units of its size. If that isn't clear, just remember the closer someone is to you in the team structure, the more their score counts for you.

Officially there were two teams of sixteen, but we only had twenty-eight kids, so in each group of eight, two kids would be double-paired to make up another score; they got the average of their two separate scores. (This would really be easier to show you with a diagram.) Dr. Niwara always said those would be randomly assigned, but in fact she always put the dumb kids into the extra pair slots so they'd get lots of help.

(You do the same thing, Dr. Lovell, and we all know it, so let's admit it, okay?)

Anyway, the point of the whole thing is that in Pyramid Math you need to get a good score yourself, have your partner get a good score, have your foursome get a good score, and so forth in that order, including finally that you want everyone in the room to get a good one. Usually I enjoy it a lot because we all have to cooperate so much.

I just wasn't lim, pos-def sure that I wanted to cooperate with Randy Schwartz. We sat down next to each other and didn't say a thing while our first problem sets came up.

I knew I was in trouble by the third problem. "Randy?"

"Need help? Okay, let's see . . . um, negative proof? Assume it's not true and show the trouble it gets you into?"

I looked at the problem again; it was obvious. "Thanks—I think I have it."

We went back to working, but it seemed like I needed help every other problem. He kept losing his place and getting flustered when he tried to help. Finally it got so obvious that I asked him about it. "Randy, is something wrong?"

"No, um, I—" He shook his head. "I guess I just don't feel like math or something today, Mel. But we have to do it, so . . . hey, this one's easy. Look, you can prove that if it works for any two ellipses, it works for all pairs of ellipses, right? That's trivial."

It took me a minute or so, but he was right; the proof was easy. "Now what?" I asked. He had gone back to his own work, and seemed surprised that I asked. "Oh. Well, now that you've proven that, just show that it's true for two circles of unit radius. That way the complicated stuff all drops out."

"It seems like cheating."

"It is, a little bit. But it works—here's a diagram. . . ."

He rolled the mouse between his hands, a strange little trick he used for drawing. As it formed on my screen I saw the principle and was about to say I could take it from here, but then he asked, "Do you like to be called Mel or Melpomene?"

I was so startled that I had to swallow before I could say, "Um, everyone calls me Mel but I like Melpomene bet-better." I hadn't stammered since I was eight; neither of us was having a good day.

"I'll try to remember." He nodded,. "I think it's a pretty koapy name."

"Thank you." There was a long pause; I couldn't think of a thing to say and he seemed to be looking at the screen without seeing it. "Um, guess we better get back to it," I said, feeling more bokked every second.

"Yeah." He went back to his screen. I don't know what he was working on that day—he was zooming through it faster than I could follow, and it was all stuff way over my head.

I finished my problem, but my time was so slow it didn't do the team much good. There was an hour to go, and problem sets escalate, so not only was the worst yet to come—there would be a lot of it.

As the problems got more complex and difficult, we worked more and more in our group of four or even group of eight. Sometimes Randy crossed over to dig Carole or Barry out for the team as a whole as well.

I was just as glad to be busy and not have too much time to talk with, or think about, Randy. If only he weren't such a terrible bully. I wondered what made him that way, if he had a friend to talk with. He'd looked so lost after hitting Theophilus, as if he didn't understand how he had happened to do it. . . . And he *had* asked what I wanted to be called; no one else ever had, and when I told friends like Miriam, they usually forgot.

When I looked at the screen I almost gasped. The clock in the lower corner showed more than a minute had already elapsed. I'd been thinking about Randy, not math, sitting there not seeing the problem on the screen. A full third of the possible points were lost already.

And not one thing on the screen made any sense at all.

"Randy, um—help?"

"Sure." He hurried over—that made me feel better, but when he saw the screen I didn't like his expression. "Yuck. Hey guys, everyone who can get over here to help Melpomene." I could hear people gathering behind us, reading the problem aloud to each other, but I was watching Randy.

"Okay, okay, okay." He was talking to himself, almost chanting as he ran through his approach. "No trivial solution. Looks impossible. Therefore there's some kind of a trick to all this. Just have to find it. Look for something peculiar. . . ."

"All the measures are in terms of p and q," I offered. It was the only thing I had seen.

"Could be, yeah, on a more standard problem there would be four variables and nine constants, but this is all . . . Hah! Those two areas look like you could express them . . . yeah. One is p plus q squared, one is p minus q squared, when you boil it out, and the ratio between the sides is pq over pq minus q, so . . . well, try that much."

I set that up; I still couldn't see where he was going.

"So the triangle is p squared q over two?"

"Yeah," he said. "Now we have three angles on that projection, so if we define what happens to p and what happens to q in terms of them . . ."

Well, we finally brute-forced our way through it. Nobody but Randy had any ideas at all, of course, but at least I understood what he had done well enough to explain it if Dr. Niwara backchecked us—though there hadn't been much backchecking of partners in the last few years. I guess we were supposed to be mature enough. . . .

Finishing with less than two minutes left on the clock, it was a lot of work for hardly any score at all. I felt pretty bad—me sitting there all that time without working had cost the team the high point value of the problem.

I started to apologize, but Randy said, "No, I'd just have burned the time myself trying for elegance. Neat problem—I just wish it hadn't shown up on a Pyramid day, when we're working against the clock." He touched my shoulder lightly. "Anyway, if they give you another one that tough today, it means they think you're a genius, for what that's worth." He turned and went to help Ysande.

"Next time call for help when you need it," Kwame van Dyke said. "If you can't do it find someone who can."

Randy's head snapped around. "Leave her alone. She did okay."

It got very quiet, and I had just an instant to wish he hadn't done that. The other kids were staring at him, and I think he was also wishing he hadn't said anything, but his fists unclenched and he explained, reasonably, "She couldn't have gotten help any sooner because I was working with Roger."

It wasn't true, but he had been sitting with Roger, who was busy with a problem right now so no one would bother asking him. "And since none of you had any ideas when you saw the problem, you wouldn't have done her any good if she had called for you. So, we'd have lost the points anyhow."

He looked around from Kwame to the others and back to Kwame. "If you upset people when they have trouble, they have more trouble. It doesn't matter—we need to concentrate on the points we can get, not on the ones that are already gone. Now go get some points if you guys are so smart."

I thought his argument was pretty good—at least it got me off the hook. As soon as Randy's back was turned, Kwame whispered something nasty about what I would do for Randy to show my gratitude. But that's the kind of thing Kwame says all the time, anyway, so no one ever listens to him.

I turned back to my screen and punched for the next question. It looked like a variation on the one before, but now I was just supposed to say whether the problem could be solved. I almost hit "yes," figuring I had just seen one solved and the next thing it would do would be to ask me to solve it, but something caught my eye. "Randy," I said, "on that last problem—if the horizontal and vertical projection angles were specified to be equal to each other, would it be overdetermined?"

"Yeah. Why?"

I hit "no." It scored big After that last problem, the testing AI had expected me to either bokk badly or take a long time from overcaution. "Thanks," I said, "Got it." I went on to the next problem.

We didn't have any time to say anything to each other after that, because the last part was Speed Estimation. They flash these complicated pictures at you with distances and angles marked in blue and a few red question marks for some distances and angles. You don't set up the problem or do any calculating—you type what you think the value of the length or the angle is over the question mark; the faster you finish and the closer you are to the right answer, the higher the score. It's the only part of math I've got any talent for.

Final scores at the end of the afternoon put Randy second and me seventh—low for him and very high for me. Theophilus had first, and most of the high places went to the other team; Miriam even got fifth. Apparently Theophilus was a good coach, in addition to being wonderful at math.

I thought I might be able to head off trouble. "I'm really sorry, Randy," I said, catching him on his way out the door.

He seemed surprised. "About what?"

"Oh, I really p.d.'d our score, especially on that one problem. You'd have done a lot better with a partner like Gwenny or Padraic—"

He shrugged. "Doesn't matter. I can't be on top all the time—it's probably a good experience for me. I'm an awfully bad loser."

We were out in the corridor by then, and for just a second our eyes met. I said "See you tomorrow," and he smiled a little.

"Yeah, see you tomorrow. That AI must think you're pretty smart—those problems were really tough."

I nodded. "Um, thanks for giving me a dropline—"

"It was no dropline. How you do your problems isn't Kwame's business. That's between you and your partner. Kwame always coasts on his teammates' efforts anyway, and you aren't responsible for getting him a good score if he won't do his share of the work."

It was all true, but I guess I hadn't expected to hear it. "Maybe. Thanks anyway."

He nodded. Then neither of us had anything to say, so we stood there awkwardly. Finally we turned away in our separate directions. It was about the most awkward, stupid, bokked conversation I'd ever been in, like something that Olson woman might have written.

Miriam and Theophilus were walking along ahead of me, so I hurried a little and caught up with them. "Hi, guys."

Miriam had a strange expression, as if she wished I wasn't there, and I was about to disappear as gracefully as I could manage, but Theophilus smiled and said hello, so I was stuck. We walked along not talking, taking the stairwell instead of the omnivators to the center of the Mushroom. After we had climbed through several levels, Miriam suddenly said, "What were you talking to that Randy Schwartz about?"

"Oh, just the math problem sets today. He was my partner. I bokked up on a hard one and he sort of got me out of the mess." I walked along with them a little longer. "He *is* pretty good at it."

"Almost as good as he thinks he is," Theophilus said.

I didn't have the foggiest idea what he meant by that. Almost as good as he thinks he is? Who else would know how good he was? And why "almost"? With all the feedback we get, how could he be consistently overestimating?

Miriam was giggling, so it had to be a joke.

"Ted," she said, "you're lim awful. He's going to hit you again if you keep that up."

I still didn't get the joke, but I was getting bored with it already. "Ted?" I asked.

"It's what I like people to call me," Theophilus said. "I like short names. Like what you guys are called—Mim and Mel."

Yuck. One more person to call me Mel. "Oh." I walked with them for the rest of the way through the Mushroom, and then waited with them for the exit ring to crank us around to A Block.

"What do you think for Penny Graham?" Theophilus asked Miriam.

"I don't know, you pick." She was giggling. I wondered if they were going to throw a surprise party or something. Theophilus certainly seemed to be influencing Miriam—she wasn't making much more sense than he did.

"Pancakes," he said.

That got them both laughing, and Miriam said, "They really are, you know. I've seen her in the locker room and they're not just small, they're sort of empty and droopy."

I couldn't imagine why they were talking about Penelope's breasts, or why it was so funny.

"Okay, pos-def it's Pancakes," Theophilus said. "Now who else?"
"Pick one."

"The girl that sits two seats in front of me."

"Rebecca Hayakawa?"

"Yeah. Her," Theophilus agreed. "Uh—Full Disk."

"I don't get it," Miriam said.

"When they were announcing what you could see from the viewing deck, when I first got here—"

"Oh, I see. 'Both Earth and moon showing full disks. . . .' But we can do better. How about Plug?" Miriam said. "For what happens when she tries to go through a narrow corridor."

Rebecca was terribly sensitive about her weight and figure, because she was such a big girl. I was sure that if she heard any of this she'd burst into tears, but both of them were laughing like idiots.

The Block A entrance rolled up and we walked through. Since I lived on a different corridor from theirs, I started to say goodbye, but neither of them was looking at me, so I just grabbed the netting and pulled away. They ignored me, whispering and giggling to each other. Just before the door closed, I heard Miriam say something that I didn't quite catch.

Then Theophilus said, "Hey, that's great. Daddy Shrinko, Mommy Unco, and Baby Shrunko!"

When I got home I went straight into my room to study till it was time to go to dinner, but I couldn't concentrate. Okay, I was not very big for my age, and maybe I looked a little younger than I really was. And yes, Mother had quit being productive and was just staying home and deadheading.

Miriam knew how much those things bothered me. How could she laugh like that?

I was studying in my own room, with the door open so I could hear Tom if he wanted help or wanted to talk, when my comscreen whistled. I saved the essay I was stumbling through—"Abstract Microeconomics of Orbital Transfer"—and flipped the screen over to com, bringing it up to full visual. Too late, I remembered it had been rabbit lasagna in the cafeteria that night and as usual I had forgotten and worn a white tunic.

Luckily, it was Miriam, who wouldn't care. "Hi Mel, just wanted to talk—do you have time?"

"Pos-def, Mim, what's on your queue?"

"Well—say, what's on your tunic?"

"Dinner, I think," I admitted.

She shook her head. "Mel*pom*ene. Honestly."

Miriam had been doing that for years, but for some reason it felt different tonight, as if—

The door banged closed a quarter meter behind my head. Mother, making sure I had my privacy whether I wanted it or not.

Miriam seemed to be trying to find something to say, which was strange since *she* had called. Then she asked, "Have you got the stuff done for Art Club?"

"Oh, yeah, sure." I was the membership chair, and Miriam was treasurer, so she needed some figures from me on how many people had joined so that we could get our share of the Club Support allocation. We took some time to get all the numbers straight.

Then there was another very long, very awkward silence. After a few moments of looking around at everything but Miriam's face on the screen, I said, "Tom has a big toggle race coming up—the All-Ship Championship. Saturday morning."

"Oh. Does he have a good chance to win?"

"He's hoping to keep the All-Ship Championship for Shift A."

"Wish him luck for me."

"I will."

Silence.

"On the lit assignment for next week," Miriam said, "you know that question about why Nick says Gatsby's story is really about the West? Did you get that?"

"Sort of. It's like some of the things in the books my mother reads—a lot of them are imitations of Hemingway and Fitzgerald and all those. I'll transmit a copy of my answer and you can see if it helps. . . ." I popped a copy of the file to her.

She looked down to check the transmit-verification line. "Thank you."

We both sat there, twitching. I thought about just saying "Oh, well, I have to run," or something like that, but I didn't.

Finally I asked, "How are things going for Theophilus?"

She sat up straighter, and her lips pushed out a little momentary pout, before she said, "He likes to be called Ted. He told you that."

"I'm sorry. I forgot."

"He wants to be called Ted. He was just too shy to tell us before."

"I'm sorry," I said again. "Really. I just forgot."

"Well, you should try to be more careful. And why didn't you say anything today when we were walking home? It was like being followed by my kid brother. You *embarrassed* me."

I thought maybe I should apologize but I didn't know for what.

She didn't say anything either, and we sat there and looked at each other. Finally she said, "You're doing it again. Acting like a lump. Honestly, Mel, you're my best friend but sometimes I wonder about you. We were cracking all those jokes—and you just stood there like a moron. Theophilus asked me why people say you're smart!"

Miriam had never talked to me like this before. I didn't know what to do. "And today you really won the prize," she went on. "Hanging around with that Randy Schwartz. That was the most—"

"I wasn't hanging around with him." My voice sounded whiny, like I was pouting, and I hated it. "I was just talking to him. I had some math questions and he's good at math, and he helped me." And, I added mentally, I was trying to make sure Randy wouldn't hammer Theophilus-excuse-me-Ted into the corridor wall. But I was starting to wonder why I had bothered to worry about that.

"Well, it looked like you were hanging around with him and that's what counts. That's what I mean. Don't you ever think about how things are going to look? You can be so stupid sometimes—"

My voice felt mashed and dry in my throat. "Why are you talking to me like this?" The corners of my eyes stung. I was afraid I would cry in front of Miriam, and though that had never been a problem before, now I couldn't stand the idea.

"It's for your own good, Mel." She sighed and rolled her eyes. "If you can't take a little criticism . . . well, never mind." Then she smiled, a little. "I'm sorry. Really. Look, I just called to see if you wanted to meet me and Ted and some of the others for breakfast early tomorrow in Cafeteria Twelve."

"I'd like to," I said, "but you know my mother's rules. Our family always eats breakfast together at our local cafeteria. So I just can't."

Miriam glared at me. "You know Ted only invited you because I insisted. It really took me some effort. I won't tell you what he thought after he saw you in action this afternoon." She clicked off.

I leaned back in my chair and cried for a long time. Everything was wrong.

There was a little tap on the door, and Tom's voice. "Melpomene?"

"Come in." I got out of my chair and flipped it up to let him in.

He came halfway through the door. "You sounded upset. Do you need someone to talk to?"

"Yeah. Pos-def."

So he came all the way in, closed the door, and pulled down the guest seat. I pulled my chair back down and sat, but when I started to talk I couldn't think of what to say and my throat felt so swollen I couldn't breathe. I just sat there wheezing with tears running all over my face, dribbling from my nose, burning with humiliation.

He leaned forward and took my hands. "We can talk later if you need time by yourself now."

"Now you're talking like Mother."

He clutched his chest, pretending to be shot the way they do on old flatscreen vid.

I sniffed a little, pulled down a utility wipe, and sort of halfway cleaned my face. I was feeling a little better.

"I guess I do want to talk," I said. "But none of this is going to make any sense." Then I just poured it all out, starting, for some reason, with Randy hitting Theophilus the day before. "Do you think I'm crazy?" I asked. "Or reading too much into it? He did look strange after he hit Theophilus—I don't know why that matters. . . ."

Tom shrugged a little. "He got angry and did something he was ashamed of. Or he didn't know what he was doing until it was too late. Or maybe . . ." he grinned at me. "Maybe he didn't want *you* to see him acting like that."

"You've got to be—that's the bokkiest thing I ever—"

"Don't get upset. I'm just doublechecking. Does he act like he likes you?"

I started to say "Of course not," but instead I found myself saying, "Well, yes, sometimes. I mean, he *is* always really nice. To me, I mean. So I—well . . ." I told him about Pyramid Math and, as an after-thought, about the compliments Randy'd given me during aerocrosse.

Tom had that evil gleam in his eye that means the heavy teasing is about to start. "Okay. Just checking—nothing is as interesting as someone else's love life."

"He's not part of mine. He *hits* people!"

Tom winked at me; that made me even madder.

He must have seen—he got serious. "I guess this really isn't what the matter is."

"It's *some* of it." I blew my nose again. "I've tried my best to be nice to Theophilus, but I wish he'd never turned up in our class." I told him the rest. When I got to the conversation I'd just had with Miriam, I started to cry again and he had to hold me and soothe me before I could get through the story.

"That's so weird," he said. "I can't imagine treating a best friend that way. And I can't see what she's getting out of it either except hanging around this Theophilus person, which doesn't sound like any big treat to me."

I was still snuffling, but I was feeling a lot better. Now that Tom had pointed it out, it *did* seem pretty strange, not like anything I'd ever seen anyone do. "Maybe he has some kind of contagious insanity," I said. "I don't know. But whatever it is, Miriam's got it really bad." I suddenly felt very sleepy. "I think I'm okay now, at least for the moment."

Tom sighed. "Well, good, but I think you've managed to worry *me*. Are you going to have time to get your homework done?"

"I'm working on the day after tomorrow as it is. Tomorrow is No Friends Day."

"For me too. You want to see something neat I've been working on?"

"Sure," I said, though part of me groaned inside. Ever since I could remember, Tom had always used his lab allowance to build endless strange gadgets that weren't exactly art but certainly weren't engineering. Unlike most of us, he never bothered to enter any of the Projects Day competitions either.

Most of us knocked ourselves out for Projects Day—Miriam and I had been up for two nights straight getting a mural done last quarter, borrowing supplies from everyone after our lab allowance ran out. And Penelope Graham's improved fan-harness, and Chris Kim's new type of oxygen scavenger for the aquaculture tanks, had really succeeded—they had gone into use.

It wasn't like Tom to decline a competition of any kind, and this was something he was potentially good at—he could have knocked his standing hyperbolic if he'd even half tried, I was sure.

Yet every quarter he put all his lab allowance into a weird mixture of metalworking supplies and processor chips, plus an apparently random collection of other things, spent hours welding and wiring according to some strange plan that seemed to be only in his head, and produced what Mother called the Alien Artifacts—piles of bolted-together metal plates with flashing lights on them, strips of copper and aluminum tied around a tetrahedral frame surrounding something that moaned like irregular feedback, a set of five tiny gliders that pursued each other in irregular spirals and emitted little jingling sounds.

Once he had asked me to teach him how to work a CSL problem he thought was integral to his project. The problem was completely incomprehensible and so was the project.

Anyway, normally I'd have begged off, but now I owed him a big favor. And since I wasn't all that eager to see whatever he had come up with this time, he was already across the passageway between our two rooms before I started reluctantly moving.

Which is why I caught Papa standing at the edge of the share-space, listening.

He was a little startled, but he nodded at me once and turned back into the sharespace without saying anything.

I supposed I shouldn't have been surprised. Most of the CPB spent an hour or more every day listening to com calls at random, and cameras and microphones were everywhere. But for some reason I was furious.

Still, I didn't want to have a big row right now. I needed to get to sleep on time, with Compets the next day. And besides, Tom was probably wondering how I had managed to get lost on a two-meter trip. So I just went on in, resolving to talk to Papa later.

Tom's room seemed to be about seventy percent filled with a tangle of wires, clips, thin aluminum tubing, and rectangular metal plates. "Did you pull all this stuff out of the service access, or has there been a terrible accident?"

"Lucky me—such a clever little sister. Sit down in the guest chair and just watch and listen."

Then he turned out all the lights. I couldn't see anything—with the door closed there was no light at all. "Sing something," he said.

"What?"

There was a brief flicker of yellow, and then something that looked like a three-dimensional model of a spiral galaxy burst into being. Three chords like a sort of tinny organ pulsed out. With a little trill, the spiral galaxy swirled down into a sphere of blue points, no bigger than an aerocrosse hall, and disappeared.

"Oh!" I said. "That's really—"

A great fountain of reds and yellows poured up from the floor, bounding off the ceiling as something that sounded like a Beethoven duet for piccolo and banjo rang out. The fountain poured back down in a swirl of green stars, all making flat farting noises.

There was a click as Tom threw a switch. It was completely dark again. "It doesn't deal well with speech. Now if you want to really see something, *sing.*"

He threw the switch again before I could point out that I don't sing well and I'm very self-conscious about it. But if I said that out loud, I'd trigger another one of these weird displays and he'd be mad about it.

Unfortunately, the only thing that came to mind was Papa's old story about his college Alma Mater, so I sang:

> *I don't know the god damn words,*
> *I don't know the god damn words—*

It looked like a rose made up of tiny points of light but with all the petals different colors, spinning in front of me. A sound like French horns, not quite in tune, came out of it.

I didn't know what I was supposed to do other than keep singing, so I tried to follow the melody that seemed to be coming out of Tom's gadget, singing,

> *But I'm trying very hard to sing as if I knew what I*
> *was doing.*

The instruments became more like a marimba, and the rose inverted, folded, and flowed into its own center.

> *So I keep singing even though I know it makes no*
> *sense.*

The contracting swirl at the center suddenly broke through its bottom and fell to the floor, then bounded back up in a mushroom cloud. The chords got richer, deeper, moving into the sound of a piano and then toward an organ.

Suddenly the lights and music were gone. "What an incredible idea!" Tom said. "Why didn't I see it—well, never mind." The room lights came on. "You were singing *in response to* the effects."

"Sorry if I wasn't supposed to. You still haven't told me what this thing is supposed to be."

"You did *great.* That was exactly what I needed and couldn't think of." He got out from behind all the hardware, gingerly. "And as for what it is—well, it does what it does. You could call it sort of a brain in space. Microphones pick up vibrations from the struts and wires. Photocells pick up the spots the lasers draw. They all report to system-state memory. Then the processors that control the lasers and the audio outputs scan the memory and decide what to do next based on that plus the music."

I didn't want to tell Tom he had just re-invented the principle of the mercury delay tube—which Alan Turing had used in the first true computer. (I had done a report in history on it.) "What's it good for?" I asked, being as tactful as I could manage while still trying to get out the door and back to bed.

He laughed, a clear open sound that I hadn't heard in months or years. It was so wonderful to hear that I even put up with his answer: "As the piano is to music, so this pile of wire and pipe is to whatever it's good for. And I think you just helped me see what it's good for."

"You're welcome," I said. I turned to go.

"Thanks," he said, missing the irony completely. As I opened the door to my room, I could hear his keyboard starting to put out some notes apparently at random.

I almost went back to see what he did. Some of that had been sort of pretty, even if it was otherwise useless. But I had already opened my door, and Papa was sitting there in my room, in my seat.

"Come in," I said.

"I thought you might want to talk."

No one was understanding irony tonight. Well, even two days ago, this wouldn't have bothered me—but still, just like my bokky mother, I could feel my privacy being violated.

I wonder how children who are born blind feel, after the artificial eyes are installed, when they see clashing colors for the first time.

"What am I supposed to say?" I asked, finally.

"Whatever you want."

I thought I was going to tell him to get out of my room and leave me alone. But instead I started to cry, harder even than I had with Tom, and I couldn't stop. I felt my throat tightening the way it does in an anxiety attack, and tried to get my breathing slowed down and regular to head that off, but for the first time I could remember, I couldn't do it, and I stopped breathing and began to panic.

He stood up and put his arms around me. "Breathe," he said, "breathe." But I couldn't.

Then he whispered something—you never know what phrases they plant during hypnosis—and I started to sob, crying as hard as ever but breathing and less frightened. "I don't understand *anything.*"

"You've been excluded," he said. "Shut out from a group of people. That doesn't happen very often here, and you're not used to it."

"Does it happen a lot on Earth?" I was hating Earth more than ever.

"All the time." He sighed. "When I was in high school, my classmates and I put a lot of time and effort into excluding each other."

I sat back down the guest seat. "Is this something you engineered, too? Because if it is I think it's really stupid and cruel."

He shook his head. "We've sheltered the *Flying Dutchman* kids from it till now. It's absolutely pathological—hurts everyone it touches, including the ones doing the excluding, and doesn't do anything for anyone. Earth kids feel hurt by it just like you do, but because it does happen more often there, people are more used to it and they've developed more ways to handle it." He leaned forward and looked at me with one eyebrow raised, his lips flat and compressed. "I'd like to know the whole story, as you see it, from the beginning. But you're upset, Melpomene, and we can talk later if you'd rather. You set the pace."

I sighed and took stock. Crying had helped me calm down—it always does, even though it's kind of embarrassing. "Let's talk now. If I start crying again, or something, we can always stop."

Papa nodded, and leaned forward to hold my hand while he looked deep into my eyes. As I said, I don't know what any of the commands he uses for light hypnosis are, because they're blocked from me; I'm told it's some combination of several words that never would occur together in any natural context, followed by a few nonsense syllables.

He gave me the sequence that lets me remember everything, or at least think I do, and then said softly "All right, tell me all the relevant things that happened in school today. Take your time, digress all you want, don't prejudge what's important. . . ."

After living all my life with him, I can recite those directions as well as he can. I told him the whole story, without embellishment because I was under hypnosis, about Randy and Pyramid Math and how he stuck up for me, and about going home with Miriam and Theophilus and being shut out of everything, and all the rest of it.

Because you can't suppress detail in those things, it was almost 2330 when we finished up with the routine suggestion that I let my feelings out. I cried for a little while, felt much better, and then saw the clock.

"Have I kept you up too late?" Papa asked, of all the dumb questions.

"Well, yes. I have Compets tomorrow, and school starts at 0745."

"Would you like me to plant a suggestion so you'll have more energy?"

"I think you've messed around with my brain enough."

"I'm sorry I took so much of your time."

"It's all right," I said. It was—I was feeling much better now even though I still didn't know what was going on. "I just need to get to bed. I can take being a little tired tomorrow."

He hugged me again, and we said goodnight.

As I got into bed, I didn't feel too bad—I had cried myself down to emptiness.

Just as I was about to jump up to the stretchout handles, I had the stray thought that I might dream about Randy Schwartz. I had no idea why, but suddenly I had a terrific fantasy about him. I lay down on the bed, and got an orgasm almost as soon as I touched my clitoris.

It was great—it put me right to sleep. I don't remember whether I dreamed about Randy or not.

Stupid werp. I've defined clitoris three times and it still keeps asking if it's audience-appropriate. I'm sure girls on Earth have them. Oh, well, going to bed, fix it later.

FIVE

December 22, 2025

I don't know why this is going so strangely for me. Every day I write a little more, and yet every day it seems like there's more of the story to tell. Also, I'm finding it harder and harder to just set down what happened. I keep wanting to explain that I didn't understand this or I was going to be wrong about that, because I'm sure whoever is reading this is thinking things like that and I want them to know that I understand now, too. It was just so hard to understand at the time.

It's also ruining my studying for the FA, not so much because it's taking lim time as because I get all weirdwired and then I can't study. Last night I got so upset from writing that for the first time since I was eight I went to class unprepared. It felt horrible.

Right now there's a big pile of undone work beside me, and I'm still working on this instead. I can't seem to stop, or anyway I'm not stopping. I just hope Dr. Lovell knew what she was talking about.

Thursday was Compets. We all call Compets "No Friends Day" because you have to work in a little booth by yourself and you can't give or get any help. You just sit there and do what you can with what the AIs throw at you.

They always shoot for your weak zones, so I got hardly any CSL or history and only a little English and Esperanto. They hit me hard on Japanese, math, physics, and chemistry, so I stayed busy all day.

They must have decided that I had a flair for projective geometry, based on the problem I did with Randy's help, because for once I didn't get any, but I would just as happily have passed up the additional diffy-q.

(Oh, not again. The werp flagged that; I think there's something wrong with it. Okay, let's see if it will take this definition: diffy-q is differential equations, and it's part of calculus, the boring part that's just a bag of tricks. I hated it then and I still do. The only person in class who's any good at it is Randy, damn him.)

Now and then they threw some Spanish, economics, or bio at me, and a few times they hit me with Earth Geography for the good of my soul or something—tell the truth, do *you* care where Block B is? Then why did *I* need to be able to find Australia on a map? It's all Earth to me. . . .

The whole day went to that nonsense. Everyone hates it, but you can't slough off, because Compets weigh so heavily in your overall academic standing, and when you lose standing everybody knows. So I just kept pounding away at it. . . . "Write five hundred words on 'The Economic Feasibility of Tri-Modulating the *Flying Dutchman* Orbit to Add a Jupiter-pass.' " . . . "Prove that natural-language gender cannot be mapped onto a rigid hierarchy of binary rules." . . . "With which nations does the Unaffiliated Soviet Republic of Kurdistan share boundaries?" . . . "Create a program of less than two hundred lines, to be implemented cellularly, to model the range of probable absorption rates of Resisting Protestants into the Ecucatholic movement. Specify initial and boundary conditions for the model as a whole.". . . The proctor brought lunch by. I set it by my elbow and kept working.

"Write a program, self-replicating with mutations, that will grow into a stable aggregate which can learn and solve the four-color problem." At least that one was sort of fun. I rechecked it twice, and then prettied it up a little when I saw that the clock was low. Just as I sent it and got back the score, a perfect-plus on that problem, time ran out on the day.

I stuffed the candy bar from lunch into my mouth, suddenly hungry, and looked around the desk to make sure I wasn't leaving anything in the Test Center—it always takes forever to get anything back after you do that. I flipped my cup of chocolate to WARM, then gulped it cold when the proctor stopped in front of my desk and opened up. I dropped my mostly-still-full tray and cup into the slot, and it rolled on to the next booth.

Out in the hall everyone was standing around comparing notes. Even though problems are all individualized, most people still believe in "hard days" and "soft days."

I looked around for Miriam, but she was over talking to Theophilus, Gwenny, and Kwame, and I felt funny about going near them. They seemed to be watching for something too.

Randy came out the door as if he were looking for someone. The four of them walked toward him, coming up behind fast.

I had no idea what they were doing, but there was something about the way they moved that I didn't like. I started toward Randy, the high grav making it easy to move quickly.

He looked up, saw me, and started to smile. Then Miriam tapped his shoulder.

When he looked back to see what it was, Theophilus spun on the ball of one foot. The other foot reached up, head-high, and hit Randy's face a dozen times harder than any punch I'd ever seen. Randy seemed to fly sideways, falling clumsily to the deck. I had never seen anything like it.

I started to run—everyone did—when there's a fight, if it doesn't stop quickly, they punish the whole class for it. Because I'd been headed that way already, I got there ahead of most people, and I saw the whole thing.

Randy clutched his face, rubbing it. "I'm sorry I hit you," he said. He sounded like he was choking with anger, but he was holding his voice level. "It was a rotten thing to do, and I really had this coming, so I guess we're even."

"Oh, you're sorry," Theophilus said. "I just bet. I bet you say that to anybody who can knock you down, Your Majesty."

Randy sat up. He still looked a little dazed. "Isn't that what this is about? I mean, I hit you, and I know it was wrong. Wasn't that why you kicked me? Isn't that what this is about?"

"Isn't that what this is about?" The mockery in Theophilus's voice made me wince. "Oh, good, good, *good*. You hit me, I hit you, now it's all o-*kay*. Is that the way it's supposed to be, Your Majesty? Well, get this clear: I don't want your apology. I don't want to be friends. I took five years of tae kwon do. They won't let the kids here study any martial arts so I know you don't have any idea how to really fight. I just wanted you to know I can do this to you any time I want. Have you got that?" He stood over Randy, poised, waiting to hit or punch him if he moved. "Say you understand, Your Majesty."

Tears streaked Randy's face. "I understand."

"You thought you could treat me the way you did everybody else and beat me up for being smarter than you. Because you've always been the big king of the class, haven't you, Your Majesty? Well, you're not any more. You were never anything but the plain old class bully, and now you're the ex-bully. And the only reason people are bullies is because they're stupid." As he smiled down at Randy, I couldn't remember anyone I had seen so happy—or any time I had been so frightened. "Say it."

Randy didn't seem to know what Theophilus was demanding. He looked puzzled, and scared, and about to start really crying.

The Earth kid turned sideways and his foot snapped out, catching Randy in the side of the head. "You really *are* stupid. You don't get it, do you! Say you're stupid."

"Why?" The whine in Randy's voice made me want to vomit.

"Because you are. Do you want another one?" Theophilus faked another kick at Randy's head, and Randy backed away, scooting on his hands and knees, keening under his breath and snuffling. Theophilus took a step forward and stamped on his hand, holding him where he was. "You know the only reason you have such high standings is because everyone is afraid to do better than you."

I hated to see Randy's face, but I couldn't look away. He didn't say anything, but from the way the anger went out of him he'd been hit harder with those words than he had with Theophilus's foot.

"Now say you're stupid or get another one. I'm going to teach you what you are."

Randy looked for a moment like he might defy Theophilus—but then that foot cocked back and Randy looked down at the deck. "I'm stupid," he said, quietly. "I'm stupid, okay? I'm stupid."

Theophilus stood there with his hands on his hips and a smile that made my skin crawl. "That's much better. Now you know what you are, Your Majesty. King Stupid."

"So how does it feel, Your Majesty?" Miriam said. It was the same tone of voice she had used on me the night before. I hated her then, more than I'd ever hated anyone. Gwenny Mori laughed, and then Theophilus and Miriam laughed, and then Kwame joined them.

A few people in the surrounding mob of kids laughed as well, more from nerves I think than from anything being funny.

"All right, everyone get moving," Dr. Niwara said quietly. She had come up behind us.

Randy stood up and walked out of the center of the crowd. I could hear a couple of people whispering, "King Stupid," and "Your Majesty" at him. He didn't look to either side, just went straight to the omnivators.

"I said everyone." Dr. Niwara's voice was colder and flatter than I'd ever heard it. We all started walking; as I turned the corner I looked back and saw that a lot of people were crowding in close to Theophilus. They seemed excited, nervous—*happy.*

I got on an omnivator by myself, keyed my destination—all the way to my Corridor Commons, even though that ties up an omnivator for much longer than necessary—and left in it without waiting to see if anyone else wanted to come along. It was the first time I had ever done such a thing. I wondered how many times you'd have to do it to be declared an unco.

I swam out of the omnivator to the wall of our corridor, and hauled along the net as fast as I could. It felt really good—I almost bruised my hands stopping at the living unit.

Mother was sitting in there, at the reader as always. Usually I'd have said hello, she'd have said hello, and I'd have gone to my room, but this time she pushed the reader away. "How was school today?"

I shrugged. "Mostly okay—it was Compets." I didn't want to tell her about what had happened to Randy; Mother never gives you sympathy when she can give you an interpretation instead.

"I finished the turnover to Mrs. Harrison. She's *very* interesting, but I'm glad I won't have to go back to that office now."

"Oh." I unslung my werpsack and tossed it lightly against Tom's door, letting it bounce into my room. Guess it had been stupid to hope that she'd decide to go back to work.

"She said that a bunch of the other children—a 'real gang' she said—got together to visit with Theophilus this morning over breakfast. I understand your friend Miriam Baum was with them—"

"Yes, Mother," I said. "I was invited but I thought you wouldn't let me go. You know, breakfast with the family?"

"Well, for something like this, of course I would. If he does it again—"

"I don't think he'll ask me. We're not getting along very well." I plunged into my room; for once I really did want some of that privacy she was always talking about.

Five seconds after I closed the door, she banged on it. "Melpomene."

"Yes?"

"He would really be a good person for you to get in with. He's from Earth, and you could get more of a perspective—"

"You mean a distortion. No thanks. If I want to be an unco, I'll ask for advice here in my own family."

"Melpomene!"

She started to open the door; I kicked it shut. I sat in my chair, rubbing my face. More than anything, I wished my homework was already done—it would have been if it hadn't been for all the nonsense yesterday, and now with this . . . it didn't seem right. Today had been more than long enough already.

After a while Mother tapped on the door.

"Go away," I said.

"I will. I know you need some time by yourself." What I needed was time away from her, but close enough. "Your father and I are going to one of the little cafeterias over in the Mushroom. If you want to come along you can, or you can wait for Tom and go to dinner with him."

"I'll wait for Tom." I could tell from her tone—that was the right answer. "See you."

"All right, Melly. Take care." I heard her and Papa go out; she probably hadn't told him that we'd had a quarrel or that I was upset—she would think it was "none of his business." I'm still not sure I understand what she means when she says that. Since they were gone, I pushed the door open and went out to sit in the sharespace. I could have pulled out the werp and gotten some studying done, or maybe meditated—our family is cybertao but it's been at least a year since I've even looked at *Forks in Time*.

There were lots of things that might have been sensible, mature things to do, but fortunately I wasn't so old that I always had to do those things. Instead I turned on the reader and called up a book—good, old, familiar *Beat To Quarters*. After a minute I got myself a hot cup of coffee and chocolate, and settled in to read.

I was feeling a lot better half an hour later when Tom got home and called me back to this world with a touch on my shoulder. I guess he was kind of surprised to see me at the reader—he and I usually only use it late at night when we can't sleep, and on weekends and vacations of course. "Something new come in from Earth?"

I raised the reader's screen away from my face, brought the seat back to upright, and turned off the back massager. "No, just something old. I was waiting for you and didn't feel like doing schoolwork. We're on our own for dinner—want to bum some of my discrets and go get a pizza?"

"Baby tilapia and rabbit sausage?" he asked—his favorite kind.

"You drive a tough bargain. Can we skip the fish and just do straight rabbit sausage?"

"It's your treat—but how about mushrooms then, instead of tilapia?"

"Pos-def. Bunny and fungus, large. I'll order; grab whatever you're taking with you." The pizza cafeteria is down in the promenade area beside the entrance from the Mushroom. It would take us a few minutes to get there, so I flashed the request ahead.

We didn't talk much on the way, and a couple of minutes after we settled into a booth the pizza came out of the slot, so there was a long time there of not talking and just being with Tom. That helped too.

"I missed you," I said suddenly, not sure why I had happened to think of it. "All those times you were having dinner with Susan the Rodent." He tensed. "I mean, Susan, your girlfriend."

He shrugged. "I'm sorry." He could have had the decency to say he'd missed me too. "I know you don't like her. But since you bring it up, I'd better mention that we've started seeing each other again. In fact," he leaned forward and winked at me, "part of the reason I was late was we did a quick sneaky."

"Koapy." I was in a nasty mood. "Did you execute the docking maneuver?"

"No. we just had time to touch each other a little. It was fun, though. She's got breasts. Why don't you grow some?"

I stared down at my food and tried to make myself eat.

"I'm sorry," Tom said. He reached over and tagged my shoulder. "I know you don't like Susan. I won't talk about her."

"It's not that. Well, it is, but that's not the big part of it. . . . Things just aren't going very well. They haven't all this week, and they really didn't today."

"I knew something was on your mind," he said. "You've been feuding with Mother a lot."

"Yeah." I sighed. "Something really awful happened today, but I don't exactly know how to talk about it." I took another bite. "Theophilus organized an audience for himself and then beat the living shit out of Randy."

"You'd better tell it a little slower."

I did, calmly at first, but then seeing it again in my memory, coming near tears at the end of it. "I never saw anything like it except on vid. I mean, when people hit each other sometimes someone gets bruised or shaken up a little, but he *really* hurt Randy. And he wouldn't accept the apology and be friends afterward or anything. I know a lot of kids are afraid of Randy and they probably liked seeing him get beaten, but this is too much. Theophilus doesn't stop after he's won. . . ."

He chewed his way through his whole next piece before he said, "Bad. Real bad. You talked to Papa, too?"

I nodded. "Last night. He'd been waiting in my room when I went back. Before that he was listening to us at the door."

Tom nodded. "Earning his salary, I guess. Did he say anything about what was going on?"

"I get the impression it's some kind of a bizarre Earth custom. Like human sacrifice and slavery, you know, in the history books. Oh, Tom, it just makes my head spin. I feel bad for Theophilus and for Randy and maybe even for Miriam and don't know what to do about any of it. Thanks for listening but let's change the subject. How was *your* day?"

He shook his head. "The thing is, I really don't know how it was yet—I'll have to see how it comes out. This should be good news, but I can't just relax and enjoy. it—it feels like I'm being set up for something." He stopped to take a big bite. "I got this colony-hold of CSL problems today, and all of a sudden I knew all the answers. Nothing like that ever happened before. I must have p.d.'d ten kids."

"That sounds wonderful," I said. "I always knew you had talent for it—you just never seemed to be able to use your talent."

He shook his head, stuffing in another bite and chewing quickly. I love my brother but the way he eats . . . "The trouble is that I didn't really know how I got any of the answers—I just got them. Flash of light, blind intuition, whatever you want to call that. So there's no guarantee I can ever do it again—"

"And now the machine's going to jack your difficulty level. Ouch."

"Yeah. Ouch. Unless of course they're all going to be like these today."

"Maybe there's some trick all these problems have in common, and you're doing the trick without knowing that you're doing it. If I can figure out what it is, and show it to you—do you remember any of them?"

He gave a gusty little tenth of a laugh. "That's another weird part. I remember them all perfectly. Usually I sweat over a problem for ages, and then I can't remember any of it—but none of these took me as long as a minute, and I could practically recite them all verbatim."

I had him key all the problems onto my werp to look at later. At first glance, there was something strange about them, but I couldn't see what.

"You know," Tom said, out of nowhere, "it sounds like Randy was never very popular before. Your new kid seems to have figured that out in a hurry."

I nodded. "And he's getting a lot of use out of it. But for what? He seems to be after something, but I don't have any idea what it is."

"Maybe he just wants people to accept him, " Tom suggested.

"Maybe. But this doesn't seem like the way to do it." I shrugged. "Maybe it'll blow over," I added, trying to talk myself into the idea.

"It might. Do you want that last piece of pizza?"

"Take it, it's yours. You need it for the big toggle race; you have to impress Susan."

He gobbled the last piece of pizza as I watched—or rather, as I avoided watching. "Melpomene, it's okay. You don't have to be nice about Susan. It's even harder to take than when you call her a rodent."

"Sorry. Just trying . . ."

"Yeah. It's okay." He stretched and yawned. "Between the rumors going around about Mother, and the fact that Susan is so impressed by Papa's job that she can't talk when he's around, it's pretty hard to get her to come for a visit to the living unit. And I really wish she would. If you do want to help, just act like you're glad to see her the next time you meet."

"Do or die tryin', bwana," I said.

He leaned forward and kissed me on the cheek. "Were you reading Rider Haggard earlier?"

"C. S. Forester."

We tried to talk about small things after that, but it got more and more awkward. The problem was that Tom was so close to FA that getting it was all he could think about; he'd even lost interest in toggle racing, which at one time I'd have thought could never happen. He was going to stop being a kid in less than ten weeks; I had two years yet to go.

There just wasn't as much to talk about any more. That thought made me really sad, and I got quieter and quieter. At last we went home, not saying much, shy and awkward with each other for the first time I could remember. Tom went straight into his room, and to judge from the noise, the Alien Artifact was progressing nicely.

Papa and Mother were still not back. I didn't care about Mother, but I knew Papa would want to talk about what had happened between Randy and Theophilus—well, I knew I would—and I couldn't afford to be up late two nights in a row.

I got my homework done and they still weren't back. I put a trace on them, and of all things they had gone to Ballroom Dance Club, out on the rim of the Mushroom. When I was little, they'd done that a lot, but it had been years.

Well, if that was their idea of fun, they were welcome to it. We had tried it in rec and the best thing I could say for it was that I got to do an up-close inspection on a couple of boys I kind of liked.

They were sure to be late, but I still wasn't sleepy, so I decided to wait up a while.

Tom had gone to sleep, and it was past Lights Down, so I couldn't go out, and it was too late to call anyone in A Shift on the com, and I didn't know anyone in B or C. I didn't feel like I had to get way out ahead on my homework either, and though re-reading the old Hornblower had been comforting earlier, I didn't especially want to read any more just now. I wished Tom were awake to talk to.

That reminded me—his problem set. There was nothing else to do, anyway.

When I looked at the problems carefully for the first time, they certainly looked intriguing—difficult and tricky, but not at all beyond me. I was probably doing CSL at higher level than Tom was—birthyear doesn't determine the level of what you study, only who you study with—so I was sure I could do them.

Forty minutes later I was wide awake, and more frustrated than I'd ever been with a set of CSL problems. I had almost forgotten I was waiting up for Papa.

Tom said he had come up with right answers in less than a minute for each problem. So far I hadn't made a dent in even one of them. Yet they were all well within my level. Something was drastically wrong.

I got myself a container of fruit drink from our food dispenser, punctured the top with the straw, and sucked it down, half-finishing before I got back to the screen.

Twenty more minutes, and it was really late, and I still wasn't anywhere. I gave up and tried setting up a feasibility-proof algorithm for every problem. Usually that's the dullest, slowest, and dumbest way to solve a programming problem, but the one way that always works. I hadn't thought of doing it because, if Tom was getting the answers in an intuitive flash, it seemed unlikely he was subconsciously solving the problem by the *slowest* of all possible methods.

It was such a big job that there was actually a little bit of a delay; apparently even with an allocation for four kiloprocessers this was a struggle. When the answer finally came back, it took me completely by surprise; all the problems *did* have something in common.

They were all incomputable.

(The werp just hit me for another explanation. I'm afraid I have trouble remembering you don't take CSL. Well, it's important for things I'm going to tell you about later, so let's try:

There's a thing called Godel's Theorem that shows that not every true proposition can be calculated—some problems can have just one right answer with no logical pathway to it. You can guess a right answer, or you can try lots of answers and hope it happens to be one you try, but you can't really "solve" such problems at all. You can only get answers.)

Somehow or other, Tom, who couldn't do the easiest problems without sweating blood, could just "know" the right answer to all these impossible ones. That had to be what the software was looking for, and it had found it. Well, he could stop worrying about getting harder problems—what he was doing was already impossible.

It didn't make any sense, but not much did any more. God, I was tired. I folded everything up, pulled down the bed, jumped up, stretched, let go, and was asleep before I hit.

SIX

I got to class a little later than usual Friday morning. There had been some changes.

Miriam, who always sat by me, was next to Theophilus. I knew he wanted to be called Ted—Dr. Niwara had even announced it—but somehow I kept calling him Theophilus anyway, maybe mental revenge or something. Gwenny and Kwame and Carole were clustered with her around Miriam and Theophilus. Well, that was no surprise, since Kwame was probably following Miriam, and Carole went wherever Gwenny did.

Usually Randy was a little separated from the rest of us, with only Barry Yang close to him. Randy was in his usual seat, but Barry was across the room from him, in back of Theophilus's crowd.

And there was no one near where I usually sat.

In a way it was a continuation of No Friends Day, because we started with Individual CSL. My mind was wandering but I got top rank anyway; the problems on the screen just flew by, more like I was just completing sentences than actually figuring anything out. Of course, after I had spent more than an hour the night before trying to do the provably impossible, this stuff was bound to seem easy.

Toward the end of the time, Dr. Niwara notified us through our werps that the afternoon would be pyramid CSL; the screen paused a moment, and then added:

—YOUR PARTNER: CHRISTIAN KIM.

Lim koapy. The guy was dumb as a rock. There went my top standing. . . .

—PAIRED WITH: PADRAIC MONAGHAN AND ANGEL CASTAGHENA.

Well, maybe we could all gang up on him.

I got engrossed in the last bonus problem and was last in line on the way to the cafeteria; I seemed to be about thirty seconds behind the present all the time today. Theophilus and his "real gang"—thinking back to some old flatscreen movies I'd seen I could see why they called it that—were all up front with Dr. Niwara.

While I was thinking about that, the people in front stopped to let a class of little kids get through an intersection, and I bumped into the guy in front of me, suddenly realizing it was Chris Kim. "Sorry," I said. "I wasn't looking where I was going."

"It's okay." He smiled at me, a little shyly. "I guess you're in charge of de-dumbing me on CSL this afternoon." It didn't sound like he was challenging me. I almost wished it had.

"You shouldn't say you're dumb." I was still thinking about Theophilus and his "real gang." That was such a good word for it . . . not like they stuck together out of friendship and loyalty, like the pack of wolves I saw once when my window was tuned to a camera in Denali Worldpark . . . more like a school of sharks . . .

Chris had just said something and I had no idea what it was. "Sorry, I'm completely weirdwired today. What did you say?"

"I said once you see me try CSL you'll say I'm dumb too."

"Well, look, give me a chance to make the discovery for myself. What's so bad about CSL, anyway?"

"Nothing except it's gibberish." He sounded just like Tom.

We went through the door into the cafeteria. Our lunches were waiting for us as always, and somehow, with all that had been happening, that was wonderful. No matter what people thought of you or who you had trouble with, your lunch was always there with your name lettered on top "—because you belong to the ship," I heard Papa's voice say, and I suddenly realized how many times I had been told that when I was younger. Thank the ship for your dinner. Love the ship because it feeds you . . . because it loves you.

Suddenly I knew whatever was in the lunch, I didn't want it. Oh well, everyone always ended up trading anyway. . . . "Ugh. I can't imagine why I ordered guinea pig fried rice."

"Trade you crawfish cakes for it," Chris offered.

"Pos-def."

We took a small table together. I wanted to see if I could figure out what the matter was between him and CSL before he actually had a problem in front of him. I scraped my fried rice onto his tray, and he flipped the crawfish cakes onto mine. "There," I said. "We've pushed out our indifference curves."

He wasn't listening; he was watching Miriam go over to sit with Theophilus. "Uh, what did you say?"

"I said you're hardly indifferent to the way her curves have pushed out."

Chris laughed, a nice big friendly sound, nothing like Theophilus's evil-minded giggle. "Okay. I *did* hear you the first time." He shrugged. "I used to think Mim was a little bit interested in me. It looks like that's over."

I watched too. She was hanging on every word Theophilus said, laughing at all his jokes.

"You're tying a knot in your fork," Chris pointed out helpfully.

I straightened it on the edge of the table, giving it all my attention.

"That Ted person really has changed things around here," Chris added.

I nodded, glumly, and looked around the room. The crowd at Theophilus's table was whispering and talking, and sometimes they'd laugh that funny way that sounded like it was meant to be overheard. Occasionally you'd swear that some of them pointed at you and said something, though you could never guess what.

At the tables around their table there were a lot of other kids, all trying to listen in. Some of them, like Barry Yang and Paul Kyromeides, seemed to be trying hard to get invited to Theophilus's table; others didn't seem as directly interested, but they too tended to lean in to listen whenever there was a roar of laughter from the table.

There were other people, besides Chris and me, who weren't sitting close to the Real Gang. Randy Schwartz was all by himself, across the room from them. His concentration was all on his tray, but his shoulder blades were pulled back like he was expecting an arrow between them. Bekka Hayakawa and Penelope Graham were at another corner. They seemed to be ignoring it, but they both dove into their food whenever the laughter got really loud. Rachel DeLane was all by herself too, reading something on her werp, but now that I thought of it, she had always done that. There were other people scattered away from Theophilus's table, but it seemed to me that all their ears tipped toward it.

Padraic's voice rose a little above the rest of the Real Gang. "Well, he is *kind of* ugly, and *sort of* clumsy, but he makes up for it by being *completely* stupid."

Aside from Randy, he might have been talking about Robert, M'tsu, Ichiro . . . as the roar of laughter came, every one of them tensed up. I looked at Chris, and he was clenched like a fist.

"Even some of us who are friends with Miriam think she's out of her mind," I said. "Some of us still think it's more important for a guy to be kind, and good at a lot of things, and a hard competitor, than it is for him to impress people."

His smile was thin. "Well, I'm a hard competitor, and I'm not _un_kind. But I'm certainly not any good at CSL, or any school stuff."

"Wait till I'm done with you," I said, only half teasing. Dr. Niwara had told me more than once that I was a natural teacher.

Chris was looking off into space, as if he hadn't heard me. "A lot of it probably is that I'm just not motivated, so I get bored. You don't need CSL for agtech. I want to work the aqua side; that just means I have to be able to do a few numbers and read graphs. This other stuff, it's all right I guess, but sometimes it just feels like it's there to make me feel bad. I can't wait to get FA and never have to look at it again— I just want to get down to the tanks and work."

I took a big gulp of milk; I had the urge to ask Chris if he was sure he was smart enough to outwit the oysters. Papa always says there's room for everyone, but some people certainly take theirs up without making it interesting.

After that, the conversation drifted over to sports. That was more fun—I had noticed before that although Chris was small, he was wiry and very agile, but now I realized he had a real eye for strategy, and his opinions about people's hidden strengths in the class and who he would pick if he were a captain (not likely, with his low standings in everything) were really astute. (They agreed with mine almost completely.) He wasn't as dumb as I'd thought, I realized—just not interested in the same things I was.

That thought gave me a little flash of insight. When Chris offered to take both our trays back, I took him up on it. As soon as his back was turned, I called up the Fink Board on the werp.

The Fink Board (the official name is the Shared Instructor Information Bulletin Board) is where you post things you've noticed to help the teacher. It's supposed to be anonymous, but I'm sure the CPB knows whose i.d. things are coming from, just as they monitor the private channel com.

I typed in "C Kim probably more interested in CSL if app problems were from ag ecol & econ esp aqua." I cleared my screen before he turned back my way, and called up next week's schedule as a cover.

Sometimes you can really do someone a favor with the Fink Board, but nobody appreciates it.

We talked a little more, mostly about toggle racing and six-wall handball, and then it was time to go back to class. I felt a lot better.

The afternoon did not start badly. Pyramid CSL is always a lot easier on me than any other Pyramid competition. I dug Chris out of a few problems, bailed out some of the others on the team, and once gave Randy a couple of hints—though CSL is usually a good subject for him.

We were milling around outside the classroom at the end of the day, and I was saying encouraging things to Chris while trying to get him over by Miriam, who was still hanging around with Theophilus, when it started.

"Randy. King Randy. Your Majesty." It was Gwenny that time. Randy ignored her and walked straight toward the omnivators.

"Hey King Randy," Kwame chimed in. "You came in second again, Your Majesty." There was a nasty titter among a lot of kids. I still didn't understand that style of joke, and I was getting to be glad of it.

"Hey Randy." Theophilus stepped out of the crowd. "Randy, boy, I'm talking to you." I didn't know why he stressed "boy" so hard; after all, none of us would even *take* the FA exam for more than a year.

Slowly, as if he'd rather have done anything else, Randy turned around to face Theophilus. "What?" he asked, sullenly, his head down.

I wanted him to hold his head up and stare Theophilus into silence, but Randy just stood there looking at the floor.

Theophilus stepped up to him confidently, waiting for him to look up before he said, "I thought it would be really funny if you did that howling noise for everybody."

I could see Randy didn't know what Theophilus was talking about. Neither moved or said anything for a couple of long breaths.

Then Theophilus, very slowly and deliberately, turned his back on Randy and walked a few steps toward us. He looked around and said, "Since I have to 'get adjusted,' they make me go to this psychiatrist. Randy goes too. His appointment is right before mine. I always hear Randy in there before me, yelling and screaming, and then he makes these lim weird howling noises. So I was wondering if maybe King Randy would do them for all of us to laugh at. . . ."

Randy stood there as silent as if he'd been stunned. Tears ran all over his face. He didn't move to wipe them away.

"Come on, King Randy." Theophilus took a step back toward him. "Don't you remember? It goes like this. . . ." He put his head back and howled—a long squealing inhale erupting into an open-mouthed falsetto moan, sharp sobs and deep grunts breaking into it as it collapsed into a slow, wretched wheeze. Even in Theophilus's mocking imitation, its misery pierced me from throat to gut.

It got so quiet I could hear Randy breathing. Miriam, who ought to be slowly gutted, gave a nervous little laugh. Then a lot of kids did.

Randy wasn't really trying to hit Theophilus, I don't think. I've never asked. It looked more to me like he just charged blindly at him, too furious, too outraged, to make any kind of a real attack.

Theophilus was ready—probably had started out ready. He did another of those pivot-and-kick things, hitting Randy in the face, then stepped in for a solar plexus punch. Randy sat down, hard, and Theophilus grabbed his jaw and slapped him across the face again and again. It sounded like aerocrosse balls slamming into the safety pads, and Randy seemed to fold around the blows like a soggy towel.

I didn't even know I was running toward them. If anybody yelled, or said anything, I didn't hear it. Papa had hammered at me, as soon as I could speak, that whatever I heard or saw of his patients, I was to say nothing to anyone, ever. Chris and Barry have both told me since that I was yelling, not words, just a loud, open-mouthed yell, the whole way to Theophilus; I don't remember doing that either.

I would have hit him squarely in the middle of his back, except that he reached out, grabbed my wrist, snapped it downward as he kicked me high on one thigh, and flung me upside down against the wall.

Papa says they teach all of you how to do that in rec, and it's one more reason I'm never going to visit Earth.

My back stung like being burned, and my thigh was numb, but then I slid down the wall and landed on my head. A dull curtain of pain shut off the world. I was barely aware of Dr. Niwara bursting in on us, and by the time things quit hurting enough for me to focus, Papa was there, sitting with me and Randy in the empty classroom. "I think," he said, "the time has come for a long talk. Randy, I've called your father, and he knows you're with me, so if you'll just come with me . . ."

After everything that had happened, I was expecting some sort of a big revelation, but I was completely disappointed. Papa had just wanted to make sure Randy understood what was happening to him, and he had wanted me there "to supply observations and comments," as he put it.

There wasn't much to say. Theophilus Harrison was about as well-established as he could possibly get. What Papa called "adolescent power games" were replacing "the mutually supportive neoconstruct." I'm sure half of it went right by Randy, since a third of it did me and I'm used to Papa.

Finally, Randy said, "Um, Dr. Murray? I can follow most of this—I think—but I don't see what I can do about it. Or Melpomene either. We're just kids, you know."

Papa scratched his head; I always liked the way he did that. The great brown expanse of his bald spot shone as if it had been waxed, and I found myself looking at him and thinking about how old he seemed to be getting, rather than listening to what he was saying.

"—not sure you are 'just kids.' In a lot of ways, you're the only people who really do understand anything." He sighed. "We have a very small number of adults trying to raise a very large number of you into a culture that we just made up, one we don't have any emotional attachment to ourselves. We're doing about as well as anyone does in a completely unprecedented situation. We're screwing up right and left."

Randy scratched his head too. I had the funny image of it being contagious. Since then I've learned that Randy does that when he's trying to find a polite way to tell people to cut the bullshit. "Um, sure. I see. But what can we do?"

Papa leaned back and seemed to be thinking, harder and harder. I had a little time to think myself, and I was losing my temper. This man had programmed both our brains to think what NAC wanted us to think. Now it turned out he'd done it wrong and didn't know what to do. So who did he ask to dig himself, and NAC, out of the mess? You've got it. Us. The people they had crippled with their plan.

So here he was calmly talking about it with Randy as if it were the most natural thing in the world. Then again, Randy was just sitting there listening to it—of all things, having had this done to him by this man, Randy was asking him for advice.

I was about to say something—maybe yell something—when Papa shook his head, as if something sticky had landed on it. "Pfui. I had a bunch of answers and none of them really tells you to do anything—only to 'be this way' or 'be that way.' Typical shrinkspeak. I'll tell you both what I want you to do, and especially you, Melly."

Melly. I hated that.

"Follow your hearts."

Follow *our* hearts? In just what way were they supposed to be ours? "That's it," I said. "This is all I can listen to."

I got up and left; they were too startled to do anything about it. I think my father called my name.

I scooted into our living unit, slung my werp into its bin, and shut the door. I wasn't sure what time it was but I couldn't get up enough ambition to push a button and find out. Instead, I just put the desk and seats up, pulled the bed down, and stretched out on it.

Drained and empty as if I'd cried for a week, I was asleep almost at once.

I always know when I'm dreaming, so nightmares hardly ever frighten me. But this one did.

In my dream, I walked around the outer edge of the Mushroom, along the central corridor that rings the rim. The gravity was too high, somehow, and I'd been walking for a long time, so my feet and ankles and knees were aching. No one else was there.

I was whining to myself—I *never* do that in real life.

At first, I thought, "In this dream I'm going to look for someone and not find them." But I couldn't imagine who I was supposed to be looking for, and besides I'd have been allowed to rest if that was how it worked.

Footsteps behind me. I must not look back and I must not let whoever it was catch me. I always hate chase scenes in the old flatscreen films, and I like them a lot less in my dreams. It seemed to be gaining on me, and I broke into a run, my legs aching and sore from my thighs on down. For some reason I could not turn off into any side corridor either.

At first I seemed to be getting away, but then the footsteps behind me broke into a run and caught up rapidly. I ran harder, gaining space again, and again they caught up. Finally, when I ran as fast as I possibly could, my pursuer also seemed unable to go any faster.

Up ahead, I heard more footsteps, retreating from me. If I could just get to that person, I would be safe. But the footsteps in front of me stayed the same distance away, their source hidden by the upward curve of the floor in front of me. Just as I could not lose the terrifying steps behind me, I could not catch up with the friend I could hear just ahead.

In the same part of my mind that knew I was dreaming, I realized that both sets of footsteps were my own. That didn't stop my running—

nothing could. The fear I fled and the hope I chased had to be obeyed, even though the sounds themselves were mere echoes circling the outermost ring of the Mushroom.

In that senseless logic, it was my running that kept the Mushroom turning, like the little animals I had seen on treadmills on the vid. Without my running there would be no grav and our calcium balance would go, our skeletons dissolving. The ache in my legs was from the terrible effort of pushing the great structure, half a kilometer across, a hundred thousand tonnes, with only my two legs.

I saw myself from outside, face darkening, stumbling. Either I would master my irrational fear and hope, and stop, or I would not, and would keep running.

If I stopped, I would fall into an exhausted sleep on the floor. Slowly, as I slept, the Mushroom would run down and stop turning. There would be no more grav, and because it would all be my fault, the disaster of everyone's calcium loss would fall on me all at once. My bones would dissolve, urine white and thick as yogurt pouring from my body, the flesh collapsing. The ribs would soften and bend, and I would wake only in time to feel my chest muscles give their final spasm, the bones crumbling, my lungs collapsing, unable to breathe, to move, even to reach outward, pulsing on the deck, turning blue-black, face and brains sucking down into my windpipe . . .

Or if I kept running, like the "Wonderful One-Hoss Shay" in the poem, my whole body would finally go to pieces at once, every blood vessel ripping along its length, every membrane rupturing, all the tissues turned instantly to thick jam, the skin going next to last as my screaming face dissolved. My juiced body would splatter forward in a long red iron-reeking streak.

I both watched and felt the last of it—the nervous system remained intact. My brain, trailing an immense tangle of nerves, lay in that red pool, dying for hours as pain messages flooded in through the still-intact spaghetti of nerves.

Both my deaths, shapeless collapse and dissolution, were impossible, as impossible as my turning the Mushroom by myself or hearing undistorted footsteps through almost two kilometers of corridors. I said this to myself over and over again, as I said to myself that I was dreaming.

But I didn't stop running and I didn't wake up.

"Uh, Melpomene?"

I sat up screaming into Randy Schwartz's surprised expression, my face sticky with tears.

"Uh," he repeated, staring. "I'm sorry I woke you up if you were sleeping."

"Hi," I said, not sure what else I could say. I grabbed a wipe from the dispenser and rubbed my face frantically.

"Hi. Uh, Dr. Murray . . . you know, your father—"

"That's what Mother says."

"Yes, well, he—what did you say?"

"It's an old joke I heard in an old flatscreen movie, so old it was in monochrome. The movie I mean, not the joke." I blew my nose. I was so glad to be out of the nightmare that I couldn't yet remember what I had been upset about. "Have a seat, if you can find one. What did Papa say?"

Randy sat down next to me on the bed. "Well, uh, he wanted me to see if you were okay. He said he was afraid that he would just upset you more, and he didn't want you to have to wait for your brother to get home."

"Well, I am okay," I said, sitting down. "How are *you?* I thought Theophilus was going to kill us both."

"I half wish he would." Randy shook his head. "Kill me, I mean. At least they'd give him some brig time and I wouldn't have to be afraid of him anymore."

"I see what you mean, pos-def. Did Papa say anything after I left?"

"I wanted to go after you but he said you probably needed time by yourself I thought that was a pretty weird idea, but he's the shrink, so . . ." Randy shrugged again. "Anyway, I'm glad you're okay."

"Did he say anything else?"

"Not about you, exactly." He looked down at the floor and that was the first time I realized that he was shy. "He—um, I guess you know I see Dr. James once a week about some problems I have." He made himself look me in the eye. "I guess everyone knows."

I nodded. "I still like you."

Randy turned two shades redder and I was afraid he was going to cry, but then he smiled this big, beautiful smile—I'd never seen him do that before—and even laughed a little. "Thank you! I'm always afraid people won't like me. Like anything they knew about me would be one more thing to hate me for." He was looking down again. "It's lim weird, Melpomene. It used to be people hated me for being the class bully, and at least I could understand that. Now I'm not much of a bully anymore, and they hate me even more."

"I don't hate you," I said. "As far as I'm concerned, you're real koapy. And I don't think very many other people really hate you either.

It's more like Theophilus has invented this new game and everyone wants to play."

He sighed. "Maybe."

I couldn't think of anything more to say, and he looked so tense that I was afraid if I touched him he'd jump head-first into the ceiling. I sat there for several long breaths, just watching him.

On the other hand, this silence was worse than anything I could possibly say. "You were talking about Dr. James," I said.

"Yeah."

"Are you happy to be changing doctors?"

"Yeah. I don't always get along with Dr. James." He shrugged again. "It might be because he's pompous lim bokkup and cryo besides. Just for example. But your father—he's pretty koapy, I think, I mean just from meeting him this once, so I asked if I could be his patient instead of Dr. James's."

"That's great," I said. I meant it, because I knew Papa was supposed to be very good, but at the same time it made me remember what I had been angry about. "When are your appointments?"

"Mondays after school. He said if it was okay with you, I could come home from school with you, then he'd see me, and then I would come to dinner with your family?" Randy made it a question, and I could tell he was ready to back out if he thought the idea annoyed me at all.

"Pos-def it's okay," I said. My stomach rumbled, and I remembered. "Speaking of it, have you had dinner?"

"No, I spent a long time talking with your father. He said he didn't want to impose himself on you for a while. I think he and your mother were going somewhere together."

"Well, let's practice for Monday, then," I said. "Let's eat together, maybe some cafeteria where nobody knows us so we can talk about this."

"Pos-def." He got up, grabbing his werpsack, and I got mine from the bin.

We decided to go to the cybertao cafeteria out on the Mushroom, Randy because he'd never done ceremonies and me because I was hoping doing this could get me out of CT on the weekend. Papa and Mother weren't especially strict but I usually found myself at Copy Transference most Sundays, bored and annoyed. Maybe if I bought the guilt off now, I could sleep in on Sunday.

It was fairly far—about as far as back to school—so we caught the omnivator together. When the high grav hit us, down in the outer edge of the Mushroom, I found out how tired I really was, trudging limp and hungry down the hall to the cafeteria. I looked at Randy, and if anything he looked worse.

To my surprise, the attendant at the cybertao cafeteria was Bert van Piet, Sylvestrina's father. Usually the attendant doesn't have much to do, since everything is automated, so after we sat down and ordered meals, he came over to talk with us. "Good to see you here."

"Just wanted to try something new," I said noncommittally. Miriam and I had hung around with Sylvestrina quite a bit when we were younger, but I hadn't really gotten to know her father.

He nodded and smiled. There was something just a bit weird about it, and I was suddenly glad that this was a public place and that Randy was here, even though I wasn't sure why. "Have you done Ceremonies before?" he asked.

"Only on the wire—I'm afraid I don't have them memorized. Is that all right?" I knew it was, but I might as well get authority to confirm it and make Randy comfortable.

"Oh, yes, of course. I take it you liked the Ceremonies or you wouldn't have come back."

"They're very soothing," I said. It was the most neutral, bland remark I could think of.

"You'll find they're even better once you have them from memory." Obviously he was no better at taking hints than his daughter was. He said it with this big, beaming warmth that looked sort of like Earth politicians on the vid, or come to think of it like Dr. James. Turning to Randy, he asked, "You're Randy Schwartz, aren't you?"

"Yes, sir."

"Silly talks a lot about how much help you give her with her math. We really appreciate that." He had switched to beaming at Randy now.

Silly. And I thought Mother calling me "Melly" was bad. I guess there's always someone worse off. . . .

"She's really pretty good, just lacking some confidence," Randy said. He was lying. She's dumb as a rock and lazy besides. But I guess Randy wasn't going to tell her father that.

I had missed something Mr. van Piet had said. Randy was explaining, "Well, um, actually, Dad is Ecucatholic, kind of, but we don't go to church much."

"Well, if you enjoy yourself this evening, be sure to come back and try it again. And if you do have any questions—"

"I'll be sure to ask." Randy looked at me a little strangely. I realized that he was probably wondering if I had lured him down here to be converted; you don't get many people like Mr. van Piet up here, but there are some everywhere. (Papa says Earth is infested with them.) So maybe Randy thought I was another one. This was getting embarrassing.

Mr. van Piet talked to both of us about trivia for a little longer, then went off to bother someone else. "Sorry about that," I said. "I wasn't really thinking. I should have realized they'd have a Pathmaker in here to try to save us heathens."

"I thought you *were* cybertao."

"Not enough for people like him."

Randy made a strange, sour face. "Maybe this is why Sylvestrina is so quiet. Probably her parents want her to try to make converts, and she's too nice a person to do it, so she just doesn't say anything."

The thought hadn't occurred to me, but it explained a lot. "I guess you never really know what goes on in someone else's family. Dinner will get here soon; if we're going to do Ceremonies, we should start."

"You're the expert here."

That made me laugh. "Just remember this is the infidel leading the heathen." I pulled the earpiece up from under the table. "Pull this out, put it in your ear, and do what it tells you to." I stuck mine in.

He pulled his earpiece up, looked at it curiously for a moment, and put it in. I touched the cue spot. "Tell your companion you are happy to share a meal with him," the voice in my ear said.

"I'm really glad we're eating together," I said. "I hate eating by myself."

Randy listened to his earpiece for a moment, then said, "I'm glad too. It's a real treat to have somebody to talk to."

My earpiece said, "Tell your companion something you like about him."

"I like the way you smile," I said.

He turned purple, but after listening to his earphone he managed to say he thought I was a genius at CSL. It was kind of cute.

It went on like that; the First Ceremony, which a lot of people memorize, is a directed conversation about how much you like each other. Papa says that's what really converted him to cybertao.

At the end of the First Ceremony, the cart rolled up and we took our food. I was surprised at how heavy the trays felt until I remembered the grav was almost .5 here, ten times what it was in the cafeteria where I usually ate dinner. You get used to the idea that breakfast and dinner won't weigh much but lunch will be heavy, and this kind of put everything off rhythm.

"Second Ceremony now," I told Randy, "while we wait for this stuff to cool. Then we eat and talk, and we do Third Ceremony before we get up from the table." We put our earpieces back in.

Second Ceremony is an individual experience, and it's always done on the wire. The machine directs you in a Random Appreciation of Circumstance, which is the official language for sitting there thinking about how the food got to the table, how many people worked in the process, how much the plants and animals and you had to evolve to make this particular meal a possible event, and so forth. "Try to see the wheat in the pasta," or "Remember somehow the table had to get there," or "Consider protein compatibility," are the kinds of things it throws at you, about thirty seconds apart, usually five of them.

I always want to ask what questions other people get, like after a test in school, but that's a Minor Discordance and you aren't supposed to do it. I just hoped Randy wouldn't ask me, because if he did I'd never be able to resist trading information.

He didn't ask, though, so I had no opening as we picked up forks and ate. "It's different, but I like it," Randy said.

"The Ceremonies?"

"Yeah. We 'say grace.' "

"Like in the old flatscreen movies?"

"Yeah."

We went back to eating. I'd never been so hungry. There's nothing like a brawl, an emotional crisis, and a late dinner to boost your appetite.

Finally, Randy said, "Um—Melpomene . . . I guess I ought to talk with you sooner or later about one thing. Your father says you got really upset after he told you about the social engineering for the *Flying Dutchman*. . . ."

I nodded, too unsure of myself to speak. He sat still for a couple of long breaths before saying, softly, "That happened to me, too, but I didn't have anyone to talk to about it."

"Really?"

He nodded, but then there didn't seem to be anything more to say. He made a thorough scrape of his tray for the last of the gravy.

I ate my last couple of bites, and said, "Are you caught up on your homework?"

He looked startled, smiled crookedly, and said "That wasn't exactly what I was expecting you to say."

"I thought maybe we could go do something together where we could talk. It is Friday night, you know. We could get a room for rec someplace."

"Yeah, I'd like that. Sixwall?"

"Pos-def." Sixwall is a speed and coordination game, where his being a big guy wasn't going to matter so much.

We talked a little about schoolwork, did the Third Ceremony, and said a quick goodbye to Mr. van Piet. I was really afraid I would end up promising to make it to CT and thus blow the whole point of coming here.

With food in we weren't as tired as we had been, and back in the Main Body we played sixwall for more than two hours (it was Friday, so curfew was late), mostly without talking. We were fairly evenly matched, and it was good to just concentrate on playing, and to have someone there who was making sense—a lot of my old friends hadn't lately.

He had won the last two games. I was getting tired, and it was late. I asked, "Do you want to play more, or is it time to talk?"

"Let's talk." He pulled himself over to a strap. "What was it like when your father told you about it?"

I told. him everything, just letting it spill out, about talking with Papa, starting with Tom because that seemed to fit in too. Every so often he stopped to ask me, in detail, what Papa had said or how he had reacted.

It felt so good to just talk about it and have someone understand me. Sometimes while I talked, I cried; sometimes we laughed about something together—I don't remember about what. Finally I wound down, drained and tired, but feeling less alone than I had in days.

He said, "This is going to sound really bokky."

"If it does, Randy, you're forgiven." I moved over and sat next to him against the wall, almost touching. He didn't move away, but he didn't put the arm I'd been hoping for around me either. He rubbed his face with his hands. "Okay. Here goes. I know this sounds dumb, but I wish somebody like your father had told me. Dr. James just told me flat out in the last two minutes of one appointment. He practically shoved me out the door."

"That's terrible."

"Pos-def. 'Oh, by the way, everything you think and feel is part of the conditioning that NAC designed to make you a good employee. See you next week." He shrugged. "Pretty much the same way he does everything. I keep wondering if he's planning to transfer out or some- thing. That's why I'm so glad I'll be your father's patient."

"He didn't do *me* any good. I hurt too."

"Yeah." He nodded once, slowly, looking down at the floor. "I know you do." That was such a stupid thing to say.

"He's a lot better with other people than he is with his own family."

He folded his arms around himself, closing up tightly. "A lot of people are."

"It's not really all that wonderful to get told something like that by your own family, either, you know!" 'I took off my gloves and kneepads with awkward, fumbling fingers and rammed them into my werpsack.

"I'm sorry."

"You should be."

He stripped off his gear, wadding it up, dropping it carelessly into his werpsack. And we had only half talked—he hadn't really gotten to talk at all. I had really done it this time, absolutely lim bokked.

He closed the werpsack and said, "I'm really sorry I upset you. I'll try not to bother you again."

There was a tear trickling out of his eye. Two people had ever made him cry as far as I knew—Theophilus and me. I felt so stupid. "I'm sorry too." It seemed about the only thing to say. "And you don't bother me at all. I like you. I just lost my temper, and got upset, okay? I still want to be friends."

His head dropped, but he said "Yeah, pos-def." He looked at me sideways over his shoulder. "I'm sorry," he said again.

"About what?"

"Um, I just am, I guess, that you got upset."

I was bokking, but I wasn't the only one. "You're upset too," I pointed out. "Can we stop apologizing?"

"Maybe *you* can." Randy sighed. "Barry used to say I apologized for everything . . ."

"He was right. Let's talk about something else, though—anything else."

"Pos-def." So of course we stood there with nothing to say to each other. Miriam had been telling me this always happened with boys and I hadn't believed her.

Finally I thought of something I *had* wanted to say. "Randy?"

"Present, ma'am."

"Cute. Uh. What are we going to do about all this?" Randy looked

very startled and embarrassed. It's only now, writing this more than a
year later, that I realize what he must have thought—and now *I'm*
embarrassed.

I did figure out that he didn't know what I was talking about, so I
said, "This whole social engineering thing."

I'm trying to remember now whether he looked relieved or disappointed. Probably it was both.

"I don't know what we could do," he said, sitting back down. "I
figured we were just talking about how to live with the idea."

"Well, I'm curious, anyway. I want to know how much they actually hardwired me. Do I *have* any feelings of my own? And there's a
bunch of stuff I can't believe they could design, like I don't see why
you would design people to be lazy or rude, but some people sure are."

Randy shook his head. "I've been wondering about all those times
I got lim weirdwired and started beating on people because I was jealous of them for something. Was I just doing what the CPB wanted me
to do? Did they want those kids beaten up? Then why do *I* have to feel
guilty for it? Or if they wanted me to have the experience of being a
bully, why did the other kids have to get beaten up?"

I took a deep breath; I'd had an idea, and if Randy went along with
it I was ready to think it might be a good one. "That's exactly the kind
of thing I wonder about. And the other thing is, I don't see how they
can ever try to do it down to fine structure. Maybe they just did something like set up the Three Laws of Robotics in us, or something—
remember those old stories?"

"Yeah. 'An employee cannot harm NAC or through inaction allow
NAC to come to harm.' And so forth. But—I just realized. What makes
a bunch of groundhogs think they know every situation that can possibly come up? What if someday we all need to be able to leave the ship
or something?"

I stared at him, my clever idea gone completely. "You're right. If
they've limited the options, sometime in the future that could put the
Flying Dutchman in danger." It was almost too horrible to think about.

"And now all of a sudden it's not working," Randy said. "Your
father told us so." He kicked upwards to the ceiling, flipped over,
pushed back down, and bounced between ceiling and floor. If I'd
known before that he was a ponger—

Another flag from the werp. All right. Ponging is the same thing as
the "pacing" I've seen people do in Earth plays and films, but adapted
to low g. It's a way to burn off energy when you're thinking hard. A lot
of people do it.

On the other hand, a lot of people get driven crazy by it. "Will you please stop that!"

Sheepishly, he caught a loop and pulled himself to the ceiling. "Sorry, I do that when—"

"When you think. I know. Mim does the same thing." I sighed. "Sorry I snapped at you. I'm a little edgy myself." My idea began to come back to me, but I wasn't sure I wanted to involve Randy in it. "Do you have any ideas, anything we *can* do?"

"No. I just know we need to do something." He shook his head. "I'm sorry."

Randy looked so guilty, and for nothing, that I couldn't help laughing.

"What?!" He glared at me.

"You! If the sun went nova and cooked us all, you'd apologize."

"Well . . ." he looked like he was getting angry, then like he was going to apologize. "Well, um—somebody should."

That was so silly we both laughed, and I felt a million times better. I was about to tell him my idea when the speaker came on. "Attention Melpomene Alice Murray and Randomly Distributed Schwartz. Estimates show you need to check out of the six-walled handball room and begin return trips to your living units within fifteen minutes."

"Acknowledged," we said in unison, and turned to finish packing our werpsacks.

"Tomorrow's Saturday," Randy said. "And next week is languages."

"Yeah." There we were again, standing there without anything to say. "What do you do on weekends?" I asked him, for lack of anything better to ask, and then I realized how perfect my idea was.

"Usually I study," he said. "Barry and I used to get together for glideboarding sometimes, but . . . you know . . ."

He sounded so sad, and there wasn't really time to explain, so I said, "If your studies are caught up enough, do you want to get together for some time tomorrow? I think I have an idea about how we could do something about the problem, and I really only need Sunday to get ready for next week."

"Well—I want to get in a lot of practice on Japanese—"

"I can always use some too. Maybe we could just speak it for a lot of the day?"

"That would help, but I really need to work through the readings." Then he made that strange face again, like he was laughing at himself and not enjoying it. "This is really silly. I'm dying to spend the day with you. I'll find some study time somewhere this weekend. Let's spend Saturday together, and you can tell me all about your idea."

"Better than that, we can actually get started. Let's just meet after breakfast and—oh, no."

"What's the matter?"

"I really have to go to Outside Club tomorrow morning. My brother Tom is toggle racing. It's for the Juniors All-Ship Championship."

Randy gave me an even bigger grin. "That's what I was going to suggest. I've been dying to meet him."

"You follow toggle? Do you do it?"

"I'm no good at it," he said, "but I love to watch. I've seen your brother a lot. He's terrific."

"I think so too." We stood there stupidly.

"Well, then, it's settled," I added after a long pause.

We stood there some more, until Randy said "Yeah. Meet you at the Block A Commons, 0900?"

"That will be fine."

"See you then."

Another very long pause. Then, quite abruptly, he kissed me on the cheek.

I was really startled, and he started to back away, so I hugged him. He hugged back.

It would have been even better if we hadn't both been too embarrassed to look at each other or say anything. Finally the loudspeaker broke in. "Attention Melpomene Alice Murray and Randomly Distributed Schwartz. Estimates show you need to check out of the six-walled handball room and begin return trips to your living units within five minutes."

We let go of each other, both of us smiling and flushed and looking at everything except each other. "Randomly Distributed?" I asked.

"Dad said sooner or later he was bound to lose a paternity suit, and more likely than not it would be to an unfit mother." He seemed to be very serious.

"I think Randy is a really nice name." And that was how I got kissed on the mouth for the first time.

December 23, 2025

Today is bizarre.

I've never missed school before.

When I finished writing I had only left myself three hours to sleep. I really did try to get up—crawled almost to the dressing corner before falling asleep again, and now that I'm finally awake, there's less than an hour left in the school day. Bokky thing to do—close to FA exam.

I guess I'll call the postings board, get the assignments, get them done, back to bed. Really wrung out.

Wish I could just sit down and get back to work on this, feels like it's too important not to finish first, but I'm not thinking lim clear just now; might do same thing again, miss two days.

Writing about yourself is addictive. I hope all you kids notice that. If you feel like autobiography, try heroin. Lots safer and easier to control . . .

Schoolwork. And a night's sleep. Then we'll see if I go on. Might be a while.

SEVEN

January 2, 2026

Well, it's been ten days for me, but I don't suppose it seems like much to you. I've been re-reading all this and it seems like I haven't told you a tenth of what happened, at least not of the important things. And sometimes I've gotten way off the subject. I mean, getting kissed by Randy was my first and all but it happens to a lot of people and it doesn't have much to do with what I was going to try to tell you about.

I guess I started to recognize the problem when I was talking with Dr. Lovell yesterday. She always struck me as 100% cryo, efficient and so on, maybe someone you'd turn to in an emergency but never for sympathy. Yet there I was, sitting in her office, voluntarily putting up with half-gee grav for half an hour after school just so I could talk to her.

"I feel like if I write more I'll say too much."

"There's always that chance. And you might say it wrong." She leaned forward, looking into my eyes with a sad little half smile.

That wasn't exactly the reassurance I had wanted. I looked at her window; like Papa, she left it always tuned to Outside whether there was anything interesting or not.

Today it was just a black field of stars. "I guess I need some idea about how important this is really supposed to be," I said. "I mean, you asked me to keep writing. Is this therapy, or does the whole future of the *Flying Dutchman* depend on it, or what?"

Her smile widened. "Easy question. Somewhere between."

I wasn't in the mood to be teased and said so. She apologized, but there didn't seem to be anything to say afterwards, so I got away politely and went home.

Tom wasn't in yet but Susan was. That was okay. Usually, if not exactly a source of unending joy, living with Susan is okay. We accept each other and sometimes we even like each other. Later in this I might mention some of the stuff that happened between us in the last year.

She was sitting in the sharespace, in what had been Mother's usual corner, finishing up some report or other on her werp. She's really very talented at what she does—internal logistics architecture—and I guess they think a lot of her in her office. Susan doesn't talk about her work except when I ask, and then only for a minute or so.

She finished an entry, looked up, and said, "Hello, Melpomene."

"Hi. Anything exciting happen in your day?"

She yawned and stretched. "I talked them out of two traffic corridors that they were going to put in. Too much logs of structural strength for too little cargo handling."

"That sounds big to me." I sat down, dropping my werpsack beside me.

She smiled and shrugged. "Yes and no. Remember, the *Flying Dutchman* won't be finished until 2059—and then it probably won't be running at full capacity till 2120 or so. And problems like the ones I solved today won't show up significantly except across several orbits at full capacity. So it's 120 years till what I did today will have any measurable positive effect."

"With what they're finding out about life expectancy enhancement from low grav," I pointed out, "we'll probably both still be alive. I'll buy you dinner."

She winked at me. "I'll hold you to that. All the same, I can't get rotated soon enough, even though my next job is really just the opposite of this one—proposing new structures for my old team to shoot down. Kind of like getting paid to be in Debate Club." She sighed. "And now I'm whining and complaining again. That drives you crazy, doesn't it?"

I know a cue when I hear one. "I like you, anyway."

She got that silly glow she always gets when I say something like that, even if she has to fish for it. It must be awful to need to hear all that reassurance all the time—and to be so shy that you blush when you do get it.

"There were several months last year when you didn't complain at all, and you certainly had a right to," I added. I'm never sure whether I say these things because they are true and I need to remember what a good person Susan is really, or because I know they make her squirm and I enjoy that. Probably both.

For once, she just accepted it and changed the subject. "How's the book going?"

"Not that well. Or too well. It's chewing up a lot of time for something that's not that important."

"It's *not* important?" She sat up straight and looked at me with this lim intensity.

"Well, no. I've got FA exams coming up in fifty-three days." I couldn't believe she could forget that. She could be so dumb sometimes. "That's what I have to focus on," I added, in case she still couldn't see the connection.

She bit her lip, hard enough that mine hurt watching her, and said, "I'm trying not to annoy you."

Oh, god, why did Tom have to have a sensitive kid like her for a lover and a bokkup like me for a sister? "You're not annoying me—I'm just getting annoyed. Much too easily, too. It's the damned FA, I worry about it all the time, but that's not your fault and I'm sorry." By now I was sitting facing her, holding her hands in mine.

We always end up like this, lately, trying to talk around the awkward problem that we both love my brother but we can't talk without drawing blood.

Susan nodded a couple of times, being a good sport because I was trying, I guess. "Melpomene, look, all I meant to say was—listen to me, because I don't always get these things right and I want you to get what I *mean*—when I see you working on that book, you concentrate harder than anyone I've seen, except Tom when he's doing a spatial, maybe. I guess I don't know really if it's that important, but I can certainly tell you feel that way."

I hugged her. "You just said exactly the right thing."

"I *did?*"

"Yeah. Don't let it go to your head." I even kissed her cheek. "And I think I'm going to go work on the book. I've got fifty minutes till Randy meets me at the cafeteria."

"I hope it goes well." She really meant it.

Okay, it shouldn't have been such a big deal to me, but it was. Besides, whose book is this anyway? I felt like telling you about all this stuff, so I did. And Randy is late as usual, so I'll get back to the real story I'm working on now.

Breakfast the next morning—I'm back to telling you about last year again—was amusing, if you're the kind of person who's amused by slow torture. As always, Mother started it. "Are your friends having breakfast together today, Melly? Would you rather have gone with them?"

"I'm meeting a friend after breakfast—we're going to go to Outside Club and then study together. And I thought it was 'important for a real family to eat together.' " Okay, I was being lim snotty . . . but on her part, she was really pulling out all the stops on her deeply-concerned-mother routine.

Papa started another one of his jokes and it died, like they do ninety percent of the time, so all of us were off to a jolly start.

There was a long pause while we all just shoved food into our mouths, but that was too good to last. "Tom, you're barely eating," Mother said. "Is something wrong?"

"The less I eat now, the less I'll spew onto my faceplate in three hours," Tom said, talking with his mouth full.

"Tom!"

He shrugged. "It's true. And don't tell me I'm spoiling your appetite. You brought it up."

"You are, but I'm less concerned about that than I am about your hostility," Mother said primly. She was getting just what she wanted. "I'm honestly worried about you. You don't eat, you pay so much attention to sports and the Alien Artifacts . . ."

Tom dropped me the slow wink that we've always used to say "Watch this—and back me up if I need it," and looked Mother straight in the eyes without smirking. "It's Art, Mother." You could hear the capital. "It's just going to take a while for you to learn to appreciate it."

Mother was so quiet that at first I thought he had actually stumbled on the magic formula to shut her up.

Finally she sighed. "I suppose you could be right. It *is* in the family. . . ."

And she was off into telling us about her dead kid brother James. James was a poet, which may or may not have involved writing any poetry. He was constantly lonesome and depressed and had no friends. I could easily see why—he made fun of the athletes (I guess in Earth schools only a very small fraction of the students are allowed to play sports, and those kids aren't allowed to study, or something like that—it sounded so stupid I could never make myself listen), and the athletes beat him up. He fell in love with girls who didn't know him at all, and they rejected him. He hung around with the brainy kids, but he annoyed them so much they got rid of him too. (Since according to Mother he refused to learn anything about anything except poetry, I can see why, again.) I'm really not sure that any of that had anything to do with poetry, but Mother seemed to think it did.

It sounded to me like a classic profile of an unco, but of course on

Earth it's not a criminal offense so people can't be given the therapy they need. In that way I guess it was kind of sad about James—up here they'd have treated him, and he'd probably have been fine.

Anyway, James wrote a lot of things, all very short, in which he talked about being an isolated screaming X in a vast indifferent Y. Like X=pebble, Y=beach; X=tree, Y=desert; X=iceberg, Y=ocean. You get the idea. I know those Xs don't really scream, but Mother says that's part of the point.

In every photo of James I have ever seen, he seems to be wearing the clothes of about a decade before, say of 1985 or so, in gray or black.

Anyway, he was twenty-six when he got mutAIDS and died. It was after the main Die-Off and the Eurowar, so maybe around 2005 or 2006, as if he couldn't bring himself to go with anyone else in any normal way. Probably about seven or eight years before I was born, I'm not really sure.

I think, but I'm not sure, that what my mother was trying to say was that since she had been the only one who understood James's poetry, if there were anything to understand about the Alien Artifacts, she would really have understood it.

Tom got more and more quiet as this went on; Mother seemed encouraged by that. She elaborated on all the ways he was different from James. Apparently the major one was that Tom wasn't "sensitive." Since surely she knew Tom as well as I did, she couldn't have meant any of the normal meanings of that word, but as far as I can tell, she was using it to mean "clumsy and a bad loser," since the reason Tom wasn't sensitive was that he liked sports.

Several times Papa tried to get her going on some other dead person we were related to besides James, but without success. As far as I was concerned, they were all dead groundhogs. What was there to talk about?

Finally, finally, finally, breakfast was really over and we'd had enough home and family values for the day. I'd eaten about half my meal, Tom even less. Papa sort of steered Mother out of the cafeteria to something he said she'd be interested in, mentioning that they would catch Tom's race on the vid.

Tom went down through the Main Body toward the Men's Suit Room. It was still half an hour before I was due to meet with Randy, and it was sort of on my way, so I went along for company.

The corridors were deserted—no more than half a dozen people in sight. Tom hauled along ahead of me, without looking back.

Finally I asked, "Um, Tom—are the uh, Alien Artifacts *really* art, or did you just say that to hassle Mother?"

"They have to be art, Melpomene. Remember the First Law of Anthropology—if they're doing something you don't understand, it's either an isolated lunatic, a religious ritual, or art. I'm not religious and since I'm the Great Cornelius Murray's son I can't be crazy, so it must be art." His voice was so harsh and so bitter that I thought of just turning and going, but it seemed like everyone was letting Tom down lately, so I couldn't.

Keeping my voice as even as I could, I asked, "Are you worried about the race?"

He squeaked out, "Kind of."

I put an arm around him, and he turned to hug me. We dropped a long way down that corridor before we realized neither of us was hanging on. Luckily we hit feet first and it was only about fifty meters of drop on a low grav day, so it was less than what you'd feel jumping off a chair on Earth. Still, it was a jar, enough to get us out of it.

As he leaned back, he was smiling a little. "I feel better. I'm glad that wasn't our heads. I think we missed our turnoff."

We hauled back up; when we had taken the turn we meant to, he said, "Susan will be watching. She made me promise that if I win, I'll show her the gadget I showed you—how it works and so forth."

He paused. "I've made a lot of changes and improvements and really learned how to use it," he added defensively.

"Has she ever seen any of your other things?"

"All of them." He hauled on ahead of me. I sped up to catch him, since the entry to the Men's Suit Room would be coming up soon. "Tom."

"What?" He looked back at me. "Do I have to spell it all out? She liked some of the other stuff—she even talks like she understands some of the things I'm trying to do, trying to say. She's the only one who ever did. And this one is the most important one. So, yes, I'm nervous and I'm a little tense. There's a lot riding on this race."

"It will be good work," I said, "whether or not you win the race. You'll see, and so will she."

He didn't speak for a long time, then, just hung there by his hands and feet from the netting, upside down, a few meters from where I sat on the floor of the corridor. "I'm serious," he said at last. "What if Susan doesn't like it?"

"She's going to love it. Then she's going to explain it to me, and

I'll love it. Really. Now go win the race so you won't have an excuse to put this off any longer."

He gulped, nodded, and hauled away to the Men's Suit Room.

As I headed back up to meet Randy, I found myself thinking that, half an hour after breakfast, it had already been a long day.

Randy was waiting for me at the Block A Commons, a little early but so was I. I suddenly realized we hadn't planned to do anything other than watch Tom race, and we wouldn't have to suit up for that for at least an hour.

Well, based on the experience of the night before, maybe we could stand around awkwardly and stammer. In fact, that was almost certainly what we would do.

As I approached him, weaving my way between tables of chess players and kids studying together, watching out for little kids flipping through the air, I realized he hadn't seen me yet. He was doing about as much ponging as you can get away with in public, bouncing in a little triangle in one corner, rising up half a meter to bump his back on the wall, then turning his back against the other wall, then sinking to the floor; from floor to wall to wall, to floor to wall to wall—after watching him through a few cycles from a few meters away, I was getting dizzy.

He was either thinking really hard or he was really nervous.

I bounced over and said hello. He hit the ceiling. Nervous, I guessed.

"Ouch," he said, rubbing his head as he came back down. "I must have been drifting—you really startled me."

"Let me take a look at your head."

"I'm okay. Koapy. Really."

"How can you tell? Can you see the top of your head?"

He bent down and let me look. There was a red spot showing through the thin fuzz of red-blond hair. "Here?"

"Ow! Don't touch!"

"Must be. Looks like just a bruise—no broken skin and you won't get a bump. Thanks for letting me check, though—otherwise I'd worry about you."

Randy touched the bruise gingerly. "And to think I always wondered what it would be like to have a mother."

"You can have mine if you like. But I warn you I'm not taking her back." It came out much more seriously than I intended it to—all of a sudden we were staring into each other's eyes, and now *he* looked worried.

So we sat down and he heard all about my troubles, and Tom's troubles, with Mother. He listened the way he always did, with his full attention, and somehow after enough of that, although Randy didn't say anything much at all, I began to feel a little silly about all my fighting with Mother.

After a long time I sighed, wiped my eyes, and decided to stop feeling sorry for myself. "Well, now that we're all done with emotional first aid, I guess we should go suit up."

"Yeah." He got up, and without either of us quite intending it— well, I didn't and I don't think he did—he took my hand and held it. I was very proud of not hitting the ceiling myself.

I hoped no one would see us.

I hoped everyone would see us.

Especially Miriam, so she could see what it was like with a *nice* guy.

As we went down to the locker rooms together, I remembered. "I never did tell you my idea, Randy. And it's the kind of thing I think we could talk about better off-radio Outside."

He looked a little puzzled, but he said okay.

I knew I was getting paranoid, and I kept telling myself that, as I suited up and went through medcheck. But I had no idea how the CPB or Security would look at what I had in mind, and if they didn't approve we could both be in real trouble. So with so many cameras and microphones around, it just seemed wiser.

As always, the race started late because some of the racers had to be walked through the toggle course extra times. Tom says that's what a toggle racer does when he's losing his nerve but it's too late to back out.

The course is always a zigzag circumnavigation of the Main Body, and it's always nine kilometers, but they change it every time, so it can always be used as an excuse to add more toggle stations to the Outside. I suppose that's a demonstration of how bokky people are—instead of just saying that the people who work Outside can always use more toggle stations, they justify it by recreation.

In the race itself, everyone has a series of stripe-coded toggle lines, and they toggle their way around—

The werp just pointed out that you don't do toggling on Earth.

Well, okay. Toggling is the basic man-powered way of moving around on the surface of the Main Body. A toggle station is a collection of extruded steel poles about five centimeters in diameter, each with a ring on top, about as big around as your fist and as thick as your thumb. A toggle is a simple locking clip that fits over the ring, and a toggle line is a spun monomyl cable with a toggle at each end.

To toggle from station to station, you pick a cable that runs between the two stations. You take the toggle off the ring and clip it to your chest harness; then you clip the replacement cable from your backpack to the ring, and make sure the line is running free so you won't yoyo backwards. (Yoyoing's not a problem for racers, because they don't have to run replacement lines.)

Then you jump straight up and wind in the cable to pull yourself toward your destination station, wrapping the cable onto the lugs on your chest harness and slowly pulling yourself down onto your destination station. When your magnetic boots grab surface at the other end, you flip down the lugs, put the wound-up cable onto your back harness, take the replacement cable off your backpack and toggle it to an empty ring, and there you are. If you need to make multiple jumps to get somewhere, you just keep repeating the process.

Toggle racers have a pre-laid set of cables, one set per racer, forming a nine-km course around the Main Body. Some of the legs are long, some short, because those pose different problems. The objective is to get through all your toggle stations and back to the one you started from first.

There were about fifty spectators today on the surface tram, plus I suppose a couple of hundred others on the vid like my parents. When you see it on the tram, you watch the takeoff, then ride around to some station roughly in the middle of the course, and finally ride back to the starting point to watch them all come in.

While you ride between points, you can either watch the monitors to see the rest of the race, or you can just look out into space, which—sorry Tom!—is what I usually do.

As I came out of the lock, I saw Susan already standing by the tram, boots clinging to the rail, and waved to her. She stood still for a long second, then waved back enthusiastically. I guess she was surprised that I had paid any attention at all to her; well, if being nice to her was what it would take to make Tom happy, I'd be so nice it would choke her.

She jumped over—down, really since the tram is above the lock—with a neat flex of one ankle, the safety line to the tram shaking out behind her, and said "How was he this morning?"

"Jumpy as a fat rabbit before Celebration Feast. How was he last night?"

"Completely impossible." You can't really see faces through the faceplate very well, but I could imagine the face she was making. "Do *you* know what it is he's going to show me if he wins?"

There was an unidentified snicker on the com. Silently, I held up my private link cable; Susan took it and attached it to hers. I tongued from open freke to private link. "Test?"

"Check. Don't you *hate* it when people listen in?"

"Yeah. I suppose someone would get all worked up about it, though, if we cut his air line or pushed him off and let him walk to Mars."

"That's morbid," she said. It was also from that bokky Earth vid show, *Pirates of the Asteroids,* but I guess she hadn't seen it. "But it's an idea. Anyway, what *is* this big secret of Tom's?"

"It's hard to describe." I hedged because I really didn't know what would be the best thing to say, but that embarrassed me because we were trying to be friends and I thought I should trust her. "It's not like anything he's ever done before, and I don't understand it very well myself, so I don't want to bias you."

She nodded. "But did you *like* anything about it?"

"Oh, pos-def. A lot. But I didn't really know what it was that I was liking." It was an exaggeration, except for the last part, but with a little luck it would be what she had wanted to hear.

She bought my answer, anyway, so I was off that hook. "I just want to make sure *I* like it at first glance."

"Tom said you like a lot of this stuff."

"I do," Susan said. "But this is different. He's got an awful lot wrapped up in this whatever-it-is. And he's decided that how I react is the same as whether it's good or not. So I've *got* to love it. I just thought if you could tell me something about it, I could get myself pre-set. Because he's *got* to stay with it."

"He does?" I said, startled, not just by what she had said, but by the way she was holding both my hands, facing me, and by my realization that I really knew nothing of her beyond my vague impression that she was quiet, always hanging onto Tom, adding nothing, *boring*—and as I saw her now, glad that my suit gloves kept her from crushing my hands, she was someone else entirely. "I know it matters to him," I added, stammering, "but I don't see—"

"I can't explain it. I just feel it. He's doing something we all need, even if we never understand it." She shuddered with frustration. "Shit, if I could explain it, everyone already *would* understand."

So I hugged her. That's very awkward in a suit, but I had absolutely nothing to say otherwise. I'd probably never get to like her but for Tom's sake I was going to love her if it killed me.

There wasn't much to say after that, so we both agreed, in this lim bokked half-conversation that I can't even begin to re-create (it sounded like neither of us had exactly learned to talk yet), that we both hoped he won and we both wanted him to do well. Then we unclipped, tongued back to radio, and got on the tram.

By now almost everyone was on. I felt guilty, as I looked for Randy, that I didn't know what his suit looked like. Most of us have all kinds of patches and markers, especially if we're in Outside Club, and then we do custom coloring, so that the total effect is this patchwork map all over your body.

It's as distinctive as a face, so you can identify people Outside as easily as you can when they're sitting across the table from you.

That is, you can if you know what they look like. And I had no idea what Randy looked like.

Fortunately, at first glance there were only four people Randy's size. I knew who two of them were, and thought vaguely I'd seen another one in the Women's Suit Room. The last one was a kid-sized Outside Crew uniform, vis-orange with no colors, just VWU Junior Auxiliary patches and black hashmarks for Outside experience. I knew, vaguely, that Randy's father did something on Outside Crew, and that was in the union. Besides, the kid in the vis-orange suit sat like Randy—all by himself.

I sat down next to him. "They've given them a really complex route," he said, "seventeen stations, but two legs more than a k long. It zags all over the place. One long leg is practically straight down."

"Hunh," I said. With lesser racers, that could be really dangerous. On a long downward toggle, if you didn't jump right, you could end up "trailing out," unable to wind in before the motion of the ship pulled you down into Main Engine exhaust—the purple glow that eddied and vibrated down below us, ions streaming out a shaved fraction below lightspeed. But this was a Championship, so they must have figured people could take care of themselves. "Tom should be fine, then—he likes drops."

"Yeah, he has that funny trick he works with yanking on the extended cable. I tried to copy that once and slammed up against the side."

"I can't do it either," I admitted. "He says it's all timing—which is like saying that playing piano is all in the fingers."

Tom's stunt—I had heard, with secret pride, some kids in my class calling it a "Murray takeoff"—was to leap straight back, stretching the cable taut, and then give a hard yank exactly along the line of the cable. If you did it right, you put yourself on a ballistic trajectory for a point close to your destination station. Then, if you wound cable in fast enough, you would again have a taut line when you were near your destination, and could wind in quickly. It was much faster than staying taut the whole way, and going down toward the engines it could be incredibly quick, almost a direct bound.

"The tram will be going out to Station Nine," Randy said, "which is right at the bottom of the longest drop. And the next leg is only two hundred meters, sideways, so we get to see all of that hop too."

Lots of other people were chattering on the com, too, and it was getting hard to hear each other, so we cabled up to talk privately.

The racers came out at last, stretching and bouncing around as they always do before takeoff, on the short tether from their starting rings.

A thought hit me, and I felt stupid again. "You know, Randy, the way you talk about it, you must have been following the whole toggle-racing season for the last fifteen weeks, but I've never noticed you out here."

"I hardly ever talk. I never had anyone to talk to."

"Oh." I didn't know what more to say; his voice had been so flat.

"I go Outside every chance I get. My dad teases me about it, calls me the Junior Space Ranger Five Star Cadet, whatever that means. I go anyway. Do you ever make the Wednesday night excursion?"

"I never have," I said, deciding right then that I would soon. "Isn't it just a tram ride around the Main Body?"

"Yeah." There was a warm enthusiasm in Randy's voice, like he had wanted to say this for a long time. "But they do it with no roof on the tram, and there are so few people, you can just strap onto the bench and look straight out from the ship the whole way. It's just— well, I don't know how to describe it. Koapy. You'll have to see it for yourself."

"Now that you've told me about it, I *will* have to," I said. "It sounds beautiful, but it must get pretty lonely."

"Actually that's part of the attraction."

"Um—well, anyway, if we're not both too loaded down with homework on Wednesday night, let's do it. I really want to." I hoped Randy wouldn't notice that I was sounding like a moron.

There was a soft chime in the earpieces. "Race begins in two minutes. Racers prepare for toggle check."

Mother always said Tom's suit looked like he'd stolen it from a poor family's scarecrow, though why anyone would own both a scarecrow and a space suit is beyond me. Anyway I knew what she meant. The whole surface had so many patches attached, and had been re-

colored so many times over the old patches, that except for two recent
ones—"Shift A Glee Club '24" and "Block A Commons Redecoration
4-2-24"—there couldn't have been five contiguous square centimeters
of the same color or patch. Tom preferred shimmery re-colorings and
shiny patches, so in the glare of Outside sunlight, the total effect was
iridescent.

The main opponent he'd have to worry about was the B Shift
Champion, Karol Kysmini. Karol was a big, strong guy who favored
heavy horizontal lines on his suit—he always looked like a piece of
heavy machinery to me—but B Shift had lost the spin, so the race
started four hours earlier than Karol would ordinarily have gotten up.
Furthermore, Karol wasn't very clever. Tom always said he must have
put a lot of time into perfecting his headstop.

C Shift had won the spin, and was competing in their early
evening hours, but their champion, Inga Blanc, was really just the best
of their weak field. She might have been a little stronger than Tom, and
she was surely smarter than Karol, but she wouldn't have made third
on the A or B Shift teams. Her suit was patched only from waist to
shoulder on her right side, with the rest re-colored silver-gray. She
wasn't much of a competitor, but she looked lim koapy.

I didn't know any of the other racers from B or C Shifts. The other.
A Shift racers were Tswana Carmen at second, a girl from Tom's class
who I thought had a good chance at second overall, and Levi Yang, one
of Barry's older brothers. "I wonder where Barry is," I said. "You'd
think with a racer in his family—"

"They hate each other," Randy said. "Levi is the Yang family
'good kid.' Except for him, none of the Yang kids spend any more time
in their living unit than they can help."

The opencast spoke again. "Racers to starting stations please."
There was a little flurry of motion, and the starting position lights
rolled over from red to yellow at each station.

"Racers signal ready please." Nine right arms went up. "Get set.
On green—go." The lights went green.

Tom and Tswana shot straight out seventy meters from the side of
the ship, snubbing at almost exactly the same distance. Their lines
snapped taut, they heaved, and they plunged toward the horizon of the
Main Body. In less than ten seconds their lines formed graceful curves
in the sunlight with darker dots at their tips. I clicked up my distance
lenses and looked at Tom. He was winding the loose cable in quickly
and steadily. He would probably only have to wind under tension for
the last twenty meters or so.

Meanwhile, Karol had bounded up only about thirty meters from the *Flying Dutchman*. He yanked hard, but it was obvious that he'd have to do more than half the trip on tension rather than ballistically.

Everyone else took off in the old diving style, leaping forward rather than back and winding under tension close to the surface. "Bokky, lim bokky," Randy noted. "Levi even knows how to do your brother's takeoff but he won't because his father said "You can jump further with your feet than your arms." Brains don't exactly run in that family—they sort of dribble slowly away."

I laughed, and then realized. "That's the same kind of joke that Theophilus and the Real Gang have been making," I said.

He made the "shot through the chest" gesture and admitted, "I've always *thought* things like that. I bet other people have too. We just never used to say them till Theophilus came up. Probably in a few months even the little kids will be doing it."

The tram started its slow crawl around the outside of the Main Body, gliding a few centimeters above the iron track so slowly and evenly that most of us only noticed we were moving by the slow motions of the stars. "Well, midpoint next," I said. "I always think coming in is more exciting than takeoff anyway."

"Yeah. More to see. Um—we're on private link and it will be a while. Do you have time to tell me about this plan of yours?"

I sighed. "I wish it were more than it is. I was just thinking that if there really is some kind of master plan or design for the society they're fitting us to, then there must be a copy of it somewhere, proba-bly in the CPB's files."

"Those are *private!*" I had been afraid he would be shocked.

I gave him the argument I had used on myself. "Are they really? They're *about* everyone, they concern everyone—that seems pretty public to me."

Usually suits hide headshakes or nods, but he was shaking his head so hard I could see it plainly. "No, *no*, Melpomene. It's—well, it's not like—well, shit. I understand what you said, but that's not how you decide whether files are private. It's not."

He was stammering like a moron, and I hated to hear that, because it made me realize how much I had upset him. But if I backed out now, we might never find out. And I still thought we had been right the night before—this might be important for the whole future of the ship. "What makes a file private?" I asked him, stalling while I thought of more arguments.

He didn't answer for a long time. "All right, Melpomene. I don't know why you're making me explain something everyone knows by the time they're six, but all right. A file is private because the person who created it says so. That's the only way there can *be* any privacy. If anyone else were to decide, they'd have to look at it, and then it wouldn't be private, would it? So if the creator says it's private, it's private, and that's all there is to it."

By now I had thought of a lot of arguments. I could have asked whether I could copy one of his files, label it private, delete his original, and then say he couldn't read it. I could have pointed out we were mad at the adults exactly because they wouldn't tell us anything. I could even have insisted he back me up because we were friends. Lonely as he was, that would have worked, though I'd have felt like an unco for it.

I didn't say any of those things. You can't really win an argument against somebody's feeling that something is just plain wrong. Papa always says that.

So I let the whole thing drop. I leaned over against Randy and watched the stars wheel around us. After a minute he dropped an arm around me. "Sorry, Melpomene."

"For what?"

"Oh, getting upset, lecturing you, being a bokkup, being born. Things like that."

"I'm glad you're here, anyway." I attempted the nearly impossible—snuggling in spacesuits. It must have worked; he seemed to relax and we just watched the stars and talked about some of the recent races as the tram crept around to the dark side of the ship.

The Earth and moon were still visible, low downship as we crossed into the shadow; the Earth was a half-disk, the moon a rounded dot. Together, they were the size of a pea and the period on this screen, a handsbreadth apart and an arm's length away.

Then they fell below the horizon. A few minutes later Mars rose upship, a bright red light not yet showing any disk.

"Tell you what," Randy said. "Let's go there next."

"Pos-def. It's a lim koapy red. Wonder if it will turn green or blue when they're done with it?"

"We had a problem set on that in my old class. It's supposed to depend on how much water they put into it. If they do fill all the big lakes they're talking about and use cloud cover to hold heat, it will probably turn white sometimes the way Earth seems to. But it's going to stay at least half desert, so all that will still be red."

"I did some numbers on my own, and I think we'll be in position to see the first comet strike on Mars. That will really be a sight." I drifted off into a daydream, happy thinking about watching that with Randy . . . and with all my other friends, even with Susan—and then I remembered Miriam, and I thought about how much trouble there was, and that got me back to Papa and the way they'd engineered us, and in two minutes I wanted to cry. I couldn't imagine how it could all work out.

The tram glided into place, and we all turned to watch the ship horizon for the racers. "This toggle station is really far down toward the engines," Randy said, breaking me out of feeling sorry for myself. "And the leg is almost the full length of the ship, nearly vertical. They're putting a lot of challenge into the course, even for an All-Ship Championship."

"I guess they figure they can handle it." I had a brief twinge of concern for Tom, but he was better on the toggle than most people, and not the type for idle risks.

Still, the ship length was more than a kilometer, and a lot could happen in that distance.

The opencast spoke. "Racers are now arriving at the previous station, and can be expected to be visible within two minutes. First racer down at the previous station: Thomas Murray, A Shift Champion. Second: Karol Kysmini, B Shift Champion. Third: Tswana Cannen, A Shift Second."

Probably it was just family arrogance but I was so sure Tom would win that I was actually worried more about Tswana's chances for second place. How had Karol gotten ahead of her, anyway?

We clicked up distance lenses, set them for infinity, and watched the upward horizon.

The first indication that anything was wrong was how fast Tom rose over the upward horizon. He shot up like a line-rocket does during a rendezvous, appearing to go straight out from the side of the ship.

Whole seconds crawled by as Tom reached an impossibly high peak. Then Karol and Tswana bobbed slowly up over the horizon, arms wheeling slowly as they wound on cable, and another few seconds went by before slower racers, using the old technique, came into view low on the horizon, wrapping cable quickly to keep it taut.

I looked upward again to see what Tom was doing and I couldn't find him at all. "Where—"

"Near Cygnus's head," Randy said, his voice low but tense. "He must be five hundred meters out from the side at least. What's he doing?"

"I don't know." Now that Randy had pointed him out, I could see Tom dimly when I clicked in for a closer look. I saw that he was winding his toggle line with both hands, not in the big easy loops he usually used, but keeping it hard and tight on the lugs by pulling it taut with one hand and winding with the other. I had no idea why he thought he would want neat, tight wrapping—his takeoff technique was effective because he didn't have to put much muscular effort into winding against tension. And he wasn't even getting the benefit of winding in— he was shortening the line, but it still hung limp, and in fact he had to use his free hand to keep it pulled taut as he wound it on the lugs.

The other racers neared the station. Tom continued at that amazing distance from the ship. Everyone watched him.

"Look at his line," Randy said quietly.

Near us, it was visible in the ship's floodlights. It was no longer completely limp, nor taut yet either, but bulged in a long, single, unwinding curve.

"There must be some kind of potential energy in that," Randy said, "but I can't see what it is."

I told him how Tom was winding it tightly for no apparent reason. "He's up to something, but it had better work fast—Karol and Tswana aren't long from coming in."

I had never seen a toggle race so hard to follow. Normally all the racers are in one small area of the sky, lighted by the sun or the floods depending on which side of the ship it is, not more than one hundred meters out. But Tom was ninety degrees or more away from the rest, and where they were mostly within fifty meters of the surface, he was out at around three hundred, covering only three percent as much sky and reflecting only three percent as much light.

Randy gulped audibly.

"What?"

"The cable. Look now."

It was still bowed—but now downward toward the engines. Tom had dropped down below the station and would have to work his way back up.

This couldn't be some new tactic. My brother had bokked and was certain to finish last. I felt terrible for him, even for Susan . . .

As I thought this, he brightened against the sky. A weird, flickering light suddenly played across his suit, multicolored fire dancing on its iridescence.

"What—" Randy began.

I knew. "Main Engine exhaust. The light from it." I had seen it through vid cameras and on dinghy excursions—but now the light of its flickering, dancing sheets of thin plasma played over Tom's body. My stomach felt like I had swallowed a brick of iron. "He's got too much line left. He's going to trail off into the exhaust."

I heard Randy's breath catch. Tom was now very bright in the exhaust glow, flickering and shining. Just before he trailed off he would probably pass out of the ship's shadow and I would see him flare in the sunlight before he dropped into that deadly radiation bath.

"The cable looks like—" Randy began.

Tom jerked, hard, with his whole body.

He leaped upward, back toward the station. He jerked again, and again. Abruptly, the flicker of Main Engine exhaust over his body stopped as he shot back into the shadow of the ship.

Randy laughed, a weird torn sound of relief. "God, your brother has nerve. He timed that snub perfectly, yanked the cable right at the bottom. Just like he does in that takeoff. And it catapulted him forward. Want to bet he lands fully ballistic?"

"No." I was breathing again myself. "He jerked more than once— I guess he could catch the line because he could see it in the exhaust glow."

"Watch the station!"

Karol and Tswana were within a few seconds of landing, with the rest of the racers trailing. Karol was a bit higher up than Tswana, and I gave her the edge—

Tom shot straight in, almost perpendicular to the side of the ship, landing so hard his heels seemed to bump his butt. In an eyeblink he had handed off his coiled cable to ground crew, reclipped, sprung upward, and snapped the new line hard. He shot forward and slightly upward toward the next station, a short leg of only about one hundred meters.

Before Tswana even came in, Tom was halfway to the next station. She did a neat turnover, and Karol came in as she launched herself. Before either of them had finished the short leg, Tom had come in again, taken off, and gotten over the horizon.

The rest of the field was just straggling into the station in front of us.

"That's the most amazing thing I've ever seen," Randy said. "He might even beat the tram to the finish line."

As if the group super had had the same thought, the tram started. Since there was little more to look at, we spent most of the trip to the last station arguing about the physics of what Tom had done. Randy eventually got me convinced that he was right—all the advantage came from the added acceleration of dropping below the finish station, so it was only likely to be effective on really long downward legs.

When we got to the last station, we had to wait less than a minute before Tom hurtled in, far ahead of everyone, and made a neat landing by his station, boots clamping to the side of the ship. The clock registered his time—not a record for the nine kilometer toggle, because the course had been unusually tough. Still, he had come in before the rest of them cleared the horizon, which had to be a record lead, anyway.

He shoved his card into the reader, registering out, and came over to join Susan. From the way he waved to me, I guessed he was pretty happy.

The rest of the racers came in with Tswana leading Karol by four full seconds. As the racers and spectators gathered around and on the tram, Randy and I clicked over to listen on the general band.

They were all talking about Tom's maneuver, some of them making him explain slowly to them what Randy and I had already worked out. Apparently the really dedicated people who watched the whole race on vid had seen him do the same thing on another long downhill leg. He had to explain the basic idea several times—that the long free fall past the toggle station stored up a lot of energy, and all of it could be redirected by snubbing hard because monomyl line was so elastic. The additional energy was large enough to more than make up for the longer path if some formula he had worked out was satisfied—it depended, obviously, on the length of the leg, the extent to which it ran downward, and the acceleration of the ship.

The opencast's voice crackled in our ears. "Announcement of standing for today's toggle race. First place and All-Ship Champion: Tswana Carmen. Second place, Karol Kysmini. Third place—"

The machine read through all the placings, down to the last straggler from C Shift, before it finally said, "And one special judges' ruling. By unanimous verdict, Thomas Murray is disqualified by use of a dangerous technique. The judges' ruling has been posted for inclusion in RULES FOR TOGGLE RACING in the following form: 'No racer may at any point pass below a plane extending perpendicular to the ship from a line drawn around its circumference equidistant from the lowest station and the highest engine exhaust port.' Text copies of the rule will be available for examination and comment on the Outdoor Sports Bulletin Board, available via commoncast."

My head hurt. Everyone was talking. I couldn't sort out the comm. Randy gestured to me, I clicked over, and we went back on private link. "Test."

"Check. Melpomene, that's so crazy. They just stole the race from him. And that technique is no more dangerous than being out here in the first place is."

"Yeah." I was numb. "I guess I should try to talk with him or at least—"

Susan was suddenly there, standing in front of us. She extended her private line, and we piggybacked it on my clip so she could join the conversation. "Tom is going in to get out of his suit. I'm going to catch him on his way out. Do you want to meet us at the pizza cafeteria? I think it would help if you did."

"Pos-def," I said, as Randy started to say "If you want—"

"Both of you," Susan emphasized, knocking her standing hyperbolic with me. "We'll probably need to gang up on him. He's going to be in an awful mood."

"We'll be there," I said. "Be sure you catch him—when he's really upset, especially when he's been badly p.d.'d, he goes off and hides."

"You're talking about him like he's four years old." Her voice was back to its normal pouty whine. Maybe she was embarrassed at having behaved graciously or something.

"Whatever. But he'll try to go off and hide. We'd all better get moving before he gets a lead on you."

She unclipped and went, not saying anything more. Maybe she was angry. I hoped, though, that she had taken me seriously, and was hurrying.

"Well, Randy, I guess you've been invited to a family crisis."

"You *do* want me along?"

"Pos-def." I was surprised at how much I emphasized that, and then embarrassed at having shown so much. "Meet you at the big viewing lounge, soon as we both get out?" It was about equidistant from our Suit Rooms.

"Right. See you there." Randy unclipped and the roar of chatter on the general freke came back. He brushed me with his arm—probably an intended hug—and we both headed in.

It takes a while to check a suit back in because you have to put all the things through pressure check and all the pieces through the UV sterilizer. Furthermore, there were a lot of people ahead of me, and worse yet some were adults, who never trust the machines for some stupid reason, so they always double and triple check everything and bother the attendants with dumb questions about how to tell if something needs replacing. (The suiting room administrators won't even *let* you use up ten percent of the rated duration on a component.)

Anyway, at least Susan was up near the head of the line with no adults ahead of her. She waved at me as we waited. Naked as we were, with our suits in our bags, I could see she was really developed, even more than Miriam, and though I guess I was glad for Tom, I felt my little-girl body more acutely than ever. I knew Susan was older than I was and for all I knew when I hit that age I'd look like that too, but right now I was so tired of looking like a kid.

Susan got through checkout, and waved again. I waved back. She really did support Tom, and he seemed to like her. And I hadn't thought of her as The Rodent for almost an hour, either.

She bounced off to get dressed, my envy following. Maybe puberty would hit me instantaneously and I'd just wake up looking like that.

When I got to the viewing lounge, Randy wasn't there yet and the place was deserted except for one adult couple sitting at one of the small screens. They weren't tuned to an outside camera or telescope— they were watching the view from a Mars polar orbiter, a low one.

I had noticed a lot of adults doing that lately. Maybe there was a contagious Mars fetish going around or something. Usually hardly anyone except old people like Papa and Dr. Lovell ever look at the Outside very often. A couple times a week does it for me and I bet I look more than most people.

Randy finally turned up and we grabbed net and hauled up to the Mushroom.

The pizza cafeteria is crowded most of the time, and it's worse on weekends, so it's not easy to find anyone there. We made one complete trip around the room before Susan spotted us and managed to get our attention, among all the other people waving and shouting at *their* friends.

When we sat down, I sort of officially introduced Randy, since Tom had only heard of him and Susan had only met him in a spacesuit. Tom surprised me by winking and flashing me a covert thumbs up.

"Just to get it on record," I said, "they really robbed you."

Susan glared at me and I felt bokky, but Tom just said, "Yeah, but they do have a point." He shrugged. "It *is* tricky and dangerous to do that. But I'm glad I developed the technique, because sometimes they need to get around fast out there and the risk be damned."

Randy nodded. "My father's been using your takeoff for months. I'm sure he'll be excited about this trick too."

I had a sudden embarrassing sensation. "You know, Randy, I don't actually know what your father does."

"Vacuum extrusion. Mostly he works Outside."

Tom said, "Tell him to be careful if he does use the new trick. There was a lot of darkening on my film badge when they confiscated it—apparently you get a lot more sidescatter rads than I thought you would. And if somebody didn't practice enough beforehand, they *could* trail off and get roasted. It's probably just as well that they won't let people mess with it." He got up. "I'm going to hit the head before the pizza gets here. Hope you don't mind if it's—"

"Baby tilapia and rabbit sausage," I said, "the same as you've had on every pizza since you could pronounce it."

He grinned at me. "Ah, but I've been reformed. Susan has a bunny allergy. It's sliced quail and mushroom." He kissed her on the forehead and was gone.

She smiled. "I do hope you don't mind."

"No problem," I said. Quail tastes like an old boiled sock without the flavor.

"I'll eat almost anything," Randy said. Since then, I've realized he was lying too, about the "almost." "Do we need to throw in discrets?"

"Tom insisted it was his treat," she said. "I'm—well, you know him, Melpomene. He's really acting weird. He was taking off to hide, just like you told me he would, when I caught up with him. He said today was the only day the museum was open for general visitors and he wanted to see it."

I couldn't help laughing. The museum is where they keep a lot of old junk from Earth, pictures and clothes and so forth. *Nobody* our age goes there, except when they force us to, in school.

Susan obviously didn't think it was funny at all. I thought she might start whining at me.

"I'm sorry." I swallowed several painful giggles. "It's just I've been tracking down his hideouts ever since I was a little girl and that's the strangest one he's ever picked."

She nodded, looking a little thoughtful. "Well, then it's one more really strange thing he's done. I was dragging him back here and he was being really sullen, and then something, some idea or something, just hit him and he got all weirdwired. But very cheerful and excited, too, which really didn't make any sense."

"I don't know him," Randy said, "but isn't it true that when some people get really hurt, they'll kind of react the opposite?"

"Yes," I said slowly, "and Tom does that."

We were all quiet for a long time. Then Randy said, "I still don't understand it. There's half a dozen moves that are legal in toggle racing that all have some serious risk of trailing off. Why did they pick on this one, especially when it's so effective and gives such a big advantage to the best athletes and the people with the most guts? The ruling itself just doesn't make any sense. The reasoning behind it is silly. It doesn't really fit in with the other rules for similar situations. What made them decide to do that to him?"

I wanted to get Susan back to how Tom was acting. "I don't think it was personal."

Randy nodded, but I saw his mind went elsewhere. He was thinking really hard about something, but I had no idea what.

"Did Tom say anything about why he was feeling better?" I asked. Normally when he's in a good mood he dumps his heart out to everyone about everything.

"No, and that's not like him either. I even had to ask what he was thinking about, and I've never had to before because he tells you right away—"

I was afraid she was going to pout. "What did he say?"

"Either he was crazy or everything was fine. That's exactly what he said. And that he had to work on it. And all of a sudden that thing he was going to show me that I asked you about—well, I guess he still is going to show me—he said he was sure I'd like it and he wasn't worried and we'd probably just do it this afternoon. And that's all except he's been sort of happy and silly and disconnected ever since." She paused and took a sip of water. "Could he really have cracked up from disappointment or something?" She gnawed her lower lip again. With those thin lips, it looked really rabbity.

I quoted Papa. " 'Just because people do go crazy doesn't mean they do it often.' Maybe he's just come up with a new Alien Artifact?"

Susan seemed startled. "You call them that too?"

"Yes, why?"

"It hurts his feelings when your mother does. He's told me so a lot of times."

I felt like a cockroach.

"I'm sorry!" Susan said.

"No. It's okay. I'm just glad I found out."

Then one of them changed the subject, I'm not sure to what or which one of them it was, but after a while I quit feeling guilty and joined in. We just talked about trivia like school and families.

Since Susan had four brothers and five sisters, she naturally did most of the talking about families. I found myself thinking, as I often had, how odd it was on the *Flying Dutchman* for Tom and I to be the only two kids in our family. And now that I thought of it, I hadn't heard Randy mention any brothers or sisters at all. Hadn't he said he'd wondered what having a mother was like?

Just when I was really beginning to lose the thread of the conversation, Tom got back, even more obviously cheerful. Then the pizza arrived, and we all ate quietly for a while.

Or it would have been quiet if it hadn't been for the strange little thoughtful "hmms," "aahs," and "yes!es" Tom was making.

We finished up with the guys making such a fuss over trying to give each other the last piece that Susan abruptly snagged and gobbled it. At that moment I really loved her.

We talked about the latest batch of movies up from Earth for a while, all of us watching Tom closely, until, out of nowhere, as if he had finally given in and agreed to surprise us, he said, "You all really should see Main Engine exhaust."

He looked around the table; none of us said anything. "That must have sounded lim bokky."

"Pos-def," I said.

Susan asked, "You mean the glow—"

"Yeah, but not on a vid or from an excursion dinghy a kilometer away. The way I did. The glow is—well, hard to describe. That's why you should see it." He sounded like he was politely trying to explain something obvious to a very small child.

That seemed to end the conversation. Presently Tom dragged Susan off to go see the gadget. He wasn't making much sense, but he still seemed happy.

"That was the weirdest I've ever seen him," I said, after he'd gone.

"Well, not knowing him," Randy said, "I'd have to say he was either a saint or completely crazy. I mean, he's too smart not to see that they're doing something to him."

"Doing something?"

"Yeah, pos-def they are. They're really working him over for some reason." Randy wasn't looking at me. He seemed to be squirming, and I wondered if our day together was about to get cut in half. "Would you mind if I ordered another small pizza and ate it, as long as we're here? I didn't get much of that last one."

"Me either," I said, "how about splitting a medium? Anything as long as it's not bird-and-fungus again." We settled on rabbit sausage with extra cheese; it came fast, so the awkward silence didn't last long after we'd ordered, and then we could just concentrate on eating. Mother always said the great thing about young love is that when you run out of things to do or say you can always eat. Maybe this was the first sign of love . . . or maybe not being able to talk was.

After a while, I decided to just tackle it head-on, the way Papa would. "Randy, I think you're one of the smartest people I've ever met, and I like you, and I trust you. So even though it obviously makes you uncomfortable, I wish you would tell me what you think is being done to Tom."

He took an enormous bite of pizza and chewed it very slowly. After swallowing a couple of times, he seemed about to speak, but then he took another big bite, chewed it, swallowed . . . drank some water . . . at last, he sighed.

"There's not exactly a word for it. But if they arrange so much of what happens to us, why are they arranging such bad luck for him?" Another drink of water. My fingers felt like drumming, but I didn't let them.

I saw him force himself to look into my eyes. I looked back as steadily as I could.

"You know how I really felt when Dr. James told me about the social engineering they've done on us? Scared and mad." He said it with almost no expression, like he was typing it onto a screen. "A lot of times when I feel like this I just start looking for someone to hit. Like if I could just hit the right people and hurt them bad enough, they'd have to stop."

"Stop what?"

"The thing I can't name. That I just feel they're doing. Whoever they are." He sighed again. I was getting to hate the sound of it. "That's what the world needs, more responsible people to hit, I guess. I don't know.

"About your brother. Number one—when have you ever seen a new rule announced as a disqualifier? I know they *can*, but have you ever seen them do it? They watch everyone practicing so they won't have to. If anyone does anything they don't like, they warn them way in advance. And that couldn't have been the first time Tom ever did that. So they knew he was going to try that long-drop-and-bounce-back maneuver. And they gave him no warning. On a technique they claim is too dangerous?

"They can't dropline fast enough to make that look right." He tore into another piece of pizza, as if trying to murder it with his teeth.

"Don't choke on that," I said. "I'll wait to hear the rest."

"Grmph." He swallowed. "Sorry. When I don't hit people, I eat. The two basic solutions for all problems. Okay, so the judges' ruling doesn't make any sense, and all by itself that looks like they're out to get Tom. Now, put on top of it that you tell me he's been really upset by the CSL problems they give him—and it turns out they've been giving him *impossible* problems. And all this right before his FA."

"He did those problems."

"I would bet they didn't know he'd be able to. I think they were really trying to throw him for good, have him get a zil he couldn't work out of." I had seen Randy angry lots of times, but always before it had been a wild lashing-out."

Now he sat here, talking to me without raising his voice or tensing a muscle, but angrier than I had ever seen him.

"Probably fifteen weeks ago Tom was a real leader in his class, lim high standing, am I right?"

"Pos-def. Except CSL he was terrific at everything."

"I wonder how they held his CSL scores down—"

That sounded just plain paranoid. "Maybe he just doesn't have the knack."

He snorted and shook his head. I hated the twist that came into his smile.

"It could be," I insisted.

"How? At least nine-tenths of CSL overlaps math and language, and you told me he's good at those. And everyone knows CSL performance has big correlations with music, art, and science performance. Remember what it says in the fourth year CSL text—'in a sense, doing CSL is synonymous with being intelligent'? So how can he possibly be doing so well at everything that overlaps CSL, and so badly at CSL itself?" He crammed in more pizza, gulped more water.

"You're going to make yourself sick."

"Yeah." He drank again, more slowly. "Or something will. About your idea, to took at those files . . . have you ever tried anything like that before?"

"Not really. It didn't seem like it would be difficult."

"It's much harder than it looks. I know. I'd hate to see you get in trouble because you didn't know some of the tricks."

I nodded. "Thank you."

"If we're both done eating, let's go back to my living unit. We won't be interrupted."

The whole way there we didn't talk much, but for some reason I felt very close to him, and better and safer than I had all week. And that was truly strange. You'd think I'd have been afraid of all that fury I could feel in him.

EIGHT

Randy's living unit was really small, and of course since it was Saturday and most of B Block was asleep or just getting up we had to stay fairly quiet, too. So it was natural to keep our voices really low. It made me feel like a secret agent in one of those silly flatscreen movies we get up from Earth.

He slung his werpsack into the bin in his room, saying, "It's easier to wipe i.d. off a house terminal, so we'll use that."

His room was completely undecorated, and everything he had visible was standard issue—not one thing an extra discret would be spent on. It was clean and neat, but there was no Randy in it at all.

We went back to the sharespace. "Where's the rest of your family?" I blurted out, feeling stupid as I said it.

It didn't seem to be a sensitive subject, though. "Dad's probably with the Earth Sports Club, watching soccer or baseball or something, so he'll be gone all day. And there's just me and him."

We sat down at the house terminal, and in about ten minutes I realized that though I might be better at CSL in theory, Randy knew far more about the ship's system than I did, because I had rarely gotten into anything restricted or prohibited.

"I hate to ask and show you how dumb I am, but why are we doing this?" I asked after a while.

Randy touched my shoulder lightly. "I'm certainly glad I'm your guide on this one, Kemo Sabe."

"Who?"

"Old flatscreen. Lone Ranger. Show you some time." His fingers were flying over the keys, pausing only to grab the mouse and roll it. "Just meant you'd have been in lim deep shit if you'd tried it on your own." He sat back and gestured at the screen. "Now it's running a program to set up a chain of virtual terminals. Each virtual terminal controls another one on out to a few hundred of them."

"What's it for?"

"Well, you can't use your own terminal because they read i.d. and attach it to everything in every dialog, right?"

It was right, now that he pointed it out. I'd have been caught right away. I leaned a little closer to him. "Okay, so why so many?"

"The sys register for this class of terminal only tracks virtual parents fifteen deep, but you can chain up to 511 of them. So when it's chained out to a couple of hundred, we're disidentified. And at that point we're free to mess around."

"Why not just sixteen terminals in the chain?" This was getting interesting; maybe Randy's CSL talents were as sharp as mine, just differently directed.

"Well, there has to be a bridgeburner in the chain if we don't want to get caught. So we'll work at a depth of 250 and set the bridgeburner to start at number eighteen." He pounded at the keys again; he must have been replacing his keyboard every week.

I was dying to know what a bridgeburner was, but I felt like I'd bokked enough already. By watching what he did, anyway, I figured out that a bridgeburner watched events further down the chain. The register showed only the last fifteen terminals in the chain, so you couldn't get caught in a direct jump, but Security could still trace you back in jumps of sixteen. If they started, the bridgeburner would destroy all the other virtual terminals, leaving no pathway back to the controlling terminal.

It was lim clever, and sneaky too. "That's brilliant," I said. "Where'd you learn all this?"

"A lot of techs pick it up. Self-defense against management, you know. It helps to have the real numbers at contract time. And B Shift has most of the techs. Any knowledge that's any kind of use transpires after a while." He brought up a dump of the registers, studied it, and nodded. "That's a good start. But if we're going to try to penetrate the CPB's files, we better load on some other stuff too, say a pepper shaker and a false continuation."

I took a large bit of my pride and swallowed as hard as I could. "I don't know what they are."

"The AIs that trace chains of virtual terminals are called bloodhounds. A pepper shaker viruses the bloodhound, turns on all its error bits, and reports it as damaged code to the system, so the immunity AIs attack it. It can take as much as eight milliseconds for the bloodhound to get back on the track, and by that time the bridgeburner has us out of there."

I watched as he set it up. "Shouldn't you optimize the algorithm more?"

"Where can I?"

"That induction engine should use a discrete geometric in its comparison space, instead of a continuous one." At last I felt almost sort of useful. "And in that case you can change the comparison from numeric to linked-OR, add the matrix will be a tenth the size."

"Yeah—got you." We worked on it together for a few minutes. When we had a finished version, Randy installed the pepper shaker in a dozen virtual terminals. "Mind if I post it too?"

"Post it? Where?"

"The *Unofficial Organ*. It's a good trick, and other people could use it."

"Sure." I didn't really know what I'd agreed to, but he obviously thought I should do it. I had heard of the *Unofficial Organ* a few times, but always as a pun in a punchline. I had no idea what it was.

He tapped out a key sequence and a couple of unfamiliar icons appeared. He triggered two of them, and a copy went somewhere.

I could also help with the next step: corrupting a newly copied generic AI to do the penetration. That's tricky—you have to override some deep-level prohibitions, because if an AI is smart enough to do the penetration it's smart enough to suspect something and call Security.

The real barrier is supposed to be the password, but in fact we were already past the hard part. Password protection up here isn't all that effective because everyone's complete bio is required to be available online to anyone. So you can always find mothers' maiden names, relatives' names, what a person reads, anything that would normally be there in a person's Security dossier.

For example, from some past minor tinkering, I knew that when Papa was in "high school" on Earth, his friends sometimes called him Horny Corny, and that on his first date with Mother he had been arrested by Sergeant Joseph Clifford for driving at sixty-four miles per hour in a forty-five mile per hour zone. (I converted those numbers to kilometers and decided everything moves much too fast on Earth.)

So you could set up another corrupted AI to search relevant biographies and see what it could pull out. Besides, very few files were password-protected. Most people figured the "private" flag was enough, even on a file where they had recorded some higher level password.

We were into the files of the clerical staff at CPB almost at once, and sure enough, some of them had recorded passwords for more secure files there.

As soon as we got into the high-secure CPB stuff Randy said, "Okay, now for a false continuation. In fact, we can make it do something really clever. . . ."

It was clever—and with a little help from me it was elegant. CPB has the highest clearance on the system. So Randy extended the virtual terminal chain out from CPB and into Security, using the CPB's high-level clearance to override Security's protections, and put monitors on the ends of the chain. In effect, he bugged the police station.

We ended up with lots of time to work because of that. First we pulled copies of twenty or so files that we thought might contain something we'd want to know, and downloaded copies onto my werp's backup memory block, where Central wouldn't be able to see that we had them. Then we went through more systematically, picking up any file that shared more than eight keywords with the ones we'd gathered. Finally, mostly for amusement, we pulled the files on ourselves, Tom, Theophilus, Miriam, Gwenny Mori, and Barry Yang. "Let's pick up Susan the Rodent while we're here," I suggested.

Randy laughed. "Who?"

"Susan Rodenski. We had lunch with her and Tom."

"One rodent added to the menu." The file copy dumped it into memory.

The living unit door opened.

My heart bulged against my larynx. We were in lim shit—it would take almost a minute to fully close down.

Randy squeezed my hand with his right hand and worked the mouse with his left. An icon spun—an old-fashioned cartoon burglar, wearing a black mask and carrying a bag. Randy clicked again.

We were looking at a reading assignment in Japanese, with a notepad below.

In Japanese, Randy typed "all clear" and wiped the screen, bringing up the next page. He passed the keyboard to me.

"Hi Dad," he said, as calmly as if we had really been doing homework.

Mr. Schwartz was *huge*—close to two meters tall, and heavy as well. I suspected two of me could have sat comfortably on one of his shoulders.

He was wearing one of the standish vis-orange coveralls most techs seem to prefer. It had a bunch of really koapy patches, mostly construction project ones, going back to Quito Geosync Cable in 2009 and right on up to the *Flying Dutchman* Outside construction patch, the Vacuum Workers Union, and a couple of union office badges. On the left front, just below the seam, was a black XV with two bars underneath—seventeen years total time in space.

I wondered if it bothered him that Randy and I already had twelve.

"Hello, company, I see."

"Dad, this is Melpomene Murray. Melpomene, this is my father. She's a friend from school, and she's singlehandedly saving my Japanese grade."

"Brave young lady."

"It's nice to meet you," I said. "And Randy doesn't need that much saving."

Mr. Schwartz nodded, smiling, and said to Randy, "If you can believe it, they're showing four hours of cycle pursuit. Can't stand to watch a bunch of guys in tight shorts chase each others' butts, so I thought I'd get a scrub and a change." He nodded to me again. "Nice to meet you."

He reached into his room, pulled out a small bag and a change of clothes, slung them over his shoulder, and bounced out the door in one neat motion, letting it autodog behind him.

"I hope I didn't just chase your father out of his own living unit."

"No, he always goes to the public baths anyway. He likes to have people to hang around with—most techs are that way."

I sort of knew that the baths were there, but I had the impression from Mother that there was something disreputable about them. "Do you go there?"

"Sometimes. There aren't many people our age. Your friend Miriam is there with her folks now and then."

So he had seen Miriam naked, but not me.

Yet.

I was annoyed with myself for feeling so jealous, so I said, "Well, let's see what we caught while we were burgling. And where did you find that coverup program?"

"Just a little trick from the *Unofficial Organ*. I'm surprised you know computing so well and you've never run across any of the good tricks. Most of the real wizards are—" The funny expression that crossed his face bothered me, and the nervous laugh bothered me more. He took my hand. "You don't know why."

I felt hurt, but had no idea why. I shrugged and shook my head.
"Your father's on the CPB."

I couldn't have been more surprised if he'd said the problem was
my horns and cloven feet. "What's that got to do with it?"

Randy gestured at the list of secret files on the screen.

"Oh." There must be millions of things no one had ever told me
because of that. I must have been left out of stuff for years. Suddenly I
could remember lots of times I had felt like a conversation died when I
came up to join it.

I cried. It went on for a long time. He held me, and rubbed my
back and neck gently, and after a while I stopped, but still we sat there
for a long while, holding hands facing each other and saying nothing.

Finally, Randy said, "There's snot or something hanging from
your nose. Would you like a wipe?"

"Y-yes." I sighed—and it turned into a giggle. "Ah me, what a
romantic you are, sir."

He bounced over to the wall dispenser and fetched a wipe, handing it to me with an exaggerated bow.

I felt morally obligated to honk, which got him laughing too.
When we finally calmed down, I said, "Now maybe we'd better take a
look at those files we've gotten."

The CPB has a lot of strange jargon. Scanning keyword lists and
abstracts didn't do us much good. Finally we just worked through it
sequentially.

Most of the afternoon went by as we alternately read and argued
about what it all meant. It's not easy to turn shrinkspeak into English—
"Japanese would be easier," Randy said. "A lot easier."

"Hai soo-desu, ne? At least it's *starting* to make sense. And it's not
as bad as we were afraid it would be—"

"I don't know about that, Melpomene; there's stuff that would
make a lot of techs explode." He was pointing at the list of "Values for
Inclusion in Semiotic System at Age 8."

"I thought that was just a list of platitudes."

"Looked like it to me, too, at first. But look at number three: 'On a
space ship or in a society, the fundamental interests of everyone are the
same. We must all cooperate with corporate policies and directives
regardless of position, rank, standing, or title, to fulfill the objectives
of the ship.' How do you square joining a union with that? In fact if
you take away the high principles, it boils down to 'everyone should
shut up and do what NAC tells them.' "

I read it over and over, trying to see what he meant. "I guess you could read it that way. The applications list on that value would probably tell us whether that's the intention. Do we have any docs of the rule applications it refs?" I hit a few keys and the list came up. "Looks like we do—two abstract reports, our case reports, and Tom's case report."

"That's weird. Why us three and not any of the others?"

We found out in about five minutes that that was the key to all of it. This is where NAC will probably erase everything I write, so I'll just put it down for my own sake:

Unions were supposed to disappear within twenty-five years.

Elections would be replaced by an "organically developed consensus process" before 2040. (We were thrown off the track at first by "organically developed." We thought that must mean it was up to the people on the *Flying Dutchman*. After enough poking around in the supplementary material, we realized it really meant that the CPB wasn't sure what people would accept yet, so they were going to wing it when they had a better idea.)

And most importantly, when we began to examine our own files, we found that Randy, Tom and I were all labelled "Special Category."

"What *do* we have to do with all this?" Randy asked. "There's the mystery."

But just as we brought up the file and began to read, the door latch turned. We had to flip back over to the Japanese assignment.

I swallowed hard for one second. I suppose I imagined Papa and the whole CPB bursting in with guns blazing or something. Of course it was just Mr. Schwartz again.

"Hi. Hope you got a lot done. Anyone want to get some dinner before the party starts?"

I hadn't heard anything about a party. I looked at Randy. He was blushing a deeper red than I'd ever seen.

Mr. Schwartz looked back and forth between us a couple of times and broke into a broad grin. Then he whooped, bounded up to the ceiling in a tight flip, shot straight back down, caught himself on his hands and kipped back upright. He was roaring with laughter.

Randy was almost purple, looking down at his lap.

"So you didn't get around to it," Mr. Schwartz said.

Randy shook his head.

"Randy?" His voice was suddenly gentler.

Randy didn't move or speak.

"Uh-hm. Uh, sorry." He turned back to the door. "Uh—" he winked but Randy didn't look up to see it—"I just remembered I have to go check the vacuum hold to make sure the vacuum isn't leaking out into space. So I'll be back in maybe ten minutes or so, okay?"

Randy nodded.

"I'm sorry. I really am. Don't feel like *you* have to act like an idiot just because your old man does. It's not a big family tradition or anything."

Randy looked up, finally forcing a sort of wan smile. "Pos-def. See you in a few."

Mr. Schwartz was out the door in a single bound and had it dogged faster than you could say it. You'd have thought there was a francium hydroxide spill in the room or something.

I didn't really know what was wrong with Randy, so I put an arm around him. He moved, a little and then settled back. I waited.

"See?" he said, finally. "This is his idea of lim hilarious." He snuffled. "I can never bring anyone home. He's always going to barge in and say something stupid. Always. He's so fucking bokky. And it's like it rubs off on me."

I bounced up, grabbed a wipe from the wall dispenser, and handed it to him. He blew his nose and sighed. "You'd think I'd be used to him. I mean, I know he thinks he's the life of the party. But somehow or other I always end up in a corner looking at the floor while he laughs at me. If I could just look up once and explain—I don't think he'd even hear me." He blew his nose again. This was a big day for crying. "The truth is I just forgot. I meant to, but I forgot. It wasn't because I was scared or anything, but he's going to make it into a funny story now—"

I handed him another wipe, and watched him wipe his eyes. "Forgot what?"

"Oh . . ." He started to turn red again. "Tonight, or this afternoon and night, on B time—well anyway, it starts in a couple of hours . . ."

He took a deep breath and started over.

"It's the B Block party, the big one they have after every perihelion and aphelion. Because after an Earthpass or a Marspass, the big rush is over—most of the Outside crews and techs are on B Shift. It's kind of a big thing, I mean, everyone goes, all my old friends will be there, and I kind of thought . . .

"Well, you know, I don't eat with Dad that often, maybe once a week at most, but this morning we had breakfast together, and for once we were talking, really getting along. And he was asking about school and friends and things. I wasn't going to tell him about Ted and getting beaten up, and so I mostly talked about . . . you, Melpomene."

I gave myself a mental hug. "So what did he say?"

"It's what I said. Well, kind of. He started teasing me—I mean, not really cruel the way he does sometimes, but just teasing me like a friend—about asking you to go to the B Block party with me. . . ."

I hugged him, hard, and said, "And you forgot to because we got so involved in everything else. Well, it's okay, I accept."

He started crying again, harder. Guys can be really weird.

I grabbed another wipe and handed it to him. "I mean I accept if you still plan to ask me. For both dinner and the party. But I'd really appreciate about forty-five minutes to get presentable. Since all your old friends will be there, I think the least I can do is be devastating, don't you? Or should we settle for stunning?"

He finally started to laugh, which was a relief because I wasn't sure how long I could keep this line of nonsense up. "Okay, formally, Melpomene, do you want to go the B Block party with me?"

"Pos-def."

He sighed. "Well, it wasn't exactly what I imagined it would be like, but it worked anyway. I feel like a moron."

"But you're such a *likable* moron." I kissed him on the cheek. "See you in a little bit."

So I zoomed back to my living unit, probably flattening fifty little kids without seeing them, heart pounding, practically singing, plunged into the shower, and finally found myself pulling out the new white coverall I had been saving to break in on School Awards Day.

Papa and Mother came in as I was looking at myself in the mirror, trying to think of something else I could do along the lines of looking wonderful. Crewcut, coverall, and blue slippers wasn't much to work with. . . . I kept trying to decide whether I wanted to wear a belt or a sash.

Papa headed straight for the bathroom. Mother stood and watched me for a while.

She finally said "Melly, if I didn't know it was impossible, I would swear you were primping."

I don't know why I thought that was funny, even with the "Melly," but anyway I laughed and told her what was on the queue.

She seemed a bit startled, but then she smiled at me, this great big wonderful smile that I hadn't seen in years. "Melpomene—dear—no doubt this will come as a complete surprise to you, but I do believe you have a *date*."

"Uh, Mother, I'm really just going to a party . . . uh, with a guy, to meet all his old friends . . . hunh. Maybe I do." There didn't seem to be much else to say. "Well, umm."

She looked me over. "Not a bad effect, a little different from what was fashionable in my day, but skirts aren't really practical in low g and heels always hurt my feet anyway. Let's see what we can add—"

"What else is there?" I asked.

"Hold on for just a minute." She darted into their room; in a moment she was back with a small box. "Let's see what we have."

I gaped at the box. "It's wood. Natural wood. Not tank-grown."

"Yep, brought from Earth." She passed it to me carefully, and I took it with a strange sensation that there was something terribly important there. "That box, and what's in it, was about ten percent of my weight allowance," she added, nervously, as if afraid I'd laugh.

"It's so smooth. But the grain is so . . . swirly, random, like a picture in a fractal geometry lesson. And so warm to the touch . . ."

"I got it from my grandmother when I was a little girl. The clasp slides to the right. It's silver."

I had never seen so much silver in one place, even in the chem lab. It was a strange shape that I couldn't quite name, but had probably seen in a biology text. A leaf or a seashell or something. I pushed it over to the right and gently lifted the lid.

"Jewelry! I saw some when our class went to the museum. I never even knew you had this. . . ."

"It wasn't time yet. Or something. I'm not really sure why I didn't show it to you before." She took it back carefully. "You know, you and I really have similar features, so all this should work for you, but you don't have pierced ears or long hair, so . . . let's see. This pin was my grandmother's." She lifted out a little rose of metal and fastened it gently on my chest, a few centimeters below my left shoulder. "And-hah. Of course, I'd almost forgotten it, but it's perfect."

She pulled something tiny and crumpled from a little compartment in the box. "Short hair, really short hair, was very in fashion a couple of years before we came up. Your father gave me this."

It looked like a tiny piece of metal netting. "What is it?"

"They called it a 'coleman.' Maybe that was the designer's name or it was based on something coal miners wore, or something." She held it loosely in her fist and breathed over it several times. "Once it gets warm . . ."

She eased it out; now it was a rumpled flat sheet the size and shape of Nathan Roswald's yarmulke. She spread it out and laid it on the left side of my head, just to the side of the crown. It gave me an odd prickly feeling in my hair. "Now shake your head hard."

I did.

"Good." She breathed on it again, her breath warm and moist on my scalp, and waited a few seconds. "Shake your head again. Right. Okay, one more time . . ." Her breath was warm on my scalp. "Wait . . . now shake." I bobbed my head around vigorously; I could no longer feel the coleman. "Is it still binding anywhere?"

"No."

"Now it will stay on as long as you want it to, and it won't pull your hair. They respond to temperature differences somehow—I don't really understand it. Have a look at yourself in the mirror."

I was amazed—the whorl of shining metal spread against my dark hair like a tiny galaxy, catching fire from the oval gleams on the rose-shaped pin . . . "It's beautiful."

"You are." Mother said it briskly, as if correcting me. "It's a family trait. Now hurry—traditionally you're supposed to be a little late, but up here five minutes is a long time."

"How late did you used to be?"

"Just as long as you will. Exactly long enough for him to really want to see you, and not one second longer . . . unless you're absolutely determined on a career as la belle dame sans merci."

I laughed, but her expression just got stranger. "Do you know . . . do you know that you look, oh, five years older? Like a woman?"

I felt something swirl in my stomach. "Like a very small woman, maybe," I said, and felt how flat the joke was.

But she smiled anyway, and we hugged. It had probably been at least a year since we had done that.

I took an omnivator by myself, partly because I was running a little late and mostly because I wanted Randy to see me before anyone else did.

He opened the door right away. He had changed too—into his company uniform. NAC insists we all have them in case our parents have to entertain some plutock tourist and pass us all off as real corporados. I guess a lot of groundhogs who come on Ship Tour think we wear those all the time.

Randy, like everyone else, wore a kidsized version of his same-sex parent's uniform. For Randy that was vis-orange separate shirt and pants, broad black cloth stretch belt, black slippers, and black neckerchief. My father always called it the "Halloween Boy Scout look," for some reason, and referred to our light-green professional uniforms as the "Hospital Boy Scout look." Sometimes adults don't make any sense at all.

Randy looked terrific, very grown up and handsome. The only thing that spoiled the effect was that he seemed to be staring at me. "You look really . . . good," he stammered, after a moment.

"Try not to be so surprised. You look great yourself," I told him.

There was a long, awkward silence, before Mr. Schwartz spoke from somewhere behind Randy. "Your next line, son, is 'Come in.'"

From the way Randy blushed, I guess it embarrassed him, but he stammered out the invitation and I came in.

Mr. Schwartz was in uniform too. He was holding a camera and grinning. "You two stand together."

So we did, and he took pictures of us.

It was so startling we both laughed. He laughed too, but he kept shooting pictures. He set the camera into the reader slot in the house terminal, and hardcopies rolled out. He bent to tap at the keys for a moment. "Might as well send your mother the full set, Melpomene," he said.

"My mother?" I asked, startled.

"She called while you were on your way over. The pictures were her idea, but I thought it was a great one. So the hardcopies are for me." Then he tapped at the keyboard for a couple of minutes. "Soon as I get this last thing done, we'll go to dinner. Hope you guys don't mind hitting the Soup Bar." He finished whatever he was typing and picked up one of the pictures. "I've saved permanent copies, but you guys really should take a look at this." He held it up.

I saw what my mother meant about looking five years older. Believe me, when you're twelve, that's lim koapy.

I had only rarely been to the Soup Bar. The first thing I noticed was that there were a lot of Outside techs in there. When his father went up for his fourth refill, Randy explained, "You know how dry your throat is after two hours of Outside Club? And how hot and sweaty your suit gets if you have to piss while you're Outside? Well, they don't drink anything for several hours before going Outside, and they work most of the day on just sips of water. So they really get dried out. I always make up a couple liters of flavored gelatin and put it in the living unit refrigerator as soon as I get home from school—and he gulps half of it down as soon as he gets in."

"Here's another thing that's weird," I said. "If we're all supposed to be so equal, how come I don't know anything about techs?"

Randy's father, coming back, heard this, and after he'd had a few more spoonfuls of goop, he said, "Well, in theory the ship is supposed to be classless, but it doesn't work that way. People just experience life differently, depending on what their work is. Life feels different if you get sweaty every day or if you've always got to look good, or depending on whether management cares about what you do in your offtime." He snorted. "Perfect example right there. When I think 'work,' I think of being managed—I never think of managing as work."

Mr. Schwartz finished his soup. A thought came into my mind from what we'd just learned from the stolen files. "I know one big difference between tech and professional. All the techs are in the unions, but I don't think anyone I've ever known, except Randy, has liked unions."

"Or their parents haven't," Mr. Schwartz agreed. "Most kids just echo their parents. Randy's lucky enough to have figured out his old man's a fool at an earlier age than most people do. Some of 'em'll change their minds when they're working."

I hoped he'd go on, so I said, "I guess I've never heard the case *for* unions. The official NAC channel isn't very sympathetic."

"Well, you can't expect them to be. I suppose it's—" he glanced sideways at Randy. "Hey, I don't want to take up your first date talking economics with your girl. You ought to kick me under the table or something."

From the way Randy jumped, I guess that was when *he* realized it was a date. "To tell the truth, Dad, I'm interested myself. I've probably been in three or four fights on behalf of the union, and I don't really know what it's all about."

Mr. Schwartz sighed. "I swear it's something in the schooling they give you kids. And maybe it doesn't matter, because with your grades and all, Randy, I think you're more likely to go professional. But anyway, I see it like this. As long as people do different jobs they have different interests. Sure, sometimes, in a real crisis, like a sea-ship in a storm or a small company about to go bankrupt, everyone's interests really are the same, because saving the whole thing is more important than any one part of it.

"But most of the time it's a lot more complicated." He paused to take a sip of coffee. "See, if you're on top, it's easy to think that what's good for you is what's good for the organization. In the short run it might even be—a company does better if it gets more work for less wages paid, or if it spends less on health and safety.

"In the longer run, though, workers do the work. Management doesn't. If workers are sick, hurt, pissed off, or broke, they don't work as well."

As Papa's daughter, I'm a pretty good debater myself, and cross ex is one of my strong points. "But then there's no problem. Doesn't the company have an interest in keeping the workers working?"

"Sure—but for as little as possible. Suppose a manager got us all to work two extra hours per day for half pay. Who would get the added profit?"

"NAC," I admitted.

"Well, that's what I'm trying to say. Management works for the employer, and at least in the short run your employer's interests are exactly opposite yours. No matter how nice a guy your manager is, he still gets paid to be your enemy.

"But that's not the whole story. Otherwise I suppose they'd just make slaves of us or we'd kill them. The fact is, they don't dare win— because if they destroy the worker, who will make the product or buy it? The union limits how much management can win. So in a sense the union looks after the long run. Or justice, which might be the same thing."

He finished his coffee. "That's all I'm going to say. Actually I kind of hope neither of you ever needs to join one—as far as I can tell, management and professional jobs are a lot softer. And in the long run I don't think there will be many of us working with our hands in space, anyway, so maybe no one will be union in a few decades. But the family's been union for four generations, Randy, and I guess you're entitled to have some idea why." He stirred his coffee; there was something sad about him, like the way my mother gets when she talks about Grandpa or Miriam's father does when he talks about Manhattan before it was domed. "Now let's get going. You kids need to dazzle your friends, and I need to prove I'm not too goddam old to some of the young snots on my crew."

We hauled down the corridor to the party together, going comfortably slowly so we could talk. Mr. Schwartz told us about things years ago, jobs he'd been on, like how they hung the geosync cables, and about Earth before the Die-Off. He had run away from home when he was ten, in February of 1994, and managed to wander thousands of kilometers around North America, just as the old society was collapsing. When he decided to go back home, that June, his parents, like so many others, were dead of mutAIDS. We'd heard mutAIDS stories before, of course, but it shocked us that things could get bad enough to make you go out the door and take your chances.

He shrugged. "No psych intervention teams, no CPB, and it was an unscreened population—up here the rottenest apples are a lot less common. Just one of a lot of ways it's a lot better up here. Still, Randy, I wish you could have seen San Francisco or New Orleans or even Cleveland before the domes, or just taken a trip on the old interstates through the industrial belts. The lights and flames from the mills, factories, and refineries used to glow like dawn—it was beautiful, just beautiful."

"I've never even seen dawn," Randy pointed out.

"Well, you *will* have to see Earth someday. I'm sure they still have dawn. But the factories are gone. Now it's just a dome every few hundred kilometers and everything falling to rust since heavy industry moved up to orbit. The old highways are empty except for freight disksters, and the undomed towns are empty except for the crazies." He sighed. "A lot of people used to think the old cities were ugly—but they were *human*. It's like people are disappearing from the world."

Then he grinned again. "So here you are hanging on the nets listening to an old geezer reminisce. You kids today sure know how to have a good time. Anyway, let's get there before I'm senile."

"Have a good time, Dad," Randy said as we reached the entryway.

"It's been very nice meeting you," I added.

"You too. I'll be over on the gaffer side if you need me for anything." And he was gone.

Randy shook his head. "Well, you sure bring out the charm in him. He was practically human." He took my hand as we floated over toward a crowd of people our age. "Whatever it was, I'm glad it happened— I'm angry at him a lot of the time but I do want you to like him."

Shit! Shit! Shit! Shit!

I set the werp to give me a warning bell when it got too late, so I wouldn't miss school again. So of course it went off right when I was getting to the good part.

And it *is* pretty late. I was going to go a little longer but now my concentration is gone, too. And all of a sudden I feel like I'm lying to you. I write down what I remember, but I think I'm "remembering" things in much more detail than I probably really perceived. Like I don't think Mr. Schwartz really said everything exactly the way I wrote it down, but I'm sure I'm pretty close, so I'm not sure whether that's false or not. A lot can turn on one or two words or on an intonation that might not show up at all. Not exactly *not* true, but not *lim* true either, if you see what I mean.

And the trouble gets worse telling you about the B Block party, because I remember all kinds of things perfectly, which ought to make it easier except I really can't remember the order they happened, or how they all connected.

And if I can't write it down just like it happened I don't want to write this part at all. Because I've noticed I'm starting to remember things the way I wrote them even when I know they happened differently. Like every so often I improve somebody's joke, or sometimes I make somebody say what the whole problem is when actually he just sat there and sobbed and sniffled until I practically had to beat it out of him. And then after I've done that, when I think about it again, I seem to hear them saying the words I wrote just as if it had really happened that way.

And when it comes to the B Block party, I want all my memories to be real. It was the only completely good thing in all that bokky lim stupid time.

So there's no order, but I'm quite sure I remember people running up to say hi to Randy; resting my head on Randy's shoulder while we danced (and finally being grateful that they made us learn how in rec); Mr. Schwartz doing the Boink or some other prehistoric dance with some older tech, both of them laughing and her very drunk; Randy just touching my face lightly like he didn't think I was real and wanted to be sure; talking with two of his old friends while he was getting us drinks, both Terry and Henri trying so hard to be superpolite and superintelligent as if impressing me was the most important thing in the world.

I remember the way the music sounded louder than any I'd heard before and I could feel it pulsing down in my belly, and the gentle pull of the magnets in my slippers against the floor while we danced. That funny warm smell from a crowd that big, every one of them with a fresh shower—they must have really put a strain on the water budget.

It was so strange to look down and notice we were on the Blue Spot, in the same Big Commons where we play aerocrosse.

The punch tingled and foamed in my mouth; Randy's father roared with laughter as he held some woman over his head.

Whorls and spins of soft color drifted lazily across the floor.

One wonderful rich maroon color shone at me through Randy's hair, giving him a halo close to his head. I laughed at it because I was so happy, and he looked so confused I had to explain, and I couldn't, and that was very funny too.

I was giddy and dizzy a lot.

When our pocket phones went off to let us know we had half an hour to get home, we both jumped half a meter. It took us by surprise because the party wasn't going to end for another six hours—after all, most of these folks were on B shift—but more surprising than that, we had lost track of the time.

Mother says it happened to her a lot when she was a girl. But it never happens up here—you live by the clock. It would be like forgetting to breathe.

Nevertheless, we did it.

Now it *really* is late. Setting a warning bell doesn't do much good if you ignore it when it goes off.

Anyway, Randy took me home, and we decided the next day we'd study Japanese together, and he kissed me good night at the door.

I feel like making up the detail that he whistled as he clambered away on the net, but that's not true. He ponged from side to side of the corridor a couple of times, but he didn't whistle.

I went in and everyone—Mother, Papa, Tom, and Susan—was sitting in there with these silly smiles. I had one myself, probably.

Late. Late. Late. Well, maybe I should have another talk with Dr. Lovell about doing this stuff. It's beginning to weirdwire me.

WERP: MAKE NOTE. get appt Lovell tomorrow. END NOTE.

I'm going to bed now.

NINE

January 3, 2026

Today Dr. Lovell tried to talk to me about the writing and the FA. I got so upset I wasn't really sure what it was about, to tell the truth. As far as I could get it, maybe they don't know what to do with me. I think that's what she meant but I could be wrong.

She said, I think—god, why couldn't I stop crying long enough to listen?—she said I should put in as much time writing as I want, and I don't have to come to class anymore.

That's not what upset me so much as what I learned—if you're Special Category, like me and Randy, your FA doesn't really count. They make us take it so we share the experience with our peers, but they expect our hobbies or quirks to take over and make us whatever we're supposed to be, the way Tom's did.

When I think about it, I should have known after last year, but I guess the idea didn't sink in or something. But it makes sense. I mean, they don't raise us like everyone else, why should they treat us like everyone else?

Maybe the trouble is that now I get what it means. It's like a fairy tale. Once, upon a time there was an ugly duckling. Everyone made fun of her. She was miserable because she had no friends. Then one day she saved the whole flock from a tiger or whatever it is that eats ducks. And everyone said, "Wow! What a duck!" And they were much more polite to her.

But she still didn't have any friends, because when you come right down to it, she was still an ugly duck.

Maybe I'll write later. Just now I don't feel like it.

*   *   *

It's been an hour since I last wrote. There was a werp flag in some of
the text before this, but I want to tell you about this before I get back to
the stuff that happened last year.

Tom came in. He's been teaching Mandelbrot Pointilist technique
to an adult art class in C Shift. Susan was taking a nap, having given up
on trying to be nice to me, and I don't blame her.

When he saw me sitting there looking miserable and asked what
the matter was, I told him as best I could, and he acted like a complete
moron, trying to tell me how I shouldn't feel that way because it was
"better and freer" to be a "real individual." "Even if you feel like no
one understands you. Especially then. Because that's when you can
see things no one else sees, *understand* things and bring them into
being for everyone else. You're really important and special—"

I burst into tears. It's the best defense ever found against well-
meaning people who are telling you something stupid "for your own
good." He stammered, patted my arm, hovered around ineffectually,
and, when the sobs got louder, fled into his and Susan's room, closing
the door behind him. I went into the bathroom to dry my eyes.

After a good look at myself, I decided the rest could use work
too, so I stripped, threw my clothes into the freshener, got into the
shower stall, and turned on the spray and vacuum. I was about a day
and a half early for a shower, but I felt like I needed it now. The
warm, sudsy water-alcohol mix felt wonderful as it squirted in over
my head and slurped away through the screen by my feet. It was early
in the week, so the charge was fresh and didn't yet smell of other
people—Tom had used this only once before me, and Susan only
twice.

I clicked the filter into place and stood in the warm rinse, swishing
it over me and letting the unhappiness wash away. I pushed the finish
button and the mix went back to the storage tank.

The towel smelled like Tom. He must have showered right after a
workout again. The scavenger just can't seem to handle that.

I clicked on the vid to get some news while I dried myself. Everyone was rich and getting richer and everyone was happy. NAC was
lying again—once we're far enough out from Earth, the onship independent news channels have no way of getting information except
from NACFlash. Supposedly someday Tass or the BBC will set up
directional channels out to the ships and the bases, and we'll get accurate news all the time, but we've been up here a lot of orbits and it
hasn't happened yet.

Why they think all we should get from Earth is "HappiNews" and "Progress!" is beyond me. Maybe I didn't steal the right file to find out.

I tossed the towel into the scavenger and put my freshened clothes back on. Susan was waiting in sharespace. "I sent Tom on ahead to dinner. I'm meeting him there—you can join us if you like or I can pick up a workmeal for you."

"What would I do with a workmeal? They as good as told me not to bother doing schoolwork anymore. And I don't really feel like eating." I pushed off and glided toward my room.

She intercepted me in a sort of gentle version of a flyball tackle, hugging me and bringing me up against the wall. "No you don't. I'm sorry you feel bad but you're not going into your room to feel sorry for yourself. Tom doesn't get to do that anymore and neither do you."

I really cried then, no strategy about it. I hated her.

But it was so comforting to be held that I didn't try to get away.

"It's going to be all right. It is. Now, listen, I know I don't really understand you, but I do know that for a couple of days after you get some writing done you're easier to live with and you don't seem to hate yourself so much. And I think all that's because you're happy.

"I want you to be happy.

"So sit down and write. You'll be hungry in about an hour and a half and by then I'll be back with a workmeal. No arguments. Just do it." She gave me another hard squeeze on the arms and let go, pushing back and looking at me for a moment from the entry. "By the way, right now Tom thinks he's solved all the problems in his life. So he's really unbearable to anyone who's at all unhappy. You might want to stay away from him until he gets over it."

Then she popped out the door.

So I'm here at the werp again, anyway, and I just realized that what it flagged before was my reference to Special Category.

That even fits into the story, but I guess I'll get there when I get there. For right now I'm just setting things down in the right order and hoping it will mean something. Here goes.

The next day, Sunday, shortly after breakfast, Papa retreated into his office and Tom to his room. They said they couldn't take any more.

Mother and I had started talking about the B Block party at breakfast and continued it all the way home and back into the living unit. I told her what everyone wore, and who danced with who as far as I could remember. She seemed to have almost guessed everything that happened as if she'd been there.

Papa muttered something unpleasant about "girl talk" just before he disappeared. "Don't forget you married one," Mother called after him.

"I *can't possibly* forget," he groaned, and went in.

That was wonderful. We must have laughed for five minutes. Anyway, while we were laughing, Tom got away too.

I was having such a good time I was actually asking Mother about when she was a girl.

She had a recording of all her old family photo albums, and we looked at pictures of her going to "proms" and stuff like that. It was funny to think that probably all the buildings in the picture were crumbling now, or already collapsed—her home town was too small to dome.

But she didn't dwell on that or get all maudlin as she so often did. This time she had a lot of stories to tell that were really funny, not disguised sermons about how bad it was up here. And not like I was being entrusted with some big important "family heritage" or any nonsense like that. These were more like things she would just share with a friend.

We finally had to quit the "girl talk" because it was time for me to go over to Randy's to study. When I left, she was bringing one of that Olson woman's books up on the screen, but it didn't bother me like it usually did.

The whole way to B Block I kept thinking of things I wanted to ask her about when she'd been a girl. What wearing skirts was like—maybe Randy and I could take Ballroom Dance, down in the bottom of the Mushroom. They wore skirts for that. And what would it be like to breathe open air and see the sky at the same time, or have no temperature control and animals wandering around wherever they wanted?

Mr. Schwartz was out again, leaving Randy by himself. In case the CPB had been monitoring us and might be suspicious, we decided to do our schoolwork first.

So we talked in Japanese, Spanish, and Esperanto for a while, and we got some papers written, and spent a lot of time just holding hands and reading. When lunchtime came, we went up to A Block cafeteria, picked up workmeals, and came directly back to work some more.

About 1400, Randy stretched his arms, reaching high over his head, and said, "Well, do you want to tackle the stuff we got yesterday?"

I tickled his extended belly, which made him jerk so hard he bounced up a meter. He squawked, flipped over, came back down, and wrestled me into an armlock. "Ar there, me pretty, now I've got yer, ye scurvy wench—"

It didn't seem possible but his pirate accent was worse than his Japanese accent.

"Unh-unh," I said. "You've got to finish the pillaging first. Those are the rules."

"Well, scuttle me barnacles, the wench is right," he said, rolling off me and letting me go. He suddenly sat up, jerking awkwardly at his coverall.

"Are you okay?"

"Uh, yeah, just something surprised me. Do you want to take a look at those files?"

"Pos-def."

We called them up, and started looking to see what a "Special Category" was. "As far as I can tell," Randy said, "it's a person without more than one brother or sister. So we both are I guess. But I don't see what difference it's supposed to make."

I was shuffling my way through the technical papers. "This is like learning a whole new subject. Supposedly we get some of every subject in school, and we're close to graduation—so why does this all look so unfamiliar?"

It was another hour of arguing and trying to understand, and we still hadn't gotten around to reading our own files, before we pieced it all together.

What we found was this:

In a society that really works by consensus, no one wants to lead, because the job has none of the privileges it does in a more hierarchic or representational society. And nobody raised that way wants to act until they know what other people want. So even though you need a vast majority of consensus-seekers, if you are going to have any ability to make a difficult decision quickly, or to delegate an important job, you need a few eccentric cases—the "Special Category" children.

Almost by definition they have to be able to function without popular support, make hard choices, and rely on their own judgment. It's great when they're right, but when they're wrong (and if a society is basically functional, the eccentric individual will be wrong most of the time) they're what we call uncos. They may have friends, and a few of them might even be popular, but they're never secure in their friendship the way kids who grew up normally are. They question every decision, the group's and their own. They often try to do something differently just to be contrary.

But even though they're a public nuisance, you always have to overproduce them, because some of them are going to end up too weird, too bokky, too predatory—*uncos*. And besides you need to have alternatives for jobs like captain, chief agronomist, mayor, and so forth.

What happens to the extras, the ones you produce and don't need?

A few really do become uncos or some other kind of criminal. More of them become miserable people who do their jobs badly. Many end up work addicts, doing a good job but hating everyone.

There's a great demonstration of this available—Earth doesn't try to control the number of "Special Category" people, and if you look at the way they live down there, you can see they really overproduce them. Which explains practically all of Earth history if you ask me.

You create people like me and Randy and Tom (and probably people like you, if you're from Earth) by using some stuff they found in the 50s and 60s of the last century. Apparently the USA was going through some kind of national spasm about the disappearance of "individualism," whatever they meant by that, and they thought they needed more uncos or something. Anyway, they found out how to make uncos: Raise kids in small families so they get more attention, think of themselves as special, and don't learn to share. Force them to spend a lot of time alone when they're young. Manipulate their social lives so that their status with their peers changes a lot and they get used to "earning" the acceptance most people just get naturally. Give them to articulate parents with deviant values so that they grow up distrusting other people's ideas.

I don't really remember what we talked about after we read that. Or even if we talked. I think we were kind of stunned.

Finally we got up, washed our faces, and decided that since the academic work was done and we both felt like the whole world had p.d.'d us, maybe we'd just go to dinner and then do some rec. It might all look better in the morning. I called Mother to let her know we were going to dinner; she dropped a big wink at me, and suddenly I felt better without really knowing why.

At dinner, we were sort of practicing Japanese offhandedly, telling every silly joke we knew, and giggling a lot, when Randy suddenly switched to English and said, "I was snooping a little before you got there. Remember Dad was typing something after he took the pictures? It turns out he sent copies of them, and a letter, to my mother."

"Where is she?"

"Supra Berlin. She's married to some plutock that moved up permanently. I haven't ever seen her since I was five, when she came up to visit during Earthpass, and I don't really remember her. She used to dance in the zero-g clubs for tips." He took a swallow of milk. "Usually I only think about her around Christmas, when she transfers some money to buy me a new coverall and a new uniform, and Dad makes me write a thank-you note. He wishes I'd write more, I know, but she never writes back when I do.

"I think Dad really wanted her to come along and marry him, but she didn't want any kids. At least that was what she said at the time. I've got two half-brothers now; Dad says when the oldest gets to be about five I should start writing to them. I can never remember their names, though. . . .

"Anyway, I was being a typically nosy kid, checking in the recent activity file, and I found a transmit copy addressed to my mother, so I pulled it up to read. It was real short—I can recite it. 'Just wanted you to know he's growing fast and he's a good kid. I'm very proud of how he's turning out. Write for details.' " Randy shrugged. "Anyway, I thought it was neat. It was about as nice as anything he ever does, you know, the way he is—rude but well meaning." He looked off to the side, at the wall.

"He upsets you a lot." I tried to say it as plainly and gently as I could, the way Papa talks to patients a lot of the time when he meets them socially. And I hated myself for being so shrinkspeak with Randy.

"Yeah, he upsets me," Randy said. "Things are a lot better since we both got into therapy. Just not as much better as I wish they were. But we talk now." He stretched. "Dad was so nice this weekend. You know? I mean I kind of saw him through your eyes. Maybe that made all the difference. He can be really charming when he wants to. The thing is, it made me think about the way it used to be when he'd just suddenly hit me—"

"He *hits* you?"

"Hey, quieter. I want to tell you about it for some reason, but I'm not going to tell the whole cafeteria. And he doesn't hit me anymore—that's part of what getting therapy was about. But yeah, he used to."

I was still so shocked I blurted out a really stupid, irrelevant question. "Where?"

"Uh, usually a slap across the face."

I tried to imagine it. I'd been hit a few times by other kids. When I was ten, Gwenny Mori and I had traded black eyes. But the idea of an adult, a big strong man like Mr. Schwartz . . .

Randy took my hand. "Look," he said, "it's not so bad anymore. I know it sounds pretty terrible, but it was just something that happened.

Okay? Dad feels a lot worse than I do about it, I think. It's just, back when it was happening, right around the time we had to change shifts, I felt really bad because there was no one I could tell. I wanted someone to tell it to, you know, a real friend. So now . . . anyway, it isn't going to happen again. He's a lot better since we started therapy and I feel safe around him again. Okay?"

I nodded and squeezed his hand hard. "I just don't want anything bad to happen to you, ever. Even stuff that's already happened."

"I feel the same way about you." He sighed. "But I don't think we're going to have much control over it. Well, want to go play for a while?"

"Sure." We held hands walking out of the cafeteria. I felt like I was more alive than I had ever been, and the whole way to the Free Rec Lobby, it seemed like every time I grasped a line my whole body sang like a guitar string.

We played a couple of good games, and we kissed goodnight again. We were really getting good at it. I knew Miriam would have teased me—she'd been doing sneakies since she was ten, and she claimed she'd actually completed the docking maneuver with three guys—but it was wonderful to me and I wasn't in any hurry. It's not how far you go but how much fun you have on the way.

Hey! It's still early! I wrote a whole day up in just a few hours. I'm going to pop out into the sharespace and talk with Susan a little, and then get to bed so I can go to school tomorrow.

Maybe I'll have another talk with Dr. Lovell. Or maybe I'll just sit in the back of the room and make obnoxious noises. Since it's not supposed to make any difference, maybe I'll just try to find a way to enjoy it.

More tomorrow, pos-def, okay?

TEN

The next week was a languages week, and Monday was mostly conversation practice. That's kind of a holiday if you're any good, because it's just talking. When your birth family language comes up, you join a group to work on your optional language, which is the most fun since you don't get graded on that at all. My optional is Swahili, and I'm really good at it; it's a lot easier than Japanese and more interesting than Esperanto and Spanish. Theophilus, I was relieved to see, was over in the French group, away from me and from Randy (who does Russian).

I'm really lousy at translating, but I'll try. There were only four of us in Swahili that day, and M'tsu and Lisa got into this lim boring argument about the airgym, so Miriam and I were left facing each other. You have to talk—that's about the only requirement there is—so we were stuck.

At first we started to just talk about class work and tell old jokes, but suddenly Miriam said, "I don't know what's happened."

"You were telling me about—"

"I mean what's happened—you know, with being friends." She looked down at the desk. "I can't believe some of the things I've said to you. Or what I keep doing."

I said it was all right. We both knew I was lying. I wanted to ask her how Theophilus fit into all this, but I couldn't think of a way to ask without starting a fight, and after all we had forty-five minutes left in the practice. "Sometimes things change," I said, hoping it would get us to a safer topic.

She looked like tears were coming up in her eyes. "Did you ever just want people to notice you? I mean lots of people? The way they used to notice Randy, or the way they notice Ted now?"

I nodded. "We probably all do."

She shook her head. "I really want it a lot. I always have." She looked down at the desk. "I'm sorry about everything," she said again. "I really am, Mel."

There wasn't much to say to that, so I said it was all right again and changed the subject. After a while we were talking about all the usual trivia, and it was almost like it had been.

That afternoon was Individuals Japanese composition, which is always a battle for everyone, even our three Japanese kids.

That kept us busy most of the day, except during rec, which was in the airgym—board hockey this time.

Theophilus was their goalie, and I drove one in past him, to my deep satisfaction. Randy and Theophilus were nominally teammates, but they were avoiding each other.

I had almost forgotten that Randy had an appointment with Papa. We didn't say much on the way there; I think he was nervous.

Papa was waiting for Randy, and they went straight into the office. I tried to get some work done in my room before dinner. Every so often I heard Randy's voice, which meant he was getting pretty loud since Papa's office is soundproofed.

A half hour had gone by while I sat there, idly daydreaming about Randy and not getting any work done. I couldn't afford that—I had a fourdeep report to get written and multi-translated by Friday. With a sigh, I replugged the search program and started calling up papers from the library again, slotting them into the bottommost level and putting their keywords up as markers in the third. It's pretty brainless work but it certainly takes plenty of time and attention, and that was what I needed.

Miriam had been about to tell me something, a couple of times, in that conversation. I was sure of it. Probably it was something important, but what?

Maybe she just wanted to be friends again. I forced my attention back to the paper I was working on.

I had most of the plan for the paper laid out and most of the notes in place and was beginning to get a little bit of work done on the second level when Randy came out. His eyes were red-rimmed and there were tearstains on his cheeks, but he seemed all right now, maybe even a little calmer than usual.

"Well," Mother said. "Since we are all here, let's go to dinner."

She sounded formal somehow. "Randy, we usually eat at our local cafeteria and the whole family eats together. We use the local cafeteria because it's not quite so crowded, and we can have a whole table for just our family." There was something about the way she was talking that I didn't like, but I couldn't quite identify what. I took along my werpsack, instead of just my phone, so Randy and I could compare homework over dinner. Tom brought his werp too; Mother always talked about the family being all together, but a lot of times we were all just using werps and readers while sitting at the same table.

The corridors were almost deserted and we had the netting to ourselves; most people went to dinner right at the end of their shift's Work Period II, and this was more than an hour after that for A Shift. At the cafeteria we took a table for five.

That night it was a rare treat—chicken!—so nobody said much as we ate, except the usual comments about wishing ag would get better at all this.

When we finished, Mother said, "Randy, how many brothers and sisters do you have?"

"I'm it," he said. "I'm an only child."

"Oh. Your parents must have—"

"No." He shook his head. "It's just me and Dad."

Mother smiled. "And what does your father do?"

"He's on Outside crew. Vacuum extrusion. And he's been vice-president and secretary of the VWU local off and on."

It sounded like Mother was leading into p.d.'ing Randy's standing, but that's a game only kids play—never adults or at least never in front of us.

Papa broke in with a long funny story—at least I think it was supposed to be funny, though none of us laughed—and then he and Mother were off into one of those quiet fights that never looks like a fight unless you know them as well as I do. That meant they'd be ignoring the rest of the world for a couple of hours.

"Say," I said, "Tom, do you know what was interesting about those problems of yours?"

"No, what?"

"I looked them over and they all turned out to be incomputable."

Tom snorted. "And people wonder why I have problems with CSL. How can the problems be incomputable when I computed them?"

I shook my head. "No, that's just the point. You didn't. You just knew the answers—there was no rational, computable way for you to get the answer. You just got it."

Tom shrugged. "You mean like the proofs of incomputability in the book. I never have been able to do one of those. In fact I don't see how a problem that has an answer can even be incomputable."

I looked at Randy for support; he was looking up, apparently at the Roswalds dining overhead but probably at something in the back of his head. "Let's go through this slowly," Randy said. "You got a whole assignment of incomputable problems? Not just determine solvability, but they actually asked you to solve them—no labels or warnings? Nothing to tell you there was anything unusual?"

"No sign at all," Tom said. "Looked like any other assignment to me."

"And you solved them. Hmm. Do you have a copy, Melpomene?"

I did. Randy scanned my proofs. At last he said, "Well, those certainly are incomputable problems."

"I still don't see how you can know that," Tom said, "especially not when the answers are obvious."

That got us both into trying to explain the idea to him. By that time, Mother and Papa had wound down the fight. As many times as I've seen it, I still don't quite understand how when they're out in public they can have these fascinating arguments where they both keep smiling and talk so softly.

We all went back to the living unit together. I think Mother was a little surprised (and maybe not pleased) that Randy stayed with Tom and me, but since all of us went back to Tom's room there wasn't much for her to say about it.

For an hour, Randy set up various incomputable problems in math, and I set them up in CSL, and Tom got answers to them in five minutes or so, just sitting there and thinking at them. It was the weirdest thing we'd ever seen—weirder still because he couldn't understand how we wrote the problems. "They just seem like puzzles with only one piece missing," he said. "Of course you know what shape it is and what picture's on it—what else could it be? But how you guys come up with these—all those steps you write—that I can't follow at all."

So we started to show him, and on the way I learned a lot of math from Randy, not so much the procedures themselves, which I knew fairly well, but just how he looked at a problem. Randy claims I did some of the same thing for his CSL, which is not only nice of him but probably true.

For some reason, Tom responded a lot better to Randy and me than he did to me by myself; we really got somewhere with him. "Hmmm," he said, after working several problems successfully for the first time in his life, "I think I'm beginning to get the hang of this. You guys ought to think about being teachers or professors or something . . . you make a great team."

I don't know why Randy blushed; I don't even know why I felt so embarrassed. But Tom didn't manage to notice either of us. He was wading into yet another problem. "I can probably do a dozen more of these before bedtime. If you guys want to get on with your own work—"

Randy looked as sheepish as I felt. "I didn't start my presentation for Esperanto tomorrow yet."

"Me either," I confessed.

Tom looked at the clock in the corner of his screen; it showed barely an hour till Lights Down. "I'm sorry! I really kept you guys!" Now *he* was embarrassed. "What do you have to get done?"

"We each have to give a five minute talk in Esperanto tomorrow," I said. "It has to be arguing for or against stepping up the cargo bay building schedule. We have datasets on it, so it wouldn't be so bad, but we have to hand Dr. Niwara a copy of the speech before we give it."

"You don't have to have it memorized, do you?" he asked.

"No, we can read from a prompter screen, but neither of us writes Esperanto very well," Randy explained.

"Well, I'm top in my class at Esperanto comp," Tom said. "You're allowed to use a rough translator, right?"

"Sure."

"Okay, hack out something in English, rough translate it, and I'll help you polish for style. It's the least I can do."

So that's what we did. In English I'm just fine—remember they decided I should write this silly book—and Randy's okay, so we got done quickly; then we ran them through the rough translator and they came out in Esperanto. That doesn't work well with any other source-to-target language combination, but English has a very linear structure, and Esperanto is perfectly regular, so it was very close to right. Tom made a few corrections and adjusted them for style and we were done.

Central flashed Lights Down warning to Randy just after we got our final drafts into our pocket werps. "I'll have to go," he said, with a little regret in his voice. "See you tomorrow in class, Melpomene. Nice to see you again, Tom."

Tom smiled. "This was a big help, for me anyway. I'm glad we'll be seeing you at least once a week—and I wouldn't mind if Melpomene brought you home more often."

I wasn't sure whether I wanted to hug my brother or kick him;

Randy flushed again. We all kind of shrugged and said goodnight, and he went home.

I was going over my presentation when I heard my parents arguing; I know that even Papa doesn't like it when I listen in on them, but after all he listens in on people professionally, and besides it says right on the sign in the classroom that "the concern of one is the concern of all." I don't see why that shouldn't be true in your family, if it's true for the ship.

Papa had that ultra-reasonable voice he puts on when he's afraid Mother is going to start shouting. "Helen, you always knew this was possible when you signed up. Remember, you were the one that quoted to me the fable about the fox and the lion. Well, this is the kind of experience that's going to produce lions. I know they're not as attractive as other kids—"

"Not as attractive! That Schwartz kid is a bully, and his father beats him. Sounds like he deserves it, too! Wendy Harrison told me all about Randy Schwartz. I had to talk with her on the com for an hour today." I heard her breath rasping in her throat. "What kind of pair-up is that for Melpomene?"

Papa sighed. "Keep your voice down—these kids have nothing like our idea of privacy."

"That's another thing! Melpomene—"

"Is a moderately well-adjusted kid for the environment. With a big need to be liked, too much empathy to ever be very happy, and a certain amount of quiet charisma. That's the kind of personality our mayor is supposed to have when the ship's fully operational. And being on warm terms—"

"Warm terms!" There were two thuds about a breath apart; when Mother is really upset, she stamps her foot, forgetting that the floor is hard and her slippers are thin, and that in low grav that slams her right up against the ceiling. I imagined she had hurt herself, and was trying to rub her foot and head at the same time, waving off Papa as he hovered over her. I almost didn't hear the next thing she said. "Why don't you just admit it? You've made your daughter neurotic on purpose, and now you're going to pander her off to a psychotic kid."

Papa's voice was getting lower, which usually means he's about to be angry. "Helen, we're not just talking about the plan here. No one is going to hold a gun to Melpomene's head and make her marry anyone, any more than we're going to run her for mayor without her consent. And we aren't going to brainwash her, either. She is just what either of us is—a product of her experiences. The only difference—the *only* difference—is that more of hers have been planned for a particular effect. If you went into her room right now and asked her what she'd really like to do in 2038 or 2040, she might very well say run for council—to get ready to run for mayor in the 2050s. And if she hasn't thought of it yet, she will. We may have planned her decisions—but she's still making them. I doubt she'd be upset if I walked in and told her what we'd done."

That showed how little he knew me. I was furious! If he had even halfway explained things, Randy and I might never have gone to the difficulty and risk of snooping. One thing was for sure—when I was mayor, there wasn't going to be any of his stupid privacy business anymore. No more private files. If I could get people to go along with it, we'd take all the doors off living units and rooms.

I almost missed the next thing Papa said.

"And as for Randy—he's a good kid. The best, really. We've hyperstressed him to the limit the last year or so, and the worst he's developed is a little extra aggression. When we shift things over to give him more acceptance, his personality should just about match the ideal profile for ship's officer. If you've got to play matchmaker, think about him as a future captain."

"Ha. Extra aggression? Wendy said that he—"

"Yes, he does get into fights with her son. Small wonder. Just at the moment, little Ted Harrison is, in my opinion as a mental health professional, an asshole."

Mother snorted. "You really don't pay any attention to anything, as much as you like to lecture me. I can't believe you've looked at the Harrison family profile—"

"Yes, I have, and it *explains* why that kid is an asshole. But he'll get socialized eventually. What's happening now is just that our kids are scraping the stink of Earth off of him, teaching him what they've learned from birth—the hard way, because he needs to learn fast."

The idea that we were affecting Theophilus more than he was affecting us lim weirdwired me. I couldn't see anything like that. I was half tempted to barge out there and tell Papa how wrong he was, but I had a feeling they'd both get all upset.

Pos-def it would have been the wrong time. Mother was crying and yelling at him, that yammering whining that she goes into when she's lost an argument, and Papa was just trying to get a word in edgewise. When she gets like that, I can barely understand her even if I'm in the same room, but Papa usually seems to be able to.

When she'd gotten down to just sobbing, he finally said, "Helen, what do you want me to do? Or all of us to do? Earth is gone, the Earth we knew anyway. Nothing will ever look like it did before the Die-Off and the Eurowar. And these kids don't have any obligation to make it look like that, just because their parents miss it."

She mumbled something, sniffling, and I barely caught any of it, just fragments about "freedom" and "human spirit" and a lot of other words.

"That's a question to leave to them. Maybe you're right and people can't live like this for very long. But the best evidence—with so many people dead, and so much lost—is that they can't live the old way at all. Individualism is dead because it didn't work."

I heard her leap into their room. The door slammed. I knew Papa was in the sharespace by himself. I should have gone out to him, but I could think of nothing to say.

January 5, 2026

I showed all that stuff to Dr. Lovell. "You really think we should just let this come out this way? I mean, for a whole planet of uncos to get upset by?" (Sorry, if you're from Earth. But all the stuff I've read says practically all of you are.)

She shrugged. "Other people can decide that, Melpomene. How do *you* feel?"

"About writing it? It kind of brought a lot back. At first, I thought I'd explode with happiness. My god—mayor, if I just stayed on course. And maybe the captaincy for Randy."

She nodded a couple of times. "Why didn't you?"

"Oh, a lot of things. I got weirdwired, maybe, lim angry because of everything that had happened. And on top of that I just didn't think much of the plan anymore. Maybe I didn't want to get it like that."

"You wrote at the beginning you were going to be mayor." She sat directly in front of me, looking me in the eye. "What was that about?"

"I *am* going to be mayor. Just not the way they had scripted. I like the story but I think us kids will write it better for ourselves."

She nodded, reached forward, and squeezed my hands. "Here's what I'm wondering about, Melpomene. Is it possible that after what happened the next day—which was sort of when you and Randy got a taste of the leader's job—you decided you just don't want to do it, and this is just a way to lose it gracefully? Are you kidding yourself now?"

That was the first time I remembered that Dr. Lovell didn't seem phony to me. So I really had to think about what she had said, and that's what I've been doing all this evening, instead of writing. Susan and Tom are already in bed, and it's close to Lights Down, and I still don't have an answer.

So tomorrow I'll tell you about the next thing that happened, and how I felt, and maybe that will help me figure out what I really want to do.

ELEVEN

January 6, 2026

I still don't have any idea. Dr. Lovell's question really did something strange in my brain. So here's what happened. Maybe you can decide.

The next day in class we did our reports—both Randy's and mine went okay. Then Dr. Niwara weirdwired us all by announcing that there would be a speed math contest to find out who team captains would be for aerocrosse. Every so often they do that—make you do math in the middle of a verbal week. I guess it's supposed to keep us on our guard or something.

It was going to be seven teams of four again. Since team captains had been chosen in a math contest, I wasn't really expecting any surprises. Sure enough, Theophilus was made captain for Team One, and Randy for Team Two—he stiffened suddenly when Barry Yang whispered, "Team color should be Royal Blue." I mentally marked Barry for a good, hard body check.

Gwenny Mori was captain for Team Three, Kwame for Team Four, and Padraic for Team Five. You could really tell who had been hanging around with who lately—little as I liked Theophilus I had to admit he was a math wizard, and obviously a good coach as well.

"Team Six," Dr. Niwara said. "Miriam Baum." Another friend of Theophilus. He really could teach.

"Team Seven, Melpomene Murray."

Miriam getting it was pretty good; *me* getting it was beyond belief. But there it was—I would have Team Seven, the team that started without a goal. Some of Randy must have copied over to me.

Then we did Pairs Esperanto composition, and finally went to lunch. I was a little late getting into line, so I was one of the last ones out, behind Chris Kim, who tended to trail behind anyway. I had been sort of talking with him—I had already decided to make him my first choice for my team, because he was a much better player than most people realized—so I dragged him along when I went to join Randy at a table in the corner of the lunchroom.

That put the three of us sort of off by ourselves. Theophilus and the Real Gang were occupying the center table. Most other people were packed around that, some in close to pretend to be part of it, others farther away but close enough so that they could still hear. One thing you could say for Theophilus, since he had gotten here we'd all had a lot more to talk about.

We sat down and talked about homework and assignments, in Esperanto because it was a good way to lube Dr. Niwara, who always wandered around the lunchroom listening in.

Chris had always been a little afraid of Randy, I think, but now he was more afraid of Theophilus; after all, he wasn't going to get a math score Randy would beat him up for, but anybody could be the target of those nasty jokes.

After a while, the two of them warmed up to each other. It turned out they both were going to play airball for the VWU Youth Auxiliary team, and they both agreed that their coach, Bob Mori, was still thinking too much in terms of two baskets and playing on a plane.

I was excited from coming in so high in math and getting picked for captain, and—how I knew this, I'm not sure, but I was sure of it—Chris and Randy were both excited about becoming friends. We were all talking and laughing really loud and getting kind of silly.

I happened to look over toward Theophilus's table and saw Miriam look at me for a second; she looked really upset. What I'd been thinking of as the "inner circle," Theophilus plus Kwame, Gwenny, and Miriam, were all whispering to each other and ignoring everyone else. I didn't think much of that at the time—it was common enough, after all.

After lunch we had to go back and do dialogging—lim boring!

—HOW ARE YOU FEELING, TODAY, MELPOMENE?

—JUST FINE, THANK YOU.

—IS ANYTHING SPECIAL ON YOUR MIND?

—I'M VERY EXCITED ABOUT THE AEROCROSSE GAME TODAY.

—WHAT ABOUT THE AEROCROSSE GAME IS SO EXCITING?

—I'M A TEAM CAPTAIN.

—GERMANE? (I hate that! The stupid AI didn't see what being captain had to do with being excited.)

—TEAM CAPTAIN IS A POSITION IN AEROCROSSE. I AM VERY EXCITED TO HOLD THAT POSITION.

—APPROVED. (Gee, thanks.) WHY DO YOU LIKE BEING TEAM CAPTAIN?

After an hour of that, we all jumped up pretty fast when Dr. Niwara announced time for aerocrosse.

Since Team Seven got to pick last in each round, the only real luck I had was I got Chris. I picked Penelope Graham because I thought she would be okay, not special but a good team player, and Dmitri Onegin because he was the only one left. He tried hard but he was just kind of clumsy.

Randy, with Team Two, got Barry Yang, certainly one of the best players in the class, even if he'd sort of betrayed Randy's friendship in the last few days. His second pick was Rachel DeLane, who can throw straight as a laser all the way from bottom to top of the Big Commons. He also got Rebecca Hayakawa, which was odd because she usually got picked much earlier for her strength and brains.

Things got weird within two minutes of the start. Normally the high-numbered team faces a hard defense, but there was something beyond that, as if everyone was waiting for something that I didn't know about.

The headset crackled in my ear. Captains get both a common channel to their team and a channel to all the other captains; that way we can cut deals. We listen to both channels all the time but we can pick which one we want to talk on.

It was Miriam. "Hey, Melpomene. If Seven wants to gang on Two, Six is holding two balls." We were holding the other one at the moment and just trying to pick a target—one ball is pretty easy to defend against.

"You got it, Mim."

We bracketed Two's goal pretty well, closing in tight on it right out in the center.

The captain had posted the grav at .0006, and nothing was moving much—you could really swim. Even from a standing start treading air, it was no work at all to kick your way upward.

Miriam detailed M'tsu to guard Team Six's goal, and he took it down below where he could also help retrieve stray balls—a moderately risky move that could turn sour if the alliance broke or someone else got a ball. With that done, Teams Six and Seven were all around Two's goal, taking shots in when we could and passing the balls among seven of us. Everyone else had scattered themselves around the top of the Commons, far away from us in case we decided to do anything tricky.

It was really fine play—Randy's team was hard pressed to do anything but keep getting in the way of the balls, and I knew they'd have some bruises to show later. I was busy being captain, and the game is what counts, but I still had to admire the way Randy kept Team Two in position—I don't think I could have held goal, even with a team that good, for half that long.

Chris justified my faith in him beautifully; he kipped over suddenly, intercepted a pass from me to Dmitri, and snapped a shot in past Barry Yang. The bright "7" replaced the "2" on the goal, and Randy's team dove away from it, doing reversals on the platforms and shooting up to where the big concentration of targets was, hoping to get lucky soon since all the balls were temporarily in the crosses of Miriam's Six and my Seven.

I caught the carom shot, noted that Penelope had grabbed another ball, and clicked captain's freke off so Miriam wouldn't hear what came next.

"Dmitri and Chris, take the goal up to the top and guard it, right now. Penny, we're going to doublecross Six. Get going on a catcher platform like you're going to do a long jump up, but dive on Team Six's goal when I signal. I'll take the other side—let's see if we can take it and pun off a crosscatch."

Miriam's voice crackled in my ear. "Okay, Mel, let's take your goal up to the top. We're bringing ours up too."

She really should have known better than that. We were the first team to score, which meant we had a temporary lead—we had one, Randy's Two had minus one, and everyone else including Miriam's Six had zero. You always try to widen a lead.

Well, if she was going to be that dumb, we might as well use it. "You got it," I said. I clicked my mike over so I was talking privately with my team again; Chris and Dmitri moved our goal up, safely out of range.

I let myself drift down and over to one of the platforms, as if I were going to one-jump it as well. Penelope was already in place and nearly invisible, flattening herself back against the wall.

I flipped to captain's freke again. "Hey, Mim, why don't you just pass that goal straight up?"

A second later, and M'tsu threw the goal up toward Miriam. It drifted up slowly toward her, and she treaded air more slowly, sinking to meet it. I flipped my mike back to team freke.

"Penny, ready?"

"Ready!"

"One, two, *go!*"

We both kicked off and headed straight for the goal, its big green "6" glowing at us. Miriam caught on fast, but she was centered and had no way to work up speed but swimming as hard as she could. We had kicked from the wall, and in one deep breath we were on top of the unguarded goal as it drifted lazily upward.

"Don't throw, Penny, we'll just tag it." She acknowledged and locked the ball into her cross just before she spread-eagled and caught the goal, drifting with it toward me. I spread-eagled too and met her, the goal squishing between us for an instant before my slightly greater momentum carried it.

It was now hopeless for Miriam—we had a big lateral motion, plus an upward one we were adding to with our kicking, and we had the goal about two-thirds wrapped between us. She couldn't possibly get enough speed from swimming to catch us, and because we hadn't tagged her goal yet, hitting it with the ball she was holding wouldn't change the situation.

So she snapped her ball as hard as she could into the back of my helmet, and I found out first hand what I had done to Randy a few days before—my ears rang, my neck ached, and my teeth tingled where they had slammed together. I didn't see where the ball caromed off to.

Penelope popped the ball out of her cross and touched the goal, making it ours officially, then retrapped her ball. "You okay, Mel?"

"Yeah. A bit shook up."

"Cheap shot. She aimed right at your head. She wasn't even trying for the goal. She couldn't have been."

"It's legal," I said.

"Still . . ." she let it hang as we reached the platform. "Which way?"

"Straight up—wrap it and bounce on three." I counted off and we shot up toward the top.

"Melpomene, that was the last straw." It was Miriam's voice; she was mad, but after all, doublecrosses are a big part of the game. "I tried to get you in with everyone, and you stuck me in the back. You could have been on the same side with everyone else against Two and all you could think about was getting a cheap point."

I was starting to get irritated. "It was pretty expensive for you," I pointed out.

"Not as expensive as it's going to be for you," Theophilus chimed in.

I didn't see what Theophilus had to do with it, and his having spoken made me even angrier. Penelope and I were kicking hard, gaining speed as we approached the top, and the big yellow "1" of Theophilus's goal was directly overhead. I killed my mike entirely. "Penny, do you think we could get lucky and rivet One's goal before they caught on?"

"It's just a game of aerocrosse, Mel. Why not?"

I nodded and said, "Wait till we close in, then we'll give them both balls and see how they hop."

At that moment, all but one of Team One dove straight down at us. There was no sign that they were trying to kidnap the goal, grab it physically and try to get a ball to claim it with later. To do that you push off the top and then spread-eagle. They were flutter kicking straight down at us, getting speed for a really hard body check.

I let them get closer. "Now!" We both threw as hard as we could; I'm not sure which ball got past, but the yellow One rolled over to our Seven.

Three goals—if we could keep them.

We waited another breath, then braced our feet against the goal, and when I said "Now" we pushed off, downward and outward. Team One shot past without managing to check either of us, and the goal wobbled on up to the top, where Dmitri grabbed it.

I saw all that as I shot across the space, head first, toward the wall. I flipped over and treaded air against the motion, slowing down before I hit between two platforms. I slapped feet on the wall, caught myself with my hands on the underside of the upper platform, shoved myself down, and pushed off hard back upward toward the goal we'd just zapped from One.

Penelope, I saw, was headed the same way, and Chris and Dmitri were bumping the other two goals along to join us. It wouldn't be easy to hang onto all those goals, even up at the top.

I knew our two balls had caromed wildly and were shooting around down below, as members of several teams tried to get one. But where had the third ball gone after bouncing off my helmet?

There wasn't time to give it much thought. Penelope and I, with Chris and Dmitri, got our three goals penned up against the ceiling as tight as possible, as you have to do when you're guarding short-handed. None of us would get a chance to catch a strap and rest.

The teams who still had goals, Three, Four, and Five, scattered wildly away from us, swimming hard to push their goals against air resistance. When they caught the balls down below, we would be the focus of attack.

That was when the third ball showed up. Randy's Team Two dove out of nowhere on Kwame's Team Four. Randy and Barry plowed into them in hard body checks, sending Kwame and two of his teammates spinning down toward the bottom, and Bekka sailed in and tore the goal from Sylvestrina's hands. Then Rachel DeLane nailed it with the ball, and Randy grabbed the ball on the carom as he returned from a catcher platform—a beautiful play.

But it could have been a lot more beautiful. Randy whipped a pass to Barry, who took a shot at the exposed upper side of Three's goal— but it whizzed past the goal, past Gwenny, and into the cross of Theophilus.

I didn't quite understand what I saw. Very plainly, to me anyway, Theophilus and Barry nodded to each other. It just didn't look right— they weren't on the same team, and Barry wasn't a captain. Communication goes only through the captains, normally, though when teams are allied sometimes you'll talk to someone within earshot.

I didn't have much time to think because suddenly Theophilus's team had all three balls and was swimming up at us fast. They couldn't get as much momentum as you can get in a dive, of course, but they were building up speed pretty well and besides we had a lot to do with keeping three goals penned in the small space.

"Hey, Seven—alliance?" Randy's voice crackled in my earphones.

"Pos-def. Pull on in," I said, and clicked on private freke. "Okay guys, Team Two has joined us." Rebecca and Rachel pushed the goal into our cluster and we turned to face Team One, which was still rising.

Theophilus still didn't know the game at all well; he threw much too early, probably not listening to his teammates., The ball was slowing down, and I was closing in on it. "Yours," Randy said, next to me. I reached for it—

Something hit me in the back. Randy and I both lost our positions and tumbled as Barry Yang shouted "Got it" and grabbed for it, knocking us away.

He tried to catch it with his hand—real dumb because it doesn't change the marker on the ball—and it glanced off and took one of my team's goals.

I righted myself—Randy was still next to me, but we had tumbled about four meters. I heard an "oof" as Theophilus crashed into Rachel, knocking her up against the top and scattering the goals despite our best efforts. In a moment, Team One had gotten all of them.

Something finally connected. I flutter kicked over to Randy and leaned into his ear, turning off both frekes. "Randy, I saw Theophilus give Barry a signal. Barry bokked on purpose."

Randy stared at me. "I saw it," I said. "It's true."

Randy clicked on his team freke. "Barry, get to me right now," he said into the mike. "Melpomene, if you could . . ."

I nodded and started to take off, but Barry swam up and grabbed my arm. "What did she tell you?"

I flipped over, twisting out of his grip, and turned to face him. "I saw you get that nod from Theophilus when you passed the ball to him. And you tipped their ball into your own team's goal on purpose."

Barry started to say something, but Randy said, "I believe Melpomene, so don't bother. But what really gets me—"

"Are you going to hit me?"

"I don't hit people any more."

"Ha." Barry was starting to snivel; his eyes were wet.

"I haven't hit you yet and I'm not going to. Now listen. What I really can't stand is that I picked you for the team because—" Randy gulped and I saw his eyes were starting to run too—"Because you—I wanted to be friends again. We used to be friends. . . ."

Barry started to cry. I felt really awful for him and looked away. My head still hurt from Miriam's ball, and I thought I was bringing up a couple of bruises from where Barry had hit me from behind. We were flat at zero along with most other teams, Randy's team trailed, with minus one, and Team One now had four goals.

But the other teams weren't attacking. Team One was holding all the balls, and it took me a while to realize they were "sitting on their lead"—I've seen teams do that in the Earth sports flash-channel, but never here.

It was really a groundhog thing to do, acting like the final score mattered more than the game, p. d.'ing the other side's numbers without having to really compete with them team to team.

I knew, without being quite sure how, that if Theophilus won the game the way he had planned to, there would be a lot more quarrels, a lot more bad feeling, a lot more getting left out.

I turned on the emergency open channel on the helmet. Usually a captain's supposed to use that only for an injury or something like that, but this didn't seem like a good time to worry about the rules. "Barry Yang has just admitted that he was helping Team One against his own team. We don't know if he was the only one doing that. You'd better make sure that all your teammates are playing on the same side you are—and watch your captains especially. We all know who they're friends with."

There was a long, long silence. Then Theophilus's voice came in on the emergency freke. "You know she's never liked me ever since she found out I liked her friend Miriam better. She's even friends with the class bully now because she hates me so much. She's just complaining because she isn't popular . . . *she just doesn't belong.* She's just not one of the crowd, and she's mad about that."

My eyes stung with tears—

And Barry Yang came off a catcher platform in a hard swimming dive that slammed Theophilus spinning, clawing crazily at the air to get back his balance before he hit the wall. His head hit the edge of a platform with a nasty, sharp thump, and he tumbled back out into the middle.

And then suddenly everyone was hitting him, kicking at him, diving in from all sides to shove him and throw him against the wall. Even the ones who had been in his crowd, Kwame, Gwenny, all of them except Miriam, were on him, slapping him and punching him, keeping him spinning and dizzy and unable to defend himself or even get to the wall. Blood squirted from his nose in a corkscrewing trail, and I could hear him sobbing hysterically.

The ones who were hitting him were laughing, an ugly aggressive fuck-you-in-your-face sound I'd never heard before.

I had never seen anything like that before in my life. I hope I won't see it again. I clicked both captain's and private freke on. "Randy, we've got to get him out of there. I'm going to try to dive in and get his belt. Chris and Dmitri, come along too. We have to get him to the Blue Spot." Half of me was still in the game—the Blue Spot was where injured players went until time out could be called and they could get out. I don't know why, given what was happening, I expected anyone to respect it.

We did get him out. It wasn't easy because he was scared and he was hurt pretty badly—bleeding from some cuts and bruised all over. No one hit his kidneys or his neck hard enough to do any permanent damage, but he was a mess.

When Chris, Dmitri, and I caught hold of him, the other kids started cheering. I didn't know what it was about so I ignored it; as soon as we had him halfway stable we started moving him. He was struggling and fighting with us—probably so scared and disoriented he thought we were going to beat him up too.

When they saw what we were doing, people all talked at once, their voices very tight and high, echoing around the space. Then they all swam toward us, some of them very fast. Every one of them had the same strange expression, as if they were all running a copy of the same program.

Randy dove between us and the crowd, Rachel, Penelope, and Bekka following him. They hit the rebound boards and rose to meet the crowd head-on. Randy's voice came over the emergency open freke. "No, no, no more. Leave him alone."

I wasn't sure what he said after that, but it was pretty soothing; he sounded like he was really in charge of everything. He kept talking and we got Theophilus down into the Blue Spot; once he had a firm surface he was less panicked and we could hold him and try to calm him down.

Meanwhile Randy had gotten the others to go to the locker room and change out, sending Bekka and Penelope along to make sure they did. He came back with Rachel to see how Theophilus was—which surprised Theophilus a lot, I could tell, but he didn't say anything. We called a med capsule, put Theophilus in it, and sent him to the infirmary.

Another reason I'll always love Randy—he saw me home. I really needed someone with me, because I was having a lot of trouble remembering what I should be doing. I didn't even change out of my gym clothes, which is really rude when you're going to be out in public. He put his arm around me and hugged me at the door, then went home himself.

Mother was waiting for me. "What happened?" she demanded.

"I don't know. I don't know where Dr. Niwara was or why she didn't do anything," I said, starting to cry, "and I don't know how it happened at all. I just—"

"You beat that boy so badly he had to go into the hospital!"

She shouted it into my face; I was so surprised that I didn't even try to explain. "I keep hearing about what healthy little fuckers you are. Just different. Just a little more socialized. You ganged up on that little boy and you would have killed him if you could. And you're supposed to be—you're the ones who are going to—" She was gasping for breath.

She grabbed my shoulders and shook me so hard my neck hurt. "I should have done this a long time ago!"

And then—well, I write it, but I hope you don't believe it even though it's true: she turned me around, grabbed my gym shorts, and pulled them down. I screamed. The neighbors heard it even through the soundproofing.

And then she forced my head down over the house terminal and slapped my bare buttocks again and again, harder and harder. She was yelling at me, calling me names, and sobbing while she did it. I felt naked, more naked than I'd known I could feel, and powerless, and completely humiliated. I wanted to vomit, faint, die, anything but this.

And then all of a sudden Papa was there, and I got away and pulled my pants back up and tucked up in a little ball to cover myself, and then med capsules came, two of them, one for Mother and one for me.

They released me that evening; she hadn't hit me very hard, and there wasn't even a bruise, but they gave me a bottle of happy pills to take for the next couple of days. They were mad at Papa—I could tell, though of course they tried to hide it in front of the "boss's daughter." I figured out after a while that they didn't think he should be doing my counseling; it was against all the theories and so forth. The nurse seemed to be angriest of all; I heard him outside the door. "What kind of responsibility is that? He's been shielding his wife for years and now even after his little girl gets beaten up—" They shushed him and tried to move him farther down the hall. "I don't care what the Plan calls for," I heard him say, and then there was some more low, urgent talking to him, and I heard him again. "I don't give a fuck about the fucking Plan, it's not right." There was more talking, and then silence; they left me alone till Papa came and got me. I was drifting in and out on the happy pills, thinking about being mayor and about Randy being captain, wondering if we should visit Theophilus or something, as long as we were here . . . but of course it was just me here; Randy would be coming to visit me, though, and maybe then we could go down the hall—

I was asleep when Papa finally showed up. He woke me up and handed me my clothes; I got dressed without saying much, and we went home. Mother wasn't there. "She'll be along in about three or four days," Papa said. "She'll need a lot of patience and understanding; she's feeling very guilty right now, and they've got her under light hypnotherapy to boost her acceptance."

I nodded; the year before, when I had gotten caught masturbating in the restroom and the other girls had made fun of me for weeks, I had gone through that. They just give you a light dose of drugs to calm you down, stick you in a sensory deprivation tank, and play a recording of your own voice reading the things they told you to—mine were "I'm pretty normal," "I enjoy touching myself and I'm not ashamed of it," and "They don't mean to hurt me. If I politely tell them they're hurting me, they will stop teasing."

Of course I was wondering what they had Mother listening to. "I enjoy hitting people and I'm not ashamed?" So I almost missed what Papa was saying, and had to ask him to repeat it.

"I'm sorry, Melpomene," he said. "I didn't realize you—"

"I'm okay," I said. "Just daydreaming. Why did she do it?"

He sat back and looked at me. "Why do you think she did it?"

I hate shrink games. "Because she's crazy."

He nodded. "I can see that it might look that way to you."

"Like shit." I was only beginning to realize how angry I was. "That was the most humiliating thing that ever happened to me, and you want me to see her side of it? Well, forget it. As far as I'm concerned, she's crazy and a moron and if the guilt is bothering her, it should."

He sat quietly, then, for a long time. Finally he said, "I don't really know what answer I can give you, Melpomene. There's nothing much I can say that will make any sense to you."

He pushed up from his chair and kicked over to the viewscreen, switching it on. The stars hung still in the darkness; I could see the red glow of Mars, not to be a disk for another couple of months, in the lower corner. He *never* does that. Shrinks don't avoid looking at you, not the good ones, anyway. . . . I didn't know what was wrong with Papa. I didn't know what was wrong, at all.

"Melpomene," he said finally, "I know you got into the CPB Plan files. On Earth, information like what's in the files—if it were published—would result in rioting. Revolution. Anarchy in the streets. What do you think would happen here?"

I shook my head. "I don't know."

"I don't either." He held out his arms, as if to hug me. "Try to understand your mother. She thinks like the people back home—back on Earth, I mean. She sees the world the way they do. That was part of why she was your ideal mother . . . she helped you get more individuated. Theophilus might well have been killed if you and Randy hadn't been there.'

"I suppose it's possible."

He nodded. "So what are you going to do if you're mayor? Give good jobs to all your friends and have them get you re-elected?"

"Why?" I asked. "Are they going to be the best people for their jobs?"

He shook his head. "I mean, just give them to them. Because they're your friends."

"Why would they want them if they're not the right people?"

He smiled at me, but I could see tears glistening in his eyes. "Melly," he said softly, "I love you."

It was a strange thing to say, but at least I knew the right answer to it. "I love you too, Papa."

He nodded. "I—twenty years ago, when I was just out of school and NAC hired me, this was doomed to happen. But I never understood it up to now." He was smiling, still, and I hugged him again. "There's something you probably should hit me for," he said. "But I have to tell you about it."

"I don't think I'll hit you for it this time. Whatever it is."

"Dr. Niwara was ordered not to be in the Big Commons. We heard Theophilus and his friends on the mike at lunch time, planning it all out, and we needed to see how you kids would handle the situation with no adult guidance."

I sat back and stared at him. "You *knew* that was going to happen?"

"Not at all. We didn't have the slightest idea how offended most of your classmates would be." He held up his hand to stop me from interrupting; I hadn't actually had anything to say. "Melpomene, I just thought you should know that we fucked up very badly. And as more of you kids have been getting older, we've understood you less and less and fucked up more and more. So . . . well, we're debating something. And this is something I shouldn't even ask you, but you're my daughter, and I find I have to know this before I can begin to think reasonably about it.

"What if we said you *weren't* going to be the mayor?"

"Well, if it's better for the ship . . . I mean, I'd be disappointed but if the *Flying Dutchman* needs someone else—"

"What if we didn't *pick* anyone else? What if we just gave up the whole idea of the Plan, because it's clear we don't know what we're doing, and turned things over to you kids—because you understand more than we do?"

I was stunned. My head spun. "Would you really do that?"

Very softly, tears began to run down Papa's face. "If it's the best thing . . . I guess we'll have to. But oh, Melpomene, it won't ever be as simple as that. . . ."

Then I hugged him again, and he sighed a lot, and stopped crying and dried his eyes. I had all kinds of questions, but I didn't ask them. We just sat there for a long time.

There was a pounding on the door. Papa keyed it open and there was Tom, grinning like a maniac. "I did it! I did it!"

"Did what?"

"Top score in CSL!. The best in my class!" I heard Papa suck in his breath, but I didn't know what the matter was. Anyway, I was too happy for Tom. Papa congratulated Tom, and said he and I were done, so I went out to join Tom.

"Call Randy," he said. "Let's celebrate together somehow. You guys coached me—that's the only reason I got it at all. It was just like a light going on—all of a sudden I understood all this stuff that had been a complete mystery."

"Call Randy?" I said. "It must be close to Lights Down."

"Just 1903," he said.

Then I realized; I'd left school early, and hadn't been asleep for all that long at the hospital. "Sure!" So I called Randy on the com and we all went down to the snack facility in the Mushroom and had pizza, splurging on our discrets to add a bunch of ingredients. I even enjoyed being around Susan, which at the time I thought was amazing.

TWELVE

The next day in class we were back to working on Japanese verb constructions. I'm told those have simplified a lot in the last couple of centuries—no offense if you're Japanese, but I'm certainly glad. Randy and I were sitting with each other, not because we were trying to exclude anybody, but because no one else seemed to feel comfortable sitting next to us. After a while, Miriam came over and joined us; it was kind of strained, but we did talk. I wondered if anyone had seen that she got some help—what had happened the day before must have been terrible for her—but I didn't quite feel comfortable asking in front of Randy.

Miriam must have broken the ice or something, because in short order Chris and Dmitri joined us, and then Rachel. After the first awkwardness it was kind of nice to be in a group of friends.

Miriam's Japanese is pretty good, so we did pretty well on the oral competition—she was a captain and picked all of us, plus Penelope and Bekka.

I was kind of afraid we were launching our own Real Gang but that's not what happened. Everyone was very quiet and no one seemed to want to talk much, but by lunch time people were at least smiling back when I smiled at them, and in the locker room, getting dressed for the airgym, Gwenny made a point of talking to me and Bekka.

It looked like things would eventually heal. The rest of the day went by quietly; I went home, did homework, talked to Randy and Miriam on the com for a while, and got to bed on time. It was lim normal—which was completely koapy with me.

The next morning, B Shift's bedtime and C Shift's noon, they made the Plan available for anyone to read it who wanted to. There were a lot of arguments and I guess some people were pretty upset, but within a week or so it was just one more ship's policy question on exams. Dr. Niwara had us write papers about it. You'd have thought Randy's and my head start would have helped, but it didn't seem to at all.

Within a month everyone was bored with it, and the Committee to Draft a New Plan, made up of people from the first couple of birthyears to grow up here, quit meeting after six weeks due to lack of interest.

It was about a week after the aerocrosse riot, which was what everyone was calling it. Mother had come home a couple of days before, so I was avoiding our living unit most of the time. Tonight's excuse was that Randy, Miriam, and I needed to go to the infirmary for Psych Wing visiting hours. "Did you tell him we're coming?" Randy asked Miriam for only about the eighth time.

"Yes," she said, "I really did. He knows you kept the crowd off him, Randy. He's not angry with you. He just said he wanted to see you and Mel, so I asked you two to come. That's all there is to it."

The three of us were sitting in the snack bar burning discrets and waiting for infirmary visiting hours to start. Randy was about as nervous as I'd ever seen him.

"Fidgeting like that isn't going to make it any easier, especially not for Ted," Miriam said.

Randy grimaced. "I know. I'll be fine once we go in there. But right now I'm thinking about all the ways things could be really unpleasant, and getting myself generally worked up over nothing."

"As usual," I said, squeezing his thigh under the table.

"Thank you, Dr. Murray. Your whole family keeps telling me to relax. If I took one tenth of your advice I'd be comatose."

"If you took any of it, we wouldn't have to give it."

"Hey, no brawling, kids. Don't start something and get us all brigged." Miriam winked at me; at least we were sort of getting Randy's mind off it.

"That's a bizarre thought," I said. "Even though everyone makes jokes about it, I've never known anyone personally who actually went to the brig. Have you?"

Miriam shook her head, but Randy said, "My father."

We both stared at him, and my stomach sank like a lead ball in ten. "Really?"

"No big deal," he said. "Last year when he was really angry, sometimes he would hit first and think later. So when he felt like he was going to have a real bad night, he would go to Security and have them lock him up for the night."

I was trying to think of something to say when Miriam said, "He must really love you a lot to have himself locked up that way."

Randy nodded, slowly, and seemed to relax. I decided that I had always had superb taste in friends, all along.

We didn't say much after that; a few minutes later, Miriam's werp beeped, letting us know that visiting hours were about to start. We got up and walked down the stairs; they had thought Theophilus would re-orient a little better in the high-grav infirmary, with over a quarter gee weighing him down. That seemed strange to us, of course, but I guess if I visited Earth and got hurt, I'd want to go to a hospital at Supra New York or someplace where the gravity wouldn't bother me while I was recovering.

The bruises were faded to a nasty yellow-brown. I still couldn't believe how many of them there were.

"Hi," Miriam said. "I brought some friends."

He smiled, making a special point of smiling at Randy. "I'm glad you came."

"I hope you're feeling better, Ted."

"Quite a bit." He sat up. "How are things with you? Still holding the top of the class in math?"

Randy stammered something, choked, then laughed at himself.

"You know, that was one of the worst things you could have asked. Gwenny Mori just took over first standing, and I think she's going to get a permanent resident contract on it."

"Not after I get back she's not. And if you want to work together, I'd love to have you come down here for evening visiting—you wouldn't believe how tired I am of hearing my father talk about bal-ancing the B-complex in the new strain of tilapia."

"After you get back?" Miriam said, "Dr. Niwara said—"

"Yeah, I know what they decided. But they didn't ask me about it, Mim. How am I supposed to be able to work with any of you after I get FA, if the last time you saw me . . . well, you know."

"So you'll be back," I said. "That's going to be tough for everyone for a little while, but I guess you're right."

Randy added, "I'm glad. I really am."

Theophilus sighed and stretched; his arms stuck out of the bed bag he was in, and we could see more bruises. He saw us staring and quietly tucked his hands back in. "It's okay," Randy said. "Sorry we were rude."

"That's all right." Theophilus sat very quietly for quite a while;

none of us could think of anything to say. I was trying to imagine what the first day with him back would be like; maybe like having a new kid but a hundred times worse? How would the ones who had hit him—especially Barry Yang, who had started it, or Gwenny Mori and Kwame van Dyke, who had been his friends—how would they react?

Then he cleared his throat. "I have something to say. Back on Earth . . . well, back in Georgia. At my school in the Atlanta Dome . . . I sort of had a special role in my class. You know what it was?

"I was the class jerk.

"That's Earth slang, and kind of old fashioned. I guess you'd say I was the class unco. I put a lot of effort into lubing the teacher, and a lot of time into hiding from kids who wanted to beat me up. I hurt people's feelings, I sneered at everyone, I was lim superior because I was better at school stuff than they were. . . . I was the outsider. Always. I didn't have any friends except a couple of ding-y weird kids who followed me around, and who I picked on harder than anyone else.

"When I came here . . ." He turned toward us; tears were streaking down his face. "At first I thought it was all a fresh start, and here I was with a class I could run. I could be the popular kid. But I found out the same kind of things happen—especially if . . . if . . ." He gave a long sigh. "You know something? I wasn't really called Ted back in Georgia. They called me Theo. I hated that name."

"Would you rather be called Ted?" I asked.

He nodded.

"Then you're Ted to us."

He started to turn away, but Randy asked, "Are you going to do stuff like that again?"

"No."

"Then it doesn't matter. As long as you stop doing it, and try your best to make up for the damage you did, it doesn't matter what you used to do." Randy squatted on his heels by the bed so he could look directly into Theophilus's eyes. "Trust me, Ted. I have experience. I get along fine with people now, but I used to hit them."

We all tried to laugh, but we weren't quite ready to. We will one of these days, though, I think.

January 28, 2026

I got into another argument with Dr. Lovell. She seems to have moved from teacher to shrink to book critic in one short month. "But all that stuff afterward is boring," I said. "And it was all bound to happen if you just think about it. The Plan was dead, and anyone who would be interested in this book is going to know who Tom is. 'Fountains of Dark Vacuum' has been seen all over the place."

"It's popular right now," she agreed. "And it may well stay popular for a long time. But I think people are going to want to know how your story really came out."

"Okay, I'll tell them in two paragraphs. Two sentences. One: 'When the Plan broke, NAC decided to transfer all the adults to the Mars Terraforming Project and turned the ship over to us, so they're doing it, and by the third Marspass from now, everyone left on the *Flying Dutchman* will have been born here.' Two: 'Tom got famous because he came up with this moving light sculpture that forms interactively with a piece of music, so the whole thing looks like Main Engine exhaust and sounds a little like Beethoven.' I write that down, and I'm done."

I got up to go, but she put her hand out to hold the door closed. "*Are* you done? What's this book *about,* anyway?"

"I don't know. How things happened I guess. Or what happened. Or just what I happened to write down."

"That's all? Things just happened? Don't they mean more to you than that?" Without quite knowing how I knew, I suddenly realized something I'd never have imagined—I was one of Dr. Lovell's favorite students. Somehow that made me feel like I owed her something, but I didn't have any real answer.

So—like Papa says, when in doubt, tell the truth. "A lot did just happen," I said. "But while it's happening, you're too busy to think, and after it's happened, you don't really know what you were thinking anymore. That's all. Like at the B Block party, I know I spent some time thinking about my calculus homework, so maybe I was bored for a while, even though I made it sound like it was exciting all evening. Or in the middle of the riot, when Randy came in to stand down the crowd so we could get Theophilus out of there, I know part of the reason it worked was because Bekka and Penelope and Rachel were all there backing him up, and nobody wanted to fight all of them at once. I mean, it took courage for him to do it, and he was the leader, but they had to be smart and brave enough to follow him. And see, if I told it all, it wouldn't mean anything. I mean, am I supposed to write about every time I urinated that week or something? It would all disappear in the details.

"So I'm not going to write those last things. I see what you mean that it's supposed to be what the whole book leads up to—how my brother Tom got to be an artist, the first professional artist born in space and all that stuff TimeMurdoch and OBSR-CHANL and NACFlash hung on him. And about how the adults left and we ended up in charge a decade before we were supposed to, because we were the people who belonged here and they were the aliens. But now that it's obvious, why write the scene?"

She sighed "All I'm really asking you to do is write two more scenes. And I know you'll write them well. Besides, that visit to Theophilus in the infirmary was part of what it all led up to, so you could say you're one-third done with the ending already. Why don't you want this book to have an ending?"

I shrugged. "What the book is about doesn't have an ending. If the low grav life extension research is right, we'll all live for several more centuries. There's so much in front of us. The story will keep going because we'll keep going. So putting an end on—well, it's a lie. A bigger lie than all the lies I told when I cleaned up the story. And it's my book and I don't want any lies that big in it."

She shook her head. "But it's not just *your* book. It's for the good of the ship. It's supposed to introduce Earth people to the new culture that's developed up here, so they'll sympathize with it and understand it. So far it's all right, I think—it will work for NAC the way they want it to—but how can you cheat your readers like that and expect them to like it? They want to see where it all leads, and see that it all makes sense. That's part of your responsibility, to them and to the ship."

I thought about that one for a long time. It made sense, I guess, but I still don't want to write those last scenes. There's no point in describing art, and you know enough about me and Randy and Susan to know how happy we all were when Tom's project swept the awards for Projects Day and then went on to that special exhibit and all those broadcasts. We had kind of a party for him, and everyone danced and talked a lot.

And as for the adults leaving . . . well, Tom and I had a long, upsetting talk with Mother and Papa about it, the same talk all the kids did with their parents, really, because there wasn't anything else to do. The CPB's final report showed what you'd expect, when you think about it.

People get older. They get more independent, more different. You can't plan what they'll do so well anymore. Then it's either point a gun at them and make them follow the Plan, or turn it over to them and let them do it their way. You can't make people grown-up at fourteen and then tell them they won't get any real say in things till they're sixty.

Especially not when they really know their environment, the way fish know the sea, and you're the immigrant, the one who came as an adult.

So what else were they going to do, if they loved us? What else was NAC going to do, if they wanted us to work?

I guess maybe there is one last scene I want to write, though. Because now I just made it sound like we all sat down and made the decision calmly and carried it out and that was that.

Of course that's not exactly what happened. It's just what we told ourselves afterwards.

All their stuff—including that poor silly old copy of *Catcher in the Rye* that once belonged to Mother's father—had already gone into the shuttle. "One of the big advantages of living up here," Papa said, hefting his duffel bag, "is you never acquire enough stuff to have any trouble packing." I think he was having trouble believing that small bag was all that was left.

Mother was dabbing her eyes and looking terribly confused. "You'll take care of your sister?" she asked for the twentieth time.

"Right up to midnight, June 30, 2026," Tom assured her. "After that, she's the problem of the *Flying Dutchman* as a whole."

I had been afraid he'd be insufferable once he got Full Adult, but in fact he'd been a lot easier to get along with—he was under so much less pressure since they'd created the job of "Resident Artist" for him.

Since Mother and Papa were leaving, Susan would be moving in on a renewable trial contract—something Mother didn't quite approve of but could only talk about obliquely, mentioning that Living Unit Six would stay in the family and I could keep my room; Papa's office would become Tom's studio.

Now we all stood there feeling uncomfortable, trying to think of some last thing to say that would make sense.

"Vidphone whenever you can," Mother said.

"I'll even wash my face before I get in front of the camera," I said.

"Oh, you." She hugged me; as she pulled away I saw tear tracks on her coverall and realized I must be crying.

"It's okay," she said. "I know we don't get along, but I'll miss you too."

Then Tom had to hug her, and then I hugged Papa, and after that we all just babbled about how much we wanted each other to do well.

"Send me a picture of your first garden!" I said to her.

She laughed. "I'll be eighty before we have that, and it will look like green refrigerator scudge. We won't even be moving down from orbit for twenty years."

I nodded. "You'll just have to live a long time."

She smiled. "Come visit. It won't be as pretty as Earth, but at least you'll get to see a sky and some plants growing outdoors."

I promised I would. That was silly, of course—a ticket to visit another station or ship cost more than a year's salary, and I could hardly imagine what they would charge me to visit the Mars Terraforming Project's surface colony once it was built. But I'd never really had to say good-bye to anyone before and I said a lot of dumb things.

Papa was growling a lot of advice at Tom, mostly in fun. "Remember, you're the Chaucer for these people; try to occasionally get your mind out of the gutter."

"Chaucer didn't."

"And Anglo-American history shows it," Papa pointed out. "And no political satires about your sister, either." Tom looked baffled; Papa winked at me. "Don't tell him. Let it come as an appalling shock."

Tom looked from me to Papa and back again, scratching the back of his head. "Well, it'll certainly be easier dealing with just one of you." He stuck out his hand and Papa shook it. "But I'll miss you a lot."

That got us all crying and hanging onto each other again. No one else in the boarding bay had any dignity either, though.

Finally it was time. Mother kissed me one more time and said, "You won't think I mean it, but I do. Just do what your heart tells you—I know it's a good one."

I held her for a long time. "I hope you're happy on Mars," I said.

"Even if I'm not, I promise I'll do my best there. I'm not going to even look at another Olson book until I've got a corn crop of my own!" She let go of me. "Good-bye, Melly—Melpomene. I love you."

"I love you too."

Then I hugged Papa and words wouldn't come at all, so neither of us said "I love you." But we knew.

They picked up their duffels and went in through a door in the side of the big passenger compartment on the shuttle, among the first in a long line going aboard. Dr. Niwara went in a little after them; Randy's father was far back in the line. I had come here to say good-bye to a lot of people, but in the end I talked only to Papa and Mother.

Later, when I talked to other kids, I found out exactly the same thing had happened to all of them. In fact, Randy and his father hadn't said a single word—just held onto each other and wept for the whole hour while Mr. Schwartz waited to board.

The last of them went in, and the siren sounded. We all went out through the big freight doors and back to our business.

An hour later, the brief shuddering of the *Flying Dutchman* told us that the catapult had cycled, and they were on their way. Even though it was against the rules, Randy and I held hands the rest of the afternoon, under the desk.

February 2, 2026

Papa says on Earth you all get raised like Randy and me and Tom, maybe even more so. You're kind of all Special Categories.

It's nice that we're needed more up here, because there are so few of us—but I can't pretend it doesn't make us lonely. Really lonely, sometimes, even having each other to count on. So I *am* going to get this in shape for Scholastic or some publisher, or if that doesn't work I'm going to selfpublish it on the Copy Access channel.

And then I'm going to ask you to write to me, okay? Even with as many friends as I have shipboard, more are always nice.

                    With love,
                    Melpomene Murray

KALEIDOSCOPE
CENTURY

For Liane Treiman: Because it's dark,
and I think she'll like that.

ONE

What Rough Beast

i

I wake up for the fourth time I can remember. The first two times were longer ago. Each time I got up, drank water, and took a piss. I think the third time I was looking for a dark-haired girl, maybe ten years old. I might have known her name, and called it. I don't think she was there. I'm not sure.

I know the third time, the time before this, I wandered around the room. There was a battered old werp in the corner, its case dented and scraped, all sorts of stickers and slogan plates pasted and glued to it. I didn't get farther than noticing it was there and wondering if it might be mine. I felt sick and tired so I went back to bed.

I'm awake and much better now. The dreams from before are fading. I sit up in bed and think, My *name is Joshua Ali Quare, and I have a whole life behind me, but I don't remember much of it*. This is normal. I think.

In the mirror by the toilet, my image is hideously thin, muscles wasted as though by a long fever, immense dark circles under my eyes.

My hair's gray, face lined, beard grizzled. I had thought I was about twenty or twenty-five, possibly younger. Clearly not.

I wish the girl would come back and explain. If I could remember her name, I would call for her.

What baffles me most is that I seem to be in Martian gravity. Not as low as the moon's but lower than Earth's, anyway.

How do I know how much gravity the moon, or Mars, has? The Augmented Shuttle Mission never even left for Mars, and that was just an orbital mission, a near approach to Phobos that would have arrived on my thirtieth birthday. I was planning to get drunk with my friends and watch it.

Inventory of the room:

One steel door, with handle, unlocked, leading into a kitchen.

In kitchen: airlock door with stamped logo that reads SEARS MAR-SHACK. SEARS OF WELLS CITY, LTD.

One window looking out on a darkening pink sky and reddish dunes streaked with gray and brown, beyond which a lake—or an arm of the sea?—rolls with lead-dull waves impossibly big and slow.

Bed. Smells like I had a bad fever in it for a long time.

Toilet. Foul. Probably missed it a few times while I had the fever.

Sink and drinking glass—christ, I'm thirsty. I take another glass of water before I continue.

Rack: ten shirts, four pairs of pants, socks and underwear on top shelf. Most of it still in the package.

Bathrobe hanging on corner of rack. I put that on.

Fresher in the corner. I must remember to stuff the sheets into it soon.

Recycling shower, must use that too.

Mirror over toilet.

Werp in the corner, in a case that looks more like an old-fashioned portable typewriter than anything else.

Small box, beside the werp, with a key in its lock. A space allocation box, what they give you before you get on a ship, it fits into the slot at the end of your bunk, you have to fit all the belongings you're taking into it.

They *used* to do that. Nowadays spaceships have a bigger space and weight allowance than airliners had when I was young. I just use it because it's a convenient container. It's mostly empty. I know because it's mine.

I feel a rush of memory, much of it confusing, little of it useful. I thought at first that I recognized low gravity because I read so much sci-fi when I was a kid. I don't seem to remember anything reliably after I was about twenty or so, though all sorts of things lurk at the edge of memory. Most of my past seems to be in the corner of my mind's eye, vanishing if I look directly at it.

No, I know about low grav, had experience with regular, no-, micro-, and low. Definitely.

When?

I think, *that box contains seven things*. A brass key, a Boy Scout knife, a bar napkin with a name and phone number on it, a book of matches from Gwenny's Diner, a picture of a young girl, an Army dog tag for John Childs, and a plastic white knight from a cheap chess set. At once I have to know. My fingers scrabble over the surface, find and turn the key. Tears in my eyes—I don't know what that's about.

They are all there, inside, and the first thing I do is lift up the Boy Scout knife and press my face to its cool handle. I recall that it is rusted shut and I can't unfold the blades anymore. Touching it makes me feel better, but I am still crying. I heft the brass key in my hand. My mother gave it to me the last time I ever saw her—a key to the kitchen door. I squeeze it so hard that it bites my flesh, and that feels good, and comforting.

The name on the bar napkin is Anastasia, and I know that wasn't her real name, but I don't remember anything else. The phone number's an old-fashioned ten-digit one, from back when there was local and long-distance. The area code's for Supra New York. I don't remember when phone numbers changed to twelve digits, either, or when SNY was built.

I have an odd feeling that I might be John Childs. The dog tag feels strange; it's on a chain and I slip it around my neck for a moment, before taking it off again with a shudder that I can't quite explain.

I don't know what Gwenny's Diner was, but handling the book of matches (they are very deteriorated and I don't think they would light) makes me feel sort of warm and safe.

When I hold the white knight in my hand, my fingers begin to do a strange little maneuver, like a magician passing something, so that the knight flows around the fingers. I don't understand why I do that. I feel nothing much emotionally but I keep the knight moving.

The little girl is the one I was looking for. I'm pretty sure of that. The picture is a color holo, not the ribbed kind I remember used to be in cereal boxes, but just a flat piece of paper, about two inches square, no slick surface, into which I can look and see a three-dimensional image of the girl. I turn it over and sure enough, there's the back of her head. By angling it around I can see the picture was shot in a basketball gym, using three cameras, and that the photographer was trying to squat in one of the blind spots and not quite managing it—I see one of his sneakers, his checked pants, his red jacket, and just a little of his curly brown hair and mustache. I'm sure I never met him.

Over the girl's right shoulder, with the paper almost perpendicular to my eye, I can see the other kids waiting to be photographed.

I turn it back over and look at the girl. Long dark hair hangs limply, most of the way down her back. Her chin is just a little prominent, though whether that's a feature she will keep when she grows up, or a freak of being about eleven and very thin, isn't clear. Just a bare suggestion of breasts shows through her thin pullover. She looks uncomfortable, like the gym was cold or perhaps she just didn't want to be photographed. Maybe it's not a school photo but a shot for a refugee i.d. or something.

I can't remember her at any other age. I don't know whether, when I woke up the time before, I was looking for her because I could reasonably expect to find her, or because I was out of my head and raving about things that had happened long ago.

More things are pressing into my memory, and for one moment I'm breathing hard, afraid of being overwhelmed . . . but the surging memories never quite break through to the surface and explain themselves.

I turn to the battered old werp case and open it up. Inside, the werp looks like it's seen better days; there's a prominent dent in the keyboard and the screen has two stains that won't wipe off with my bathrobe sleeve.

The touch of my thumb on the security plate activates it. Must be mine. The screen clears. Words swim up:

YOUR NAME IS JOSHUA ALI QUARE. HIT RETURN.

I do.

THIS IS YOUR WERP. MANY OF YOUR MEMORIES ARE IN HERE. PASSWORD CHECK: WHAT DID YOUR FATHER CALL YOUR MOTHER THE VERY LAST TIME YOU SAW HIM?

The question startles me. I speak the answer aloud, "A Commie cunt." I reach to type it in but apparently the werp has voice processing because it's already responding.

When did werps get voice processing? And when did werps come along, anyway? When I was younger there were only laptops, and I sure couldn't afford one.

The screen scrolls up:

WELCOME TO 2109, JOSHUA, YOU MADE IT AGAIN. READ THIS NEXT PART CAREFULLY.

2109? But that would make me one hundred forty-one years old. . . .

Memories flood back, now, more than before, and I bend forward to read the document:

YOU ARE ON MARS. THE YEAR IS 2109 AND YOU NO LONGER WORK FOR

THE KGB, MURPHY'S COMSAT AVENGERS, NIHON-AMERICA, OR THE ORGANIZATION. THERE IS NO MORE SOVIET UNION, NO MORE FREE SOVIET ASSOCIATION, NO MORE EUROPEAN COMMONWEALTH, AND NO MORE UNITED STATES OF AMERICA. EARTH IS COMPLETELY CONTROLLED BY RESUNA. YOU ARE PHYSICALLY JUST OVER SIXTY YEARS OLD. YOU HAVE ONLY FRAGMENTARY MEMORIES OF YOUR FORMER LIFE AS JAMES NORREN, NOR DO YOU RECALL MUCH OF YOUR FORMER LIVES AS JASON TESTOR, BRANDON SMITH, ULYSSES GRANT, FRED ENGELS, EURIPIDES FREDERICK-SON, ELISHA TESTOR, OR KINDNESS O'HART. A NEW IDENTITY HAS BEEN ESTABLISHED FOR YOU AS "REAGAN FOSTER HINCKLEY," A JOKE WHICH YOU AND MAYBE A DOZEN HISTORIANS WILL GET.

Below that: directions. On the morning of Thursday, June sixth, if I haven't reported in yet, someone will come to see me and take me to Red Sands City, where I can get a hotel room, activate a bank account, and get my new life underway.

June 6 is ten days away. Today's Memorial Day, I think, then laugh. Who would remember?

The werp says there should be food in the kitchen. I open the door. Fridge, stove, cabinets, sink. Pressure suit on a rack. The air-lock door has an elaborate warning sign about conserving air and proper airlock procedure, so I guess whatever's outside isn't fit for breathing. I still don't remember Mars having water, let alone a lake.

In the fridge I find a lot of packages with labels that don't match their small square shapes: things like "rabbit," "peas," "onion soup," all of them in packages the size and shape of the small package of Velveeta Individual Slices. I look around and see that the gadget that I had thought was a microwave is a "Westinghouse *Foodzup! Reconstitutor.*" Taking a wild guess, I toss a square labelled "tomato soup" and another labelled "Four grilled cheese sandwiches" into it—it looks like a microwave inside, but who can tell?—carefully putting "tomato soup" into a large bowl first.

The readout on the reconstitutor says "select finished or prep for manual." I have no idea so I select "finished" and push the button.

It hums for about two minutes, then chimes. I open the door. In the large bowl I had put the square package of "tomato soup" in, there's a small, covered bowl, and it's full of hot tomato soup. A stack of four grilled cheese sandwiches sits on a plate, though I had not put any plate in there with that package. And there's no sign of the wrappers from the food packages.

I move the food to the table, sit down, eat. It's wonderful.

After the meal, I'm tired. I go back to bed. When I wake up again, it's dark, but I remember everything from before. I check the clock on the werp and find that I am up at 5:00 A.M. local time, or whatever time the werp was set to.

I've slept a long time. No hope of getting back to sleep. I turn on the lights—strange to see pools of yellow light on the Martian soil outside the windows—and go into the kitchen.

Plenty of square packets labelled "coffee, one liter pot." A dozen labelled "eggs," "hash browns," "bacon," "toast." I put one of each into the reconstitutor, not putting a plate or bowl underneath this time. I set it for "finished" and start it running. A coffee cup? A few in the back of one cabinet, all white, small circle on each side of them, and fine print in the circle. I hold the cup at almost arms' length to see the print clearly—I wonder if I have any reading glasses anywhere? And why I'm not surgically corrected?

The text reads: "The use of coffee is associated with bowel cancer, genetic damage, and several disorders of the nervous system. If you are a proven frequent and/or irresponsible coffee user you can be denied health benefits under the Uniform Care Act of 2094."

So some things have changed a lot, others have gotten more the same. I rinse out the cup. The reconstitutor pings.

I move the hot plate of breakfast and steaming pot of coffee to the small kitchen table, sit, and eat. I have to work on gaining back some weight. Whatever's going on, you can't fault the chow.

After I've finished the solid food and poured the second cup of coffee, I get the werp from the other room. Supposedly my history's in here; so far I have a list of seven names, besides my own, apparently aliases I've used at one time or another. And I have my seven objects.

I get up and get the space allocation box, so it's sitting next to me as I begin to read at the werp. I don't want to let the box get far from me, or the werp either.

When the sun comes up I am still reading and scanning. Tens of thousands of separate documents in the werp. Doesn't look like I've been much of a diary keeper, more of a collector, just grabbing up anything that seemed interesting. The werp camera seems to have been used mainly to take short videos of friends. Mostly they just wave and say "Hi" without identifying themselves. Also homemade porn—several shots of women, mostly undressed, right after sex, looking bored. A couple of them are saying things like, "That will cost extra." Several holograms of enormous, sagging breasts, shot up close so that all I can see is the breast.

I find four more pictures of the little girl whose picture is in the box, one each at ages nine, ten, thirteen, and eighteen. Her name was Alice.

The text documents don't reveal much. I wasn't much of a writer. When I do write it's mostly things like shopping lists. From these I learn I like Iron City beer.

Every so often, I find my own voice, usually just audio, sometimes with the video focused on my face, always talking urgently and urging me to remember, not to forget . . . something or other.

I try identifying the dates on all the documents. Perhaps if I read them from earliest to latest, I will learn something.

The one hundred and fourteen earliest ones all have the same date and time, Friday, October 8, 2021, 1745 GMT. One says "Guide note." I cue it up. It says all the other documents were copied from a stack of loose paper, video tape, photos, and cassette tapes that "Brandon Smith" had been carrying with him for a long time. I look about thirty in the note. I say I hope the "Reconstruction-issue" werp will hold up. The werp I have is not nearly that old, I'm sure—werps in those days did not have built-in cameras or holography. Or at least "Reconstruction-issue" werps didn't.

I keep working at it, as the sun comes up over the Martian beach outside. I take a minute to get up and stretch, look out the window at a bright point in the sky—Deimos, probably. I can't see it moving visibly. The small white sun climbs up out of the water toward the moon. It's a windy day and the waves out on the—lake? bay? sea? whatever—are bouncing about crazily. I feel ill looking at them.

Pull the curtains. Reconstitute another pot of coffee. Keep going. I have more than one version of my early life. They can't all be true. But the different versions all seem to be supported by fragments of my memory.

Taking a break from the early documents, wandering at random through all the others, I see a note, dated 2093, called "Inconsistencies." I call it up and discover it's a short clip of myself—looking not much younger than I look now, though it's twenty-six years in the past—talking earnestly into the camera, stopping every now and then for a pull on a beer. "Start with a list of questions. Is the girl in the picture named Anastasia, Bambi, or Alice? Is she my daughter, a girl I befriended, or perhaps my wife or girlfriend at a younger age? Could she have had more than one identity and more than one role?

"Did I get the Boy Scout knife from the body of John Childs, as I seem to remember, or was it a gift from someone? If a gift, who from? And how did it get rusted shut? I remember both finding it after several years of not having it, and burying it in the ground once. Did I do any of that?

"I think I make up stories based on the few documents I have and the few memories that leak through. Some of them are dreams I think. Then the stories end up in the document files looking just like everything else. Wish I was better at keeping records. Even with stuff from within this lifetime, I'm not even sure which files in here now are by me and which ones I edited when I moved them to the new werp. I just don't know. Sorry."

My image clicks off. I sit, stare at the screen for a long time, get up, look out the window. Late afternoon. Don't know any more than I did by mid-morning, just know it more ways.

At least I have some idea what's behind my being here. One of the earliest documents, if it's a real one, says I come back into the world differently every time a "transit" happens. Maybe this time the transit made me a better writer. I'm not sure, but I'm sitting here typing.

I wonder when and where I learned to type. I don't recall being able to when I left home. I couldn't do shit when I left home, if you want to know the truth.

I want to know the truth.

I sit and type as the sun sets on the other side of the building. Now that the waves aren't so big I leave the curtains open.

The water never gets blue here on Mars—except right at sunrise and sunset when the sky is sometimes briefly deep blue and the water reflects it. I keep looking up at the window, away from the werp screen, because I don't want to miss the moment when that happens.

ii

I was born in 1968. Till past 2000, you could say practically everything about me by saying that my mother was a black lawyer's daughter and my father was a white ex-con with a political history. Grandpa got Daddy out of jail for the ACLU, and lived to regret it (I heard him say that himself). Mama was an activist, passionate in her battle to overcome everything about the past, in her early twenties in 1966 when they married. She was ten years younger than Daddy, and Daddy was the big, strong, handsome, innocent man that had written two books in prison.

Except he wasn't innocent. He liked to rub Mama's nose in that. He had brains, looks, and a lot of charm when he wanted to, but he was guilty as all hell of the rapes he'd been convicted of. He hadn't been convicted by a proper procedure, was all. It was only that *if* he'd been innocent, he'd've gone to jail anyway. Hence the "matter of principle"— which is a "technicality" you agree with, as Grandpa used to say—that was known to lawyers as *Quare v. Tennessee.*

He was huge—a tall man, with a deep chest and arms like iron. Gray-blond hair in tight curls. Fine-boned face always red from the sun, from drinking, and probably from whatever he was doing to his lungs with all the Camels he smoked, lighting each one off the previous, so there was always one clenched between his bared, yellow teeth. From the time I was able to remember him, he had a permanent squint, as if he always looked into the sun.

I remember his voice was soft, even, and polite around Mama's parents, and that whenever he got onto a tear working on a book, he'd barricade himself into his little office and just type away for hours. He never finished one after getting out of the pen, though. He claimed that without being locked up he didn't have the incentive to revise.

My mother was light-skinned, anyway, and as a result I was one of those people of no definite race that you see everywhere now. Call me ahead of my time. When Daddy would get drunk and mean, he'd sometimes call me "that little half-nigger" in front of Mama, just to hurt her, which was why he did most things as far as I could tell. I don't think I invented my memories of him hitting me, or her; I don't think there's much exaggeration in my believing he raped her twice a week during all the years they were married. Maybe it was different back before I could remember.

Mama stayed. If there were a god, he might know why. Maybe the shame of the mistake she'd made, a bright, talented, beautiful woman giving herself to a big, vicious ape with a smooth line of talk? It couldn't have been fear it would come out. It *was* out. I saw Grandma Couandeau bandaging Mama up when I was seven, and I already knew that was nothing you wanted to ask about.

I was never close to Daddy's size. I had Grandpa Couandeau's build, slight and small. I hated Daddy as much as I would ever hate anyone, and I fell asleep dreaming of beating him up and throwing him out of the house. It never happened.

I was a third-generation Red Diaper baby. Andre Couandeau, my grandfather's father, had joined the Party in the 1920s, and, at least according to family legend, died under a cop's nightstick during the sit-down strike at Firestone ten years later. Mama, in her stroller, had attended Paul Robeson's last concert in America, claimed she remembered the backs of the longshoremen and truckers as they stood down the Legionaires "for free speech." She always told me, "You get free speech when you get the power to stand up for yourselves. Till then all you have is *tolerated* speech, Josh, no matter what they tell you in school."

We argued a lot about what I got taught in school, because I saw no sense in arguing with teachers. I was perfectly willing to agree with Mama that it was all bourgeois lies, but I didn't see any reason why I should have to correct it. Not when I could quietly drift along in the back of the room, ignored by everyone, and keep my concentration on basic issues like saving up for a car out of my job at McDonald's. It was okay with me that we went to CP stuff all the time, and the demonstrations were kind of fun, but it was like being born a Witness or a Mormon—you weren't exactly like the people around you, but you weren't *not* like them, either. You just had a slightly different set of adult friends and links to different families than other kids did.

When I was little, Mama's cell used to meet at the house, but that stopped pretty soon because Daddy was not what you could call "reliable." I get the impression he was never invited to join the Party. Anything that excluded him rankled him, but he mostly confined himself to claiming he was going to turn Mama in (even though the Party had been legal for years) "for the reward." Then he'd laugh and say he was just kidding.

Now and then they'd ask him to talk to a meeting about his time in prison. He'd tell the same stories, all from his first book, over and over.

He was also jealous, I think, of Mister Harris. I think of him that way, even now, *Mister* Harris. In Mama's and Grandpa's eyes, this was the most important person they knew. Mister Harris "traveled," which meant he drew a stipend from the Party and went from cell to cell on regular visits. Kind of a circuit preacher, kind of a beat cop.

Mama and Grandpa were both on the state Central Committee. Grandpa was known on sight to Gus Hall. Mama had shared a hotel room once, at a conference, with Angela Davis, but somehow Mister Harris was more important. It took me a long time to figure out why.

I left home forever on my sixteenth birthday. Two of the earliest documents I've got—both audio recordings of me reciting as much as I could about my own past—agree that it was my sixteenth birthday.

I passed the driver's license exam at 3:50 P.M. that day—the earliest moment after school it could be managed. My score was perfect, which was no surprise since driver's ed and auto shop had been my only "A" subjects. That meant I had to run to make McDonald's in time for my job, with so little time that I couldn't even pass by the house, just a few blocks out of my way, where a beautiful little silver RX-7—merely 120,000 miles and only six years old—was parked, for which the owner wanted just $1600.

The guy was holding it for me—$2200 in my account, $1600 for the car, $45 to register it, $12 plate fee, first insurance payment $130—two days and that car was mine.

Like most kids I knew, I was working five hours a night, piling up cash so I could have things. Might as well. They didn't teach shit in school. If you took General Math and General Science you didn't need to learn anything after eighth grade to pass, and no one needed to stay up all night studying to "express feelings" in English class or "give opinions" in American History. Half the class never read the books and got B's, anyway.

I wasn't expecting anything real big for my birthday—there never had been before. Turning sixteen was about the best present I could have had, anyway.

I trotted home all the same. Mama had told me there'd be a cake and a gift or two. I did take the time on the way home to swing by and make sure the RX-7 was still there.

Mama had made a cake, chocolate since that was my favorite—something from a mix, she was a lousy cook but could follow directions. There was a new shirt, wrapped, and I put that on.

Daddy had been drinking I guess. He usually had. I have no idea what started it. Like always, it happened too fast.

I was still in the chair, but leaned back on the back legs, my not-quite-finished cake spilled into my lap. His hand was on my shirt and he hit me again, several times, hard, beating my face so that it went numb and soft, as he explained to me that I didn't fucking need a fucking car and it was about fucking time for me to start fucking supporting the family. "Fuckin' kid thinks he's too fucking good to be one of the family," he said, and threw me backwards. The chair flipped out from under me and my tailbone hit a rung.

My head banged on the wall but I wasn't dazed or stupid enough to put my hands up. Once he started one of these, trying to protect yourself just made it worse.

He grabbed me again, dragging me to my feet, tearing my shirt—a new one, a gift I had just put on (why is it I remember every button of a plain blue shirt so clearly?). His thumbs digging into my armpits, he shook me back and forth and said, "We're going to fuckin' start chargin' you rent, boy. It's a good thing you saved up for it."

He cuffed me once more across the back of the head, slapped my face once more and said, with the exaggerated sarcasm of a mean drunk, "Oh, he's not happy. Oh, he's mad. Well, he needs to say 'Thank you, Daddy,' for putting a fuckin' roof over his head, that's what he needs. He's got no fuckin' business being mad, does he. Say 'Thank you, Daddy.' "

I don't know if I was too dazed or too mad. I didn't speak.

He drove his knuckles into my face. "Say 'Thank you, Daddy.' "

I still said nothing. Too numb. Or couldn't think.

He started slapping my face, with his open hand, one blow after another. My left cheek took about ten blows. It was bruised almost black for a week afterwards. Then he threw me on my back and said, "Your rent's due tomorrow, boy. I'll let you know how much." He stood for a moment, breathing hard, and then added, "Here's your cake," and threw the rest at me. Then he laughed a stupid-sounding half-laugh as if he were about to decide whether or not to tell me it was all a joke, or kill me.

I stayed still. After a few seconds his office door slammed. He shouted through the door that he could never get any fucking work done, he fucking had to put up with a lazy free-loading half-nigger and a Commie cunt.

Mama stood by uselessly. Typical. Daddy was crazy, mean, and dangerous. But I hated Mama more. She was useless.

I cleaned myself up, pulled on a sweatshirt, threw what remained of my new shirt in the trash. It didn't seem worthwhile to do anything about the mess in the dining room.

All the clothes I wanted to keep went into two gym bags. I'd never read much and there weren't any books I cared about, but I threw a bunch of tapes and the Walkman in, figuring it might help if I got lonely. It wasn't cold out but I put on my leather jacket.

The passbook for my bank account was in my jeans pocket. Thank god there had never been an ATM card, or he'd already have the cash. I figured the bank opened at 8:30 the next morning and hell if I was going to let the old bastard bully Mama, the co-signer on my account, into getting the money out for him. Probably he'd lost some cash gambling, or wanted to go on a spree with some of his barfly friends, or maybe go hit the whorehouse a couple of times so he could come home and tell Mama about it. Probably he hadn't been able to get the cash out of her because she didn't have it. That would have been all he needed to set him off on this "paying rent" business.

When I got downstairs, I could hear him snoring—he usually passed out in his office, ten minutes after he would go in there, because before he started working he'd have a few off the bottle in his desk.

Mama was trying to get the cake up off the rug by picking up the crumbs one at a time, too scared to turn on the vacuum and wake him up. I didn't bother to say goodbye. She'd figure it out.

But as I opened the back door, I felt her hand in the middle of my back. "You should go to an emergency room," she said. "I can give you some cash for that. What if you have a concussion?"

"I don't," I said, pulling away from her, but she caught my hand and pushed something between my fingers. I looked down. A hundred dollar bill and a house key.

"You know what times he's not in. Come in and take food, clothes, anything you need," she said. "And you know he sleeps real sound. Help yourself. You're entitled."

I nodded and went out the door. I kept the hundred and the key in my hand, inside my pocket, for blocks, just holding them. I knew I would have to part with the hundred soon.

Years later I regretted not having kissed Mama goodbye that night. I guess maybe I figured I'd be back.

The old bastard had locked me out a few times. Never for two nights running, fortunately. But I'd gotten pretty good at knowing how to keep myself out of serious trouble for a night. I knew what places in town would be open at 11 P.M., and would stay open.

So I headed straight to Gwenny's, a diner out toward the edge of town. My face was hurting with every step, and I could feel it swelling. A couple teeth felt loose, but more like I just needed to be careful than like I was going to lose them. My nose was bent and bruised, but probably not broken. Years of drinking had sapped the force of those arms, so the muscles were still big, but they were filled out mostly with lard. He was in pretty shitty shape, and the thought crossed my mind, if I wanted to chance getting killed, maybe I could take him.

Not worth it. So far I didn't have any damage around the eyes, or probably even any broken bones. It would cost something if I got hurt worse. And what would I want to fight him for anyway? The right to leave?

My face pulsed with pain as I crossed the river. The bridge was long and not high, and when I was younger I used to stand on it and look down at the trout behind the pillars. The moon was coming up now, over the willows in their tangled masses, clinging to the sandbars downstream, and I paused for a moment. No longer numb, my face ached pretty badly. I could feel tears and snot streaking over my cheeks and lip, but it seemed like too much bother, just now, to wipe any of that off.

My hand was still in my pocket, digging that old brass house key into my palm like I was trying to drive it into the bone. It wasn't much, but she had defied him more, just now, than she ever had before.

I knew I wouldn't use the key. Sure, I could get in and out and take stuff, but I didn't want liquor. After smelling him all these years I figured I'd never touch it. Anything else I took would just make Mama that much poorer.

The front of my knuckles was brushing something else. I let go of the key, gripped the hard lump I had found, and pulled it out, careful not to lose the key or the hundred.

In the moonlight it shone like magic. The eagle was worn down, and the ring for clipping it to your belt was gone. I opened the blades and checked; I had kept it sharp.

When I was eleven, every boy in my class became a Scout. Not me. That's not something a Red Diaper does. I also couldn't hang out with the kids who were too cool for it. They were *lumpen*.

So Mama threw her fit, and I gave up on it, like I had on a dog, or a BB gun, or youth hockey. Then one afternoon, early in the spring, Daddy gave me a brand-new Boy Scout knife. Told me to keep it in good shape and it would serve me well. It had never been out of my reach since.

I looked at it. He'd won it at cards or dice. Or maybe he'd been feeling too ill to get a pint, he'd seen it in a pawnshop and been generous in the spontaneous, random way of a nasty drunk. I thought about how a thousand times since I'd heard him tell the story of the knife to his friends, and how they—drunken pigs all—had nodded for the thousandth time and agreed what a great guy Daddy was.

It was the only proof I'd ever had that that man had given a shit whether I lived or died. Not worth carrying the weight.

I was crying harder now—maybe my face hurt more—but I could

see plenty well enough to hit the river with that Scout knife. It made a low-pitched reverberating *plonk,* right where I knew there was a deep hole.

The splash made a ring-ripple that drifted downstream maybe a hundred yards before it faded into other disturbances on the water, and the moon wavered and flickered in fragments and bits all over the silver surface. I shuddered and was glad to be wearing the jacket.

Not midnight yet, still my birthday.

I kicked the post a couple times, bounced back and forth. Maybe, once for a second, I thought about flipping over the railing.

Sure. Give the old fuck twenty-two hundred. That'll show him.

I wiped my face on my coat sleeve, pulled out a handkerchief, cleaned up as well as I could without a sink or mirror. I looked once more at the pool of black water where I had thrown the knife, just off the nearest pillar and behind the boulder that always stuck out late in the summer. I sort of thought a goodbye at it, and headed on over the bridge, walking fast to warm up.

Somehow, having done that, I felt lighter on my feet. I cradled the key in my fingers, squeezing it hard until it was warm as my own blood.

There were three reasons I was headed for Gwenny's. One, it was open all night, and Gwenny, the owner, generally took the night shift. I'd been in there some nights when I was locked out, drinking coffee and slowly eating chili, watching the big TV screen in the corner, and she'd been friendly and concerned in a not-pushy way.

Two, she had furnished rooms for rent, or she had had them last week, anyway, and maybe I could talk her into taking the hundred down and the rest in the morning. I had no idea what rent might be but it would sure be less than Daddy would have taken.

The most important thing was that her place was close to the bank. Whether or not I got a place to stay for the night, I needed to be there on the dot at eight-thirty.

Besides Gwenny, her cook Paula, and Verna, the older woman who waited tables, only three other people were in Gwenny's: a couple who sat with their arms around each other looking like they were trying to stay awake, and a guy who talked endlessly to them. That group was in a booth far over to one side, out of sight of everyone else. The rest of the Formica tables and Naugahyde booths waited, napkins, silverware, and cups laid out, for a crowd that there was no sign of. Probably it would fill up more later that night.

"Jesus, Josh, how did you do that to yourself?" Gwenny asked.

"I didn't. My father did," I said, trying to sound tough and failing. Anyone could have heard the tears in my throat.

"Don't look like nothing's broke," Verna said. "But you're gonna look like hell for a while."

"You going to press charges?" Paula asked. She was big on knowing the official way to do everything. "What he did's illegal, you know. He can't be hitting you that way. You're his son."

I shrugged. "Mama would lie for him. He'd get acquitted. And they'd make me go back to live with him. Do you still have furnished rooms, Gwenny?"

She looked at me closely then, a piercing stare that seemed to see farther into me than I had known existed. "Yes," she said slowly, "I do. You know if you rent a room and then move back home next week, the money's gone? And you're going to have to pay for the whole term of the rental agreement, even if you don't stay that long?"

"Yeah, I know all that," I said. "It doesn't matter. I'm not going back there, ever. He'll kill me if I stay there. How much is it?"

"My smallest one's eighty-five a month. If you and what's in those bags is all you're gonna have in it, it might suit. You get two towels and two sets of sheets and things, and keeping them clean's up to you— laundry-mat's round the corner. One shelf in the common fridge, privileges to use the stove, but you got to get your own pans and dishes. Usually I get some student at the university who's really broke to take the deal."

"Well, I'm a student, I guess," I said, "though I'm not sure how safe it'll be for me to go to school. I want that high school diploma for a job. . . ." The world suddenly seemed to reel, and I almost fell.

Gwenny caught me, in her strong arms—she was taller than I was and muscular—and said, "You've just had a pretty awful shock. I think we better get you up to the room, get you settled in, and then in honor of your being a new tenant and all, we might just find you a meal on the house, or some coffee if you're not hungry."

I felt myself blushing all over; I hadn't meant to faint, and now I could feel tears burning down over my cheeks. None of the women seemed to notice. Gwenny guided me back outside, up the exterior steps, and then down the hall to my new home.

In a room about fifteen feet square she had a small bed, two end tables, an old kitchen table, two chairs, and a wardrobe without a door. We got the business of money and keys taken care of, and she told me not to worry about the security deposit. "I'm not worried, Josh, I mean, where would you go?"

Five days later I stopped going to school because I got another job in addition to the one at McDonald's. I was a mechanic's helper at a gas station; at least it meant I could work on cars. Between the two jobs I could afford my car, insurance, and room, with a little extra left over. Mostly I put that extra in my new, me-only bank account. If I wasn't exactly set for life, I had the RX-7 to drive around in.

I kept the brass key Mama had given me in my pocket all the time. I was always pulling it out when I meant to pull out my building key, car key, or room key—but I didn't mind. At night, I put it in a special place on the end table, so that if I woke up I could see the key from my bed, by the light of the diner's sign.

iii

I sit back and look at what I've written. I can't believe how long it took, and it all looks stupid and wrong. I know what story I meant to tell, but all the first paragraph says is "Mama was black, Daddy was white, and he used to hit us both a lot. So I left when I turned sixteen and he said I had to pay rent. I stayed with a woman named Gwenny." There's too much about fixing up the RX-7, and a list of the kinds of bowties Grandpa Couandeau used to wear, and like that. I set down all these details but it doesn't make a story.

And there's just two and a half pages and most of what I remember isn't there. Maybe I write more, this time around, but I sure don't write any better.

I stretch, yawn, feel the way my shoulders cramp. God, I didn't get down a thing about Harris. And I don't know how much of this I'm making up. I suppose the thing to do is to put today's date on what I just finished writing, so I do that. Now at least I'll know I wrote it long after the fact—god, more than a century—and that it's a mix of things I remember, things I think I remember, stuff I figured out from older documents, and god knows what-all.

Maybe tomorrow I'll just talk into the machine. Meanwhile I'm tired and I've had too much coffee. I get up and pace around, wondering if there's any equivalent of TV. If they've got flashchannel or something somewhere, maybe, then I could get caught up on what's going on.

It's also high time for a shower. At least the water seems to be on its first trip through. I use the bathrobe as my towel and spread it out so that it'll dry.

If I were at normal weight the clothes would probably fit pretty well. As it is they hang on me in a loose, baggy way that reminds me of the "gangsta" clothes a lot of kids my age wore, back in the last part of the twentieth century. That makes me laugh, looking at this old man in too-big shirt and sagging pants in the mirror.

Still much too awake and wondering when I'll feel like sleeping, I put the makings of another big meal into the reconstitutor, and then put some more effort into looking for a television, a holobox, or even just a flashchannel reader. Finally I have a vague memory that things aren't separate anymore, and I sit back down at the werp and play around for a minute on the menus.

Sure enough, the werp's also the receiver. I turn it to the "News and Views Basic" channel, since that has no surcharge and I'm not sure who is picking up the bills on any of this, or how much money I have, if any. Then I set the werp a little distance away from me. One thing TV had that these don't, you could take up a whole room with a TV so nobody had to talk and it didn't feel empty. This way leaves you sitting in a lonely little spot, just you and the werp screen a couple of feet apart with the rest of the room empty. Not to mention I have already looked at the werp all day.

The reconstitutor rings, and I get out the meal—goat meatloaf, potatoes, asparagus, beets. Probably healthy as all shit but what do I know? I remember Woody Allen had a movie, a real old one I saw once. A health nut woke up in the future and it turned out all the things like hot fudge, steak, and cigars were what was really good for you.

No hot fudge or steak among the stacked meals in the fridge. No beef at all, in fact. Are cows extinct or am I Hindu?

I dim the room lights and power up the werp. It's almost like TV. Sort of comforting, but I wish the screen were bigger so I could put it farther away.

Well, one thing hasn't changed: whenever you tune in to a news channel the first thing you get is weather from someplace nowhere near you. In this case it's a weather report for North America on Earth. There are no borders. It sounds like whatever runs the Earth is called Resuna. At first I think Resuna is the name of the government, then that maybe everyone on Earth is named Resuna. When they stop talking about it I'm more confused than when they started. A lot of what the voices are talking about is storms blowing in off "Hudson Glacier" menacing the "Floridas." That makes me take a second glance, and now I see that there's a splash of big islands where the peninsula used to be. To judge from the square shape of some of them, they're probably doing something like the old Dutch dike-and-polder system to get the land rebuilt, and it looks like it must have been going on for a while.

Now that I am looking for changes in the land, I see that the Great Lakes drain through the Ohio and the Hudson; the big white blob at the end of the St. Lawrence must be ice? Pretty clearly Lake Ontario has expanded enough so that Oneida Lake is just a bay, and Chatauqua Lake has been gobbled in the same way by Erie. The main drains must be through the Mohawk and the Beaver.

I wonder when I got to know that area so well, and I have a sudden flash of tents pitched in the snow, of men on skis with rifles. Murphy's Comsat Avengers, that's who I was with. I was in that outfit with Sadi.

I noticed, when I was first browsing through and looking at all the pictures, that there were a few of me from when I was Yuri Frederickson, around 2060-something. I call them up now. The pictures show me grizzled, middle-aged, on skis, wearing a pale blue uniform under an open white parka, rifle in hand.

They switch to a weather report for South America. I don't remember anything about the geography there except that I am pretty sure that the passage between South America and Antarctica wasn't ice-covered when I was growing up, and I don't think there used to be big glaciers in the middle of the continent.

A little box pops up in one corner to say "Option Point" and I reach out and push a key combination on the keyboard before I can think about what the box means or what I might be doing. I sit back, take a big bite of meatloaf, and wonder what my fingers remembered that I didn't.

The screen clears and there's an anchorman sitting there, saying "Hello, Mars. Here's the quick break—"

What follows is much like any smalltown covers-the-county FM station, back in the 1980s. A fire in Red Sands City, inside the main habitat. They had to vent some atmosphere and re-pump to pressure. Olympia reports a rash of petty theft. The Planning Council of Marinerburg announced yesterday that the sea level had risen another 120 cm in the last year and that within ten years the water should be up to the piers. Today local elections are being contested in several places, and the current General Coordinator of Mars is in minor political trouble over some complex financial dealings years back, when she had headed up the Port Authority for Deimos.

I can't tell how long people have been living here, but at least I get some idea where the water and air are coming from. They broadcast a list of times and targets for the next day—scheduled impacts for about a hundred chunks of comets and carbonaceous chondrites.

I have to spend a long minute thinking how I knew what a carbonaceous chondrite is. Despite my best efforts I still have no idea where that knowledge had entered my brain from.

But I do know: it's an asteroid made up of a lot of rocky and tarry stuff, along with the usual bits of iron. They are being used as feedstocks for life on Mars. The Development Corporation's crashing fifty-metric-ton chunks of them, dozens at a time, into the South Pole, to make feeding grounds for the oxyliberators. It also releases vast quantities of planet-warming CO_2 and water. Later in the Martian year, at the equinox, they will switch to the North Pole—they always bombard the pole that's having winter, forcing much of the carbon dioxide and water back into the atmosphere.

I hoped the big meal and a little time watching the news would knock me out, but it hasn't helped. I'm still wide awake, trying to piece together memories, documents, memories of documents, and documents of memories. . . . "History is a dull party at which we struggle to fall asleep," I say, out loud, quoting Sadi, then realize I've thought about him ten times, and I don't know—I ask the werp. "Who's Sadi?"

"Reference document list appears offscreen, want it brought up to front?" the werp asks, in my voice.

"Yes," I say. I didn't know it could do that. Considering it's more than twenty years old and obviously it's used to me, it looks like the memory holes are bigger than ever.

I read the documents it pulls up for me for ten minutes or so. Sadi was my best friend, maybe my only friend, for forty or fifty years at least. The documents are all from the middle of the twenty-first century.

I remember one time Sadi and I got a special mission: the last time we ever talked face to face with Murphy, and one of the few times we had any direct conversation with One True. That was in the War of the Memes.

The thought is so sudden and so unasked-for that I don't quite know what to do with it. I ask myself, "Who is Sadi?" again, and bust right out laughing there in the Marshack, with no one else to see me or share the joke.

Not know Sadi? Might as well ask who was Mama or who is Santa Claus or Ronald McDonald. There's a lot I can't remember, of course,

about him, but he was so much—I reach for the memory, and this time,
for once, more impressions come, the confusion lifts like fog in the
sun, and the story hangs together in my head.

Murphy was the colonel—that was the title he gave himself, anyway—
of Murphy's Comsat Avengers, Inc., the private mercenary regiment
that Sadi and I were in during the War of the Memes. Instantly my fingers are flying over the werp keys: what's a meme, when did we leave
the organization, what's a comsat avenger—
    The answers don't make any more sense than they did before,
right away, but I have a feeling that a few things from 2064 are falling
into place, documents fitting to memories and vice versa. I keep thinking and reading. "Comsat Avengers" because Murphy was an old vag
(*vag?*) who had been in a business selling access to comsats before
the supras (*supras? just a minute ago I knew what those were*) were
built.
    Supras put comsats out of business, right. So Murphy, crazy as a
syphilitic ferret, started out to destroy the people who built the supras.
Gotcha. Complete losing cause. Trying to kill the whole world government. By the late 2040s Murphy was down to fifteen aging nuts like
himself, all hiding out in a UN Mandated Wilderness Area, pretending
to be Castro or Robin Hood or somebody like that.
    Then 2049 rolls around and we're in the War of the Memes. All of
a sudden there's money for a guy like Murphy, as long as he'll let
someone else tell him what to attack. He goes to work for One True
and the Organization orders Sadi and I to join him—
    One True. Something about that term made me shudder.
    So we worked for One True in the War of the Memes. That sounds
like whatever One True was, it was a meme, whatever a meme was.
    I ask the werp, "Do you have a dictionary?"
    "Of which languages?"
    "English will do fine, I think. Define meme."
    "There are over thirty definitions."
    "Give me all of 'em—uh, no, hold on—give me the ones that are
nouns."
    "Meme. Noun. Obsolete meaning coined originally by Richard
Dawkins, twentieth century, by analogy to 'gene,' to mean fundamental communicable ideas, such as melodies, pottery patterns, literary
forms, taboos, fashions, superstitions, customs, et cetera. Also obsolete: fundamental force opposing gene in Walter Koch's philosophic
formulation ELPIS. Also obsolete: compelling musical motif, in neo-

jazz and parahop styles of music. Also obsolete: fixation, addiction, compulsion. Also obsolete—"

"Uh, how about just the meaning in the context of War of the Memes?" I ask.

"Meme. Noun. Any of several thousand very large self-replicating artificial intelligences capable of functional copy transference across operating system boundaries, including but not limited to electronic, optical-switching, biological, and text-record operating systems."

I think about that. "Smart viruses?" I ask. "And does 'biological systems' mean 'human brains'?"

"The term virus is long obsolete in a context applied to computing; in its biological sense it is inapplicable here. Biological systems in this case is not limited to human brains as chimpanzee or dolphin brains theoretically—"

"Close enough," I say. "It's coming back now, thanks."

I remember it now. In what had been upstate New York, in 2064. The War of the Memes was down to about twenty-five competing memes worldwide, and just over half the world population was carrying some dominant meme—some program running in their heads had replaced whatever personality grew there naturally. One True was doing pretty well. It had North America east of the Missouri and north of the Tennessee, plus little scattered bases everywhere else.

It was the best deal going. Because it was so secure, One True had an area it could set aside for R&R for its mercenaries—so we sometimes got a real break. And though most troops had to worry about getting memed by putting themselves under a meme's control, we at least had Murphy, who was crazed and paranoid and did everything to prevent One True from communicating with us directly.

"Oh, I'm glad he does all that," Sadi said. "I mean, I have no desire at all to end up as one more copy of One True, and I don't want to see it happen to you either, bud. But I can't help being a little sorry that we never get to talk to it."

"Why? What do you or I have to say to a meme? 'So why is it you want to run my body?' "

He laughed, leaning back in the sun. God, he was a handsome man even then, past his prime; the white streaks in his brown hair ran along his temples like a comic book hero's, his blue eyes still looked deep into you, and his long, slim body didn't have an extra ounce of fat. "But there's that other side. Memes live forever and have such a variety of experiences. Which isn't a bad way to describe us longtimers."

Longtimers? I think to myself. *I knew what those were a minute ago too.* I get up, stretch, relax my muscles and shake out my body, then stretch out on the bed, trying to daydream the experience back into my body, trying to forget I'm on Mars and reach fifty years into my scrambled, uncertain memories. Where and when did we have that conversation? And since it was pretty much the kind of idle chatter that Sadi and I shared all the time, what made this one stand out? I was thinking something about the only time we talked to Murphy and to One True . . . I relax, shut my eyes, try not to force it, try to just listen inside my head—

We were sitting outside our cabin in Put-in-Bay on a nice June day, a few weeks after the Battle of Minneapolis Ruin, when we'd thrown the forces of Free American back from the edges of One True's territory, pursuing them all the way back to Fargo Dome.

That had been fun; Fargo Dome hadn't been hit significantly before, and the loot was terrific. Not to mention Sadi and I had grabbed one whole sorority house at the University of North Dakota, turned the ugly ones over to One True and spent three days serbing the pretty ones before Murphy called the unit back in and we had to hang all of them. Not the way we'd have done it—Sadi always said that when you played with someone like that for a while the least you could do was give them an individual death and then remember it forever. Not really esthetic or special, but still there was something about doing them all in an hour, in one mass hanging, chick after chick hoisted kicking into the air, all of them naked, the ones yet to be done cowering in the corner, bruised, bloody, crying for their mothers—I still got stiff thinking about it.

I fall back out of the memory, sick to my stomach, thinking at first it was some hideous nightmare, but no, I'm quite sure we did that. I want to say Sadi did it but the fact is I was right there with him and I loved it too. Even now, when I think of those terrified kids and how long it went on—high as we were on a triple dose of gressors we didn't sleep or leave them alone for three days. And that last hour—the tall girl with the brown hair that started to pray—

I sit up, breathing deeply, wishing for a pill to make it all go away, thinking of putting on the pressure suit and going out and pitching that werp with all its pictures and sounds into the water, think of—

How good it would be to have Sadi here. He always knew what to do when I was upset. He was much more use to me than Mama or Daddy ever was.

The memory crawls back now, not of Minneapolis but of the R&R camp in the Erie Islands. Nice day, we were sitting outside. I had been going through You-4 withdrawal—a little, the way I did after every big battle—so I'd had two days of dreadful depression, but then I'd woken up that morning feeling fine. Sadi never seemed to be affected the way I was; he took at least as many drugs as I did but he shook them off easier, and he rarely took them to get over the things he'd done. Good thing, too, because when I woke up sobbing or screaming he could be right there to take care of me.

"You just have to get your balance, bud," he'd say. "You had a rough childhood or something. You have a hard time remembering that when it's happening to them, it's not happening to you. Freud said that, you know. What makes a thing funny is when it happens to someone else and not to you. And de Sade pointed that out, as long as you get bothered by hitting other people's noses you'll never really have the freedom to enjoy swinging your fist."

I was sitting there listening to him, a big mug of coffee and a slice of fresh hot bread at hand. Made by Sadi. Naturally. The man could cook. Not like a fag or anything, he could just *cook*. At least as well as he could talk, and I loved to hear him talk.

So I sat and listened; no point interrupting something I was enjoying. Between bites of bread I practiced passes with the white knight. The only worthwhile thing I ever learned from Daddy, something he'd done in prison, practiced all this stuff from *Everyone's Big Book of Magic,* all the ways to make things appear and disappear out of your hand. That little plastic white knight from a chess set had been dancing around between my fingers a long time, going away here and popping back there. I almost always did that while I listened to Sadi.

"Look, Josh," he was saying, "it's the simplest thing in the world. People make a big deal about the War of the Memes as some big tragedy. The only tragedy is someday a meme will win, and then we won't have our freedom anymore. But you listen to Hobbes. What he said was that the state of nature was the war of each against all. In other words we're just doing what's natural, you got that? It's all that old repression and stuff that makes you feel bad, not what you did."

"I don't feel bad now," I pointed out.

"Yeah, but you know what's going to happen, bud. Another mission's going to come up, and we'll have a good old time serbing somebody One True wants serbed, but then after we've laughed ourselves sick on it, you'll start crying and babbling about some German bitch you serbed fifty years ago, or about your Mama, or something, and I'll have to nurse you out of it. And I don't mind taking care of you—hell, you've taken care of me more times than I count. We depend on each other and we're friends and that's what that's all about. But I just wish it didn't put you in so much pain. I worry about you."

I shrugged. "Not much to be done about that, I guess. I don't think I'll get over it, but I manage in spite of it. And it could be worse—if Murphy had signed on with Free American or Unreconstructed Catholic, we'd just be fighting all the time. Neither of those memes will let you hurt a prisoner, let alone serb the civilians. At least One True lets us do the fun part."

A runner came up to us, a kid who didn't look much more than twelve years old, with a note saying that Aristophanes Jones and Euripides Frederickson were wanted at HQ, in person. We glanced at each other—because it was getting so dangerous, we hadn't actually met our CO in more than a year, even though he controlled most of the buddy teams individually. The runner himself was a sign of how bad it was getting; no electronic or fiber optic could be completely trusted anymore.

A few minutes later we walked into HQ, past all kinds of guards and technicians. Through the pulser to fry any electronics we might be carrying. Finger and iris scans to make sure it was us. Getting to be a suspicious world. Finally they showed us in to Murphy.

He hadn't improved in the last year. He still had a square head with tightly cropped gray hair, and a lot of wrinkles running through his deep tan. And he still had the same mad stare. The Organization had not chosen to back people like this because we thought they were good; we picked them in hopes of keeping things stirred up, of not letting any one meme win, by making sure that all of them had a few units like MCA: competent enough but hopelessly crazy.

Murphy grunted. "Here's the deal. We finally located the source of the Freecybers, and you're not going to believe it. Right back in our home territory, near Oneida. And part of the reason we couldn't find it was that it was never any kind of organization at all. Two freelancers, a husband and wife, working back channels off an old bounce antenna pointed at Supra New York. We finally busted the encryption on it. Well, I didn't, but One True did." He giggled, hard, and looked around to see if either of us got the joke. We stared back at him. "I can never remember which one of you I made a special ops captain and which one I made his body guard."

First either of us had heard of it. "Him," Sadi said, his face perfectly straight.

Murphy wasn't the type to ask for clarification, so he nodded. Then he giggled again. "See, the stupid thing is that they'd have been

fine and had my protection if they'd just worked through the old comsat system. If they weren't doing this through an antenna on one of
those fucking supras, those giant peckers of the one world government
sticking into the planet, shit, no problem, I really approve of them
fighting off the memes since those are all agents of the one world government. But they had to go and use that antenna and give themselves
away as just one more representative—"

He went on like that for a long time, which was usual. The longer
he talked the more he'd remember whatever his goofy principles were.
Finally, though, he gave us our transport pass, specific orders, and
directions for finding the house. "And there's one more little surprise.
One True thinks this is so important that it wants to talk to you
directly."

"No," Sadi said.

"Unh-unh," I added.

"Tape delay. Thirty seconds," Murphy said. "And I understand the
fear, I really do. But remember we've worked for One True for a long
time and it's got no reason to sell us out."

Sadi's fists clenching and unclenching, feet scuffling, angry, drawing the attention of Murphy's bodyguard—"I'm afraid I'll end up running a copy of One True. I don't want my personality replaced with
another copy of that program."

"It just wants to talk to you," Murphy said reasonably. "And you
know that the reason it hires us is because we *aren't* copies of it; the
shit we do is stuff it doesn't want to remember or have copies experi-
encing. The other thing you can do, both of you, is turn it on and off, so
you discuss your replies to One True each time. So you can interrupt
the interaction—and that should keep you safe. Remember it has to
have a dialogue with you, with nobody else present, to get into your
mind."

I tried real hard not to think about the arguments about whether
that was true or not. Most people believed it, anyway.

I thought we were going to walk right out; Sadi and I kept arguing.
But the bonus for the operation was huge, with a strong hint that if we
didn't want to do it he just might have us shot in order to stay on One
True's good side, and usually the longer you talked to Murphy the cra-
zier and the more arbitrary he got so that prolonging a conversation
was always a risk, and besides I had to admit I was a little curious and
Sadi was very curious. Finally Sadi figured that as long as we were
careful to talk to each other and pass notes while One True talked to
us, we might be okay. Upshot, we agreed.

The face that popped up on the vid was the first surprise: One True, for some strange reason, had decided to look like Dan Rather, or like Harrison Ford—then I realized it was probably an intermediate morph of the two. Kind of like what everyone wanted an American president to look like back when there had been American presidents. Lots of signs of having lived and thought and felt, none of which it had done really, if you were a hardcore humanist, which is what I was trying to be while I talked to the thing.

Chitchat at us for a while. Missions and all that. Sadi talked a lot about killing and inflicting pain, I think because he was mad at One True for not wanting to have memories of that kind of its own.

Out of no place, One True said, "I haven't seen weather like this since I was a kid in Ohio."

I froze; it felt like my guts were tied in a knot.

Sadi's foot lashed out at the wall plug connected to the terminal, tearing out the connectors. The screen went blank as he lunged forward and pressed a set of keys, dumping the program out of memory—

The place filled up with guards and they marched us off. I didn't care if they shot us right then, though. "Thanks," I whispered to Sadi.

"You'd'a done it for me," he muttered back.

There were at least two bad things about this. One, One True not only knew that I was Organization, but had penetrated far enough to get my Organization password. Two, clearly because I had it memorized so deeply—one of the few things I could count on coming through each transit with—

Transit, I think, getting up off the bed to pace. *That's what just happened to me, I've transitted again.* I throw the curtains open and stare out at the dark face of Mars, lighted by the one tiny brilliant moon that never moves. God, I need sleep. Maybe I got a lot in the last few months or something. Maybe I shouldn't have had the fourth pot of coffee. Maybe I'm afraid I'll dream, now that I know what's in memory. Maybe this is all a hallucination while Sadi and me wait to be shot.

Well, we weren't. Though I don't know how or why we weren't. Memes don't have a trace of sentiment so it wasn't that.

Still, if One True knew a deep memory to touch, who knew what it might have done next? From that deep memory it could well have proliferated and taken me over. Not the first time Sadi saved me, wouldn't be the last, and he was right, I had done it for him and would again.

Still don't know. Did One True just let it all go? Did Murphy talk it into letting us live? Or what? My next memory is of the mission itself, gliding over snow weeks later. Fell early in those days, by August on the south shore of Ontario. Glaciers were growing.

Four in the morning, moon high in the sky, gliding over the snow on skis silent as owls, Sadi's lean racer's body shooting along ahead of me. The house was only three miles away but we couldn't be sure what protection they'd have. Maybe none; electronics were now so detectable that some people relied entirely on concealment.

Sadi was carrying our gear. As we topped the last ridge, he gestured for me to crouch low and follow him. We swung into a clump of pines, running the risk of hitting something in the dark. "Totally fibered system," he said. "Probably optical switching and all. No signature worth talking about but as we got closer, One True's monitoring spotted a slowdown in communication between Freecybers—which means the machines here were paying more and more attention to us."

"So what does One True say we do?"

"It's going to stage some kind of diversion, then an outright attack, and we go in while they're busy dealing with the attack."

"Attack through the net, right, not something physical coming in?"

"Right. We're supposed to wait till—" He had his hand on his earpiece. "Okay, One True's put their system in an uproar. That happens several times a day, their security won't even bother to wake them up if they're asleep. We should move up to just below the crest of the ridge."

We herringboned up; it occurred to me that right now, with our skis pointed at this ridiculous angle, would be a really bad time to have someone step over the ridge. Unaccountably, I shuddered, as if it had actually happened somehow, or as if I remembered getting shot here.

Sadi waited a few long breaths and said, "Okay, the virus attacks are underway; One True is barging in the logical door, we go in the physical. Time for fun, bud."

Just before an op started I always got a sinking feeling in my stomach, and then a wild, crazy whoop of joy in my soul. I don't know where either one came from; either I was going to get hit or I wasn't, and with modern weapons there really wasn't any such thing as "wounded"—you barely had time to notice you were dead. So the thing to do was keep going until you won or the lights went out.

They didn't go out this time, either. We skimmed down the ridge, dodging among the trees, and onto the lawn of the big house, one of those huge white sprawling places that was all gingerbread and frouf and was supposed to remind people of the old days, a century before any of them had lived.

As soon as we were on level ground we put a push on, skating to build up speed, then crouching low to shoot up toward the window where One True was telling Sadi we could get in. One True called that one right, anyway—not a shot was fired at us as we zoomed up to the space under that window.

We dropped skis. Sadi nodded hard at me, once, and I scooted up close with the charge. I slapped it against the corner of the window frame, and we backed off around the corner of the house. Thumb on button; boom before thumb touched bottom; back around, hole in house, burst in, shooting.

They had trusted their security system so well that they hadn't even set it to wake them; they first knew that One True had penetrated and we were coming in when the explosion tore a hole in their wall, and the wife was wounded by a stray round while still getting out of bed.

Their weapons cache in the bedroom wasn't much, either; the old guy was bending over his wife when we caved in the door, and still trying to pull the shotgun up to where it could do some good when Sadi kicked his feet out from under him. I grabbed the shotgun and that was that.

Long pause. He breathed hard. Finally he said, "I didn't get a good look at her wound. She may be bleeding seriously—"

"Good. I'd hate to have her putting us on," Sadi said.

He could always make me laugh.

I checked her out, though; no point in killing them, at least not until we knew what they were good for. The round had been spent by passing through walls; it had hit her over the kidney but had only penetrated the muscle, not even all the way into the abdominal cavity. I dug it out with forceps from the first-aid kit, making a messy job of it so that she jumped and moaned a couple of times.

Once we'd sealed the wound we got down to business with them. "You're going to talk to One True," I said. "Who's first?"

For a long time neither spoke; then the man said "No."

I looked at him closely. Ring of white hair around a pink domed head, squashed features, sort of a goatee; looked like a parody of an old-time professor. Just sort of experimentally, I hit him a few times, enough to get some blood flowing from his nose and lips, and then asked if he was ready to talk to One True.

He said "No" again, so I slapped his wife around some. He still said "No."

So Sadi pulled the nice cop bit—he was always better at it than I was because he could think of things to say—and sent me out of the room "to cool down." I sat just out of sight so I could listen.

"So are you the nice cop?" the old guy asked, sneering.

"Unhhunh. So I'll just cut trying to get sympathy and so forth from you, and making you feel like I'm your friend, because I can see you know the routine," Sadi said. His favorite opening. "What we can do is talk about what the deal is, what you will and won't do under your own power and what I can and can't offer you. Then if there's a common ground in there we can do that, and if there's not, well, then no doubt you've figured out that we're authorized to kill you and to do anything else we like before, so at that point I'll give you to Yuri and he'll get to do what he does. I mean, it's not an accident that he's the tough cop and I'm the nice one; this is all just a job to me, but he really enjoys it. Okay?"

Long silence.

"Is that all right?" Sadi asked.

The old guy said, "As far as I can see we're already dead, whether you kill us or feed us to One True."

Sadi said later that one rocked him back a minute; he realized only then that these two weren't carrying any memes, that though they had been making and running Freecybers they were as much themselves as any mercenaries, ops, or elrefs. But he at least had the old guy talking. "So you'd rather just die? I mean, I can do that for you if that's what you'd rather. I can always just say we demanded that you talk to One True and you wouldn't."

"Can you be quick about it?" the woman asked.

"I can but I won't. My own ass is in the sling if I don't make a decent effort. It's you or it's me, so since I have the gun and you're tied up, it's you. Should I just bring Yuri back and get started? We won't ask again if it offends you, we'll just work until there's a good scene for the follow-up team."

"Not yet," the old man said. This was the point where Sadi usually got them; we'd gotten a bishop this way, and a couple of politicals. It was one thing to be tortured to make you talk, and try not to talk; it was another thing to be tortured to death without any ability to stop it. Sometimes they got up the nerve but usually they wanted to delay a few more minutes. That was what was happening to these people. "Not yet," he said again. "I—can we talk—"

"About anything you like," Sadi said. "I just need to look like I'm trying to persuade you. If you want to delay a while to tell me about why you won't cooperate, then delay. Tell me about your fucking childhood if you want."

He was in, I thought. It never occurred to them, once they saw that

Sadi was unmemed, that he'd be carrying a microphone so that One True could listen in. And the only way to take over a system, be it mind or meme (how much difference was there, now, anyway?) was to know it well. They were about to give themselves up, know it or not.

The old man sighed. "I don't suppose you'll understand this, but in a certain sense I'm on your side. Not on One True's, but I can tell, you're a mercenary, right, from one of the free companies? Mind if I know which one?"

Sadi would have had a big grin as he said, "Murphy's Comsat Avengers. Great unit, fucking-A."

"Bet it is. I've heard of you all. Well, you all know that you could retire any time by deciding to start running One True. And One True takes pretty good care of the people who run copies of it; you'd be comfortable."

"I might do that someday," Sadi said.

"You might but you probably won't. Mostly people like you live free for a few years and then die. That's the choice you all make, isn't it?"

That bothered me a little, as I sat listening in the next room. Close to what Sadi and I had been saying to each other. I had a sudden intuition that this old guy was much more dangerous than he seemed to be.

The old guy went on. "Well, I can understand why a lot of people choose to run a meme, to invite it into their existence. Really, I do; there are plenty of people out there whose own personalities will never allow them any happiness, who tie themselves in one knot after another, people for whom the biggest curse in the world is freedom of choice because they're programmed to keep choosing wrong and blaming themselves for it. There's no meme out there that's as cruel to the people running it as their own personalities would be. They should have the choice to pick up one, even though that's the last choice they can ever make.

"But you and I—or you and this Yuri, if that's really his name, and Monica, and me, probably your Murphy if he's still alive, all of us— for some reason we're fussy. We want to make those choices. The thought of not making them makes us even more unhappy than our own failures. We can't help it, we only want happiness we can get for ourselves, as ourselves, by our own efforts and choices. And if it's not possible we'll go right on being mean and miserable rather than accept a meme to alter us. Do we all have that in common?"

"I'm listening," Sadi said.

"Well, that's what the Freecybers are about. They're memes that respect individuality, personhood, the soul, whatever. Memes against memes, or liberator memes, or whatever you call them. You get a Freecyber, and if you aren't already memed, it won't invade; if you are, it attacks the one you have and tries to put you back together. If you don't like it you can always get back into contact with the one you had. Freedom for the mind . . ."

"Now I understand," Sadi said. One strange crunching noise. Two low *spat!*s. He had shot them.

Rushed in too late. Sadi was a deadly shot, and this was point blank with the target tied up.

He had crushed the microphone in his pocket; that had been the crunching noise. Then he had put the pistol to their heads and pulled the trigger. They hadn't cried out or anything; they looked peaceful. "Think they understood?" Sadi asked. Tears running down his cheeks. I'd never seen that before.

"I'm not sure I did."

"They won the argument," he said. "Though I bet One True got everything it needed already, anyway. But it didn't get them and that's something."

"We work for it," I reminded him.

"We work for us," he said. "At least I hope so. Come on."

As we skied away, the sun was just rising. Early September, but the snow on the ground was already a month old. Someday soon this would all be under a glacier.

Low boom behind us. We turned to see the walls falling in and fresh flames lashing up from the wreckage; we'd spent some care and effort in planting charges.

Tears, still, trickling from under his goggles. "It was a whole house full of books and comfortable places to read," he said. "And it, and they, are out of the world. But One True didn't get them. That's something."

"Was what they said about Freecybers true?"

"I doubt it. Everything out there in the noosphere mutates pretty fast. Whatever they started out to do, I think the Freecybers are probably just like any other memes now, replicating because they can, spreading out any old way, taking over and running things, no doubt believing themselves to have the best of intentions. But those two people in that big house, surrounded by all that civilization, sitting in there trying to keep some of us free . . . well, I think *they* believed it. That's the other reason we had to kill them. Not just that One True would have taken them over, but that they'd have found out they were wrong, and I wanted them to believe right to the end." He sighed and wiped his eyes.

We didn't usually touch much; Sadi got weird about it. But I reached forward and started to rub his back, and he leaned back against me. There's hardly anything more awkward than embracing on skis, but we managed. He sobbed a long time, and I held him, still not really understanding, watching the burning wreckage of the house behind me, the leaping flares lighting the snow in oranges and reds against the pale indigo glow that clean snow gets at dawn. I wondered if all those books were in flames yet, and that made me think of Mama and Grandpa Couandeau and their houses full of books, and damn if I wasn't crying myself.

I'm sitting here looking at the wall, into space, into the empty spot in front of my eyes, at any old thing; tears are running down my face and I've been sitting in one position so long that my rump is stiff and I feel cold, though the Marshack seems to have perfect temperature regulation. I get up, stretch, put up with the cramping, stinging annoyance of a leg gone to sleep. "To sleep, perchance to dream, aye there's the rub," I say out loud. Sadi used to say that when I would get afraid of falling asleep because I knew I would have nightmares. And then he'd rub my back. It's a quote from something I think.

Since I can't sleep, I brew more coffee, and ask the werp, "Help request, uh, how do I record audiovisual?"

"Turn me sideways so my camera points at you," the werp says. I wonder if they all talk like their owners, or if they imitate whatever voice they hear, or what.

"Okay," I say, "Record this as an AV document. Put a date, time, and place on it."

"Ready to record, no editing," the machine says, in my voice. I swallow the first hot sip of coffee and begin.

iv

I had been living over Gwenny's for some months and it wasn't the worst deal in the world. By now I had three jobs, or four depending on what you counted. The garage was full-time, but I still worked at McDonald's three evenings a week, and in the morning before I went to work, I did some mopping and scrubbing at Gwenny's, getting things ready for the breakfast shift. She gave me breakfast and a few off on the rent for that, and the cash piled up higher in my bank account.

The fourth job wasn't exactly a job, but if a job is work and work is doing something you wouldn't usually do, to get things you want, it was a job. A couple nights a week Gwenny would come up to my room; we would say nothing about it, before, during, or after, but she would undress, stretch out on the bed beside me, undo my pants, and then finger herself while she sucked my penis. Sometimes I'd stroke her breasts or put a finger inside her, but usually I just lay back and thought about girls I knew from school or ones I knew from hanging out at the mall. It took my mind off Gwenny's fat old stretch-marked body, badly done makeup, and graying hair. She never asked me to do anything, though I would have if she had.

Sometimes, when she'd done as much as she wanted, she'd finish me with her hand, and her other hand would rest on my cheek. Then she'd usually tell me I was a "beautiful, beautiful boy." Just like that. Always "beautiful" twice.

If I wasn't feeling well or said I was tired, she'd kiss my cheek and go away without doing anything. But I rarely turned her away. It felt good and she seemed to like it. I never did know what she was getting out of the experience, except that she called me a "beautiful, beautiful boy." She wasn't jealous—I had girls up in my room now and then, the kind that are impressed with a boy their own age who has a car, money, and place of his own. That never made Gwenny jealous or anything.

I don't think she was sentimental, either, though sometimes when I got in late from a McDonald's shift, and there were no customers in the diner, the two of us would just sit in a booth and watch CNN, her hand resting on my thigh and her head leaned on my shoulder. Verna and Paula never said a thing about that.

Not love, but I liked Gwenny better than I liked anyone else on Earth.

One night we'd just finished, and she was pushing her heavy, soft breasts into place in her too-small bra, sitting on my bed. My hand was still wet with having gotten her off, and I had just tucked in and zipped up. I knew I smelled of her scent, and would need to take a shower tonight; I was considering whether to go down to the diner with Gwenny and catch the news and some coffee first. About as normal as nights were in that little room, with the light from the diner sign coming in through the thin yellow curtain bright as day.

I got up, switched on the light, stuffed my shirt down into my pants. Gwenny was struggling around getting her bulky sweatshirt back on over her head.

A knock at the door.

We glanced at each other. I opened the door a crack and found Harris—the guy who traveled for the CP, the one that Mama and Grandpa were so impressed with. "Hi," he said.

"Hi, I'm not dressed," I answered, improvising.

"Okay. I've got a proposition for you, something you might want to think about. Meet you downstairs in the diner in a few?"

"Sure," I said, figuring I needed to get the door closed and this would get him away.

"What's good there? You eaten yet this evening?"

"I've eaten, but I'll take coffee when I join you," I said. "Try the pizzaburger. See you in a few." I closed the door.

Footsteps thudded down the short hallway, then the scraping of him padding down the steep stairway on the thick lumpy carpet. "Who's he?" Gwenny asked.

"Friend of my mother's. He travels in business," I said. "I don't even know how he knew I was living here."

"Oh, your mom knows," Gwenny said. "She was pretty frantic until she found out you were here and had a place to live and so on."

"How'd she find out?"

"I called her and told her, silly. I just thought, if I had a beautiful, beautiful son like you, no matter how estranged we got, I'd want to know he was all right. She doesn't know much more than that you're here and you have a job. Maybe this guy Harris will have some work for you?"

"Very likely," I said. I hadn't thought about it till then. Once I left home I'd dropped everything connected with the Communist Party. Now, if I wanted to, I could let the Party go completely. They couldn't make me do anything; if I wanted to leave the Party forever, I could just listen politely to Harris and send him on his way. I resolved to keep that in mind as I talked to him. "But I've got three jobs already, and I'm not hurting for money. It would have to be something worthwhile."

Gwenny nodded. "He's not a fag, is he?"

"I don't think so."

She smiled. "Good. I don't mind telling you, I hate fags. They do things to young boys, ones that aren't queer, I mean, so that they're never quite the same again. The money can't be worth it."

"It wouldn't be that kind of thing. He's a very old friend of my mom and my grandpa."

She nodded, obviously relieved, and got up, giving me a quick hug on her way out the door. I followed her out, locked my door, and crossed over to the common bathroom to wash.

When I got down there, Harris had ordered a pot of coffee for the table and two cups. He was taking small, neat bites off his pizzaburger.

He wore an old but good suit, the kind that shows just a little bit of wear for a long time before it stops being presentable, dark blue with pin stripes. His tie was bright red, which wasn't exactly a signal any more, but it wasn't *not* a signal to the older members of the Party, and by that point in "the development of the historical situation," the Party was mostly old people. For some reason, I noticed that his black wingtips were older, but well-cared-for, polished mirror-bright, and obviously expensive. I took a seat across from him.

"Your mom asked me to look in on you," he said. I suppose that might have been true, but I also knew that in the little world they both lived in, Harris was too important to do something like that just for niceness or as a favor. And I'd always thought he seemed like a pretty cold fish.

"I'm fine," I said. "Probably about time I did this anyway. Life's a lot better since I'm out of that place."

"I think your mom would agree with you," Harris said, "but she couldn't help worrying. It's good to know that you're all right." He took another couple of bites of the pizzaburger and chewed systematically. "I guess you've got a job, or maybe more than one?"

"Three," I said. "Two of them are just part-time."

"Still in school?"

"Nah. No time and I wasn't good at it. I figure I'll wait a while and then get a GED or something, maybe after that do some time at a community college. For right now it's more important to get established so I don't have to go back to that place."

Harris nodded. "Your mother and grandfather seem to agree with you about that. Some of the other members have been trying to persuade your mother to do something more permanent about her situation."

"Like get a divorce?"

"Just exactly like that." He took another bite, chewed and swallowed it, and then delicately lifted a couple of french fries to his mouth. "There are those of us who have been telling her that for years."

"She won't leave him," I said, glancing around the diner. "I wish to god she would but she won't." Gwenny was back at the cash register, conspicuously a long way from being able to hear us. No one else around. Probably Verna had been warned off. "Nobody will hear us if you say anything," I said quietly, "and it will be a lot less conspicuous than if you go up to my room."

Harris nodded. "Good thought. All right, here's what you might want to consider. Legally your whole existence would get a lot easier if you were two years older. You could get a chauffeur's license and drive a cab or limo for a living, you could take the GED right away for a high school diploma, in general it would be a better deal. And with your technical aptitude, there's something you could consider doing for us. I don't need to mention that we're generous to our friends, but let me add that if it works out right, there'd be very few ties to us and not much chance anyone would ever know. It's money and a good start in the world if you want it."

I shrugged. "What do I have to do?"

"If you say yes, about two weeks from now you'll get a big package in the mail. None of it's classified stuff for anyone. In fact you'll also find there are a couple of math and science books in the package so you can look things up as needed. You're going to master a lot of stuff about radar. Since you'll be studying more, you might want to drop one job—we'll be glad to replace whatever you were making there, with double the pay, cash, so no taxes get taken out.

"Learn the stuff in the package thoroughly. A couple of months after you get the package, you'll meet a man named Brian who wants to sell you fake i.d., as if it were just for getting into bars. You can recommend Brian to a friend or two if you like.

"The trick is, that i.d.'s going to be a lot more solid than a normal get-into-bars one. You're going to be exactly two years older, which means you'll be eligible to do what we want you to do—enlist in the Army."

I half-laughed; it certainly wasn't what I'd been expecting.

He smiled too. "You're going to ace all kinds of aptitude tests, thanks to the studying," he added, "and thus you will end up, sooner or later, in one of the Stealth programs. Money will quietly trickle into a couple of accounts we'll set up for you. And then one day we'll ask you for some things, which you will provide."

"Got it," I said. "How long do I have to think?"

"I'll be back by here in about a week," Harris said. "If you're interested, talk to me then."

We shook hands, and he paid for the food and left. "Was it any kind of offer?" Gwenny asked.

"Something Mama set up for me," I explained. "I don't think I'll take it—a lot of travel and stuff. I'm sure I'll be around here a few more months at least."

"I'm kinda glad. I'd miss you," Gwenny said.

I had decided to take Harris's offer. But since it would be months before I enlisted, and everything up till then was under wraps, I figured I might as well preserve the deal I had. "It would involve a lot of traveling," I said. "Like he does. He'll be coming back in a week with some more details, but I don't think I'll take the deal."

"It's not selling drugs, is it?" Gwenny asked.

"Naw."

That night I lay awake—not long, as I worked hard in those days and it was never much trouble to get to sleep—and let my eyes rest on the key Mama had given me.

I guess regular American guys would have been shocked, but I grew up understanding that the USA had to fall, that it was the center of world capitalism and the target. And then as I got to know Party members, I was exposed to a lot of cynicism too, because by the 1980s the CP was running short on believers and long on opportunists. So I don't think I had much in the way of patriotism, and I'd never had it, and I knew perfectly well that if Harris said the CP would do it, you'd have to go to the Mafia for a better guarantee.

Figure a few years in electronics as an enlisted man; after that, well, if the CP wanted me to stay in the Army, of course I would, and money would keep piling up till I retired at half pay—and with the age jump I was getting out of this, I'd be thirty-six and well-off. Lots of time to do more stuff. Or if Harris's bosses only wanted some specific things, they might cut me loose, at which point I could use some GI Bill dollars to go through college in a lot of comfort—there would be a fat, untouched, hidden bank account out there.

In just the weeks I had been on my own, I was already realizing how much I liked piling up money. Shit, if I'd known how much I was going to like being out of my parents' house, I'd have been *planning* to run away.

Good deal all around. Some risk, but I didn't have much to lose. When Harris came through the next week, he took me out to a business-type steak house, one of those Fakey Olde Englande places, and as I tucked in a twenty-ounce slab of beef, I told him yes. I came back and told Gwenny that I had said no.

That night she asked me to undress all the way, and spent a long time kissing and touching my body all over, working herself furiously with both hands before she finally took my penis into her mouth. I stroked her breasts; they were saggy and covered with stretch marks, and the nipples were too big and too red, but I liked their soft, baggy weight in my hands. When she finished, she curled up beside me and we slept next to each other that night, the only time we ever did. I woke up with her scratchy old gray hair in my face, some of her drool on my chest. Though she was asleep, her hand was already stroking my morning erection.

v

I finally finish talking. It's been three hours. At last I'm sleepy, though my throat's dry. I toss out the last of the cold coffee and reconstitute an orange juice. Food for a month here, if I want.

I talk to the werp. "Give me a table of contents or whatever it's called nowadays."

It shows me a list of about seventy topics, each with anywhere from a dozen to a hundred channels in it. I look over the list, and say, "Give me the ads, just the ones for Mars, and make it a general random browse."

For half an hour I find out what bread costs, what jobs are hiring, what the housing options are. Then I get an urge and say, "Show me the personal ads. What are the categories?"

The list is long, but it's almost all subdivisions under "Sexual Partners—No Emotional Connections Expected" and "Long-Run Relationships with Sex and Emotional Connection." At least it's gotten easier to find what interests you.

"Connections and Memories" is the last category: a bulletin board, mainly, for locating relations and friends, because what with the Die-Off, Eurowar, Diaspora One, War of the Memes, and Diaspora Two, humanity has gotten pretty scattered and there are a lot of cousins out there who have never met, heirs who couldn't be located, friends who haven't seen each other in twenty years. "Can we plug into that?" I ask the werp. "Are we online here?"

"Yes, we've got a new account in your new i.d.," the werp says. "It's intended to be perfectly secure."

"Okay, then scan for any ad seeking any member of the Quare or Couandeau families, or referencing any of my prior aliases."

"Shall I prioritize your criterial parameters, and do you want aggregate score order?"

"Uh, define terms."

"Specify terms to be defined."

I end up spending another half hour, while I get tireder and tireder, before the machine can make it clear to me that what it means is that it wants to know how it's supposed to compare indices to decide which ad to give me first.

Once I understand that, I sit and think for a minute, and then finally, tossing my empty orange juice glass into the trash, I say, "Uh, how many people are there on Mars right now?"

"Three million one hundred fifty-four thousand eight hundred twenty-two as of one hour ago. Crews may have departed on space-craft and there has almost certainly been a birth or two, and perhaps a death, in the interval. Should non-citizen personnel on Deimos and Phobos be counted as well?"

"That's an adequate approximation already, thank you." Once they start picking nits, nothing picks nits like an AI.

I doubt that I have thousands of doppelgangers, first cousins, or people using my old aliases anywhere on a planet with a small popula-tion of mostly younger people. "Just 'OR' all the conditions together, no priorities, and give me everything you get."

"Very well. Stop if I hit what number?"

"If you hit one hundred, I guess."

So after all of the trouble it has put me through, it pulls up a total of six ads. Two Quares, no apparent connection. One Ulysses Grant, ditto. One ad for a Couandeau, but it looks like the family came to Mars from France via the Vermont Reloc Camp.

And one that is just a phone number, followed by, "Joshua Ali Quare—when you get to Red Sands City, call this number. I haven't seen weather like this since I was a kid in Ohio."

I remember exactly where and when I learned that phrase. I don't even need the help of the werp to pull it up.

That phrase, always part of always losing always finding Sadi. Our identities changed: full-fledged deep-cover ones changed at every tran-sit, temporary ones constantly. But our Organization passwords never changed because it was the one sure way to find each other.

"When I see places like this I always wish I was back in New Orleans" was Sadi's phrase. In newspapers, on walls, little notes . . . we put them everywhere, and we found each other.

I remember once, sometime in the middle of the Gray Decade when practically everyone was living on dolework, we'd gotten sepa-rated the usual way—he'd had a job to go do in science control, and I'd had a straight strong-arm to put on some politician, way out in the sticks around Spokane Dome, a guy named Bizet who was into good government and no corruption and like that, and who needed it explained to him that he could run his own territory as clean as he wanted it but Spokane was going to have prostitution because that was ours. He was one of those progressive good boys that can't believe you can do it; he had called the cops, found out who they really worked for when they wouldn't come out. I beat him pretty good where it wouldn't show, and he seemed to get the idea. Probably if he was like most of them he'd retire real soon now, start drinking or something.

I caught up with Sadi in Boston Dome; maybe 2044 just before holding the ice back got impossible? First I saw of him, I was sitting on a bench and he was going by on the other side of the street, silhouetted briefly, between two buildings, against the wet, white wall of the glacier a couple of miles away. "Hey, did I see you at Mardi Gras?" I yelled. He turned to see who it was and I asked, "Don't you wish you were back in New Orleans?"

He turned and walked toward me. "Naw. I haven't seen weather like this since I was a kid in Ohio," he said, getting closer. "Jeez, Josh, they really did you up right this time. I'd never have recognized you."

"I think that's the idea," I said. "Figured you must be in town here since I knew the guy you were controlling was at MIT; so I arranged to have the restoration surgery done here so I could catch up with you."

"Well, your timing's perfect. I hadn't quite bought a ticket back to the house in Kansas yet, so we can go back together after your surgery." He looked me up and down. "Cheekbones, lips, hair color . . . looks like they added some weight?"

"Yep. It's a good job this time. But shouldn't take too much to put me back together."

Over lunch in a quiet place we knew, where we could talk without too much risk of listeners, we compared notes. My little escapade with Bizet had been pretty dull, and besides I didn't want to talk about it much because Sadi and I disagreed on tactics a lot. Knocking Bizet around hadn't bothered me much, but that wouldn't have been Sadi's way. Sadi would have noted that Bizet had a wife, a sister, and two teenaged daughters, and would have done things to one or two of them, for fun, in front of Bizet; he thought that always increased the pressure, because there are a lot more men who can stand to risk another stomping but there aren't many who can stand to risk seeing something like that again. Maybe he was right but I didn't like it. I figured the only asshole screwing up the Organization's business was Bizet, and it ought to be him that took the damage.

Call it a point of esthetics or ethics or something. All I knew was, I slept better doing it my way. And I didn't like it that Sadi would sometimes pick on me about that.

So I turned the conversation straight to the job Sadi had done. "How'd it go? Did it get wet?"

"Not very. He's still alive and he'll keep working. This time we had something better than threats to use."

"I thought threats were your favorites," I said, teasing him.

He poured a tall glass of beer and took a long sip. "Now that really depends on how you define favorites. For carrying them out, sure. I like getting turned loose on people, especially civilian dumbfucks. So do you, you know. That's how we ended up staying with the Organization, it wouldn't have been that hard to leave—at least if you believe the retired longtimers like Peter, and I do. So sure, threats are my favorite for fun. But for effect—for getting what you want—give me bribes every time. And I had a great bribe for this guy.

"He was working on CTCs—and you know that's priority one for us to control or suppress."

"Unhhunh. Lucky bastard—what was your bonus on that?"

"Enough so the next vacation's on me, bud. Maybe we'll go up to the Supras and tear things up a little, hunh?"

"Maybe we will," I agreed. For some reason I didn't understand, research into CTCs—closed timelike curves—was just about the biggest deal going for Organization bonuses. They didn't want anyone to be working on them unless that person was in the Organization.

The trouble was that as research piled up they were becoming easier and easier, and they were fascinating. A CTC was a loop forward into time; that is, you did something or other to make a "singularity," and it created a little loop of time sitting right next to our timeline, with one end of the loop at the moment the singularity was created, and the far end of the loop somewhere out in the future. It didn't provide us with a way to reach the past—the loop could not be thrown in that direction. What it did provide was a way for the future to reach us; within the time loop, you could move on the forward leg of the loop toward the future, at a faster speed than normal time went, then follow the loop till it bent around, traveling rapidly back in time, all the way to the singularity. At the singularity, you got off the loop, into your own timeline—and your own timeline split, into a new one that contained both you and your original self, and an old one in which you vanished the moment you got into the loop.

Right now it was mostly theory, but the year before the Joule

Box—the big collider particle accelerator on the back side of the moon, which could put a full joule of energy on each particle—had managed to make a subatomic singularity. I wasn't real sure what that was except that the flashchannel kept saying they had put "a billion uranium atoms into a cubic fermi." Sadi said a fermi was a unit of measure, which helped make a little more sense than the picture I had produced in my head, but I didn't have any idea how small except "real tiny." Anyway, they had thrown about one hundred electrons into the three-second time loop which that opened up. Ninety thousand electrons had popped out of the singularity, *before* the hundred went in— meaning that we had somehow captured nine hundred universes' worth of that set of 100 electrons.

That was the basis for Sadi's theory about why the Organization was so interested in CTCs: he said the Organization wanted to have a system where they could send in a few diamonds, chunks of plutonium, or kilos of You-4 tomorrow, causing tons of them to appear today. In theory, he pointed out, you could even use the ones you got back today as your starter.

My theory was that they wanted to own the first singularity, because it would give them a monopoly on the farthest travel back in time possible (since you couldn't travel to any time before a singularity had been created).

Either way, CTCs were an interesting game. The rules were, nobody got to play except the Organization and the physicists it controlled, and we got paid a lot any time we enforced that rule.

The catch to all that, of course, was that as time went by the science and technology just kept getting better. It didn't look real promising for keeping everyone else behind forever.

"So what did you do?" I asked.

"The Organization told me to offer him a unified theory of something or other, which I had in a notebook. He didn't believe it, of course, right off the bat, but I told him to take the notebook, free, for a few days, copy it if he wanted, and it worked like a charm. Which I think is one of the things it was a theory about. Anyway, he says it will be years just to work out the implications—and while he's working on that, he won't be anywhere near CTCs. Case closed." He held up his beer and I clinked mine against it. "No more science that we don't need."

"Amen," I said. Even if I didn't see much point in the whole CTC thing, I sure knew I wanted the Organization to keep its monopoly on the longtimer technology.

He grinned at me. "I haven't seen weather like this since I was a kid in Ohio."

Automatically I responded, "When I see places like this I always wish I was back in New Orleans."

"Perfect," he said. "After your restoration surgery, you and I recover in New Orleans and spend this bonus."

And so we did. The 2040s, the Gray Decade, was hard on a lot of people, of course—worst depression since the 1930s—but we had cash and an employer that was never going out of business. When you've got all the money, everyone else is for sale. If I remember New Orleans right, I think we killed somebody.

I have been staring at the werp for several minutes while I thought about that. The ad is still in front of me, still with its phrase. "I haven't seen weather like this since I was a kid in Ohio." I shudder. I'm not sure I want to live that way again, do those things again. It's turning my stomach to remember a lot of it. But I want to see Sadi, if it's Sadi. I have to see him if it's him. I tell my werp to copy the ad but not to respond, and then add, "Set up a queue of documents—everything that includes the phrase 'I haven't seen weather like this since I was a kid in Ohio.' Wake me at . . . what time is it?"

"Nine thirty-four P.M. local."

"Wake me at five A.M. local." I go to bed, and I go to sleep, but I have horrible nightmares and get no rest. The alarm throws me out of bed at five, still tired.

I reconstitute breakfast, sit down, and start talking to the werp. This is how every day starts for four more days.

vi

Some guys say they never forget Basic. I guess I can understand that, if it was your first time away from home, and you weren't used to people abusing you physically and screaming into your face. For me, it was a lot more consistent and friendly than I was used to. My biggest problem was that I could tell the sergeant was actually concerned about us, and I ended up liking him more than I should have. I felt guilty about what I was in the Army for. Not enough to overcome me with guilt and make me turn Harris in.

A few months later I was in a tech school, living off base in an apartment I shared with four other guys, with my RX-7 parked out front. I don't know whatever became of that car, I had it for years, but there's nothing in my werp to tell me when I lost it or how. I feel a little sad about not knowing where and when it went.

The promotions came reasonably fast, and I got security clearances without much trouble. Since I didn't answer letters from my mother, sure enough she complained to her congressman, who relayed it to the Pentagon, and my company commander called me in. When I explained that I was trying to get Communism behind me, my file got all sorts of good things in it.

That was the last time I was ever to hear anything of Mama. Guess I thought there would be time to reconcile, because I didn't know it was "the last time" yet.

Money was building up in my secret accounts, and I liked working on radar. By the time I was really eighteen (and officially twenty), I had a place of my own a couple of miles from the base, and whenever I was off duty I was in civvies and off to Phoenix for fun. I still didn't have to touch the hidden account—I was even saving money out of my military pay. Might've been the best years of my life.

One day in November 1989, when I walked into the base lounge, a bunch of men were glued to the screen. "What's up?"

"They're tearin' down the Berlin Wall, Josh."

"*Who* is?"

"The Germans. Both sides."

I stared at the screen. No trace of a border guard. I remembered that years ago, when they'd told us about the Wall in school, Mama had tried to "straighten me out" about it, pointing out that "oh, sure, some young romantic students that fell for the propaganda are getting killed, and that's a shame, but most of the people defecting from the East waited to finish advanced professional degrees at government expense before they 'fled to the *freedom* of the West.' "

The contempt in Mama's voice when she said that phrase had amazed me, left me without words as she went on, "Get real about it, Josh. If they were suffering so much they'd have run for it when they were sixteen or twenty or something. But they stay there for year after year, getting free tuition and advanced training. Then when it's time for them to start paying back the benefits they received, to be a doctor or engineer for the people who paid to train them, they skip over to the West because the salaries are higher here. The year before they built the Wall, the German Democratic Republic lost practically the whole graduating class of every medical school. Don't try to tell me doctors have some special love for freedom. We know what doctors love, and it ain't that. But what they do love—I mean *money*—oh, there's plenty of that over here. That's what they come for. Because they want to make cash, not make people well."

Something about the thought of the argument with Mama made me think about the kitchen back home, the way it smelled, the rows on rows of books she'd read, and the framed pictures of her father and grandfather. A little lump rose in my throat. No one here was going to notice. Everyone else was getting choked up too.

On the screen a couple of blonde girls were sitting on the Wall, prying off chunks with a crowbar and tossing them down to the crowd. They looked like any two girls you could find in any bar in Phoenix, any weekend. Probably they were just as political.

"That's fucking *it*," one of the soldiers said. "But I bet we all end up unemployed. Three years from now the Army's gonna be half its size."

"You mean *our* Army?" another asked. "Dream on, babe. There's plenty of ragheads out there that still hate us. We'll just be switching who we fight is all. More sun and sand. Kind of a beach Army."

"Shut up, I'm trying to hear," came from a couple corners of the room.

I watched them dancing and waving flags, all the stuff that's now familiar in most people's history lessons, and I kept thinking how much it was like what Mama had told me the Revolution would be like.

I felt sick and sad and sorry. I didn't even know if Grandpa was still alive, and I couldn't quite bring myself to call them and tell them I was sorry. So I never picked up the phone, just went home to my apartment.

It wasn't that big a surprise when a couple of months later, the deposits into the secret account stopped arriving. I didn't let it worry me, much. I could sit on the money I already had, while the trail got colder. Meanwhile I had a good job and I could keep doing that.

By the time of the First Oil War, in 1991, it no longer seemed strange; the USSR was just another nation, more like a big run-down Sweden than anything else. I went over to Saudi, spent some months of boredom at a station that fed data to a Patriot battery, and came back with a good tan and a lot of extra pay. They threw a parade for us.

As I did every quarter, I checked the balance in the secret account, using a bank-by-modem system. This time, there was a new deposit.

I don't think I was surprised, or not surprised. It seemed to imply nothing, other than, perhaps, that the KGB had gotten its act back together. I leaned back and looked over the place; comfortable apartment in a big bland complex, cheap but new furniture, blue Arizona sky outside, framed beer-company prints on the walls (mostly of women who weren't old enough to drink legally, not wearing much). The audio rig was big, new, and expensive, the television huge. I was thinking about buying a house to hold all my stuff. Life was probably not going to get better.

I was watching that big TV a few months later, when all the channels were carrying the news of the Second Revolution (they were still calling it a "coup" that day) in Moscow. The tanks had Parliament surrounded, there were crowds everywhere, and no one knew what was going to happen next.

It happened I was watching at the big moment, and on CBS rather than CNN, so I saw it from the rear view and therefore saw the famous picture of Captain Alexei Nemonynov before I knew that he, and the picture, would be famous.

God knows what Yeltsin was thinking. Probably nothing at all. He was said to be stubborn. But he climbed up on a tank, like he was going to walk right up to Parliament, right over all those massed weapons. He had gotten two steps when Nemonynov climbed up from the other side and stood in his way.

No microphone picked it up, so we have only Nemonynov's word for what they said. He said later he ordered Yeltsin to get down off the tank, go home, and stop making a fool of himself. I've often thought how much better things could have been, for the world and everybody, if Yeltsin had taken that advice.

But he didn't. From the camera behind him, you could see him nod firmly, twice, and then take a step forward, his silver-white hair shining. The pistol in Nemonynov's fist barked, a hard flat sound. Bloody flesh sprayed from Yeltsin's back. He fell backwards, off the tank, to the ground, shot through the guts.

The cameraman must have been so startled that he didn't point the camera down at the dying Yeltsin for a long moment. Instead, I—and millions at the same time, and later almost everyone—saw Captain Alexei Nemonynov calmly put the pistol away, heave a sigh, take two steps forward, and spit twice on Yeltsin's twitching body.

As if that had been the signal, four soldiers rushed up, rifles reversed, and surrounded Yeltsin. Methodically, with the full force of their bodies, the soldiers put their rifle butts to work on him. The rifles rose and fell, rose and fell. The audio channel picked up the thuds on wet flesh. The soldiers' backs blocked the cameras' view— we could only guess from the dull, heavy impacts, and little sprays of blood.

Nemonynov drew his pistol again and pointed it. The CBS camera went dead.

For the next hour, I flicked from channel to channel. Some cameras were still on to show the incendiary shells tearing into Parliament. Even the next morning one guy was still uploading footage to satellite of the bodies strewn all around the streets from Red Square to the Moskva.

I figured my phone would ring sooner or later, but it didn't, though the payments kept right on rolling in, as Bush moved troops into the old Warsaw Pact nations that September. The cash continued to flow when Oil War Two flared and I was temporarily loaned to the ayatollahs to train their technicians for the defense of Teheran. The money kept piling up during the Christmas Crisis when Red Army units started to defect to the various Free Communist governments and Marines went ashore in the Baltics.

On December 19, 1991, one week after getting back stateside from Iran, I parked my RX-7 in longterm storage in Fayetteville, reported at Fort Bragg, and got on the plane for Klaipeda. We were going to be setting up radar pickets for the UN's No-Fly Zone over western Russia, and everybody was figuring war in April.

The Rising might have been inevitable, but it didn't look that way then. It was nearly as big a surprise as everything since the autumn of 1989 had been.

My memories of the big celebrations all over Europe in January are a pleasant blur, but I still remember how amazed I was to realize I would be back in California in plenty of time to vote in the primaries. Not that anyone could work up much concern about the elections. Nobody could have beaten George Bush that year, and Bob Kerry didn't seem to try. It was the first all-state sweep since George Washington's second term. They didn't even interrupt television programming for it much.

And still the money continued to come in, and still no one called me. So I just let myself enjoy fiddling around with radar. Every time clearances were reviewed I got closer to my goal of working on Stealth detection.

Not like I was bored. I had a couple of acquaintances to go for a beer with, and there were lots of movies to rent. And the early nineties were great years for music, all the bands stopped playing boomer shit. I got a lot of new CD's and a great rig to play them on.

Best of all, I was good-looking and didn't mind spending money, at least as long as the girl put out. So I didn't have much trouble getting the kind of girl I was interested in. Generally I'd go out with a girl until I'd fucked her enough times to deaden my curiosity, then drop her—if she hadn't already taken herself out of the picture once it became clear that I didn't talk much, didn't care much what went on in anyone else's life, and was mainly interested in sex. The ones who were looking for someone like me sometimes ended up as semi-friends; the ones who were looking for a "relationship" usually hated me afterwards, like they hated any guy that didn't give them what they wanted.

There was AIDS, but the old, easy-to-prevent kind. I used up a lot of rubbers.

When the visit I had been expecting came at last, I had just gotten Cyssi out of the place that morning—another high school girl, I was getting old for them but they had such perfect little bodies and they were so afraid of acting young that they'd do anything to prove they were grown up. Probably high school kids thought of her as average or even plain, but that's because high school kids are only looking at each other. She had a tiny waist, big tits, a dark tan, and a big pouf of dyed-red hair, and that had been more than good enough for me to overlook the zits and crooked teeth.

I gave her a long kiss at the door, getting another good feel in under her loose, flowing top, and she did one of those pouty little poses. "Call me?"

"Of course," I said, and let a hand slide down over her hip, probing at the cuffs of her cutoffs, stroking her through her black hose. "You're not in any trouble with your folks?"

"Oh, as if. Like they give a shit. Not." She pouted again. "You didn't call till Thursday last week."

"I was working."

"All the time?"

"All right, I'll call." We kissed again and she went out the door, walking quickly away on the concrete walkways that made up the second floor of Park Electra, the complex I lived in—I heard her Doc Martens clomping into the distance.

I had just gotten the dishwasher going and the vacuum out when someone knocked.

Harris, with a man who didn't look like anyone. I opened the door wide for them, and the nondescript man turned to Harris and said, "This is him, right?"

"Right."

"Go wait in the car."

Harris left without saying goodbye, or even hello. I never saw him again.

The nondescript man turned back to me, came in, closed the door and said, "You've got a pretty comfortable life. It's time to start earning it."

I nodded. "You need a drink or coffee or anything?"

"No thank you. I've got a lot of ground to cover today. Let me just fill you in, tell you what's going on, and then go. Feel free to ask questions about any part you don't understand of course."

"Of course."

He gestured for me to sit on my couch, and then sat beside me and opened his briefcase. "As you know, things got unsuitable for the organization during the last year. Large parts of our infrastructure had to be sacrificed, not just because our assets were in the USSR and were seized by the New Provisional Government but also because for security reasons we had to cut traceable connections. But the procedure is complete—we no longer have significant overlaps with the Party, State, or Army. In fact we're no longer even based in Moscow.

"You might say we're doing what Bush wants us to. We're privatizing and moving into being a purely capitalist enterprise. We have a number of clients interested in Stealth, and our penetration is good enough to assure us you will be on one of the detection projects soon. When you are, you will begin to receive brief communiqués, mostly questions, in a brown manila envelope that will be on the upper shelf of your kitchen cabinet. Check that shelf once a day after your promotion comes through. Give me your apartment key for a moment."

I did. He took it off the key ring, dropped it into a box, and pushed a button. A loud beep. He handed me the key back without a sound, and I returned it to its ring. I didn't appreciate them coming in without asking, but I had decided long ago to let them have as much of me as they wanted. After all I had no gripe about the pay.

"When you find a list of questions, write out the answers—in handwriting—and put that in the envelope, along with the list itself. Make no copies of anything. Do not ever use a typewriter or word processor of any kind for this. Answer the questions by the indicated date, but don't compromise yourself to do it. If there's something you can't find out or don't know by the date, include a note to that effect.

"That's it, for that part of the work. Any questions? You'll get a copy of the same instructions in every envelope."

"No questions," I said, and got up to show him to the door—but he caught my wrist.

"There's one other thing," he said, and pulled out something that looked like a ray gun from a cheap sci-fi movie. He saw how startled I looked. I think he smiled. "It's an air-injector," he said. "You're getting a vaccination. Give me your arm."

Figuring that these people could arrange for me to have a life sentence, or maybe a lethal injection, whenever they wanted, I didn't give him a fight, not even an argument. I wonder about that. If I had, would he have said, "Fine, die of mutAIDS?" Probably not, since CDC had not named mutAIDS yet, and besides that wasn't the Organization's term for it. For that matter, I don't remember whether anyone was calling it the Organization officially yet; I think they'd dropped the term KGB since that stood for Committee for State Security, and the Organization was no longer a committee, there was no longer any such state, and it wasn't interested in anybody's security.

Probably I didn't think at all. I just stuck out my arm. He pushed the injector against my bare skin, not roughly, but firmly enough to make sure he had contact. The little gadget made a poofing sound, my arm stung for an instant.

Done. Just like that.

"What's it a vaccination against?" I asked.

"Three things," he said. His inflection was flat, and he spoke fast, like he'd said this a lot of times before. "You won't believe me at first, but because you had that shot, you will never come down with AIDS—though within a few months you'll begin to test HIV-positive. Don't worry, it won't kill your job with the secure project—one of your old girlfriends has gotten infected recently, and it will be assumed that's where you got it. But *don't* worry. You couldn't get AIDS now if you tried, nor can you transmit it."

I nodded. "Thank you." At least I could be careless when I felt like it, or when the woman wanted to be.

"Secondly, it's a memory enhancer. You will find for the next several years that you don't forget anything. You'll remember every word you read or hear exactly, and everything you see exactly as it is. You'll still have to study to learn new things, because you have to be able to use the information as well as recall it—but you won't have to memorize anything again. As a side-benefit, you'll be able to learn languages very rapidly."

"You said for several years. Then I need a booster?"

He shook his head. "No. That's the third effect, which is caused by the same stuff that improves your memory. Some years from now—we don't know exactly when—you're going to come down with a bad fever, muscle aches, nausea, the worst case of flu you've ever had. It will last a few months. At the end of that time, your body will have done a fairly complete renewal of itself. You'll have dropped several years in biological age. But you will also have lost most of the memories from the years since this injection. That process will repeat indefinitely—live fifteen years with perfect memory, drop ten, lose all recent memory. So make sure, this time and every time, you keep good records of everything important in your personal life, all the time." He got up to go. "Good luck. Welcome to active duty. Your pay will triple, and we're seeing what we can do about the eighteen months when we didn't pay you."

I thanked him because it made as much sense as anything, and asked, "Where did you get all these things?"

"Which things?"

"In the injector."

He shrugged. "They don't tell me much more than they tell you. My guess would be that it's the results of some of our special research and development work, and we probably got most of that out of the USSR before the Rising. It's not at all perfect, obviously—life extension and memory enhancement is great but the side effects aren't desirable for our purposes, let alone yours. If things had gone better, I'm sure we wouldn't be trying it yet."

He closed his briefcase, got up, and left. A couple of days later I noticed a squib in a newspaper about an unidentified body found in a parking lot, money still in his wallet. The description matched Harris, but I wasn't about to call the morgue and offer to come in and identify him. And maybe I'm remembering a dream about something I was *afraid* happened. After all, Harris was a small fish.

vii

For the rest of it, there's the history books. First reports of a rapidly acting, airborne mutant HIV, December 1993. Riots and panics all over. South Central LA blew up. Then on January 28, 1994, President Bush was found dead in bed. He had been ill for about three weeks before, and probably contagious since July.

There's a principle that most people are only about six contacts away from anyone else in the world, and it's true, but the reason's that few people are more than three contacts away from their national leaders. Think about it; chances are you know some local politician, who knows some national politician, who knows the national leader, and all the national leaders know each other.

My guess is the Organization targeted Bush. Having that on the werp, if they're still around, ought to draw some attention. Why I want their attention, I have no idea, except that fifteen years from now I will be back in this position again. What if I'd just as soon die? Who would be better at killing me than the Organization?

Morbid thought. But that advertisement *could* be the Organization. I have enough memories, and the werp has dragged up enough fragments, to convince me that they're probably still around.

Anyway, when Bush died of mutAIDS, since most of the US was only a few contacts away from him, it meant everyone was infected, from babies to grandmothers, everywhere.

Every schoolchild now learns three things about it: fatalities were concentrated in those over forty years old. MutAIDS confers permanent immunity to AIDS, which is why nowadays they give it to newborn infants deliberately. And in 1994, the year of the Die-Off, Planet Earth lost 10 percent of its citizens between February and August. All that's in the books.

viii

It took a while to get leave. I had not expected how easy it would be to drive across the country—but then most of the people who did things connected with the highways were young enough to survive. Only the major cities had had to use mass graves, and the only places that had really collapsed were ones with a lot of people past forty: Rust Belt cities like Pittsburgh and Detroit, and Sun Belt places like Miami or Phoenix.

For the rest, a couple of backhoe operators and a few people who had already gotten over the disease could toss the bodies in, so that if a town of twenty thousand lost two thousand people in two hundred days, they only had to dig ten extra holes per day. You could even keep the graves marked and allow people to hold graveside services if they wanted them.

I made good time, and when I got to my home town, sure enough, Gwenny, Daddy, and Mama were already gone. I might have figured it would be that way.

I walked over that river bridge one more time, and something gleaming in the stream caught my eye. It seems like a vivid, accurate memory. Just possibly a Boy Scout knife. Just possibly I climbed down the bank, stripped to the waist, and dove for it, bringing that knife up like a trophy only to get chewed out by a policeman, as I stood there in the hot July sun, shivering with the cold of the river.

Just as possibly I saw a Scout knife in a shop, had a fit of sentimentality, and bought it. For that matter maybe I just needed a pen knife and bought a Boy Scout knife without thinking, not even in that town, but a year or two later. I can't trust my memory.

I don't know about the matchbook, either. Maybe I went into Gwenny's, found the diner under new ownership, and picked up an old matchbook, because they were trying to get rid of them. Maybe I had carried one of those matchbooks for all of the ten years since I'd left.

Maybe I left a flower on Mama's grave, but several documents on the werp say I dreamed that, later, a recurring dream that wouldn't leave me alone for weeks and months. Of course you can dream a memory as easily as remember a dream.

I'm pretty sure I didn't creep into the emergency burial ground at night, find the right numbered marker, pull down my pants, and take a crap on my father's grave, a huge, wet, sour-smelling one that left my butt smeared with shit, despite my best efforts with the paper towel I had brought, till I could get back to the hotel and clean it off in the shower.

Pretty sure I didn't.

TWO

Its Hour Come Round at Last

i

It's the fifth day and I've got all kinds of crap recorded, but when I read it or play it back, it doesn't seem to be what I intended it to be. And I already have a sense that I was at least dimly aware of lying while I was doing it.

I changed the truth. Sometimes I maybe made something up to fill in a gap and forgot to say that's what I was doing, and sometimes I left something embarrassing out. I don't know. It's already getting hard to keep straight and I've only been awake for less than a week.

I guess now I don't blame myself for the mess that was in my werp when I woke up. And I sure as hell wish I'd been able to write as well as Sadi could talk, or something, because I look and I find it took me a whole afternoon to write: "Then the man came out from the KGB with Harris and he said go back to the car so Harris did. He told me about the AIDS vaccination and the memories and the long life, and then he left. I don't know what he looked like, I don't think I ever remembered, I don't think there was much to remember. Later I heard Harris was dead and I kind of wondered." And then the story shows up three more times, different each time I talked it into the werp, and it's not any better in any of those versions. I can already see where in fifteen years there'll be another mess to get through but I don't know how to do any better.

I keep thinking about that ad. "I haven't seen weather like this since I was a kid in Ohio." Password the Organization assigned to me in the first envelope I ever found in that cabinet. I think. Or maybe sent to me on a secure channel scramble. Or something like that. Or something else. But anyway it's definitely my old Organization password.

Somebody knew I'd be waking up on Mars right around now. I checked and the ad started to run two months ago. The documents in my werp don't show that *I* knew so precisely when I would transit. Somebody knows me better than I know myself, but they don't know exactly where I am, and they want me to call them.

Maybe "exactly where I am" is the only information I have that they don't. In that case I shouldn't give that up.

I watch some stories on the werp, drink some orange juice, and read over a lot of what I have written and recorded in the last few days, checking new documents against older documents, fixing them up, which makes them sort of lumpy and awkward, but I don't care about that much, even though some of it might be confusing later.

Later I'm sitting and looking out the window. Maybe today I will figure out the pressure suit and go outside. Seems like a lot of bother just to breathe air that smells stale and too warm. Getting back into city air was always a treat in all my long years as an ecoprospector. Was I one? I check the werp, and yes, I was, for more than twenty years in two different i.d.'s.

I have to assume I did my best to tell the truth to the werp. If I didn't at least do that much, there's no hope.

I am standing by the window. It's a change from sitting. The waves roll across the water and onto the beach. Air pressure's clear up to eighty-five kilodynes per square centimeter, and temperature here on the equator has reached 6 Celsius. The air out there isn't breathable for us—too much carbon dioxide and not enough oxygen—but it's getting there.

A motion catches my eye. I look to see what it is, and the oncoming bug seems to come straight at my face like an arrow. Involuntarily I flinch away, then laugh. Stupid reaction. Thick glass.

The bug flips up sideways, big wings spread wide in the thin air, and air-brakes its way to the window.

It might have started from dragonfly stock, or maybe grasshopper; I'm no expert. For all I know it's a honeybee or a butterfly, heavily genaltered. But the body looks more like a dragonfly's than anything else. The wings are big and gauzy, with a jointed "rib" so they can furl like a bird's, and huge in proportion to the body. I see tissue heaving back and forth inside the big holes that stud its body. A science program on the werp said that Marsform bugs can "scavenge the five percent free oxygen and two percent free methane from the atmosphere comfortably, metabolizing them internally as a primary energy source."

Marsform. That's the word for what this bug is. Adjective or noun, meaning "genaltered Earth organism created as part of the terraformation project." Another part of my memory whispers that there's another word floating around out there, "Moonform." Are they terraforming Earth's moon too, then?

I am fascinated, watching the bug. It sits, breathing-holes heaving and whatever's inside them squirming, on the glass, for long minutes, and I stare at it. I want to move to see if it will react, but the only reaction it could have would be to fly away, and I don't want that. And though its ruby red compound eyes point toward where I stand, a neglected cup of cold coffee in my hand, I have no way of knowing whether or not it sees me, whether the glass is even transparent to it.

Finally it flies away. I check via werp. Yes, Marsform is a word, has been for a long time. Yes, Moonforms are now developing and the first ones are beginning to spread out over the face of Luna, where the first rains have already fallen for a decade or so. The moon is the colonies' major base against Resuna. Yes, Resuna's Earth. No, Resuna's not a new name for Earth. It's all very confusing. Just the name Resuna invites too many puzzles.

I find myself drifting through, thinking about words that came along in all those years. Marsform and Moonform, PSCs and dolebirds, vags and tagrats, supras, One True, MAM . . . I start to ask the werp, and somehow every definition seems to bring up Sadi. What I remember more than anything else is this: my parents were useless. Gwenny was in it for what she could get. The little teenage pussies were useless, and the Army buddies, and the KGB. I had two friends, maybe, this Alice girl that I'm trying to track down in the werp, and Sadi.

So I think about Resuna and I remember when Sadi and I first heard of it. Sadi was scared to death of memes, hated them, every so often he'd start crying about our having killed the Hughsons, the couple that had run the Freecyber movement, because "Honest to Jesus, Josh, Hughson was the last hope maybe we all had, and I shot him. I let One True get his basic ideas. And it's turned the Freecybers that were supposed to protect us and liberate us into Resuna."

So I was always slow, I guess, so I asked him again what it was, and he said, "You know how superfast computers are MPPs, massively parallel processors?"

"I'd forgotten what it stands for, but yeah, I know they work by doing a lot of stuff at the same time. Millions or billions of little computers dividing the problem up between them and pretending to be one big computer."

"Well, years ago they found out that any algorithm a serial computer can do, a massively parallel one can do using cellular automata. You know what those are?"

"Sadi, I do electronics. Or I used to. Sure. All those little computers have a simple program that doesn't do much in just one of them, but by passing results to each other they produce an effect. Like people doing the wave in a stadium; the program is just 'stand up when your neighbor does, and then sit down' but you get these big complex patterns moving through the stadium. Or like ant colonies; the individual ants don't know much, the queen doesn't know much, but the colony pulls in food and fights wars and all. Satisfied? I know this stuff."

"Easy, Paladin," he said. "You'll break your toy."

I looked down to see I was almost crushing the white knight between my fingers. "Guess I'm more upset than I thought I was," I said. "Or maybe I don't want to know what you're explaining. So that's what Resuna is? One identical personality for everyone, human or AI, on Earth, that will add up to One True?"

"You've got it all right," he said. "Every other meme you can at least destroy, locally, by killing a carrier, and every other meme requires a long time to download, you have to get tricked into talking to it for hours in realtime. But Resuna is so simple, it'll spread like a bad cold in an airport. And the more it copies, the bigger and stronger One True gets."

I remember dropping the knight. I had been doing magic tricks and sleights of hand with it for so long, so unconsciously, that I hadn't dropped it or even fumbled it in years. I guess I was realizing how close to the end of it all we were getting. Not long after that the thing in our tent—no, I don't remember the thing in our tent. I check the werp, seeing what's there, and I find two different confessions from Sadi that he killed me, three confessions from me that I killed him.

I sigh, stare at the screen, think that maybe I'll look into that Alice problem next. Who was she, what happened to her, why did she matter to me? I'm sort of hoping that story will have just one ending.

I look at my list of mystery words and I didn't mean to, I was going to do something else, anything else, but I spend the afternoon going through the documents on the werp yet again, and talking into it again, and even typing though I know now that my writing's even worse than my talking. It comes out badly, always badly.

ii

Got back from my long leave. I'd seen enough graves. Things were getting back to normal.

The Pentagon had decided that Russia was still Soviet even if it wasn't Communist anymore, and that the Unaffiliated Republics didn't look as unaffiliated as they first had—especially after the coups that added Afghanistan, Pakistan, and Romania to the Free Soviet Association. Lots of panicking and running around in circles screaming among the brass and at the State Department, I guess. Down at my level, it just meant that we would be moving "forward"—closer to Russia—and that meant the base outside Prague.

Maybe that's when I gave up the RX-7. It was some years old when I bought it back in 1984, and it was a lot older now. I'd given it a lot of loving attention. I loved the weirdness of its Wankel engine, the way it looked. And it had carried my RADARGUY plate a long time.

I maybe figured it wouldn't stay in any kind of condition in storage, and sold it to a guy, or I wrecked it, or it broke down for good. Hell if I can remember. Or rather I remember two different buyers, two different wrecks, and one time a kid torched it on the street.

My stuff went into about ten crates. One of them would have had the key and book of matches, in a little jewelry box with a lock I think. Probably the knife too. Hell if I can remember that either.

"The Central European Union was always a pretty silly idea," Sadi said, years later, just babbling about it while we were getting drunk. The Organization had a line on some guy that wouldn't stop doing longtimer research after plenty of warnings, so they gave him to Sadi and me. We had tied up him and his family, trashed his house, serbed his wife and daughter in front of him and cut up their faces, reminding him it was all his fault, then given him a direct shot of PCP. Probably he'd be raving mad the rest of his life.

We'd also liberated a lot of good wine, and now we were drinking it while we admired those two women's bloody underwear, nailed as trophies to the wall of our house in Kansas.

Whenever Sadi got into the second bottle he would get off on one of his explain-the-world-to-me intellectual tears. "All the CEU was was the re-creation of Austria-Hungary with the capital in a nicer town. And on top of that buying Slovenia from Yugoslavia, and Lithuania from the Free Soviet Association, bankrupted it before it began. It was one of those stupid ideas only politicians could come up with."

I was drunk at the time, and I didn't argue with him. If I had, he'd have made fun of my argument. He always said I argued stupidly, like a kid, always "but I like this" or "but it doesn't look like that" and never used logic. Sometimes we'd shout at each other about that.

So I didn't tell him why I didn't agree, but my reason was true all the same. I *liked* living in the CEU for those five years, and especially I liked living in Prague where the capital was. One of the best places I've ever lived really.

The spirit of the CEU was sort of like old-fashioned American city politics: pave streets, collect garbage, divide spoils, believe nothing. Without the threat of the FSA, they'd never have come together; with it, they just barely did, and got up the guts to ask for American help.

Although officially the Organization no longer existed, it had a lot of fingers deep into the FSA, and just about as many fingers into the CEU leadership. From our standpoint it didn't matter a rat's ass who won. We were in it for ourselves, by ourselves.

That still sounds so much tougher than life was. The CEU, from Poland down to Slovenia, was a place where you could afford about anything you liked if you had hard currency, especially if you could spend your whole paycheck like I did (knowing my Organization pay was piling up). I had a small house in the Nove Mesto, which came complete with Maja, a fat blonde girl who did the dishes and laundry, swept out, tidied up, and stayed the night (for a little extra) whenever I wanted some ass.

In 1996 I barely paid any attention to JFKJr getting elected, just enough to get all the jokes—most servicemen pronounced it "Juh Fuck Jer." Far as I could see he only got elected because who else would anyone recognize that had survived mutAIDS? And maybe it was a lingering effect of Mama and Grandpa's influence, but it sure seemed to me that one white law-school grad in a suit was a lot like another, and it didn't much matter which one was the President. The big event for me that year was deciding to bail from the Army and start being a private contractor, which meant doing the same work for twice the pay and most of the same benefits, not to mention getting access to a lot more material for the Organization since now I could work on all kinds of additional projects.

It also meant I was under a lot less restriction on how I led my life, and so usually any party was at my house. I guaranteed dope, pills,

coke, whatever, and plenty of young women, and got people used to
the idea that I was always shooting pictures—they were still used to
film, it didn't occur to them that a wireless digital camera makes a lot
more than one print if you want it to. I would tack up the pictures that
rolled out of the printer on the bulletin board right away, and most
people forgot to take theirs home, forgot they had ever existed.

Since you never knew who might get promoted, or what might
come in handy, every couple of weeks I'd label the pictures stored on
my hard disk with who was in them, date, and whatever other information—"That's Captain Gerry Clemson and the girl's fifteen"—and
send it off by Internet to an address in Iran.

In the fall of 1999, the election of 2000 was shaping up to be a lot
more interesting than the previous one, and that afternoon there was to
be a big news special on the Armed Forces Flashchannel, a "Meet the
Candidates" thing, where the six Republicans and four Democrats that
had announced after Kennedy was indicted would all be talking about
themselves. What with mutAIDS and most of the Senate being in their
thirties, it was a race between people you'd never heard of, and what
with better information tech, the one thing you were sure to know
about them was the dirt. I had just bought a flashchannel set and everyone wanted to play with it. So I had a pretty good party over at my
place. I expected to get some pictures and get some people talking
about stuff they weren't supposed to.

What everyone liked about flashchannel in those early days was
that you could call up a commentary in the inset screen, so that you
could juxtapose a senator making his pitch with a couple claiming he'd
molested their children, or with footage of bands playing and troops
marching, depending on how you felt about it. *Later on* people started
to claim flashchannel was "better" news or "more complete"—the
original sales pitch was "news the way you want to see it."

So it was kind of fun to get some liberals and some rightwingers
over, give them a lot of beer, and let them fight it out with four separate
remote controls. They were all whooping and hollering in there, and I
was out in the kitchen getting Maja and her two friends started on serving the goodies—I had them naked in heels, one each to serve dope,
beer, and pills—when the shouting started to sound different, like
something was going on.

"You all got that?" I asked Maja. She nodded. I gave her breast a
squeeze for luck and walked back into my living room to see if the
flashchannel set was on fire or something.

AFFC had broken into the "Meet the Candidates" forum and they had some old gray-haired dick up there looking worried. "What? What?" I said. "Where's the show?"

People made a "shhh" sound, forgetting whose flashchannel set this was. Then I heard what he was saying.

"The fourth major coup in Moscow in the last decade took on a more sinister turn as related coups occurred in Belgrade and Tirana, and German authorities moved to contain anti-government rioting in the former East Germany—"

Someone had clicked up all four inset screens; two of them showed tanks rumbling through streets, one with rocks and bottles ringing off it. Another showed some city—somebody said he thought it was Talinn—with the scary guys in black with shades marching around looking intimidating. The fourth showed President Kennedy looking worried and answering questions. "Depth it to Kennedy," I said, "maybe he can explain things."

"He can't even explain his check stubs," somebody muttered, but then the inset screen zoomed up, leaving the main screen—the one that showed the newscaster—running in the upper left corner.

"We don't know about that," Kennedy was saying. In the wide-angle screen you could see it was a press conference. "Right now all we can say is that everything looks bad. We're in constant touch with our NATO allies about this, most especially our newest NATO members, Finland, Latvia, and the CEU. We think whatever's going on, there's a lot that needs to be explained, and we call on all sides to remain calm and *not* to try to exploit any opportunities."

One of the reporters in one of the inset screens put his hand up, and his voice came through the main channel. "Mr. President, what can you tell us about the uprisings in Berlin, London, and Rome?"

"I can tell you that they started hours before word of the coups d'état in Moscow, Sofia, Belgrade, Bucharest, and Tirana had reached anyone in the West. We're proceeding on the assumption that they are not coincidental."

"And if they're not, Mr. President, then what—"

"I'm sorry, there's another hand up and I'm not taking follow-ups—"

The black woman who stood up was subcaptioned "People of Color Alliance Radio," and the room groaned, but then they all applauded when her question was, "That's all right, Mr. President, I'll ask the same question. If the uprisings are not coincidence, what are you prepared to do about it?"

"Let me just say this. We have clear evidence that trouble was about to break out in Helsinki and Prague this morning, but fortunately our intelligence service was able to alert local police and matters are in hand. It's now becoming clear that there were large underground organizations in place. We'd have to assume, I think, that if it turns out that those organizations are linked to Moscow, to the uprisings in the West, and to the assassination of Prince Regent Edward and several Cabinet ministers this morning, we will move hard and fast, because this looks like the first few shots of a war. If that's what anybody has in mind, well, it's a war they'll get. And I call on those who may oppose us to think again. We've been prepared to fight in Europe for more than fifty years now, and we're as ready as ever. I call on those behind the coups, the rioting, and the senseless violence, to think again and back off. Because we will not be frightened. You know my father once said he was a Berliner; I say now, I am a citizen of Europe—and I mean of Riga, and Helsinki, and Prague—and we'll fight for every inch of ground."

"Fuck, here it goes," someone said. Others were babbling about what might have happened in Prague that morning, and did anyone know anything?

"Hold it," I said, "I'll talk to somebody I know in Base Security that can fill me in. After that I gotta call family in the States. And then if we don't all have to run off to get blown up, let's at least make this a party to remember—'cause it's gonna be the last one."

Everyone applauded. I gave a holler: "Maja, bring on the goodies!" and when the three girls came out of the kitchen with the stuff, that was more than enough distraction.

I picked up the phone in the bedroom and dialed a number I had memorized years ago, but never used. "Who is this?" the man's voice at the other end said.

"Hi mom," I said. An easy-to-remember password that you could let people overhear.

"Tomorrow night, go to your regular work period. 'Eagle' is on unless you hear a cancel from us. Acknowledge."

"Sure, mom," I said. "Tomorrow night unless I hear from you."

The man hung up.

We had no operation code-named Eagle, and no message I received over that line was actually an order. The line was intended to be overheard, and to put them off my track.

"Tomorrow night" was the phrase that meant that I could expect arrest at any time; I was to destroy any evidence, do whatever harm I could quickly, and get myself under cover, to one of the safe spots we had pre-arranged. Mostly just filler to confuse the NATO counterintelligence guys; probably there were a hundred more references to "Eagle" scattered through Organization channels.

I dialed another number. "Hiya, Linda. It's me, Josh."

"Oh, *hi,*" she said, her voice getting warm and friendly, "I can't talk right now, things are crazy, and I can't tell you anything about it—"

"That's okay, Hot Ass," I said—figuring I'd at least get something embarrassing into her files; she giggled—"I've had the news on, and I know. I just wanted to make sure I had clearance onto the base—I'd rather come in and work, where I'll be underground in a bunker surrounded by guards, than sit in a wood-frame building in a city where fighting could start any minute. Can you clear me onto the base for that? I'd have been coming in tomorrow, anyway."

"Sure, no problem. Anything else?"

"Just two. One, you might want to have counterintelligence come down and talk to me, I've got something for them. And two, I'm crazy about you."

"You're sweet. Okay, get here as soon as you can, and I'll have someone go down and interview you at your post. That'll give the officers more time to figure out where to use the extra hand, anyway."

"You're an angel, Linda. And you've got the tits to prove it."

She gave another shriek and giggle, said, "Oh, you," and hung up.

I'd been fucking Linda, and then relaying everything she said about life on the base to an Organization drop. She'd never let anything slip that seemed valuable to me, but I wasn't an analyst. For all I knew what I was getting from her was vital.

I had gotten her drunk enough to compromise herself a couple of times at parties—I had a great shot of her topless, dancing in front of several men—and I'd been commended for maintaining such a good contact.

The two possibilities were that she was unaware, and merely a bad security officer that I was taking advantage of, or that she was counterintelligence herself, and they were on to me. What I had just done was to put them (with luck) off the track no matter what. They might think I'd decided to turn myself in, they might think I was coming in early to get started on whatever "Eagle" was, or they might think nothing at all. In any case, they'd be waiting for me at the base rather than sending a car out to get me.

Back in the living room, everyone was getting high and drunk as fast as they could, except for a couple of nerds and straight arrows who were just leaving, heading back for the base, like they might miss the war or something. I saw those guys out the door as quickly as I could—they would have spoiled what I had in mind next—and then turned back to my other guests. "It's what it sounds like," I said. "According to my inside contact, fucking war for sure. Already starting down in the Balkans, and both sides are moving forces up to the line around Michalovce and Krosno. Lots of violence in the city here. Linda said on your way back, you're authorized to shoot if any civilian does anything even a little bit weird."

"How often you *been* inside that contact, Josh?" somebody shouted.

"Jesus, why do you care? With Linda there's plenty for everybody," I said. That brought a roar of laughter. "The deal is, the way I see it, probably nothing moves till tomorrow night, and they don't want to make the situation worse by moving too fast, if there's any chance the Sovs might back down. So we probably won't be called up till close to regular time. But that's all diplomatic bullshit, and nobody thinks it will work. There's a fucking war on as of tomorrow. So—might as well make this a fucking *party,* hunh?"

Everyone whooped.

"Maja!" I said. "Come here, babe. Set down the tray."

She looked nervous, but she probably felt safer coming to me than she would have trying to get away, especially since she was naked. "I figure," I said, "we're all out of here in a day and nobody's going to come looking for us, so we might as well have some fun." I grabbed Maja by her shoulders and pushed her forward onto all fours. She cried out in fear and I slapped her butt, clutching her head under my arm. "Quiet, piggy. We're going to all get some pork."

The place roared with laughter. Maja tried to stand up. I shoved her ass back down, swinging her around so that her bare bottom was toward the crowd. "Now who wants some?"

One of Maja's girlfriends tried to break for the door, and two men tackled her, spilling the tray she was carrying everywhere, forcing her to the floor. One of them, shouting "Pig, pig, pig," grabbed a beer bottle and shoved it into the girl's ass, making her shriek; already another man was kneeling behind Maja and undoing his pants.

That got it started; the third girl was pulled down onto the floor, crying "Ne! ne! ne!," her heavy breasts shaking as she struggled against the men holding her wrists. She started screaming when two big men pulled her legs apart. I heard my coffee table go crunch as someone climbed over it to get at Maja, and thought, *well, fuck it, I'm not packing the furniture, anyway, and it'll all be gone soon.*

In the other corner they dragged the girl up onto her knees by the hair, the bottle still protruding from her ass, and the men were lining up; one of them was forcing her jaws open. I looked around the room with satisfaction; nobody was watching me, they were either on the women, or watching the others. Left to themselves they'd probably kill one or two of the girls before they were done, but they weren't going to get that much time. I slipped off into the bedroom again, dialed 158 (the equivalent of 911), spoke my address into the phone several times, and then let the phone dangle over the edge of the bed. The screaming in the background ought to get the cops here in a hurry.

The way the men were whooping rhythmically told me they were doing something to one of the women, probably Maja to judge from the steady sobbing and the oinking noises they were making at her. I didn't bother to look out; my bedroom window opened on the alley, and all I needed was my jacket from the closet.

There had been rumblings and rumors all summer, and the last week had been a pretty tense one, so I had my basic "evacuation system" ready to go: a nice, powerful charge in a metal Macintosh case. I opened the slot I had cut in the box, slipped in the single folder that held everything incriminating, and set the detonator for fifteen minutes or whenever someone touched the box, whichever came first. With luck the Czech cops would be in the middle of busting the place when the bomb went off. Make some chaos. Good deal. Get going.

I turned to my closet and slipped on my heavy leather jacket, though it was a warm day outside. Inside pocket: already packed and zipped with all the documents I had to have. Left front pocket: Czech papers for false i.d. Open jewel box on dresser, get out key, Boy Scout knife, and book of matches, zip into right front pocket. Touch pocket once for luck. Check watch, forty-two seconds, better than any rehearsal. I stepped out the window to the alley.

Fifteen minutes later, sitting on a bench in a public park, I had been hearing sirens for about ten minutes. The distant explosion came right on time, and if the timer had run all the way out, they hadn't been very hot on my trail. If they had been, they'd have conducted a real search, and set the bomb off earlier.

"Do you know what the sirens are about?" an old guy asked me, in Czech.

I said, "American soldiers raping Czech girls. All over the city. This is how they help us. This is their 'democracy.' "

The old man's eyes gleamed crazily. "It was better in the old days.

Vanya was a better friend." (Vanya: diminutive of Ivan, equivalent of "Johnny," nickname for Russians anywhere in Eastern Europe.)

"Yes," I said. "I hear too that the Americans have been given one last leave to go out and rape and rob in the city. Some of them are shooting civilians for fun. They gave them all their pay for the year in advance because so many of them won't be coming back. I think I may take a knife tonight and see if I can get some of that."

I watched him toddle off with his cane to spread the gossip. That ought to get some things going and maybe give some people ideas. Meanwhile, I needed to pass the time till dark, so I got up from the bench and took a long, wandering stroll through that beautiful city in the autumn sunlight, staying away from everyone and from all the sounds. Not hard—most people were hiding inside.

Prague was wonderful then, just days before it was wrecked. It had missed being bombed in the two big wars of that century, and in the golden glow of an Indian summer, it was like something out of a picture book. I was there later after the bombings and the fires, when they had put a dome over it, but to me, Prague always remains the beautiful medieval "city of a hundred spires," trees blazing with fall colors, warm with buttery sunlight. I still kind of miss it.

iii

Late. The shadow of my house reaches out toward the beach. No more bugs. I wonder, if I go for a walk tomorrow, if I'll find algae floating in the water, and why the water's not ice—it must get cold enough at night.

I'm not sure whether my memories of the black, dark skies of Mars are projections, or whether I've seen it. I don't know why I'd have been out at night. Or why I visualize an airliner with an open top, like an old twentieth-century convertible. Must have been a dream.

After all, I was an experienced ecoprospector, I knew the back country well, and I wouldn't have been out at night. Though pressure suits are heated and well-insulated, being out at night is not really safe: if anything goes wrong, you're a lot harder to find in the dark, and there are a lot fewer people standing radio watch. So it must have been fairly odd circumstances that had me out at night.

The moon I thought was Deimos has been in exactly the same position each time I've looked for it, so I ask the werp. It turns out that decades ago the two moons were brought into areosynchronous orbits 180° apart, so that each now hangs over a single point on the Martian surface forever, like the old comsats or the supras around Earth. I ask the werp. It says the moon I've been looking at is Deimos, and that Phobos is not quite visible from here—I'd need to go a couple hundred kilometers west before it would hang above the horizon.

While I'm asking questions I find out that the water in front of me is Lake Argyre, and that I could easily walk the two kilometers over to the station—from there the maglev will take me to Red Sands City in only about an hour. Closer than I had thought.

I'm feeling disturbed. I've picked up that brass key and started playing with it again. I guess part of it's the strange way memories get reconstructed; I have four written notes and a couple of verbal accounts of the day I bailed in Prague. I know it was October 1999, anyway, and that fits fine with the start of the Eurowar according to a history summary I called up on the werp. In one of the documents I found an account that had been swiped off a database somewhere, the report of a surviving cop, who said three women had been gang-raped and that they were all down in the ambulance at the time the bomb went off. Three cops and six suspects killed, two cops and four suspects wounded. They were looking for me, and all of the women swore I had raped them as well. I'm pretty sure I didn't.

The funny thing's I feel this urge to apologize. I want to say (to three women who have been dead for at least thirty years, even if they lived to ripe old ages) that it was nothing personal. The Organization needed a public outrage committed by American servicemen, and some dead Czech cops, to add fuel to the fire. The excuse sounds weak in my mind.

I think about that for a while. I wonder what the women thought they were getting into. They knew they'd be waiting on drunken soldiers, stark naked, and for that matter Maja at least was planning to turn a few tricks in the course of the day. Of course that's different, agreeing to do it. Probably I could have handed each of them a couple of hundred and told them to lie down and spread for a gang-bang, and they'd have done it—but that wouldn't have served my purposes. It wouldn't have gotten rioting underway, nor sent the Czech, CEU, and NATO authorities on a wild goose chase.

But I still feel bad about it. I've felt bad about it in the past, too. One of the voice recordings in there seems to have been recorded when I was drunk and weepy about it. That's where I got some of my idea of the things that were done to the women.

Yet it's a long-ago crime done to long-dead people. Apart from my records the only thing left of the crime is a few old police files—and so many of those were wiped or altered during the War of the Memes that they might not be true anyway. No way to verify it against Earth records because they're all controlled by Resuna now. I don't see why I should feel guilty. But I am bothered that I can't stop being bothered.

By now the sun's going down. Tomorrow, if I wanted to, I could get up early, make a trip into Red Sands City, scout around, and come back.

But to do that I would have to go to bed early—I'm still sleeping a long time every night—and I don't. I sit up, zap through records in the werp, drinking coffee and eating an apple pie I reconstituted. Try to pull a story together. The records of five other times I have tried to do this—the earliest in 2080, the most recent just last year—don't agree with each other. Maybe some of them have memories in them that I've now lost, or maybe some are based on documents that I decided were false and threw away. Or is it possible that some of my memories at any given time are not really lost, but just inaccessible?

If I search on "Weather-Kid-Ohio" as a cluster, I turn up too many cases to read and view tonight; yet I don't give up.

"I haven't seen weather like this since I was a kid in Ohio." I can count a good dozen times I heard that expression, just in my memory. The dark outside the window starts to give me the creeps. The glow off Deimos is a funny color, maybe caused by all those lights I see glowing on its gleaming metal skin. I stand up, draw the curtain, reconstitute more coffee, pour a cup, and continue.

iv

"I haven't seen weather like this since I was a kid in Ohio," the man next to me said. "Jesus, this train station's cold."

"Fuck it," I said. "If it gets hot it'll get hot real sudden, and we won't like that either."

Pretty standard remark after so many nukes had gone off, three years or so into the Eurowar. I knew he'd said my password, but I figured I'd make him sweat for the acknowledgment.

"Do you think we'll get more snow?" he hinted. Must be amateur, new recruit, couldn't have much experience. Way he was doing things, wouldn't get much older.

I looked sideways at him. Coat fairly new, outermost sweater almost clean, shoes insulated hightops, shredded by long wear, that

were a strange shade of brown-gray from a lot of walking in ashes and
muck. They maybe were originally waterproof, but they sure weren't
now, not with one dirty black big toenail sticking out of one of them.

"I'm from Ohio, myself, and the sky always looked like that
before it snowed," I said, giving the countersign. I had amused myself
about as much at his expense as I wanted to, and even after my three
years of active duty I didn't know how much fucking around the Organization would tolerate.

He slid an envelope into my pocket. I waited half an hour, got on
the first train that seemed to be headed somewhere, hoped a rocket
wouldn't hit it for a while, and then went into the bathroom. The first
bathroom I picked held a dead conductor. Close that door, walk farther
down. Next one was unoccupied. I put a newspaper down on the seat,
sat down on it, and opened the note the guy had given me.

A short note like all of them: a British regiment in Amsterdam was
showing signs of effectiveness. Go there and kill any two men I
thought would do max damage. No more than that. After you bagged
two, odds they'd bother to retaliate went up, and we had assets in Amsterdam that they might know about. Just two, preferably in the same
incident, could be put down to random sniping or even tourist psychos.
Further orders at a specific bench in a public park in Brussels.

On the way, look in on a missing agent who had married a German
politician in Essen. Find out why she'd sent no reports in two years.
See why he was still alive.

This schedule could easily get me killed—I'd have to stay on the
same trains for *hours* to get to the right places at the right times. And
every minute a train rolled was a chance for overhead satellites to get a
fix and dispatch a deathbird. Usually all one did was stop the train—
but now and then a train got wrecked seriously and passengers died,
especially from the new Soviet deathbirds that could take out a group
of ties just ahead of the train, derailing the works. Besides there were
so many tourist psychos out there, playing at being "Resistance Fight-
ers," it seemed like more trains wrecked than not. And you could
always worry that someone had virused the train's automated driver.
That happened a lot too.

2001 was a year. Nothing worked and 90 percent of the engineers
on Earth, probably, were busy figuring out how to keep it from working. Two doctors in Japan announced that they thought they had a way
to induce successful immune responses to everything—the "make you
well" shot—and the next day one was thrown from a high window and
the other was run down, and backed up over, by a dump truck. The

physicist in Einstein's old job published a paper about closed timelike curves—limited time travel; most of his family died in a fire, the rest were shot trying to run out of the burning house. The Nobel Prize for Peace was not awarded. This upset half a dozen ayatollahs (who had felt that they had earned it for brokering a peace between India and Pakistan), so Stockholm was hit with 100 missiles on Christmas morning, seventy-eight people died, and it only made the prime slot on the flashchannel because the *motive* was novel.

The price of teenaged slaves in Benelux fell to 1500 rounds of whatever the seller's weapon took. Police departments couldn't get new applicants for anything less than the pre-war pay of brain surgeons, usually payable in a mix of gold, offshore electronic funds, antibiotics, and food. The file in my Organization-issued palmtop computer, listing what bonuses were paid for different categories of assassinations, was 75 kb long. Good year for money. Bad year for people.

The train bumped past a burned-out column of tanks, big old Abramses that must have been hit in the first week of the war. Not safe to try to clear stuff like that out, so they'd been left where they burned.

I wondered idly if I knew anyone who was rotting in those hulks. Very likely I did. I'd been doing some work on counter-battery-fire control systems, including a system to be installed on the Abrams, at one point, and that meant traveling around and meeting a lot of Abrams crews.

No helping them now. Or any of the hundreds of thousands of unburied dead still lying around Europe.

The First and Second Oil Wars had taught everybody a lot of lessons. Mainly how to write SMOTs, Simulation Modeling Optimizing Targeters, ultrafast programs that ran on microsupers and could make "smart weapons" into "brilliant weapons."

Smart weapon: a munition that hit the target more often than not. Old-fashioned bullets and bombs, the kind you saw in WWII movies, were "dumb"—meaning that it took 10,000 rounds to kill one enemy soldier, and a bomb came down within one kilometer of the target. With dumb weapons, misses outweighed hits by factors of hundreds or more. Smart weapons hit more than 50 percent of the time. The number of shots you have to fire to get the target is 1, divided by the percentage of hits; 50 percent means you get it in two shots, instead of a thousand.

Brilliant weapons: the smart weapon went after the most important thing on the battlefield. A smart artillery round would jump out of a howitzer, look down below it, find a tank, and land on that. But a brilliant artillery round would look down below and pick out the tank that contained a general. Dumb bomb landed somewhere around a power plant, smart bomb went through the roof in the right place to hit a generator, but brilliant bomb hit the generator that was carrying peak load.

Essentially in the split second before the weapon was launched, the SMOT simulated a thousand, or ten thousand, possible hits and consequences of those hits, picked the one whose result was best for its side and worst for the enemy, and reprogrammed the smart weapon to go do that.

Nobody realized *both* sides had SMOTs. The NATO nations had been developing them right along after the First Oil War, confident that they had the only ones. The FSA thought they had invented the idea after studying Western weaponry during the Oil Wars, and had been scrambling to get them working, especially after the new government had come to power and achieved some kind of stability.

Pretty soon the pilots and gunners gave up aiming at anything in particular; the SMOT, with its faster reflexes and better ability to evaluate all the data flowing in, could pick out the preferred target within several square miles. So you'd just pop up, fire, and get out of there, not even really knowing what you were shooting at.

SMOTs got better, and faster, and able to think about more issues at once—tech evolves quickly in wartime, and software evolves faster than other tech. After a while you didn't really need people in the loop at all; you just sent out a drone to carry the SMOT, weapons, and sensors, linked to a network of SMOTs via encrypted tightbeam, and told it to go make life miserable for the enemy.

One time, in the middle of getting drunk and high together, Sadi said "every big war begins by slaughtering privates to educate generals." The Eurowar was different. We slaughtered generals, and presidents and ministers, corporate executives who knew what they were doing, and lately both sides had been nailing engineering talent.

There were rumors that this new Pope, Paul John Paul, was going to do something for world peace. One of my contacts had laughed and said he must have some divisions no one had heard about. I looked at him blankly, and he tried to explain it was some kind of old joke going back to Stalin. I guess he'd been in the Organization a long time.

The train rocked on through the winter landscape. At least we had heavy cloud cover and only had to worry about radar satellites. Nowadays most trains were carrying jamming rigs, just like the few airliners still flying. Next year they'd probably have those on city buses too.

I looked out the window at land that got flatter and flatter. We'd be crossing the Rhine in little time unless—they used to say Murphy hears you.

I saw it coming—bright silver, like a model airplane with a three-foot wingspan, zigging and bouncing a couple of feet off the snow, skating in toward the train. A deathbird, maybe fired by a mine miles away, dumped in from orbit in a container, or shot out of a robot sub off the North Sea coast. Probably it had started after the train within a few minutes of our starting to move along this line—deathbirds had enormous range but they were not fast, and it might have taken an hour or more on its way, easily.

I had needed to see only that flash of silver and the strange swirl in the air of the electrostatic propulsion system. I rolled off the seat and down onto the muddy, grimy floor of the railroad carriage.

The jolt was pretty bad—it took out a group of ties—and derailed us. Floor bucked, slammed against me, belly-lurch of weightlessness before things settled out. Then I was sliding on my stomach over the grit and mud of the train floor, several feet face-first toward the door.

As soon as the train carriage came to rest, with the car canted over to the side but the door mercifully on the up side and the little lights indicating the power was still on, I jumped up, scrambled back, got my valise, made for the door.

Only a few people on the train. Safe way to get anywhere nowadays, walk slowly by yourself. So I'd had the carriage to myself.

As I was opening the outside door, the door to the next car slid open, and a man, in a three-piece suit, came in, already reaching inside his coat. Reflexes kicked in. Draw and fire, fire, fire, fire. He fell over backward.

Nice. All four shots in the head and chest.

The man lay sprawled in the up-tilted bank of seats, dead. Something clenched in his hand—his weapon? Might be worth trading up.

A pocket watch. I shrugged. Call it education—he would not make that mistake again.

His pocket held a Boy Scout knife, like the one my father had given me, which I had lost sometime before. I took that. He also had an American passport, which I took for resale, and a Missouri driver's license, worth nothing here so I left it on his body to identify him. The authorities would probably get his body home. Better deal than the conductor was likely to get, since he had looked like a Turk, and they'd probably just cremate him and mail his effects to his relatives.

I wondered if I was the only survivor of this train. Three men got on alive, one got off alive. The story of Europe lately.

I climbed out the door onto the side of the train, then down past the overturned wheels to the ground. No sign of any other passengers, so they were hurt and still on the train, or had already gotten away— either way, none off mine. Or they might be already out of the train, waiting to kill me.

I slid on my butt down into the ditch beside the embankment. Nothing shot at me. I waited a few minutes. Still nothing. Either they had more patience than I or there wasn't any "they."

I climbed back up the embankment and started walking up the track toward the Rhine. Sooner or later I would cross a main road, which would take me to someplace where I could steal a car.

Stealing a car was getting really tough now that most civilians had White Flag transponders—radio gadget that told satellites and mines that this car was promising to be a noncombatant, give aid to neither side, and obey whoever won. Normally a White Flag wasn't abused because if they found you driving something with a White Flag on it, and contraband inside, they hanged you on the spot and relayed the owner's i.d. to everyone, and whoever could do it, on either side, would kill the owner.

That made it tough to steal a car, but not impossible. Civilian protection systems were far, far behind the military stuff that had been developed during the three years of war, and the Organization had the latest from both sides.

Twenty minutes later I walked into a little German village, a quiet, sleepy kind of place that had a couple of gas stations, an old shut-down movie theater, and one tiny Catholic church next to one tiny Lutheran church, all surrounded by about fifty houses.

I needed a car I could work on without being observed. I set the low-energy scanner to look for household protection software it recognized, and my cellular datalink to see what it could find out about security systems purchased here.

Most of these German households were in hock up to the eyeballs with buying all the various security systems, plus enough guns and ammo to back up the alarms. A good, fully trained Doberman nowadays was renting for more than a chemical engineer made.

But since these poor bastards just wanted the war to go home and leave them alone, that was what they had predicated their defense on— protecting each individual house. So I could walk right up the middle of the street, in the middle of the day, and though almost everyone telecommuted now to avoid the weapons targeted on transit, nobody was patrolling the streets; they sat in their individual cocoons and waited for the blow to fall on one of them, even though probably half the houses in the village had picked me up on sensors, and the house-holders were undoubtedly sitting with their hands on their guns, wait-ing with sweat staining their armpits. If one of them had just not waited to see what I would do, seen what I was and taken one good shot, it would all have been over. But they lacked the balls. They always did.

The cellular data link spotted my chance a half second ahead of the scanner. Side street not far ahead: integrated home security system with known bug, plus hole in his camera system, angle of approach uncovered.

I checked again—jackpot—systems analyst for the German gov-ernment. One of those obscure ministries, likely intelligence work. Probably a small fish, but all the same I could expect to collect a bounty on this one. The Organization was currently under contract to the Sovs, just as if it were the old days, so a German who worked in that ministry was bound to be worth something.

He probably had gotten this system cheap, and then never bought upgrades because the old one was still keeping people out. The report said he'd registered a marriage to some girl half his age, address unknown, two years before.

I walked up the path my computer told me to take, and when we were close enough it seized his house's cellular link and dropped in a bunch of tranquilizer viruses. Suddenly the house was as dead as any old building. It wouldn't call the police for help and it would sound no alarms when I broke in. And it would not tell the people inside that its status had changed, either.

Of course he would know what was up when his door caved in. But I knew I was going to shoot at anything that moved. He had to decide. The advantage was still mine.

I didn't have any explosives to do the job with, so I gave the door a good old-fashioned roundhouse kick. The cheap lock broke and it swung open with a ripping, booming noise as the veneer facing on the door tore to shreds and the bolt of the lock cut through the wooden doorframe.

He came out naked. I pulled the trigger and he went over dead, onto his back. They'd have executed him anyway for letting me steal his car. So what the fuck.

In the bedroom his wife trying to load a shotgun; she was cute, a brunette with nice little breasts. Probably she'd been out on the street, a runaway or war orphan turning tricks, and he'd bought her services permanently with his techie salary and nice safe house—though she might even think she loved him now. That was pretty common in those days.

"Put that down," I said in German.

She did, and I said, "Kneel. Open your mouth. Shut your eyes."

She did, again. Tears were running down her face and she was mouthing some word; I told her to shut up.

I wanted her to think this was going to be an oral rape. Most women complied, hoping to survive.

I couldn't let anyone who had seen me live—composite pictures got more accurate with every witness, and, if I let witnesses live, the time would come when an AI checking street camera records would recognize me. But I could make it quick. I shoved the gun into her open mouth, the muzzle forcing her palate back and up, and pulled the trigger. It made a hideous mess, and the sound hurt my ears in that little room.

The girl had had maybe one minute of terror from the time the door caved in, tops. No physical pain other than the instant of the gun thumping on the roof of her mouth. A lot better than most people got nowadays. Still, that made three I'd killed today—more than in the month previous—and that made me feel funny.

That was when I realized the word she had been mouthing was *Kinder.* Children. Shit.

I violated a lot of rules. Stupid stupid stupid. It wasn't like I'd just done them any big favors, I'd just orphaned the little bastards. But the twins looked to be about two. *(Stupid shit. Probably she was pregnant when he took her in, and they weren't even his.)* I didn't think those kids could contribute crap toward identifying me.

And after all we were expected to improvise. So I did. I picked up the phone, called for help, and told the emergency dispatcher that I was monitoring him on datalink (I wasn't—my cellular wouldn't patch through), that I had handcuffed both of the kids to a remote-controlled charge, and that if he fucked with the White Flag on the car I was taking, or tracked the car, or if the cops got there in less than an hour, the kids would be blown to the moon.

Then I took the car from the garage and peeled out for Essen. I figured the dispatcher would behave for an hour, mostly, though I expected cops were tracking the car one way or another. But they wouldn't dare try bombing or blasting the car—too much chance I had a deadman program running. And an hour was all the time it would take me.

Those kids had had it made, I thought, as I shot down the highway, doing top speed because there was nothing else on the road. That little house had been wall-to-wall toys. Father had had a telecommuting station, so both their folks were always there.

Probably they'd even gone outside in the backyard a lot. Dad probably loved the hell out of Mom, because she was so beautiful and he'd never thought he'd get a pretty teenager for a bed partner. Mom probably loved him for taking her in, cleaning her up, giving her a place that was safe and secure. Probably those kids had no idea about a war, thought the world was one big warm friendly.

Well, welcome to reality, dumbfucks.

Still, I hadn't liked the way they'd looked when I'd left them in that house with the bodies of their parents.

Our agent in Essen turned out to be dead—caught and executed the year before. I nailed the politician to collect the bounty. The Amsterdam gig was routine—a good CO with one sharp staff officer. I bombed the car they both were riding in. One of those trips where all the bad stuff happens up front.

The guy who talked about the weather in Ohio with me, in Brussels, gave me a jar of something to pour into the Seine above Paris. A complete milk run, or so I thought at the time.

The first sign that the Eurowar was entering its last and worst phase came on that mission, and it wasn't much just yet. As the bus headed south out of Brussels, I saw long rows of men and women filling sandbags. It was winter, after all, so one might have expected some flooding, but the river wasn't particularly high. And it did seem strange to see so many people risking their lives by being out in the open. I was bored, so I asked.

The bus driver grunted. "The worms, they say."

"The worms?" I asked.

"Eating through dikes and destroying levees, far upstream. They're having to spray poison but the worms don't die easy. They look like ordinary earthworms, you know, but when they get a chance—poof, solid banks of earth become mud overnight. Not a good thing, you know, there aren't many to work on these things with a war on. I don't like being near it myself, I keep thinking what if the worms are somebody's trick to get people into the open. I just can't imagine what will happen next, you know, if this keeps up."

I sighed and said something about the damned war and the politicians. I didn't want to draw too much attention to myself since there were only four people on the bus, and once we reached the city of St. Quentin I was planning to get off the bus and leave a bomb behind me. In an abstract kind of way I admired this man's guts, and anyone who could keep an old pile of rust like this running through three years of a war deserved some respect, but the existence of reliable transportation in an area where we had only sporadic control had to be dealt with. I'd get a substantial bonus for identifying and eliminating this one.

The bus rumbled on south, bumping and slamming over the potholes of three winters without road repairs, as it wove its way through the smaller roads and every little cowpath, never repeating a route, like an ant or bee that knows roughly where it's going but may jog and wander all over the map before getting there.

There were more and more rows of sandbaggers. If the worms were Organization work, we'd done a fine job.

Even then it didn't occur to me, really, just how bad the emergency must be if they were exposing so many civilians to attack. But things changed fast—three months later it was no surprise when the Netherlands and Belgium signed a separate peace to get a chance to evacuate. Another typical dumbfuck move in a war full of dumbfuck moves, mistaking their allies for their friends. All they did was trade FSA deathbirds and mines for NATO deathbirds and mines. They still lost thousands who tried to take buses, trucks, or trains. After the first day, people just moved any way they could. June of 2001 saw the great refugee swarms pouring into Germany and France, walking or cycling to high ground with whatever they could carry or drag, and the beginnings of internecine fighting in NATO as the fleeing populations became too large for the refugee camps.

By that time, though, the Sovs were too busy to exploit the opportunity. Prague and Budapest had to be abandoned within a week after fire-roaches appeared, with their terrible stings and single-minded attraction to anything that smelled of Russian gun-oil. The first tailored potato blight showed up later that fall, across Poland and Ukraine, and simultaneously the other potato blight swept Ireland. First one to jump the Atlantic.

Individual things happened, at first all over Europe, then around the world. No eels here, no robins there, turf that turned to black slime in one place and deer who became inexplicably aggressive and migrated in great destructive herds like lemmings in yet another area.

The flashchannels kept trying to come up with names for it—

ecowar, environmental terrorism, all sorts of terms that mostly told us, as usual, that the news people were the last to get what was going on.

After all, it was a logical consequence of having SMOTs plus good remote sensing on satellites. An ecosystem's more complicated than a rail net, electric power grid, or market, but it's the same kind of math, you can study it the same way if you can get enough data, and therefore disrupt it the same way. The only thing that had kept both sides from waging ecowar right from the beginning was the problem of learning how to translate the targeting into DNA. Both sides had raced to get the genetic code up as a piece of general engineering; they had finished so close to each other that from our perspective, in the twenty-second century, with so much history lost, we can't even say which side "won."

The SMOTs running on thousands of microsupers in tiny little labs, a few freshly trained microbiologists in each one, wrote script after script for ecological disaster. Here a new fungus to attack a particular set of roots; there a bacteria that locked up soil phosphorus in an unusable form for a few weeks out of each growing season. Here the supergrasshopper, toxic to birds and especially attractive to them; there beetles that fed only on the leaf buds of trees in the spring. Everywhere, as vegetation lost its grip, mud and slime replaced soil, and the living parts of the continents bled down into the oceans.

Hawaii and Cuba seemed almost in a race to see which could have worse things happen to sugar cane; California, South Africa, and the Crimea all had the same mad proliferation of insects; cabbages died equally well around the Baltic and around the Great Lakes, destroyed by modified loopers.

The final blow, the one that forced all the politicians to sit down and talk straight, came in the West Pacific War, one of a dozen little brushfires that flared up as we got the allies involved. Japan and South Korea had no desire to attack the Soviet Far East and face being turned into another helpless, prostrate Europe. China had been quietly feeding Russia. Neither side felt like getting involved on the home ground.

Hence Indonesia, backed by China, was brought to attack the Philippines, backed by Japan and South Korea. The bio labs were hit with precision munitions on the first day. And what escaped from the two labs was so identical that no one could tell who had "originated" it—not that anyone wanted credit. Tailored Rice Blast was going to wipe half a billion lives from the Earth.

The best brains in the intelligence communities went to work on that. How had labs more than a thousand miles apart, working without any direct knowledge of each other, created two things so identical genetically that they couldn't be told apart? To the analysts that was a lot more interesting than the mere starvation of hundreds of millions, which after all was new only in scale.

The answer they found was painfully simple. The tendency had been noted in the 1970s for public, not secret, labs to move faster and farther. More heads and hands on the problem meant greater speed. Leaked information diverted other researchers toward itself, and multiplied the effect of research in that area. By 2001 the side that won the scientific race was almost always the side that kept fewest secrets—the rewards of getting there first were always outweighed by the dangers of being second.

Once the smart guys figured that out, everyone published nearly everything—so military inventions were appearing on both sides of the conflict at almost exactly the same time. The software you distributed to your troops this morning would be in the other side's hands before nightfall.

The idea that you could attack an ecology using the same algorithms as were used to attack railroad systems, communications nets, or power grids—and tailor organisms to do it—wasn't any one general's idea, or even any one SMOT's. SMOTs had been told to look for systems on the other side that could be disrupted. No one had told them to stick to highways, water pipes, and warehouses. The SMOTs copied each other. Became more alike. Got brighter and more destructive. As if the war itself had become an intelligent being, with purposes all its own, which didn't include human survival.

"By the next spring the people at the top of the warring nations were finding out what any sophomore in college ecology could have told them"—that's how Sadi put it, once, in a file he was filling up with his personal history of the twentieth century. Why was a copy of it on *my* werp? "Release anything in large enough numbers, and not all of it will die on cue. The next spring saw all the bugs and germs spreading back from the infected zones into the places that had launched them, and also revealed the (now obvious) point that what's easy to modify is apt to mutate."

From my standpoint, the summer of 2002 was the summer when I was getting rich. Bonuses were raining into my account, and though collapse was coming on fast, and with it the war's end, if I lasted out this last winter, and if the final collapse came in the spring, then I could live like a king in the aftermath. Plenty of the world's fortunes had gotten started in wars. No reason why mine shouldn't be one of them.

Meanwhile we were busy. Targets we had been trying to hit for years—especially scientists and engineers—were popping out of their protection like pheasants out of a cornfield, as the spreading ecological catastrophe made their hiding places and secure areas uninhabitable.

One night, I met two other Organization agents under a bridge in Germany, to swap data between our computers (the major secure way of trading information by then). We all stuck around to get drunk together, and in the course of talking and bragging, we discovered that every one of us had nailed at least one Nobel Prize winner. The blonde woman whose name I didn't get had bagged three of them, one while in bed with him.

It gave us all a good laugh. But considering how much wine we'd had, almost anything would have.

I was sitting next to the blonde woman, and we were passing the jug back and forth. Peter, the other agent, whom I'd worked with a few times, was passed out on her other side. We had begun to get maudlin, about things like sausage stands and the good beer there used to be, and I was thinking about not having gotten any ass in a while. I sure wasn't going to try with the lady beside me, though. If she didn't like what I was doing, I'd be dead before I knew what hit me.

The damp of the ground was soaking through the seat of my jeans. Mostly I was thinking about what I would do after the war was over. With all the money I could get a big, defensible house somewhere, with servants. There would be a lot of desperate young women—so I could probably find a pretty one that would do what I wanted for a safe place to sleep and enough to eat. Hell, I could probably keep a harem if I wanted. In a couple of years, I'd be sleeping in a great big warm bed, eating huge hot meals, waited on by naked bitches. . . .

For right now I had a jug of red wine, this spot under the bridge sheltered from the drizzle, and the touch of the blonde woman's leather bomber jacket against my shoulder. It was less lonesome here, in the damp dark, than it had been for a while.

"So, you gentlemen want to show a lady some fun?" she asked.

"You mean sex?" I asked stupidly. God, I was drunk. I just hoped I'd be able to function and remember it afterwards.

"That's the idea, fella. It's been a while since I got the itch scratched just for fun. And I'd like to refresh my memory about what it's like to do it just because I want to."

"Fuck," Peter said.

"Unhhunh," she said, nodding emphatically.

"Fuck," he repeated. "Fucking killing kids and cops and teachers. Murder the poor bastard firemen. Poison in the wells. Fuck." He fell silent. Passed out again.

We rolled him over on his side so he wouldn't throw up and choke on it—as much privacy as we were going to get. We each had a ground cloth, and that gave us a surface that, if not comfortable, was at least tolerable.

The kissing was the best part; the rest was just relief after getting worked up. When we had finished, and pulled our pants back up, she held me for a long moment, and then whispered, "There's something else I'm supposed to communicate to you. It shouldn't matter that Peter's around, I think he's out. Memorize this—the name is Jason Testor, that's spelled with an 'o,' and here are the account numbers and passwords."

She rattled off some long character strings. By now I was used to my enhanced memory, and not surprised that I could recite it back on the first try. Then I asked, "So who is this guy? Am I supposed to partner up with him, kill him, what?"

She laughed, and folded her fingers around mine. "No, stud, you're going to *be* him."

"It's an alias?"

"Yes. For after you transit."

"After I—"

"You remember a shot you got, just before you went active for the Organization? The one that let you repeat all those twenty-digit numbers back without a hitch, and kept you from dying of mutAIDS?"

"Sure." It came back to me. "I'm going to lose my memory and get ten years younger."

She nodded. "We know a lot more about the special treatment than we did when we first gave it to you. About three months from now you're going to come down with something that feels like the worst flu you've ever had. Then for about six months you'll be pretty helpless, raving with a fever, not aware of your surroundings. You want to be somewhere where people will take care of you—you won't be lucid. At the end of the six months, you'll emerge about ten years younger, biologically, than you are now."

I was thirty-five now; physically I would be twenty-five. "How do you know it will be in ninety days for me?"

"I have orders, you goof. They can figure it to within plus or minus three weeks now, because they've had a lot of experience with it. In fact I'm part of the experience—I was one of the first tests in the field. Believe it or not I'm just over forty years old if you go by the clock." I'd have pegged her thirty at most.

She went on. "Anyway, the important thing to remember is that your appearance will change enough—due to weight loss and youthening—so that you can take on a new identity easily. But make sure you've got everything you need written down, and with you, by the time it hits. Start keeping your records with you right now, if you aren't already. Make sure they contain everything you want to remember—*especially* the account numbers with all your cash in them. And try to make sure you come down sick near a charity hospital, or with a private duty nurse around, or something like that."

"And the Organization will take me back on afterwards?"

"Oh, yeah. You'll be younger and have an airtight false i.d. And your motor skills will stick—you'll still be a good shot. They'll want you. Don't worry."

So I didn't worry. We had more wine, and then tried to have sex again, but I couldn't get it up so we just messed around for a while until she was satisfied. The whole time Peter stayed asleep, as far as we could tell, and when we were done we got a blanket out of his pack and covered him, shook the cold and damp off ourselves, and walked back along the canal to the town, holding hands till we parted company, with a gentle little kiss, in the white-green smear of harsh light under a streetlight. Just as if we had been any other couple, or known each other's names.

V

I rise and stare out into the dark. My first lifetime wasn't even my worst. In my memories—and many of my notes and text—I seem not to be bothered by it at all. That worries me, or ought to.

I guess.

For right now I just want to get the bare facts down. I find several tearful confessions in here, drunken maudlin babblings where I rave on about how delicate and pretty that very young German housewife was. I talk about her breasts so much that I think she must have been naked to the waist—perhaps they were making love when I burst in?—or something unusual must have happened that involved them.

But in my memory now she's wearing a black sweater and a long skirt. As if maybe I'd kept her alive for a while. Or made her strip and then—

Did I actually serb her? I'm sure I accurately remember killing her. But did I serb her first? If I did I think that was the first time. I'd heard other agents talking about it; the nasty little Fourth Balkan War had given us the word, because it had been the Serbs who had discovered and exploited the same thing everyone had always known, that rape, destroying a person while leaving the body alive, was often more effective than simple killing, just as wounding enemy troops had always cost the opposing general more than killing them. Some Organization people regarded it as a perk, some as a trademark, some as just one more tool. All of them said, "You gotta try it."

Was that the first time I tried it? Am I forgetting that? Surely not. I was in a hurry. I needed that car. I couldn't be completely sure that all the alarms were out. I didn't have a second to spare. Even if I had wanted to, or been the type, surely I wouldn't have, not that one, not then.

But then, how rational was I at that moment?

I can't settle it out. The blonde woman who gave me the information—what was her face like? It tends to blur into Gwenny, into the German housewife, into Sadi if I'm not careful. Sometimes I think she was there, that the two of us tied up the German housewife and I raped her while the blonde woman watched. It's all slipping away from me as I grab at it, and what I write to straighten it out makes it worse.

I seem to remember every document I read or see, now, from my werp, exactly, as if I had a perfect movie with sound for the whole time since I woke up. The memory enhancement must still be working. If I had just, while the memories were perfect, managed to set down some, accurately, for every year since about 1990 . . . well, I didn't.

And I can tell that I don't have the skills to do that this time around, either. The records I am making don't look like my memories, but like all the other records in the werp.

It's late now, and I don't set the clock. When I get up there will be sun. I will make coffee and see if I can get further with my memories.

Tomorrow for sure I will go to bed early, so that I can catch the maglev into Red Sands City. "I haven't seen weather like this since I was a kid in Ohio." The phrase in that personal ad just keeps coming back to me. If I were to pull out of here, move my bank accounts, jump to some other town, and *then* answer the ad . . . would I be safe? From what?

vi

Several of the documents I have on the werp use the same phrase for it: "I missed everything." I suppose you could say that. I went into a Catholic Worker hospital in Madrid in March 2003, war still going. I had ditched all the i.d. except the stuff that was going to go into a locker at the hospital, plus an envelope that I told them was a letter from my mother that I wanted in my bedside table.

Late in September I woke up for the third time I could remember, exhausted, seven kilos lighter.

Ten years younger.

No war.

Two thirds of the beds on the ward were empty. The TV by my bed didn't have any flashchannel controls but it could get the main screen signal for AFFC, CNNFlash, NYTFlash, and ObsrChanl. But they were useless—I had no idea what the Mutual Surrender was, or that there had been a war, or what a Public Services Corporation was, though I got from context that it had something to do with the UN.

More puzzling was the fact that the American President, the Soviet General Commissioner, the Japanese PM, and half a dozen other people were in Rome at a meeting chaired by Pope Paul John Paul (American media loved to call him PJP) and it sounded like fighting—*what* fighting?—had stopped everywhere.

Every Japanese and Korean shipping company that could manage it were putting the few ships that had survived the roving air torpedos—and weren't needed to feed their own people—to the job of getting a couple of million American soldiers home, along with all the millions of refugees who had been invited to help resettle North America. There was a new mutAIDS outbreak in the States, so there was even more room once people were vaccinated.

Lots of reference to "indocoms," to the "Global Habitability Report," and to "the coming Rebound Winter in which we expect to lose millions despite our best efforts." As far as I could figure it, an indocom was an apartment building linked to a mall linked to a factory, where you had to be a member to live and work there; the Ecucatholics, who were apparently Pope PJP's people, were building a lot of them, and it sounded as if, mysteriously, there weren't many other churches anymore, though the few there were didn't like the Ecucatholics much. I wasn't sure who wrote the Global Habitability Report, or who they wrote it for, but it must be highly respected because every politician referred to it at least twice per minute. For some reason it was going to get really cold this winter. That was about all I could get, even though I had nothing to do but lie there, eat soup and bread, and watch the TV.

The Catholic Workers were nice about letting me stay until I recovered more. The "letter from mother" told me why I wanted to get my metal box from hospital storage and look through it. A few days later, I had read everything scribbled into several notebooks, and listened to five audio tapes. I was in shape to move around, so I tried going to the three addresses I was supposed to check in Madrid.

First: empty, door hanging open by a single hinge.

Second: bombed out.

Third: street number that had never existed according to everyone in the neighborhood.

I had ten phone numbers. Tried dialing all of them, all disconnected.

Well, supposedly I had money. I already knew what was likely to happen, but just the same I went to the Estacion Chamartin, the biggest train station in Madrid—they had just restored service to Paris two weeks before—and got into line for an ATM.

When I finally got to the head of the line, I punched in my new codes to access my bank accounts in the name of Jason Testor, and much to my surprise, the banks *did* have a record of Jason Testor. All the account numbers were valid—but all the accounts came out overdrawn. Besides the valise (two spare shirts, some socks, underwear, the jewelry box with its keepsakes), the clothes I was wearing, and the change in my pockets, I owned *less* than nothing—fourteen thousand dollars in bad checks were out there looking for me.

I did a general query, and it showed that all my accounts had been cleaned out on 9 June 2003 between 5:08 and 5:12 GMT, from an ATM in Stockholm. Four months ago. While I was lying in the hospital, not knowing where I was. Then about twenty checks, all dated 8 June 2003, had come in between 9 June and 11 June. The checks had all been written to Stockholm businesses as well, and the businesses with English names all had names like "Reality Associates," "Information, Incorporated," and "Business Operations, Limited." The blonde woman—or Peter—or anyone in the Organization, who had access to the account numbers, had also had access to the security codes. Somebody had decided they needed that money more than I did.

No good pissing off the growing line behind me. I knew everything I needed to know. I logged off and walked out into the echoing railroad station.

Before the war they'd had card tracers, I recalled vaguely, a system so that if you checked in with a bad card the cops nearest you were immediately alerted. I didn't know whether they still did, or whether the Spanish authorities were even interested in catching debt skippers, but anyway the Jason Testor papers were no use at all, and I still had my old Joshua Quare papers.

You lose almost all the facts, you don't lose motor skills, you don't lose attitude. I went around a corner, pulled out a pencil, and wrote down all the ATM codes in the back of the Jason Testor passport. Then I wandered down a couple of alleys, talked with a few guys on the street, and eventually met Raul, who looked something like me and thus like the picture of Jason Testor on the passport.

After we'd haggled a while, and he'd pawed over the passport thoroughly, I agreed to accept the price of a week's hotel room for it. He asked where I'd gotten it. I told him I'd taken it off an American who was drunk and passed out in an alley.

He asked if I was selling ATM cards, and I said I had been planning to take them to a hack shop, one of those places where they could jack into the net illegally, submit the card code, and then break data security to watch the machine try to check the number—thus getting the access code. Usually at those places they split the proceeds fifty-fifty.

"I will give you triple what I've paid you already," Raul said, "for the cards. I think I have a way to hack them more economically."

He was an amateur; he couldn't help touching the pocket where he'd put the passport.

I let him talk me into the deal. He was off like a bunny to the ATM the minute he'd handed me the cash and I'd handed him the cards.

The cash in hand wouldn't get me to Paris by itself, but it was a dandy start. I figured if I could get to the main American repat center in Paris, with luck, as a civilian in a needed specialty, I could get repatriated within a few months. After I got home, either the Organization would find me again and I'd have an income, or I could take my skills and go make a living—radar and electronics were going to be in demand for decades. For that matter I wasn't a bad hand at software, either, though they said hand-coding was about to die out for good.

For tonight, anyway, and maybe for a couple days following, I'd check into a YMCA or whatever other kind of secure shelter they had—no sense spending cash when I didn't need more than that. Meanwhile I figured I'd take a look around.

I had been walking only a few blocks when I saw the big banner on the side of the building: SALVATION ARMY REORIENTATION LIBRARY. I went inside and discovered the guy at the desk was an American, a wrinkled guy with white hair, thick glasses, and a heavy accent in his Spanish. He seemed relieved to have someone to talk to in English, and he was proud and eager to talk about what they did. "It's really the most useful thing we can do for people right now, since there's not much actual starvation anymore, and with so many dead there's plenty of housing, you know. So we run a temporary shelter around the corner, and we provide this place because so many people were so cut off from their usual information channels by the war that they're having a hard time adjusting."

"Er, I think I'd like to apply for the temporary shelter," I said. "And a hard time adjusting how?"

He shrugged. "The world has changed a lot. Plenty of people were unhooked from the news for long periods of time. They need a place where they can just look up what all happened and read about it."

I grinned at him and said, "I think I've found where I need to be. Can I get set up in the shelter and then come back here?"

"Sure, we're open hours yet. We close at five, dinner at the shelter's at six—"

"Prayer service's at seven," I said. "I can tell some things haven't changed."

His eyes twinkled. "When were you—"

"Oh, my old man used to hit me and lock me out," I explained. "I slept at the Salvation Army some when I was a kid."

His smile was warm and friendly. "Well, we're here if you need us. But I sure hope your luck changes."

"Me too."

I got myself checked in at the refugee shelter, stashed my gear, kept my cash with me, and came back to the Reorientation Library to read. For the next several days I stayed at the shelter, ate thin soup and bread there and food from sidewalk vendors during the day, and spent my time reading in the library. They never even really hassled me about going to prayer service.

One of the ways I had always frustrated my mother and her father was that though I was quick enough at learning, and bright enough, I just never saw anything all that interesting in books. But for those few days, I was a great student. I *had* to know what kind of world I had ended up in, especially since, besides my missing six months due to fever, most of my memories from 1992 forward were gone.

The Reorientation Library was mostly just books and newspapers on CD-ROM, with older issues and books available over the wire. I read pretty fast—a perfect memory helps—and thought pretty hard. And now that I had a better handle on things, I could see that I had been more right than I knew: with my technical skills I was going to do pretty well in the new world that was forming, now that Pope PJP had apparently put some peace together.

I would always be able to get work because you can't operate in space without radar, and humanity was going to space—no choice about it. Even with all the deaths thus far, there were way too many people for the food we could grow, and the various blasts, blights, worms, sterilizers, viruses, and so forth were still mutating rapidly, so no crop of anything was safe on the ground—space offered the only perfect quarantine.

Besides, the American and Soviet weather weapons had apparently blown a bunch of methane into the atmosphere, caused teratons of carbon dioxide to dissolve in the oceans, moved the jet streams and created some condition they were calling the Super-Niño . . . the list was long and I couldn't follow all of it, but the weather was going to set records for hot and cold, drought and flood, wind and snow and hail, everywhere for the next few decades. You couldn't count on a factory or a power plant on Earth's surface—before it was finished it might be buried under ice, the river that cooled it might dry up, it might not be able to get materials over the sea or via roads.

They were caught in an even deeper bind: the plants they needed would have to be *big*—bigger even than the giant ones in East Asia that had been built in the last few years—and there could be no more giant plants. The total ecology of the Earth was now "thrashing."

I spent a day looking up "thrashing," tracing its meaning from the time I had been in high school forward, and that was an interesting little education all by itself.

The word "thrashing" started out in computer science, migrated into music and fashion, and had now become a stock term in environmental news—which had changed a lot too while I had been unconscious.

Back at the dawn of computers, when they first invented parallel processing and time sharing and all the other ways for a computer to run more than one program at once, they discovered that as the work load got bigger and more complex, the system spent more and more time just moving work in and out of the processors, until eventually you hit the point where system management was taking up so much time and space that the system wasn't doing any work anymore. That was called "thrashing."

Kids with skateboards and guitars in Silicon Valley picked it up from their nerdy fathers and used it to mean "going out of control"—especially going out of control by switching off the outside world, and just banging to the rhythm in your own head. For them it was a *good* thing. When I was in Army tech school, I used to say that some of the programs we had to work on were headbangers—you could tell because instead of doing any useful work, they'd rather thrash.

"Thrashing" had become a bad thing again while I had been lying in the hospital. Just as a computer system, when it was working right, used some power and processing space to keep itself running, but mostly processed outside stuff, Planet Earth, when it was working right, used some of its energy to keep nutrients and vital materials moving around, but plowed most energy back into binding more energy and making more life. Wild, natural ecosystems, left to themselves, ran sizable surpluses of bound energy, which became essential to other ecosystems.

Not now. Huge flows of heat and chemical energy, almost none bound in the biosphere. Like a computer that couldn't decide what to do next, frantically busy while nothing got done, the Earth as a whole was thrashing. "Thrashing" was about every tenth word in the *International Herald-Tribune* environmental news section.

"Environmental news" was another measure of how much things had changed. It had started as a back-page thing in newspapers, read mostly by kids, and now was the thickest part of the paper. At a corner newsstand one day I saw an issue of *El País* with front-page news that four whales had been spotted in the South Atlantic and that the *USS Rickover* was on its way there—the world's biggest submersible carrier to save four animals. The same front page also featured a long, complicated story about bottom temperatures and dissolved oxygen in the Mediterranean.

The world had awakened to the environment beyond the dreams of the Earthies I could remember from ten years ago. We could hardly help it—because taken by itself, the environmental news was a death sentence. The four and a half billion people left alive after mutAIDS and the Eurowar couldn't afford large-scale agriculture or industrial facilities anymore, at least not as we had known them in the past. Zero surplus production from Earth's environment anywhere anymore. Anything we did might make the situation worse. No risking big industry or big agriculture.

But we had way too many people to just turn into hunter-gatherers and survive. In fact, because they needed more land, energy, and minerals per pound of stuff produced, the Third World was much more expensive to operate, in *per capita* environmental terms, than the First World. If we wanted to live, somehow we had to achieve a living standard far above that of Japan or pre-war Germany, for everyone on Earth, without building industrial facilities anywhere on Earth—and as fast as possible.

That was the loophole: "anywhere on Earth." Everything we needed—energy and raw materials—was available in space. Apparently people at NASA and a lot of other space agencies had been studying that since 1975, and they knew it would work. As I was sitting in that library, the leaders of the Earth were meeting in Rome to figure out how to do it. Fast.

A couple of new gadgets that had come out of the war would make it easier—the protonic/lithium reactor, which didn't emit neutrons and therefore didn't make materials around it radioactive, meant at least we could build nonpolluting power plants on Earth to drive the launchers, which would give us a temporary (but risky) way to keep the lights on while we moved everything into space.

The other thing, which reporters were making a huge deal about, was that we were close to "phase reversal MAM." I had to hop around flashchannel recordings a lot to find out what MAM was, but it turned out that some bright guy at Tsukuba University had finally explained why surplus power was coming out of the old "cold fusion" experiments; in just the right electromagnetic field, the quantum numbers of a proton could become indeterminate enough so that some protons would flip over to being anti-protons. It didn't take many of those to get something hot.

The scientist who had figured that out had been "killed by a prostitute still at large." I had a sudden memory of my friend under the bridge, and a moment of admiration; she'd bagged a *big* one. Then I spent half an hour that day looking through my notes in my werp, to make sense of the memory. All I really figured out was that if she'd ripped me off, at least the person I was looking for was one hot piece.

The hope was they would have MAM working as a practical technology within five years. At least the surviving best brains in physics were on the job, and money was being thrown at the problem like there was no tomorrow. Of course if they didn't solve the problem, there wasn't.

Meanwhile, whether or not they'd have MAM to power it, they

were going to be putting up space stations, and huge spaceships, and starting to colonize Mars and the Moon.

So with all that going on, a guy who had a pretty good background in radar and electronics ought to do fine, even if the Organization no longer existed or didn't want me. I just had to get back to the States, where it would be easy to get hired.

After a few days of reading and studying, I thanked the nice old guy behind the counter at the library, checked out of the shelter, and went for a long walk. Around noon I had lunch and stashed the valise in a coin locker (using the last of my coins to do it), and started wandering around in the back streets near the Calle San Jeronimo, where if there were any tourists, they would be likely to be drifting around. Sure enough, there were a couple of kids, a man and a woman in their early twenties, wandering along in the narrow streets. I let myself shadow them for a while, listening in.

I don't know exactly what tipped me off that the guy had been a tourist psycho. One of the most bizarre features of the Eurowar: rich American kids who dodged the draft through any of the wide variety of legal means, then got themselves over to Europe, armed to the teeth with all kinds of weapons they'd bought privately, and wandered around attacking things and people in the areas controlled by whichever side they didn't like.

Weirder still to me was the fact that so many of the tourist psychos were Japanese, South Koreans, well-off Arabs, or Brazilians—people whose nations were not in the war at all.

The favorite explanation seemed to be that entertainment had been so violent for so long that these kids thought an opportunity to go somewhere and commit random mayhem was better than Disneyland. Everyone denounced them but because almost all of them were anti-Sov and doing a lot of random damage in the Soviet-controlled areas, the West had done little to curb them. They were a great deal for their home governments: volunteer soldiers who paid their own way and who could be abandoned with a clear conscience if they were taken prisoner.

Of course from reading through my notes I knew I had been no angel, but still, I had been professional; civilians I had killed were "collateral damage"—I hadn't gone out of my way to kill them, their killing had just been incidental to my mission.

I suppose I hated tourist psychos the way a call girl looks down on a streetwalker. Especially tourist psychos who were now walking around, hand in hand with the pretty girl from back home, showing her where they murdered Communist labor organizers and shot people they thought were Soviet agents. And most especially when the tourist psycho and his girlfriend were obviously carrying wads of hard cash.

Late in the day. They still hadn't noticed me. That might have been because they had each had a liter of wine in a café. I was hungry, I'd heard more sweet little nicknames for "Margaret" than I ever needed to hear again in my life, and finally they were taking a turn into a dim alley.

He probably wasn't armed now. Even if he was, he was drunk, and he'd more than proved he was unaware. Still, no sense taking chances. I came quietly up behind him, and at just that moment he stumbled.

The note said I'd keep my motor skills, and that's when I found out what they were. I sidekicked him a hard one, right into one kidney, as he was still catching his balance. He went down without a cry, probably too startled, maybe already in shock, and I gave him another hard kick, with everything I had, on the point of his chin.

Little Princess Maggie Margie-pie Meggy Meggums turned around in a swirl of sharply styled red hair, her black-lipsticked mouth gaping to see him, knocked flat and still, with blood running out of his mouth. I grabbed the mass of big dangling earrings in one of her ears with my left hand, yanked her head toward me as hard as I could, and drove the heel of my right hand into her face. The earrings tore out and her mouth gushed blood. I closed in while she was still staring, not believing what had happened, and put her out with a solar plexus punch. She fell to the ground like a sack of wet sand.

I got both their wallets and her purse; one of his loafers was lying by his foot, and I saw the money in it. More in his undershorts. These were the kind of people who put it everywhere.

Sure enough. Two hundred dollars in Amex Universals—those traveler's checks you could redeem for gold—tucked into her bra. Three little "microingots," the pea-sized chunks of gold carried by nervous travelers these days, in her panties.

I looked them over. His pants down to his thighs, her clothing pulled aside and ripped. Both still breathing, but I figured I'd concussed them good. Days at least before they woke up lucid.

I drew my Boy Scout knife and slashed her clothes apart, flung her legs wide open, took his limp hand and scratched the nails all over her thighs and belly. I pulled his passport, city visitor permit, and i.d. papers from his inside jacket pocket, taking them with me. I dropped the bloody tangled mass of earrings into his open palm and folded his limp fingers around it.

On my way back to the train station, I phoned the 091 emergency number, claimed I'd foiled a rape in progress and the girl was unconscious, told them where the two of them were, and left the phone dangling.

I walked away whistling. As long as the cops got there before either of them woke up, she'd go to a regular hospital for treatment, and he'd go to a police hospital for interrogation. It could well be days before she was coherent enough to say anything about what had happened and get him out of there. Meanwhile the Spanish cops might kill him while questioning him, without anyone ever finding out who he was. By the time she woke up he might already be in a hidden, anonymous grave. I loved it.

Maybe he had only been pretending, making up stories about his exploits. A lot of tourist psychos had gotten over to Europe, found out they had no balls, and spent their time in hotels or wandering the streets within a few safe blocks of home.

Better still. If he wanted to pretend to the role, what could be better than his having to pay the price for it? And on the other hand, if he really had been a tourist psycho, we were well rid of him. I decided the same policy covered girls who dated tourist psychos, especially girls who encouraged them to brag about it.

After cleaning out the money, I pitched the wallet and purse down any old alley that didn't have anyone in it; I figured they wouldn't stay there long—someone would see them and move them. His i.d. went down a storm sewer grate.

I got my bags out of the coin locker, changed the cash, blackmarketed the gold behind the station to get some more cash, bought a ticket, and was on my way to Paris with a stake in my pocket. I splurged for a compartment all to myself, so that I could sleep on the way.

The next morning I was at the USA Repatriation Office, seeing if I could swing a berth to the US. I figured that given how fast they were going to be moving into space, a radar whiz would be high priority.

Apparently a lot of people were in my spot, or a similar one, to judge by the long line for "critical specialties—no papers."

I got in that line, told them my name was Ron Richards—such an ordinary name they'd never notice it—and half an hour later they parked me in front of a terminal to talk to the AI that would check me out on radar and electronics.

Ever have that nightmare about knowing you studied for a test and not being able to remember anything? I knew everything up to when I'd had the injection. After that, maybe I knew and usually I didn't.

And when there's been a major war, tech development has gone far and fast in ten years. Suppose you'd been an airplane mechanic in 1937, gone to sleep for ten years, and then tried to get hired in 1947.

1 might as well have come in qualified to shoe horses, run a key-punch, or troubleshoot tube radios for all the good it could do me. The AI administering the test noted that I had a lot of aptitude, and said that whenever I got my clearance to come over, I'd sure be welcome to take the test again, and even if they couldn't use me just as I was, they'd be happy to train. But—(and I could swear that I heard regret in the artificial voice)—the need was for existing skills with state of the art equipment, and humma humma humma. Out the door, kid, and come back when you know some stuff.

I had told it Ron Richards was twenty-five years old, so I was surprised that it didn't bother to ask how I knew so much about radar from the years between my ages of six and fifteen, but it didn't. Apparently they hadn't yet asked the testing AIs to look for anomalies. This might be useful to remember.

I wandered out into the bright daylight of Paris—a city that was already working hard. The French hadn't bothered to worry about how they were going to pay for Reconstruction, so they'd just started rebuilding, because to them it was obvious that Paris needed to be a great city rather than a great ruin. Most of the workers were getting paid in scrip that could be redeemed somehow, sooner or later, in the sweet bye and bye, in theory. What the hell, the French always liked theory better than reality.

The only place you could spend scrip was in the tent cities, or for soup and bread at the kitchens.

It would at least conserve my cash. I was swinging a pick within the hour, helping to clear rubble from a caved-in Metro entrance.

By the end of the day my hands were pretty sore—it cost me more scrip to get a pair of gloves from the little store at the camp, for the next day—but I had a bed in out of the rain, all mine, and food enough.

The French don't trust banks. Or at least they don't trust French banks, and who can blame them? Paris has more safes, lockups, private storages, and so forth than any other city I've ever seen. I spent more scrip to lock up my cash and the jewelbox of keepsakes in a rented strongbox at the camp's central office.

I worked all fall, got into great shape. I wasn't going anywhere, and meanwhile I got fed. When the first hard snow came in October, we all started to find out that they hadn't been kidding about Rebound Winter. The Northern Hemisphere was about to start growing glaciers again.

They moved our tents down into the Metro, but it was still cold. There was a new protonic power plant running outside the city, so they could afford to power space heaters for us. When they had space heaters. Different tents got them on different nights for a while, usually every other night but now and then your turn would come for two nights without heat in a row, which was bad. They were promising that by March there would be a heater in every tent.

On nights when your tent had no heater, your choices were to lay out more scrip and rent additional blankets or towels (if you got there early enough), or huddle up with everybody and watch television together on the big screens they'd set up in the Metro stations. The trains roared through all night, but we were used to that; a lot of times I fell asleep wedged in between half a dozen other people. It beat freezing your ass off in the tent.

The trouble was you could get shoved to the outside of the huddle, and then it was really cold. Usually I was big enough and aggressive enough so that that didn't happen, but when I got in late, there I'd be, butt on the cold concrete, back to the windy tunnel, huddled up and trying to press into the people in front of me.

One night in February when that happened, my second night without heat, I finally gave up in disgust. I decided to go do something, anything, that I might enjoy. So I got some cash from the strongbox, and got on a Metro to the Place de la République. If you wanted anything people didn't approve of—alcohol, drugs, pussy, violence, whatever your action was—you went to République.

Fairly bright, outside the station. With so much power available, they had all the streetlights on. Far below freezing, but no wind, a crisp night. For a little while I just walked around the big, open space; the Place de la République is one of those places Paris is made out of where several major boulevards converge around a pillar with a statue. Before the war it had been kind of upscale. Now it was where several long corridors of rubble and a few choked streets emptied into a squatter's encampment surrounding a shattered pedestal, the statue long gone, and *the* place for contraband.

Around one corner I had to wait for a long convoy of trucks to pass. Their tires ground on the icy grit, plumes of exhaust roiled in their headlights.

I thought of waving but probably only the lead truck was driven by a human. So many surplus robot vehicle controllers around after the war, price down to almost nothing, usually only the lead truck was driven by a person, the rest just programmed to follow it.

When they had rumbled by, a girl, thin, with stringy black hair, wearing a cheap plastic raincoat over a bunch of sweaters, stood under the light across the street. I crossed the street. As I passed her at the corner (keeping a wary distance in case she had a gun or something) she said, "Wanna get high? Get laid? Get some travel i.d.?"

I looked at her closely. She couldn't have been more than nine. "Uh, you're pretty young to be selling any of that stuff," I said.

"You're telling me. Wish you'd tell it to Pop," she said, in English. Obviously she'd recognized my accent.

"He doesn't make you—"

"He doesn't make me have sex," she said. "And I don't handle the dope, either, or the i.d. I just bring guys in for him, okay? And don't think you *can* do anything with me, either, he's got you covered right now. Make a wrong move and you'll see a laser designator spot on your chest; keep moving if you want to see a bunch of holes." Her chin was up and her lower lip stuck out a little.

I didn't believe her, but I was curious. It beat wandering around and getting colder, and there were a lot of ways to kill time that I didn't like as much as I liked getting high or laid.

"So how do I meet this solid citizen and president of the Chamber of Commerce?" I asked.

"Don't make fun of me just because I'm a kid and my old man's a crook," she said.

"I wouldn't dream of it."

"He's over there in the shadows," she said, pointing into a crooked alley. "Talk to him. He deals everything. Good prices, fair prices, he doesn't care as long as you pay him something he can spend. But he discounts scrip ninety percent."

That was the normal street discount, easy to figure and the traffic would bear it. My scrip would count for one tenth of its face value.

I followed the kid into an alley. If someone cracked my head, right now, I would probably lie in the alley and freeze to death, but they'd be wasting their arm strength on the job—I was carrying about enough cash for a round-the-world with one of the young girls who sold themselves over by the statueless pedestal, or for enough synthak—receptor-addressed coke—to be extremely happy for five or six hours. Enough for an evening's fun, not enough for anything else.

The man who squatted on his heels at the end of the alley turned on a rechargeable lantern between his knees. The blue-gray light, washing over his face from beneath, made him eerie the way a kid's face in a school fair "haunted house" is—that is, you could tell he was trying to give you the creeps and not succeeding. Probably forty-five, definitely overweight, and he'd be strung out on a bunch of shit for sure. I stopped well out of arm's reach, but near enough to see both his hands clearly, and said, "Your daughter here said you got some merchandise."

"Yeah," he said, wiping a blob of snot from his nose. Something glinted at his neck in the dim light. I wasn't sure of what it was, but it looked familiar. "I deal a lot of stuff, man, you just gotta say what it is you need. If I ain't got it, for a finder fee I can put you on to a man that does, someplace. The little chick will take you wherever I tell her to, to whatever your thing is, and bring your finder fee back as long as you're satisfied. So there's like no risk if you want something I don't got. But I got most anything."

He talked like an old boomer, though the real born-in-the-1940s boomers were almost all dead. He looked like something that would grow gradually, over years, in this corner—or in any other dank, cold place, if there were enough dirt.

"What's your specialty?" I asked. "Just now I happen to be bored and cold. I want to be warm and amused."

Face wrenched sideways in an angry smile, he coughed like a sick dog. Definitely coming down off synthak. "How about a fucking cup of hot chocolate, a fireplace, and a nice storybook to read to the little chick?" The sneer in his voice was thick and loud; the attitude said synthak, the way he was just blurting it out said screamies. Bad mixture—coming down off them together made people paranoid and extremely horny. One very screwed-up staff sergeant I had known back in Prague got himself arrested on that mix, fortunately not too near any party I had thrown, and had tried to hump the cops' legs. We all thought that was pretty funny. "You can read her *Alice in Wonderland,* and you can both have chocolate and marshmallows, and then you can make her eat your mushroom."

"She says you don't sell her," I said.

"Does she? She's a liar *and* a whore. If she's what you want, I'll take your money and give you a place to do her, but I ain't holding her down for you."

"Is she what's on special?" I said. "I think that poor kid's all you've got, and I don't buy children."

"Ha," he said. Probably in daylight his teeth were brown and yellow, but in this light his mouth just opened and closed like a hole. The tips of the stubble of his beard glinted silver. What the hell did he have around his neck? Quite a chain it was on—something he wanted to make sure he kept. His mouth gaped wide at me in a grin that I think was meant to let me know we were getting down to serious business. "I got a bunch of goodies. You want synthak, you want screamies, you want hemp, you want Big Angel or Little Angel or even old-fashioned heroin . . . it's all here. Just say the word and I'll say the price. Screamies cheap enough so you can hire a chick to relieve you on the down side—that's pretty special."

"I'm thrilled," I said.

"Got these," he added, and his arm stuck out as far as he could comfortably reach; something clinked and tinkled at the end of it, in the shadows. "No picking but I'll give you whatever's closest to a match."

He brought his hand nearer to the lantern. Seven DoD-issue dog tags hung from his hand; I was looking at a fortune—it would get most people to North America and into their new lives at least two years early.

"Real?" I asked.

"Real enough," he said. "Twenty kay in pre-war francs, or one hundred gold dollars, Amex same as hard stuff."

I was carrying thirty kay of pre-war. "Fakes," I said, bluntly. "The real thing's worth sixty times that, and you know it."

"Can't fault an old dealer for trying," he said smugly, his hand still holding out the glistening tags. Probably they were solder copies—the cheapest way to make a fake tag was to press a real one in a wet flour and salt mixture, then pour liquid solder into the image. You could put an ordinary black shirt button on the back for the readout.

It wouldn't fool anyone who saw it in good light—but that wasn't what you had here. These were to be sold to some poor bastard who was so high that he was throwing money around at random; he'd buy the tag, have a grand dream that as soon as he came down he could go to a repat camp for a comfy bed, good food, and a ride to the States . . . and then wake up hung over, minus his money, with a chunk of solder glued to a button. "The special on screamies is real," the man said, "and I got a little hooch here where you can wrap up in some blankets to stay warm. Go for a nice ride on a screamie, ten kay, and on the down side, the little chick's not bad—and she's just eight kay."

"Let me see the fake tags again," I said. "I might want to deal some of them myself if you can cut me a wholesale price."

"Twenty per cent discount," he said, "if you take them all." He extended his arm, holding them out to me.

I grabbed his wrist and yanked as hard as I could, whirling to drive my knee hard in the face. His nose and lips made a wet squash against my knee cap.

He cried out, and when I stomped down in the blanket by his side, his hand was already on something heavy and hard. But I'd hit him hard enough so that he didn't have much of a grip, my foot had smashed his fingers, and in a second I'd reached under the blanket and wrestled the heavy thing out of his hand. I gave him a couple more kicks and ordered him to lay quiet and keep his hands stretched out in front of him in the light.

Just putting my hand under that blanket had made my fingers smell bad. My knee stung. For nothing. Of all the useless things, the weapon he'd been concealing was a NATO 9mm, at least ten years of no maintenance, clip empty, corrosion visible in the light of the lantern. He tried to pull a hand back. I ground my heel on it. He sobbed and said, "Please."

I told him to behave.

Well, this was a fiasco. I'd hoped to get a usable weapon out of this, which would have been the first step to getting out of the tents. I felt like using the useless thing to club him senseless, especially because something about the way he was treating his little helper pissed me off.

A thought grabbed me. I reached down and under his collar, took a grip, and yanked hard, pulling the loop of thin steel chain over his head. Probably I scraped his lips, ears, and nose with it.

"Give that back," he whispered quietly, "please give that back."

"What did you do to get it?" I asked. "Kill some GI? You don't look like you've got the nerve, unless you killed him while he was sleeping. You a tagrat, shit-boy?"

"No, no, I . . . I just found it."

"Found it on a body, I bet," I said.

"Yeah, that's it—"

"A body that just happened to be in a casket you dug up, by any chance? A casket that just happened to be at Chartres?" I asked. Part of the fun of this was that he had no idea what was really affecting me— which meant he didn't know what answer might make me pissed off enough to stomp him to death.

The joke was, I didn't give a shit, except for the pleasure I was taking in his terror. He could be killing and eating GIs for all I cared, or strangling them in alleys to get their ears for trophies. I'd killed them myself, during the war, for worse reasons.

And it looked like I had guessed right about him. The one place for getting a tag that was easy, no matter how gutless you were—as long as you weren't also squeamish—was in Chartres. Close to where four thousand American paratroops had all been hit in midair with Soviet body-temperature-seeking bullets was a big burial ground that the French had thrown together in a hurry, using the least possible money and effort, after the bodies had lain out for a couple of years. Being French, or busy, or just bureaucrats, they had ignored the request from USDoD to return all the tags. They'd crammed the bodies into pine boxes, stacked those five deep, and bulldozed a lot of broken concrete over the whole thing. There would be a lot of campaign mileage made off that in the States, for sure.

Anyone who wanted a tag only had to throw concrete chunks aside for a while, then start breaking open boxes. Somewhere amid the remains in there, there very likely was a precious dog tag. Sometimes more than one. Our heroic French ally hadn't been too careful about getting it one boy to a box.

If that tag matched you well enough, and your English could pass, presto, a ticket to the land of opportunity.

"That's what I make my living with," he said. "Please."

"You've still got six fakes to sell," I said, "if I didn't break them. They'll be lying around in the alley someplace. And all those drugs, and the girl."

"Fuck," he said. I could hear tears in his voice.

"Ain't life a bitch," I said, and walked off a couple of steps, just in time to turn around and kick him hard in the ribs as he went to get to his feet. He rolled over and bellowed, "Ow! What was that for?"

"For fun," I said. "I just like having you know I did that, and you never got even. You never even had the guts to *think* about it. Remember that. Think about it when you get around to jumping from that high window or opening your wrists—and be sure you go ahead. I'm keeping the gun, too, I'm afraid you'll bruise yourself with it."

I strode out of the alley, and heaved the gun in a high arc into the dark. Likely it would land on a roof. Chances were the tag wouldn't match me, but I could sell it to a dealer for good money.

It had been a great evening. Besides getting the tag, I had come out looking for excitement, I had found it, and I hadn't spent a dime. I enjoyed making him think I wasn't afraid of him, but of course what I was dealing with here was a cornered rat, and I could just as easily have gotten myself killed fucking with him like that, especially if he had been carrying a weapon that worked.

That was the whole appeal; if I'd picked the wrong guy I'd have gotten shot. My ears were ringing from adrenaline and I thought maybe now I would go find something to get high on, or maybe a whore.

I was aware of the girl just when she came up beside me. "You really did him right."

"Not much of a way to talk about your father," I said.

"Him? Shit."

"He's not your father?"

"Naw. Dad was GI, or that's what Mom said. She was a college student over here, and she got pregnant. Too ashamed to marry the guy or maybe she never knew which one it was." She said it so firmly that I was sure it was a lie; probably her mother was one of those "students" who just lived in Europe on parental money for several years, not bothering to enroll anywhere, let alone study. That used to be fairly cheap. "Spent all her time getting high and listening to music. She never went out or learned a word of French. Mom didn't last long in the war."

"How long have you been on your own?" I asked.

"Mom died in the first missile raid on Paris. But I'm never on my own. I always find somebody I can work for."

"Did that old bastard really—"

"He'd take the money, then we'd both run and split up. I got caught a couple times. But it's not like I *did* it for the money. Just a couple times someone paid him, and then caught me. It wasn't like he *meant* to sell me."

We came up on a streetlight, and I turned and lifted her bony little chin. She might be eleven. Go hungry long enough and puberty gets delayed. Maybe even twelve. I bet she didn't know, either, by now. Her American English was pretty good, so I figured her mother probably was what she described. I just didn't think her father was; probably her mother told her that to give her another claim to American citizenship.

Yeah, that was a mother for you—anything you needed, as long as it was a lie that didn't cost anything.

There were a lot of kids like this scrawny brat in front of me, kids nobody kept track of, who either found some adult that was nice to them, or just died.

I turned away from the girl and looked down at the tag. I could manage to match it—at least this guy John Childs had my blood type. I pressed the little dot for a read, and projected it on the snow in front of me, shading the image with my body. I could match Childs for height, weight, and age, near enough. If they checked prints or DNA of course I was dead but I heard they were loading ships pretty fast.

And then I saw the dependent list. He had a daughter; his wife in the States was an unfit mother, and he had sole custody. "Hey kid," I said, but then I looked around and she was nowhere in sight. "Hey kid," I said again, louder in case she was walking away. "I need a little girl to be named Alice."

Long silence.

I thought, *fuck me, I'm going to have to find another kid,* but then she reappeared in the glare of the streetlight beside me. "Are you gonna do father bullshit?"

"You mean like make you clean your room?"

"Like that. Do I *get* a room? All my own?"

"Possibly," I said. "I wasn't planning to have a daughter. But you know, you're going to die if you stay over here. It's a miracle you've lasted this long. And the food and bunks will be better in the repat camps."

She thought for a moment, and then took my hand. Unselfconsciously—probably no one had ever told her not to—she put her other thumb into her mouth. We walked some way before she said, "Yeah, I would like to be named Alice."

THREE

Slouches Toward Bethlehem

i

Did I really get Childs's tag that way? It makes sense, but I seem to remember what he looked like. Wait. Pull up the file on the werp. The read button on that tag has long since gone dead, but somewhere back there I copied the image onto the werp. Sure enough, the face and expression I remember is the one in the werp. Probably I was talking to the image from the button, the two times that I have recordings where it sounds like I was talking to him.

I'd rather not have been a target. And besides, GIs learned early to avoid being alone with anyone who looked like them.

It's the seventh day I've been awake and able to remember. I'm up early again. After probing around in the werp, I find myself thinking I'd rather get moving. The werp shows that I have a good pile of cash, enough to live on a year or more if I have to, even in comfort.

But Martians, like most space people, despise idle wealth, so I probably won't do that. Never make yourself too noticeable to the neighbors. So off to find my funds and then find a place for me to be and a thing for me to do. Ecoprospecting, maybe, that wasn't so bad the last time.

I don't know if I will come back here or not, so I run all the clothes through the fresher in the corner and pack them in my valise. Then I put all the mementos back in the space allocation box. I seem to know the list of them without trouble as I check them off. Matchbook, key, knife, picture, dogtag, chess piece, napkin. I look over them one more time, close the space allocation box, and slide it into the valise. Still plenty of room in there, so I slide in the werp also. The valise has a shoulder strap and I can carry the whole works without difficulty—it masses only about twelve kilos or so, which means it weighs only as much as five kilos does on earth.

I will leave nothing of mine behind except the Marshack itself and the food in the fridge. Maybe I'll be back—free food and a free place to stay, just a short ride away on the maglev, and the fact that nobody's here yet means no one has found this hideout. But more likely I won't come back. It's not a good habit to come back to where you've been. I have no trouble remembering that, either.

I'm pulling on the pressure suit as the sun comes up. I go through the written checklist carefully, even though my hands are executing all the moves faster than I can read them and think them.

When I open the outer airlock door, the first rays of the sun are glowing on the boulders, and a few little patches of shore grass are twitching in the light breeze. The sky's pale pink. I walk farther and crank up the helmet's outside mike so I can hear. Wind in the grass, slap and splash of waves, wind whistling around the little shack by the shore. Like the beach at home, if Earth's home anymore. If my records are right I haven't been there in about forty years, not since One True went cellular and massively parallel, converting itself to Resuna.

I wonder if that little girl in the hologram's Alice. I think so but why didn't I write it down?

I think that at other times, when I had a slightly different set of memories and more of them were about her, I missed her terribly. By now, of course, she's long dead of old age—I have a short note from the day I heard that she died, in 2095, or 2096—why is there a discrepancy? Anyway, she was a hundred two years old.

The trail hasn't been used in months but there's so little growing stuff that it doesn't matter—it's only wind and the occasional rainstorm that erases the passage of people, so far, on Mars. There would have been a time when it was only the wind. . . . I wonder idly, remembering the one time I visited the Apollo 11 site, if they're doing anything to preserve that from the moon's new wind and water (in fact, it was on low ground . . . might it end up at the bottom of a lake or something?).

Jesus, I think, I was one year old when that happened. I was born when no one on Earth had set foot on another world. Can't be many of us left. A few physical freaks, a few plutocks who got the very earliest life-extension treatments, a few Organization longtimers. Maybe they should just let the Apollo 11 site sink beneath the waves. Would it matter to anyone?

The trail climbs at a gentle angle over a high ridge. Loose gravel and stone around. Not much on the path. I have a vague memory of a machine, something called a "thumper," that you use to make these paths.

I sit down on a boulder by the path, reach into the valise, pull out the connector, jack it into the werp and then into the data port on the pressure suit. Zip up the valise, pull it onto my shoulder, get going again. Now I can talk to my werp if I want to.

Encyclopedia search shows that yes, there's a gadget called a thumper—it looks like a lawnmower and slams the dirt hard enough to compact it. So much of the Martian surface can be mistaken for other parts that even though it's firm enough in its native state to walk or drive on, it's important to have a pathway to follow. I look down at the trail and see that every few feet there's a little number "166704 1842" fused right into the sand, probably burned in with a laser.

It makes sense—that way if paths cross you know which are yours.

It's only going to be about fifteen minutes to the station, then half an hour or so to wait there, supposedly, and finally just about an hour's ride into Red Sands City. Plenty of time to think and remember.

I tell the werp to read me some more about Alice.

ii

"Yeah, *college,* why the fuck not?" I said to her.

"You're not my Dad."

"You tell me that all the time, but I notice you don't mind it when I buy you school clothes and groceries, you don't object when I pick up the whole rent, and—"

"Oh, fuck off, Josh." Alice sounded tired. "I've told you before I want to get a full-time job, and split expenses." She extended her hand and studied the nail silvering; it looked perfect to me, but I suppose the real point was that she didn't have to look at me.

Alice hadn't grown up beautiful, but I doubt she cared. She'd learned how to get boys with the body she had. And she liked what anyone likes at her age—frying out brain cells, fucking around, and sneering at everybody that isn't young and good-looking.

She was wearing her hair in a NeoFormal, which is what I could have told her was known as "Big Hair" when I was her age. Her lips were painted vivid pink, her eyelids almost black, and she had just set a streak of Confoam over her breasts and snugged on a pair of gauzy pink oddy pants, dressing for a typical Saturday night in the foreigner section of Quito.

I'd never complained about how she handled her life. I remembered being in my teens, and how much I liked getting into pointless trouble. The clothes and makeup were coming out of what she made at her after-school job, serving booze in a topless bar near the cablehead. I covered necessities but they didn't come to much. I had just asked that she not make too much noise in her room, and keep most of the trash in there.

Hell, we were just roommates—it had been a long time since she'd wanted an adult to pay any attention to her. I was tough on only one point: I expected her to go to school and I expected her to do her homework. Naturally that was what she got herself into a snarl about all the time. Well, in another three weeks she would graduate, and then we'd have to find something else to fight about.

I sighed. "Okay, okay. I know. I didn't go. And there are lots of good jobs now that don't require college, or even a high school diploma. That's what happens when you kill everybody over forty, and then ten years later you kill the best-educated people. It's a big world full of opportunity. But there are still more opportunities with the degree than without, and kid, I like you, for god knows what reason. And the situation won't last—colleges are reopening and those diplomas will start to matter again. All I said was I'd pay, not that I'd make you go. Hell, I *can't* make you go."

She nodded. "That's sweet. But I've got a job that pays plenty."

"Showing men your tits."

"Yeah. Is that why you come in there with your friends all the time?"

"Point to you, Alice."

"Shit, you know where you found me. You never tried to make me behave myself. I hope you don't think I'm blushing and fainting about it all." She faced the mirror and fluffed her dark curls, then put in the little static-electricity clip that would keep it all inflated for the night. "Josh, you made a kind and generous offer. I said no. If you want to know why not, it's because I'm not going to fit in there or be comfortable. I know I'm an okay student in high school, I know I *could* do college if I wanted to work at it, and I *don't* want to work at it. I want to do my own stuff. I love you, you know, and I owe you my life, but I've got things of my own to get done, you know?"

"Yeah," I said glumly. "Well, it's okay, I mean I'm not just saying that—but the offer's open as long as I've got the money."

"I know," she said. "Look, uh—friends?"

"Always."

She hugged me—I was always afraid the foam would end up stuck on my clothes, but that never happened—and said, "Okay."

She was out the door a couple minutes later. I quit worrying about it and got into the shower.

Scrubbing in the hot shower, I told myself that I was thinking too much about the fact that in just under six years, I would slip into another six blank months. I had never told Alice about all that, and for some reason I didn't want to.

We had had to stay together for several years, because INS was a bunch of suspicious bastards. By the time I had gotten the job on the hang crew for the Quito Geosync Cable, and we were down in Ecuador where nobody would have paid much attention, we were used to each other.

Well, all right, I would miss her. If I paid for her schooling she might leave earlier but she'd stay in touch for longer afterwards. And I just plain wanted to know what was up with her. Sentimental dork, I know, but might as well admit it.

Then too, if she'd take my offer, she could be two years into a good job—an engineer or something—by the next time I was going to transit. Maybe by then I could tell her. That way I'd have somebody to take care of me through transit and help me recover memories afterward. That would be good. That would be the *best*.

I turned off the shower. Supposedly next year, when Quito Geosync Cable was built, they'd be moving a lot of us on to build Kilimanjaro, and from there on to Singapore. A few guys were going to be shipped up to space to build Supra New York and the transfer ships, and a few others would be moved over to the Deepstar Project.

There was more work in the world than there were people to do it, but we still had millions living in refugee camps because there weren't enough people to teach them the needed skills, or enough transport to get them to where they were needed. Still, every month you met guys fresh from the camps, and they said that though life was hard there, there was plenty of hope—they needed people so badly that everyone's number would come up sooner or later.

Funny thing. World full of crime and violence. A lot of people had lost everything. Civilization wrecked. Ecosystem still thrashing. And more hope now than at any time in my life before. Hope is weird.

I pulled on my own gear. Physically I was thirty-five, and the work on the cable was keeping me in great shape. We had finished the steel up into the stratosphere earlier the year before—the great truss like a six-legged, hex-shaped Eiffel Tower that thrust nineteen miles into the sky, clutching Mount Cotopaxi like a huge talon.

If the world had had the time and resources, the way to do this would have been to design the special equipment and the robots, and only then begin building. But we didn't have the time, so we built it anyway, climbing around on that crazy spiderweb of girders in our heavy, awkward pressure suits. The project killed workers now and then—suit leaks, falling stuff, squashed between moving members, every so often the Long Dive. But I never heard of anybody quitting because of that.

All of us got to be muscled like apes because there weren't machines to do the special jobs. And if you were thirty-five, single, ready to party till it killed you, and had great muscles, Quito in 2012 was the place to be. The Ecuadorean government knew a pile of loot when they saw it, and NihonAmerica, Global Hydrogen, and the other big PSCs had bought everybody right down to beat cops and garbage collectors. If we did anything that endangered the project, provoked mob violence, or was just too big to ignore, they could throw us in jail forever or just have us shot behind the barracks. But if it wasn't anything big, it wasn't anything at all.

Saturday nights were the nights when you could buy anything if you had the money, and anything short of a major civil insurrection was regarded as blowing off some steam.

So my little squabble with Alice was nothing, really, as far as I was concerned. I wanted her to have the best things that could be managed, but I knew she could look out for herself—she was smart and would work. That was all it took during Reconstruction.

I suppose I still miss those times. What I remember of them. At least the documents from the werp seem that way.

I pulled on my going-out clothes: big white Cavalier shirt, tight black ringmaster coat, plush burgundy clingpants that started about as low as was practical for trousers, and spiked black boots. I put in a couple of big hoop earrings and checked myself in the mirror, pushing back the black hair falling in loose curls around my face. "Arrrrgh," I said, grinning at my own image—a crazed pirate.

I wondered idly for a second if the Organization was really gone, or if it had just lost track of me somehow. That reminded me of my looted account from nine years before, but it was only a shadow of a resentment—I was comfortable and well off now, and I had time to get more socked away before another transit.

Well, time to go out and strut my stuff again. I took the air injector and gave myself a power dose of my personal mix: Immunobooster so that I could fend off any new strains of AIDS or syph, of which there were still plenty. Wake-me-up shot of gressor. Slow-acting alcohol metabolizer so I could get drunk and not wake up hung over. Performance lifter because I knew that even in great shape, I wasn't necessarily able to keep up with some of the younger girls. To-the-limit dose of You-4, which was just coming in that decade and was already the Big New Drug Menace.

One good thing the war had done was that not only had it caused molecular tailoring develop a long way, it had forced the technology to disperse into millions of garage labs, and nothing and no one had been able to shut them down since. Labs that had been making ecoweapons in 2003 and 2004, getting cash from any of a dozen governments, were still in business—but now they had moved over to the private sector. There were still drug laws, and people who took the old shit, but the only reason for either was tradition.

I swallowed a candy bar in two bites to give the shot something to run on, rinsed my mouth, and headed out.

Everyone knew Spanish by then, but the language of the Calley Alley had stayed English. Plenty going on—a lot of girls, standing around waiting to get money spent on them. A few of them might actually be whoring, but most were just out for fun and didn't see any reason why they should need to carry money when so many nice men would buy them everything.

A lot of guys dressed like me checking them out.

Gaggles of new workers just down from Norty or up from Argentina, still in their issue coveralls because they hadn't yet gotten out to spend the wages in the shopping district, wandering around with their eyes and wallets wide open.

The BFH Lesbian Brigade were out in their cammies, holding hands or clutching their bats, but so cheerful about it all that you'd have to be pretty stupid to be afraid of them. Sure, if you tried raping some poor girl around them, you'd wake up with a fractured skull, but it would serve you right.

One of them I knew from my crew waved and dashed over to say hello. "So what's the news, Josh?"

"Flat zil so far. I just got out. You check the posting for next week? The crew's all the way topside."

"Yuck," she said firmly, running her hand over her shaved head. "Extra half hour commuting each way."

"Positive-definite," I said. "We've gotta lean on Joe Schwartz about that portal-to-portal thing—what kind of a shop steward is he, anyway? And I think since we've gotta suit up at the bottom we should get the pressure suit wage for it."

"Yep. Joe will whine, you know—he's always trying to be reasonable with the PSCs, as if."

"Hey, Syd!" one of the Brigade yelled.

"Gotta run!" she said, and scooted back to her group with a wave of her bat.

I waved after her and turned back to look over the Alley. Right on the equator, the sun goes down bang at 6:00 P.M. and comes back up bang at 6:00 A.M., every day, all year round. So the sky was already dark, the narrow strip I could see of it, anyway. The street glowed in the red and yellow glare from the long rows of advertising signs. I'd already had a good blast from the injector, so I wasn't up for either of the chem bars I was facing; the next shop over was a restaurant but I wasn't planning to eat just yet, either. A couple drinks might be nice. . . .

The You-4, starting to hit, made all the women dead solid gorgeous. Not that they needed any help. Those were great years if you had the body to get any—besides Confoam, there were oddy pants, those wonderful little poufs of gauze that went from just above the crack of the butt to an inch or two down the thighs and swished like poetry, and great thigh-high cling boots, and everything else you could think of. It was also one of those great periods when there's no VD they can't treat, and everyone has the time and the money.

Four girls, classmates of Alice I think, all waved at me as they went by, and although objectively they looked about like any other teenagers, under the You-4 they were the four hottest pieces I'd ever seen in my life. I drifted into the bar—the most wonderful bar, filled with terrific people who I was dying to meet—and ordered a marvelous bottle of Bud from the bartender. He brought it right away—so fast! the man was a saint!—and the first sip told me that this was the best bottle old Augie Busch had ever made.

The You-4 hit harder. I worked hard not to start giggling. I loved this stuff but I didn't want other people laughing at me. I sat down on the bar stool, which caressed my bottom like the firm hands of a trained Thai masseuse, and let the Bud soak into me and blur out the acute edges of pleasure.

Great to be alive. After a while, the band started up, and my Bud was about gone, so I decided to dance; those were the years of the

Boink, so everyone had an oversized belt loop on each side of their clingpants or oddy, to give your partner something to hang on to. And if you were on You-4, so that sensations were enhanced hundreds of times, the Boink was the best dance ever invented.

I spent an hour or so floating from partner to partner, watching as the women got themselves off on me, sometimes feeling the little surge of a pseudorgasm—one of You-4's better side effects—hit me as well.

About the time I was thinking seriously that I was hot and wanted another beer, this girl Myndi, a school friend of Alice's, came up to me and asked me to Boink. They were starting kind of a long number, and I was tired and hot—but on the other hand, Myndi was a nice-looking redhead, one of the tall, rangy, horsey kind, with big floppy tits on a totally fatless body. So I said yes.

She really pushed hard into the grinds. I might have wondered what someone that young wanted with someone like me, but between You-4 and gressor, I couldn't imagine, just then, that any woman didn't.

She came on me a couple of times when the music hit crescendos, and at the end she wrapped her arms around me and jammed her tongue into my mouth. My hands slipped under the cuffs of her oddy pants, caressing her butt, and she pressed closer.

So after that it was natural to get her a drink—Myndi was seventeen, a year younger than Alice, but there wasn't much concern about age along Calley Alley, for drinking or anything else. And then after she'd put down a couple of pink things with little paper umbrellas, and I'd had another couple of Buds, it seemed pretty natural to go back to my place. We staggered in trying to be quieter than usual, because even though Alice and I sure knew the other person was having sex, I wasn't sure how she'd feel about my nailing one of her school friends.

It was one great fuck, and it lasted a long time. The enhancer let me manage two more times before I settled into kneeling between her legs and licking until she finally said she was satisfied. By the time she said that, I was sore and tired like I'd spent the night boxing bare-knuckled—and losing—and I didn't care if I never saw that devil's-mouth tattoo that she had in her crotch again.

I woke up late the next morning, to discover that I was being had again; she had climbed aboard while I was asleep. This time I wasn't on all the drugs, and I could see that she was young, but also that she didn't seem to be involved with *me*, just pumping away (though she certainly seemed to be enjoying it). I came in a minute or so. She went down on me to clean it up. When she came up she kissed me and started to get dressed.

"That was great," she said, as she sprayed a fairly modest Confoam top on, "I thought I was doing Alice a big favor but that was pretty nice. I guess older guys do know more. Maybe sometime again, hunh?"

"Uh, wait a sec," I said, trying to figure it out, but she had already given me a little wave and gone out the bedroom door. I grabbed a pair of sweat pants and yanked them on, but by the time I got out of the bedroom she was gone. I stood there for a stupid second before I recalled that she had said she thought she was doing Alice a favor, which meant Alice had asked her to—

I turned and looked around the apartment. Light was coming in from the three big windows, and sunlight was splashing in from the kitchen window, so it must be past 3:00 P.M.

No spill of makeup bottles across the coffee table. No laundry basket full of filmy nothings. I knocked on her door—an odd, hollow sound. When I looked inside the bed was made for the first time since I had stopped cleaning in there. Closet open and empty. Plenty of dust and stain on the end tables and dresser, but nothing else.

The note on the bed said she was going to be staying with Joe Schwartz, the union guy for my section. I looked at that and started to laugh.

Syd had been right. I'd have to talk to him. Well, I could hardly fault his taste—let alone that after all, he was only ten years older than she was, and considering how much older than Myndi I was, I was hardly in a position to pick on Joe about it. I wondered if Alice had set Myndi on me as a going-away present, or a diversion? She'd certainly been diverting.

It bothered me that she hadn't told me what she was up to. But then, being Alice, she was probably afraid she'd get my blessing.

iii

I am sitting on this bench at the maglev stop, just thinking and letting my eyes roam around the red sand hills of Mars, with dark brown streaks from which a thousand tiny stars glint and glitter. The bioextractors are replacing oxygen with sulfur and creating surface deposits of pyrites wherever the dust is deep enough. A lot of Mars will glitter for a few years, until the wind and rain spread soil over it, and then those cracks and pits where the dust used to lie will become the permeable beds through which groundwater will rise and fall. At least that's what the werp tells me.

I wonder whether, a thousand years from now, when the glittering pyrite beds are being covered up, there will be people who will miss them. Right now, this century, it's pretty.

The sun's warm through the bubble helmet. Suit temp control's good, I'm not really sweaty. Where was this back when I was doing space rigging? Oh, well, that's the nature of things. As long as it was just working stiffs, nobody was going to bother making suits comfortable.

I wonder about what to do with what's in the werp. One part of me argues that I ought to wipe the works, write ten short paragraphs, and bury the werp and the space allocation box someplace. Next time around start clean—after all, the poor bastard, whoever I have become, will be sixty-five physically. I know he could live a long time after that, but why not just let him live comfortably confused, troubled only by the occasional nightmare or haunting dream?

I can't bear to part with the space allocation box, or with the tangle of stuff in the werp. It might have been different if I had never known it existed, but now that I do it seems like it's the one thing that absolutely has to go on.

Once my life gets back underway, then I'll be less hung up on this, I'm sure. Part of the problem was having nothing to do but this. It must have been even worse that first time, when I just had the paper notes and had to fake my way through the hospital without knowing what was going on. I think I remember I was afraid and upset, but of course that vague memory could be nothing more than my making it up. It seems convincing, but maybe I just know myself well enough to know what details will make it convincing to me. After a long life, even with six memory erases, you know what a hospital smells like (bad) and how doctors and nurses treat people without money (like frozen shit on a stick).

The notes say the Catholic Workers were pretty good to me, but I don't really believe it. I've been around too many handout windows to believe anybody gives you decent treatment unless they're going to make cash off you. It isn't the poor they buy off, but their own oversensitive consciences. Probably I was just too young to notice them being condescending.

The maglev arrives almost silently, even with my outside microphones amped up. A shimmer of white above the trough-shaped metal track, far off in the distance. Something flashes bright white in the sun. Breaking out of the distant hills, there it is, slithering to the station at high speed. A voice in my earphones says, "Please acknowledge that you are the passenger who requested a train stop. You have twenty seconds to acknowledge. Twenty. Nineteen. Eighteen . . ."

"I acknowledge," I said.

"Number of people in your party?"

"One."

"Number of bags you are carrying, and will you need extra time for loading?"

"One shoulder bag," I said, "and once I'm aboard you can start again."

"Thank you, sir. Please stay behind the blue line until the train comes to a complete stop."

I walk up to where a blue line appears on the ground, as if it had been painted there very precisely. The train keeps coming. I take a moment to kneel and lift a pebble from the blue line. It turns red-brown as soon as I pick it up; I throw another pebble onto the line and see it turn blue instantly.

Oh, well, I wasn't planning to work as an engineer this trip around. I only need to know what things do, not how they do it.

The train comes to a stop with a low hiss, making less noise than the brakes on some cars I've owned. It's huge—at least forty foot wide by a hundred long. At first, coming in at such speed, it looked pure white, but now I see it's smeared with fine dust.

One of the last cars stops in front of me, and the whole train sinks a few inches as the pedestals settle silently onto the track. "You may board now. Please board quickly. Thank you," the voice of the train says in my ears.

I walk forward and enter the car's airlock; the door snugs tight behind me. There's a thud I feel through my feet as the train shoots air into the lock, and then the inner door opens. I walk through, unlocking and lifting my helmet.

My cabin's the third one on the right. It's supposed to be for up to four people, so it has two fold-down beds, a long bench seat attached to the wall facing the windows, a small washstand, shower, and toilet, and a table that folds into the wall. I pull down the table and unfold the seats.

Red Sands City is a few hundred kilometers away, I would judge, since it takes something more than an hour to get there. The maglev pulls up inside the enclosure, so I won't need the pressure suit there; I strip the suit off, shower, and dress, which kills half an hour of the journey.

By the time that I'm clean and dressed, we are passing a lot of "ranches"—the word doesn't mean exactly what it would on Earth, because these people don't raise things to sell, they tend the genetically tailored wildlife that is slowly populating Mars. They get a salary for that.

My memory twinges. On Earth, for most of my life, "ranchers" were guys who looked after whichever buffalo happened to wander across their land. The older meaning's nearly gone except in books and movies.

I order soup and a sandwich. About the time I toss the napkin aside and drop the tray into the return slot, the enclosure of Red Sands City is dancing in the heat rising from the plain ahead. I straighten things up, get the pressure suit into its bag, and wait for the warning bell that means we're decelerating into the city. I get off onto a wide platform, no different from any other train platform, looking out over the treetops inside the enclosure, from which hard white spires and steeples occasionally poke up, to the blackened sky, much of the harsh daylight screened out, where the city enclosure arches.

iv

"It took us a long time to find you," she explained. "By the time we did you were about ready to transit again."

"Transit?"

"The age reversal thing. So anyway, we just watched you to see what you set up, and here we were, waiting for you. You have a heap of back pay and interest coming."

"I'll say." I took a long sip of coffee and a bite of doughnut. The first time I had come out of transit starving and broke, this time I was rich. At least if I took this deal.

I had awakened facing the blonde woman I had met under the bridge years before. She looked maybe five years older than she had then, and I looked five years younger. Aging at different times and in different directions. Confusing.

Now, a week after waking up, here I was, spending May 2017 in a big, comfortable hotel room, eating like an ox on an unlimited room-service tab. The Organization had found me again.

While I was unconscious they had moved me here and done the

coverage on "Brandon Smith," the new i.d. I had established for myself, so that the i.d. was a lot more airtight than what I'd done.

I still had not learned this woman's name. From what I could read of my past experiences in the pile of letters, still photos, holos, and scrap paper, I had never known her name. Apparently I had thought she was "the bitch who ran off with everything I owned," except when I thought it was somebody named Peter, except when I thought it was the Organization itself.

"Not that I don't want to work for the Organization," I said. "I'm confused because looking me up to give me the money that was owed to me, and then taking care of me during recovery, doesn't sound a lot like the Organization in my notes, or what I remember from back when we were the KGB. I mean, we *used* to be the KGB, but here you are acting like the Salvation Army."

She smiled. "We haven't been the KGB for a long time, and we absorbed a bunch of other outfits, so we don't really have a single origin anymore. When your home country joined the Pope's Global Concord in 2008, we picked up a lot of good people, sometimes whole offices, from several of their agencies. In other places there were existing groups that merged with us."

"Like the Mafia?"

"Yes, and national liberation movements that had lost their mass base but not their cadres and weapons. Smugglers with no borders, Mercenaries with no rogue governments to hire them. The world was full of people who still had means but no ends, Joshua—I guess we should practice calling you Brandon."

I was sure she had pretended to slip and use my real name so that it would seem more like we were old friends. Or had I—seen her with her head shaved, in coveralls—I wasn't sure what that memory was.

"So I know you can't *prove* that I should trust you, but make me a case," I said.

She fluffed up her thick blonde hair. Who'd have thought that style would keep coming back? "All right, I'll tell you the whole story. It happens I was there for a lot of it, so you can believe me—but if you'd rather not, well . . ."

"Let's hear it."

Something flew by the window—a big private car, somebody with a license to fly inside Manhattan Dome, I figured—and I glanced sideways at it, watching it descend to land on the roof of the old World Trade Center, a kilometer below. When I looked up, the blonde woman was staring off into space, toward the translucent wall of the Dome some miles away. Two thirds of the way up one of the central pillars, we could see a long way in all directions, but since vags tended to cluster by the dome wall, people looking out tended to stare into the distance, the way you'd put on a thousand-yard stare when you passed a beggar on the street, when I was a kid.

"Well," she said, "the Organization, capitalized, works a lot like any other organization, not capitalized. So we favored seniority, and like the military outfits, we tended to value combat time, and of course people with more energy and vigor . . . so longtimers, people like you and I tended to do better."

"Makes sense," I agreed, "except that our experience all goes away every fifteen years."

"Not all of it. We have each other. We can be each other's memories. Do you remember a quiet little guy that traveled under the name Peter?"

"I have notes about him in my own records." *As you goddamn well know.*

"Well, he made station chief for Paris, right when the old people up at the top were getting to be afraid of us. They were looting accounts and erasing i.d.'s while longtimers transited, hoping to slowly eliminate us. They thought if they killed us it would leave more trail than if we just vanished, the way a lot of agents were vanishing voluntarily and going to work for the Reconstruction." She sighed, turned her head, stretched like a yawning kitten—sexy as all shit and intended to be. "So . . . Peter and a few others he could find made their move. Peter pulled a coup about two years after you were cut loose. And then we started the long, difficult process of finding all the other longtimers who had been thrown away."

"It just went from 'them' to 'we,' " I pointed out. "You're with the longtimers?"

"Oh, pos-def." Kidslang. It made sense for her to use it—she must be past fifty but she was clearly vain and playing at being young. "To the lim."

Trying to needle her, I asked, "Uh, just how old are you right now?"

She grinned. "Chronologically I'm fifty-eight. Just went through another transition two years ago. Not bad, hunh?"

"Not bad at all. So the longtimers are in charge now?"

"Pos-def, and we're slowly adding more of us, both by recruiting new young people and by finding our lost ones. We want every single longtimer to come in with us, and we're prepared to offer a lot."

"This is probably stupid of me to ask," I said, "but just what happens if you get one that won't come in for any reason at all?"

"I don't know."

"It hasn't happened?"

Shrug. "It has. When it does I report it and go on my way."

"The old Organization, the one I knew, would have killed them," I said. I had about made my mind up to throw in with them, but I wanted to *know* the worst thing they might do.

She nodded. "No question. The old Organization would. And I don't suppose you remember Peter, but I worked a couple cases with him, and I shudder when I think about things he did. He didn't get to be a longtimer till he was past forty, so he spent a lot of time in the old KGB, back before it was the Organization. I cant imagine he's changed that much. But I don't really know. What they tell me, and tell me to tell you, is that the last thing they want to do is draw attention to their existence, and so the next best thing to a longtimer that works for them is a longtimer who goes quietly through life without raising any eyebrows. Mysterious murders of people who have only recently established i.d.'s would trigger all kinds of investigation. We don't want that. So supposedly we leave them alone, keep tabs on them, wait fifteen years or so, and try again when they're waking up again."

I thought about that. It might even be true. When the truth works just as well as a lie, sometimes people tell you the truth. It made me wonder—"Did you contact me after my last transit, and did I say no?"

"Everyone asks that. No, we didn't find you until about a year and a half before this transit. By that time you were working construction on Supra Tokyo, and we don't have many ins up there. We were trying to figure out how to get to you when you conveniently came back down to Singapore and established a new i.d.—damn good job for working all by yourself, by the way, the trick with setting up credit card records for your fake father was brilliant. We only cracked it because we were watching you. We figured we owed you a decent room, at least, so we moved you here—and here we are."

I would never know if that story was false, or true. Just one more thing to take on faith. You wake up ten years older, with a few scraps of evidence for a thirty-year life you don't remember, and here you are. Over and over, if this was all to be believed.

She stayed the night. I suppose it was standard practice; she told me that I was a lot better in bed than I'd been under a bridge. I had only remembered that we'd talked.

I took the job.

Two weeks later, early in the morning, I was on a high-speed diskster to Atlanta Dome. First-class compartment. The disksters were new—I didn't remember them, but I might never have ridden one, since I had mostly been up at Supra Tokyo for a couple of years.

A diskster was an electrostatic aircraft that took advantage of ground effect, and looked a lot like a flying saucer. The little MAM power plant in them—about the size of the engine in my old RX-7—could put out more power than all the engines of three 747s, and the radar and AI pilot let the diskster move along at close to 300 mph on the old freeways, since it could dodge obstructions faster than any human driver, run over river surfaces, fly short distances, and at last resort brush things like deer aside. They were a great ride—the kind of luxury that had last existed on the old ocean liners.

As we cruised out the 57th Street Door (I turned around like any tourist to gawk at the five-story-high door rolling back down like the garage doors of my childhood) and across the river into Weehawken Ruin, I saw a flash off to the side. I turned to look and saw men running for cover. A moment later, a rocket, probably out of a patrolling helicopter, had blasted the place where their mortar was set up. The diskster, meanwhile, stepped sideways hard, sloshing the coffee on my tray and making the tray itself slide along the polished wood table, so that I had to catch it. I didn't see the shell splash—I think it landed behind us.

I muttered "Nice shot, guys," and went back to my breakfast. Vags were making the best efforts they could, which wasn't much.

I sat back to enjoy the ride. At first we ran down the Hudson, close to the Jersey side to avoid the rougher water out in the bay, but shortly we were rounding the Statue of Liberty, what was left of her after the blast that had hit Jersey City just after the war—no one ever seemed to settle whether a smuggled bomb, a delayed long-range cruise missile, or just a whoopsie with a piece of surplus hardware had converted Miss Liberty into twentieth-century art. You could tell what the shape was supposed to be, but rusting steel stuck out here and there, the surface was strangely mottled where parts had melted and run, and the skeleton had twisted hard as the statue lost its torch, so that now it looked more like she was doing a dance of mourning over New Jersey.

We zipped up the earth ramp onto the old Jersey Turnpike and we were on our way south. I poured more coffee from the little pot they provided, and settled back to read with my new toy, a brand-new Reconstruction Standard Issue Werp.

My previous life, apparently, I'd concentrated on having fun. I had gotten on to Reconstruction work early, and adopted a daughter for some reason I couldn't fathom, though it looked like we'd been out of touch for a while. She was listed as Mrs. Joe Schwartz, Supra Berlin, though the last note I had from her, four years before, said she was planning to get a divorce because apparently Schwartz had decided to accept a permanent post on the *Flying Dutchman,* and besides she'd found "a new guy, a really nice guy, I mean Joe's kind and he works hard but this is so different from anything I've known." She'd had to give up her visiting rights to her kid, who I'd never seen. Reading between the lines, it sounded like the nice guy was a plutock, and I figured I'd done a good job of raising Alice. Given a choice between a five-year-old son and a rich husband, she'd made the choice that made sense. That was sort of a relief since I remembered her as kind of sentimental.

With an inward groan I turned back to review the material for my mission. I already knew it thoroughly but I kept hoping it would look better. The job was so bizarre—an Organization guy in charge of getting a bunch of libertarian bandits to join a new religion—that the better I understood it, the more confusing it got.

The reason we'd gotten into this business was that Reconstruction was going too far too fast. We had no problem with rich people—they make better customers or better victims, take your pick. But the refugee camps and the indocoms, where our power base was, were shrinking rapidly as the main economy began to absorb people faster and faster, and we were having very little luck with keeping our low-level people once they moved into the domes or up to the supras.

And we couldn't seem to get a toehold outside Earth orbit. There'd been a genuine lynching at Ceres Base the year before. The locals had pushed nine of our organizers naked out the airlock. Worse still, our reprisal strike against EuroNihon had been caught before it accomplished anything and the whole team was now in jail.

Behind the whole disaster that Reconstruction was turning into was PJP, Pope Paul John Paul. He'd gotten his prestige by brokering the peace settlement that ended the Eurowar, which is to say, he'd started out by costing us plenty. But the Ecucatholic Movement he had launched at the same time was the kicker.

The policy documents frankly admitted the Organization had misread Ecucatholicism. They had thought it was mere PR, or a recruiting method. By the time the Organization learned how much more it was, it was too late for shooting the Pope to solve the problem.

By canonizing practically every Protestant leader since the Reformation, and then establishing the principle of "surface forms and deep
forms," whatever that was (apparently a lot of theologians were turning out book after book explaining it), PJP had somehow gotten millions of Protestants to come back under the Roman umbrella.
Realizing that there was now a Saint Brigham Young and a Saint Mary
Baker Eddy gave me an idea of how far things had gone.

The result was what everyone else was calling a "new moral
force." The Organization didn't concern itself with that kind of crap.
What we knew was that UNRRA-2, Global Hydrogen, NihonAmerica,
EuroNihon, AmericEuro, and all the other Reconstruction PSCs shut
us out no matter what we tried to do. From the top down everyone
insisted on squeaky-clean operations. There were more stool pigeons
and straight arrows than the world had ever seen before, and those
dumbfucks were ruining it for everyone else.

We still had a finger in the indocoms, the old factory/mall/apart-
ment complex setups that had emerged right after the war, but the ones
that couldn't afford to get domed were shutting down, and most of
them were losing people into the domes anyway.

So we were left recruiting where we could and not where we
chose. That meant the vags—pissed-off people in the woods, many of
them useless lunatics, thugs, and cranks of course. Most were people
who had had a comfortable life before the Eurowar, wanted compensa-
tion, and weren't coming in till they got it.

They were usefully stupid. Driven by their "right" to their old
houses, businesses, jobs, prestige, whatever, they would fight to the
death rather than accept that all that was gone, united by the conviction
that the Reconstruction authorities had cheated them of their "freedom." You take your malcontents where you can find them.

The other force in the mix was cybertao, the only religious movement that looked like it might challenge Ecucatholicism. Of course
nobody knew who the author of *Forks in Time* had been—the cybertaoists believed it had somehow grown in the net itself, like primitive
life forming in the primordial soup—but it had spread rapidly among
Western agnostics and atheists, and seemed to be absorbing (or being
absorbed by) Buddhism and Taoism in the Far East.

Even when it began to recruit some Christians, mostly Protestants
who had lapsed after their churches re-merged with Rome, Pope PJP
had been careful not to condemn it too harshly, apparently not wanting
to start any new religious wars, and the cybertaoists referred to Ecucatholicism as "special case literalism," meaning as far as I could tell

that the viewpoint was okay with them, if narrow. Unfortunately all that tolerance meant that thus far there had been no overt clashes, just some garden-variety bigotry.

Even the appearance of a second cybertao text, accepted at once by virtually all cybertaoists as authentic, last year, had not led to any further clashes. *Surfaces in Opposition* was just as tolerant in spirit as *Forks in Time.*

In the briefing I was reading, the Organization admitted neither group was much to work with. Most of the vags could have been richer now than they had been before the war (assuming they were all telling the truth, a pretty big assumption) if they had been willing to go to work for the PSCs. They were genuine losers, misfits who couldn't forget that they had once thought of themselves as superior. And the cybertaoists were highly principled and at least as pacifistic as the old Quakers. (Who, of course, were all Ecucatholic now.)

But if the two could be put together, so vag rage and cybertao influence could somehow merge, maybe we could get something going again. As a program it wasn't a boil on Bolshevism's butt, but it was a better bet than anything else.

Something thudded off the diskster window; I looked up from my reading. Might have been a duck, passing through, or might have been a rock, thrown by some vag. No trace of it now. Might as well not have happened.

The view out the window was dizzying at 300 mph, but I sat and watched it roll by a long time. Everywhere, empty crumbling buildings. Twice, smoke, from campfires perhaps. Once a diskster going the other way. The world had gotten empty, outside the domes.

A month later I was squatting in a field with five of the most unpleasant people I've ever met. And I'm not fussy, either. But for me to hate you more than I hated these guys, you'd have to be my blood kin.

I was giving them a one-more-time-through on the drill. The Condor would come in from the south, like they always did, gliding gently down to its landing field. Most of the Condor pilots took pride in landing with the tanks full; the engines were only supposed to be auxiliary.

Karen, a squat, dark-haired woman, wanted to argue that the Condors didn't have to come from the south and might not come from the south—after all they were really just space shuttles, space shuttles the Japanese had stolen the plans for from us, and space shuttles flew out of Cape Canaveral, didn't they? Which way was Cape Canaveral from here?

"South," I said firmly. "And it's not coming from Canaveral. It's taking off from the drop station attached to the Quito Geosync Cable, about a hundred miles above Quito, Ecuador. Which is also south. So it will come from the south."

"Are you sure?" Karen asked. "That doesn't sound right. I think I learned different in school. They've changed everything in school nowadays but that doesn't make false true."

"Quite sure," I said. "Okay, now, James, when do you lock onto it?"

"When he starts final approach. When his landing gear are all the way down."

"Why not sooner?"

"Because they'll get a fix on me and we'll all get blown up, Brandon. Everybody knows that."

I doubted it but didn't say so. "And then what?"

"Put the rocket through the landing gear, so that the shrapnel will probably get a control surface too. Then when it undershoots the field and crashes, because the pilot didn't pull out, we run forward and get stuff."

"What kind of stuff?" I demanded of the others.

"Gold, silver, hard currency, hostages if any are alive," they all recited. The hard part. I didn't have much faith it would come out right.

Our lookout, in the tree above us, whistled. He'd seen the bright flash in the blue sky that meant a Condor was coming in.

The part of the plan that was up to James went perfectly. He snapped his rocket launcher to his shoulder, sighted, locked the radar on, squeezed the trigger, and dove for the ground as soon as the rocket got off. The little rocket, no bigger than a paper-towel tube, zipped out to the Condor, now just spreading its wings to their widest position, and nailed the landing gear. Fragments streaked in all directions. Suddenly the big ship flipped over on its back and fell out of the sky, its tail section whirling off toward the landing field. The vags got up and ran to the crushed, broken body of the plane, more than a mile away, getting strung out and separated. Didn't matter much since there was no one to shoot at us.

Then it all turned to shit. Too much loot of the kind they really wanted, the things they thought were theirs by right—so instead of going after the hard stuff, the jewelry, safe deposit boxes, or even wedding bands and gold teeth, they swarmed into that shattered fuselage, kicking the dead and the dying aside in order to grab Italian shoes, Rolexes, pre-war hats, anything at all that stood for the vanished world.

When Karen ran out the door with dozens of shoes, I shot her. Even that didn't restore discipline; they weren't paying enough attention to notice.

I walked back to camp. I'd be in trouble with the Organization if I shot my whole cadre, but if I stayed I'd have to.

Three months later I helped them lug a four-hundred-pound rocket up a godforsaken hillside to launch into a fortified village full of corporados and their kids. We scored a direct hit on the duck pond. I'm sure it was a crushing defeat from the ducks' point of view.

We blew a couple of disksters off the road, and they got back on again, unhurt. Since a diskster was not in contact with the ground, the impact got used up moving the diskster, not crushing it. Probably we spilled some people's dinners.

At the end of eight months we had murdered about two hundred people—most of them on the two Condors we had brought down—and blown up or otherwise destroyed a hundred million dollars of property. And they still weren't bothering to send the Army after us, since the Georgia state troopers already had us mostly licked.

I used some of that initiative we were supposed to use, slipped away in the middle of the night, and dropped a self-repeating message into the net that would circle around the world a few times (to lose its connection to me) and then pop up in the Georgia Patrol's in box and tell them where to get my particular group of vags. Total achievement, as I reported to the Organization, was some pointless pain and suffering (not even fun to inflict), some trivial robbery, and a precipitate drop in the Georgian vag population.

I spent another pointless year around Louisville Ruin, trying to be a cybertao prophet and get a Stochastic Jihad going. Lots of luck; it seemed to be difficult, within cybertao, to say much in favor of hurting people.

I wish I remember when I hooked up with Sadi in all that time. I don't think he was with me at the first but I'm sure he was around by the next time I transitted. He was another longtimer with the Organization, brown-haired, blue-eyed, tall and slender, an elegant sort of guy, the kind we all wished we were when we were sixteen. He had seven thousand books on his werp, all from the Everyman's Library, and had read about half of them, in cliffotated editions. He looked sort of like an old Nazi poster.

He had read more books and knew more facts than anyone I'd ever spent any time around, but I don't know that he could do more than dredge up stuff he'd read. He tended to remember one or two sentences

about everything; I had a feeling that things were probably more complicated than that.

I do know he was there more than once when I woke up after tran-
siting. I saw him transit, more than once, too. I don't know if you'd call
that love, but when I think how much it would have helped to have
Sadi or someone like him this past transit, waking up here on Mars, I
think being friends all those years with Sadi might have been the closest to love I ever got. Him or Alice. Fuck if I know.

V

No time at all to get my accounts moved and recoded—could have
done it over the wire, didn't want to take chances; in person means you
can code fingerprints and DNA, nail it down every possible way.

I'm rich, this time, but I have no friends.

I could reply to that ad. If I wanted. But what would I be getting
into? I call up an AI and start asking questions.

When I think about it, personals are surprisingly *scarce*. So much
of the human race has vanished one way or another, and so much of it
didn't exactly exist in the first place (figuring there must be a lot of
false i.d.'s in there). Why aren't more of us looking for each other?
There should be *zillions* of personals.

Finally I find out why not. There are several references to the
Copy Transference Recovery Database. Since "copy transference" is a
cybertao term for what happens when you die but your ideas live on
(like Jesus or Elvis), or for what happens in a religious service when
people "get the spirit"—I'm not sure which—my first thought is that
it's a religious thing, but it's showing up as a government function.

The Copy Transference Recovery Database turns out to be what I
was looking for—a giant database with all the data known about every
human being who ever lived, compiled as a chronological list of facts
with the inconsistencies noted. Access is free to anyone.

I play around at first. Find somebody there have been thousands of
biographies of—Hitler. There's a huge, almost day-to-day account,
tons of film, all flat and almost all black and white. Zeus shows up with
a note that not all the stories fit together and he probably is entirely
mythical. Holden Caulfield, who I remember from some book in
school, is in there with the note that he's known to be fictional, though
the name has been used as an alias at least eighteen times. Well, at least
they seem to be getting things straight enough.

I grit my teeth and try JOSHUA ALI QUARE.

My service record includes a note that I was suspected of having killed those men in Prague, a further note that I was believed to be KGB/Organization, and a final note that I might have been the Josh Quare that turned up in Quito, but if so I was unusually well preserved. No notes about my possibly being Brandon Smith or the later lives; instead it just notes that I checked into private care, that a woman named Katrina Triste checked me out and moved me to some place unknown, and that I vanished. One cop dropped in a memo titled "Speculative Note." He thought the Organization found and killed me.

Katrina Triste. So that was her name. Then. If she's still alive, she's older than me, but only by about ten years on the average. At worst she's had to make it through a couple of years of being eighty-five.

I check the other aliases and sure enough, a lot of it agrees with at least some of the stuff in my werp. I download it all to the werp and set up an automatic cross-reference. It only takes four minutes and next time after transit will be that much easier.

1 check out Alice Schwartz, back up to find her as Alice Childs and Alice Quare. I had no idea about the number of times she'd been arrested while living with me, always for something she could pay a fine for (mostly selling a feel to a vice cop). Looks like she stayed married to Schwartz for a few years, just like in my notes. So good to confirm *anything*.

Then there's a period when she's married to Hutchins Dyen, one of the Dyen MicroIntelligence family, a family of Supra Berlin plutocks. She has twins by him, the marriage lasts awhile. He gets rid of her and keeps the twins. Probably losing her looks, not the breeder she was, getting into the bottle too often.

The record notes that she disappeared during the War of the Memes, like a lot of people and records. But I'm ahead of the records on that—she departed on the *Flying Dutchman*. I drop the note in and after a moment it says the records do link up validly, and thanks me.

Of course. Sadi. I type Edward Sadi Trichin. Then all the aliases that my records show he ever used. Then I search by every incident I know Sadi was involved in where cops or soldiers got called in. Zil every time. Nobody and nothing can vanish that completely. Can it? But Sadi, who is all through my records from about 2020 to just before 2078—a man who lived for decades, spent money, committed crimes, made contracts, forged i.d.'s, enlisted in armies (even voted a few times, god knows why)—Sadi is gone.

vi

"Hey, buddy, every time you transit, somebody either stops a war or starts one," Sadi was saying. We were sitting out on a back porch on the little house he had built way out in one of the bison ranges. Hard to believe all this had ever been farmland. Now they tracked the bison from orbit, and robots harvested them.

The land-use regs said your house couldn't be right on a migration route and had to be at least a mile from all other human structures. We'd had good-sized herds passing by all fall. Maybe the bison had changed their migration route without telling the government.

"Yeah, I suppose." I pulled down another beer. Notre Dame was playing OSU in low grav—with the new hoseline systems it only took a day to go to the moon, and the forty-three-man lunar version of the game was a lot more exciting since it allowed for real aerial work, leaping over the opposing line, and the pop-up QB. "I don't know, though, Sadi. How long have we both been with the Organization? And people I knew back when are chiefs now. We're still a couple of dumb field grunts. The money's not bad, the life's not bad, I'm not complaining. I just wish they'd ask me, once, for the hell of it, just to make me think they care what I think, before they threw a war. Especially since I don't get what this one's going to be about."

He reached for the chessboard. "Okay, let me see if I can show you what's going on."

"You don't know how to play chess," I pointed out.

"I'm just going to use the pieces to show you."

I shrugged. "Okay. But you still don't know how to play chess."

"I'm just going to use the pieces to show you. Then if you want to play chess, you can play with yourself. You've been playing with yourself a lot lately, bud, and so have I, so after I get this explained to you about the war, let's talk about what we do about getting laid. Talk about violence, gotta talk about sex to balance."

Late October, 2048. I was due for transit in three weeks. I had been living under the name Ulysses Grant, which was a small joke for me, and since the USA was long defunct and anyway Ulysses was such a popular men's name in the late 1990s (which people would have judged to have been when I was born), not many people noticed. The occasional history buff was about it.

This transit was going to be the same old drill: Sadi would check me through a bunch of phony aliases and hospitals for six months, then help me get restarted once I recovered. We'd have eight years till Sadi transited, and then I'd do the same for him.

The only complication this time was that it was about time to relocate. I hated giving up the house out here on the Plains—we'd been coming back to it for more than twenty years, by switching ownership between our i.d.'s—and I hated, more than that, to see things coming to an end, but according to the Organization, it was just as inevitable as the Eurowar, Long Boom, Great Crash, and Gray Decade had been. They had a team of experts some place that figured out what was inevitable, I suppose.

Sadi and I had bought this place early in the Long Boom, shortly after the Organization re-found me and we partnered up. When the Crash of 2032 had hit, the house was paid for and most of our money was in cash, the ideal way to go through a depression.

"The thing to remember is that in a deep depression, the prices will fall to historic lows," Sadi had often said. I'm sure he'd read that in a book someplace. He always made it sound like he was my investment counselor or something, and his foresight was why so much of what we owned was cash in safes in secure places. When the real reason was to keep cops and tax guys off us.

Well, whatever the reason, all that cash would buy eleven times as much in 2048 as it had in 2031. At least we'd had some fun during the Gray Decade even if no one else had. It had made us richer than ever, and who's going to argue with that?

"Did you ever pass through here in the old days?" Sadi asked, "back when there were still interstates and McDonald's and little towns and that? When you could get your kicks on Route 66?"

"You didn't either," I said. "We looked it up, remember? Route 66 was all gone before either of us was born."

"Ahhh." He drained his beer most of the way, grabbed a You-4, popped it under his tongue, dissolved it in the beer still held in his mouth, and swallowed it in a gulp. "You still want me to show you why the war's going to come, just like the Organization says, just like those worried-looking buroniki on the flashchannel keep threatening?"

"Do I really get a choice?" I asked. "Shitmaryjesus, look at that."

The holo we were pulling off flashchannel was projected right in front of the porch, lifescale. Looked like six meters in front of the steps was the fifty yard line of the game being played on the moon—see right through it if you just unfocused your eyes. One September afternoon we had watched a herd of bison charge through a porno movie, their hooves shaking the earth and their thick, hairy hides brushing against the walls of the house as all around them fifty-foot women with tits the size of automobiles sucked on seven-foot dicks. It had been a sight to see, especially on a lot of You-4, gressors, and beer.

What was happening now was almost as much fun; a kick line of OSU cheerleaders right there, a bunch of sweet little honeys with perfect bodies.

We whooped and cheered and had another beer each, and I thought that had gotten rid of the stupid subject of the war, but as soon as the holo went back to the game, he was setting up that chessboard again.

"Okay, now pretend this tall white one with the cross on top of it's the Pope—"

"It's the king," I said.

"In this game, it's the Pope. Now the one we've got's pretty talented and pretty tricky and all that, but he just *isn't* PJP. He doesn't have the moves. So all these little guys—"

"Bishops. And the sides go by colors—"

"Not in this game, and bishops is perfect. All these guys are trying to get their own corners and run that, you see, exclude everyone else. See, four corners and four bishops. But they can't sell their ideas for shit. Which didn't used to be a problem, because old Paul John Paul kept them in line so they didn't need to have any ideas, and *he* did the selling. They're finding out that while they've just been taking orders and processing the bodies that PJP brought in, the cybertaos"—he pulled out the queens and rooks—"have been getting fucking good at recruiting." He put the rooks and queens around the center of the board and dragged the pawns into piles around them.

"So they don't stand a prayer. *Unless.* You see, unless? Unless they can enlist the cybertaos to go in with them. And the cybertaos would just love that, because any idea that gets too *close* to cybertao ends up *being* cybertao, which is why the Jews and Muslims and Hindus have all gotten so paranoid about cybertao—because they've all lost millions of believers overnight. The poor fucking Buddhists and Taoists just disappeared entirely, you know?"

"I lived in this century too, Sadi, and right now I remember more of it than you do. So what's your point? Yeah, everyone knows that the Ecucatholics are ripe to splinter, there's a lot of bishops ready to break with Rome, and when they do they'll ask the cybertaos in to help them move their brand of EC. So what the fuck?" I handed him another beer.

"I know we'll get into it, buddy, the Organization's always there when shit goes down."

He laughed. " 'When shit goes down.' Talk about blowing your longtimer cover!"

I laughed too. "Well, yeah, but in such a groovy way." That cracked him up, and then we had the bands out for halftime with some majorettes, so we walked out into the holo and followed their butts up close, talking about them (of course they couldn't hear us or see us, they were just holos, but it was fun anyway), and that time I thought for sure he was off the kick.

No such thing, pos-def no way, unh-unh. The game started again and there he was fumbling around with the knights. "Well, see, here's the thing. You can do a lot with psychorrects and shit, and a lot with combined CSL tactics and all, but when you come right down to it, if you don't want a brain to think the wrong thoughts, the surest way is to put a hole in it. You can do all you like with intelligences that aren't in bodies, but it's the ones that *are* that call the shots. If you shoot those bodies, that settles the question. And who's got the expertise in shooting? Us horses."

"Knights."

"Even better. Samurai." He tossed me another beer and I took a long gulp of it. "See, the struggle isn't going to stay diplomatic and religious forever. It can't. It won't. And then there'll be a real market for us. Not just around the edge like dealing You-4 and shit. Not just loans and construction and running hos. Real work. Kick some butt. Make some bucks. And fun too. Remember what it was like to have a woman all by herself, no cops, and do whatever you wanted, kill her right in the middle if you wanted?"

I almost choked on my beer, and then I started to tell him about that little German girl I'd murdered, the one that was living with the computer nerd ten years older than she was, she was bare-naked and sobbing over the nerd's body, how I'd made her eat the gun to the trigger guard, pulled her black sweater up around her neck, how small and perfect her breasts had been as I stroked them just before I pulled the trigger and how her head had gone apart. It made me feel so bad that I just lay there crying and sobbing while Sadi tried to get me out of it.

The comedown off You-4 can be like that, and once it starts, a diskster load of them won't get you back up. You get crying and you can't stop.

I thought the little German girl's name was Alice, and that was the name I was calling in my sleep all that night, according to Sadi, but when I checked my werp I had no record of her name. I was sure I had seen it on the marriage certificate on her wall. Anyway, the next morning I was feeling better, having sobbed it all off in my sleep. Besides it was pretty hard not to feel better when Sadi fixed one of his monster breakfasts.

"Just the same," Sadi said, "we know what's coming, bud. Time to start the disappearing process and get you under wraps. You got an i.d. even started?"

I yanked out my werp and grinned at him. "Here we go," I said, and pulled up the master for it.

He looked over my shoulder. "Fred Engels? You're on a history kick. No more of those after this one. You don't want to get a pattern going, you know."

"Tell me about it, Joseph Andrews. Who was Tom Jones before?" Sure, he'd had to explain it to *me*, but who said a *cop* couldn't be an English major?

He shrugged. "Well, I won't call myself 'David Copperfield' next time. So is yours all in order, bud? Can you give me a file to take care of?"

"Jack the werps together and I'll do it for you right now," I said. "Now, you were saying—"

"Well, I thought maybe we'd take some of the throwaway cash and go throw some of it away up at one of the supras. It'll just go to waste otherwise." We had hit on the tactic, when it was time for one of our i.d.'s to disappear, of establishing a pattern of wild spending just before, leaving a substantial wad in the bank to just lie there, and scattering a few blank checks and credit numbers around to insure there'd be withdrawals after we disappeared. It made the exact date of disappearance hard to identify and also made it look like the fake i.d. had been killed and robbed, by the time it came to any police AI's attention. That made a nice, cold confusing trail to nowhere for anyone trying to follow us.

"You're right," I admitted. "We need to make Ulysses Grant look like he's off on a spree."

"You know I'm right," he said, and put through a signal for a robot cab. "One spree coming up. Got your keeper box and other junk in order?"

"Always. Ready to jump to the next life when you are. What kind of spree did you have in mind?"

"Well, the supras are expensive, and lots of vice is legal there. I was thinking Supra New York. We can get it onto your debit accounts that you're gambling and losing, and maybe have a serious ho habit and a tendency to gobble You-4 like popcorn. Which you do of course. That should make you look like a small-time hood who got careless on a spree."

" *'Louie Miller disappeared dear/After drawing out all his cash . . .'* " I sang.

"What's the matter, Lassie, is Timmy caught in the fence again?" He poured another large mug of coffee and plunked it down in front of me. "Drink that and let's get some more potatoes and bacon into you. You're not as young as you used to be and we need to get some extra weight on you before you transit. But yeah, in fact, I had another idea, we can maybe help each other out on this. Suppose it looks like maybe I looted your accounts—a couple of them, missing several others— shortly after you vanish. Make the AI suspicious."

"And then what? Getting yourself watched by the cops isn't exactly—"

"That's the beauty. If they just *think* maybe I did you, I go into the back-burner file as the guy to arrest whenever they find Ulysses Grant's body or other evidence he's dead. True?"

"If you say so. We can hack Interpol's system, scan a bunch of files, and see if that's true."

"Way ahead of you, I've already done it. Answer is, they like to solve murders with minimum effort, especially when it's social scum like us, bud, because us killing each other is a *low* priority. So as long as it just looks like one of us doing the other, they leave it to the AI to remind them, once there's a body."

"Hmmph. So . . . I *get* it! When the 'suspected murderer' disappears, it makes it look like they can close the case on the 'victim,' right? Every time one of us transits the last police records of the other go inactive. Slick. How long before they notice that chain of victims?"

"Length of four or so I guess. Thirty-plus years. A lot can happen in that time. Why worry?"

"Unhhunh." I gulped coffee and shoved in a mouthful of the scrambled eggs he'd plopped down in front of me. It was never fancy but Sadi could cook. I thought about our plans some more. "Yeah, a spree in Supra New York, I think. Then we make it look like our boy Tom Jones did something rash."

The biggest advantage of losing your memory every fifteen years is that there's a limit to how sentimental you can get about anywhere or anything. I took just the bags for a vacation (clothes and my werp), plus my space allocation box. On my way out the door, Sadi turned and picked something up. "See if I'm not right, bud. Try to remember it for the next trip around, and note it in your werp."

I switched on the recorder and said, "What have you got there?"

He walked in front of the werp's camera eye, and said, "Okay, official prophecy from Sadi, currently Tom Jones, and your old buddy. When you wake up in 2049, I'll buy you a steak dinner if there's not a war on, and if we're not in it somehow, Paladin." He held up a white knight to the camera, then tossed it to me.

I clicked off the werp and muttered, "That was pretty goofy. It'll just confuse me after transit." The chess piece went into a pocket, or my bag, or something. I don't know when or how it got into my space allocation box. I'm pretty fussy about what goes in there.

We joked around a few more minutes. Faint hoot from outside—the robot cab out of Tulsa Dome. We grabbed the bags that were always packed, and our keeper boxes, and went out the door, leaving it unlocked with all the home security software wiped. Better if the place got burgled; it would destroy and scatter more evidence.

The diskster that hovered a few inches off the grass was a first-class job—no point in being cheap—comfortable, spacious, and all ours. We figured we'd catch it all the way south to Mexico City before we got on the maglev to ride down to Quito—a splurge, but this was *supposed* to be a spending rampage.

We took more You-4s and gressors and ordered a big onboard meal. With the extra time to swing by the pickup point for the diskster to grab our meals it would be five hours till the Mexico City station. We left the windows sealed and told the robot to give us lim speed. That meant every so often it lurched wildly when it dodged a bison, didn't see a cactus till the last minute, or had to jump a fallen overpass, but it also meant we would get to Mexico City way ahead of normal schedule, and kind of splashed up with liquor and disheveled. A few cameras were bound to look at us. If they checked the tapes we'd *look* like two guys on a spree.

From Mexico City we took the express maglev to Guatemala City and then the high-speed undersea tunnel to Quito. Since it would take two days for the train up the cable to orbit, no matter what, being in such a hurry to get to Q-town looked pretty goofy too—just as we wanted it to. We partied some more in our compartment with a couple of disposable girls who had just wanted a ride from Guatemala City, Japanese I think, if the recording in the werp of two naked Asian girls was made when it says it was.

We knew we'd done a pretty good job of establishing ourselves as scum on a spree when we got held at the cablehead for a couple of hours and NihonAmerica made us put down a return-ticket deposit.

The train ride out to orbit was just like it always is. You pass the Condor station, outside the atmosphere, in twenty minutes, at the speed you're making, but then it's still forty-five hours till the train pulls in at Supra New York. As you climb the grav falls steadily, which is kind of fun, and there's a couple of hours there in the middle where you can look back at the Earth and see that it's far away, SNY isn't more than a bright star just yet, and the kilometer-wide cable seems to stretch to infinity in both directions. Okay view.

But mostly you just take drugs, hire a girl, or go down and play in the casino car, once you're beyond the atmosphere and it's all legal. Most people on board are tourists; the corporados and plutocks flaunt their money by taking fast private-track cars, or the even more expensive rocket service that leaves from the same station as the Condors.

I spent my time in the cabin by myself, sorting through the mementos, getting drunk and reviewing old records on the werp. I got to feeling extremely sorry for myself, and for the whole world. Maybe I just had some weak You-4 and was coming down off it harder and faster than I expected.

Because I got all sloppy and regretful the whole way up, I read through the werp and found out who Alice was. Thank god not that German girl. Naturally then I checked, hacked a netwide search on her global i.d., and in about an hour found her working—at least pulling wages—in a dance bar up in Supra New York.

When I mentioned that to Sadi, he grinned and said, "Now there's something you can play with."

"Play with?" I took a long sip from a big bourbon and ice.

"Well, you know for all practical purposes you're her dad, bud, am I right?"

"I don't remember her."

"But she remembers you. Except she'd figure you ought to be about eighty years old, right?"

"Something like . . . yeah, that's what she'd figure."

"And she's gotta be what, fifty-two? Good shape, too, if she's still shaking her titties for the crowd, especially in a high-price joint like they have up in the Supra. Well, you're in good shape too, and you don't quite look fifty. Wanna see if she's got an Electra complex?"

"What's that?"

"Like a female Oedipus complex. See if she gets hot for guys who look like dear old Dad?"

I shrugged. Reviewing the records had brought back some stray memories, mostly things when she was a little girl. Nothing that would get me all hot for her or anything. "Sure, I guess. You got something in mind?"

"Just an experiment. Let's see how she takes it when you walk into that club . . . you can't know till you try. It won't be boring I bet."

Nobody ever figured out why the supras were so much like the originals. Supra Tokyo was crowded, rude, and bewildering, but clean and safe. Supra Berlin was badly lighted, cold, and decadent. Supra New York was where everything and everybody was completely for sale, like some old analog sound recording I had when I was a kid said "where they roll you for a nickel and they stick you for the extra dime." I used to love the freedom there.

The dance bar was called Titswingers. The women flipped around in zero g and shook their breasts. Usual lez show. Usual dildo show. Usual bid board so you could buy what you wanted. I got restocked on You-4 and then sat back to see what came out, brushing off a couple of bims that were trying to B-drink off me. Not that I couldn't afford it or that it wouldn't have been good for my cover. Just that I wanted the table free if Alice was working tonight.

Sadi had said he wouldn't come along the first time but he admitted one reason he had pushed me on the idea was that after looking at some of the shots of Alice in my old werp he was a little hot for her. I said she wasn't eighteen anymore and I wasn't so sure that picture was even her but he said he liked her attitude, not her body.

Anyway, so I was in there alone, riding on You-4, though a longterm user like I was doesn't get that great glow a lot of people do—it didn't seem like the place was wonderful, just that I was happy. They said if you kept using it you'd have to take it, like a vitamin, just to avoid depression when you got old. I figured I wasn't going to get old for fifty years. Meanwhile it made me happy.

After a while a bored-looking woman, a fat blonde wearing a pair of fake fox ears on her head and a fox tail on a short stick stuck into her ass, swam by and asked what I wanted to drink. I said lots, didn't care much what. She suggested their champagne, which was going to be outrageous in price, so that's what I took. She asked me if I wanted any company at the table, probably hoping it would be her.

I said I'd know what I wanted when I saw it.

At first I didn't recognize Alice. All I remembered was the pictures, and she'd had herself genaltered, the popular new form of cosmetic surgery, and then surfaced, so that the flesh had grown back according to the new genes. That had given her two big firm tits, a flat belly, and vivid strawberry-blonde hair, but she'd kept her basic face with just a lift. Maybe she liked it, maybe she'd just been afraid of what might go wrong with having that surfaced—every so often you saw a bad regen, a woman who looked like the troll dolls they had when I was a kid. Some women, especially an old bim like Alice, would be scared pissless of that.

She looked as good as thirty-five-year-olds that took care of themselves used to look. I watched her loop around in the central space. She mostly just shook those big tits, no art to it at all, so I figured if I flagged down the fat blonde in the fox rig and sent word that that was my choice, it would be no trouble.

Figure again. "Anastasia never B-drinks," she said. "Is there anyone else you like?"

"Can I just send her a drink and have you point me out to her?" I asked. I had assumed it would be easy, but when had anything connected with that girl been easy?

"We can try that. She *might* take a look at you before she just takes the drink and stays in the dressing room. Then again she might *not*. She tends to treat customers like shit, you know? Like the bitch is too good for anybody. I don't mind telling you the owner's pissed because Anastasia turns away business, and she won't peddle ass on the bid board, either. Treats the place like a fuckin' *job* if you know what I mean. No kind of ho-*stess*."

About five minutes later Alice came out, in a dressing gown, and sat down next to me. She didn't say anything right away, but she took another drink when I offered one. I flagged the blonde in the fox rig, who seemed to be pissed at Alice. Younger women always seem to think they have the right to be the most attractive person present, and they get mad if a guy wants somebody older.

After a minute or two I said, "You remind me of someone I saw in a picture a lot, a real long time ago."

She sipped at the little ladylike drink—something that looked like lemonade—and said, "Funny, you remind me a lot of somebody I knew a long time back, myself. I don't know if he ever had any kids or anything. You any relation to Josh Quare?"

"Uh, you could say that. He was my dad but I never knew him all that well. Wasn't home much."

"What happened to him?" She leaned forward.

"He died working outside on one of the transfer ships, trailed off into the exhaust. I don't even remember which transfer ship. It was a long time ago." That ought to be vague enough, if she checked, but for good measure I added, "I think he was working under some other name."

She sighed. "My first husband's retired now, on Mars, but he was an officer of the Vacuum Workers Union a few years back. He'd have a record of a guy who died outside. Maybe I could track him through that. Or do you know any more about him?"

"Not a thing, and I'm not even sure that's right. My mom's dead too and the thing about Dad dying was one of the last things I heard from her, so I never got any other information. Like I said, I didn't know him well anyway."

"Well, you're the image of him," she said. "When were you born?"

I was in the fog of booze and You-4, just coming down off of it, but I had to answer that one fast, and I couldn't think of a thing to say. I also knew I'd picked up Alice in the Eurowar and she'd left before she was twenty, so I said, "2012, it's just the gray hair throwing you. I'm just a kid really. And of course I've been outside a lot, on the ships and the supras. Would you be, uh, Alice?"

"I used to be. Yeah, I guess so. Alice was the name I grew up under. Your father was my stepdad." She peered at me closely. "You look a lot like him but you sure didn't inherit his genes for aging. It took me a long time to figure it but just from stuff he let slip I figured out he was ten years older than he looked. But you're ten years younger than *you* look. You don't mind my saying that, do you? I mean, you look okay, distinguished and everything, but if you're only about thirty-five . . . well, you've had a hard life I guess, or something."

"Or something. No offense taken." I took a long, slow sip of that cheap champagne—to really appreciate it you had to have your hand on some bim's leg, I guess—and considered. "Yeah, Dad had a lot of pictures of you that he'd taken at one time or another. Four or five, I mean." That was how many were in my werp. "When I was growing up there were five pictures of you on the wall."

"Well," she said. "I guess we can both see how we've turned out. I work in these places, and you come into them."

"Probably his influence," I agreed. Long, awkward silence. I tried thinking about things I could do next.

Start with the craziest possible idea: tell her.

No.

See if I could take her to bed—or even get her alone and make her do something, just to see what it was like? No again. "You ever have any kids?" I asked.

"Three," she said. "Two of them by a rich guy that wanted me for his toy, but didn't want his kids raised by a bim. He handed them over to the nanny, first thing. One kid that used to write now and then, that I had back when I thought I was going to get on the *Flying Dutchman* and travel with my first husband. I think that kid gave up on me."

To fill the silence I asked, "So what became of them?"

"The older boy's exec officer for the *Dutchman* now; you remember those officers that stopped the mutiny last year? Well, he was one of them. That's how he got promoted up from the engine room really fast. I guess that if he was one of the loyalists, that means he probably helped push some of those mutineers out the airlock like they showed on flashchannel. I scan the ship news for his name; I never wrote back to him so he stopped writing, I think after his dad stopped making him write. Last picture I have of the kid, right before he stopped writing, is from his first date, some kind of a prom or something. I sure hope he didn't marry her because she looked like the puddle you'd get in the road after a four-day ugly-storm. But still he turned out better than the other two. The boy I had by the rich guy is working on drinking himself to death, last I knew, and messing around with a lot of You-4 and all that, middle-aged and fat at thirty and looks like hell and never had to do a useful thing in his life. He'll probably dry out after his old man dies and he inherits. The youngest is on about her fifth divorce. 'Fraid I'm just a pile of fucked-up genes. Murderers, drunks, losers . . . must be my genes because I didn't raise any of them."

"You don't seem like a bad sort to me," I said.

"You haven't seen much of me. Just those pictures and whatever Josh told you."

"He always spoke very kindly of you," I said. It sounded like a line in an old movie. Like something I ought to say.

She nodded, sniffed. I saw her eyes were wet. "He would have."

In zero g, if you want to get out of a chair, you have to unfasten the belt, and though my hand groped tentatively for the fastening, I didn't unlatch it. The moment passed too fast for me to reach and touch or hold her. Don't know why I wanted to. Must've been a memory or something. Probably when she was little I'd had to do that a lot. Maybe because I liked her or maybe just to keep her quiet. Kids are that way.

It made me feel disoriented. Already I was thinking, right now I'm about her age physically and next year I will be ten years younger. It's like everyone's falling down into the well where you start as a baby at the top and you end as a corpse at the bottom, only I get to climb back up every now and then, so I see people whizzing by, people who start out behind me and plunge on down into the darkness ahead of me where I can't see where they go. And here she goes, into the dark ahead.

I have a memory of introducing that kid to her first bathtub in years. It was weeks before I could get her to spend less than an hour in it every night. Alice used to scrub in that hot water till she looked like she'd been boiled. I have another memory of that harsh-smelling Reconstruction soap in her thin black hair, and the feel of her bony arms wrapped around my neck. I think she had a nightmare and I needed to get her back to sleep.

We had a couple more drinks. She proposed a toast "to Josh." It made some kind of sense. The guy she was drinking to *had* been a better guy than me.

It got later, I got tireder, and after a while we had nothing to say except we both missed Joshua. That was all poetic and stupid like a movie. Still, I was drunk enough to appreciate it.

I paid to walk her home early—which meant the owner thought I'd bought her for the night. Probably it got Alice slightly out of trouble and anyway it got her out of there early. The way she thanked me, over and over, on the way, was pathetic.

I let Alice go home by herself when we got to the tram station. We were already out of things to talk about. At the tram station, she hugged me once and said I was a prince. We knew we'd never hear from each other again.

The whole thing had cost me a pile of money, but spending a pile of money was what I needed to do just then. Call it a good night's work. When I got back to the room Sadi and I were sharing, I told him that Alice had been on vacation so I'd just stayed in the club and gotten some action off a dancer. I didn't think Sadi—or anyone else—would get a chance to hose Alice while he was here; "sorry about that," I added.

"Oh, well," he said, and got that faraway look in his eyes like he always did when he was going to make a joke that I wouldn't get, usually jokes about philosophy and that, " 'The best-planned lays of mice and men,' you know."

FOUR

To Be Born?

Sadi's gone from the records. Must have been erased during the War of the Memes. Likely a traceraser—whenever he died or went undercover, a self-replicating program woke up and hunted through the net to destroy any reference to him.

Usually you can still find the person afterwards: gaps in serial numbers, money flowing in and out of banks without specific accounts, parents who wrote down one child more than the system can find, all that. The Copy Transference Recovery Database has nine hundred million numbered trails in the records without names—tracks left by tracerasers. Some of those must have started as fake i.d.'s, some as real people. It doesn't matter to the system. The name has vanished, but the chain of holes in the records still says "someone was here, once."

I run a big search across all nine hundred million. Even with a superMPP built into everyone's werp these days, it takes three full minutes to get back to me.

Not one of those numbered personae could have been Sadi. Not one probable hit in the search. Must have been a damned good traceraser.

Most can only wipe a name, but this one, after it nailed all the names, went back and built false continuers—hundreds of fake i.d.'s linked to points all over the chain of recorded events that was Sadi. It not only erased the name and made a hole in the records, it went back and filled in the hole.

So Sadi was important enough for the Organization to send a very sophisticated traceraser after him. Maybe he's still alive, maybe even still with the Organization. "I haven't seen weather like this since I was a kid in Ohio." Sadi himself? Some cop who cracked an Organization file? Most likely, the Organization has found me again.

One problem with having a screwed-up memory, and only the kind of record that I can manage to keep in the werp with my lousy writing skills, is that I don't know who I did what to and when. Sadi, or the Organization, or a cop, or for all I know that German chick's kids, might be out to kill me, hire me, anything.

I have to reply to that ad, but the idea scares the hell out of me. What if it's Sadi? What if it's not?

I hope his password's as burned into his memory and as scattered through his records as "I haven't seen weather like this since I was a kid in Ohio" is for me.

My little white cubicle has no window. I need to get out. If there's a rebate for not using all my time, it'll track my account down sooner or later.

Walking around Red Sands City, letting my mind drift. Weird stuff I'd rather not think about. Put an audio tour guide on the werp.

Red Sands City is a third-generation Martian city, settled mostly by native-born Martians. It looks down onto the crater floor below, so that one edge of the enclosure's much higher than the other. The whole town's on five excavated ledges plus the rim—the transparent enclosure is in the shape of a gigantic slug just crawling up over the cliff, so water will gather in the top part of the enclosure, filling the little artificial lake on the clifftop.

Within the giant slug: tidy square straight streets, staircases, escalators, all the buildings squarish, pink concrete, Disney cliff dwellers. Outside the enclosure: disorderly mess of q-huts, little pressure domes, pressurized c-block buildings, trash heaps, Sears Marshacks like the one I woke up in. The jumbled heap's plastered all over with solar collectors and baby MAMs, interwoven with thumpered dirt trails, rutted and pitted because nowadays it rains every couple of months.

I watch for a while. Not much difference in the activity inside or out. People in pressure suits outside don't look any more busy, or any less, than people inside on the walkways. Probably there's more illegal stuff out there, and probably the illegal stuff in here is worth more money. That's usually the pattern.

I could go full legit this time, retire, drift through the next fifteen years without doing a thing. Today I'm feeling that lazy. I sit on a park bench up by the top-level lake, stretch my legs out, and look over the city.

After a while I tell the werp "Place an ad. 'Connections and Memories' section. 'Seeking tall male comma thin comma brownish hair comma uh probably gray comma uh vet colon Murphy's Comsat Avengers comma we had a house once in Kansas comma Louie Miller disappeared dear comma quote marks When I see places like this I always wish I was back in New Orleans close quote marks.' Finished. Take out the uhs. Post that and alert me if anything comes in on it."

I sit back on the bench and bask some more. In a while I'll take the elevator down; I can afford any of the three hotels in town. I wonder how I got such a large pile of cash together as an ecoprospector. Reviewing the werp I see again that the life before this, as James Norren, I woke up from transit with my accounts intact but no sign of the Organization. I got into ecoprospecting for no reason I can find evidence of, made a lot of big strikes, spent almost nothing.

There are fewer records of my most recent life than there are of my first two lives, before I had a werp. I think about that. I can prove it was quiet. I can't prove it was unhappy.

I've gone legit before. And life wasn't half bad, if the werp is to be believed. But I know the werp can't be believed. I hope not, there's three places in there where I confess to killing Sadi, one where I say I killed Alice, one where I say Sadi did.

But that doesn't mean any particular thing in that werp isn't true.

But it can't be trusted.

But.

I laugh at it all and stretch. A mother walking with her kid stares at me for a second, as if I might be dangerous. Well, that's the way, I guess.

Somewhere down in Red Sands City I could probably get some gambling, some You-4, gressors, a whore. It would be something to do, but it would take energy. I'd rather sit here on this bench and soak up energy.

People move fast on Mars. A lot of them in here are half running. Out beyond the enclosure the dust plumes of the trucks streak along. Funny, it's not like life's short. With extension technology everybody makes it to 100 or so, and before the transfer ships left the solar system talk was *they* had found a way to live to be 250 or 300.

Probably all the scurrying around, the way people run out to meet the trucks and race up staircases, is a combination of low gravity and just the way Martians are: everything needs to get done right now. Figure they're making a whole living world out of a barren one, there's a lot to get done.

Then suddenly I remember a very dark night on Mars, years ago when they were all very dark, when there was so much less air that it wasn't much different from the moon . . . darker still because I was sitting, with hundreds of thousands of others, on Olympus Mons. And as the thought comes back, I remember the rest of it.

With the collapse and disappearance of the Organization, our suppression of closed timelike curve research must have stopped. And apparently it was an area pretty ripe for study, because the people on the transfer ships got it figured out in just the short years it took them to get out of the inner part of the solar system.

The big barrier to time travel was always causality, the same reason nothing could go faster than light. You can't have the effect modifying the cause, just as people traveling back in time and shooting their grandfathers before they had any children was unworkable. But there was a kind of loophole—you *could* travel into the future faster than regular time. Traveling close to light-speed would do that. And it didn't matter, really, which time you traveled along as long as you traveled along some time or other.

That part confuses me, so I ask the werp. It explains time splits and curves back: where there's a singularity, a place where matter becomes so dense that it isn't exactly in the universe we know anymore, but the *place* it occupied still is. I don't get that part very well.

Anyway, out of a singularity come a whole bunch of lines of time, very much like the line of time that we and the whole universe are in, except that for the "subtimes" both their beginning and their end is at the moment the singularity was created. Those little subtimes start out into the future just like regular time, but they gradually curve backwards until finally they are going all the way backward (relative to our time) and end up at the place where they began. It's sort of like we're on the only highway that goes anywhere, and there are all these big looping exit ramps that come off the interstate of time, but then just swing around and feed back onto the highway right where they left it.

What that means in practical terms is that while you can't reach your own past, you can make it possible for your future to reach you. When it does, there's no grandfather paradox—because what happens is, you get two futures. So you make a singularity, and later have children, and they have children. One grandchild decides to get rid of the rest of the family, gets into that loop, rides it forward as it curves around until it rejoins his own past, and then shoots you. Then, as an adult, he lives on into the future that you never see, which doesn't contain his parents. But because on the whole trip nobody ever moved backwards in the time line they were in, he has parents and grandparents in his personal past, and he continues to exist.

That's why it's called a closed timelike curve. It's "closed" because it only runs through one part of time, eventually bending back to its origin (where our universe is open—it keeps moving forward in time). That bending back is the "curve." And since you can follow it and exist in it just as you can in regular time, it's "timelike." If I got that right.

Anyway, the transfer ships had set off the bomb to make a giant singularity out at 100 AU, way out where the comets come from, and then scattered out to settle five solar systems. A thousand years or more in the future, they would send ships back from those colonies, a whole huge fleet and army, either to retake Earth from Resuna, or at least to seal up Resuna on Earth forever.

We'd had one message from that fleet already—they had informed us they'd be arriving in just about 300 years, and would need permanent accommodations for one hundred million people. *That* was why everything seemed so urgent here; the whole population of Mars was currently that of a city the size LA had been when I was a kid, and somehow in just 300 years they had to get ready to move in the whole population of Japan. They could do it, no doubt—but it was going to be a push.

And that probably percolated down from planners to politicians to managers to bosses to foremen . . . so that everyone got in the habit of running around like they were part of a kicked-over anthill. Hence all these people rocketing by me, or scrambling around out there outside the enclosure, and the occasional dirty look I was getting from people who were walking fast and looking worried.

When I lived at Gwenny's, she used to have a cartoon on the wall, one of those things that migrated from fax machine to fax machine, of a bum on a bench saying "Work is fascinating, I can watch it for hours." Well, it's true.

I sit through the long afternoon, watch the sun go down, and catch the elevator down to the Radisson Red Sands, which is about like every other pricey hotel in the last 150 years, right down to the same room service menu. I order a pizza, watch the news, and go to bed early without setting the clock.

The next morning there's no reason to check out so I don't. I grab a shower, change clothes, toss the dirty ones into the bag to be freshed, send the pressure suit in for routine maintenance, and I'm out the door, just me and my werp, to take a long stroll around the city. I can walk down every street in this town today, if I want to. There are worse ways to kill time.

I eat a long breakfast at a place doing its best to look like a European streetcorner café. As I'm having the third cup of coffee, the werp beeps. An answer to my ad.

It could be something I don't want just anybody to hear, so I take it on the screen rather than putting it up on voice. The message comes up. I HAVEN'T SEEN WEATHER LIKE THIS SINCE I WAS A KID IN OHIO.

My heart jumps up. Has to be—

IF YOU'D STAYED PUT I'D HAVE COME OUT FOR YOU.

I grin. Glad I managed to make it a little tough. I'd hate to have him think I'm getting soft.

LOOK BEHIND YOU.

Oh god. Oldest werp trick there is, sneaking up on someone and then contacting him via his werp. Kids do that all the time. I turn, ready to say "Sadi."

It's not.

She's wearing a plain black dress, a little out of place on Mars where coveralls are more usual. Her hair, amazingly enough, is still blonde. I can't see her eyes behind the dark glasses—

It can't possibly be Katrina. She was at least ten years older than I was, couldn't look more than five years younger than me now, at best. *This* woman doesn't look thirty.

"It's been a long time, Josh," she says.

It's definitely, really her. I close up my werp case, stand, extend my hand; she gets up, takes it, shakes firmly once, then pushes her dark glasses back off her face. She's smooth, unlined—maybe twenty-five in appearance. "We need to talk," she says. "Your hotel room."

She must know where I'm staying. She heads straight for it though I say nothing.

When we get to my door, she presses her thumb to the doorplate and it opens. For some reason the hotel thinks she's staying with me, I guess. Maybe she is.

I follow her into the room. The maid's already been there. My bag and the returned, tuned-up pressure suit sit neatly in the corner, but the rest is anonymous like any hotel room. She turns and smiles. "You must be hopelessly confused."

"It's been pretty baffling," I admit. "Are you really Katrina?"

"I have been. Look closer. Study my face . . ."

Like I have no will of my own, I walk toward her, mind blank. My eyes follow the curve of a high cheekbone, the thin lips that seem to be about to make faces at everything, the big, wide eyes. You'd think if she's really 160 or so, and especially if she's been with the Organization all that time, it would show somewhere, around her eyes, in her expression, somehow. But even around the eyes she looks like a twenty-five-year-old.

"You've known me under another name," she says.

I look more closely. Did I read or do I remember that something like this has happened before? Yes. More than once. Not recorded in my werp, but it did.

Shit, I think, looking at her, never wondered what a rejuve job would do on top of that anti-aging stuff. Genaltering and surfacting has gotten so far along that if you're willing to spend six months dreaming in a tank, doped up on painkillers and drifting in a deep virtual reality hallucination, you can come out looking like anyone they can recode you to, but I thought your age caught up with you within a year or two. God, she looks good.

Something in her voice, too. She knows me. Her voice touches me like a hand gloved in soft leather, and holds my heart like—

Then I feel my right hand begin to turn, ever so slightly, the fingers begin to work, and I know that if I held my white knight in my hand, it would be appearing and vanishing between my fingers, neatly, quickly, never where you would expect it.

"Sadi," I say. "Jesus."

"Right on the first guess," she says, and steps into my arms. My cock gets so hard it hurts. Her tits are soft, heavy, warm against my chest. The muscles of her back are hard and strong. She's undoing my belt even before I sit back, pulling her onto the bed beside me, our mouths still locked.

ii

Scuttlebutt in Murphy's outfit was that the ice dam across the St. Lawrence wasn't going to breach this year at all. We had been wandering uselessly around Syracuse Ruin since May, supposedly waiting to make an attack on a major node across Oneida Bay as soon as the lake drained back and the land was exposed again. But now it looked like what everyone had been saying—that the St. Lawrence was due to stop flowing for good sooner or later, because every summer the time it flowed got shorter—had been true.

This year we were fighting for One True, because it had offered us more money than any other meme had. We were contracted to destroy the Carthage Ruin node—an Un-reconstructed Catholic memo running on it was re-infecting millions of AI's and thousands of people. Supposedly if you got infected you'd start hearing PJP's voice telling you that Ecucatholicism was all a mistake and you had to kill everyone who wasn't a strict Catholic, plus you'd suddenly have all these false memories of growing up in a very uptight old-fashioned Catholic school and of being the star student there.

Anyway, if the ice dam wasn't going to break, we'd have to walk around the bay instead of across it. So in little groups of twos and threes, passing word to each other when we met, we had begun to drift south out of Syracuse, up into the hills, then north toward Carthage Ruin. Moving slowly and carefully, doing our best to look like scattered and isolated travelers, Murphy's Comsat Avengers might be able to assemble near the node by late September. Months late and some of us wouldn't get there.

That night in our tent, Sadi was talking. As usual. I was working some passes from the *Boy's Big Book of Magic*. Found it in the storage vaults for a public library, and that white knight I always carried in my pocket was exactly the right size for doing all the little palm-and-finger tricks, which I was getting good at.

After all those years and lives together, Sadi and I didn't really converse. Sadi talked and I listened. I liked it that way. The knight gave me something to do with my hands while I listened to him.

"Trouble is," he said, "we're still losing people. No question about it."

I made the knight slip into my sleeve on the thumb side, out on the little finger, brought him through the middle, popped him into my palm. Years before I might have said, "How do you figure?" or "I don't see how you can know that," but nowadays Sadi could just assume I wanted him to go on.

"Figure our last twelve rendezvous, right?" He totted them up on his fingers. "Four times we met with a party and fought. Twice they snapped out of it—must've been a weak meme. Once we killed them. And once we all had a meme and we attacked each other. Good thing we had a pistol shot that time to jar us out of it. And a real good thing it wasn't you or me getting shot. You saw how tough it was for the guy's partner."

I knew that as well as he did. He liked to tell stories. I liked to hear them. Mama would have called it division of labor. I kept the knight moving.

"So figure one in three times we make contact a meme activates, right? And what, maybe one in four is a strong meme then? So in twelve contacts, about six months, out of a total of, let me think, I guess thirty-one guys counting you and me, three died. That's ten per cent per six months. Toss in no new recruits anymore. Not figuring what happens at headquarters, ten per cent dead per six months, figure it's twenty percent or so per year. Used to be if an army had ten percent killed it stopped functioning."

"They're not like old armies," I pointed out, letting the knight slip around and into my other hand, covering the drop by bending my fingers. "The memes just contract us to do a job, and they hire the size unit they need for the size of job. Besides, we're not organized in fire teams or anything; really we all fight on our own. An outfit could die till nothing was left but the headquarters company, and *that* could keep fighting."

"Yeah, but unless they know how many men they have left—"

"They know," I said. "That's why Murphy's sitting behind a wall of bodyguards that are never allowed net access and a bunch of AIs that run on continuously re-encrypted operating systems. So he can use his werp all the time. Sure, *we* stay offnet for safety's sake, but when we check in or when we make our contacts, the count gets relayed to him. He knows."

Sadi sighed. "Right as always, partner. Want me to read you anything?"

I shrugged. "Go ahead and read if you like, but you don't have to read aloud. I'll just sack out."

"Yeah." The way he said it made me think he would go on, but then he didn't. Any time Sadi stopped being talkative something was wrong. I looked up at him.

In the light of the little flickeret, he glowed sort of flame-color. His brown hair was streaked and spotted with gray, now, as if he'd been painting a ceiling not too carefully, and his thin face and high cheekbones made him look like one of those elf-warrior guys on the covers of the books I used to read when I was squatting on my ass in the desert during the First Oil War.

He looked good. Three years till his next transit, five years since my last, we both looked like we were in our mid-forties, though I was almost a hundred and he might have been a bit over.

Sadi stared off into space, started to speak, thought again, stared. Usually when he did that I'd catch him watching me from the corner of his eye, seeing if it was working, if I was about to start saying "What? *What?*" Though a lot of times he just talked, Sadi liked to have my complete attention for something important. So he'd stare off into space to make me ask him.

But this time he really was staring off into space, which I hadn't seen him do much. Finally he spoke again. "Do you suppose that we're going to know when to bail? I mean, get real. The War of the Memes is winding down, bud, has to be. Nobody new joining the armies, memes merging and consuming each other, someday there will be one meme and no soldiers."

"Uh, it's a small world after all," I said.

For years after that I tried to remember whether he had blinked, winced, flickered, had a twitch in his face, anything. I still don't think so. He just smiled as he usually would and said, "Better luck next time."

"It's a small world after all" was our trigger phrase. We'd used some of Murphy's memeware and built a binary chaser for each of us. When one of us said "It's a small world after all," normally it activated an old Disney meme that both of us were carrying, followed by a simple chaser to turn it back off. The whole process of calling it up and getting rid of it took a tenth of a second at most. But if there were a new meme in either of our heads—if somehow we'd been penetrated by something we saw, read, or heard—the meme-and-chaser cycle would trigger something that looked like an epileptic seizure. That would give the uninfected person time to get us tied up and treated. The most common memes out there nowadays were ones to make you attack the person you were with. If you didn't catch it in time, your best friend could kill you.

Sadi had passed the test, and I sat back. "Okay, I admit, when I thought you'd been memed, I wasn't paying any attention to what you were saying, so what were you saying?"

He shrugged. "Oh, a leading question, I guess—whether we'll have any idea when to get out of the war and go do something else, because pretty soon either One True, or maybe one of its competitors or a mutation, will take over the whole show. The armies aren't getting anybody new and they've attritted like crazy. And think about the way a meme works—basically it's a set of ideas with a compulsion attached, right, that ties into the deep structures, all those places where the brain and mind overlap?"

"Thank you, Doctor Science."

"I'm saying this out loud because I'm trying to think it through. Really, honest to god, Josh, I know I lecture too much but I'm just trying to get this to make sense to me so we can think straight about it. Now, look, the way they work is they attach to existing beliefs. And it's easier to attach to an existing meme, but by now everyone has at least some small memes. Right? And as the number of different kinds of memes goes down—because they combine with each other and take each other over—it gets easier and easier for one meme to sweep the whole system. Right?"

"Makes sense," I admitted, because it did and because I was tired of him lecturing me. I worked a tough faked pass to cover a simple real one. The knight slid around in my fingers like a trusted old friend, always everywhere you want him.

"So the armies are shrinking and there's just a few kinds of memes left. In a pretty short time, there will be just one and it won't need armies—it'll need cops. And the cops will have one job—make sure everyone has the master meme. Right? You know I'm right. It's coming, Josh, I told you this war was going to start, back in Kansas, and now I'm telling you it's about to end and once it does there will be no place for us to hide, whether we're on the winning or the losing side."

"So what's your point?"

"We've got to get out past radio delay," he said.

I didn't know what the hell he meant. But non sequiturs were like the biggest red flag of all. "It's a small world after all," I said, and triggered the backup as well, "To sit in solemn silence in a dull dark dock."

He shook his head as if he'd had a neck crick. Was that the sign? If I had been a little more clever . . .

The trouble was, people were only as clever as they had been during the Paleolithic. Perfectly good brain for mating and whacking animals and running away from tigers. All gravy beyond that.

But memes were getting more and more clever. In the middle of war they evolved as fast as weapons or generals. Of course in a way they were both.

The war had been raging ever since some bright guy had figured out how to write a program that could analyze any operating system it talked to, figure out how to penetrate, and get in and take over AIs. Whoever it was, he'd probably never realized that to a program like that, a mind's just one more operating system on a slow-running massively parallel processor—probably he only meant, as a loyal cyber-

taoist in the chaos of religious violence sweeping Earth, to make all
the banks, autopilots, navigation software, and medical robots go
cybertao.

Whether he intended it or not—and for that matter I had no idea
whether or not it was a "he"—he'd about conquered the world for
cybertao before Ecucatholic memes had turned up to fight back,
quickly joined by Sunni and Shi'ite memes and the mad-dog guerrilla
memes called Freecybers. Now the whole First Generation—cybertao,
Ecucatholicism, RPs, Newcommies, Freecybers, Slammers, every
meme that had begun the battle—was long extinct, except copies in
museums.

It had to go that way; the most effective thing for a meme to do
was to take over, copy, or digest another meme. Competition was
fierce and fast; nothing lasted long.

Mercenaries like Sadi and me, and everyone in Murphy's Comsat
Avengers, worked for memes but didn't talk to them. We did what they
told us to do and they paid us.

Probably three quarters of the world's human population was now
running One True or one of the other memes. They weren't exactly *not*
themselves but they weren't exactly themselves either. Like after a
religious conversion, kind of.

I stared at how Sadi rolled his neck after I triggered our chaser and
our backup chaser. Strange move for him, but it really looked like just
a crick. No use *asking* him. Memes could lie better than people.
"Well," I said, "what is it you'd like to do?"

"I want to power up a werp and check the situation. If the numbers
don't look good we bail. And from now on we watch for when we
should get out, before it's too late."

"Too late for what?"

He shuddered—or maybe it was a spasm. "I don't think the
memes—or the meme, let's face it, One True or something descended
from it's going to win—will let any uninfected minds exist after the
war's over. I think once the profit's been made from the wars, we want
to get out to where the radio delay's significant."

"*Space?*" I asked. The memes had not been able to take hold in
the terraforming projects, the asteroid cities, or the transfer ships
because radio lag provided a natural barrier. A meme needed to inter-
act with what it was infecting, quickly enough so that the person or AI
under attack would accept the responses for an instant or two without
question. An AI or person who was more than a few light-seconds

away had too much time to think between responses for the meme to get a grip. It helped too that when the War of Papal Succession had turned into the War of the Memes, the space people had seen what was coming and started all kinds of quarantine measures so that nobody could send them a whole copy of a meme.

"Space," Sadi agreed. "And the question is, when is it time to jump? Figure Earth is going to be effectively cut off from space at the end of the war. This Resuna idea that One True has won't work if ideas are dribbling in from space and stirring the pot, because the idea of Resuna is everybody gets the same personality, and if some of them are talking outside the system they won't stay the same. So no question in my mind, once Earth is all Resuna. there's going to be an embargo, blockade, call it what you want but money in our Earth bank accounts won't be worth crap. The question is *when* we want to take our muster out, catch the next transfer ship, and end up rich out in the solar system somewhere. And if we wait too long, we'll end up here as happy little processors running One True, thinking One True thoughts and doing whatever it likes."

"Well, then maybe we should jump now," I suggested.

"I've thought about that too." He glanced down. The flickeret shone off his face, making it look warm, though nowadays in upstate New York it rarely got above freezing on a summer night. "But let's be honest about this one, bud, hunh? If we wanted to play it safe we'd have gotten out a while ago. We're as rich as we could ever need to be, you know. We ought to just bag it."

"Let's."

"You're kidding, right?"

"Naw." I hadn't thought about it for anything like as long as he had, of course, but then thinking about things for a long time was something he did for fun. I didn't want to be one more copy of One True, and as soon as Sadi pointed it out it was obvious—stay on Earth and I would be, sure as all hell. Yeah, when I left there'd be no coming back. But that doesn't matter when you really *have* to leave. I've had houses I loved but if they were on fire I left.

He sighed. "Just like that. Should've figured you would. Can we still run the werp real quick? I just figured out what numbers would tell us when to jump, I think. We could just pop onto a flashchannel for a second, depth it to get statistics—and you know stats are safe, they have no power to compel attention at all—and be back out before anyone knows we've been in."

I shrugged. "Suit yourself, but why bother with the numbers? No point in waiting around when running out now will work just as well. And it seems to me that any number you get off a flashchannel has probably been buggered a dozen ways by memes, for their own purposes."

Sadi said, "You're right in principle."

Sadi always said "You're right in principle" just before he did something dumb or pointless. "You want to check?" I asked. "Keep it short."

"Sure, sure." He uncased his werp, set it up so we could both see it, turned it on, passworded it, waited a second. A picture sprang up on the screen, I don't know what of. I sat back for a long breath. The edge of my little frame cot pressed my leg, my pants were rubbing my thighs, I could feel the very slight tingle of some grain of pollen that I was just a tiny bit allergic to in my left sinus, the one that runs between your nose and your mouth—

I knew!

Sadi was not my friend he had never been he had never intended to be what he was was a useless parasite who talked too much and always talked down to me like I was a goddamn *moron* or something and he'd shat all over my memory of what I had done to that German girl that poor kid I'd raped her mouth in front of her babies and then shot her dead with my sperm still dripping from her lips and that had made me feel like shit like total evil I had been burned by guilt and he'd just laughed at that laughed at my guilt at her babies just encouraged that just wanted to hear about it because it got him so fucking hot and horny to hear about that girl she was so young and so pretty and she was probably devoted to that poor stupid fuck who rescued her I blew his head off and then I found she was just getting fucked when he got up to see who had kicked down his door so I was hot to see her like that and I kidnapped her and killed her kids except I kept the girl and raised her and named her Alice and that was all Sadi's fault he wanted me to tell him those things and that Alice left home when I raped her like I had her mom and Sadi made me take him to the club at SNY and afterwards he fucked Alice and told me how it was she was a snotty bitch he said so he had to hit her and hit her and then it felt so good when she sobbed he got done he cut her up bad and then slapped her around and humiliated her he married her that summer and they didn't invite me he made all the guests do her on the floor he spread himself out and had them all do him he had eaten my shit and deserved to that was what he wanted I had had such a good time been such a good boy done good things done things good grew up killing and raping he made me feel bad about it I wasn't innocent when he was done I was always in fear of him that was why I did it he made me ashamed of what I had done he made me like it he did it all because he knew it was bad for me he did it all to make me evil to make me not guilty to leave me without the love of God and now I saw Little Lord Jesus look down from the sky Jesus and Lenin and my mother Sadi raped Mama Sadi raped Mister Harris Sadi raped Grandpa Couandeau Sadi made me say I wasn't sorry Sadi kept me from going home Sadi was evil Sadi was all evil Sadi evil Sadi evil Sadi evil Sadi evil Sadi evil

flashed into my brain in less time than it takes a breath to catch. Just as I was vowing to Jesus that I would not let Sadi lead me astray anymore, just as I was understanding that I had a personal commission from Comrade Lenin to deal with Sadi's betrayal, just as I was calling Mama and telling her I'd be home for a visit—

That son of a bitch grabbed my throat and tried to choke me.

I struck back, hard, with everything I had. We got our grips and sank them in. Our little shelter went crashing and rolling. He tried to dig out my eye with his thumb; I got a hand free and slammed him in the side of the neck. He beat the back of my head against the hard edge of my cot frame; I kicked him in the belly, turned him over, got a full nelson, and pressed with the whole strength of my body . . .

The human neck is strong, and Sadi was a big, strong man in good condition. It takes a lot to break a neck, but I did it.

His neck crunched like a joint of frozen beef breaking in half, and I wrenched and twisted his head, bucking it back and forth to make sure the spinal cord severed.

I felt his body go limp. For good measure I slipped into a carotid grip and held it for a two-minute count, as hard as I could. When I finally dropped his battered, twisted body onto the floor of our shelter, among the strewn mass of our possessions, his face was contused by the internal blood pressure I had cranked up on his neck.

I put my head back and laughed, laughed, laughed, for the pieces that made me up had at last found each other again, after migrating into these two bodies and then calling up the third piece, and it was a good trick on Sadi and me, and it was *funny* to see him dead like that—

And then, too late, the chasers won out. Sadi was dead. My hands were still warm from where they had clutched his body to squeeze the life out of it. The last laugh strangled as I fell to the floor of the tent, weeping, screaming, clawing my face with my nails.

iii

It's past lunch time before we're really done with each other's bodies. We call up room service but otherwise we just lounge around in the afterglow.

No question. Katrina and Sadi are the same person, and physically she's in her mid-twenties or so.

"All right," I say, "You owe me some explanations."

"Oh, I agree," she says, her voice purring and warm. She snuggles against me and adds, "After a nap, you know."

Drifting off to sleep I think I will wake up and discover that this whole thing's a hallucination. But when I wake Sadi's in my arms. Her eyes are open. We rise without speaking.

It's three in the afternoon. "Let's get dressed and take a long walk," she says. "I'll tell you everything, but we have tons and tons of time. There's no reason to rush *anything* anymore."

We end up on the bench, up by the lake, where I sat yesterday. I suppose if anyone looks at us they must think I'm her grandfather, or maybe her customer. She checks something on her werp and says, "Okay, there's no listening device within a hundred meters, and we have the net bugged—if anyone starts recording us the werp will sing out. Say something distinctive."

"Uh, clap your hands if you don't believe in fairies?"

"That's if you *do*. Every time some child somewhere says 'I don't believe in fairies,' a fairy falls down dead."

"Well, you would know children's literature better than I would. It looks like you just got out of childhood. It's been awhile for me."

She giggles. "Yeah, I suppose so. All right. I have three great big bombs to drop on you, things that will change everything, and I'm just trying to think what order I should go in. I guess I'll start with the smallest bomb first, the obvious one. If it had been entirely up to me I'd have always worn this female body, but I got the surgery in the early years of the Long Boom, because when I got assigned to go out among the vags, back in 2021, it just seemed like being an attractive woman would be dangerous. So I figured, well, here's one whole lifetime as a male and then at the next transit the sex change will undo— that happens, you know, as part of the regeneration—and that will be fine. But instead I ended up partnered with you, and—well, it's hard to explain. You got to be important to me."

"That's not hard to explain," I say. "You got to be important to me, too."

"Yeah, I know. Well, anyway, the thing was, it was a male-to-male friendship and I wanted to make sure it kept going. So I managed to get some stuff through a back channel to keep the sex change from undoing, and I went through transit, and there you were, taking care of me."

"You looked like hell," I said, remembering, "but it felt good to care for you. And it was such a relief when you finally were lucid and could talk again."

She nodded. "That's what it's like for us, isn't it? We need the care and the help and we need it from someone we can count on. Anyway, then once I'd done it the first time, decided to be a man, I found there were other advantages. The male body is clumsy and awkward but it's a good body for violence, and that was mainly what we were going to do. And obviously it's the only body for serbing. I never much cared for sex like this but you know all those old feminist bitches were right, it *is* about power. I love the way they look after you're done with them, you know, girls or boys, you've stolen their soul, left your mark on them forever. Do you remember some of the things we did?"

"Just what comes up when I look in the werp." I look out over the terraces of Red Sands City, full of quiet people doing their quiet business, and say, "I know I enjoyed a lot of it but all that stuff's behind us now. Earth is two billion Resunas without crime or violence, and the space cities and the ships were never very violent or dangerous. I don't see what there could be another war about. I think it's probably about time to put all that shit behind us, don't you? And to tell you the truth what I remember, and read off the werp, of my past two lives is that I slept a lot better and it didn't feel awful to be me."

She sighs and snuggles against me. "Yeah," she says, "it was always a little trouble to get you back into having fun whenever you transitted. You'll see when we take you through revival."

"Revival? Is that what the process is called that makes you, uh—"

"The apparent age I am? You bet. Congratulations, you just set off bomb number two, the middle-sized bomb. Here's the short on the deal: you get to live a lot longer than you thought you would, and do it with a young, healthy body. Not available commercially and with luck never to be discovered elsewhere—we've got people working on making sure that it's not discovered independently, you remember, the same kind of work you and I used to do on CTCs." She giggles. "Remember Doctor What's-his-dick and his little wifey and their daughter? That kind of thing. Every so often just for kicks I go along on one. It's almost as much fun to watch, I think; like I said I was never into that male body but I love that feeling of male power.

"Anyway, yes, we have the revival technique now. Works on any longtimer. I don't understand a lot of it, but apparently if your body already knows how to transit, then they can push you into a transit, and then make the transit go all the way to completion so that you end up with a completely new body, instead of about a ten-year regeneration. While they do that there's some stuff they do with the brain so that not only do you keep all your memories, you get all your old ones back."

"You mean like now, you have a perfect memory till the next time you transit?"

She beams at me. "You don't suppose the Organization stopped doing research after the longtimers took over? They found a way to bring back *all* your memories—except for the transits themselves—completely accurately. Including your memories of what you thought happened while you were still reconstructing them after every transit, if you see what I mean. You'll be able to remember both what you believed and what was actually true, and keep them sorted out, just the way you know the difference between what was a dream, what was real, and what you remember from someone else's stories. Not perfectly—most people get a few false memories out of it—but good enough so that you can figure out what actually happened to you. Your past life's going to make some sense to you, finally."

My eyes get wet, yet I don't feel much inside. She holds and cuddles me for a little while and though I still don't feel much, I sob a few times. "Completely normal," she says. "You never forgot those things, you see; it was more like every time you transitted, the pointers got reset so that you couldn't find most of them. It's all still in there, wanting to come out, and you want it back, so even though you don't 'know' what's in there, you're emotionally overwhelmed by the possibility of getting it back. It comes out physiologically but you can't touch the feelings yet. It will all be a lot clearer and easier to deal with once you go through revival."

"Does it hurt?" I asked.

"You go into the tank for six months and have a lot of nice dreams. The time passes like nothing. Then you come out and you'll remember everything. And you'll be physically somewhere between nineteen and twenty-five. For maybe a month after that you'll need to sleep a lot to sort it all out. And even though your memories are very clear at that point, you'll spend a few years finding which ones you want to access—there will be just too many to go through all at once. But that's all the trouble it is. And after that you're just like anybody, except of course that you're living for hundreds of years, physically in your mid-twenties. You're going to love it, Josh—I've talked to you in the future, and you're going to have so much fun."

"*You've talked with me?*" I take a very deep breath, lean way back onto the park bench, and let it out.

She smiles at me again; she has hardly stopped smiling. "I said I was going to drop *three* bombs on you. Number one was my being a woman. Number two was revival. But number three is bigger than both. Have you gotten around in your reading and remembering to recalling where the transfer ships went?"

I think about it and I do remember—and once again, I'm over-whelmed. The fleet of five transfer ships, out at 100 AU from the sun, set off a matter-compression explosion that created a singularity, the base point of a "closed timelike curve"—a thousand-year loop into the future. Now any spacecraft could simply take a turn over into the adjoin-ing, backward-running temporary universe which had extended out into the future from that singularity. And once in that backward-running universe, anything could move back in time as far as the orig-inal singularity, re-cross to our universe, and thus enter its own past.

Of course you needed a really big nuclear bomb for the initial energy to establish the singularity. Bad idea to make a big singular-ity—one large enough spatially for the five-kilometer by one-kilometer cylinder that was a transfer ship, and extending a thousand years or more into the future—anywhere within the solar system, so they'd waited to construct their singularity for a couple of years until they got out to 100 AU.

With the singularity in solar orbit, the transfer ships would be able to return to that point in solar orbit at any time within the thou-sand years before it merged back into ordinary time. It was the door-way back.

That doorway built, the five ships—each with its crew of ten thou-sand—had scattered to the nearest stars where the light-speed probes, launched fifty years before for Deepstar, indicated solar systems which had both habitable worlds and minable asteroids. Drives running flat out, the transfer ships would reach the star systems they were heading for in a couple of centuries. That would give them some more cen-turies to get civilization under way around the new stars before dis-patching fast ships back to the Earth system, traveling toward Earth backwards in time around the closed timelike curve. The hope was that a huge, technologically advanced force from the future could at least help the colonies to confine One True to Earth, and perhaps by the time the ships came back, they might even be able to think about invading and freeing the Earth itself.

If they didn't do it, sooner or later One True would find a way to break out of Earth, swallowing up the solar system colony by colony, bringing them all into Resuna. In a few thousand years One True might even spread to the stars.

According to the fast probe that had popped out of the singularity a decade ago, the ships from the future were still three hundred years away, but when they got here they'd need accommodations for a hundred million people. That was the last that had been heard from that source. Meanwhile, observations of Resuna from covert flybys seemed ominous; at a minimum they were putting up fifteen more supras, and why build a space port if you're not planning to go somewhere?

I realize I've been sitting here slackjawed while all of recent history runs through my head. I had read it a bit and a piece at a time, to explain parts of newscasts or to understand fragments of memory, but this is the first time I've thought of the whole story.

Sadi's still looking at me, smiling patiently. At last I say, "Yeah, I do remember. The first time I remembered was the other day. I was just wondering why Martians always seem to be in such a hurry, and then all of a sudden I remembered why everybody's just trying to get it together for when the ships come back, three hundred years from now or so, and they aren't sure they can get their terraforming done in that time. So it's all focused into the future and hardly anybody pays any attention to what it's like now."

"That's it." She stretches, yawns, and pulls my arm around her. "All right then. You're about ready for bomb number three, the big one. You'll probably guess it as soon as I say, making a singularity was something almost anyone could have figured out how to do ever since the first atomic bombs and the first rockets that could get outside the atmosphere, right? Because all you have to know is how to position the reflectors to form an infinitely regressing perfect virtual image. When the image gets dense enough for phase reversal, the whole thing instantaneously converts to exotic matter; it's not really any more complicated than an ordinary hydrogen bomb, phase reversal MAM, or single massive-photon laser, as long as you know what you're trying to do.

"Right." I suddenly realize what the truth must be and blurt it out. "So the *Soviets* made a singularity and used it?"

She nods. "Back in March 1987, when the Soviet Union was decaying fast but they still had an effective space program—and while the Americans were pouring all their effort into dealing with that space shuttle that exploded and had no time for anything else—there was a semi-covert robot mission, carried out by teams from the space program, weapons research, and KGB. The weapons research people had only figured out that they might be able to make a singularity, that it was dangerous, and that therefore they might be on to a new weapon; the KGB was in it because they were into everything."

"You said 'semi-covert.' "

"Unhhunh. You can't hide three missile launches in a period of days, especially not ones big enough to leave Earth orbit. The Japanese, Europeans, Chinese, and Americans watched it leave and monitored the transmission but they still didn't know what was going on.

"The Soviets put three satellites into solar orbit. The first one was just a relay station, something to relay signals back to Earth, concealed as an unannounced, failed Venus mission. They leaked information that the second one was supposed to be a secret solar observatory for the Soviet Navy to provide early warnings of solar flares that could cripple their communications. That one was really a scientific station that went all the way 'round the sun, to a point just short of 180 degrees from Earth in its orbit, so that it was hidden by the sun. And right at that 180-degree point—"

"The third one must have been the singularity constructor," I said. "So they fired that off on the other side of the sun. Of course. It took them what, more than a year to get there? But it was too dangerous to try on Earth and you couldn't hide it in near-earth space, so it had to be somewhere where the traces would be lost in the glare. So that's how they found out how to make one?"

"That's how they made one. The singularity implosion didn't look very useful as a weapon, so they gave up on it and left the data in the files, not knowing what they had. But they had produced a closed time-like curve, just like the ones the transfer ships made for themselves, though much smaller—only 144 years in diameter and only big enough for a small ship. They didn't know how to use it at the time, of course—because the theory of a singularity producing a CTC wasn't yet developed. And they thought their data was hopelessly scrambled because it looked like a lot more matter came out of the singularity than had gone into making it—but there was nothing wrong with their instruments. What they were seeing was a steady dribble of spacecraft sailing out of the singularity. All very small craft. And a lot of those were *us*, Josh. You and me. We just keep going around the loop, making the twenty-first century more and more the way we want it."

I thought about that for a second. . . . "How long do we actually live?"

"Oh, well, when the Organization figured out how to use a CTC, back in the early 2000s, we went back and looked at the Soviet observation satellite's records of the singularity, and we put up an observation satellite ourselves. And the answer seems to be that about fourteen thousand ships went through. Figuring most of them are you, me, or both of us, say we each make ten thousand trips through a loop of a bit over a hundred years, that's a million years." She shrugged. "Once you get used to the idea you stop caring. But you're always you, and from your own local perspective time is always running forward, so what else matters? Maybe somewhere in that sequence we find a perfect version of the twenty-first century, and decide to fire off another singularity constructor so we can do a billion times through the twenty-second. The point is, thanks to relativity, we can skip over the bad parts, and thanks to revival, we never get old. We get to be together at our favorite times in history, *all* the time."

She's looking at me very intensely, like it's important that I be happy with this. I don't know why I'm feeling funny about it. Finally I say the first thing that pops into my head. "That seems like a lot to do for a couple of employees. The Organization must really have changed while I wasn't watching."

"Oh, you were watching," she says. "You just didn't *know,* the first few times through. While the struggle was still going on I had to conceal my operations from both you and my earlier self, mostly for your own protection since there would have been people looking for you if they knew you were important to me. But nowadays, Josh, since around 2070, all there is to the Organization is me, plus the hired hands. I own it, it's all mine, now."

iv

Every time before, Supra Tokyo had been grim, orderly, quiet. You knew you didn't fuck around, they knew you'd behave.

Today the air stank of fear. My ears ached with the cacophany of thousands of people trying to argue a reason why they should live.

My best reason had just failed—I'd pulled out enough platinum to make anybody a billionaire and Captain Space Prick had just sneered and gone on the next. I'd been smart enough not to try drugs, the people on the transfer ships never used them much—a few decades before when the Organization tried to get an in that way, our organizers got massacred.

So though I didn't understand it, I knew they didn't like drugs there. I had never realized they didn't like money, either.

Fuck 'em then if they didn't want to make any sense.

I passed back through the crowd to the waiting area. Lots of people were trying more than once but since the only people at the admissions table were the same two spacers—a snotty rat-faced bitch named Rodenski and a pompous fat bag of shit named Harrison—and they seemed to have good memories, it looked pretty stupid to try to get in by iteration.

The year before, the transfer ship *Albatross* had been almost grabbed by the Unreconstructed Catholic meme on its last Earthpass; they'd had to kill twenty of the crew in the process of keeping it out of the control of that meme. That freaked the *Albatross* crew—there's practically no violence aboard the transfer ships, usually nothing worse than a punch in the nose, and what with all they had all been teenagers or younger when the adults left the ships in 2024, and with life extension, whole decades went by without anybody dying on one of the ships. Twenty in a day, shot, left them in hysterics, though any realistic person would've known that was nothing.

The hysteria was really unnecessary anyway, because the Unreconstructed Catholic meme was extinct by the time the next transfer ship arrived. One True had won the war and taken control of the Earth—which it was rapidly turning into Resuna—but the transfer ships had vowed they'd never trust a meme again, no matter how many assurances One True gave them. They were all modulating orbit so that they would not pass nearly as close to the Earth as they had before, which meant a longer radio delay and hence made infection much more difficult. But it also meant it was going to be much more expensive to get to Mars, Venus, Ceres, or the Jupiter or Saturn systems.

But they had been willing to strike one very limited deal with One True. They would take all the people they could carry in one trip to the colonies—any refugees who did not want to join Resuna. All you had to do was be at one of the supras during the last pass of a ship, and get far enough up the list.

All you had to do.

All the people they could carry was hardly any, compared to how many wanted to go. The bottleneck: short time to load—the transfer ships didn't even come within the moon's orbit. The shuttles to and from them could only run for about six weeks (four weeks before and two after the Earthpass) at most, and it took a shuttle around a week, round-trip. Fifty shuttles times five passes times six round trips per pass times 1800 passengers per shuttle worked out to 2.7 million. About half a million on each of the five transfer ships.

Total. One-way trip. Coming back for nothing.

There were at least twenty million people packed into each, supra during each pass. And out of the sixty million who were lucky enough to get to a supra, 2.7 million—fewer than one in twenty—would actually escape. The rest would go back down the cable into the One True society where everyone would be Resuna.

The trick was figuring out how to get to be one of the 2.7 million, especially since I was older, male, single, with a criminal record two meters long if they happened to check my thumbprint against their database. Which they were bound to do. They *needed* reasons to reject refugees.

All that was why Supra Tokyo echoed with keening, wailing, shrieking. People pleading. Showing pictures. Rejected families selling their children to those yet to apply. I had been in this vast steel cave before—it had been advertised as "the largest dance floor in the solar system," on the flashchannel. (They cheated, in zero grav you could count all the surfaces.) I had never seen it so crowded or so loud.

The queue was messy. You can't keep kids still anyplace. In zero gravity it isn't even worth trying. The line wound around the inside of that giant box like a spring coiled in a can, people hanging on handholds, and with the person on one side of you a thousand people ahead in line, the temptation to muscle in got pretty strong. There were fights and squabbling all over all the time.

The Supra Tokyo cops were already One True, and that helped, because One True was fairly gentle, for a meme, and took better care of bodies than some of them did. Still, the cops had their hands full and if you looked around at the coated walls along which the long spiral of humanity ran, you could always find a fight someplace.

As I drifted through the center—the exit route—I thought, my platinum coins might as well be chewing gum wrappers for all the good they were apt to do. Not sure why I was doing it yet, I pulled out a couple handfuls of platinum coins and flung them all around me, letting myself tumble as I went and not worrying. I hit the catch net at the end and scrambled out. The noise behind me had just started.

I guess I'm sort of sorry. There were fifteen dead or so from me doing that, most of them kids. Once people saw that much money—one platinum coin was worth more than most people made in a year—they went for the coins. But their place in line was just as precious, and a lot of people grabbed places rather than coins, triggering fights. I hadn't pulled myself more than a hundred yards along the corridor outside before the screaming din behind me got even louder.

Then the screaming was drowned in thunder.

A long life of healthy habits had me moving fast before I thought what the hell that might be.

I had heard something like it before, but not as loud. I remembered. People zero-g dancing, when a place was really crowded. They made that sound by springing off the sides. But this was a thousand times louder.

Feet and bodies, slamming into the walls. Those with some zero-g skills were leaping back and forth, grabbing coins and places. Those without were getting beat up and thrown around. Most of the thuds were made by feet and hands as people bounded against walls, springing off to change direction. But a lot of them were people ramming into the walls at high speed, smashing on protruding handholds or thudding heads onto the unyielding metal. The inside of that room rang like a giant drum.

I moved faster. No idea how many people had seen that I was the one responsible, but for sure once they figured out platinum coins had started the riot, Rodensky and Harrison would tip Supra Tokyo cops off and they'd be looking for me.

Then I realized why I had done it. Instinct, on my side again. Nineteen shuttles docked at Supra Tokyo. Major riot underway. Not enough cops to guard shuttles, for the next few minutes anyway.

I had no idea how anyone could stow away. But I would.

Either I was going to find a way to get on board one of those things in the next couple hours, or they would catch me. Supra Tokyo was a few kilometers across nowadays—maybe a tenth the width of a full moon from Earth's viewpoint, not the mere bright star it had been when it was first built—but it was still a space station, with so many internal checkpoints, airtight doors, cameras, and microphones around, that anything I did I'd better do quick.

Or I could always go back down to Earth and become part of One True, be Resuna. Like shit.

I wished Sadi were here. According to my werp he'd always been quick with an idea when you needed one. And I had expected him when I last woke up from transit, eight years ago, but the Organization (before the memes had destroyed it) had only said that he was busy and it would be a while before we could be assigned together, on the werp it said I'd killed him, but also it said he'd killed me—he said he needed my werp to help me and had to kill me to get it.

Well, he'd never showed up, and my Organization pay had stopped coming. One True had killed four Organization agents that I knew about. And we'd never been able to hit back. Why it hadn't killed me, I had no idea. So I was all alone in the world, just me and my wits, like back when I was starting out.

It worked out simpler than I had thought it might, once I decided to trust my gut and improvise. I found a big secure area, with many waiting rooms for people cleared to board the shuttles. Then I heard alarms going off and realized there must be twenty other people trying to slip through and setting off guard beams. I slid under a guard beam that no cop was backing up and I was in the secure area.

The people in the waiting rooms kept their boarding passes where they could watch them. Small wonder, they were worth killing for.

I slipped into a men's room by the waiting room nearest the next shuttle to depart, and waited in one stall, floating in a curled ball so that it might look like it was just locked for maintenance, carefully maintaining a position where through the crack of the door I could just see the entrance.

Guys came and went. Lots of them. Mostly just from boredom, I suspect—taking a piss is about the only thing you can always do. A lot were in groups; forget them. Guys way older than me. Little kids. All that. A very tall blond guy, my age but nothing like me. Ditto two dark black men, one after the other, and an Asian. I sat, floated, waited. Relaxing all my muscles, getting ready to move when I had to, I watched through the tiny crack as men came and went.

Finally a good one: by himself, about my height and weight, near enough my hair color. I sealed the toilet and flushed it as if I were just finishing. He had just pulled out a length of disposable hose from the dispenser, slipped it over his penis, and plugged it into the vacuum urinal. He was pissing, not looking at me.

As I went by him, I grabbed the urinal hose and yanked as hard as I could. It probably didn't hurt much—the things were lubricated to fit comfortably—but it startled him and the spray of urine droplets caught him in the face. He cried out, half a breath, half a scream, a little sound lost in the slurping roar of the urinal drain sucking air.

I pulled the hose off its connection and whipped it around his neck. Legs around his waist so that I was riding his back, I arched my back to stretch him out as I hauled the hose as tight as I could, snugging it up under his jaw.

He was in lousy shape and had no idea what to do in a fight anyway, so his arms just waved around ineffectually, and he didn't manage to push me against a wall hard enough to do anything, as we rode around the room. His face got all screwed up and funny looking, and I couldn't help noticing that what they used to say when I was a teenager was true—getting strangled really does give a guy a massive woody.

He passed out in a few seconds. Carotid cutoff is a fast way to go. I took his limp body and slammed the back of his head on the wall a couple times till I felt something give. Then I stomped his larynx, kicked his kidneys, and knotted the urinal hose tightly around his neck, to make sure he wouldn't be waking up later. Didn't matter which he died from as long as he died.

I shut off the roaring vacuum urinal so it wouldn't draw an attendant, and searched my pigeon's corpse. Sure enough, he had a boarding pass and an i.d. that I could use. Better still, nobody traveling with him. I floated the corpse into the stall I'd been in and locked him in.

That would sure be a surprise for whoever cleaned this place later. Well, Supra Tokyo had always been kind of dull. This would liven it up some.

Only took a few minutes. Nervous about it anyway. If anyone had walked in I'd've been in deep shit.

Instead of a thin mist of piss, I thought to myself, and giggled. This was going so well.

His i.d. showed this was Dr. David Stroup, M.D. Most people just went to medical AIs but there were still a few M.D.'s who did research, and to do research they had to treat patients. I suppose the idea was that his skills shouldn't be lost to the human race. Well, they were. On the other hand the human race would be keeping *my* skills. Win some, lose some.

Stroup's i.d. showed he was traveling alone. Nobody would come looking for him, which meant I could use this pass and wouldn't have to wait and try for another one.

I checked his boarding-pass time. Thirty-eight minutes away.

Forty-one minutes later, precisely, having established by watching that three minutes was really close, I raced up to the gate, looking like I was panicking, jammed the i.d. and boarding pass under their noses, said I'd been caught short in the bathroom. I figured if they smelled piss on me so much the better. It would seem more like a guy who'd been in a panicked hurry in a zero-g bathroom.

They waved me aboard.

I wasn't going to go to Stroup's berth—for sure they'd find and i.d. that body within hours. So I looked around for one that had a "still vacant" light on, and found one for George Pillbrenner. I put Pillbrenner's name plate on Stroup's berth—no passenger would ever check the number against the name—and wedged Stroup's name plate, and the urinal hose I had used to strangle him, down between the bunk and the wall. Maybe I'd get lucky, and when they found Stroup's body, they'd check the berth number he was supposed to be in, search this berth, find this stuff, and waste a couple days interrogating George Pillbrenner.

Next step: find somewhere to be during acceleration, and ideally for two days afterwards. I could steal water and food, or since it was just two days manage without them. Save the problem of getting off the shuttle and onto the *Flying Dutchman* for later. Right now, get somewhere to not get caught.

Every acceleration couch in every berth would be full, one way or another. The shuttles didn't boost hard—nothing like taking off from Earth's surface—but they still pulled a good two gee for the first twenty minutes, and you could crack an ankle or get a hernia in that. I wanted somewhere soft to lie down.

I ended up sacked out on top of a pile of wrapped meal packets in a storage bin—they were all being held to the wall by a piece of cargo net. I wasn't sure but figured that probably they'd put them on the engine-side wall, which would be "down" whenever the engine was on. I tucked my feet under strands of the netting, grabbed two more, and held on.

I waited a long time. It got to be an hour past departure time. Nervous, breathing slow to calm myself, more nervous. Always possible they'd found Stroup, put together the timing of the riot and Stroup's death and maybe some evidence I hadn't been careful enough about, were searching for me, were just about to open the door . . . right now. . . .

The catapult shoved us and I lurched into the pile of meals, Then the engines cut in. It felt a little weird as I sank into the slippery pile of wrapped meals, but it beat being dead or back on Earth.

When I slipped out of the storage bin, I had half a dozen meals tucked into my werpsack, along with my werp and my space allocation box. That, the clothes I was wearing—and maybe thirty million in platinum coins—was all I owned. It would do, if I could get anywhere with it.

It was easy enough to fix those meals. You just had to get some water from a bathroom, put it in the vent on the meal, and microwave the meal a few seconds. This shuttle had been a luxury liner—there were a lot of little lounges with microwaves. No problem that way, if I could avoid getting caught.

Mostly I just circulated around, looking like I had somewhere to be, talked to no one. Lots of people still in shock. Easy to avoid conversation.

Late that first day I overheard some of the passengers talking about a stowaway. Some poor bozo had killed George Pillbrenner for his boarding pass and then tried to take his cabin. He'd disposed of the evidence of Pillbrenner's murder, and he had Pillbrenner's i.d., but for some mysterious reason he hadn't gotten rid of the urinal hose he used to kill Dr. Stroup, as well.

The shuttle captain gave him a two-minute trial and then tossed him out the airlock. The shuttle was moving at above Earth escape velocity, so the stowaway's freeze-dried body was on its way into solar orbit. He'd be out there a good long while.

Anyway, with him gone, they stopped looking. The second day they weren't checking i.d.'s in the mess, so I got regular meals. I still tried to stay out of sight a lot.

Poor stupid bastard. Going to sleep in the berth of the i.d. he'd stolen. Obvious amateur. They'd have had him for murdering Pillbrenner, anyway, eventually. No skin off mine if they threw him out the lock for Stroup, instead.

V

Revival is kind of fun. If you've led an active life imagine literally having six months to catch up on sleep. After that, with my new twenty-year-old body to play with, Sadi and I settle down to a "honeymoon" in a big private house she has way out in the Martian desert.

I'm still troubled by all the memories. Now that I know what happened, I feel it, it doesn't seem so bad to me, but it doesn't seem so good either. I don't want to take antidepressants to get rid of the feeling. Sadi's very patient. For some reason this bug or blues or whatever it is makes me horny all the time, and she's willing to have sex with me as often as I want.

Many nights I put the heated suit on, go out, lie in the rust red sand, look up at the stars, and finger the emergency venting valve. Hit that one twice, speak the right codes each time, and I'd be fresh out of air instantly. The transponder would summon Sadi but I'd be dead before she could suit up and come out to me.

The thought's not exciting or comforting or anything. Just a thought.

I've searched the records more completely in the last couple of months. Alice died of old age a while back. Her transfer ship officer son, the one she had with Joe Schwartz, paid for her to come as his permanent guest on the *Flying Dutchman*. The odd thing is, I came to Mars on that ship, though they kept us in the cargo hold and wouldn't let us talk to the crew for fear of memes. I was maybe three hundred feet from Alice and neither of us ever knew.

The report that she was dead came from the *Dutchman,* en route to Epsilon Indi, a few years ago. They were fourteen years out from Earth, then—around 63,600 AU, almost a light-year away. That's a long way from anywhere.

She was a hundred two years old, not bad for an old bim that never took care of herself, when she died.

With my memories back I realize Alice and Sadi were the only people that ever counted worth shit to me.

Alice has been dead, now, for twelve years. Thirteen, I keep forgetting about radio lag. That is, dead in this time line I am living in. There were many other times when I believed she was dead, when I have vivid memories of having seen her dead. Sadi says those are false memories, like the way I remember her killing me and me killing her, or that I remember so many different Boy Scout knives or two different times decades apart when I learned magic. Sometimes I just lie out there in the desert night, staring up at the stars through that thin atmosphere, and try to sort out all those memories.

There's a small river named for Alice, most of the way around the world from here, where I found a good artesian vein while prospecting, during my years as Kindness O'Hart, just before I transitted, time before last. Mars Development Inc. paid me to open it up and let it flow.

The Alice River winds south from the equator, across the highlands, before plunging down a two-kilometer fall into the Mariner Sea. There are Marsform frogs and otters and trout in it. She always liked animals, so I guess she'd have liked that. And since I did that about twenty years ago, if she ever looked at maps of Mars, she might have seen it. She wouldn't know that she was the Alice, of course. I'm really sorry she didn't.

I named it during the time I was Kindness O'Hart; right after I did that, I started to work really hard to make the James Norren i.d. full legit. When I woke up as Norren I spent fifteen years wandering around in the desert by myself, just thinking things through. Didn't like what I thought. Never saw any way to think different. After a while I was just kind of "present," not really thinking at all. So I didn't write much down.

I liked that a lot. I wish Alice could have seen as many Martian dawns and sunsets, as many great plains thinly dotted with green and brand new seas and rivers rolling, as I've seen.

I wish, instead of Quito, we could have shared my years as an eco-prospector in the Martian back country. T hey were good years. They were miserable years of loneliness. Both.

I wriggle to get a bit more comfortable. The iron sands crunch under my butt and shoulder blades. The stars are as bright as ever—a clear night on Mars is like the Arizona mountains, squared and cubed. I sigh, think about it all. More trips through will mean a chance to meet more people, but am I going to care about any more of them?

I never had any friends.

There have been times I've been so tired of Sadi I've wanted to kill him. Her. I guess it'll be her from now on. We've got a million years together. I can see what she likes about me: I listen. I do what she says. I'm all a god needs, an audience.

And she's a god. Every trip through she gets to fix more things and try more experiments. The world's getting to look like what she likes it to. Lucky me that I'm part of it. I mean part of what she likes. Because the parts she doesn't like are going away, and she's really enjoying getting rid of them.

The valve's right there under my finger. I'm very tired. I lie there and finger the button. I feel the words rehearse on my tongue, I know what it would be like to press twice. Then I wouldn't be able to breathe and I'd be panicky and thrashing, and then the lights would go out.

"Josh?" Her voice in my headphones.

"Yeah."

"Just wanted to see how you were doing. Want to come in?"

"I guess. Anything up?"

"Not really. I just kind of missed you. It's been a lot of years without you and now I want to see you all the time. But if you need time to yourself, say so."

"Guess I'll come in."

We get into a fight over something stupid, and we end up sleeping separately that night. It's always the same question—why I don't want to jump back to 1988 together and start it all over again. I point out that if she knew me before, she must know when we will. She won't say a thing about that.

She gets into her Doctor Science mode of lecturing me about the jump for the hundredth time. Never did know when to shut up. Like the problem's that I don't understand the deal. I mean, I understand it just fine. What I haven't decided is whether I want to take it.

"You're just impossible," she screams. She's dressed the way she likes to dress around the house—like something out of a porno movie. Looks uncomfortable to me and I don't see how you can get horny from what you're wearing—I mean, if you're inside, how can you tell?—but she says it makes her feel good to do that in front of me. Don't get me wrong, I like to look, but I wish I knew why she does that.

So I'm looking at this bim screaming at me in a little leather swimsuit and a pair of thigh-high boots, and I'm thinking that maybe I should've just opened that valve.

"One more time," she says. "There's nothing irreversible about this. You can just do it once and then decide not to. You can just be a timeline that only went around once. But just try it. Get on the ship with me, and with relativity it will only be about a year subjective, and then we arrive more than a hundred years back. And then we can do whatever we want for a hundred years, or come back forward if we get bored. I swear to god, Josh, I don't know why you won't try it at least once."

I won't try it for the same reason I won't suck cocks—I'm afraid I might like it, I think. *I don't want to be locked in a tin can with Einstein the Psycho-Slut,* I think. Neither of those is the real reason. I don't know the real reason. But it has something to do with remembering too much.

She's shown me holos and everything else about this. I understand it completely, I understand everything except *why* I would want to do this. You get on the little very fast ship with some dingus on it. As soon as you're far enough from large masses, the dingus goes "bing" and then you're moving backwards in time—or you'd be seen as such to anyone outside your ship. Since there's nothing close to you out in space, from your standpoint it just seems like a hundred-year space-ship ride—at relativistic velocity so it only seems to be a year—while the planets go backwards and broadcasts from Earth are time-reversed.

When you re-enter the inner solar system and pass through the singularity, there you are, back in whatever year you aimed for.

She repeats it all twice, screaming. Her makeup runs all over her face from tears. It's like being reamed out with a physics lecture by a hysterical streetwalker. When she's all done, I just say I haven't made up my mind and maybe she's in the wrong timeline.

vi

The big night, half of the population of Mars gathered on the slopes of Olympus Mons, in our pressure suits, to watch. Of course there were better views on the vid, but so what? We wanted to see the actual flash.

It took a big bomb for a singularity that size, and a lot of matter got sent through some very strange changes. Even out beyond Pluto's orbit, the bomb that could make a big enough singularity—forty gigatons—would be more than visible from Mars. So we all sat and watched, knowing that near that flash would be the five transfer ships, now starships, bound outward.

They would have to get to where they were going on their own, at their miserable crawling acceleration of about one percent of a gee. That meant it would be centuries to reach the star systems, and even with life extension it would be the current generation's grandchildren that would get there.

But if this technique worked, they'd have a way back. A singularity opened up a big loop in time, a "closed timelike curve" so that there would be a backward path in time available from the moment of the singularity until the loop's farthest reach, a thousand years in the future. They could go out, settle the new systems, build a civilization, and then send a ship backwards in time, back to our solar system, to enter the past. The resources and knowledge of the future would be available to civilization back here—and with those, perhaps Earth could be taken back from Resuna, or at least the colonies could be better defended against One True.

Some people were watching because it was going to be an important event in human history. Most of us were watching because it was the last naked-eye-visible sign of the transfer ships, where so many of us had friends and relatives. Alice was on one of those ships. Lots of people had such reasons. I read later that there were four hundred thousand of us on the side of Olympus Mons that night.

True, the flash would not be *exactly* where our friends and relations were. They were firing off the singularity ten million miles from the ships—but ten million miles was nothing at all compared to nine billion miles from us to the ships. That flash would be as much of a wave goodbye as we would get.

Strange to think, too, that the die was already cast—when the light at last reached us, it would be fourteen hours since it had already happened.

Even after this flash, I could theoretically write to Alice, of course—the ships and the home system would still be in communication for decades to come. But I had had to scramble a lot to establish an i.d. The only thing that had saved me was that so many of the refugees had decided to give themselves new names for Mars, it was like a fad, and that made a lot of noise and confusion in the records, giving me somewhere to hide. It had been tough enough getting onto and off of the *Dutchman,* and creating the i.d. of Kindness O'Hart (the kind of silly name that went with my previous forged i.d. being from Frisco). Because I'd had to improvise I hadn't done it at all well. My i.d. as "Kindness O'Hart" was already shaky enough, all too apt to connect me to Stroup's murder and god knew what else, without giving any possible listener a clue to who I really was.

But god, I wanted to write to Alice.

The flash startled me because it was over so quickly; the bright light burned for an instant, like a star that had been turned on and off with a switch, a dot underlining Casseiopeia's W. That was all.

Everyone had been told it would be like that. I was glad that we had only digital com. I didn't have to listen to people who had missed it by looking away at the wrong time, or kids griping, or anything.

I had two years to go before I would transit again, and the i.d. I was building for that transit would be a good, tight, solid, clean one. Not good enough to allow me to write to Alice, never good enough for that, sorry Alice, sorry. I'd have had to explain being alive at my age, especially since she thought she knew when and how I had died.

Well, the choice would be out of my hands soon enough. She was old, she'd die. They figured it was hopeless for the ships to communicate with the Solar System after about a light-year or so anyway—though that distance kept getting rolled back as the technology improved. The old Deepstar probes had had to come all the way back, but the new series were good out to a light-year.

I got up and walked down the mountain to where the excursion planes were parked, showed my ticket, got aboard. The plane was weird looking, built with seats on top in a passenger compartment open to the air. Usually it transported hikers and climbers. The open rows of seats on top, where we sat, took up about as much room as the passenger area of an old Earth airliner, but this ship had eight times the wingspan. The wings themselves formed one big delta wing, extending almost as far behind us as out to the sides, and looked all the stranger because that giant wing was not a solid structure but a hydrogen-inflated balloon. With so little oxygen in the air, there was no fire hazard, and hydrogen lifted more and leaked less than helium.

The electrostatic pushers cut in, vectored downward, and we rose from the side of Olympus Mons, then glided silently away at a gentle angle, headed for a railhead a thousand kilometers off. We weren't taking off from the top, but we were three times higher than the peak of Everest, and Olympus Mons is steeper; it was like sliding into a night sky full of stars. The dark bulk of Mars hung below us, and the sky—now empty of anything but stars—was all around.

In a way this voyage into deep night was the best part of the excursion. I was glad I'd decided to do it. Probably just that I'd been thinking of Alice, especially the way she'd been when she was a kid, but I thought about how exciting she'd have thought it was when she was nine or ten.

She'd have made a good partner for an ecoprospector. She was always really into all the enviro-stuff, and wandering around finding places to help life take hold would have appealed to her. Ecoprospecting would have been a better job for both of us, really, than the ones we actually ended up with. We wouldn't have talked much or anything. Just had company for the sunsets, and sunrises, and all the wild Martian landscape.

I had an expedition coming up, ecoprospecting for a place where I could plant a bomb and start a river. And maybe Alice looked at a map of Mars now and then. I thought maybe she'd get a kick out of it if she happened to see her name on a map, though of course she'd never know that it was me, or that I meant her.

I sat back and enjoyed the long, slow, silent crawl across the Martian sky, said hello to Phobos when it rose, drifted off to sleep a while before we touched down. One of the best naps I ever took, I think.

vii

Sadi and I stopped yelling at each other, gradually, a while ago. I guess Sadi, as a woman, doesn't like to yell. I don't like to yell at women. Reminds me too much of my old man.

So we circle each other in that house, getting close to each other, avoiding, getting close, avoiding. We sulk, so the other one can see we're sulking.

We don't fuck much anymore.

I keep wondering about the memories of killing him, of him killing me, her killing me. I think about the memory problem a lot because now that it all links together, I notice that if I try to recite any long block of it to myself, I get—loops.

Loops, like continuous timelike curves, I find myself thinking.

A million years of time. And she's been around the loop many times, had to have been to have changed the world so often.

And I finally ask myself the question that I should have asked before: am I that sure that this is *my* first trip? I try out the perfect memory: I think about my fortieth birthday, in 2008. I remember Alice and I went to a movie, I remember Alice had a bad cold so we didn't go to the movie, I remember a little blonde girl, not Alice at all, I remember— It falls into place, right there and then, as I'm sitting with my arms folded trying to think of a way to carry the argument on. We're having a big joint sulk-off. "Sadi," I ask, "how many times have I been around the loop?"

She starts to cry, and won't let me hold her or touch her. Finally she says, "I thought you were ready, I thought it was all going to work out. I thought this time we could be really together, that I wouldn't have to hide the memories from you anymore, that I could let you have the revival treatment so you wouldn't get old. That's what I thought. I thought, you change the world, you change the person in it, and I thought I had changed the world enough."

"So you *have* taken me around the loop before?"

"I wouldn't have gone without you, Josh. I mean maybe I'm kind of crazy and I know you sometimes get bothered about things that I like, but you know, you've got to know, I have always loved you. I never felt any other way. You can't say I didn't love you."

"I believe you."

"Well, I tried, Josh, I really tried. And this time I thought yes, yes, he's ready, let him have revival, it's time to be really together, to stop picking you up and trying over every trip through. I really thought that."

"But it didn't work out," I say. I am thinking about what is in my memory. Sometimes we killed each other. Sadi has killed Alice more times than I know. Sadi did get me to kill Alice, and I was remembering that on the night I killed Sadi. It's the opposite of it all falling into place; suddenly it all falls apart, and I realize that "apart" is the only way it fits.

"It didn't work out," she agrees. "But you can come around the loop anyway, Josh, just take the ride on the CTC with me, and then we can work it out together through the rest of the century. We have lots of time. It can be good, we just have to use the time to work it out."

"Let me think," I say.

Then she won't talk about it anymore, but that night she comes down to the small side bedroom I sleep in now. She's naked. She hands me some short lengths of rope.

I'm not sure what she wants, and I stand there with those in my hands, till she says, "You're angry with me."

"Yeah."

"Tie me up and hurt me. Do what you want. I worked so hard to get you here, like this, you, young, with all your memories. I love you so much. I'll let you do whatever you want with me. You can hate me, you can kill me. Just don't ignore me."

I throw the rope aside, hold her, cry into her beautiful soft hair, let her cry on my shoulder. We cuddle for a long time, and then it turns into giggles and flirting, and finally into wild, screaming sex. It's very late when we fall asleep.

When I wake up the gravity's all wrong.

I get disoriented and dizzy when I stand up, the way it used to be confusing to walk in the Mushroom, the high-gravity area of the *Flying Dutchman* where they made us work out to keep us healthy during the voyage.

I don't remember much. The prick of a needle? The shot of an airgun? Where is Sadi? (Where's Alice? I think, and then I know how stupid that is).

My werp's there, and my space allocation box. When I open it, the napkin, the holo, and the old dogtag are gone. One thing has been added: a holo of Sadi, as a young woman, naked, positioned for doggie style so that her tits look huge from the front side and in the back you can see right up her vagina. A note clipped to it says *Remember this is waiting for you.*

The kind of funny sideways feel to the gravity can only mean one thing, I realize. I'm in a spaceship that's using centrifugal gravity.

She'll have left a message. If there is anything she *can't* do, it's *not* explain. I turn to the werp and say, "Play the message."

Sadi's face comes onto the screen. She hurried about her makeup, didn't get the lips right.

"I really do love you," she says. "By now you've figured it out, haven't you? I would think you would. While you were still asleep from the drugs, the time shift was initiated. You're on your way back to the singularity, Josh. You were never going to make up your mind, and you know it. But you have to do this. It's taken me centuries—all the twenty-first" (she giggles at her own joke) "to get it to this point, where I could offer you a chance to really share the century together, where I could let you have a permanent revival and all your memories and know you would come back to me. You can't just give up on it now.

"This is costing a third of the budget of the Organization, and it's worth it.

"So you're off at near light speed, going out almost sixty light-years and coming back, 120 years that will pass like fourteen months. The ship you're in is not under your control. Don't try to hack the control systems—you could screw up life support. Besides you're not an astrogater.

"When you pass through the singularity, after your return to the solar system, I'm sure you'll be happy to find yourself in 1988. The ship will drop you off on a low hill in the New Mexico desert. Head *west* on the two-lane road at the base of the hill. Take everything you need from the ship, because as soon as you're out of sight, it's going to take off and go hide in a long orbit.

"You will be three miles from a small town with a Greyhound station. You will arrive there, at a normal walking speed, about an hour before dawn and three hours before any business opens. In the ship's safe—which is keyed to your thumbprint—there are six ATM cards, each with a million dollar balance to draw upon. You've also got an apartment in San Francisco—keys and details also in the safe. Use them and enjoy them, bud.

"I finally realized how unfair I'd been. I've been around the loop thirty times with my memories, several before I ever found you. Of *course* my mind's made up, and of *course* you'll need time to think. So I'm giving it to you. The ship will give you five years back there— right up to when the mutAIDS plague hits—to play around and think. After that there will be a message for you, mailed to that San Francisco address, so if you move be sure and leave a forwarding address. That message will be a letter from your ship's AI setting you up for pickup and return.

"If you're ready then, fine. Come on back and we can talk about what it would be fun to do together. Or if you want to stay longer—why anyone would want to do mutAIDS or the Eurowar again is beyond me—go ahead. The ship can park in a long orbit, way away from anything that might detect it, for as long as you want to stay. After the first time it returns for you, in 1993, the ship will place itself under your command. You can even repeat all or part of a loop.

"Enjoy your trip, Josh. Take all the time you want, because you have it. I won't be lonely. Whenever you get back, in your time frame, it'll be just minutes for me. Sorry to pull a trick on you, bud, but you know, you'd never have done it otherwise, and we had to do it. For me it's always been you."

She blows me a kiss and waves. My werp clicks off. Alone, in this metal box, fourteen months to go.

I'm sure she has provided plenty of ways of amusing myself; I can probably dream most of the time away in virtual reality, and there's probably a big library and a lot of movies and music and so on. Any kind of food I want. Some kind of gym. All that. I don't bother to look just yet.

1988. I can go see Mama, Gwenny, Grandpa Couandeau. Ambush Daddy someplace and kill him if I want—I have all kinds of skills now. Be a serial killer, billionaire (I remember the brand names on about ten things that ought to make me rich if I want to pick up a quarter million in stock), politician, anything. Go to college and spend a hundred years reading to see if there's any worthwhile shit in books—not that I need that long to find out there's not.

Wonder if the information in my werp and my memory is adequate to find Alice's mother? Get her out of Europe early enough, might make big differences.

Other thoughts hit, and I start to really smile. That little German housewife. All the places where there's going to be no law at all. Or set up a pickup with the ship so I know when and where I'm getting out of Dodge, go do ten things for the hell of it, go catch the ship, presto, twenty years into the future or past. Never take me alive, coppers. Never even take me *existing*. I have total, complete, freedom to be me, to be as many kinds of me as I want. All kinds of chances.

Sadi was a fool. (Love does that.) She figured if she gave me this century to play with, I'd get bored and run back to her. Or maybe she thought I'd be so in love I wouldn't give a damn for all the stuff that's here.

I laugh and slap the steel wall of the ship. "Yes sir?" the AI asks, in Sadi's voice.

"Steady as she goes and hold your course," I say.

"I am not authorized to alter this flight plan on your commands, sir," the AI says. "Would you like something to eat, or some entertainment?"

"Not just yet." I lean back and consider failing back asleep. Lots of time. Worlds of time.

I can do good things for Mama, Gwenny, Alice, everyone, if I want. I can party for a hundred years. I can kill someone every month just for fun. And if it ever starts to look too hot for me, I can always get on this ship again.

Knowledge is power and I've got that. Power is being able to touch and not be touched, and I've got that.

Hell of a century coming up, I realize. Best one so far. I have to wait fourteen months to get started, but even that's okay. More time to plan, think, dream. Then off the ship and all my dreams come true.

Yeah. It will be the best century so far. This time it will all be different. The next century is fucking *mine*.

CANDLE

For Paul Edwards.
"If you live
in this country long enough,
you get colorful."

One thing you have to say for the Colorado Rockies, you sleep good, these days, now that there's nothing to worry about. I was dead solid asleep when I woke up to a voice saying, "Hey, Currie."

I didn't recognize the voice right away, but that wasn't so unusual; One True speaks in different voices. I sat up in bed, facing into the bright moonlight. Mary and me, we love to sleep with the curtains open so we can see the sky and wake up with the sunlight, and we can do it nowadays because nobody ever looks through a window anymore unless they're supposed to. Probably we could've done it in the old days anyway because Sursumcorda, Colorado, never had more than a thousand people anyway, and we live a ways outside and above it.

Our house up there is a nice old twentieth-century A-frame with lots of glass. With that southern exposure, on a full moon night, you wouldn't need electricity to read in there.

"Hey, Three-Cur."

Nobody's called me that in a long time so I was wondering for just a second if I was having a waking dream, like I used to just after I retired. But Mary didn't even twitch, and since we always leave our link on while we're at home, when I have a bad dream, or she does, we both wake up. And my copy of Resuna seemed pretty calm tonight— nothing out there but the usual traffic of assurances and friendliness.

"You're wide awake, Currie, and we need to talk," the voice said. Now I knew it was One True. It had chosen to come to me through my auditory nerves, instead of as a voice entirely in my head. I reached to my copy of Resuna and it reached to Mary's; sure enough, One True had already put a block on her so that she'd sleep pleasantly through any noise and light we needed to make.

"Yes, it's One True," the voice agreed, responding to my thought. "Do whatever you need to get comfortable and I'll talk to you in eight minutes and thirty seconds."

"Eight and thirty," I said. In the back of my mind, my copy of Resuna started the countdown. I got out of bed.

I sleep ten hours or more every night in winter, especially late winter. Not that I don't enjoy skiing, snowshoeing, hunting, ice fishing, and all, but at forty-nine years old, a few hours of anything outside tires me pleasantly out, and then a decent dinner, with a small glass of wine, and a good book after, usually put me out by eight or nine at night, and I get up with the sun, *not* before it. So from the way the full moon hung in the southwest, I guessed it was about five in the morning.

Five eighteen a.m., Resuna said in my mind. *Seven minutes forty-four seconds remaining.*

I shook off the last drowsiness, climbed out of bed, and threw on a dressing robe and slippers, wincing at the way the cold hurts my bad toes these days—I had led a little too vigorous a life when I was younger, breaking most of my toes and getting a touch of frostbite a few times, so that between one thing and another, my toes are lim sensitive, and that cold floor just sets them off.

I went into the bathroom and peed into the recycler, stretched a couple more times, and finally said aloud, "Bob, coffee now, please, and warm rolls for one in twenty minutes?"

"Sweet or plain?" Bob asked. This was out of the household software's experience—Bob had been installed after I retired—and it wouldn't necessarily trust the data files it had copied from its predecessor.

I took a moment to clarify—"Sweet. If I get a call that gets me up before sunrise, pritnear always, I'll want sweet rolls."

I splashed some water on my face. Since I was up, Bob would already be warming my clothes for today, so I didn't bother with instructions about that.

As I was buttoning my shirt, I could hear the gurgle and gush of coffee into the carafe, and by the time I got my shoes on—*one minute forty-four seconds to go*, Resuna assured me—I felt pretty decent. Resuna was grumbling, where I could just feel it, about having to adjust my serotonin levels when I was going to throw caffeine at my brain as well, but I knew perfectly well it could do that without any trouble. Your copy of Resuna picks up your traits to some extent, and I'm afraid I've always been a griper.

I went to the kitchen to get my coffee. I didn't know why I was so sure this would have something to do with my old job. It *could* be something else. One True calls everyone a few times a year—always on your birthday, and on your region's Resuna Day, and then there's all the routine business stuff that everyone has to do—but something about this call had made me think at once that it would turn out to be about the old job.

Three-Cur. He addressed me as Three-Cur. That was a nickname I hadn't heard since my days as a cowboy hunter. I got coffee from the kitchen, enjoyed the pleasant odor of sweet rolls under way in the foodmaker, and went downstairs to the big room. In the moonlight, there was no need to turn on a light. I sat down and took that first long slow sip of coffee that helps a lifetime caffeine addict see that the universe, on the average, is a pretty good place.

Aside from the moon and Orion, and a few scattered other stars, I could see no lights through the window. The dark rectangles and trapezoids of Sursumcorda lay far down the mountain from me, with no streetlights—no one was out, so they weren't turned on. Pritnear everyone in that little town sleeps like Mary and me in winter—we're a community of old-timers.

I leaned way over sideways on the couch for an angle through the window. Just as always, I saw the bright tiny oval of Supra New York hanging in the sky. In all my eleven years on the job, I had seen SNY in the sky from camps in the wilderness just before I went to bed, and from canyons and mountaintops while I waited on stakeout, hundreds of times, and always taken comfort in the sight. Seven million people lived up there, nowadays, almost directly above Quito, Ecuador, all running Resuna, all part of One True like me.

The wilderness just didn't seem as lonely, as long as I could see good old SNY. I saluted seven million fellow citizens with my coffee cup. They didn't wave back, but I still knew they were there. I took another sip, sat and waited.

Three-Cur. Nice that One True still remembered. I didn't really know what had possessed the woman who abandoned me at the Municipal Orphanage in Spokane Dome to name me Currie Curtis Curran, but at least it had furnished an endless source of amusement, first to my squad mates back during the War of the Memes, and later to my team of cowboy hunters.

"Bob, I'd like it a little warmer," I said, quietly, and felt the faint hum of the baseboard heaters an instant later. Was I more sensitive to temperature, or was it just unusually cold on the other side of the window? A moment later, Resuna told me that it was minus seventeen out there, quickly translating that to half a degree above zero, Fahrenheit, before I could ask. So it was cold for February, even up here. Year 26 was shaping up to be the coldest on record; supposedly that trend wouldn't begin to reverse till around Year 35.

The meters-deep snow in the moonlight was crisp, with hints of pale blue, and wind-sculpted into knife-edges, untouched by anything more solid than a shadow. It was nice to sit and look and wait for things to begin.

Just as Resuna counted off "zero," One True came back to me.

"Look at your wall," One True said.

I turned to look at the white wall. To download information to a copy of Resuna, and thus into the person running Resuna, One True must move so much information that polysensory ways are the only way of doing it in a reasonable time. It was like a vivid dream from which I would awaken knowing everything I needed to know, or like I would imagine a religious revelation would be, or like falling into some other life, or like being One True myself, for a few minutes. Once I woke up, I would have to talk, to One True and to my own copy of Resuna, to activate the knowledge. For the moment, though, it wasn't too different from being asleep, and for a cranky old guy like me, up too early on a February morning, that was pritnear perfect.

I was standing on Fossil Ridge, right along the Great Divide, looking east toward the Arkansas Valley. I had no body, but my point of view was its usual height off the ground. Something behind me was not right—frightening, but nothing I wasn't willing to turn around and face. I knew the difference between the fear that comes with ordinary caution and the fear of annihilation or worse. This was something— no, someone—physically dangerous, not anything that might destroy who I was, just someone I might have to fight.

I turned and looked down toward where I could see the falls of the Taylor River, splashing over the old dam in Taylor Park, where there had once been a reservoir. It was many kilometers away and hundreds of meters below me; I couldn't see much more than the sparkle and splash of the falls, and the thin snaking blue curves of the river winding through the park and then plunging into the dense forest below.

Then, in the intense illusion, I *could* see that far. My eyes were like telescopes or like an eagle's. A man was running as swiftly as he could, but with precision and care, on the old dam, as if he feared some accident. My view swung overhead. I was hanging on a surveillance satellite like a nosy angel. I dove at the man on the dam, and his image expanded.

He was fit and healthy, but looked like he had missed plenty of meals over the years; his belt was fastened a third of the way around his back. Through my satellite eyes and One True's databases I perceived him as six foot two, 145 pounds. I descended to the crumbling top of the dam, directly in his path.

He kept coming my way. His clothes were handmade, doubtless from cloth he'd looted from some abandoned store. He wore a simple blue pullover shirt with several pockets; black trousers, slightly dirty with much wear at the knees, fastened by a drawstring with a two-button fly; an ancient belt with a dozen hand-cut notches; deerskin moccasins with old-radial-tire soles; and of course the hat, the thing they could never resist. He'd camo-painted it pretty well, but it was a Stetson.

Here in the Rockies, we called people who lived outside One True "cowboys" because for some damned reason they all wore those stupid creepy-looking hats. One True had decided that no one else on the Earth would have a taste for those—just as no one wanted to wear the burnoose that marked the bedouin in Arabia, or bush hats in New Guinea—in part to make the cowboys stick out more. Just the sight of it in this recorded vision was making my flesh crawl, back in my comfortable living room.

His face was bearded but he kept the beard close-cropped and it looked like he shaved out his corners. The last few cowboys I had caught had been extraordinarily neat in their personal grooming, come to think of it. One True explained that personal neatness went with being meticulous, and more meticulous cowboys lasted longer.

I looked closely at his face. I wanted my tranquilizer gun at hand, even though I knew this was all recorded and hallucinatory.

His face had not aged in eleven years. He was even wearing clothes almost identical to the ones he had worn on the day I thought I killed him. Well, perhaps he had thought he'd killed me. Maybe that made us even.

The man I was looking at called himself "Lobo." Or had called himself Lobo, eleven years ago when he was last hunted. I had been one of the leaders of the hunt for him, and the gang he led, and we had thought that he had died after taking a hard, long fall in the Black Canyon. I didn't remember ever hearing that they found his body, but cowboy hunters deal only with the living, so it hadn't seemed so odd then. Now, I was thinking I should have taken more time for paperwork.

As I stood and watched him, in the vivid vision that One True was sending, Lobo slowly turned around, removed his hat to reveal thick, short, badly trimmed, still-dark hair, and bent, stretched, and showed himself off so that I could learn what he looked like from every angle. He walked and ran around me so that I got a sense of how he moved.

Even without One True's sending me the pictures, I would have recognized Lobo any place, any time, for the rest of my life. The hunt for Lobo had been the longest and hardest I'd ever had. Lobo'd killed three of my hunters, and badly hurt five more so that it took years for them to recover, and just before his departure over the cliff and into the canyon, had left my face a gory wreck that required months of hospital time to put right. If he was still out there, we still had a score to settle.

Resuna usually doesn't approve of revenge as a motivation, and will shut down those feelings if it detects them, but my copy of Resuna was being strangely silent as I felt the rage rising in me against Lobo. *In this case*, One True told me silently, *we have someone who seems to be cunning—and therefore dangerous—beyond any of the old cowboys that you hunters hunted to extinction.* Therefore any extra motivation that One True could find for me—revenge for Abbot, Johnson, and Kibberly, desire for a good hunt, whatever feeling it could find— would be amplified by my copy of Resuna until the mission was accomplished.

In an old-fashioned reading library with heavy thick carpets, a big polished table, and walls lined with reference texts, a librarian who was One True leaned over my shoulder and set a pile of documents down in front of me. I pulled them toward me and began to read.

It looked as if Lobo had managed to dropline all of civilization, all at once, as soon as he got away from the Black Canyon, because for years there hadn't been the slightest evidence that he was still alive. He hadn't raided, he hadn't tried to contact anyone, he hadn't stolen a watt of power or a slice of bread from the civilized world for nine and a half years after his purported death. Furthermore, he had been able to unplug more completely, and vanish more thoroughly, than any other cowboy ever had, just as soon as he had given us good reason to believe him dead, which argued that he'd planned a difficult, complex procedure in considerable depth for some time before he had elected to use it. Presumably he was now eleven years more experienced and paranoid.

He'd been the toughest opponent I had ever faced. Now he was back from the dead. It gave me a shudder, especially since, perhaps due to the final exhaustion of his stored supplies, he was now raiding again, and he seemed to take a peculiar sadistic pleasure in some of what he did, almost as if he were trying, impossibly, to bait or frighten One True.

I opened a file folder. A hole in it grew out to the size of the table; I fell through into someone's memory. It took me half a second or so to realize that my name was Kelly and I was a twelve-year-old girl, living with my mom in a big cabin, high up on a mountain.

One True had decided that Mom's nerves would be better if she were living in a quiet cabin in the woods, and that I needed a calm mother. Resuna patiently reminded me, now and then, that we had to live way out here because in past generations Mom might have been abusive, alcoholic, or both; she'd led a hard life before she turned, and I had a few ugly memories myself—we'd been living as wild squatters in Vegas Ruin until I was three, when the team found us and turned us, and the world suddenly got all better.

I was sitting on the floor, in our house up in the mountains, playing Parcheesi with Mom. We both thought that game was a pleasant way to kill time while you watch snow fall among the aspens early in an October evening. We were discussing whether we wanted popcorn, hot chocolate, or both, tonight, when we were startled by a terrible crash.

A man in an outside suit, the kind that rescue workers wear out here in the mountains, came running up the stairs from where he had smashed down the door. He was holding something in his hand—I didn't recognize it, but Mom did and I got a vague sense that it could hurt us badly. The impression through our linked copies of Resuna was only in my mind for an instant before Mom screamed "My god, don't hurt us" and her strong surge of emotions shut the link down.

The man in the suit came a step forward, and said, "Shut up." Then he said something horrible to us—something that I can't remember now, mercifully, because Resuna and One True have erased it from me, but once he said it, I couldn't receive Mom's thoughts or feelings, and Resuna was not there, and I had no way to call One True to help us, no comforting voice in my head to tell me I could get through this. I had no way of knowing what Mom needed from me, or of telling her what I needed.

The man in the suit slapped Mom, hard, twice. She fell away from him, barely catching her balance, staring dumbly at the hand that was raised to strike her again. Blood flowed out of her mouth.

It was like a nightmare, except that Resuna wasn't there to wake me up and tell me it was all right. I was frozen, not moving, unable to think, just endlessly screaming for Resuna in my mind.

The man slapped me too; I didn't know why. I hadn't been hit at least since Mom had turned, and the sensations—flesh crushed against skull on one side of the head, teeth stinging in suddenly swelling gums, one eye running with uncontrollable tears—were a thousand times worse because nothing explained them to me, and I had only my own body's natural shock response.

The man pulled back his hood and said, "Medicine synthesizer. I need your medicine synthesizer. I need you to put your hand in there and have it diagnose and prescribe for me."

"Will it do that?" Mom asked. Her voice was timid, shy, high-pitched, like a little girl's.

"Oh, it'll do it," the horrible man said. His hair was as long as mine, matted to his skull with sweat, and his rough thick black beard was wet, almost dripping. He reeked like spoiling meat or a dead animal under the house. His eyes were too bright and his lips reddish purple against his too-pale skin. "I'll show you how. All you have to do is do it. I want the medicine, I want a good meal, and maybe some other things. I just hurt you so you'd know I'm serious and you'd do what you're told. Now do what you're told and I won't have to hurt you any more."

I fell out of Kelly's mind for a second, and everything froze into a still picture. Below the image of the man, One True inscribed a positive identification of Lobo, from voiceprint and DNA. A moment later it added that according to information and samples recovered later, the disease he was suffering from seemed to be a strain of measles, aggravated by mutAIDS. Both diseases were supposed to be extinct, but Earth's a big planet and you never know what might yet be festering in its untended corners.

Then—I had just an instant to wish this wasn't necessary—One True commanded, and my Resuna dropped me back into Kelly's memories.

As Kelly, I watched Mom put her hand into the medical synthesizer, and the man stood close to her and pressed a bare shoulder against the sampler. Then he spoke some codes aloud; in the old days communication between people and machines hadn't been perfect, and whoever this man was, he still knew how to use the old accesses that had been there, for example, so that parents could get medicine for their babies.

The man winced briefly as it gave him a pressure injection, but when that was done he sighed with relief.

He ate practically all the ready food in the house, and reconstituted three meals, each of which was supposed to be for four people, and gobbled those down as well, along with more coffee than you'd have thought could go into a human being. He seemed fascinated with our reconstitutor; with a faraway look, he calculated for a few seconds, and finally decided to take it with him, along with almost all the food in the house. "The rescue crews will bring you more," he assured us, but I didn't believe him. I still wanted Resuna worse than I had ever wanted anything.

When he had finished eating, he said, "There's one more thing I need. I'm very much from the old days, I spent a long time as a mercenary during the War of the Memes, and you know what that means. You and your daughter have cooperated just beautifully, and been very helpful, but there's something I want to do to both of you, which you are not going to like. I hope you'll do your best to cooperate so it isn't any more painful than it has to be."

Mom was starting to cry, and I was afraid about what was going to happen.

The man said, "Resuna is supposed to be able to erase everything, afterwards."

Mom shook her head. "It doesn't really work that way. I still have lim too many memories, from the old days, and they still hurt me every day."

The man nodded, several times, as if he were thinking carefully about that. "You know, part of me is very sorry to hear that. Another part of me is real happy to know that this is going to be in your head forever."

Mom was crying really hard now, and that was so frightening that I started to cry too. The man grabbed us both by our arms and took us down to Mom's bedroom; he told us to take our clothes off, and left the room. Mom said we had to do what he said, so we did. I was cold and felt really strange about being naked.

A moment later he came back, with a tube of skin lotion from Mom's bathroom. He undressed, and told us where to put the lotion; it felt weird and icky. He had me watch while he did things to Mom, and then made her watch while he did the same things to me.

Then he got dressed. We were both crying. Mom was throwing up. It looked like he was crying too.

He grabbed up his pack of looted food, and the reconstitutor, and said, "Hey, I'm the last of my kind. I'm not going to ever come back. And it was nothing personal. Both of you were just here. Like getting hit by lightning, you know."

He went back through the shattered door, and out into the snow; when he turned and saw us staring at him, he yelled, "Get back upstairs out of the cold! And make sure the alarm is thrown!"

We did what he said. When we checked, the alarm was already going off. It was only maybe half an hour until the rescue crews got there in the disksters, and gave us new copies of Resuna, and took us to the hospital.

My new copy of Resuna is very kind and patient, like they're supposed to be, and supposedly I won't have big problems later, because all the bad things were dealt with so soon after they happened, and because Resuna is always there helping me. Sometimes One True itself checks in to see if I'm all right. Eventually, in a year or two, what happened will just make me sad, now and then, and maybe not very often if things go the way the doctors are hoping they will. I know it will work out, because Resuna says it will, and how can you do anything but trust Resuna?

All the same, the copy of Resuna that tells me things and comforts me is the new copy that the rescue crew put in, and I still miss my old Resuna. The new one doesn't know me as well as the one that had lived in my head since I was a little kid. I know that it will get better, but I miss my old one.

I fell backwards out of Kelly's mind. I was back in my comfortable chair at the table in the library; the hole in the table closed up, contracted into the folder, and became a dot no bigger than a period. I could go back there, if for some reason I ever wanted to.

I didn't want to. I could feel the picture of what he'd done to that mother and little girl building up inside me, a thing to be avenged and taken out on him, like the destruction of my crew a decade ago, like the deaths of Tammy and Carrie during the war, like all the good friends I had lost too young, like all the evil that the cowboys and their spiritual ancestors had worked in the world.

I had not felt such a passion for a hunt in many years; maybe I had never felt it before at all. The anger hurt, physically, in my chest, but I knew Resuna *needed* me to be that angry, and I accepted the pain.

I opened another file folder, from the still-tall stack of them to my left. There was more, but there wasn't worse, and I was grateful for that, at least. I seemed to be there for hours reading all the accounts of what he'd done since his reappearance a few months previously. In those visions you have perfect concentration, and time passes much faster than it does in the outside world—but it still takes a while to digest such a catalog of human evil, perverse cruelty, and solid constant nastiness. By the time I had finished my reading, I was feeling tired and sick, and felt like I'd used up a full day's energy right there in the "library," even though my copy of Resuna told me that I had only been in the vision for six minutes and fourteen seconds.

I sat back on my couch, talking to One True consciously now, no longer in the dream. "Sort of flattering," I said. "There're at least five other hunters you could've picked who could've done the job. You could even've sent a whole posse of us. Why me?"

I was surrounded by warm, friendly laughter. One True was playing my auditory nerves a quad sound system. "Why 'why'?" it asked. "We don't understand your reason for wanting to know our reasons, and your copy of Resuna doesn't seem to understand either. Are you fishing for a compliment? Are you seeking clarification? Are you—"

"It was the first thought that happened to pop into my head," I said. "You have five other reserve hunters for the Rockies. They're all very good too. I was just wondering why One True picked me."

"Because we had to pick somebody," One True said. "So we picked the best one. Or at least the one with the best record. Do you think someone else could do it better?"

I thought about that. Resuna helpfully pulled up the records of the other five, and I compared those with my memories of them. They were all very good, but I had to agree that if we were just sending one, it probably ought to be me. "No, I guess there's not."

"Well, then, we'll send you. And just you—because our guess is that since one hunter will make less noise and attract less attention than six, we should just send the best one after him. This Lobo is apt to be crafty and easily spooked."

Outside, the very first hints of false dawn were starting to color the distant peaks on their east-facing sides; their west sides still shone brighter in the cold light of the full moon. It looked like a million degrees below zero out there, and I shivered despite the warmth in the room.

"Remember that excessive curiosity and doubt can damage your copy of Resuna," One True reminded me. "And because yours is such a veteran copy, it is to the benefit of all of us for it to stay in good shape. There's a lot of memory that the world needs in your head, Currie. Don't start arguing and questioning; all you'll do is hurt us all."

"I'm sorry," I said.

"We know," One True said. "Your copy of Resuna just relayed the feeling."

I felt better. The mind of the whole planet understood that my feelings were sincere and my intentions were good. We didn't need to talk about much else—all the arrangements had been there in the dream—and so I took a last look at the cold landscape outside and asked aloud, "Bob, temperature of this room?"

"Seventy-three," it answered, defaulting to Fahrenheit. "Usually you feel warmer if I bring up lights. Would you like a warm glow, heavy on red and yellow, here and in the kitchen? Your sweet rolls will be ready in about two more minutes."

"Do it," I said. The room was suddenly bathed in yellows, reds, and oranges, flickering as if there were fireplaces on all the walls. "Looks like we'll be back on work schedule until further notice. Do you still have a copy of it?"

"Last time on work schedule was January 19, Year 14, or 2076 Old Dating," Bob responded, "and the copy appears to be undamaged. Per that work schedule, shall I put on a full breakfast in addition to the sweet rolls?"

"Do it, Bob." I went out to the kitchen, dumped my cold coffee, and poured myself some fresh. Strange to be having such a morning—I had thought I'd never have another one.

I took my sweet rolls out to the little table by the main window in the big room, facing the grand view down the canyon to Sursumcorda, and ate greedily, washing the sticky sweet gooey rolls down with gulps of searing hot coffee. At least for the duration, no more worrying about calories, except maybe for worrying about getting enough. Resuna mentioned to me that my blood pressure and pulse were up and I was using more oxygen, and asked if I wanted an adjustment. I told it hell no. This was just what it was to feel really alive after so long in retirement.

I reviewed my newly acquired memories to make them conscious.

When I had hunted Lobo, he had been the leader of a gang of eleven cowboys, a huge number for those last years of hunting. His gang had pulled off several sizable raids on small towns and isolated work stations, making Lobo a throwback even then. The gangs of cowboys had been rounded up and turned first, mostly before Year 5. It's much easier to catch a gang because it's harder to hide in groups, and usually all we had to do was catch and turn one of them to get enough information to find all the rest. By the time we were given the mission of hunting Lobo's gang, everyone else that the team had been hunting for at least three years had been loners.

Lobo had survived to become the last lone cowboy himself. The rest of his gang was long since captured and turned, so far as I knew—though if he could survive so many years without One True spotting him, who knew what else he might be managing? This was going to be the greatest hunt of my career; I felt that in my old bones already.

The sun was up far enough now to turn the sky blue, put a bright shine on the distant snow-spattered top of Mount Teocalli, and bring out the color of its distinctive striations, so that it stood like an island of light and color above a sea of dull slate-darkness. In the old days I had loved this time of morning, and once I thought that, Resuna copied the memories forward, and I loved it again.

It had been a long time since I'd hunted a cowboy. I had been a mercenary soldier in the War of the Memes before I'd been a cowboy hunter, and before that I'd been a kid. When I thought of those things it always seemed so far away.

Since retirement, I had led a pleasant life of old-man pleasures—the greenhouse, the library, occasional carpentry, plenty of outdoor sports, almost always with Mary scant meters away. It was rich, fulfilling, well-earned, everything I deserved for my years of danger and hardship in One True's service—but it wasn't what I had been forged out of anger and love to do.

I thanked One True, in my heart, again, so that Resuna would pick it up and relay it. First I thanked One True for selecting me and giving me the chance to live fully one more time, hunting Lobo. Then I thanked One True for making a world where people like Lobo would be stopped before they destroyed everything, where the pain and horror they inflicted had a limit. Finally I thanked One True in advance, knowing that when Lobo was caught and turned, and I was menaced once again by the melancholy pain of being a cowboy hunter in a world without cowboys, Resuna would be able to soothe my soul and return me to the warm, mellow, soft life of my retirement here; I would never really have to feel my painful loss of usefulness.

Bob announced that the full breakfast was ready. Resuna was already tinkering with my physiology: I was ravenous, though as yet I'd done nothing strenuous. No doubt in a short while I'd be glad for all the calories I could ram in.

I had stayed more or less in shape. Skills should be okay as well. The whole time I had worked as a cowboy hunter, my copy of Resuna had been uploading those to One True and downloading other hunters' skills to me. If anything had atrophied or been forgotten, Resuna would call up One True's libraries, find it, and get me a fresh copy, and muscle memory is long-lived anyway. As I finished a second plate of eggs, home fries, and baked beans, I had little moments and flashbacks—instants when I visualized making a couple of tight turns to descend a steep hillside in the back country, or daydreamed of checking the ice on a not-frozen-enough river, or remembered creeping forward, belly down in gray slush, around a rock with my tranquilizer gun for a clear shot at the bare buttocks of a cowboy taking a dump in the bushes. All the old systems were waking up.

Besides my own skills, I would also be able to draw on the most recent copy of every skill of everyone who had ever been good at this business. On the other hand, I was still up against the unknown. No cowboy until Lobo had ever hidden out for so long completely undetected.

"All the same, it looks doable to me," I said, aloud, knowing that my copy of Resuna would hear me and pass it on to One True. "Looking forward to it."

I finished breakfast and carried the dishes to the regenner to be melted, purified, and reformed. The view over the snow-covered boulders up the hill from the kitchen window—not as spectacular as the view on the other side, out over the town and valley, but in its quiet way, something that had also grown into me—seemed to remind me how much One True valued me. Or rather, the old part of me (which had lived for decades, full grown, before Resuna turned most of humanity) always insisted on thinking of the view, and the A-Frame itself, and the many comforts Mary and I had in our retirement, as rewards for the years I had spent in the woods, tracking the last outlaws on Earth. But the part of me that knew and understood the world through Resuna knew something that was so much better; I had been preserved because in One True's estimation I had been one of the six best cowboy hunters in the Rockies, and therefore One True had created a life for me that would let me stay in shape and maintain my basic capabilities, against any future need.

I knew One True was sending these memories and feelings into me because of the question I had asked earlier, and I felt both how absurd it was that I needed it, and how willing One True was to look after my need anyway. After all, what was there to be reassured about? It was just realistic to know that I had been the best and been preserved for that reason.

In the old days, before the memes, there were things they called "pre-memes" now, in retrospect—little partial routines and programs that were shared by many people; I'd had my share like anyone else. One of them called "modesty" would have been ashamed at my saying baldly that I was the best, no matter how true it might be. Another one called "self-esteem" would have been pleased whether it was true or not.

In the sort of minds people had before Resuna, modesty and self-esteem would have fought it out, wasting great quantities of energy and effort in my mind as they struggled with each other, paralyzing me from many effective actions, creating a dangerous propensity for overestimating or underestimating my own capabilities, misleading me into foolish diversionary actions in the attempt to satisfy them both. Most pre-memes were quite capable of clouding a person's judgment, and replicated by strategies that were anti-survival for the larger mind or person.

The man I was going to be hunting probably still had dozens or hundreds of pre-memes—pride, rights, honor, self-reliance, and vengeance, just about for sure, since almost all cowboys we had ever captured and turned had been running those at the time of capture. He might even have some of the more complex, thought-to-be-extinct pre-memes, like Ecucatholicism, cybertao, or America, or even the really exotic ones like communism or fundamentalism. That was why it was vital to take him alive; though he was a deadly enemy to One True and therefore to the whole human race, he was also a repository of memetic material that might be analyzed so that useful parts could be incorporated into everyone's copy of Resuna, and defenses could be built against the bad parts—*if* Lobo could be turned and the old pre-memes extracted and copied from him.

So it was no surprise that One True, which rarely made mistakes and never abided in them, had had a superb cowboy hunter like me available, right here in the Colorado Rockies, just when the need had arisen. One True thought farther ahead than any mere person could do, and it shaped us to ends that were good for us, good for the poor old mauled Earth, good for itself. I was the product of its foresight, which is why I could enjoy being One True's superb tool.

In the same way, One True pointed out to me, a Cajun hunter still lived on a houseboat in Simmesport, and a bush-hippie hunter was waiting in reserve in a hand-built cabin in Homer.

Not having thought about either place in decades, I was startled at what poured back into my memory. When I had been born, the Mississippi had still flowed into the Gulf in Plaquemines Parish, eighty miles south of New Orleans—far east of where it did now—and most of Alaska had not been under the glaciers. Thanks to One True, nobody would ever come out of the backwoods to disturb the peace of Earth again, and there would be time enough now fix everything, now that all of humanity on Earth truly worked together. We hunters had done our small bit to make that happen, and like every other hunter, I thanked One True for having given us the opportunity.

As always, the mission was the Four Ts': track him, trank him, and truss him. One True would take care of the fourth T—turning him. I was also supposed to look for any evidence that he'd had any contact with the extraterrestrials, particularly anything that violated the Treaty of Supra Berlin. Probably there would not be any such evidence—his radio would have given him away long before this if there had been—but it was important to make sure that the wild individuals still living on Mars, the asteroids, and the moons of Jupiter remembered their obligations not to meddle in our affairs.

In broad outline, the productive parts of my job could have been accomplished in a couple of hours, leaving the rest to be mere details. Details, however, could often be a bitch. In my years as a cowboy hunter, I had been shot four times, broken one arm and both legs, gotten nipped by frostbite on one cheek, three toes, and a thumb, and had to have one eye and four teeth regenerated after stopping Lobo's cleated boot with my face in that last grim fight before he had supposedly died. A guy as tough as Lobo, and as smart, was bound to generate a few violent, dangerous details.

I could hardly wait.

Lobo had led a small band of cowboys operating out of the little ghost town of Manly, Colorado, a former three-street tin-mining town up toward Frisco on old Colorado 9. Lobo and his cowboys had set up military shelters inside the crumbling 1920's-vintage buildings, thus concealing themselves from easy orbital observation. We'd all had a good chuckle—even One True had seemed to laugh—at the fact that we were tracking down the Manly Cowboys. But it had gotten a lot less funny after three of us had been killed and five more, including me, severely injured.

As I put together my kit that afternoon, I kept turning that pursuit over and over in my head. The Manly Cowboys had seemed at first to be the usual story—mercenaries who had served one of the losing causes in the War of the Memes and now would not accept Resuna, people who thought that for some reason the rest of us owed them the right to wander around loose and dangerous without the restraint and guidance that only Resuna could give. That gang of cowboys, in other words, was a small sample of the pure evil and sheer bad attitude that had made the mid-twenty-first such a terrible time.

Luckily our side had One True, or rather our side *was* One True. Transferable experience and telepathy help immensely when you're fighting a guerrilla war, whether against cowboys in the Rockies, bedouin in Arabia, or renegados in the Cordillera. Anything the enemy could do to coordinate with other groups, or to recruit individuals, tended to give them away; they had to function in isolation, so that they only got smarter by their own individual experience, a method as slow and painful as it had been in the Stone Age. By contrast, the newest hunter among us—Sandy "Mulekick" Arthur, at that time— didn't have everything perfectly in her muscles yet, and might be slightly slow in using reflexes that were still more in Resuna than in her own muscle memories, but still, in principle, from the day she joined she could immediately track like Abbot, climb like Kibberly, ski like me, and shoot like Pinpoint Sue. And not long after she joined us, we all started to have her martial arts abilities.

We lost Johnson and Kibberly to pure carelessness—after driving the cowboys out of Manly, we'd thought we had them boxed into a coulee below Swadge Ridge. Johnson, a big rangy guy who didn't talk much and never acquired a nickname that stuck despite all our ingenuity, had gone up there with Kristi Kibberly, who could climb a rock face like a goosed monkey and who we sometimes called "King Kong" on account of that, her initials, and her build.

It was as simple as you can imagine: Lobo figured there'd be a couple of us there to hold the upper end of the draw that his cowboys would try to escape through. Being strong and fast himself, he ran on ahead, got around behind Johnson and Kibberly, and belly-wriggled into a position above them. Meanwhile all of us hunters were down there in a big, thin line, working our way along in parallel, staying in constant touch through One True, our Resunas all chattering constantly about every step and rock.

We were just closing the trap. Abbot and me were in the middle. We had just told the flanks to advance and start working inward.

Two nasty little spats, almost on top of each other, a noise like *paddap!,* just as we felt Johnson and Kibberly vanish from the telepathic web, told us we were screwed. Afterwards, from the way we found the bodies, we figured Lobo had taken the time to program his rifle, an old military make, so that it automatically re-aimed the second shot. Johnson was hit square in the back of the head, Kristi Kibberly just behind her right ear, and they were dead before they knew what had happened.

Meanwhile the shots were the cue for the Manly Cowboys to run for it, which they did, fast and hard, shaking us off their trail almost at once. Pinpoint Sue D'Alessandro got the only capture of the day, a straggler that she nailed at extreme range; we loaded him onto the diskster to be taken away and turned, and did our best to get back into the chase, but by nightfall the Manly Cowboys had gotten clean away.

We took a day to attend funerals—it wasn't that long after the War of the Memes, and One True understood that people still needed funerals.

The day after, emotionally supported by our Resunas and thus feeling no worse than mildly depressed, we were back on the track.

It was ten days of the hardest pursuit we ever had, and at the end of it the whole hunting group had to be reconstructed, both as a group and individually. Abbot stopped a sniper's shot with his kidney and died before the diskster arrived. Sue D'Alessandro took a bullet through the thigh and was out for months. Mulekick Arthur knocked down two of them and I was able to tranquilize them, in a vicious little ambush she and I walked into on the south side of Fossil Ridge; in the process she was badly cut up and was out too. Feeney got splashed with homemade napalm during the night attack when they set her tent on fire, which put her in the burn unit for a couple of months. Replenovich gave half his foot to a land mine and was in regeneration for a year. In those ten days we took more casualties than we had in the previous three years.

Looking back, if we hadn't had One True, and our individual copies of Resuna, to hold us all in the correct perspective, we'd have thought we were losing, though we were gradually capturing all the Manly Cowboys. The unmemed human mind can't really perceive success when the losses are too high.

But because we did have Resuna and One True to get us through, in those ten days we captured all the Manly Cowboys except Lobo himself. Within three months each of them was running Resuna and on his way to being someone useful—two of them later became cowboy hunters.

By the time my team was down to just me, Brock Peters, and Moonchild Swann, and the Manly Cowboys were down to Lobo, he was trying to lose us by going through the old Black Canyon wilderness. We were completely exhausted, sloppy and careless, and so was he.

Moonchild was a good tracker—she was almost as good as Abbot had been—but she missed one of Lobo's double-backs, the only one she had missed in a day and a half, but it only takes one. Peters was a young kid who normally ran like a rocket everywhere, just because he couldn't stop himself—his nickname in the unit was "Scamper"—but he was much too far away downhill, and much too tired, to get there and give me some backup when Lobo popped up out of nowhere, coming at us from behind, just where the trail skirted the north edge of the canyon.

Black Canyon is a unique place; in its narrowest few miles the sides are so steep and the canyon so narrow that it's dark down there for most of the day, even in summer. In the old days it was pretty nearly impossible for anyone to traverse it on foot, and floating it was experts-with-good-luck-only.

For the long years since, when I had thought about it at all, I had thought that Lobo had just gotten careless, and gone charging into a fight in the open with nowhere to go but over the cliff and down. Now I wondered if that had been part of a plan.

I had been running through the checklists absentmindedly, trusting Resuna, which didn't wander like my own mind did. Everything was identical to the equipment I had been familiar with eleven years ago—not much hunting in this part of the world since then, so no technical improvements, so they just faxbricated new copies from designs on file.

Mary came in, and I could feel our Resunas generate deep empathy, connecting me to her anxiety and tension. "Will it be a long hunt?" she asked. "Your last few weren't very long. I'd like it if this one wasn't."

"That's *real* unknowable," I pointed out. "Personally I hope he walks in front of me five minutes after I first arm my tranquilizer gun, falls right over, and I'm back for lunch. But I don't think it's gonna be that way. I got so many short hunts, my last year, because most loners had gone real low-tech. They were hard to spot, but once you did find them, they were so exhausted from living off the land, cold and over-worked and half starved all the time, that they didn't have much energy to run with. This guy Lobo is a whole different kinda situation, and I can't tell you how it's going to go because I've never tried to catch a guy like him before. I know he can disappear completely for ten years, but I don't know what else he can do."

"Poop," she said, sitting on the couch with a thud. "I hate this. You don't know what you're getting into, *One True* doesn't know what you're getting into! It's like back during the war, when nobody knew what was going on and everyone always had to just wing things for themselves, and you couldn't trust anyone else to cooperate. What did we fight the whole War of the Memes for?"

I could feel that Mary's copy of Resuna was having a hard time regulating her emotions. I told my Resuna to reassure it. Then I felt One True kick in; it knew just what to say, and suddenly I was talking a whole lot better than I usually can.

"It's all part of one huge thing, Mary. We did win. The whole human race on Earth is pulling together to save ourselves and our planet. Someday we'll drive the glaciers back to where they belong in the Northern Hemisphere, and we'll restore the glaciers on Antarctica, and the Gulf Stream will flow again. We'll do it all. You know One True is breeding back thousands of animal and plant species from DNA specimens, too. By the time we celebrate our hundredth, Mary, it's going to be a beautiful world. But not if we let things like Lobo keep running loose in it.

"You know the whole wreck of the Earth was probably brought on by no more than twenty thousand people, working for the old pre-memes like America and Communism and freedom and Islam. We can't let even one of them run loose anymore. Lobo has already hurt and frightened fifty-nine people since he popped back up. And I'm the one with the best chance of catching him. One True loves you, and it loves me, and we love One True, but sometimes something hard just has to be done."

I waited, confidently, for One True to exert its control and help her appreciate just how right those words were. But though I felt One True trying, it didn't work at all. I could feel her tension and fear rising faster, all the same, despite her best efforts to control them, and despite her copy of Resuna's doing everything it could to calm her. It was strange, after all these years; this had never happened while I was a hunter before.

Perhaps it was that Lobo was different from the others, perhaps that Mary and I were older and she was more emotionally dependent on our quiet life here than she had been, perhaps somehow the terror and anxiety of the war years were coming back to her in a way that they never had while I was hunting cowboys before. In the old days she would send me off with a kiss and a warm smile and tell me to bring back a Stetson to bronze for the mantelpiece.

I got up and held her for a moment, looking at the thick gray hair that cascaded down her back, feeling her heavy but still strong body against mine, but she just froze and resisted. I whispered "I love you," and "It's okay," and squeezed her tight, but she was like a plank till I said, "Mary, love, it's all right, just remember, 'Let override, let overwrite.' "

She relaxed her throat muscles, unclenched her fists, and started to sob. Then she let One True have her, and dropped into my arms in a slack faint. I set her down on the couch and kept listening through our copies of Resuna as One True healed and helped her, while I got on with my packing.

It only took a few minutes of Resuna's complete control. Mary's irrational fears were dissolved and argued away, her courage was restored, her faith in One True and me strengthened, and a wonderful calm courage and love settled into her. One True overwrote her short-term memory, so that she would recall only sitting on the couch and watching me pack, pleased that I was working again.

It's better for people to have their own memories, and their own ideas, but when those hurt One True, or cause behavior that could annoy other people, or make the person having the ideas feel unhappy—that's the time to "let override, let overwrite," and get on with the world as it should be. It was the first time I could recall Mary having to do that in a long time.

Back in the early years, when we were first married, it had been two or three times a day. I smiled to myself, thinking, *for all I know, I've been needing it, and getting it, every day all these years, and for all I know I have been overwritten a thousand times more often than she has. That's the beauty—you get the help you need but you never know.*

When she revived—all at once, and without any awareness that she had been unconscious—she chatted and laughed and it was like old times for the next hour, as I got all my kit together. When I'd run that last little paranoid check that you always run before going in harm's way, and Resuna and I agreed that I had everything, I slung up my pack, put my duffel on my shoulder, and walked down the road about seventy yards, being careful not to slip on the ice. Just before the window went out of sight, I turned and waved. Mary waved back and blew me a kiss.

I took the last few steps down to the road. It was three-forty in the afternoon. A moment later the diskster glided silently up the road beside me and settled onto its feet with a soft crackling of static discharge. I tossed my bags into the cargo hold and climbed into the passenger compartment. It was hard to believe that in the old days, I got so used to this that I used to blank the windows and just catch a nap on the way out to the job. Now, as we raced along the old highway and up the frozen river, then through a succession of mountain meadows, I couldn't have made myself look away from the jagged, snowy mountains, still months from spring thaw, or from the brilliant blue sky and the dark swarm of pines on every hillside.

It was so good to be back.

I had about an hour of daylight left when the diskster dropped me off, far up in the high country. One True and I had selected a spot, a few kilometers from where we thought Lobo's hideout might be, where the diskster could turn off the creek, up a bank, and into a little meadow close enough to walk to my campsite from, but far enough away from Lobo's main operating area in the Dead Mule drainage so that I probably wouldn't be spotted right away. With luck, in the next few days there would be a good-sized snowstorm to efface the broad scooped-out track of the diskster.

With a bumpy lift and rise, the diskster climbed the twenty feet onto the bank and drove into the meadow. I looked around to make sure there weren't any immediate problems, like sinkholes, grizzly, or perhaps Lobo himself, and since there weren't, I said, "All right, disembarking," and fastened the hood of my coverall. The outside suit we wear in the winter in the high country, most of the time, looks like an old-fashioned space suit—or "like a baggy pair of footy jammies with a built-in Spiderman mask," as poor Abbot used to say. It's not very attractive or flattering, but it works real well, and I've lived enough of my life in them not to care a whole lot about what they look like.

It took me just a moment to swing my two bags down from the

compartment and sling up, and now I stood knee-deep in the snow with all that weight piled on me. I knew I was going to hate this.

After trudging all of about ten steps, I decided that it was pointless to be miserable while walking, just to save some unpacking and repacking. I set the duffel down, got into the side attachment of my pack, and pulled out the flexis. I set the knobs for wide snowshoes, plugged the flexis into the power supply on my suit, and waited.

In a few minutes the little squares of lightweight white plastic had spread out to form wide planks with stabilizer tails, a smooth tadpole shape that would let me walk mostly on—instead of plunged deep into—the snow. I took the straps from the pack pocket, attached them, put the flexis on, re-gathered pack and duffel, and was on my way, clumping and swinging along. It was awkward, but not nearly as bad as floundering in the deep snow had been, and pos-def it was faster— which I needed badly just then. I had two kilometers to make before dark if I possibly could, and the flexis had delayed me a few minutes.

The late afternoon sky looked blue enough to burn you. To my left, faces of red volcanic rock, carved by wind and water into pipe organs, castle keeps, and giants' teeth, rose in wild defiance at the empty sky. The little black runnels down their sides indicated some thawing. It wasn't much, but the sun's northward invasion had a foothold, at least for the moment.

Resuna reminded me that I had ground to cover, not scenery to examine. I reminded it that my satisfaction was to its benefit.

Behind the pinnacles was a sheer gray cliff, brightly lighted wherever the pinnacles didn't shadow it. A distant crash like far-off thunder told me that some creek nearby, too, was starting to break the grip of winter.

I rounded the first big grove of firs, into the wide upper meadow. I was breathing hard now. This was more work than I remembered, and I could feel the little generators on my back whirring away as they drew heat from my insulated suit and converted it to charge in the electrets; they were working hard just now, but I'd be glad enough for every bit of scavenged juice later.

The swing-and-stomp rhythm of snowshoes requires pritnear nothing but pure patience. After that first 250 meters, my legs warmed up, the muscles stopped fighting each other and got into tune, and I began to enjoy it.

Soon I was pushing up a shallow draw. The flexis were swinging up and reaching out as if of their own accord, my heart was thumping in the healthy, vigorous way that means you're really working, and the blood was singing through my body. My balance had come back and the duffel on my shoulder wasn't bothering me anymore.

To my right, down slope, a wide swath of thick fir mingled with pine trees stood tall; to my left, a scraggly line of windblown firs underscored the ridgeline. The sun now stood low in the sky behind me, washing amber light across the untracked snow and making the edges of the shadows of the trees and rocks glow deep blue.

I came around another bend and saw a ruin. Though the main buildings were buried under three meters of snow, the huge, green-painted metal towers marching up the hillside off to my right plainly showed that this had been a small ski area. The stretched, sharp-angled shape in the snow before me had been the lodge, its back now broken in two places and the glass long since shattered and knocked down by the building settling under the weight of the snow that no one swept off. A couple of rings of walls nearby were probably places where hotels, restaurants, or stores had suffered a roof collapse, with the long-fallen roof now buried under this year's snow.

My first wife Tammy and I had spent one of my rare ten-day leaves at a place not too different from this, back when we were teenagers. It had cost me about three months of my earnings as a corporal in Burton's Thugs for Jesus—and it had been worth every penny. Somewhere in my files I still had a picture of our daughter, Carrie, three years old, then, in her pink snowsuit.

I stood for a long time, looking down at the ruined lodge. For a moment, I imagined the tired people skiing in from the last run of the day, breathing hard, their muscles aching, piling through the rental checkouts, and gathering in exhausted huddles at the tables and the bars to enjoy having gotten exhausted together. The lodge would have had a nice fire, and at least one of the bars would have had a band. I could almost smell the pizza, beer, and sweat.

Oh well, someday, again. Maybe in my lifetime. Maybe when things got better, with more resources to spare, One True would let me apply to create a new ski resort. Helping people have a good time would be fun in its own right, almost as much fun as tracking them down, I supposed.

I clumped on around the resort, giving it a wide berth because I didn't want to plunge into the snow-covered remains of a ballroom, abruptly feel a six-condo unit slide down the hill underneath me, or be the final force that shattered the glass roof of a swimming pool, so I had to work my way about halfway up the ridge to be certain that I was above the old resort; that took a while, and the sun was setting by the time I was leaving the ruins behind me.

The moon was just a day past full, so it would be up shortly and I'd have more than enough light to get near my campsite, but I would camp in the shadows to reduce the chances of being spotted, so the last forty meters would be in the dark. And I knew from too-well-remembered experience that pitching camp in the dark, relying on light-amplifier goggles to do the fine work, was going to be a bitch.

I thought briefly about delaying setting up camp until daylight—I could lie down in the snow and sleep in the suit, if I had to. But there's not much provision in those suits for taking a really comfortable dump, which counts for a lot with me. Furthermore, if your suit heater system fails, or if your electrets slow-bleed and lose charge during the night, it might be July before you thawed out enough to realize that you were dead.

Half an hour later, the mountains to the west were outlined by a broad streak of red behind them, and I was finally coming over the ridge to my campsite. The first stars were out, and Resuna said that the moon would be up in seven minutes. Already a silver glow surrounded the ragged palisade of volcanic tuff topping the butte to the east.

I sat down to wait for the moon, and let my mind run through the memories of the day, for Resuna to upload to One True, thus making them potentially available for the whole human race to share.

It's not easy to explain about the mountains at that time of year. The life is burrowed deep; most of the world that surrounds you seems to say that winter will last forever.

Five minutes after the sun sets it can be cold enough so that you hear your breath snap and bang as it freezes and falls into snow at your feet. That's what thin air will do for you; you're just that hair closer to what it's like to be in outer space.

And yet the days are longer than they are in December, and during the day, it can be downright hot when the sun bounces off the frozen snow into your face. You hear water breaking loose from its frozen prisons, the distant boom of avalanches tumbling down into valleys, the dance of the firs in the wind. It has no place for you; this is a world where you stick out as if an orange ring were painted on the air around you. You never feel your individual existence more acutely.

Resuna asked, curiously, if feeling individual felt good. I didn't quite know how to explain it. I had to say that it was a feeling I seemed to need every now and then, but I didn't know whether it was good or bad.

I looked around slowly. Nothing moved. Hard to believe that this time last night I had been reading an old mystery and having a glass of wine at home, without a thought that I might ever be out here again.

Here I was, anyway.

Taking just as long as it would have if I hadn't been impatient, the moon climbed over the hill, huge against the pines. I waited till it lit the up slope in front of me before I went on. I angled up the slope carefully, since even though no doubt they would rescue me quickly if the snow slid, the rescue would alert Lobo and complicate the whole hunt. Besides, my old memories assured me that even one minute spent lying half buried in the snow with a broken leg is way too long.

A few minutes later I was looking for a low-visibility way over the ridge. I unstrapped from the flexis, set down my pack and duffel, and crept belly down in the rough, crust-covered snow, taking a good ten minutes to cover the last thirty meters to the top. Looking over, I saw broken rock here and there, a few scattered scrubby trees, and a couple of bowls whose edges I could skirt. Could be worse.

I climbed carefully back down, making sure I wasn't going to start any slides, slung up, and headed for the spot I'd picked out, behind a big promontory that would give me access into a nice dark bowl. It took maybe an hour until I was clumping along in the shallow snow between the trees on the dark side of the bowl; from there, my face-screen map said I'd only have to go about 150 meters to the place I had picked out for a campsite, among some small pinnacles and broken boulders with a couple of trees to cast nice deep shadows on my shelter.

I got there without any further trouble, switched the face screen to amplify the starlight, and set about the fumbling and fiddling necessary to make camp. First I got the little disk out of the top of the duffel, plugged it into my suit, and waited for it to turn itself into a snow shovel. It took about ten minutes for it to set into shape. I couldn't do much while dragging that thing around—I made a note to Resuna about redesigning this gear so that one or more of the electrets would detach—but meanwhile I got a long drink of warm water from the suit's recovery reservoir, and looked up, through the trees and boulders, at the stars. You'd think I'd be used to how bright they could be, even with a full moon, up here in the mountains, but after so many years, I still never got tired of it.

When the shovel had set, I dug out the space where I had decided

I wanted to put my shelter. At least this snow had not been packed down by anything, and hadn't been exposed to the sun, so it wasn't particularly dense or hard to cut (there was just so much to move, and I couldn't throw it back over my shoulder where it was likely to be visible from below). But I had to throw it forward into the pile of scree, an awkward way to dig that makes you use your chest muscles too much and your back not enough. I was sweating and panting by the time that job was done.

Next, the shelter itself. I dragged out the big rectangular block, the size of two old-fashioned shoe-boxes, with an oval opening on the top. It was a structurer—it needed chon, carbon-hydrogen-oxygen-nitrogen, to operate on. I set it down with the arrow that marked the door pointing south, and heaped dead branches, rocks, dirt, and snow on top of it. When the pile was about half a meter higher than my head, the soft chime pinged, letting me know it felt enough mass directly above it. Then I touched the Structure button and stepped back, sitting down on a boulder to sip warm water and watch the shelter make itself.

First there was a low vibration as it shattered the materials directly above it and pulled them in. After a minute or so, the pile became visibly smaller, and then the black edges of the rapidly forming shelter peeked out from the sides like a doormat rising from a heap of dirty snow.

Curls of vapor were rising from the pile as the warmth of the shelter was absorbed by the melting snow, and the mounded rubbish shrank as if it were slowly falling into a trapdoor, as more openings on the partially structured shelter formed and drew in the mix.

I was old enough to remember the days before structurable molecular processing, and this still seemed very weird to me, even if it was just the same process that happened in an ordinary food reconstitutor.

In a short while that heap of junk I had made was down to being a damp black rectangle that covered about the same area as an old Sears Deluxe Tool Shed, covered with wet twigs, needles, and bark. Then the shelter absorbed the last of those, like a great squashed black amoeba, so that nothing was left but its own slick surface. It pinged, indicating that it was ready for more material.

Again, I heaped on branches and rocks, and then shoveled on a load of snow, until the self-forming shelter indicated that it was satisfied with the weight on top of it. After a few minutes, the snow and junk had flowed into the dark, lightless surface again, as if sinking into a pool of pure shadow.

The chemical changes and the rearrangement inside took some

silent time, and the only sound was the occasional splash and hiss as snow fell from the branches above and turned to steam on the hot surface. I used the time to sit down in the shadow of a big rock, not far away, where I could look out over the valley. I didn't much hope I'd see a hidden campfire, or a trail, or someone moving around, but if I didn't look, I'd never know.

I scanned for a long time, surfing through everything from infrared to low X ray, and saw nothing I wouldn't expect to see in the mountains.

On a feeble thread of a game trail, perhaps four kilometers away and 250 meters lower, I spotted one lone figure slinking along, which just barely might be a man. But switching around to get the right setting on my goggles, I got a good look at it: an old cougar, probably one who had lost his territory and was scavenging where he could (why else be out at night in February?). I felt vaguely sorry for him, but Resuna quietly reminded me that I was here to hunt cowboys, not to rescue cougars, and anyway getting old and incapable was the natural lot of cougars in the wild. He would no doubt find the death that suited him, sooner or later, without my help or worry.

That made me feel much better.

I heard a soft creaking noise that anyone any distance away would have attributed to pine boughs. The shelter eased itself upright. With a faint sigh and several loud creaks and cracks, its members went rigid. I turned to see that it had completed itself; all I had to do was throw my stuff inside, walk in after it, close the door, and I'd be "at home." It wasn't my warm, comfortable A-frame with Mary, but for the moment, it would do.

The pack went in with one toss, the duffel with another, and then I pushed the flexis and shovel in after them. Finally, I got inside, sealed the flap, and said "Light" to the pitch darkness.

The soft yellow glow came from panels on top of the shelter, and since the shelter walls were fully opaque and the light would go off if the door unsealed, I didn't have to worry about it being seen. The insulating shelter wall also kept heat radiation to a minimum—the shelter itself sent most of the heat to a recoverer to recharge its electrets. So I was now invisible except at very close range, and could relax in my new home.

Shelters are always too hot on the inside the first night, before their brains catch the rhythm of the outside temperature, so once I had done the minimum unpacking and verified that the bed and linens had generated properly, I took off all my clothes. I stripped out of my outside suit, turned it inside out, and stuffed it into the recoverer, which would clean it thoroughly, extract and purify the water from the reservoirs, scavenge the body salts for anything useful, make sure the electrets were up to full charge, and finally drop out a couple of pebble-sized chunks of waste.

Naked and comfortable in the warm little room now, I said "Lights down" and dimmed them to the point where I could just see; that always helps me to sleep. I slid a narrow rectangular mealpak into the food reconstitutor, waited a few minutes, and pulled out a tray with two small hamburgers, french fries, and baked beans, which I sat down and wolfed while the reconstitutor turned another pak—this one more cubic—into a pot of hot chocolate.

Resuna told me that Mary was happy and thinking of me. The thought brought a friendly, warm glow to my heart. The meal and the hot chocolate were working their magic, and the reassurance from Resuna was all I needed; I stretched out on top of the covers, told the bed to wake me at four the next morning, and fell sound asleep. All night I dreamed about old friends who were dead, and the way the world used to be, and the big empty spaces around the pine-covered mountains.

When the bed squeezed me gently, twice, around the knees and back, I woke instantly. The lights came on dim and red, and a soft voice said "It's time, sir."

I sat up, enjoying the pleasant warmth of the shelter, dropped the blocks of breakfast and coffee into the reconstitutor, and opened up the toilet side of the recoverer. Back when I had started as a cowboy hunter, we'd still been in tents, and had to make breakfast over a stove and dig our own latrines; the cooking was sort of romantic and quaint, I suppose, but one thing I had been glad to see the end of was the morning dash, through the far-below-freezing thin mountain air, to the slit trench. I told Resuna how much I had enjoyed waking up in camp; it might lead to One True's eventually encouraging more people to go camping.

After gobbling down the biscuits and gravy and drinking a couple of cups of coffee, I was ready to slip into the outside suit, strap on the day pack, and start the job. It was 6:20, about half an hour before the sun was due to come up. I carefully closed the flap and walked around the outside barrier that kept the brief flash of warmth from being visible through infrared scopes. For today I would be working my way down into the Dead Mule drainage, exploring this north side of it, to see what conditions were like on the ground and look for any places where someone might hide from the satellites.

I had gone only about 200 meters when what had looked like firm ground turned out to be a snowbank, which slipped away under my feet. For a weird instant, I seemed to hang in air, as if I had lost connection with the ground—the moment of free fall when the snow no longer pushes against your boots—and then a whirling tumble as I got myself turned around, spread out my arms, and let myself fall face first onto the snow behind me, trying to stay up above the real trouble. I slid down the ridge, face down and feet first, for about thirty meters before coming to a stop and tentatively dragging myself forward about three feet to get up off the sliding part of the snow. I slowly rolled over, pointed my feet downhill, and, cursing softly into the face screen, looked down to see what I had done.

The first light of dawn was just beginning to break over the mountains to the east, and the tops of two mountains to the west were already touched with the arc-brightness of sun on snow. That gave me more than enough light to see by without using the amplifier.

The snowslide had only traveled 150 meters down the slope, bumping along in a sheet rather than a rolling wave, never more than a meter deep or so. Unless he happened to look right at it when I touched it off, and saw me flopping around on top of it, the slide would look like the most natural thing in the world.

I sat up, took a sip of water, and let Resuna calm me; the worst I had been risking, probably, was just a plain old broken leg, which they fix pretty quickly these days, even in old guys like me. Something about that phrase, "the most natural thing in the world," was running through my head, the kind of clue that nags at you for days or weeks until you see what it was trying to call your attention to. Those sometimes turned out useful—and more often led nowhere.

I scanned the valley slowly, playing with different magnifications and different wavelengths, and the only thing out and moving in the early dawn was a small herd of elk crunching their way down through the snow to drink from Dead Mule Creek, stopping often to look for willow shoots, or grass under the snow, or aspen twigs that they hadn't already chomped down during the long, bleak winter. When I'd been a kid, the government used to send out helicopters to drop hay to the elk, because it upset the voters if the elk starved, and so there were always way more elk than the land could handle naturally. Nowadays, Resuna took care of public upset—and starvation, blizzards, wolves, and cougars took care of the elk—so we had sparse, healthy elk.

I watched the little herd pick their way down to the firm part of the stream bank, a step at a time, following in each other's tracks. A muscular young bull led the way, turning and sniffing the wind now and then, looking about with huge brown eyes. The elk of the Rockies look like big mule deer, I guess, to the untrained eye, until you realize they're half again as big, and until you see that wild, cunning intelligence looking out of the eyes. In the old days, good hunters loved them and lazy hunters only saw them from the road.

The bull must have decided it was okay, and began to scrape at the stream bank with his front hooves. Two cows joined him, and a yearling that looked like it would be on his own soon, and shortly they were making all kinds of noise down there, breaking ice, pawing up grass, and having what elk must think is a good old time. In the cold, still dawn air, their breath rose in silvery columns, catching the sun that sliced between the trees above them in white flashes.

I looked at them in everything from infrared to X ray, and they looked pretty much like any herd of elk, eating, in late winter or early spring.

The most natural thing in the world . . .

That was what, somehow, Lobo must be managing to look like. Even back in the 2030s, satellite optics and computers had been good enough so that they could designate individual buffalo and elk for the Doleworkers to cull from the herds. Something the size of a human being, dressed only in regular cold-weather clothing, couldn't possibly remain concealed from overhead satellites for more than a decade, and yet obviously something had.

He must still have a working insulating/storage suit, and somewhere to run a heat exchanger that wasn't noticeable. That meant in turn he had to have somewhere to charge his suit, and that meant a not-very-likely sizable power source someplace. He couldn't be stealing off the grid because that would be noticed immediately, but most kinds of generators, electrets, or batteries were just as visible from orbit, more visible even than the man himself would be.

Or maybe I was thinking too much like a modern, civilized cowboy hunter, and not enough like a crazy but very smart cowboy. I tried to come at the problem another way and think about how small a profile he would have to have to remain concealed—that is, how small must he look to sensors and screens in order to be lumped into the landscape?

What if he had gone completely wild, living out there with a flint-tipped spear, building fires only far back under rock shelves, sleeping on the ground, acting like a Paleolithic hunter who was afraid of high-flying predators that could see in the infrared?

Then where had his clothes come from, and how had his beard been trimmed neatly, when he turned up again? More to the point, human beings are *big* animals, and the satellites and databases *did* track big animals individually, so why hadn't they tracked Lobo?

Elk, bear, buffalo, moose, mustang, deer, wolf, coyote, mountain goat, bighorn, cougar—those, according to Resuna when it checked with One True, were the animals in the immediate area who were regularly tracked as individuals rather than as herds or flocks. All of them took up more than a square meter, had mammalian body temperatures, and massed over twenty kilos.

Lobo had to take up something close to two square meters every time he lay down—and you can hardly survive by hunting if you don't lie down now and then. If he was ever out of an insulating suit, he was more than warm enough to register on infrared. And even as gaunt as he had gotten, he must still mass at least seventy kilos. He was *way* over the threshold where he should have been detectable.

He must have a way of looking, to any satellite overhead, like anything else you would find in the wild country out here. He had to have had it for most of a decade. And whatever it was, it must have gotten lost or stopped working recently, bringing him out into the open.

Resuna remained absolutely quiet and let me work through it; very likely One True had already had some of these thoughts and was waiting to see if I came up with a different answer, or even a better one. After a while I was forced to concede that I still didn't have a clue, and I gingerly stood up, afraid that some of the surface under me might give again. I couldn't climb down the slide, since it was bound to be unstable for a couple of days, and death in a small slide is not much of an improvement over death in a full-fledged avalanche. Probably I should work my way down across the gentler slope to the west.

I got out the flexis and set them to configure as Nordic skis, plugging them into my suit and letting them take their time about forming up. The elk, below, finished their morning elk-business, and formed a straggly procession going back up the slope. For a moment I wondered, idly, if Lobo might have disguised himself to look, at least to overhead satellites, like some common animal; but the thought of Lobo crouching out there in an elk suit seemed just too wildly improbable.

The flexis had set and cooled into skis, so I unplugged them, strapped them on, and pulled out the extensor poles and telescoped them into position. Trying to hold it to *one* unpleasant surprise this morning, I took it very slow and easy.

This whole area had been pretty much abandoned in the aftermath of the Eurowar, when so many people fled into the cities for law and order and their share at the food distribution centers; now, ninety years later, it was "natural" insofar as what was happening out here was wild and unmanaged.

But it wasn't anything like it might have "naturally" been. The first decade or so after the war, before blight-resistant cover plants had been bred back into existence, had been bad for the land. Many shallow draws had been cut by water into deep ravines and gullies, and after cover had begun to grow again, it had taken many slopes some decades to re-shape.

The loads of silt and mud had altered the rivers as well, aging them rapidly, making them wind and twist in strange patterns that shouldn't have happened for another ice age or two—and the growth of the new glaciers on the highest peaks had put still another stress on the Colorado mountains. Add to that the fires in the dead forests, and the sudden surges and retreats of a dozen bioengineered plant species as they fought with a variety of non-native weeds and some species that were probably escaped ecoweapons, and it had been past 2025 before you could predict what might be growing where—if anything was—anywhere in the high country, and almost up to the beginning of the War of the Memes, a quarter-century beyond that, before field ecologists were writing with any assurance about what was out here.

The animals had recovered quickly enough; between the Die-Off and the Eurowar, plus the epidemics that had followed in its wake, the area hadn't been much needed by people, so as soon as there were plants for food and cover, animal populations had surged back. With so many cities and settlements deserted, and much less land under cultivation, they had migrated freely, and by the beginning of the War of the Memes the grizzly and wolf were all the way back to the old Mexican border, and the herds of buffalo were again beginning to carpet the Great Plains as they had two centuries before. And yet the differences remained: wild longhorns in Texas, a huge wolf-dog-coyote crossbreed that ranged from the Rio Grande to the Platte, bigger and stronger mustangs thanks to the infusion of domestic draft horses. Any forester could have pointed out any number of things different from what they had been a century ago, in any part of the drainage.

My first long glide across the slope was successful; the snow skidded out from under my skis no more than one might expect, the edges bit into the sun-formed crust easily enough, and by the end of that first swoop I was perhaps ten meters lower, and a quarter of a kilometer to the west. I made a big, awkward, snowplow turn like a beginner to avoid having any speed at all as I swung back east; the snow would be deeper now and I intended to take it at a steeper angle, so as not to be up here all day. Again it held, with one scary moment when I slipped sideways for a few seconds on some thicker crust, and now I was down into the heavy, partially-refrozen, pellet-like corn snow that you have to expect on a southern exposure this time of year. It's treacherous, but it can be managed. A few more wide, slow, careful turns brought me down to where the ground began to level off into a gentler slope toward the creek.

The satellite passing overhead told me, via Resuna, that nothing was visible anywhere, but I didn't entirely trust that. Many cowboys, especially the loners of the last few years of hunting, had become pretty fair jackleg mechanics, and every now and then one of them thought of something simple and effective—it had to be simple because they didn't have the resources to do anything sophisticated, and if it wasn't effective, they didn't last long between the mountains and the hunters.

Of course, Lobo was out in the open, now. So maybe whatever his miracle gadget was, it had broken down, and now it would be just a routine hunt. But just as possibly he was showing himself for some other reason entirely. I resolved to try to work as if he might be within fifty meters of me, all the time, and take it slow and easy. I would be looking for anything that resembled tracks—but at the same time I would be leaving mine, and I knew that *I* didn't have any way of hiding my tracks, whatever Lobo might be able to do.

Now that I was down in the easier country, I pushed off and skated slowly and carefully westward. There was some old sandstone in the local surface rock, and it was possible he might have found a cave somewhere, or even dug one if he had somewhere to hide his debris pile. Some mining claims went back 150 years and more—perhaps he'd found some old tunnel to move into. But that would only explain where he slept and holed up; how did he move around without being detected?

Well, when in doubt, start with basics. People eat. Lobo had to have been eating something. What he was eating had to be either stolen food, stored food, or wild food. I didn't believe he could steal for more than a decade and not come to One True's attention before this. Ten years of food is a lot to store somewhere. That left wild food—hunting and gathering. So he was relying on wild game, especially in the winter.

The best place to find wild game is where it drinks, so I decided to take a brief patrol along the creek.

I took my time getting there, going downhill in safe, slow snowplows almost as often as I paralleled. If I screwed up on this first day—twisted an ankle or something and had to be rescued—I would be humiliated by having let One True down, and embarrassed by the mess that would be made of the hunt by having to bring a diskster up here. Worse, I would be out of action and somebody else would get my cowboy.

An hour and a half later, it was almost noon. I was sweating buckets into the suit, the charge in the electrets was at 100%, all heat reservoirs were likewise full, and I had turned off the prewarmer on the air circulator because I needed the cooling from breathing the mountain air.

I only had to go two kilometers down the elk trail to Dead Mule Creek, but that was plenty. Elk do not have a skier's idea of what is a usable trail. The pathway wove through stands of trees, broke from brush on one side of a meadow and, after disappearing among a stand of young aspen, took a plunge down a bank into dense undergrowth.

When I finally came down through a bunch of beaver-felled aspen to the bank, the sun was high in the sky, and I was hot and uncomfortable. But a quick scan showed no trace of Lobo, nor any other human being. Probably there wasn't a single person between me and Mary, in the cabin a hundred and ten kilometers away—this part of the world had always been empty and in the past century it had gotten emptier.

At best I would have two hours down here before I would need to start working my way back to base, but then my opponent had only a very limited amount of time when he could move around, too. The chances of our both being in the same place during those brief periods were pretty slim. But I only had to catch him once, and he had to evade me every day. If I didn't catch him for a whole year, he could be ahead of me 365–1 at the moment I collared him—and I would still be the winner. Patience would do the job, more than anything else.

Down here by the stream, the warmer air had made a mess of the snow. When you're trying to stalk someone, it's hard to believe how many ways heavily weathered snow can be frustrating. It crunches constantly, breaks with loud cracks, and makes appalling squealing and grinding sounds against your skis. It grabs unpredictably, always threatening to dump you on your butt. If you fall down it makes a noise like a giant folding a garbage truck. If you don't fall down you still leave painfully sharp and clear tracks. Every so often it turns into sheet ice that can send you rocketing downslope, struggling for control.

Soon I was thinking too much about my skiing and not enough about my hunting. I finally got a clear view of a path down to the creek, and shot down it, alternately snowplowing and paralleling as best I could, turning often in big wide turns, bouncing around on the slope like a rubber ball down a storm culvert.

I was watching for somewhere good to pull into, and not finding it, so I kept trying to slow down—which wasn't so easy either. The snow under my skis screamed, thumped, skittered, and sprayed, giving me no solid grip; I was staying upright almost purely on balance. At least I was cooling off. The air coming in through my breather was almost clean and cold.

I turned up onto a rise to spill some speed, climbing up and then doing quick loop turns back down. The winding creek was still some distance below me, but the clumps of tall pines were much farther apart now, and there looked to be a nice, easy path at a reasonable slope. I had skied for almost a quarter-kilometer before I realized I must be on some long-abandoned road. In another hundred meters, I saw something by the roadside, and almost didn't believe it. I circled back and checked again.

There, partly covered by the snow, was a badly smudged print where something had been slipping down a gravel bank and had to brace itself. It was too wide for elk or deer, and had no claw marks like a bear; the heel was suggestively narrow where it had stamped in hard. And not far from that—again, the distance of something under half a meter suggested a lot—another smudged print, presumably where he had boosted himself back up. That clinched that it wasn't a bear—the weight, marked by the deepest depression, was much too far forward in the track. I searched in that area for another half hour and turned up three more badly smudged prints.

Squatting down till my eye was almost at snow level, I looked toward the creek. Farther down the hill a low, chaotic mess of crumpled and broken snow, less than two meters across, told me my man had taken a flying somersault after leaping the road.

Judging by what was packed into the shadow side of his tracks, he was using one very-low-tech method of evading detection—going out during snowstorms, so that most of his track would disappear to satellite observation before the clouds cleared.

The pattern argued that he had been descending when he passed this point, on the way to somewhere else, but I had no way to know how often he went there. Possibly he often took this path—or would, until the first time he saw my ski tracks leading up to it.

I skied back a short distance, feeling that odd prickle you get when it's a distant but not zero probability that someone will shoot at you. This area looked like an old-fashioned Christmas card—the vivid cobalt sky, the absolutely white snow, the greens shading from sun-spattered forest to nearly black in the shadows. The road behind me, leading up eventually to the ridge where my camp was, despite all the bright eye-stabbing daylight, looked suddenly weird, threatening, and hostile, the way a path through a public park at night looks to a young child.

Resuna steadied my nerves. I felt all my skills come to the forefront of my mind.

I found a place where I could climb the hill, just about twenty-five meters back, and herringboned up onto the bank. Remembering that Lobo himself had slipped, I stayed wide of the road.

If he didn't come this way often, the track was information but useless; if he did, the information would be useless to me the first time he saw my ski tracks. So I had to follow his trail in one direction or another, right now. The melting on the edges of a couple of the tracks had suggested that they were days old.

I picked up his trail easily enough; he was moving from rock to bare dirt to snow, stepping from one to the other in an irregular pattern, so that an AI looking at satellite photos was unlikely to see any pattern to it (especially since only the tracks in the snow would show well from orbit). But to the naked human eye, looking up the slope and just letting things have enough time to group and arrange themselves, the pattern was perfectly obvious. I could see his track or tracks—my guess was that he had been this way many times more than once—right up to where the ridgeline slashed the pure blue winter sky. I felt like whooping for pure joy. That's the way it feels when you know that One True has put you right where you most belong.

Lobo was clever, and he'd had a long run of making no mistakes at all, but all runs come to an end. Though, hell, even this didn't really count as a mistake; just one of those inevitable things that has to happen because no one can control everything. If I had the good fortune to bring him in, especially if when I brought him in he was still in shape fit to be turned, then at the cowboy hunter reunions I would have a tale to tell that surpassed anyone else's.

I checked my time. It was nearly 3:30 P.M.; the sun would be setting in two hours.

I doubted that I could follow his track clear up the hill before dark, but I had to try. This was clearly a frequent path for him, and he couldn't fail to miss my tracks when he came this way next. I had to push as far as I could, and find a place to set up an ambush the next day, or even tonight if it looked promising enough.

According to the satellite map on my face screen, his path angled slightly toward my camp. That meant a shorter haul back to base, a longer time I could stay out, possibly an easier position for the ambush. On the other hand, I would be going uphill, crossing ridgelines, and if he happened to be on this path ahead of me, *he* would be the one with a perfect ambush.

I shrugged and got going. You have to not only be lucky, but feel lucky, to hunt cowboys. And on this beautiful day, I didn't think I could feel anything but lucky.

I could be up all night, if I had to, anyway.

Herringboning is an efficient way to climb a hill in the snow, but efficiency is relative—all you can really say for it is that it is easier than boots or snowshoes. It's still lots of work. By the time I cleared the first ridgeline and could look on up the slope to the next—and to the distant white peak that gleamed over it for a moment—I was sweating as if I'd been stoking a furnace. Resuna adjusted my inner thermometer, but nothing compensated for the heat produced in my large muscles. The suit's heat storage was at 120%, which is 10% more than when you're supposed to stop and dump heat.

I moved into the shadow of a large boulder, took off the radiator, set it on the ground, and shoveled snow onto it. The snow flashed off. I did that several times, each time releasing a cloud of white vapor, which might give my position away if Lobo just happened to be right in the neighborhood and looking right at me, but if I got rid of enough heat, I would again be able to breathe and function without having a telltale infrared signature.

Besides, he'd have to be nearly on top of me to see it today. In the shade, and in the thin cold air, the clouds rose less than two meters before they turned to ice crystals and tumbled away invisibly on the wind. I was careful to make sure that the cloud of vapor didn't drift into the sunlight before it froze. He'd have to be looking right at this part of the mountain to catch me.

I gulped some warm water, swallowed a few bites of the blue-berry-flavored field rations, and systematically studied the fresh slope above me. Knowing his way of moving, I could pick out his path pretty quickly, and soon I was herringboning along his pathway, now warm without being hot, and refreshed by the food and water. I went at it hard, making good time.

Checking the satellite map, I saw that I was still angling toward my base camp; I might have only a couple hundred meters to go to get home, if the pattern held. There would be two more ridgelines before I reached the top, but I doubted that he was going all the way to the top—not with a decent pass just two kilometers west. Probably the tracks would start to angle west either over this next ridgeline, or the one after it.

I worked steadily up the hill, following the footprints closely, not cutting across his track, because you never know what additional clues might be around any one track. However, because Lobo had not been in much of a hurry, he hadn't dropped anything or torn anything off his clothes, or broken any branches. Unlike so many pursuits I'd been on, he wasn't bleeding, either.

I pushed my way over the next ridgeline without stopping, exulting in the chill taste of the thin air and the thunder of blood in my ears, but when I got to where I could see what came next, I was somewhere between muttering and swearing. It hadn't been especially visible from the satellites, being long and thin and rimmed with trees, but I was looking right at an old rockslide, and that was just where the few tracks I could see led.

If you're evading capture, old slides are your best friends in the mountains. There's all the bare rock you could ever want to put your hands and feet on, and furthermore, unless the guy tracking you knows the rockslide as well as you do, it's dangerous. A rockslide is only a *temporarily* stopped river of scree, and it can start flowing again with almost any provocation. Once you've worked out a safe path through one, by slow and cautious exploration, anyone coming along after you is going to have a hell of a time figuring out where you've gone, and will have to go very, very slowly if he wants to follow you up the slide without running the risk of getting killed.

So I stared at that dead end, trying to think of what to do next. It was less than an hour till sunset, and good as the light amplifiers were nowadays, they still couldn't find faint tracks in dirt under a tree after dark. I would have to give this up soon no matter what I decided.

It was looking like an excellent time to just turn and head for home, unless I saw his tracks leading off the rockslide somewhere. After a thorough search with binoculars, I didn't. I checked with the satellite and it was just as I had feared; the rockslide bent in an L shape farther up, and ran for almost a kilometer along the face of this big ridge; in at least fifty places, trees and brush got near enough to it to provide an invisible escape off the scree and into the woods. My best hope would be to search each of those potential escapes, one by one, probably the west side first. It would take most of the day tomorrow.

I was well and truly screwed: I had no tricks left to find him with. Probably he would find me first. Maybe he wouldn't come that way for another day or so, but that wasn't much to hang my hope on. Badly discouraged, I turned for home.

There was a deep draw on my direct path home to camp, too, and skirting around that through the woods meant that I didn't reach camp till the full moon was up again. At least it was so late that my post-sunset watch over the valley had only half an hour to go. I sat down in the snow, sipped warm water from the suit, chewed a chocolate ration bar, swept the valley in all wavelengths over and over, and—despite Resuna's prodding—felt extremely sorry for myself. Exactly on the minute, I gave up the watch, just as fruitless as the pursuit had been, and went inside.

I staggered into the shelter, tired and cold, with the ominous feeling I was getting old. Resuna crept quietly into the less-conscious part of my awareness, like a friendly old cat sneaking onto your lap, and I let it hang around there to see what it could do.

The hot soup and noodles that I reconstituted were one of the best meals I ever had, the bed felt remarkably good, and just as I stretched out, my copy of Resuna passed along, via One True, a warm, deep feeling of affection from Mary; she missed me but she was happy and comfortable at home. The warmth, dark, and silence got me to sleep right away.

I suppose that in my youth, I might have been a hero to little kids. After all, I was a cop, and there had always been great numbers of shows about cops in the days before memes.

Resuna and I have argued about this many times. I say that people were attracted to cops because so many of them were good-looking guys—young, alert, in great shape. Besides, uniforms and guns always got attention.

Resuna says what all the attraction to the cops was about was that most of humanity was looking forward to the creation of the memes and eventually of the One True meme. Resuna has a tendency to see One True wherever it looks, which I guess isn't very different from what human beings used to do when they saw gods everywhere.

What Resuna says is that the police were always the agents of order. Society runs on order. Hence the police always sent the message, whenever they appeared, on the street or in entertainment, that order was good, order should be sought, and that human beings who helped to make order were better than human beings who helped to destroy it.

Resuna never has convinced me, but we argued for years. It was a good way to while away otherwise dull time on stakeouts; it didn't interfere with seeing or hearing and it made no noise. I know Moonchild Swann used to play chess with her copy of Resuna, and it wouldn't have surprised me to learn that during stakeout, everybody was locked in some kind of conversation with Resuna. All that it was, was that the conversations I preferred were vaguely philosophic arguments, was all.

Every so often, to vary the argument, and because Resuna is always helping everyone examine their feelings and helping them to stay a valid and fully compatible unit within One True, Resuna would work through the issue with me, not as a philosophic matter, but as an emotional one: did I *wish* that I had lived in a previous era when an individual such as I might have been a hero? Did I dream about such times, or feel disappointed that I hadn't been part of them? Or if I didn't wish that I could have been a hero, did I sometimes regret, perhaps, that I had not lived in the intermediate generations when heroes gave way to role models?

Heroes were people who were idolized and admired for being bigger and better than you thought anybody could be—dreams of what a human being might struggle forever to just barely live up to. They were visions of what was beyond the human, structured in a way that called forth the human maximum.

Role models were friendlier, squishier concepts, for the friendly, squishy times in which they formed. They were people that you could imagine being; people you knew, who you were sure—given some effort—you could be like. It was the essence of a hero to be at or beyond the human boundary; it was the essence of a role model to be well within it, to be something that a human being could reasonably aspire to be.

And finally, at our point in history, there were no heroes anymore, and there were no role models, but there was what I was—for which there didn't need to be a word, because, though we cowboy hunters and other people who did dangerous, individual jobs, were *useful*, we were no longer *important*. One True could draw pieces from any of the vast number of its component Resunas and individual psyches, all over the Earth. If any child, or anyone at all, needed my approach to the world, emotional attitude, moral qualities, or any other bit or piece of my way of doing things, at any time in life, she or he could have it instantly, not by laboriously copying external actions until they became habits and then parts of nature, but by an easy direct transfer—One True would call my copy of Resuna, which would copy the required piece of my personality and upload it to One True, which would then download it via the child's copy of Resuna.

Resuna says it was really just a matter of the human race developing a more efficient process for moving information from one brain to another; the structures we called heroes were the oldest, crudest, and least-efficient system for copying virtues. If unusual courage and cunning existed in Odysseus, and the rest of his culture wanted to share them, his courage and cunning had to be told and retold at aural speeds, from mouth to ear, over and over again, until they were sharpened into a particularly clear and memorable form, and then the text had to be repeated to people until the merest mention of Odysseus would fill the mind with the drive to be clever and the self-perception of courage, for anyone who heard it.

Role models, as a way of transmitting virtues, were less thrilling and perhaps traded away some high resolution and clarity in order to be able to reach more people, more thoroughly and faster. The role-model method of transmitting virtues was to train a child to see her or his own abilities and potentials in the people around him. That didn't produce the excellence that the heroes had, since no one ever reached beyond what had already been achieved; at best it produced a competence that only degraded slowly from generation to generation. But it did provide very effective socialization. You didn't get any more high soarers, but nearly everyone took off and flew for a ways.

In this century, direct transfer of information, brain to brain, via Resuna and One True, provided greater accuracy and clarity than the "hero" protocol, *and* greater efficiency and wider accessibility than the "role-model" protocol—I could almost think I heard Resuna preening about the subject. The personal traits of people like me and the other specialists working for One True—not just the hunters but the engineers, rangers, ecologists, scouts, and all the other dedicated units that put high skill and personal courage and integrity at the service of the planet—were available to every person on Earth, whenever they needed to be like us. Ordinary people no longer had to form those qualities by long habit of practice; they were directly available just as soon as you needed them.

It was as if every Greek had been able to be possessed by the spirit of Odysseus at will, as if every athlete had an inspirational coach at his elbow and every preacher heard the voice of his god directly, and perhaps most important, in the long run, it was as if every parent could be the best parent on Earth. And so the reified, studied, carefully rehearsed and ingrained examples—the heroes and role models—passed from human memory, except as characters in old stories, for whom fewer and fewer people had any time or interest. One True had largely stopped bothering even with revising those old stories, since they no longer received the attention that might allow them to do harm, and any benefit they might exert could be achieved by more effective means.

Those were the thoughts I drifted awake with, shading into Resuna's usual celebration of morning—how good it is to contribute, how important it is to be a part of something bigger than yourself, how much one must rejoice in the strength of One True, and in the sanity that Resuna brings to your life. Resuna usually ran something like that through my head in the morning; my copy of Resuna and I shared the joke that it was a sort of mouthwash against spiritual morning breath, for often, when I was waking from sleep, my old memories crapped up my view of the world.

When I had served in Burton's Thugs for Jesus, we had been a relatively respectable outfit, but we had also been mercenary soldiers. There had been things I had seen my comrades do, and things I myself had done, that still, late at night, sometimes could disturb my sleep despite everything Resuna could do, and despite all the comfort of waking to find Mary beside me. Now, drifting awake, comfortably naked on the warm bed, with a day of challenging, productive work ahead of me—work that I knew it was terribly important to do—I drank in the sense of my place in One True, and thus in the perfection of human history, like a magic restorative honey in some old fantasy—sweeter than anything else could possibly taste, and bringing me strength, welling inexhaustibly from within me.

When I went outside in the pre-dawn, it had snowed, and exactly the wrong amount—not enough to obscure the fresh tracks I had made the day before, but very likely enough to cover Lobo's older, already partially melted trail.

It was also extremely cold, as it so often is in the mountains in the hours just after a snowfall. No stars shone, and the moon was an occasional yellowish smear in the west that never quite broke through the clouds; probably a high nimbus hanging over the area, enough to keep the warming sun out, not enough to hold ground heat in. It was going to be a real stinker of a morning.

You do your job even on bad days, so I turned up the temperature in my suit to warm the stiffness out of my joints, and sat up on the ridge for the dawn watch, scanning mostly in infrared because there was so little light in the visible band. I focused on the area where I knew his trail ran, but I saw nothing of Lobo. That could be because he had not come that way yet, or it could just as easily be because during the night he had seen my clumsy tracks from the day before, knew what was up, and was now four drainages away and running like a scared cat.

In infrared, the sun shone through the clouds as a great bright sprawling spider. The morning was so cold, and the light that filtered through the high clouds so feeble, that even after the sun had been up for half an hour, there was too little contrast to really see properly in the infrared: everything was about the same (painfully low) temperature.

It was still pritnear dark as night in the visible spectrum, but I flipped back to it, cranking up amplification to the maximum, to break the monotony. No Lobo, nothing moving, no sign that I wasn't the only thing alive that morning.

When the sun had been up for an hour, I went back into the shelter, had a quick breakfast, and suited up again. It looked like I would just have to stay on plan, since nothing better had appeared so far.

I shaped my flexis into telemark skis, let them cool, and pushed off; now that I knew where I was going, I could go much more efficiently. Fighting my way around that deep draw the night before had convinced me that I'd be better off going down and then up; besides, since that old road cut right across one of his major pathways, probably it would cut across more than one. I skied to the nearest convenient high point on the road, and started my search from there, slowly drifting down the road between the gray trees and the gray rocks, under a blurry gray sky, as the temperature continued to fall and little bits of sleet occasionally spit out of the sky and skittered down the hood of my suit. Without the satellite guidance, I'd have felt hopelessly lost in no time at all; as it was, I had to check my position every few minutes.

I was down at the place where I had found his trail, the day before, in only about an hour, and although it was now beginning to snow in earnest, at least that made a more pleasant surface for skiing, might help in hiding my tracks, and was sort of pretty in the gray, silent forest.

The tracks down here, on the lower part of the slope, were covered by the drifting snow, but I followed the satellite's guidance up the hill to where Lobo's track had petered out, going up onto that old rock-slide. I planned to cast back and forth along the west side, up to the top of the ridge, and then work my way back down the east, looking for the place where Lobo got on or off the rockslide—or perhaps even to see a print or two in the fresh snow on the scree, if by any chance he had come this way the night before.

I stamped up the gentle slopes and herringboned up the steep ones, making good time but only by dint of buckets of sweat. By the time I got up to the slide itself, it was almost mid-morning, and I stopped to open a ration pocket, take out a warm cheese sandwich and a pouch of tomato soup, and swallow those, chasing them down with a pouch of hot coffee.

This time, knowing that it could be a long day and I might not be getting home till well past dark, I had loaded all seven ration pockets on the suit with reconstituted stuff that could stay warm all day. Besides, it gave me more heat sinks for my body heat without having to vent and make myself visible in the infrared.

I made sure the next pocket from which I intended to eat was set to warm, and that the other pockets were to stay at ambient unless they were needed as auxiliary heat sinks, and got back on my way, herring-boning up the west side of the scree, gliding about in each successive little tongue of forest or brush that presented itself, until I was sure I'd have picked up any track. There was no trace.

Today, besides coping with the cold, the clouds, and the bad luck and fruitlessness, I was going to have three long gaps in satellite coverage, all in the afternoon. Normally the periods when a satellite can't pick up the signal from the jack in your forehead, even out in a less-covered area like this, were only about four or five minutes long at worst. If you were line of sight from SNY, or from the towers of the several new supras now under construction, antennas on any of them could give you continuous coverage.

But as it happened, a satellite had recently gone off-line, and the repair crews hadn't yet gotten up there to do anything about it. There-fore, today, in perfect accord with its being a shitty day, there would be three *big* holes in my coverage, each something over twenty minutes long. Most of what I was doing was on north-facing slopes, and since the supras hang above the equator, I would have no line of sight to any of them, most of the time.

Three minutes during which you're on your own, when your copy of Resuna can't raise One True, is scary enough—you could be hurt, captured, or killed with no way of calling for backup and evacuation—but in twenty minutes you could not only get killed, you could get disappeared. Two cowboy hunters from the old days were still listed as MIA—and both of them had vanished during "brief" satellite lapses, presumably either dying in some bizarre accident or killed by a cowboy, with their bodies never recovered.

Resuna was trying to be reassuring, pointing out that it was always there to help, but help from a meme running in your brain, and help from the combined minds and resources of the entire Earth, are very different. When a big, strong, clever man may suddenly try to kill you, you really want the latter.

On the other hand, if Lobo was coordinating his movements with the satellite gaps—*and* if he also knew about the dead one, and wasn't just coordinating by watching for them with binoculars and plotting orbits—then this was exactly the day and time he would be out, and the chances of my finding him were much better. The chances of catching him if I did find him were a different matter.

After climbing for another hour, and checking out three more innocent stands of trees without finding any trace of Lobo, I had Resuna contact One True and check back through the files. Kelly and her mother had been attacked during a time when two satellites were fully up in the sky and in line of sight, so maybe Lobo didn't pay any attention to the gaps in coverage. Too, the remote photos of him had to have happened with a satellite above the horizon. And twice he had been photographed crossing a south-facing slope with a direct line of sight to Supra New York. Chances were he wasn't coordinating with satellite passes, so he was *not* unusually likely to be out, today.

Just after two o'clock, not long after the first gap in satellite coverage, I was finally at the head of the old rockslide, a remnant cliff where a tower of volcanic tuff had fallen down sometime in the last century or so. I squatted down on a snow-covered boulder, looking out across the wide valley before me. The day was turning nastier, hard though that was to believe.

Far below, on the flat floodplain around Dead Mule Creek, I could see the wild swirls of the little ground blizzards. In the old days there had been auto accidents because of those things; someone would come around a bend in the road on a clear day, and a smear of white would erase all vision just when someone else, similarly blinded, drifted across the center line, or when the road turned out to be occupied by a wandering steer, or when the next bend hid a school bus that had stopped to drop off a ranch kid. People didn't drive themselves anymore, and machines could see right through a ground blizzard or call up a satellite and look over the top, but still something evil, frightening, almost alive lurked in the white swirls, a kilometer across and a meter high, that alternately hid and exposed the frozen creek.

I gobbled the macaroni and cheese, hamburg steak, peas, and warm apple tart of my mid-afternoon second lunch; Resuna informed me that this was what had once been called a "popular television dinner," but I didn't bother to find out what that meant. Every so often Resuna just hands you a fact, with nothing attached to it to explain why you should want to know. There are people in Sursumcorda, oldtimers who turned late in life and perhaps not willingly, who whisper that it's a bug in the system. I always feel bad about having my copy of Resuna report them.

The wind was rising. Minus ten Celsius, and falling. The firs on the slopes were whipping and dancing like mad drunks; the aspens bowed and bowed endlessly like compulsively obsequious servants; and even up here, high on the ridge without much snow upwind of me, the blowing snow was obscuring my view off and on.

It was senseless to try to find any of Lobo's tracks now; the weather would erase most of them before I got there, and in this miserable visibility I would not be able to see whatever trace might be preserved in a sheltered hollow, or to the windward of a rock or tree. Yet there were still nearly four hours of daylight, and I really didn't want to just ski home and sit out the bad weather in the shelter.

I could ski down the side of this ridge to where the old road joined with a larger road, far below where I had first picked up Lobo's tracks. A junction of two roads near a known sighting of a cowboy was a pretty good place to hunt. Furthermore, a check with satellite records showed that the terrain was reasonable—during most of the last portion I'd be following an old ski trail left over from one of the many abandoned resorts up here.

Once I got down there, I'd just follow the old road back to a point near my camp. That would be mostly uphill and should take the rest of the afternoon, especially if it snowed more or the wind picked up. If I found nothing, no harm done—the odds had been against it anyway—

and I would then just herringbone up the hill to my camp, get home just before dark, and turn in early that evening for a fresh start after the bad weather blew over.

But maybe Lobo used the old road down below regularly, and watched it. If so, I might be able to ski into an ambush. If he didn't manage to kill me in the first few seconds—and the suit was projectile-resistant, especially for old-fashioned bullets at long range, and I was in great shape with my fighting skills freshly replenished—then backup units would come swarming in, and all I'd have to do would be to hold him long enough so that he could be captured.

Then again, if by sheer bad luck a satellite blank spot coincided with falling into his ambush, that might just even the odds enough for him to get away—and for me to get dead. A lot can happen in a few seconds, and ten minutes can be forever in certain kinds of emergencies.

I could have waited till the next day, when there would be only two very brief interruptions—but that would mean running the risk of having Lobo see the tracks, or even of following them back to my camp and taking me. It was possible that I still had surprise on my side, and that even if I didn't, he hadn't had time to either prepare to fight or to run. But an advantage of that kind spoils fast; you use it right now or you might as well have thrown it away.

I pushed off toward the junction. Since I had the time, I treated myself to doing all kinds of hot-doggy stuff on my run down the hill, enjoying the experience as my own audience; long ago I'd have despised someone who did big, vigorous, show-offy turns like these, but back then, my knees hadn't hurt after a long day on skis.

When I got down far enough to pick up the old ski trail, it was full of brush in the center, but along the north side, where the tall pines and firs shaded it during summer and the ice lay on the ground till late spring, it was still more than clear enough. And three or four meters of powder will cover most of the rocks, bushes, and odds and ends; probably in the old days, if this much snow had fallen, the people who owned and ran that abandoned ski resort would have thought they had died and gone to heaven. Chances were they had died, anyway, at least by now.

Resuna, trying to give me a balanced view, kept talking about the ecological damage. It reminded me of the glaciers that had already eaten old towns like Crested Butte and Leadville, and might well bury towns as far south as Santa Fe before they were done, and the scablands that now covered the Rio Grande valley, caused by all the ice dams forming and breaking up on the tributaries that sent scouring floods down the river every third year or so.

Me, I just enjoyed the fact that the deepest, most untouched snow I would ever encounter was all spread out in front of me, and it was all mine. I shot down that hill feeling more and more like a teenager, bouncing and bobbing, spraying huge rooster-tails of snow behind me—what the hell, it might conceivably call attention to me, and make it more likely that Lobo would set up the ambush that I would be trying to trip.

After checking the satellite image of my path, I turned out of the old ski run with tremendous momentum and dashed across a small meadow, then shot through a grove of aspen. As I ascended the gentle slope up to a low saddle, I coasted to an almost-stop, let myself fall forward to conserve the last tiny bit of momentum, and then hurled myself up the slope in the closest thing to a flying herringbone you can do. In a few seconds I had covered the hundred meters or so to the top, and I coasted to a spot among the trees from which I looked down on the junction of the two old roads, an easy minute away, and rested for a moment.

Resuna asked me why I enjoyed this so much. I tried to make sure that Resuna understood the exhilaration of running on your own best skills, far out from any other people, in spectacular country, but I had little hope that it would be such a compelling explanation that One True would allow more people to come out to the wilderness. Better to pack humans together in cities, from an engineering and energy-efficiency standpoint, and the small amount of necessary pollution could be concentrated into a more easily handled point source. The all-but-mortally damaged ecology of the Earth just plain couldn't handle the extra load that tourists would impose, not just yet anyway. Probably, at best, I had supplied One True with something that it would want to introduce, as a "new" idea, in another generation or two when the Earth was well on its way back to health.

I thought it was possible, too, that the experience of the run through the trees might be copied into quite a few people's memories. Like the little boy in Germany whose surprise birthday party, at age eight, was now part of everyone's experience of childhood, or Katie Rafter, the young woman whose wedding we all remembered from her viewpoint, I might be added in as the perfect backcountry skiing experience. Thanks to One True, nowadays everyone who really needed or wanted an experience could be assured of having a vivid memory of the best possible version of it. It was even possible that the total social benefit from my addition to the library might outweigh the contribution of bringing Lobo in.

I leaned forward, pushed off, and slid onto the shallow slope beyond, skiing a single, big C–curve down onto the old road. In the low temperature, the fresh-fallen snow squeaked under my skis. A very dim circle of sun was appearing high in the sky in the south; you could almost imagine it might come out.

Every cowboy hunter I ever knew agreed that there had to be a tiny touch of the cowboy in every cowboy hunter, and I suppose that's true. I always had a streak of pride in me that Resuna could do nothing with. Just now, having made such a good run, that part of my nature was truly kicking in; I hoped that Lobo had seen me, partly because I wanted to attract his attention and flush him from cover, but also because—Resuna insisted that I admit this—because he was obviously a highly skilled, experienced outdoorsman, and I wanted his respect.

I started trudging up the gentle slope of the old road, planting and pushing like a beginner. This wouldn't be nearly the fun that skiing down had been.

I would have to move in an irregular pace, sometimes openly, sometimes with more stealth, sometimes rushing ahead and sometimes dogging it, to throw his rhythm off. It's easy to surprise a guy who moves along at a steady pace in a predictable path. It's harder when he's alternately rushing and dallying, hiding and showing himself, giving you too much data to analyze but not enough information to figure him out. We'd see if a cowboy could handle that any better than a hunter.

For the next two hours, as I covered about half the distance back to camp, I stuck with that plan. Now and again I'd skate hard and rush along like a rocket; every so often I'd just sit down and have something to eat. Sometimes I'd cut off a couple bends on the road by skiing across a meadow, thoroughly exposed to view; sometimes I'd climb up over a tree-covered ridge, taking it slow and disappearing for a while. Nothing happened; as Nordic skiing, it was moderately interesting, and as job performance, it was a flat zil.

Another satellite gap passed quietly as I climbed over one of those ridges; nothing happened during that time except that I really had to poke around to find a way up, after discovering a big brushfall in my path. From the top I did a big series of slow, graceful turns, killing time to throw his rhythm off. Maybe I threw it off so far that he never saw me at all, or wasn't there, I thought to Resuna.

Resuna instantly pointed out that I was playing all the odds right and my job was to keep doing that; success would come eventually. I told it I felt like I was running *Reader's Digest* instead of Resuna.

I had another cup of tomato soup. It's the most wonderful food there is, if you're skiing XC all day—hot water, salt, sugar, and a few vitamins and some flavor, all the essentials and nothing superfluous.

By the time I hit the third satellite gap, I was starting to feel like the characters in the old flatscreen movies who say to each other, solemnly, that it's "quiet. Yeah. Too quiet." I wasn't far from where I'd found his trail the first day. Still no sign of him. Maybe he was off doing whatever it is that cowboys do when they aren't stealing from society, terrorizing homeowners, raping little girls, interfering with ecological reconstruction, and congratulating themselves on what fine free people they are because they don't have a copy of Resuna to tell them that they're acting badly. Maybe he was around the next bend.

Adding to a sense of security that I knew to be false, the sun had burned through the nimbus layer, which had retreated rapidly to the east, leaving flocks of big thin mare's-tail cirrus scattered across the sky. The mare's-tails had chased after the nimbus in turn, and now the late afternoon sky was perfectly clear and blue; the sun was warming things up quickly; and at this very tail end of the afternoon, it was turning into a day I could enjoy.

I was beginning to feel a certain affection for Lobo, anyway. He'd given me an excuse to be back out here, in this season, after all these years. Now and then I heard a thundering crash, as the little added warmth undid some of the last-formed January's ice. Two ravens flew urgently, black shadows moving in straight lines against the perfect blue, wasting no time, because the carrion they eat is scattered and rare, winter kill that might be buried at any moment by another snowfall. Thanks to Lobo, I was getting one more look at it all.

I stopped all to watch a bunch of big, thick icicles that had probably been growing in the depression in the cliff face since November, dripping in the sunlight, dropping water back into the little hot spring that had spawned them; it hissed now and then as a cold drop found a spot of hot rock. A little stream of steam rose from the spring and enveloped the icicles, but it looked to me like the sun was sweeping away the steam for the most part, and the icicles must be losing more to their dripping than they were gaining from condensation. The real widespread riot of life that is Rocky Mountain spring was still three months away, but the living things were joining the resistance against winter everywhere.

Another bend brought me to a place where an elk herd had crossed; I stopped to have some coffee, being profligate with rations now that I had less than an hour to go back to camp. One set of very big tracks, three running to average, and one average set where the feet all came down closer together than they did in the others—looked like a bull, three cows, and a yearling. Probably the same ones I'd seen drinking from Dead Mule Creek the day before.

The wind had died down. Other than the gurgle of coffee in my throat, and a far off *flump* from snow falling off trees now and then, there wasn't a sound. I might have stepped, for that moment, into a photograph. I looked up at the snow reflecting off the glaciers on the peaks, and thought that I'd have plenty of time to return to the shelter. My thigh muscles were hot from the exertion, but not in pain; the only part that hurt was the part that always does, my arches and insteps— there's something about the motion of skiing that just works those muscles harder than anything else, and I hadn't been on skis enough in the last few years to build the right muscles. It wasn't agony; just an annoying ache that made me look forward to taking aspirin before dinner, with maybe some wine to wash it down, and rubbing my legs with an analgesic ointment before bed.

Well, since home was close, and now that the coffee had put more heart and attention in me, it was probably time to get going again. I pushed off and got into a nice big, slow skating motion, mostly keeping the poles tucked.

A shape didn't quite work, but almost should have, in the bushes to the left of the trail up ahead—a human shape, lying down. His cammies were just slightly off, maybe, for the dirt he was lying on, or he was stretched out just a hair too much and the line of him against the line of the bush didn't look right, or something like that. You can't always explain how you know. The figure stretched out prone on the frozen mud of a windswept bare patch, among all that gray-green crunchy, broken sage, was undoubtedly a man.

I kept skiing, just as I had been, though I felt like rough hands were squeezing my bowels. Right now I knew he was there, he knew I was here, and I was one bare point up on him because I knew that he knew. He could take a shot at me from this distance, but if he did, the IR signature to the overhead satellite would give One True an exact fix on his location, and he had no way to know that I didn't have a dozen backups waiting to jump in. In less than three minutes, there'd be the third and final satellite gap of the day, but I didn't know whether he knew that, or had a way to know that, or cared. Regardless of whether he knew or cared or not, I didn't want to move into his ambush just as my communications with the outside world went dead.

I couldn't even be sure that he had seen me, either. He hadn't moved a hair since I showed up. In my last remaining instant of satellite time before the gap, I called in a wide-angle image that covered a square kilometer centered on me over the last thirty seconds, zoomed onto him, blew it up, and saw that he hadn't moved at all for the whole time.

I slipped off the road and behind a big heap of rocks, figuring I might as well try something. People have been known to fall asleep on watch. Just maybe that had happened, or he had zoned out one way or another. Maybe he was lying there with his eyes shut, and had not yet seen me at all. If and when he awoke, or opened his eyes, probably in just a few minutes, he'd see my tracks. But it was just possible that if I skied down the steep slope to my left—flashing through his field of vision for a few seconds—I could get behind a little crag that stuck out of the hillside there, scoot around it like a bunny, climb up the other side, and have him from behind. And if he did wake up and saw my tracks, I figured he wouldn't have time to move into any new ambush position; he'd have to either run, or slug it out from where he was.

I pushed off down the steep slope, going as fast and straight as I could, to minimize my exposure.

I bounded over a couple of bumps that hadn't been visible beneath the thick layer of powder, used them to change direction so that I'd present a somewhat worse target, and picked up as much speed as I could, the skis bouncing around on the edge of getting away from me.

Normally, out in backcountry like this, to be safe, I'd have snow-plowed down a slope like this, ski tips close together, trailing edges splayed, digging in with my inner edges to slow down, so that I'd have more control; but normally in backcountry the risk is twisting an ankle, not getting shot. I was going down this slope like an old-time bump skier used to go down the trashed-out prepared slopes, just as if this had been a carefully groomed safe area, with a rescue crew standing by and the ski patrol watching. The skis slammed against yet another bump. My knees felt older than the rest of me.

For a moment, I was sliding sideways, just over the line into out of control. Then I got the uphill edges carving into the snow again, drove the pole in hard and reversed direction in a stem christie, and rocketed down the last part of the slope to slip behind that crag. I turned back and forth until I was practically snowplowing uphill, and finally finished up, grabbing a quick deep breath through my raised face screen, facing an empty hill. There had been no shot; without the satellite contact I had no way to know whether he had even moved. I felt blind.

Resuna informed me that I had fourteen minutes, twelve seconds to go until I'd be back on-line with the next satellite. That was too long to wait for Lobo to come creeping around looking for me, so I got busy. I pushed slowly downslope around the crag, taking a couple of minutes about it, sticking as close as I could to the rock face to make my tracks less apparent and keep closer to cover; some of these cowboys were so primitive, back in the old days, that they had been using old pure-projectile rifles without augmented sighting, hypervelocity, or homing ammunition.

On one occasion I remembered, a cowboy had caught Sue D'Alessandro in the open and taken four shots at her without hitting her. That failed to cheer me. For all I knew, Lobo might have stolen good modern equipment.

I was still wondering why there had been no shots so far. Was he asleep? Had he had a heart attack while waiting for me up there? I wished I had an infrared shot from the satellite.

By the time I reached the bottom of the crag, I was crouched low and just barely gliding along, getting steadily more nervous. Resuna had started to chatter, trying to cheer me up, and I'd had to tell it to shut up, and let me have my whole mind to think with. The slope down to the creek below me was streaked with the blue shadows of the scattered trees and snowdrifts, reaching far across the glaring white. In less than ten minutes I would have satellite coverage again.

Trying to make haste slowly, I got off the snow onto some sheltered gravel and took a full minute to reset my flexis, putting them into the snowshoe configuration. It drained the stored power in my suit considerably, but with luck this whole thing would be settled in the next twenty minutes, and besides, I would be putting out a heavy load of body heat soon enough, which would get me recharged.

I stepped onto the snow; I hadn't let the flexi cool enough after reconfiguring, and it was hot enough to flash some of the snow to steam. The loud hiss and puff of vapor startled me, and I said "Shit," perfectly audibly. If the burst of steam and the bang hadn't given me away already, surely my voice had.

With cover blown, speed was all I had—and maybe unpredictability. I kicked off the flexis, dumped my pack, drew my tranquilizer gun, and set about climbing up over the crag, coping with an unfamiliar surface smeared with snow and ice, with a mixture of rotten stone. That first face was about twelve feet high, broken and irregular enough to be feasible for three-pointing, but not at all easy, and I was feeling the effects of the long day.

Still, nothing happened; no shot whizzed by, or pocked the rocks, or stung me. No one shouted. When I looked out at the rough, snow-covered slope, which I did in every spare second, I saw nothing moving and I might as well have been all alone.

After that first face, the upper part of the crag was a tumble of boulders, which I could scramble over on all fours, staying as low as I could, off the skyline. It was still a terribly long way to the top, and if Lobo came around, I was going to be a sitting duck up here on the rocks. I kept pushing and I have to admit that I was starting to feel the first nasty whispers of panic; Resuna moved in to soothe that.

Less than five minutes after having stupidly let off that puff of steam and given my position away, I was ready to poke my head out and take a look toward the brushy up slope above, where I had first seen Lobo. I drew a deep breath and let Resuna have its full effect, calming and preparing me; this was frightening, and I needed the clear head that Resuna could give me.

When I peered over the edge of the rocks, he was in exactly the same position. I raised my head further, and still he did nothing. He was still out of tranquilizer-gun range, so I couldn't just put a shot into him.

I adjusted the sun filter on my face mask and kicked up magnification. He was propped on his elbows in the snow; no one could possibly put both elbows down into snow like that, in a jacket that wasn't heated, and stay in that position for as long as he had; your hands would go to sleep and you wouldn't be able to grip anything, not to mention the excruciating pain after a while. I couldn't see his face because of the way his Stetson covered it, and all I could see of one hand was—*what?*

I notched magnification still further and zoomed in for a better look. That hand was oddly undetailed: perfectly smooth, without hairs, any unevenness in skin color, or wrinkles, and its shape was long and delicate, like a female model—*or an old-type clothing-store mannequin*—

I felt the terrible blow to the back of my head, and my eyes blurred and stung. Pure training and instinct made me try to roll over. I got onto my side, curling to protect my gut. I had just time to see a boot heel at the center of the crazy star of my shattering face-screen. I sucked in a breath, trying to get my arms and legs to answer me, before a second blow to the back of my head drove my broken face-screen forward into the snow. As the darkness smeared across my vision, and a big chunk of broken face-screen forced its way into my mouth and onto my tongue through my sore teeth and bruised lips, I could taste the icy tang of snow mixed with mud.

When I woke up, the only thing that I could remember with any certainty was that someone had given me soup one or more times during the indefinite period while my mind endlessly repeated a few disconnected, frightening images—things that floated in out of a dark, noisy void, then drifted back out. I had little idea where my body had been going or what it had been doing while my mind was bouncing aimlessly through the void.

I had been eating soup. Someone had fed it to me. I remembered the soup because I had been so embarrassed about throwing it up on myself, and on the hand and arm of the person feeding me.

That was another clue. I realized that I remembered big, gentle hands cleaning me off, and then more dreams in which I wandered down trails in dark forests—not the friendly, familiar night forest in which I had spent much of my working life, where I knew what everything was and could savor the sounds and smells, but the terrifying confusion of the forests of childhood nightmares.

But now I was definitely sliding back into the real world, and I didn't remember what I had been doing when I had left. The immediate environment in which I had been sleeping was chilly, but I was warm under covers. That brought back another memory: sometimes a soft, warm male voice urged me to crawl out of the covers, across a rough, cold floor, and use a chamber pot. Afterwards the same strong, weather-roughened hands that fed me would clean me up before putting me back to bed.

Now that I was aware of what had been going on and what I had been doing, I was also aware that the same events had been repeating for a while; I think I must have been given broth, and thrown it up, at least three times, perhaps more. Well, continuity of memory is one of the signs of recovering brain function, and to judge from the pain in the back of my scalp and the dull ache in the middle of my head, I must have had a pretty severe blow to the head.

I asked Resuna what had happened and what I should do.

Resuna wasn't there.

I was so frightened, and so shocked, that I fainted. When I woke again, I reached for Resuna, and it still wasn't there. I thought about pulling the covers aside and looking around me, but that seemed like too much work, and I was already tired from worrying about where Resuna had gone. I let myself fall asleep again.

I'm not sure how many more intervals of lucidity like that I had in the next hours or days. Eventually I woke up and saw some light and heard some noise. The presence of reality was almost as comforting as the presence of Resuna would have been, and later, when I ate, the world seemed almost normal.

It was still a very long, indeterminate time—I'd have guessed at least two or three more days—until I was conscious for any period longer than five minutes at a time. When a brain takes a hard blow—and a mind loses its controlling meme—it takes days or even weeks for anything beyond the most basic functions to be restored. By the point where I remembered the last few days, and realizing that I must be still up in the mountains, my time sense was coming back, so that I was beginning to group my experiences into day and night. For some stretch of time, Lobo—I had realized that I must be his prisoner—would go in and out frequently, about one errand or another. Probably I was lying in an important work or living area of his. Then the lights would be off and Lobo wouldn't come; that must be the time while he slept. Most likely were that "Lobo active, lights on" versus "Lobo absent, lights off" corresponded to day and night—I just didn't know which went with which.

One day the soup was good but different—I found chunks of meat, jackrabbit I thought, plus bits of wild greens that he must have gathered and dried, and a flavor I finally identified as canned stewed tomatoes. With irradiation and non-reacting containers, canned stuff was good for centuries, so it wasn't surprising that it was edible, but it was surprising that somewhere he had acquired several years' stock of it. That information was vital—it helped to explain how a man could be living off the land in the high Rockies and not come down with scurvy—but there was no Resuna to upload the information to One True.

After a while I was able to look around and see the room. It was a refinished cave, probably an old earthquake crack or maybe an old mine shaft, and the part I could see was pritnear ten meters long by three high by four wide, quite a big space. Iron pipes gurgled all around the walls, and when I put a hand on one next to the bed it was very warm, though not hot enough to burn. That answered one riddle: he was keeping his place warm with a combination of good insulation and water from some hot spring, and it wasn't visible to a satellite because it looked like every other hot spring.

The walls were lined with forty-year-old canned goods, all with that silly "atom" sign that meant that they had been irradiated—in the old days, when people were allowed to have any old set of irrational fears they wanted to, with no Resuna to keep them in tune with reality, so many people had been afraid of irradiated food that the government had required those labels—I guess so that people could avoid clean, safe irradiated food and enjoy stuff that might be spoiled or contaminated instead. Nowadays the food was exactly as safe as it had ever been, and Resuna kept you from worrying.

Any place on the wall where there wasn't a shelf of food, there were portraits of people. Out of habit, I reached for Resuna to tell me who they were. Once again, I was all alone in my mind. I pulled the covers over my head, curled up tightly, and went back to sleep.

When I woke again, my eyes were focusing, my head ached only slightly, I could form more or less coherent thoughts, and Resuna was still not there. For the first time in a long time I had had many hours of real sleep, not the torment of half-waking nightmares. Almost, if I hadn't felt so lonely in the absence of Resuna, I'd have been comfortable.

Lobo came in, looked at me for a moment, and something must have been different in my facial expression. "I *did* hit the back of your head hard enough to kill any normal person," he said, with what sounded like mild frustration, "I'm sure of it. But I guess you're a hard-headed man, Currie Curran, and even though by all rights you ought to have a fractured skull, all you got was a concussion." He looked intently into my eyes, as if he thought I might explain what had gone wrong; after a breath, he said, "Looks like you're feeling better."

"You're Lobo," I said, unable to think of anything any smarter to say.

"Stupid name I gave myself when I was just a kid," he said, obviously embarrassed. "I guess I'm lucky I didn't end up as the Masked Avenger or something. My real name is Dave Singleton, if you want to use it." He was carrying something under his arm, and when he brought it closer, I saw he had a loaf of fresh bread, a cutting board, and a knife. "You going to be reasonable, Curran, and not go grabbing for the knife? If you say yes, we can share this while it's warm."

"Deal."

He sat down and sawed off a couple big slices, handing them to me. They tasted wonderful. He cut a couple for himself, ate quietly for a while, then said, "Funny thing. You might say I'm the reason for your existence. I'm the last cowboy, at least I think, and therefore, Curran, you're the last cowboy hunter. But then if you weren't hunting me, I'd just be a damned eccentric living out in the woods, so I guess you're the reason why I'm a cowboy, at least as much as I'm the reason why you're a cowboy hunter."

I let what he had said lay there between us. Too much response, too soon, kills most people's urge to talk, and I needed to learn many things that I'd only get if he told me.

I wanted to know why I was still alive; if he had been able to bring me back here, to nurse me back to life, he could just as easily have carried me far enough away so that my transponder wouldn't lead people to his hiding place, say to some stretch of thin ice on a mountain lake. Then he could have filled my outside suit with rocks and pushed me under. Probably nobody would ever have found me, and I'd just be another one of those hunters that disappeared during a satellite blackout. In the condition I'd been in, I'd never've even known he was doing it.

So why hadn't he? I could think of absolutely nothing that a cowboy would want with a living cowboy hunter. He ought to know— would know, to have survived so long—that because the individual parts of One True are nothing, there is no point in trying to take one of them hostage. One True will just lose the part, direct the individual copies of One True to comfort the mourners, and go on.

After a long while of just sitting together, during which he said nothing and I said nothing, I was unable to think of a more subtle approach, so I just asked, "Why didn't you kill me, Dave?"

The big man shrugged. "Well, I guess I had a bunch of reasons, but none of them sound all that good to me right now. Probably I'm just being stupid and acting contrary to my own interests. Most likely it's because I've got this great big phobia: I'm real, real, real afraid of dying by being hurt so bad I can't take care of myself, and starving or freezing a short way from home. It's what all my nightmares are about, and whenever something goes wrong, or I get sick or have a near-miss accident, it's the first thing I worry about.

"So I'd just hit you real hard and you weren't moving, and I checked you for a pulse, and damn, you had one. Well, I could've just pulled the electrets out of your suit, opened the heat reservoirs, and left you to freeze. I could have gone real low tech and cut your throat. Either of those would have made perfect sense. Instead I looked down at you and said to myself, *he's going to die here, helpless with no one to find him. I can't just leave him.*

"Well, I told myself I was just being silly and sentimental, but once I had let myself feel that I couldn't leave you to die in the snow far away from any help, the feeling carried over, I guess I'd have to say, to other ideas, so that I also felt funny about banging your head with that log again. Once you start caring *how* you kill somebody, I guess, you're already starting to think about *not* killing them, if you see what I mean, and—there I was. The moment was past. The blood was cold. I plain old flat out couldn't do it, at least not out there in the snow, far away from help or friends, where you might never be found. Not right there and then, anyway, not unless I really had to.

"Now, mind you, I might still take you out and slit your throat, later, but if I do, it'll be quick and clean, and you won't just lie there dying for hours, and I'll put you someplace where they'll find you and your family and friends won't have to wonder what happened. I haven't entirely made up my mind on that."

I kept my expression as neutral as I could, just like they taught us in training. "I see your problem, Dave. Is there anything I can do to, uh, influence this decision?" I was desperately trying to cue up Resuna for advice, but Resuna remained absent.

"No," Lobo said. "You can try but I'm not sure the ideas you'd have to use, and think of, would come naturally to you. How many years have you been running Resuna?"

"Twenty-six years next November, but, uh, I don't think I'm running Resuna right now."

Lobo looked at me curiously. "That was the impression I had, but I wasn't sure how to ask you. Usually Resuna has more options than the native personality, and it can recover faster; I expected to talk to Resuna whenever you finally came around, and to have to ask it to let me talk to you. But . . . you mean it's quiet in your head? Nobody in there but you, listening or talking?"

I shrugged. "I can remember Resuna's voice, but I can't seem to get it back. And I've been trying for a while, so it's not some temporary thing."

"Interesting. Who'd've thought a cowboy hunter, of all people, would be a good candidate for dememing? More bread?"

"Sure. You're a good cook."

"Not much else to do out here but please myself, and I'm sort of a fussy guy, or I was in the old days." He cut me off another chunk; I ate it more slowly than the last, savoring how good it was. I reflexively reached to store the experience with Resuna, and again it wasn't there.

Dave—I was starting to think of him as that, rather than Lobo—was staring at me, obviously curious, tugging at his lower lip with its few days stubble of beard. His hands were clean, though heavily callused, and his trimmed-short fingernails had no dirt under them. "You just tried to call up Resuna, again, didn't you?"

"Yeah," I admitted, seeing no reason to lie about it. "Every couple of minutes, I forget that I have this problem, and reach for Resuna, the way your tongue looks for a missing tooth. And every time I reach for Resuna, it's not there *at all*. Nothing like the temporary weird feeling when my copy is being replaced, and for a couple of hours I can't connect to it easily, and the new copy isn't yet using the old memories effectively—that's still Resuna, just Resuna that's hard to reach. This is just as if it had *never* been there." I ate another couple of bites. "What did you mean when you said I was a good candidate for . . . dememing, was that the word?"

"That was the word," he agreed. "Now and again, you know, people do get rid of a meme, or lose one, or it gets knocked out of them somehow. In the old days some of the cowboys were just people who woke up one day with Resuna not running, and they'd slip away and come join us. I don't imagine that's what very many people did. I'd bet that most people reacted the way you've been doing, so that soon as they woke up with Resuna not there, they called up One True on a computer or via some friend, to get another copy loaded in. But a few people would suddenly just not have a working copy of Resuna, and wouldn't want another one, and those people would run off to become cowboys.

"And—this wasn't so much the way it was with Resuna as it was with some of the older memes—sometimes you could trick a meme out of people's heads. Sometimes the drugs they used to use on mental patients would work, and sometimes shock, like an electric shock, or a big dose of insulin, or a blow to the head. Which I guess is how you got dememed. So what's it feel like to not have Resuna in your head?"

"Don't you know? I mean, you never have had it, so you must know what it's like."

"Yeah, but what I'm asking you, or I guess what I should have asked you, is what does the *change* feel like? How's it different now from what it was before?"

I thought about it, taking my time. When a guy saves your life, and would have had every reason to just kill you, you owe him at least the courtesy of a good answer to his questions. I knew if I had been running Resuna, like normal, it would have had some very convincing argument against that feeling, but right now it was just me. After the long pause, I just said, "Oh, like, uh, it feels a bit—a little bit—like it used to feel before memes, when a friend would die or leave. All of a sudden there's somebody you keep wanting to talk to and can't, you know? Not too different from . . ." I stared at the blank rock wall opposite and let the thought form. "Not too different from waking up from a dream, calling for somebody you only knew in the dream, and then knowing they aren't there and can't be there."

Dave nodded. "Poetic." When I stared blankly at him, he said, "Well, that's one effect we've identified. Clearly being dememed makes people get poetic." He smiled, and I made myself smile back, though I wasn't sure that I had any sense of humor about that subject just then. After an awkward pause he added, "I got some coffee brewing, too, if you'd like some. Do I have to tie you up every time I leave the room?"

"I guess not. I wouldn't get far, naked, and I'm not stupid enough to try anything yet."

"Glad you put the 'yet' in there," he said. "I'd have to be pretty damn dumb to expect you not to lie to me, but I'd sure appreciate it if you don't lie to me more than you feel you have to, and if you don't let me catch you doing it too often."

I considered. "Why don't you just figure that I won't pass up any good chance for an escape, but I won't do any petty shit that just makes both of us uncomfortable? I'll lie if it'll help me get away, but not just to fuck with you."

"Deal. Let me go get that coffee. Bet you're tired of jackrabbit soup by now, too; in another hour I'll be done cooking up an elk loaf with some reconstituted potatoes."

My stomach rumbled and I said, "I think I can help you out with that. How many days have I not eaten solid food?"

"Since you got hit on the head," Dave said. "Sorry not to be able to tell you more than that, but it's always possible that you have a perfectly good copy of Resuna, and what's keeping Resuna from restarting itself, and turning you again, might be nothing more than having lost track of the time—it does depend partly on that internal clock it creates inside you when it takes over. So, I can't answer that question."

I shrugged. "Well, anyway, I can tell it's been a long time, and I don't really have to have things more specific than that. And the food sounds wonderful."

Dave went out to the kitchen, and I continued to sit on the bed, not really thinking of anything, just enjoying being awake and not feeling awful. There would be time enough for more advanced pleasures, later, perhaps, but right now sitting and waiting for a good meal, and being well again, was about all I needed.

When Dave came back with the coffee, which smelled so wonderful that I was beginning to wonder if he had been slipping You-4 into my soup (maybe because making me happy all the time would help keep me dememed? I didn't know a thing about how dememing worked—hadn't even known it was possible until it happened to me), I had thought of another question to ask him. "How did you build this place? I know that sounds like a stupid question."

"Not really. What you want to know is how I got this place without tipping off the satellite, and the answer was good luck and patience. I found this old mine, a hundred yards from a hot spring, half-choked with dirt, and dug it out. I carried the dirt with me, on the regular rounds during the day, in a pack I made from a gunny sack with a few holes cut into it to let the dirt dribble out as I walked. It took a long time but I had a long time. The first couple of years I lived in a shelter like yours, basic military-surplus thing, under the overhang, where there was room to set it up. After two years of digging out a pack-load of dirt per day, I had a nice medium-sized room to live in. And now after a couple of decades, I've got a bigger house than I ever had back before I went off to be a cowboy. With ten years of a pack-load a day, if you're careful not to miss a day, you can have a pretty big hole."

"You're still digging?"

"It's something to do. I have a room in back that's going to be a warm, comfy library; it happened I found an old armchair that was in great shape, so that made me think how much I would enjoy just having that as my regular place to sit, enough to bother bringing it up here, but then I didn't exactly have the perfect place to put it. So I went looking for a rug to go with it, and a floor lamp, and when I had all of that, well, two bookcases fell into my hands, which was fate's way of telling me that that armchair needed a library to be in. And I already had some books. All this finding stuff and figuring out what to do with it was all across a number of years, mind you, while I was still digging out the hot-tub room, so I had lots of time to do my planning."

"A *hot tub?*"

"Well, I've got hot water, more than I can use. Might as well. Though I admit that I also use the tub for laundry, and dishes. Room in it, though, for three or four people to soak; I just like having the room. Anyway, once I got the tub room done, it was time to start on the library. Figure another two years and that'll be done as well, which

will be good. I ain't as young as I used to be, and a warm place with
good light to read by is starting to seem more and more important, as I
think about what kind of a setup would be best for a rickety old man."

I looked at him intently for a minute, and then finally blurted out,
"Jeez, I can see why you'd need to plan for when you're old, but you
don't look a day older than when I thought I'd sent you over the cliff."

He laughed. "Well, *you* look awful good for an old fart of your
age, Curran. Especially for one who was in a dangerous occupation for
a long time. People living a long time and people looking younger than
they are are things that happen, you know, with better medical treatment and all."

"I guess so," I said. I didn't believe him. In the first place, except
for his recent foray into rape and robbery, Dave hadn't had access to
much of that medical technology, nor could he have had much in the
last fifteen or twenty years.

Also, he was exaggerating about how well preserved I was. I could
tell you ten things that are different in my appearance, now, from what
it was ten years ago: more pounds in bad places, less hair in good
places, some lines and wrinkles. Dave, on the other hand, looked
exactly the way he had looked when I had last seen him in the flesh—
better, in fact, since now he wasn't tired out by a long chase. Somehow
nothing had happened to his face or body at all. My degree of preser-
vation might have been mildly interesting in our present world full of
well-preserved old guys; but his was dead solid freakish. That he was
trying to conflate the two suggested that he was unobservant (unlikely,
in someone who had survived so long out here) or more likely that he
was trying to put one over on me (very likely, in a cowboy).

I thought about pressing the point, but either he was telling the
truth (and there was nothing more to tell) or he was lying (and wasn't
about to tell me), and what he would say would be the same either way.

So I changed the subject. "And have you been living on canned
goods and hunting all this time?"

"If you're a decent hunter and there's just one of you in a wilderness area, it isn't that hard to keep yourself fed. Didn't even have to
work that hard. The canned stuff is good for the things I can't grow, but
I grew some of my own stuff too. I'd plant vegetables on hillsides
under upside-down aquariums, which make perfect ready-to-go cold-
frames—I raided a couple of old pet stores in Gunnison and Montrose
for those. My plantings were too small to show much from orbit, as
long as I kept them scattered out pretty wide, which meant I'd have to
do some walking, but I had time to do it. Now and then a deer would

smell something it wanted and knock over an aquarium, or a gopher or rabbit would tunnel in for it, but not as often as you'd think, because herbivores basically aren't too smart, and my growing sites were so scattered that if they raided one aquarium and figured out how to do that, by the time they ran into another one, like as not they had forgotten. And I could combine making the rounds of my aquariums with my hunting. Even doing all that stuff, I had plenty of time to dig and think. It's been lonely work, hard work, but it ain't worn me down yet."

I shrugged. "It might even be why you still look so young," I said, hoping to keep him thinking I was believing him. "Abundant exercise and a good diet, far away from all the places where there are leftover plagues from the wars—probably a healthier life than I've been leading." I took another sip of coffee. "This is as good as I get at home. Reconstituted?"

"Yeah, I stole a reconstitutor a while back."

That reminded me, for the second time in a few minutes. Since I couldn't afford to offend him, I did my best to repress a shudder.

All the same, he must have seen the change at once. "What is it?"

I don't usually like to pick a fight with my host, and I *was* naked, disarmed, and completely at his mercy. Plus we'd already had a theoretical discussion about his cutting my throat. But the unfortunate habit of a lifetime—saying whatever popped into my head—caused me to blurt, "When I was prepping for this mission, One True took me through Kelly's memory, and all I can say—" I stared at him and tried to reconcile this soft-spoken, seemingly gentle man with Kelly's vision of him bouncing on top of her and laughing at her cries of pain and fear "—shit, I don't *know* what to say. How could you *do* a thing like that to a little girl, and her mother?"

He looked puzzled and said, "I didn't have much choice; they'd caught Nancy a long time back, even before your group caught up with me, and once they found out she was a cowboy's wife, they really poured on the Resuna copies until she was completely theirs. And Kelly never had a chance—she was probably given her first copy of Resuna before she was three years old. But you know what Robert Frost said—home is where, when you've gotta go there, they'll have to take you in—and I was good and sick, so I paid them the visit. I was damn lucky to get away, and even luckier that I could dememe them long enough to have my chance to say hello to my wife and daughter; there are days when I feel like, now that I've done that, I can die easier."

I was staring at him now, unable to believe what was either an audacious lie, or . . . the thought connected. "You mean you not only raped that poor child, but she was your *own daughter?*"

Now he was staring. If there'd been a third person there cruel enough to laugh, he'd probably have busted a gut at the spectacle of two men who had suddenly dropped their brains on the floor and didn't have anything with which to think of picking them up. Finally, he sputtered, "What the fuck are you talking about, you crazy fucking idiot?"

I was not used to being called a crazy fucking idiot—with everyone running Resuna, profanity and insult are both very rare—but despite being startled, I could see that he was pretty stressed. And I knew that this wasn't a turn the conversation should have taken, but hell if I saw any way out but forward. "That's what was in her memory," I said. "I played through the whole memory copy, and believe me, I'd rather not have, and I wish like all shit that she didn't have that memory, but she does. You came in with a gun—the poor kid had never even seen one before, do you realize how much innocence you were spoiling?—you threatened them into giving you medicine and food and their reconstitutor, and then you made that little girl watch while you raped her mom, and then you raped her. That's what she remembers. And thanks to the transference from One True, I remember every bit of it, and you better believe I wish I didn't. Now *you* tell me that was your wife and daughter that you did that to. Well, ek-fucking-scuse me, and I guess now you'll kill me for saying it, but out of all the dirty, vicious, hate-filled cowboys I've ever hunted, you are the only one I've ever really despised." It was about there that I noticed I was shouting into his face, standing over him where he sat on his stool, fists on my hips like I was going to yell him into submission, with some of the effect spoiled by the fact that I was buck-naked.

Dave stared into space. If I'd had pants to throw on and a weapon to hand, I could have taken him right then, right there, without much difficulty, I'm sure. As I watched, a tear ran down his cheek. "You damn well ought to be crying," I said.

He wiped his eyes, stared at me, and said, "Of course you believe that memory."

"What are you going to try to do, pull some Freud-bullshit and tell me she *wanted* to remember something like that, and made it up?"

He shook his head slowly. "Curran, I don't have a damn idea in my head for how to tell you this so you'll believe it, but . . . hey, did you ever meet Kelly? Or just that copy of her memory?"

"Well, of course I just got the copy of her memory! What would you think? One True *never* inflicts unnecessary pain. It wasn't going to make her sit there and tell me all about it. Not when her copy of Resuna could just load the memory up to One True, and my copy could load it down to me, and I would know what had happened to Kelly far more vividly than she could ever have told it, and with no pain to her. Why would we need to meet face-to-face?"

He shrugged, got up, seemed about to speak, stopped himself, looked down at the floor, visibly got himself under control, and started to pace, gulping at his coffee, as if the solution to some hard problem might be anywhere on the floor if he could just find it. Finally he looked up; the whole silent performance had taken over a minute, and I didn't believe any of it; he'd had days to plan whatever he was going to say now.

"You ought to ask," he said, "why your only access was that copied memory. Couldn't her copy of Resuna have just taken control, so that you could have met her face-to-face? Wouldn't you have had a stronger feeling if you had really known Kelly instead of just importing that one memory? Wouldn't that have motivated you more, if you had looked into her eyes and promised her you'd catch the asshole rat-bastard that did that?"

"Might have," I admitted.

"So, One True can do damn near anything and it couldn't do that for you?"

"It might have hurt her—"

"A *conversation?* Even though it might be emotionally painful for her, it couldn't be as painful as what had already happened. And One True could erase her memory of the conversation easily enough, if it needed to. Hell, it gave Nancy a whole set of imaginary memories about being with squatters in Vegas Ruin, and being a slave there, to replace our marriage. You should've seen how bewildered she was when I dememed her and she suddenly knew who I was—and who she was—again! One True *could* have let you talk to Kelly—should have and would have—if the memory that was copied to you was accurate. Even if it had hurt Kelly at the time, her copy of Resuna could control and erase the pain as necessary. And meanwhile you'd have been just that much more motivated, and she'd have had the comfort of knowing someone was going out there to catch me. *If* One True was telling you the truth, *if* I had really done those things to her, then that was what it should have done, and if it knows us as well as it says it does, it would have done it."

"But I *felt* her personality," I said. "Real and human and twelve years old, not the kind of thing that even One True could make up—"

"Oh, I'm sure One True *started* with some memories from Kelly, when it created the one it gave you. Probably even copied over some bits and pieces from some adult woman who was raped as a child—the War of the Memes went twenty years and sooner or later pritnear every girl and woman who had the bad luck to live in those years got serbed, so One True probably had a wide selection of rape memories."

"I never serbed anybody," I pointed out, "and I was in the War of the Memes."

"I was too, and I never serbed anybody either!" Dave said. He was glaring at me, dark eyes fierce under his bushy, unkempt brows.

"Until recently when it was your wife and daughter," I said, sneering, maybe hoping he'd just kill me.

"That's what I'm fucking telling you, Curran. The memory is *false*. One True probably started with some of Kelly's fear, from when I broke into the house, which it got via her copy of Resuna. Then it fused in a bunch of rape memories. You damn well know that memes can create memories that you experience as real—weren't you ever hit with Unreconstructed Catholic, or didn't you know someone who was? And don't you remember how everyone who ever ran Unreconstructed Catholic all remembered kindly Sister Agnes and lim koapy Father Jim from first grade at St. Aloysious School? And being their favorite and feeling secure and safe with the Church guarding you? Or Real America's memory of the Fourth of July when you were in eleventh grade and went to the high-school prom in Brightsburg, Vermont, with the red-haired girl that used to pitch for your Little League team? You *know* memes can make you remember things that didn't happen, dammit."

"They *can*," I said, "but One True *doesn't*. Never, never, never. It just helps you understand the memories you have. And anyway, One True isn't a single program dominating your brain; it's just what all the Resunas together make. Your individual Resuna is a much smaller program than the old memes, and it's just a helper for your own personality. It's not going to screw things up for you by making you remember things that didn't happen . . ." My voice was getting softer and I was almost mumbling.

I hated the feeling and wished Resuna were here to help me, but it wasn't. Unfortunately I was realizing a couple of things. First of all, Resuna and the emergent version of One True were the most sophisticated and capable memes; it wasn't smaller because it had less power. Anything any other meme could do, One True could do, easily.

Then a rush of feeling and memory roared through my mind like white noise cranked to ear-bleeding volumes. I was remembering things that had been erased from my memory of my life with Mary, trivial stuff like little fights and moments of anger, that I was better off forgetting—yet still they had happened—yet I was better off not remembering—yet-yet-yet . . . and simultaneously I felt an odd quality to my memories of Mary's love and support during my cowboy hunting days . . . *in fact* she'd been very upset nearly all the times when I went out, and *actually* there were times when I came home and could tell that everything had just been cleaned and fixed up that minute, and *really* there was no Mary to talk to, just her Resuna, as if *in reality* it had been unable to make her function and had just grabbed control and straightened out a mess at home . . . I remembered her throwing the lamp at me the time she had yelled something about days spent in bed crying, and yet another memory seemed to try to crawl over it and say that she had told me that story about a time during the War of the Memes when she was a slave . . . and yet, ghosted over all that, images of my brave, supportive, smiling wife who could send me off to fight cowboys with the warm confidence that I would be back, with a total confidence and love.

Well, that had been very useful for One True to have me remember, hadn't it?

All of those thoughts and feelings rushed through my head in less time than it takes to think a single sentence in words. I hated Resuna, One True, Mary, the whole of my life, and Dave, not necessarily in that order. I hated myself for having lived for years that way. And most of all I hated the way that it seemed likely that Dave was right. "Shit," I said, flatly. "Shit, shit, shit. You might as well make me the rest of your argument."

He shrugged. "You have the same expression in your eyes that Nancy did as she came out of it. Look, I don't think One True would have put that rape memory into Kelly; it made up the memory to show to you, but it put something different into her head. That's why it didn't set up for you to meet her. Probably it told her that she hid under the bed the whole time I was there, and maybe that I vandalized the place or threatened her. From One True's standpoint, that would make sense—it wouldn't give her any more trauma than it had to for its purposes, so it gave her a false memory that would help her cope with the world she'll have to live in. Probably slightly painful but nothing she can't cope with. And I would bet that the false memory they gave her *doesn't* hurt as much as her few hours of knowing the truth and being herself did. But she did seem to like that little taste of freedom, even with the pain and all. Or maybe I'm just projecting because I wanted her to like them."

"Why would One True give somebody a false memory?" I asked. I was rummaging, hard, in my own memories, trying to get Resuna to come back; I felt so utterly defenseless without it, and I was sure that if only I had One True here, it would have a real answer to all these accusations. "And why should I trust you to be the one telling the truth?"

He looked so directly into my eyes that I sat down as if he had pushed me. For a moment, I wondered if this might not be some sort of hypnosis. "Look," he said. "You know the answer to that perfectly well, even if you don't want to admit it. One difference between me and One True is that I don't have a planet to run. And all those billions of copies of Resuna in everybody's brain are parts of One True. Now since the world began, people have been lying to themselves to get through their day, get through their job—get through their life. How many people have gone to their graves thinking that the boss really valued them, or that they were better off not changing jobs, or that their mother cared about them, or that their children loved them— when any objective observer could have seen it for pure bullshit? Sometimes it's just very useful to believe something that isn't true.

"And you don't care what your individual brain cells do or believe, except as it matters for your convenience, do you? If it makes you happy to have a few thousand of your brain cells think your wife is the most beautiful thing you've ever seen, and respond to her like that, you don't necessarily want those cells to develop the objective opinion that she's actually much plainer than ordinary, do you? Aren't you better off having those deluded little cells in your head telling you different?

"Well, that's what One True needs from its component copies of Resuna, frequently. Much as I hate to defend it, One True's reasons for what it does are not necessarily bad or crazy. One of the troubles with fighting One True, psychologically, for every cowboy I ever knew who wasn't crazy, was that—objectively speaking—we had to admit that One True wasn't evil; oh, it had done some cruel stuff and it had fought the War of the Memes to win, and like that, but unlike so many of the other memes, One True was not out to enslave the human race to some ideal that was meaningful only to it, or force people into behaving according to some crazed code that was a bad parody of an extinct set of ideas, or any of that stuff. It really did intend to benefit human beings and the planet.

"When One True took over, a billion people worldwide were hungry even though there were more than resources enough to feed them; hundreds of disasters were going their way without interference, even though humanity had the brains and resources to control them; and everyone was in fear, even though the only thing they really had to fear was each other, and very few of them really wanted to hurt each other.

"One True gave everyone Resuna, and *became* what everyone needed—something that would ensure that everyone put his whole heart into meeting the global crisis for the next few decades. Earth would be in worse shape without it." He was emphasizing his points as if trying to pound them into me; I couldn't imagine why a cowboy was talking like this.

"So, along the way, sometimes, One True needs an individual to believe something that isn't true. What if a woman wants a particular man, maybe one she got separated from during the War of the Memes, so much that she won't do her work in the farm or factory, and just wants to go looking for him? Resuna keeps the thought of him out of her mind until One True can learn if he's alive or dead, and if he's alive, maybe it's convenient for the Earth, and the whole project of saving the planet, to bring them back together—and maybe it's not. If it is, they get together and there's much rejoicing; if it's not, they don't, and their copies of Resuna keep them from feeling more than a trifling sadness now and then. Who's hurt?

"Or maybe a brother and sister both have genius-level talent for doing the math for the ecological computer models that One True needs them to do. Unfortunately, the brother molested the sister when she was a little girl, and she's afraid of men, afraid of him, and too depressed and angry to do any work. Her copy of Resuna adjusts all that, and bingo, she's functional, she's not unhappy, she and the whole planet gain. Furthermore, his copy of Resuna adjusts him so that he won't do things like that anymore. He's not only happpier, he's a much better person. And the math gets done, part of the Earth gets repaired, fewer children get hurt, and two people who would otherwise have been basket cases of one kind or another work happily side by side. Now who can argue with that? Might not be all that much justice to it but there's pritnear perfect mercy.

"So, Resuna needs to make sure that Kelly does *not* form any part of her identity out of being a cowboy's daughter, and it really doesn't want her forming any ideas about rebellion or freedom or any of that, which young brainy people are very apt to do given half a chance. So instead it creates a memory that will be a barrier, forever, against that side of herself. The minute she thinks of things that are wild and free and uncontrolled—like a cowboy—she thinks of how scared she was by me. And then Resuna comforts her and she doesn't feel so sad anymore, or hurt; all she feels is love and gratitude for Resuna. And Resuna needs you to want to hunt me down—so it gives you that gruesome memory and tells you it's Kelly's. The result is that Kelly grows up to be productive and happy, you catch the cowboy, and everyone is better off. Even the cowboy, who finally has his personality altered so that he can function in the real world. The false memories are good for her, good for you and me, good for One True, might even be good for the future of the planet. And if what you remember doesn't happen to be true, well, it's useful, isn't it?"

The strangest thing about it all, as he sat there and said that to me over our hot coffee, was that he not only didn't sound bitter or sarcastic, he sounded more as if he were just explaining, in a friendly way, to someone who didn't know, how the world worked. It was a good strategy, I realized—I wanted to believe him. And now that I was calming down, the thought no longer made me angry at Resuna or One True. I still wanted to get back as soon as I could. I just felt as if I weren't quite myself.

I sighed and asked, "How do I know, though, that you're telling me the truth?"

He shrugged. "You don't. That's what life was like before Resuna, and if I were still fighting to free the world from it, *and* I thought I could win, I'd say that's what life will be like after Resuna. One of the books I like to reread—*Forks in Time*, even though I'm not cybertao— says 'Certainty is a very overrated quality,' and it's got a point. But then *Surfaces in Opposition* says 'Certainty is what most people prefer to truth, and it cannot be kept from them.' So you slice it whatever way you want, I guess."

I shuddered, feeling as cold as if I had rolled naked in the snow. "I can't seem to make my thoughts come together, at all. And I don't mean to be rude, but I feel incredibly tired."

He nodded. "Well, just making a guess, I'd say that since you've just had an exhausting physical injury, your first good meal in a long time, and a whole big set of emotional shocks, you probably need to sleep. Let's put you to bed—I hope you won't resent that I have to lock the door—and when you're awake again, we can talk more. For right now, I don't have any reason to do anything except feed you and keep you here, till I make up my mind what's to be done."

As soon as he mentioned the idea of sleeping, I realized I'd never heard a more attractive idea. And who could say? Maybe I'd get

Resuna back after some more normal sleep, or come up with an idea for escaping and contacting the authorities . . . or I'd feel more sure that Dave was right, and then do something—the lights went out, I heard the lock turning, and I was asleep.

When I woke up, I remembered everything, and got up and carefully made my way to the light switch. I used the chamber pot, and wondered if perhaps I could get a sponge bath or the use of the hot tub soon, because I had spent enough time in a too-warm bed to be pretty rank.

Resuna was still gone, and the ghosted-over memories felt more false; you don't remember a thing as vividly when there isn't a voice in your mind insisting that you do.

There was a knock at the door, and I said, "Sure, come in."

"Saw the light on," Dave said. "You've slept from meal to meal; you want to come out and eat again, and maybe talk some more?"

We'd about finished eating when he said, "Well, I don't know exactly how to put this, Curran, so let me just say it, and say I'm sorry to have to think about this. Now that you're so much better, I'm going to have to decide what to do with you. I like having somebody to talk to, and there'd be room for two here, so if it was just you and me, I'd invite you to be my roommate and that would be all there'd need to be. However, there's a whole big planet out there, and by spring at latest there's going to be another manhunt for me, and I can't afford to have a house guest who's on the other side, if you see what I mean. Nor can I let you go—your copy of Resuna already uploaded enough to One True to give the hunters a much better chance of catching me, and what you know now would pretty much zero them in on this place, so I want the time to move my things and start over somewhere else. I'm way too old to run out in the middle of the night, sleep in trees for a year, and start all over from my skivvies again.

"So, little as I like it, I have to figure you're getting stronger every day and pretty soon locking you in a bedroom won't stop you, or even deter you. And once that's true—which might be tomorrow for all either of us knows—well, then my two choices seem to be to enlist you, or to kill you."

"Uh . . . how do you mean, enlist me?"

"Partner up. Work together. Not really for the cause—I'm not at war with One True anymore, except so far as it's at war with me—but just to live free out here. I know it's not much to offer but I wanted to have some alternative to killing you; I'm really soft these days, or something, because I could have just walked right in there and done it while you were asleep, and you'd've never known. Anyway, it didn't seem fair to just sit here, making small talk with you, and not have you know that that's what's going on in my mind."

He looked as embarrassed as a teenage boy proposing marriage to the girl next door. In slightly different circumstances I'd probably have laughed. As it was, feeling stupid, I said, "I understand your situation, and I understand that it's nothing personal, and all that. You aren't going to kill me right now if I say no, are you?"

"You haven't said whether you want to take my offer."

"Will you trust me if I say yes?"

"Guess that's up to me." He sighed. "Let's fix a big pot of coffee and go sit in the hot tub. We can talk for a while about any old thing, and maybe if I put the decision off long enough, I'll think of something else, or you'll decide you'd rather live free, or something." He got up from the table. "How *are* you feeling?"

"Pretty well mended," I admitted. "Resuna's still gone. I don't seem to miss it quite as much as I did at first, but if I said I didn't miss it, I'd be lying."

The reconstitutor pinged—he had some "refrigerator art" pinned to it, and he grinned and said, "Kelly's, of course. Nancy gave it to me. All except this one that Kelly drew for me, herself, right then."

I looked at it and was startled by memory, again. Kelly's drawings were good first- and second-grade art—basic realism, shading, stuff that looked sort of ordinary—but I remembered, then, that "Kid pictures didn't used to look like this. This is like something a talented fifteen-year-old might have done in the old days. How is it that now all children do this kind of thing at six?"

He shrugged. "Resuna pleases people as much as it can. Small children really want to draw realistically, it's just that the parts of the brain that they need for the process haven't grown in yet. So what Resuna does is, it takes control of the eye and the hand and draws for the kid, copying skills from more experienced artists. Eventually the skills do download, which is why everyone can draw really well nowadays. See, in the one picture she drew while she was free, it's supposed to be a picture of me, but you can see where the skills weren't all there and she had trouble integrating things; I think it looks sort of cubist."

"Well, you don't have five eyes, or two mouths, so I guess I agree," I said. "And I *can* see some of the cowboy viewpoint, I admit. With Resuna she draws better than she ever could by herself, but just like everybody else. This picture is the only one that's completely her—"

"Or completely Kelly except for the parts of her that Resuna had already shaped so strongly that she really can't be separated from it," Dave said. "Just like the parts of her mother and her classmates that *they* mainly got from Resuna. Anyway, the coffee's done; if you'll carry a couple of cups, the hot-tub room is right through here."

The tub was an old twentieth-century model with none of the valves or hardware; he had set it up with a pipe running in at one end and a slightly lower pipe at the other, so that water from the hot spring flowed through continuously. I dipped my hand in; it was at a comfortable temperature. "Pour the coffee," Dave said, undressing.

I did, and set the pot and cups within easy reach of the tub.

"Well, let's get in," he said. As we settled in—the clean warm water felt wonderful—and each got our coffee, I said, "You know, if I do throw in with you, and we have to run, I'm going to miss this."

He grinned. "I've got three alternate sites within three days' walk. Every one of them with a hot spring. We'd have to do some digging for a while, but we'd have this back eventually. Probably pretty fast. There's no better work incentive than an opportunity to get back something that you had and lost; you know just what you want and how bad you want it."

I must've stared off into space then, because he asked me what I'd thought of, and then I realized what it was. "Yeah," I said. "It's not just material, either. My second marriage was much more work than my first. And when Resuna turned me, I fought a far, far bigger battle to be a decent person again than I'd had to fight years before just to start out as one. And yet, somehow, that much harder fight *seemed* easier, I guess because I knew where I was going and what I was after. Sort of like, if you and I had to re-create this room somewhere else, knowing how nice it is, we'd work harder and feel less tired."

"You said you had to work hard once One True turned you?" Dave asked. "I thought Resuna just relayed orders from One True, which did what it wanted to people, no work on your part, and that if you did any work, it was in resisting it, so that it was just dragging you around like a puppet."

"Well, I suppose that One True *can* drag people around like puppets if it wants to," I said, "but that's a terribly inefficient way to work, like teaching a dog to walk on a leash by dragging it down the sidewalk—it works after a fashion but it's better to have cooperation."

"But if you didn't want to cooperate, why did you join it?"

A thought clicked: if I were to tell a story that took all night, I could buy hours of time. Not to mention maybe get some more sympathy built up. It wasn't the greatest strategy I'd ever thought up, I knew, but it was one more strategy than I'd had a minute ago. "Well," I said, "it's a complex story, which isn't a bad thing, in my situation. I never ran One True back when it was brain-native. Like most people, I got Resuna and joined One True, rather than running One True in the years before Year One, and then converting to Resuna. I got Resuna just a few months before most people did—right at the end of the War of the Memes. But all the same, I wasn't one of those that had to be forced. I accepted it knowing what I was getting into. That has to do with my second wife, Mary."

"She was running Resuna?" Lobo asked, settling back for a story. Cowboys spent their lives, until they were caught, with just a few people, out in the woods; telling a good story was probably important for them. It was that way with cowboy hunters, too. And realizing that you have a good audience, you always put on more of a show.

"Mary was one of the first fifty thousand people or so ever to run Resuna," I said, not bothering to hide the pride in my voice. "And at the time I met her, I was one of the most evil people I had ever met, anywhere in the world, and she was one of the best—and I knew I had to get what she had, one way or another. Now, when I say 'evil,' I *don't* just mean not integrated into One True, and I *don't* just mean I had bad habits. What I mean is that, objectively speaking, somebody should really have killed me and put both me and the world out of our mutual misery. And in a sense, that's what Mary did with Resuna—killed the old me. It was a me well lost, if you see what I mean."

He seemed to sink further into his chair to hear the story; after checking to make sure I was set for coffee, he gestured for me to get on with it. I doubt anyone ever had a better audience. I kept talking till the tale was told, interrupted now and then by a question or some coffee or a pee break. Judging by his expression, and the questions he asked, I don't think he missed a word of it. Funny what not hearing a new story in so long will do to a human mind.

"To begin at the beginning," I began, "I'm a foundling, like most of our generation—I was dumped at the orphanage in Spokane Dome when I was a few weeks old, in April 2038. Besides the blanket and diaper I was wrapped in, and the child's crash seat I was tied into, the only other thing I arrived with was my name, written in Magic Marker on the back of the seat: "BABY NAME: CURRIE CURTIS CUR-RAN." The world had been in a severe depression for some years, so armies of babies arrived at the orphanage more or less like me. At least I didn't have any of the common HIV strains and wasn't born addicted to cocaine or You-4, and had no birth defects caused by my mother using gressors. And I was healthy, decently fed, and clean, so I guess Mom, whoever she was, just couldn't keep me and that was all there was to it."

Dave grinned. "You and me could be brothers, you know," he said. "That's pretty much how I got my start at Denver Dome. The Gray Decade sure was no time to be a kid, was it?"

"Got that right," I agreed, "pos-def. And I was nowhere near the worst part of it."

The 2040s were one of the worst decades of peace the world ever knew. The long false prosperity that had been sustained by constructing the supras, the transfer ships, and the colonies on the other planets, and by the huge process of ecological rescue on Earth, had all been financed on borrowed money, and though the world had far more stuff than it had had before, and was a better and more prosperous place than it would otherwise have been, the re-formation of the Earth into a better home for humanity and all other living things, after the disastrous Eurowar, had been a giant, everyone-in-on-it Ponzi scheme, which had worked well enough in the 2010s and 2020s but now was absolutely out of suckers.

The whole human race, on Earth and in space, was trapped in a set of paradoxes inherited from Reconstruction. Great wealth did not provide enough revenue to pay off on the bonds; astonishing productivity made goods too cheap for anyone to make a living selling them. It cost almost nothing to feed and clothe people, but investment and development, let alone further progress in restabilizing the ecology and getting energy production and industry moved to space, were on hold for the next half generation.

Only a few people here and there starved, but only a very few worked, and almost no one dreamed. Mostly the world sat on its haunches and tried to figure out what to do to get going again. The lucky ones left for Mars, the Moon, Ceres, or Europa; a few continued the now-losing battle against the whipsawing global disaster that was the heritage of the Eurowar and now decades out of control. Glaciers formed in a matter of weeks in the fall and melted almost as fast in the spring, deserts leaped their ancient boundaries to advance deep into agricultural land, the seas were covered with blooms of organisms never seen before, and strange new diseases devastated plants and animals every few years, giving nothing alive any chance to work toward stability before the rolling catastrophes tore up the rule book yet again. Some scientists and engineers, with such resources as a world in a state of economic gridlock could throw to them, were trying to do things about that; many more would have been glad to help, but had to eat, and so they fixed potholes, picked up litter, or just collected a Dole check, while their skills went to waste.

Whenever two people who lived through them start to talk about the terrible thirty years that began with the Panic of '32 and ended with the Second Diaspora, Resuna, and forced unification, it isn't long before their minds turn to something that's too far away in time and not far away enough in memory, and they start staring into space and sometimes don't come back.

Back in the regular world, that's when your copy of Resuna shakes you out of it, dumps in serotonin and norepinephrin, and gives you a big, warm mental hug. Without that, I guess we'd have lived anyway, but in a cold, bleak world. This was what it was like without Resuna. Here I was, seated in a bath, warm, comfortable, well-fed, with pleasant idleness to tell stories (even if it was between cowboy and hunter)—able to think of nothing but the sufferings of people who had mostly been in their graves for decades, and to taste only the ashes of the lost world.

"You ever wonder how different the world might've been if there hadn't been a war, or if somebody'd figured a way not to go through the Gray Decade, or any of that?" Lobo asked.

"Yeah, always," I said. "Even when I've got Resuna there to help me through it. Well, anyway, you know what those years were like as well as I do. Let me just collect my thoughts, and see if I can just concentrate on how I got through those times, myself."

I took a slow, warm sip of his excellent coffee, looked up for a moment at his hand-finished sandstone ceiling to collect my thoughts, and launched into the story, taking plenty of time and filling in lots of details, because that's what he wanted, and you always make sure your story pleases the customer if you think he might be in the process of deciding whether or not to kill you. You might call it Scheherazade's Law.

It doesn't fit too well with your standard orphan story, but the truth is that the people that ran the Spokane Dome Municipal Orphanage were reasonably kind, and probably would have been generous had the city government given them with anything to be generous with. I suppose in a sense, looking back, that the city council *had* been generous, though not intentionally. They had kept the Dolework system running—it had had to be shut down for lack of funds in most places—so that people at least kept eating and had somewhere to stay, and because they needed jobs for every Dolebird, they featherbedded city facilities pretty heavily, which meant the orphanage, like every other city facility, had many more employees than any efficiency engineer would have said that it needed.

Of course, taking care of kids is a lot more than feeding them, wiping noses, and stopping fights, and a decent orphanage *needs* to be featherbedded, so that there's a few spare adults around most of the time for the kid who is lonely, or confused, or for some reason just badly needs some undivided attention that nobody wrote down on the schedule.

The orphanage had quite a few employees who had the makings of good parents, and some first-rate teachers. Since the public-school system had gone private, and money for vouchers was cut down to zero before I was born, we got whatever education could be worked in by the people who were feeding us and watching us; luckily that was considerably more than nothing, even if it was pretty catch-as-catch-can.

The first year I remember, I was six. The only events outside the orphanage that made an impression on me were the rolling ecological disasters that crashed across the Pacific Northwest. That whole year was a great one for watching the teams of Doleworkers through the big windows in the dome: I saw them on the outside surface struggling frantically to remove a load of snow three times what it had been designed for, cleaning centimeter-thick soot from the huge range and forest fires, battening down the exposed surfaces during seven days of 150-kph winds, and replacing panels pitted by baseball-sized hail. I think at that time I could imagine no profession more romantic or heroic than working on the surface of the dome, and if everyone up there working was just a plain old Dolebird, well, so were all the kind, considerate adults here in the orphanage, who were the nearest thing to parents I would ever have.

Life crept on, as it will tend to do, and for me the orphanage was about as much world as there was. Most days Mr. Farrell took us out to play games in the park, and we learned all those things that were pritnear extinct among better-off children—baseball and soccer, of course, but also Capture the Flag, Run Sheep Run, and Red Rover. Ms. Kirlian read to us most nights, and in the morning she'd help you with learning to read if you couldn't get along with the AI's on the orphanage werps, which were ten years old and didn't always understand a kid's speech as they should. The food was monotonous but not bad, there were enough affectionate adults to assure you of some hugs when you needed them and somebody who would seek you out and talk to you when life stank, and at least the bunks were warm and the stuff in your footlocker was yours until you outgrew it and it went to some younger kid. If it wasn't paradise, it was better than a lot of people, over the long centuries, have grown up with.

The year I turned eleven, I knew real discontent for the first time in my life. That's how I always put it when I tell this story. When I say that that year was 2049, most people immediately conclude that I encountered real discontent because of the way the world was going then. That's why I say it, for the fun of catching them wrong.

If I had been just a year or two older, and paying any attention to the way the world as a whole was going, I would have been plenty upset about it, like every other reasonably aware person on Earth. For one thing, for the first time in half a century, it was teetering on the brink of war—the slowly dying Pope Pius Benedict hadn't been able to hold things together the way his brilliant, long-lived predecessor, Paul John Paul, had, and Ecucatholicism was starting to fragment in an eerie mirror image of the Reformation as the many churches it had absorbed began to move for greater independence and less tolerance of each other.

The regional governments in Asia were wobbling under the impact of a new mutation of that old human enemy, tailored rice blast, which had devastated them at the end of the Eurowar. Moreover, a new threat to the domesticated whale herds that were the source of more than half of the Asian protein supply, CPCA, Cetacean Prionic Cephaloatrophy, informally known as "whale scrapie," had roared through domestic whale populations from India to Hawaii in less than a year.

Based on seismic testing and deep cores, the scientists gave it no more than ten years till the West Antarctic ice sheet slipped, to be followed, probably, by fragmentation and rapid calving in Wilkes Land; the oceans were now rising and falling two full feet with the summer-winter cycle in the Northern Hemisphere, but they were about to start doing it nine feet higher up, and because everything depended on the exact mechanism by which Antarctica would lose its ice, no one knew whether the world's coasts would have twenty years' or twenty hours' warning. It was horribly clear that forty years of global reconstruction were about to go down the toilet; the greatest effort the species had ever made for its common interests, and those of the planet, had turned out to be too little and too late.

All too predictably, most of the human race, having struggled shoulder to shoulder for two generations to save the planet, now that things were turning to shit, rushed about looking for ways to make matters worse. Several of the constituent Ecucatholic churches were pushing candidates for the next pope, and declaring the others' candidates unacceptable, even before the current pope was dead. A new intolerant version of Islamic fundamentalism was sweeping into the parts of the world that had been converted by cybertao the generation before. Regional governments were asserting rights over resources that in better times they would not have claimed, and making so-far vague threats at each other and at the planetary government. A political battle was forming in many parts of the world about when and where—or whether—to resettle seacoast populations.

Meanwhile, by late summer of 2049, the global weather models were forecasting that, after decades of wobbling madly, the world climate was at last going to achieve a stalemate, if not stability, for a few decades: a new ice age in the northern hemisphere, a warm interglacial in the south, and storms beyond anyone's imagining all through the tropics, including, probably, some permanent hurricanes on the scale of the Cyclone of 2021, giant storms that would circle the Earth at the equator for decades. They were seriously trying to figure out if the towers up to the supras—three kilometers thick and 36,000 kilometers tall, all anchored to mountaintops along the equator—could stand up to the near-supersonic cyclones they were expecting.

So the world had reason for its discontent. But if you think back to when you were a kid, you won't be surprised to hear that none of that mattered a fart in a windstorm to eleven-year-old me. I had reason enough for my own discontent and could have been just as unhappy in the golden days of the 2020s. What mattered to me was that I had only two shirts that were not hand-me-downs, one pair of pants without patches or stains, and since laundry day was once a week, most days I couldn't wear those "good" clothes. This is a problem when you have fallen in love with the most beautiful girl alive, even if her wardrobe is no better than yours.

Tammy Knight was probably not particularly impressive to any guy who wasn't also eleven: in holos I have from the orphanage, taken in that year, to my adult eyes her major characteristics are a thick mane of frizzy, orangish hair, the color called strawberry-blonde if you didn't go to college or auburn if you did, plus two extremely long knobby-kneed legs that end in remarkably big feet. The rest of her was a skeletal sketch of a person, with rampant freckles, vivid green eyes, and long fine-boned fingers. In fact she turned into a beauty, and I

think all of us boys in the orphanage always knew she would, but I
have no idea what power let a kid see that. As an adult I'd've never
seen it coming.

She had more immediate charms than impending beauty, from the
viewpoint of a boy her own age. Tammy could pitch like a rifle, played
forward with an aggression terrifying to behold, and was followed
around by a half dozen of the littler kids all the time, mainly because
she was always patient with them and would listen when they talked to
her, which was constant. I was hopelessly, madly in love with her, in
the way you can only be if you are not aware that this can happen again
many times in a normal life—but then, perhaps I was accidentally wise
about that, because I was not going to have a normal life.

You can't really say it was unrequited love, since I never said a
thing about it. Furthermore, she, along with the entire rest of the universe, appeared to be unaware of anything other than my friendship,
and that was mostly confined to three kinds of interaction with her:
when she pitched, I caught; when she played forward, I played goal;
and when one of her entourage of little kids would break a toy, she'd
smile at me and say "Please" and—if it were humanly possible—I
would fix it. Though none of those were the relationship I wanted to
have, I could just barely admit to myself that I wanted anything else,
and my ideas about what feelings and experiences ought to go into that
imaginary relationship were extremely fuzzy. I kept quiet, looked for a
chance to talk to her whenever I could, and lived in terror that the
other guys would find out and my life would become a hell of endless
mockery.

At least, if religious war came, as everyone was now expecting,
there wouldn't be much fighting right where I was, because Spokane
Dome was deep in a heavily Ecucatholic area. Many tiny Protestant
churches had gone Ecucatholic all at once in the Great Rejoining of
2004, and there just hadn't been enough of the highly educated computer geeks around to form more than a small minority for cybertao.

Because Spokane was such an Ecucatholic town, the municipal
orphanage almost always held a Christmas/Hanukkah pageant, carefully kept bland enough not to offend cybertaoists (who, if not driven
out, would celebrate anything with anybody). When necessary it could
be easily modified to slip in a nod to Ramadan. And in Spokane, like
any place where the population ran heavily to Ecucatholicism, 2049
was going to be a big, *big* year for the Christmas pageant.

Seemingly on the brink of death, during another false alarm, in
early September, Pius Benedict had proclaimed that Christmas of 2049

was to be dedicated to celebrating, and praying for the continuation of, the forty-seven years of world peace we had had—and the fact that no one would have suggested waiting for the fiftieth anniversary pretty much told you everything about how little faith anyone had by then that we could make it that far.

After a couple more scares, and a brief moment when it looked like he might have a miraculous remission, the pope finally died on December 7, and the first fighting of what started as the War of Papal Succession, and finished as the War of the Memes, began on December 14, almost before the debris stopped falling from the atom bomb that gutted Rome and killed the whole College of Cardinals.

The Municipal Orphanage went ahead with its plan for the Christmas pageant anyway—it's hard to cancel a plan so late in the game, it was every bit as hard to believe the world was going to go to war again as it had been that peace could last, and besides all the practicalities, people really felt like they needed Christmas, to take a break from the grim news and to try, just once more, to summon up whatever they could of peace on Earth and goodwill toward men.

The bioweapons and weather weapons of the Eurowar fifty years ago had gotten humanity on Earth into its present mad predicament, and kept it there because they were much easier to let loose than to call back. You couldn't walk a kilometer anywhere in the inhabited, or formerly inhabited, parts of the Earth without seeing the traces of some horror. This time, with a whole long generation of better technology, perhaps we really would live up to the potential pointed out by Marc-Paul Prévert, the head of the commission that was supposed to find a peaceful solution (and who would be assassinated himself in the first hours of 2050, torpedoing the last hope): "We now have the means to kill the whole population of the planet and send it into an ecological catastrophe that will last a hundred thousand years, a capability to make all our past madness seem a mere caprice." The bitter joke at the time went that this was all a beautiful illustration of the principle that "If at first you don't succeed, try, try again."

Once again, though, that's me thinking of it as an adult looking back and saying "Oh, so that's what was going on." From my standpoint, December of 2049 was a month of interesting explosions and weapons on the flashchannel, adults acting mysteriously upset—and my lucky break.

Ms. Kirlian had been appointed the director of the pageant because many years ago she had been an amateur actor, because she was liked and trusted by all us kids, and most of all because nobody else had the patience. She followed the usual rules for such things: make sure that key dramatic roles go to older kids who are less likely to panic or freeze, and try to have one of the older kids on stage at all times so that the little ones can be rescued if need be. As a practical matter, that meant that Tammy, even though she was extremely untalented dramatically (she spoke her lines in a drawling monotone like she was scared that someone might hear or understand her), was going to play Mary, since that would put her in nearly every scene, most importantly every scene that involved large numbers of small children.

I, on the other hand, was more of a force for intimidation than an influence for moderation, and therefore I was the Head Shepherd. My official role was to walk in at the right moment and say, "Behold, we have seen a great light and an angel said we ought to come here. Where's the newborn king?" (I guess Ms. Kirlian was about as much of a playwright as she was a director.) My unofficial role was to keep all the smaller boys, who were playing Miscellaneous Shepherds, from running amok backstage until it was time for our entrance.

"What does 'miscellaneous' mean?" one of them whispered to me, on seeing the program.

" 'Well-behaved,' " I lied, hoping to have some positive effect.

"Oh, does not," he whispered back. "You're just making that up so we'll behave."

"You've caught me," I said. "It's a breed of sheep. Now shut up or I'll punch your face in."

Our audience was made up of a small minority that wanted to be there and a large majority unfortunate enough to be compelled. Since we had no parents, the city dragooned whoever it could: bored kids from the schools doing their charitable bit by coming to watch us be humiliated; city officials, who were there so that someone would take pictures of them with the poor orphans, and the pictures would then appear on local flashchannel; city employees whose supervisors had pressured them into attending. A smattering of people from the local churches had either been arm-twisted by their pastors or were badly starved for entertainment. Finally, the Doleworkers whose duty station was the orphanage brought their families to see us. They were the ones who really mattered to us kids.

We shepherds had just entered, knelt, and presented a dozen badly worn stuffed toys (anything that could be presented as having once resembled a sheep) to the porcelain doll wrapped in a blanket, which was portraying the nonspeaking role of Baby Jesus. To my deep relief, my ragged gang of Miscellaneous Shepherds had pretty much held formation, knelt more or less simultaneously with suitable reverence, and not made a mess of things.

My assigned position was kneeling behind them, first of all because I was taller than any of them, and secondly because if they started to giggle or whisper it gave me a chance to do what Ms. Kirlian had said, and put a hand on their shoulders to "steady them down." I figured if they didn't steady when I did that, I could hit them in the back without too many people seeing, and I had made sure that that was what the boys figured, too. So far, though, things were going unexpectedly well. I hadn't even needed to do any steadying.

Our Joseph was played by a kid named Joseph, about my age, our only acting talent. He was a small dark-haired boy with a delivery so clear and expressive that it made the rest of us look more foolish than anything else could have. At this exact moment he was making a long speech about what a nice bunch of people the humble shepherds were, having brought all these lambs. Just what a newborn baby was going to do with a dozen lambs was beyond me.

Then Tammy's line, as Mary, was supposed to be "We thank thee all very much, oh shepherds, and so does the baby." It had been shortened and modified repeatedly as Ms. Kirlian had gotten more and more frustrated with Tammy's flat delivery, and that was what caused the problem; she told me later she just couldn't remember which version of the line she was supposed to say.

Unfortunately, that line was the cue for the Three Wise Men to enter. Our Three Wise Men were three nine-year-olds who had been drilled, drilled, and drilled *not* to jump their cues (after an unfortunate crown-crushing collision, in dress rehearsal, between Melchior and a late-entering Miscellaneous Shepherd). They weren't about to come in until they heard "so does the baby."

Seeing Mary's paralyzed-with-terror stare, I realized what had happened, and tried to feed a cue. I said, "Us shepherds are lim glad that thee likes the sheep."

The cue remained malnourished, but Joseph caught the idea and gave it a shot, too, saying, "We thank thee very much, oh shepherds."

Tammy froze all the more completely, now that Joseph seemed to have stolen one of her lines. I was out of ideas (or good ones anyway) and when Joseph and I made eye contact, he gave me a micro-shrug, as if to say, *Okay, now what?*

I stood up, to be heard better, pointed my face in the direction of the dark where I hoped the Wise Men were waiting, and said, very loudly and firmly, "So does the baby."

Three Wise Men, thinking they had missed their cue, charged in at a speed that robes made out of old sheets were never designed to accommodate. The first one fell flat, the other two fell over him, and the shepherds were bombarded with carefully wrapped shoeboxes, which were fortunately empty and contained no actual gold, frankincense, or myrrh. "Pick'em up," I whispered to the shepherds, "and give them to Mary and Joseph."

This was working pretty well, especially because my awkward whispering of directions—aided by Joseph, who understood at once and pointed the shepherds to where to put the Wise Men's gifts—was almost entirely covered by the peals of laughter from the audience. We might have gotten away with it, except that Tammy's malfunctioning memory finally fired. Maybe "detonated" was the word for it. For the first and only time, she was fully audible when she said, "We thank thee, oh shepherds, and so does the baby."

The Three Wise Men got up from their bewildered heap, where they had been lying still and trying not to be noticed. As one Wise Man, they grabbed their gifts and carried them offstage, now convinced that they had entered early. Mr. Farrell told me, the next day, between fits of giggles, that for one moment he'd had the impression that the Wise Men had been offended at being mistaken for shepherds and had taken all their stuff back.

The shepherds, animals, and Holy Family watched in amazement as the Three Wise Men took up their entry positions in the wings. A long moment crept by. The crowd noise died down to embarrassed giggles. Not sure what else to do, I whispered to Tammy, "Say it again, real loud." I must have whispered too loud, because the audience started laughing again.

Nevertheless, Tammy did as I suggested, and this time the Wise Men entered, handed over the shoeboxes per instructions, and moved to their places. The audience applauded wildly, and the show went on; other than a wing falling off one angel, we had no more trouble that night.

After the show, we had punch and Christmas cookies, and Santa paid a visit. It was an election year coming up, so Mayor Bizet was there to be seen by the flashchannel, playing Santa Claus. (We all knew that he was Mayor Bizet, and not really Santa Claus, because he explained to us that he was, and further added that Santa had personally authorized him to stand in for the night. It was a good way to keep little kids from blurting out the obvious truth.)

When it came my turn, I was much too big a kid to sit on his lap, but I walked up there to get whatever Santa had for me—the first time in my life I ever hoped for new clothes instead of a toy. To my pleasant surprise, I got a new shirt and three brand-new packages of socks. I blurted out a "Thank you" and was about to go sit down when the mayor added, slightly muffled by his cotton-batting beard, "So you are the heroic shepherd who rescued the show."

"Uh, I just kind of helped," I said.

"Good enough," Mayor Bizet said. "The secret of impressing a crowd is to do the right thing at the right time. If you do it intentionally, that's just so much icing on the cake. Now, I happen to have some things to present in my capacity as mayor, as opposed to my capacity as jolly old elf." (I saw one of the people in suits who were taking pictures of him give the mayor a thumbs-up; I always wondered afterwards how much of the speech had been prewritten.) He pulled out a small envelope. "At the Arts Center, for the whole week from now through Christmas Eve, we're having a festival of family movies—movies are sort of like the flashchannel, but with no interaction, on a very big screen that you sit in the dark and watch. So here are two free passes so that you and a friend can go to all the shows. The gift includes public-transit passes too, so that you can get to the Arts Center."

I was amazed and in awe; I didn't care a thing about movies, which I had seen a few times because the orphanage had a few of them and a projector. But it was tickets for *two*, which meant—if I had the nerve—this might be the lucky break I would have been waiting for, had I been able even to imagine so lucky a break. I stammered a thanks, put the precious envelope into my shirt pocket and buttoned it closed, and sat down. Ms. Kirlian led the applause. I'm not sure if I've ever felt more appreciated at any time in my life since that night.

Pretty much, that was how it started. Later that evening, when they were teaching us older kids how to dance, I bravely volunteered to be Tammy's partner—after all, she was only half a head taller than I was. As we shuffled around in a state of complete confusion, trying to follow Mr. Farrell's directions, I managed to blurt out that I wanted her to go to the movies with me. She seemed pretty startled and said, "But that's not fair. It was all my messing up that caused the problem in the first place."

Our feet tried to come down in the same place at the same time, and we both half-tripped. Mr. Farrell said, firmly, "*Lead*, Currie, you're supposed to *lead*."

As far as I could tell, if I did that, most likely it would be much easier for everyone to see who was making the mistakes, which was the last thing I wanted. We got back into the vicinity of the beat and I said, "I don't care about fair or not, it's my pass and I'd rather go with you."

"Really?" she asked, as if perhaps she was wondering whether I was crazy.

"Really." My nerves were shot; at least I wasn't going to step on her feet, since I was too tense to move.

"Currie, loosen up! You're holding a girl, not a block of wood!"

I could have told Mr. Farrell, I suppose, that I'd have been much more relaxed holding a block of wood, and that he had nicely identified the exact problem. But I just tried to move as if I weren't in a state of terror. It didn't seem like a good idea to beg, but on the other hand the suspense was killing me. I was trying to think of a way to rephrase the request when she said, "Well, I guess if you want, I'll go. It would be different from sitting around this place watching the flashchannel every night."

"Currie," Mr. Farrell said, "you might try bending your knees. If you start relaxing now, you might be able to get your first date by the time you're thirty."

"He just *got* it," Tammy said, loudly. The room turned to stare at us, and Mr. Farrell's jaw flapped a couple of times. I felt like I was going to turn bright purple, I hoped that I would sink through the floor . . . and I saw Tammy grinning at me, freckles, crooked teeth, green eyes, and all, and didn't care a bit.

"Well," Mr. Farrell said, after a moment's recovery, "then all the more reason to practice." It wasn't a great line or even very funny, but I think everybody wanted an excuse to laugh.

It took me three nights at the movies to muster the nerve to hold hands with her, and it wasn't till Christmas Eve that we tried kissing (with indifferent results), but from then on, in the little world of the orphanage, we were an "item," and very happy to be. Nothing much was going to break us up, ever; sometimes you just know those things.

During the next few weeks, while Tammy and I were exploring "being a couple," fighting spread through border districts all over Asia, and local governments seceded from the world government and set about raising armies. The Ecucatholics splintered so many ways that no historian ever kept a definitive scorecard. Bombs and riots and assassinations filled the flashchannel. Prévert was gunned down as he came out to talk to the press about the proposed settlement, and only a few specialists ever even bothered to learn what had been proposed. The world was crashing back into chaos, but for Tammy and me, everything was just falling into place.

Three years later, the world was still at war. By that time there were battle lines and fronts, and most people had managed to get away from them.

In the summer of 2051 the first meme had exploded into the world's consciousness, the crude and primitive thing called "Goodtimes." Two months after that, a hundred modified versions of Goodtimes were competing with each other. Six months later, that small beginning had exploded into a diversity of more than four thousand different memes, all locked in a mutual struggle for supremacy.

When I was still a kid, back in the orphanage, the whole idea of a meme terrified me; now, four decades later, though I can understand the fear of being controlled by a meme that would not take care proper care of you, I can't seem to reconstruct why I was so afraid of all memes; I was much more afraid, in Dave's hideout, when I *didn't* have a meme. But at the time, I know, people were not only afraid to go online or to phone somewhere through a head jack—the two ways you could be infected by Goodtimes—they were afraid of almost any contact with any information processor. News stories told of people throwing out digital clocks and handheld calculators, trying to "play it safe."

The historians never did finish the job of tracking Goodtimes back to its exact source, but they did identify one group of people in one shop, one of whom—but who could say which one, now?—had been two things, both important for the story: a cybertaoist, and a genius. As a cybertaoist, he or she was painfully well aware that cybertaoists did not fight cybertaoists, that the stubbornly reasonable and gentle Stochastic Faith produced martyrs but few fanatics—and yet this could not last, because either cybertao would mutate into some crueler, more vicious form, or it would be stamped from the face of the Earth less than fifty years after its birth. The one hope for its survival was to convert everyone, or almost everyone, before they got serious about killing the cybertaoists.

He or she could easily have rationalized this, anyway, because the Christian and Muslim populations of the world were both inflamed by every kind of mania all at once, and the potential for holy war, leading to mass slaughter, was building up in the chaotic conditions that were emerging as each little, not-quite-technically revolted district, region, or county of the globe made alliance with one or another of the popes or antipopes (with the apostolic succession thrown into such question, it was all but impossible to know which was which); even the Islamic parts of the world had opinions, now, about who was rightful pope. It wasn't an altogether foolish idea that if everyone could be converted to the patient, peaceable way of cybertao, a great deal of human suffering might be averted.

There might have been two or seven or twenty million other cyber-taoists with similar ideas out there, but the one who invented Good-times was unique for another reason: he or she did no preaching, no writing, made no direct effort to convert a single human being. Rather, this person—or could it have been more than one?—came up with an absolutely unique idea, which required solving a problem that had been unofficially bedeviling computer scientists for the better part of a century by that time. The mystery genius had been able to see an entirely different way to accomplish her or his purpose, realize it required a solution to a problem that had not been solved for decades, and finally solve that problem. It was very unfair that history had not given that individual a name, or any credit. The invention of the meme was as great, in its way, as fire, the wheel, mass production, or the computer, for it brought the whole world into peace, harmony, and cooperation.

The long-unsolved problem was that of the universal virus. A computer virus, in its simplest form, was just a program that would cause the computer to make copies of the program. If you allowed for much greater sophistication, viruses could accomplish all sorts of things, good or bad, from continual optimization of a network to lying dormant until they could sabotage a weapons system that did not exist at the time of their creation.

Despite all the things they could do, however, no virus before this could cross a previously unknown operating system boundary. That is, no one had written a set of instructions so that a virus could realize it was communicating with a system different from the one on which it usually ran, analyze that system, and eventually construct a virus that would do the same thing in the new system. The universal virus was the holy grail of information warfare. All the armed forces of the Earth had unique, locked, secret operating systems, to defend themselves from being virused, but to be effective, all those systems had to com-municate. If they communicated long enough with a universal virus, they would give themselves away, as it acquired enough information to translate itself and cross the boundary. Tens of thousands of engineers, analysts, and programmers had been looking for universal virus algorithms since before the Eurowar.

Yet that small team containing one or more unknown geniuses had solved that problem and created the true self-porting virus: it analyzed any system it encountered and eventually created a version of itself over on that system.

The purpose of the first self-porting virus, the now-extinct Goodtimes, was to convert, not people, but AIs, so that the intelligences that ran most of the economy and nearly all the fighting units would become missionaries for cybertao, refusing to fight against it, seeking to convert every human being to cybertao. It was designed, using the universal virus as its translator, to re-create itself onto any machine, in any operating system.

History books say that the extensive "human contact" portion of Goodtimes was set up only to allow it to talk to people; though in hindsight we know it was a crude meme, the creators thought that it was merely an advanced virus, and so they imagined that the mechanical missionary would have to work just like its fleshly counterparts; after it took over an operating system on an individual machine, it would have to argue with human beings to persuade them to embrace cybertao.

But the designer far exceeded his or her intentions, for reasons which are obvious in hindsight. From the standpoint of a meme, a brain is just a computer made up of massively parallel slow-running processors. And if Goodtimes's purpose was to spread cybertao, and the way to spread cybertao was to spread Goodtimes into every available system, then it would spread it to the human brains on the other side of every screen and speaking device.

The first human brains turned by a meme were probably the creators of Goodtimes. To test it they must have been doing many hours of interacting with its personality, seeing what they could make it do and how it would handle complex and ambiguous questions, and so forth. Very likely in one of those long conversations—especially if one of them had a skull jack and was talking to it directly—Goodtimes figured out how to take over the human brain, and discovered a rich new playground in which it could propagate.

In about thirty days it was all over the world and was being treated (in the non-cybertao areas) like a form of highly contagious madness, in just over a billion infected brains.

And a year later it was extinct except for museum copies. Working frantically, partisans of all the different sides in the War of Papal Succession had extracted the universal translator, copied it, and put it into their own memes, and unlike Goodtimes, these were designed from the beginning to target minds at least as much as computers, and to displace each other if at all possible.

By 2051, when Burton, the owner-commander of Burton's Thugs for Jesus, came by the orphanage, there was rumor of a third-generation virus that would be able to fully use all of its hosts' capabilities—that is, if it infected a brilliant general, it could use his strategic ability and charisma to spread itself; if it infected a composer, it could spread through his music; if it infected an accountant, it could embezzle for its own purposes, including relaying money to the general or the composer. Another rumor, even more grim, was that these other memes, as they were coming to be called from a term in some old technical papers, were no longer the products of military research; they were making ever more advanced versions of themselves without human intervention; for once, all the rumors were true.

Burton's Thugs for Jesus was an all-male outfit—most of the mercenary companies were, though I'd never really heard anyone explain why—but they let all of us older kids come talk to them, regardless of gender. Tammy and I came in holding hands, and sat near the back.

Burton was a physically robust man, running to fat but in good shape nonetheless, with piercing blue eyes, jet-black hair, and sharp features that had probably been very handsome when he was younger. He wore one of the lightweight camouflage suits that were made and distributed everywhere nowadays, a green forage cap, and a pair of nondescript ankle-high boots. He stood in front of us with his hands locked behind his back, as if he were going to inspect us that moment.

"Well," he said, "you all follow the news. You know there's a war on. You know that your dome has voted to ally itself with the Episcopate of Reno, which, at the moment, is at war with Real America, and there's been some fighting around Homestake Pass, over by Butte, so far just some little skirmishes and things, because Real America doesn't hold a base anywhere close to there.

"Now, it happens my outfit, Burton's Thugs for Jesus, is, if I say so myself, one of the finest fighting forces in North America today, which means it's also close to being the best in the world, if not *the* best, and because of this, the Bishop of Reno has hired us to hold Homestake. I've got engineers already digging in up there; and because it's such a big project, we're moving our permanent base to somewhere nearby—for security reasons, I can't be specific—in the old Silver Bow country south of Anaconda Ruin.

"Now, since manning trenches and dugouts is tiring, especially at high altitude, I'm going to need to rotate people in and out of Homestake, and I don't have as many as I'd like to have for what will eventually be the third shift up in the pass. At the Silver Bow camp we will have a boot camp this winter, and I'm looking to take in a few dozen recruits. If you're a male in good health, all limbs functional, over five feet two, a hundred and ten pounds or heavier, with at least one good eye and any mental illness controlled by medication, I'll be happy to take you.

"Since we are a mercenary company, I know people worry about being called on to attack their home areas, so let me assure you that our contract with the bishop is firm, and you all know that Spokane Dome is loyal to him. If you elect to enlist with me, then chances are that for the rest of the war you'll be defending Spokane Dome. If we do change sides or contract elsewhere and leave the employ of the Episcopate of Reno, you have a one-time ten-day option to resign and return home, or, if you wish, you can continue with the company from then on and take your chances about who you'll have to fight.

"Burton's Thugs for Jesus is a union shop, represented by the United Combatants, Engineers, Medics, and Chaplains, and we use the standard UCEMC contract for a battalion-sized unit. You get room and board, medical, dental if we ever get another dentist under contract, and locked-in rent control for basic uniforms and equipment. In the event of combat against other UCEMC units, you have a much better POW contract—which can make a big difference if you're captured—you keep your seniority without penalty if you elect to defect, and you fight under the strict form of the Hague Convention, so the union is a good deal for most of you, and it's a flat four percent of your pay. You also pay for your training with a five-percent deduction from your pay for your first year, which I waive if you're decorated for bravery in combat. You don't pay any local or episcopal taxes.

"Now about BTJ: we were formed out of seven smaller units in San Francisco two years ago—three street gangs, two militia companies, my old merc engineer company, and one MP company out of the old Cal Guard—specifically as a mercenary unit to serve the One True and Only Ecucatholic Church. That branch loaned myself and my vested officers the startup money, which we've long since paid off, and last year, with their blessing, we took a contract with their allied church in Reno. We expect that we'll continue to be primarily an Ecucatholic outfit, but we're open to monotheists of all kinds, and to theistic cybertaoists as well.

"We have an unusually high percentage of experienced officers and noncoms, and we're among the few fully Geneva-compliant units—we absolutely don't tolerate war crimes. So if you're looking for a chance for some on-the-side rape, looting, robbery, slaving, massacre, or torture, look somewhere else—and pray that we don't catch you."

I put my hand up.

He snapped a crisp nod at me. His expression didn't change at all. "Yes, son."

"Three questions, sir. Is there any age limit? What do you do for dependents? And can you perform marriages for anyone in your command?"

"No age limit, but I do interview, and if I think you're not mature enough to understand what you're getting into or to behave yourself and follow orders, I won't sign you. I have no brig, so the only penalties I have available are the whipping post and hanging; UCEMC limits me to thirty lashes within a month, which, believe me, is plenty more than I want to give, though I will if I have to. I don't want to have to whip or hang a kid—or, anybody else if I can help it—so I don't enlist anybody if I think that issue might come up.

"For dependents, I send whatever part of your pay you request to them, but if you want them to move around and follow BTJ, that's all at your expense. I do pay a bonus if you're killed while following an order or during enemy attack, but that's usually not how your dependents want to get money from you, and it's my opinion that the bonus I offer just isn't worth dying for." From the slight twitch of his mouth, I realized that that was probably a joke.

He continued. "And if you were planning to enlist and get married, well, son, I'll be happy to perform a ceremony for anybody, in my unit or not. It's legally binding if I'm outside any superseding jurisdiction, which is a fancy way of saying that if you and your girlfriend want to get married, we can just go outside the Dome and I'll do it for you— you don't have to enlist. Though I'd rather you did."

Mr. Farrell said, "You do know that these two are fourteen?"

Burton shrugged. "I've married a thirteen-year-old boy to a twelve-year-old girl, because he wanted to enlist and he looked like soldier material to me. So far he's made corporal and their marriage looks happy. Life is short, these days, sir, especially for the young. A couple in love doesn't have much time to wait. Not to dwell on morbid things, but chances are that a soldier and his bride won't both live to regret being married, but one of them may well live to regret *not* having married. That's how I see it, anyway. And if they're fourteen, I believe you have to throw them out of the orphanage soon, anyway, since Spokane Dome won't let them stay here past their fifteenth birthdays."

Farrell shrugged. "I won't try to stop them; I tend to agree with you, for what that's worth, much as I regret it. Just wanted to make sure everyone knew the whole story." He turned to us and said, "Knowing Currie, he probably didn't bother to propose formally, did he?"

"This is the first I've heard of it," Tammy said.

"Well, I think you've heard everything you need to know about Mr. Burton's organization. So would you two like to go up to one of the bunk rooms and talk about it a bit? I think Mr. Burton will be here for at least an hour longer—"

"And you can call me—I have a secure com for that—if you need to," Burton added. "So you have up to three days. But it would be great if you can decide more quickly."

"We'll go up and talk," I said, and Tammy and I, still holding hands, left the room. As I went, I could hear another kid asking, "Is there any officer program?" and Burton explaining that he wanted every officer to have spent at least a year as a noncom. That was reassuring too.

When we got up to the dorm room, Tammy said, "If I say yes, will you try not to be smug about it? And will you at least ask me why I'm saying yes?"

"Okay, I won't be smug, but I sure am happy," I said, "and I guess I probably should ask why you're saying yes."

She sat down on the bed, her thick mass of orange-red hair surrounding her face and hiding her expression. She counted it off on her fingers, as if she had prepared the list of reasons in advance—maybe she did. "One, I have to go somewhere, Spokane Dome isn't taking any new Doleworkers, and I don't want to starve or beg, so living off what you send me doesn't sound so bad. Two, I do like you a lot and maybe that's a good enough reason all by itself. Three, as of what the medical AI told me after doing some tests this morning, I'm three weeks pregnant." She looked up at me from under the untidy shrubbery of her hair and gave me a shy, tentative little grin; I guess she wasn't completely unhappy about it. She always liked babies and little kids.

My stomach rolled over. I knew that Tammy was more religious than I'd ever been, and she wasn't going to have an abortion; and anyway I didn't want to never know my own child. I couldn't decide whether I was happy or miserable, but I hugged and kissed her before spending any time thinking about that; either way I would want to be with her. "Well, then I guess getting married would be the right thing,

and since the only jobs on the whole wide earth right now are for soldiers, and I need a job, that pretty much answers all the questions,
doesn't it?"

"It wouldn't be the best start a family ever got, but it won't be the
worst, either," Tammy agreed, and we had a deal.

Early the next morning Burton met us, and the whole rest of the
orphanage, out in a field outside the Dome (inside, marrying age was
sixteen), and we were married in about ten minutes. Mr. Farrell was
my best man, and Tammy's buddy Linda was her maid of honor; the
bouquet, freshly picked daisies from the field where we were perform-
ing the ceremony, went to pieces when Tammy threw it, so either no
one caught it or four girls did, depending on how you counted.

After the ceremony, we had a picnic lunch, and at the end of that,
Burton swore me in, advanced me a loan so that Tammy could rent an
apartment in the Dome, and gave me a forty-eight-hour leave to find
the place, move our few possessions over from the orphanage, buy
some furniture and dishes, and "Do whatever consummating you have
time and energy for, son, keeping in mind that this two days might be
your whole marriage. Don't waste a damn minute on rest. You can
sleep in the diskster on the way out to Silver Bow."

Burton, as I was beginning to suspect and would confirm a thousand times in the next few years, was a very decent guy, probably too
decent for what was coming. Burton and Mr. Farrell, between them,
were pritnear as close as I ever got to having a father. Lots of men have
done worse.

When I enlisted with Burton, it was still the War of Papal Succession; most of the sides were either supporters of some candidate for
pope, or groups trying to avoid the war and forced to fight to keep
armies off their territory. By the time Carrie, our daughter, was walking and talking, Burton's Thugs for Jesus had moved far to the west, to
the opposite frontier, where we guarded Snoqualmie Pass, and we no
longer worked for a person or an organization. Our whole region had
shifted over to the meme called Real America, which had bought out
Burton's contract.

Even then, though people weren't yet calling it the War of the
Memes, pritnear half of the four hundred or so sides on Earth were
memes. Real America wasn't especially greedy or aggressive, but it
did insist that everyone in any government post within its reach had to

run Real America, as did the more important businesspeople. This wasn't altogether a bad thing; Real America tended to give people a cheerful, sentimental optimism and at least a veneer of generous tolerance. It was so psychologically effective that doctors who didn't run Real America would suggest it for depressed or psychotic patients (abundant in wartime).

Burton, like most mercenaries, didn't trust the meme, since it was often necessary to change sides and the meme could get in the way, so he forbade all of us to acquire Real America—and better still, Real America respected that.

Even in places where memes were not so tolerant, enrolled members of mercenary companies were immune from the requirement of being memed, because they'd fight to the death to prevent it. You'd have to be crazy to be a trained, experienced soldier and run a meme—memes, finally, existed only to propagate themselves into as many brains as possible, and in the current struggle for power, they used—and used up—every resource they could acquire. We all knew what kinds of things an experienced soldier would get used for.

Tammy was still in Spokane, in the apartment I'd found for her, with Carrie. When BTJ switched sides and I got reassigned, since it was faster by the diskster from Snoqualmie than it had been from Silver Bow, this was a pure gain. So far, for us, the war was an employment opportunity and a way out of the orphanage and out of poverty. In the abstract I knew that for others it was different—we'd beaten back several assaults at Homestake, I'd been on many patrols out of Snoqualmie, and we'd run into firefights where I'd lost a few friends—but still, so far everything had gone better for me than I could have imagined, and although I was now a combat veteran, I was also just eighteen.

By the time we moved into the Snoqualmie fortifications, the One True and Only Ecucatholic Church was more commonly known as One True Church, and its forces had been thrown most of the way back to Reno—it was a thoroughly totalitarian meme that most people were afraid of, because it did such a thorough overwrite of the existing personality, and any remaining doubts anyone might have had about the way One True Church operated had been settled by the way the Bishop of Reno behaved after it got hold of him.

The biggest worry for Real America, and for BTJ, we thought, was that Seattle Dome and the Puget Sound area around it had been seized by the Neocommunist meme, which was extremely aggressive militarily. We had an uneasy truce with One True Church, south of us, a peace agreement with the various Native groups north of us, and a de facto alliance with the Unreconstructed Catholics who held much of the old American Midwest and Ontario on our eastern boundary. Real America's frontiers were as secure as anybody's (not very), and our population was more prosperous than most (which didn't take much doing).

Aside from the Neocommies, we also had to worry about our hanging flank to the southeast. The plains and desert country beyond the mountains had been a sort of unclaimed no-man's-land ever since Denver Dome was nuked in '54. There were enough people in that big central stretch of the Rocky Mountain Front so that any government that tried to move in got into all kinds of trouble with resistances and liberation movements and so on, but it was empty enough so that an army could move through, and we had to figure that sooner or later we would have to wheel around, run southeast as fast as we could, and defend the whole Bighorn country until the citizen army could be mobilized. Fear that something big might suddenly come up the Bighorn or the Missouri kept a lot of our forces tied up around Billings Dome, which was frustrating for everyone, but that was the way it went.

Over my three years so far in Burton's Thugs for Jesus, Tammy and I had settled into an existence that might not have been the ideal way for kids to grow up, but worked pretty well for us. During my weeks on the line or in the reserve camp, she stayed in the apartment in Spokane, took care of Carrie, and got whatever schooling she could, either on-line or live, against the day when there might be regular jobs again. Whenever I got a leave, I'd hop a diskster back to Spokane— four hours from Homestake, at first, and later only two from Snoqualmie—and zip home to get reacquainted with my daughter and to spend as much time as possible with Tammy. I suppose, except for our ages, there wasn't much about the life that a soldier in any long war of the past wouldn't have recognized.

At the time I didn't know, either, how fortunate we were that most of the rules of war were still being adhered to. As far as anyone could tell, no one had unleashed bioweapons, most domes were not bombed or shelled, and geosync cableheads remained demilitarized neutral zones. Nobody was fighting to the last ditch; it was understood that the moment you knew you couldn't win, you surrendered or retreated. War, so far, was purely a matter between the mercenary companies.

On the other hand, there were some drawbacks to being a mercenary, even in a very humane war. Attrition was taking its toll, and hyperaccurate modern smart weapons meant that a much smaller number of men was needed for the same firepower. Though Burton's Thugs for Jesus had begun the war at battalion strength, and our effective fire-power had increased, in numbers we were no longer more than a rein-forced company.

By that time I was a corporal, leading a fire team, and the only way I was ever making sergeant was if my best friend Rodney, the squad sergeant, got killed. (Two squad sergeants stood ahead of Rodney for platoon sergeant, so I stood very little chance of a domino promotion.) The chance of advancement—or the lack of chance—didn't bother me at all. I could keep doing what I was doing indefinitely, and if the job was unpleasant, dangerous, sometimes terrifying, occasionally nause-ating, well, it was a war, when you came right down to it. And my leaves were practically heaven on Earth; Tammy and I never saw enough of each other to have much to fight about.

I turned twenty, Carrie turned five, and life turned to dead solid shit, all in April 2058. By then Real America had taken a hammering and was just trying to hold on. One True Church had become One True, and had successfully seized several of the older memes. Our old Unreconstructed Catholic allies were suddenly a branch of One True— so suddenly that we lost Madison in four hours of a savage attack out of nowhere. A week later we had to abandon the Twin Cities Domes after a bitter fight, and we were thrown back to Fargo-Morehead Dome, where we finally made a successful stand.

We held through a bitter winter of fighting—I made platoon ser-geant, having buried all my predecessors. We got things squared away, got the Natives north of us to come in as allies, and seemed to be mak-ing more of a real fight of it. After beating back two assaults in the sum-mer, we felt much more confident, and when we retook the Twin Cities Dome in September, it looked like the worst of it was over. BTJ held the Twin Cities Dome against another winter assault, and that spring Burton told us that if we wanted to, we could move dependents up into Fargo-Morehead, so that they'd be easier to visit on the weekend.

I figured we had the front stabilized, and I'd rather have Tammy and Carrie near. There were good reasons. I'd missed them, while there had been so few leaves; Spokane had been attacked a couple times by One True's hit-and-run raids out of Salt Lake and Boise; in the married-soldier barracks at Fargo, they could live under armed guard. It seemed like a rational decision.

To this day I think I should have been able to see that it was com-pletely stupid to bring them up to Fargo, considering what we were fighting. When we retook it, the inside of the downtown Minneapolis

Dome had been piled high with corpses—noncombatants all. One True had had no way to evacuate that group of women, children, and old men. Rather than let them be captured, and turned by any other meme, it had made them all walk off the roofs of high buildings.

It was One True that had broken all the truces and mercenary rules of engagement, and One True that had begun to aggressively infiltrate computer systems and weapons-control systems, seizing control of mercenaries wherever it could in order to copy what they knew. Then it loaded those aggregate mercenary memories into the brains of any kids it had, and sent them out with their badly working minds and their imperfectly assimilated training, to fight and die in the first wave of every attack. A regular mercenary company might kill eight or nine of those poor teenage zombies for every death it took itself—but a regular mercenary outfit, by then, wasn't much bigger than a hundred men, and One True could send three or five thousand of those enslaved kids against it. Every advance by One True made the war, and the world, uglier and dirtier; it seemed to be the one meme that didn't care what the Earth ended up looking like, as long as it got to rule.

The world tried to resist. Maddened by the fear of having their minds erased and replaced, countless people, crazy, paranoid, perhaps as dangerous as One True itself, devised memes, large and small, to subvert or attack One True, and to promote violence and disorder within One True's territory. One True hit back with the same kinds of memes aimed at the world at large, not caring who it hit. There were legends about a meme, or a counter-meme, called a Freecyber, a sort of meme-inoculation that could liberate you from One True or any other meme's control, but then there were legends about free passes to the space colonies, and hidden cities in Antarctica, and secret bases on the sea floor, where you could take your family and live peacefully forever. I didn't credit Freecybers any more than I did any of the others.

It was hard for anyone who had been in for as long as I had even to imagine the changes that were happening. One True was fighting to "win" in a sense that no one had seen since the Eurowar, now almost sixty years in the past. People with severe psychological trouble, particularly severe depression and stress disorders, were easier for a meme to self-install into—and so One True's troops were encouraged to traumatize the population wherever they went, and the all-but-forgotten custom of serbing captured women and children resumed in those last years of the war. As our electronic equipment became more and more vulnerable, we resorted to more and more primitive weapons and tactics, trying to avoid being hooked up to anything, even a phone, through which One True, or one of the rogue memes, or even the re-engineered (and much more aggressive) Real America might seize control of us. As memes increasingly were able to disguise their presence, and often to spread incrementally through conversation and ordinary daily interaction, we began to fight in pairs or trios, limiting our contact with anyone else. The almost civilized war I had joined was turning into the real Fourth World War, and it was rapidly catching up with the Eurowar and the two wars of the twentieth century for its savagery and lack of restraint—and it would probably end like all of them, in the sheer collapsed exhaustion of the losing side.

It seems so obvious in hindsight. I should have known how the world was going. I should have resigned, or deserted if Burton wouldn't let me go, grabbed Tammy and Carrie, and run like hell to somewhere; taken all my saved pay, maybe, or robbed some place, gotten enough money to pay our way onto a transfer ship, and emigrated to Mars. Sometimes I really did think about that, but at the same time I felt like I owed Burton a lot, and he was more and more shorthanded.

So I procrastinated and didn't resign, didn't desert, didn't look for a place where my family could move far away from the fighting, read the emigration information for Mars a hundred times and even realized I could probably make a living as an ecoprospector and might even like the work. I thought about it frequently, but I did nothing and just let it drift.

I had figured everything wrong. I found out just how wrong in the first week of August, 2059. I woke to the alarm in the middle of the night, rolled over, kissed Tammy, pulled on the fighting clothes, went into Carrie's room and gave her a quick hug, receiving a sleepy little kiss on the cheek, and pulled the gear out of my weapons locker. By then Tammy had come out in her bathrobe; she said, "Any idea—?"

"It's what they call an urgentest," I said, shouting to be heard over the alarm, which would keep ringing until I went out the front door. "Usually means we've got to jump on a diskster, go someplace, and fight. Get on-line and make sure all my insurance is paid up, will you, honey?"

"Is One True invading again?"

"Could be. Or maybe some ally switched sides." I checked; I had all the gear I was supposed to be picked up with. I desperately wanted another quick leak, a snack, anything for twenty more minutes with Tammy, but the alarm was whooping (I could hear most of the other alarms in the married-soldier barracks doing the same thing), and no matter how often I did this, I always wanted twenty minutes more. I could pee and eat on the diskster, going in; it was really just that I wanted time with Tammy. I contented myself with a long, awkward kiss, as she managed to fit against me despite all the hardware hanging from the suit. "I'll see you soon. Love you," I said, and left.

Two guys were already waiting at the pickup spot, and within five more minutes there were ten of us. My "headquarters" squad was a good one—I'd handpicked a bunch of experienced types to put plenty of vets around me, and everybody in the squad had at least two years fighting experience under his belt. The squad sergeant, Mark Prizzi, had been among the first squad of soldiers I'd ever trained, back when I was a corporal.

My headset popped. "Dog Platoon, come in, Currie." It was Burton.

"I'm here, sir," I said. "Headquarters squad is all assembled, waiting for pickup."

"Check your other squads."

I did; all were at stations. I reported back to Burton.

"Good so far," he said. "But it looks like the enemy has managed to virus our pool of disksters. Figure a half-hour delay till pickup, while we reload memories into all of them. You can let men go back inside if they want to do anything for fifteen minutes."

I passed the word along, but nobody went back in; once you've said your good-byes, that's just too hard. We stood around, not talking much, till the disksters showed up. I walked up the gentle slope of the gangplank and took my seat at the rear right, long-practiced hands strapping me in against the up-to-four-gee turns that these things could do—or the up-to-ten-gee jumps if something went bang too close to you. When my three squads were all loaded and strapped in, I reported back to Burton. "All right," he said. "Just a minute or so more for the disksters to pick up Bravo, and then we'll be in motion, finally. Looking bad."

"Can you tell me what it is?"

"Wait till we're on the highway," Burton said. "Then I'll let all the platoons know. But it ain't good, and this is gonna be a rough night, and I don't think we're all gonna see the sun come up." In some strange ways, competent and compassionate as he was, my CO was still a kid who had read one too many adventure books.

About fifteen minutes later we were racing down the corridor formed by the old highway, making all the speed we could for the Twin Cities, and Burton was filling us in. No intelligence outfit had yet figured out how—none of the intelligence companies from the area were even reporting, which suggested we had been hit even harder than we knew about—but somehow defenses around Twin Cities Domes had gone down, all at once, and before the garrison could mobilize, the barracks had been hit with narrow-beam ionizing radiation from overhead, cooking most of the defending troops in their beds or while they tried to pull on their uniforms, and all their families with them. The few on guard, and the few who had gotten mobilized fast enough, were now trying to hold a ragged, thin line south of the domes, with too few people, too ill-equipped, and no idea what was going to hit.

It hit before we got there, which is why we survived. At diskster emergency speeds with everyone strapped in, you could travel from Fargo-Morehead to Twin Cities in about an hour and a half. Within that time, the defenders at Twin Cities were overwhelmed by a force that was probably fifty times their size, plus more bursts from that damned irradiating satellite.

We kept going anyway, because the forces of One True zipped right around the Twin Cities Domes, dropping off a small garrison force, and fanned out toward the other important domes in the area. One big spearhead was coming our way. At least our disksters were fairly radiation-resistant, and should be proof against the ultrahard positrons they had used on their two bombardment passes so far.

Bravo Platoon had the lead, and they never had a chance at all. With onboard radar, a self-driving maneuverable vehicle like a diskster could normally dodge an artillery shell—but Bravo's disksters had had to spend a critical few extra minutes in the shop, and that was when, so far as Burton and everyone else could figure out later, they had been sabotaged with a sleeper virus that woke up when the first shells appeared above them, and they steered right under them. Bravo Platoon's three disksters flashed into smoke and debris, all of our disksters began to dodge and duck, and Burton did the only sensible thing and tried to have us pull back to form a fighting line somewhere where it might work. We swung east of the old highway in a tight, high-speed turn over the empty fields and meadows.

That was when all kinds of heavy fire poured onto us from the east; we had turned into their trap. The automated defense weapons on our disksters shot back, but we were up against something overwhelming, and we did the only thing that seemed to be an option—turned to run west and north, evading and dodging all the way, never having the spare minutes that would have been required for us to stop and deploy forces.

They pursued us for a solid hour, pushing us ever further west and further out of the battle, scattering our forces all over the landscape. Any time one of the disksters tried to turn and fight, it was chewed apart by heavy fire; we evaded in all directions, and we must have traveled more than a thousand miles in total by sunrise, while only being pushed a couple of hundred west, but we were getting beaten bad no matter how you figured it, and the most we were managing was to run away.

At sunrise, we were way to hell and gone somewhere in South Dakota, they had just stopped shooting at us and broken off the pursuit, and Fargo was naked to the enemy.

We raced north as fast as we could, and we damn near made it; Burton's Thugs for Jesus, or what was left of us, were running even faster than we had after the slamming-around we'd just taken. Most of us had families in Fargo, or at least girlfriends.

Not long before noon, we were making a final dash, moving along at almost 200 mph over the prairie and meadow country that had been wheatfields once, about forty miles west of Fargo. It might have been a nice day if we hadn't all been worried sick about getting there, but theoretically in just minutes we could be taking up positions to the east of town, and calling in all the passenger disksters available. We weren't going to try to stop them, just slow them long enough to make it possible to get the civilian population, especially our dependents, out of their way. Burton had pledged to use the whole unit treasury, if need be, to evacuate all the civilians in Fargo-Morehead Dome.

Now all we had to do was get there soon enough and hold long enough.

Burton and his four headquarters staff were in the diskster just over a roll of land from us, maybe a mile and a half away—we were staying spread out in case of attack—and so I didn't see it directly, but there's no mistaking an atom bomb. A white flash over the ridgeline blinded us for a moment, and the diskster slewed sideways and bounced along for half a mile or more in just a few seconds, before the AI got it back under control and brought it around. By the time we were back near where we had been, the classic mushroom cloud was already forming. Burton must have been right at ground zero when that went off.

While we all wondered what to do—none of us had ever had any other CO and anybody else we might have turned to for leadership was on the diskster with him—one of the disksters for my platoon flared with blue arcs as it sank into the tall grass, its balancing capacitors all discharging. Our diskster went in to see if we could help, and the surviving parts of BTJ went with us because they weren't sure what else to do, but as we arrived, our com crackled and an unfamiliar voice said, "Burton's Thugs for Jesus, this is Shultz's Rangers. We've got you. Every one of your disksters has a weapon locked on it, and we are preparing to shut down your propulsion by our control of your software, which we just demonstrated with one diskster. Please have your senior surviving sergeant surrender, so we won't have to fire again."

That was me, I realized. I grabbed the com. "Burton's Thugs for Jesus here. We'll surrender. Are you offering UCEMC terms?"

"Our employer does not permit that," the voice said, flatly, and I realized that the other unit was memed with One True, so there wasn't going to be any negotiating. "Do you still wish to surrender or shall we fire?"

I gave the order, and our surviving five disksters set down, grounded out their charges, and went inert.

An hour later, still the senior surviving sergeant, I was trying to explain the issue. "Look," I said, "we are not acting for Real America in this. It just happens that most of our family and friends live in Fargo. All we're asking is time to declare it an open city, and some respect for Hague and Geneva. And we're asking. We're certainly not in any position to tell you."

Shultz nodded agreeably, his eyes far off; probably his whole company had only recently been turned. It was said that One True would do that to you for anything that it considered to be a violation of your contract. He spoke on the com for a while, repeating our requests.

Then he stopped and said, "Fargo-Morehead has been promised to Murphy's Comsat Avengers as a reward for their services. We are not at liberty to make any other arrangements. We will hold your forces here for sixty hours and then release you."

My heart sank through the floor. Murphy's Comsat Avengers was one of the most brutal mercenary companies anyone had heard of— from a unit initiation that made me sick to my stomach just to hear about, to an earned reputation as the most enthusiastic serbers in the war, to the mutilated bodies that they left behind to make pursuers hesitate, they were the epitome of everything that the War of the Memes had turned into in the last few years. They were one of the very few not-yet-turned companies that One True had under contract. It was rumored that they hadn't been turned because One True didn't want to share in any of their memories. I believed it.

I tried to appeal to Shultz's honor as a soldier and his human feelings, and I tried begging, and I offered to sign over our whole unit treasury to ransom the city, or even just to ransom our dependents. But it was absolutely no use to argue; Shultz now thought whatever One True needed him to think, and One True wasn't going to change its mind for a few scruffy, defeated POWs, not when it had already promised to reward one of its most effective fighting units.

We sat out our sixty hours under guard, and when they let us go, we fifty-five survivors—all that were left of the 122 men who had started out—began the long, unhappy walk toward Fargo. Nobody in Shultz's company bothered to say good-bye, let alone good luck.

Four days after I'd seen Burton vanish under that mushroom cloud, I stood by two graves in the public park not far from the college.

Hardly anyone was alive in that miserable town. Looking for Tammy, I'd seen half a dozen things that I figured I would remember for the rest of my life—a pile of heads outside a hospital, a whole street with a body on every tree, a quartered baby on a park bench, a woman with all four limbs torn off floating face down in a fountain.

It took me most of the day to find Tammy and Carrie, and it was almost a relief: they'd just been running down the street, trying to get away, and been hit from behind by machine-gun fire, probably body-heat-seeking bullets, because they'd each been hit in the back and the bullet had gone out through their hearts. They had died instantly, without torture or serbing, as far as I could tell, and Murphy had not been able to use them for his legendary hobby of killing children in front of their parents. No, they had been very afraid, and perhaps hurt for just a second, and then they had fallen forward, dead, Carrie's forearm still clenched in Tammy's hand.

I dug the graves deep and was careful about it; when I finished, I rolled a matformer over from a hardware store, set it on vitrous, and started shoveling dirt into it, letting it fill its tank all the way before I dumped it into the graves, so that I wouldn't have to smell too much of what happened when the hot material hit the bodies.

When I had filled the graves with molten glass, I poured a big block of glass at the head of each, positioning it to weld onto the filled grave, and with an iron bracket from a shattered park bench I pressed their names and their birth and death dates onto the slowly solidifying glass. I figured if anyone, animal or human, wanted to defile a grave, there would be easier ones to defile.

For two full years afterwards I was a madman. There really wasn't any other word for it. I took to stalking Murphy's Comsat Avengers. Every few weeks I'd pick out a man asleep in his tent, a sentry, a messenger, or any living human target from Murphy's, as long as I was sure of my escape, and kill him with a knife or bare hands, partly to be less detectable, mostly because it was more messy and painful for the victim.

Besides, doing it that way sometimes gave me an instant, as they realized what I was about to do, to tell them why. And after they were dead, I would do some cutting and rearranging, to give their buddies a surprise when they found them.

When MCA went into battle, I would shadow a scout or flanker, and kill him in the uproar. I had a few noisy radio beacons with timers that I would sometimes stick onto a piece of their equipment, and now and then one would go off and a diskster or a heavy weapon would be hit.

I left no notes, told no one, talked to no one who wasn't already dying, gave them no clue about who was doing it. I moved from place to place, following them generally east across the Midwest.

Eventually they were based along the south shore of Lake Ontario, not far from the southern tip of the still-growing Hudson Glacier. It was cold and dreary and the cover was less plentiful, but I stuck around and kept killing them, a few per year. I lived on one kind and another of scavenging; I was barely more than a predatory animal.

Once, when I had gone hungry for a while, and I had knifed two Comsat Avengers in their tent as they slept, I took away not only their rations, but their buttocks, hamstrings, and quadriceps; that might have been the beginning of my return to sanity, because when I reached my camp, the thought of cooking and eating those was too much. I tossed them out into the snow for a cougar, wolf, or coyote. To my surprise, I could not quite descend as far as cannibalism. Still, the next night I shot one of their sentries at long range, so I hadn't exactly forgiven or forgotten. I just had some standards, I guess you'd say.

I doubt they even knew I was there. They were up to their necks in so much fighting, and so much of it was now stalk-and-ambush, that a few men more or less in a year was nothing much. If they thought about it, they must have thought that they were running into exceptionally bad luck, the way the rest of the human race had been for so long.

Dave leaned back and shuddered for a moment, more as if he were cold than afraid. "Up around Lake Ontario?" he asked.

"Yeah, not far from where the St. Lawrence ice dam used to form and break. Spent a long time freezing my butt off up there. Not much left in the ruins—so many armies had gone through, you know. But I managed."

He stared into space for a long time. "You and I have much more in common than either of us thought," he said. "I lived up there at the same time, so I guess you won't be surprised to hear that I also had one hell of a grudge against Murphy's Comsat Avengers. I don't know who could live in that area and not feel that way, you know?"

I nodded. "Yeah, I know what you mean. The strangest thing to me, right now, is that I've spent decades during which the memories didn't hurt, or at least I didn't know that they hurt—losing my wife and child, the things I saw, the things I did . . . I spent ages without thinking about it, and now, here I am an old man, with a lot more present things to worry about, like whether or not you're going to kill me—and I can't get it out of my head. I can't make it go away. I'm halfway to crying and halfway to screaming and if you told me that Murphy's was somewhere in the neighborhood and you wanted to go kill one, I'd beg you on my knees to let me come along and help. It's like none of that went away at all; more like I just had a complete lapse of memory for twenty-five years."

Dave nodded. "Well, you know, that's not an uncommon reaction in people who have been dememed. I've seen people our age crack up, or go into shock, when they're dememed, from just remembering too much. Anybody who lived through those years has a bunch of experiences he never wants to talk about, and feelings he can't get rid of, and so forth. I'm no big fan of One True, but I can understand why some people would let it turn them, or even go out and find it and ask it to turn them. My memories are bad enough, and if someone told me I could just forget them forever, at a bad moment on a bad day, I guess I just might wish to be turned."

"It's not that you forget them," I said, "it's just that you don't think about them. Ever. For a real long time." A thought was beginning to bother me, more and more—memories and thoughts flooding back, different remembered pains striking me from all sides, throwing me off balance. I realized, too, that I was no longer reaching for Resuna to get them fixed, but I wasn't sure whether that was because I had gotten used to Resuna not fixing them, or because I didn't want Resuna to do that. I wished I could make the thought come clear in the front of my mind where I could know it for whatever it might be.

"Being able to not think about it might be good enough," Dave said, "when the times are bad enough." We both leaned back into the hot water, stretching and shaking ourselves out. "Two old farts that spent too much of their lives working hard outside sure appreciate a hot bath, don't they?"

I arched my back and let myself float upward. "Yeah. You know how farts like to float to the top in a tub."

It was a dumb joke, but he stretched his own back and laughed. "You want to switch from coffee to something stronger? I've got cases and cases of wine around and I never drink it because I hate to drink alone."

"That would be real fine."

"And I ain't gonna kill you tonight, either. I'm way too soft for this job, you know."

"We're none of us what we used to be," I said. "Jeez, I don't even *need* the wine to make me say stupid things."

"It's like parabolic skis," he said, grinning, shaking the water drops from his beard as he got out. "You don't have to have them to turn, but they make it so much easier. You don't need wine to say stupid things . . ." He shrugged.

I gave him a thumbs-up. "Bottle for each of us?" he asked, pausing at the door.

"Pos. Fucking. Def."

He laughed gaily and went out. Abstractedly I considered that I could leap out of the tub, break the coffeepot, jump him when he got back, cut his throat with the shard, put on some of his clothes, and walk out and signal to be rescued. Cowboy hunters are not supposed to kill unless we have to, but I seriously doubted that I'd be in any great trouble about this in the present circumstances. Even if I were, all that my new copy of Resuna would do is help me to see that I had acted in a deluded way, that the violence hadn't been necessary, had been no part of One True's intentions.

I froze. I could barely breathe. The thought I had been looking for had come to me.

I had spent my years as a soldier—except my very earliest—fighting against One True. I had been on the other side for years. Soldiers for One True had killed my wife and child, shot them down in the back as they fled to escape serbing, torture, god knew what atrocities. One True had turned Murphy's Comsat Avengers loose on that town, and all those scattered, piled, dangling, mashed bodies had been permitted by it. It had even sent Shultz's Rangers to keep us away so that we wouldn't interfere.

One True had broken the understandings among mercenary companies, making the war much more savage. It had abrogated Geneva and the Hague. It had brought back all the nightmares of past wars, turned loose every horror from atom bombs to massacres to looting and serbing. And I had fought against it. In fact . . . a huge, dark, horrible shape rose in my mind and I was ready to cry.

Well, I realized, I sure wasn't going to kill *Dave*. He was most likely the only other person on the planet who might understand what the matter was. I just wished I had a clue as to what I was going to do.

"Well, here's the party," Dave said, coming in with four bottles of the wine, a corkscrew, and even wineglasses. "I brought along twice as much wine, just in case the first one I open turns out to have gone to vinegar," he said. "Besides which, it might just happen we need to get extra-stupid before the evening is over."

So it was evening, I thought, and wondered for a moment if guessing a time and believing it—say 8:30 P.M.?—might bring back Resuna. I didn't much care.

He fiddled with the first bottle, solemnly, and at last extracted the cork, pouring a sizable glass, which he handed to me. "Try it—carefully."

I took a sip. I'm no connoisseur, but it wasn't vinegar and it didn't taste like barrel, and it went down smooth and warm. "Great," I said.

He handed me the bottle. I poured myself a full glass, set the bottle carefully on the floor beside the hot tub, and took another sip. Meanwhile he was opening the other one, and in a minute he was back in the water beside me. "Good health," he said, raising the glass.

I clinked mine against his. "Good health," I agreed. "Well, I never did answer your question; I told you all the story that leads up to how I got turned by One True, but I never did tell you that story itself."

"I sure don't have any meetings to rush off to," he said, "and it's been a long time since I heard a new story. You keep talking and I'll keep pouring and we'll have a fine old time."

"It's not a very nice story," I said.

"The best thing about stories about bad stuff," he said, "most especially true ones, is that you can remember it's all in the past."

I wasn't so sure it *was* all in the past, but I didn't say that. I launched in, and figured we'd talk about it after I told it, or not, just as he pleased. The wine was good, the hot tub was grand, and my calendar was as open as his.

I've seen vid and flashchannel recordings of the celebrations of the Pope's Peace in 2002, the one that ended the Eurowar. People dancing in the streets, soldiers from all the sides hugging each other, the famous shot of the mayor of Paris turning a shovelful of earth to celebrate the beginning of Reconstruction. The Earth was poor, worn-out, shot all to hell. The uncontrolled bioweapons were raging across the planet, converting forests to wastelands, farmers' fields to obscene black goo, fishing grounds to empty water. Lowland soft-soil areas like Florida, the Netherlands, Bangla Desh, were gone. Tailored rice blast was threatening to make rice extinct in Asia, and if it couldn't be stopped, the expected famine might wipe out half of the human race.

And yet there was a sense of hope, faith—even a feeling that human beings had been delivered from a far worse fate—and in the pictures, still or moving, you can see the joy, courage, and faith in the faces of the people.

There are no such pictures from the end of the War of the Memes. Twelve years, four months, and nineteen days of global fighting don't leave you much energy or joy to celebrate with. What you see are two sets of expressions: the grim determination on the faces of those whom Resuna had turned, who knew that they were going to be working like donkeys for a decade or more just to get the world back to material decency, and the horror of those trying to emigrate offworld before the scheduled forcible turning of all those who had not turned voluntarily. 2.7 million would depart on the last regularly scheduled voyages of the transfer ships; the rest would be anesthetized so that jacks could be installed in their heads, and then would be quietly, painlessly, but inexorably turned to Resuna.

The billion people running One True, but without cellular jacks, would be equipped with the jacks, and then their copies of One True would be replaced with Resuna; a single One True would run as an emergent program on the vast network of cellular automata created by all the linked copies of Resuna. There was a bitter joke about One True ascending into the network, and another one about the human race being demoted—since One True had occupied the mind completely and Resuna would merely be a voice in your head and a sort of add-on to your personality, we were going from having everyone be an identical lord to everyone being an identical serf. To be sure, those jokes only circulated in the temporarily free population.

Millions of people were turned away at the processing centers up on the supras, as the transfer ships cherry-picked the most valuable 2.7 million free citizens; money, family, possessions of any kind, even genetic heritage didn't count—only highly developed knowledge and skill, and only the very finest of that. Rockefellers, Kennedys, Rothschilds, Windsors, Michelins, and Toyodas were turned back with a shrug—they had nothing of value to offer. Beautiful models, known on sight to the whole planet, couldn't get a second look. Mathematicians, surgeons, violinists, sculptors, poets, gymnasts, footballers—so long as they were the very best of the very best, as judged by the transfer ship and colony governments—got aboard, and so did the very closest members of their families, especially if the family itself was highly talented. Dinner-table conversation during the months of journey to the colonies must really have been something.

The offworld colonies and the transfer ships had absolutely no need of a fair-to-good infantry sergeant. I suppose I might have gotten aboard unofficially, using my skills as an obsessive assassin, but I was only good at killing people I hated psychotically; I didn't want to kill any poor bastard who, like me, was just trying to escape from an Earth that was about to become the sole property of One True.

By the time I even got to the cablehead at Quito, they had a bunch of space types down on Earth, rationing the train seats up to Supra New York. The transfer ships were not willing to come anywhere near any meme again after Unreconstructed Catholic's attempt to seize the *Albatross* a few years ago, so they had each agreed to take just one load of colonists out to the colonies before bending their trajectories forever away from the Earth. The bottleneck was not the capacity of the transfer ships—in the several cubic kilometers of their cargo bays, they could move whole cities of people plus all the needed food, water, and air—but the number of available shuttles, since the transfer ships were only within shuttle range for about six weeks of an Earthpass. It took a shuttle, seating about 1800 passengers, anywhere from four to eleven days round trip, between a supra and the transfer ship as it swung by the Earth, with the first shuttles reaching the transfer ship just as it came in range and the last ones being barely able to make pickup on its way out. Minor variations in exactly where each transfer ship was coming from, which supras the shuttles could return to, and where the Earth was in its orbit at the time, determined the exact number of shuttle flights that were possible, but it worked out to only about 540,000 passengers going onto each transfer ship, even though the transfer ships could easily have handled two million each. At least, if you got aboard, once you were on the transfer ship you were going to have plenty of room.

By the time I was trying to talk my way aboard, only the *Wandering Jew*, which had been the Earth-Titan transfer ship, remained; I had seen each of the other four transfer ships appear as a dim star in the night sky, grow to be ten times brighter than Venus, recede into dimness again, and then sprout a great flare of purples, golds, and greens as their MAM drives kicked in to re-bend the orbit for a new destination—the *Flying Dutchman* first, back in March, then *Mohammed's Coffin*, then *Diogenes*, and the *Albatross* just a few weeks ago. Now, in November, with binoculars you could just make out the incoming *Wandering Jew*. In a few weeks it would go from dim star to bright star to dim star to surreal comet—and it was the last ship from Earth.

I never got any farther than the cablehead on Mount Cotopaxi. A wheezing spacer in a powered wheelchair heard my story, then asked politely and gently if I had any skills or experience, anything at all, that I hadn't already told him about. I had to admit that since I'd been soldiering from the age of fourteen, I had no skills they were ever likely to need out there. He looked terribly sad as he stamped my form with REFUSED.

They didn't even have enough seats on the trains, anymore, to let people go up to the supras and try; four million people waited in line on SNY alone, in addition to the two million who normally lived there, all of them endlessly applying, applying, and applying for the few remaining seats, some hoping that their skills would suddenly be wanted after all, others hoping that an administrative mistake might slip them aboard, most just hoping. Trains took two days to geosynchronous orbit, and didn't carry enough passengers; they had to be reserved for people who were genuinely good candidates.

I walked out of the vast, echoing terminal at the cablehead, and watched for a moment as a train climbed slowly up the narrow line of the track on the vast, kilometer-wide surface of the cable, accelerating quickly to 500 mph, vanishing into the clouds in a few scant seconds. There might be fifty people, out of the thousand on that train, who would get aboard; the rest would be coming back down, after a while, to be turned by Resuna and rebuilt—*no doubt into useful, productive, helpful citizens*, I thought, savoring the cold cynical feel in my mind, *just like I'm gonna be. If Mr. Farrell hadn't been killed in one of One True's bombing raids, I just bet he'd be real pleased with what One True is going to make out of me.*

I had no idea what to do at all; no family left to love, no Murphy's Comsat Avengers left to hate, no BTJ or Real America to command my loyalty anymore. I might have known a person or two in Spokane Dome, but I hadn't been back there in years and hadn't kept in touch with anyone I knew from the orphanage. I guess that was about as alone as I'd ever been.

I walked down the road, toward the city of Quito. I wasn't planning to walk the whole way, but for the moment I was being too cheap and not in enough of a hurry to catch a public diskster, too tired to think much, not quite too numb to feel sorry for myself, miserably hot in the late afternoon equatorial sun. All along the road I could see exhausted, discouraged, frustrated people like me, in ones and twos and families, some muttering about the unfairness of it all, some trying to cheer themselves up by brightly saying that maybe everyone wouldn't have to be turned (and inventing reasons why One True wouldn't want to turn them in particular), some comforting others, a few cursing endlessly, most just walking along toward Quito because that was the only logical place to walk from the cablehead.

Beside me, a woman's voice said, "It's really rough, isn't it? People understand that everyone can't go, but all the same it's so hard to be one of the ones who doesn't go."

"Yeah," I said, as much reply as I could think of. At least this might be someone to talk to. I glanced sideways and saw a woman with a thick, single brown braid down to her waist and an aquiline nose. She was wearing a black and red sweatshirt that advertised the 2048 Olympics in Singapore, mended but not dirty blue jeans, and ankle-high hiking boots. I guessed that she might be anywhere between eighteen and thirty, depending on how she'd gotten through the war. Her head was up and she was looking around, not seeming depressed at all, and that made her absolutely unique on the road, as far as I could see ahead or behind.

"Do you have any plans for what you're going to do now?" she asked.

"No," I said. So far she was doing all the work in the conversation, and that seemed sort of unmannerly, so I added, "Didn't have any plans other than to come here and try, so that I could at least feel like I tried. I'm an old mercenary. No use for us on Earth or in the colonies.

People have given up war, at least for quite a while, and that's all I ever had any knowledge of or training for."

"It must be tough to feel like no one needs you anywhere," she said, with just enough real sympathy in her voice so that I was pretty sure she hadn't been walking up the road saying it to everyone, as someone who had been turned by a meme might do. My first thought had been that she must be one of those few people who were still independent of memes—or at least of big, controlling, take-over-the-whole-personality memes—because she didn't have the slightly flat, time-delayed, vaguely robotic affect that most people with memes had, or at least most people that I knew to have memes. It was always possible that she either had one that was cunning enough to lay low, or perhaps she was running a bunch of smaller, non-dominating ones, like so many mercenaries I had known (it could be handy to have some of the abilities they carried, like certain kinds of emotional control and skills). I was lonely but I didn't need company that was going to try to take over my personality—just at the moment that was about all I had left and there wasn't much of it.

We had walked a short ways together before she said, "I just noticed that you were discouraged, but not angry."

"I don't have much energy to be angry with," I said. "I lost my family in the war, and I got my revenge for that, and now there isn't going to be a 'me' anymore, so I guess on the whole I'm quits with the world. Whatever I was here for has been accomplished. So I don't have much commitment, one way or another, to anything except going back down to Quito, catching a diskster to somewhere else, and maybe checking into a hotel and spending all my back pay before they erase all money next year."

What I had just told her wasn't quite true. I had been thinking that a man who had survived out in the wilderness, hunting professional soldiers, as I had for two years, surely could manage to disappear and stay disappeared, maybe living somewhere out on the fringe of the settled areas or maybe around some ruin deep in the woods. It might be lonely, at least until I found other people doing it, which I figured there were bound to be. At least I'd still be myself.

I was sort of thinking of taking a diskster up to Albany Dome and walking from there up into the Adirondacks—it might take weeks or months, especially with the first heavy snowfalls starting in late September as they did these days, but if I got there soon, grabbed gear and basic supplies in a week or less, and got out of the dome without leaving too many traces, I ought to be thoroughly gone by November 30, when all of us who were still unturned were supposed to turn our-selves in.

Given just how risky the whole business would probably be, I wasn't about to confide it to a woman I'd just met. You never knew who might be listening or when she might be turned. But I did like the company, and what I had said so far was only what you might have expected of someone who'd been turned down at a cablehead.

"You're not going to try at Kilimanjaro or Singapore?" she asked, sounding surprised. "You know there's always another chance."

"Naw. Why? There's another chance if you're on the borderline, maybe, but the list of what they're looking for is the same in all three places, and nobody like me is on that list anywhere, you know? Expe-rienced professional killer? That's just about the only thing that One True and the colonies agree on—they don't want any more of them. So there's no point using up one of my few remaining weeks as myself running from cablehead to cablehead begging. I can make far better use of the time, even if I just use it to lie on my back in the grass, at night, and watch the stars turn around."

"When you put it that way, yeah, I guess there are better uses for the time." She grinned at me. "Are you planning to have any company in the grass?"

"Haven't really been interested since I buried my wife," I said, not particularly sharply. I wasn't trying to discourage her attention—right now it was the only thing even vaguely interesting I had encountered—but I didn't quite have the energy or interest to come up with an appropriate, gracious lie.

"I did say company, not ass," she pointed out, smiling.

On the equator, the sun rises right at six and goes down right at six, and so darkness was starting to sweep into the afternoon even though it wasn't particularly late. There was still some daylight left, but the very first lights were going on in Quito, down below us, and the shadows on the backs of the people ahead of us, and the faces of the ones behind us, made everyone into indistinct figures. Now and then a diskster would come up or down the road, alternately darkening or flashing as it passed through patches of light and shadow. We walked another hun-dred meters or so before she said, "My name is Mary Roder."

"I'm Currie Curran." I realized the conversation had reached a point where, out of nothing but politeness, I should be asking her a few things about herself. "Were you up there applying, too?"

"No, not really," she said. "I've got no reason to leave Earth."

"Not to get away from One True?"

"I'm part of it," she said, so comfortably and easily that at first I didn't believe she'd said that, and I must have gaped at her stupidly. "Really," she said, emphatically. "I've been running Resuna for a year and a half."

She kept right on walking along that mountain road, just as casually as if she had merely happened to mention that she collected stamps or had worked as a carpenter. It seemed too bizarre to be a joke and too pointless to be any kind of a scam; it might be the truth.

"You don't act like somebody with a meme."

"It doesn't feel like having a meme," she said. "I ran One True for years, and that whole time I felt like I was just crouched in a corner in the back of my brain, unable to do anything but watch. Now I feel like I run the show—I just have a very useful, friendly voice in my head that gets me through things. And on very rare occasions, One True calls me up, but now it calls to talk, it doesn't take over my head."

"Well," I said, stupidly, repeating the obvious because I couldn't think of anything else to say, "you really don't come across as a person with a meme."

"Neither do most of the people with Resuna," she said. "I can't promise you, when you turn, that you'll like it, but I can promise it will be different from what most people imagine. I'd think that would be sort of a relief, because most people imagine *horrible* things."

I agreed that that was true, and we walked for a while longer. Eventually, looking for something to talk about, we talked about how big the geosynch cable really was, up close—on most of the Earth, of course, the night view of a geosynch cable was just a black vertical line ascending from the horizon, suddenly turning to brilliant silver somewhere in the sky; the silver line continued on up to where it was capped by a burning white dot, the size of a BB shot held at arm's length. But here, right by it, it looked like a mountain with no top; it was almost a mile thick and went right up into the sky farther than you could see, to something that looked like a tiny half moon right overhead.

I didn't feel much for her, or anything, but Mary was company, and that was pleasant. She didn't seem to be doing any of the things that a person with a meme was usually compelled to do, like trying to persuade me to join her or acquire the meme, which meant either that Resuna was subtle and crafty, or just possibly it really *wasn't* as terrible as the other memes were.

Always assuming she was telling the truth at all.

"I bet," she said, "that you are wondering about whether my copy of Resuna is going to try to grab control of you. Am I right?"

"Exactly right," I admitted.

"Well, you aren't going to believe this," Mary said, moving just enough closer to me so I couldn't help being aware of her compact, slightly heavy body. "But it's true, anyway. Resuna is a sterile meme, by design. It has to be loaded into people. It can't load itself or spread by itself. Like a seedless orange or a mule—purely a useful creation, not an independent form of its own."

"Why?" I asked, really curious about something for the first time in a long time.

"Because reproductive neurocode for a meme, not to mention the neurocode for reproductive motivation, takes up enormous amounts of space in human memory," she said, "and Resuna no longer needs to be able to reproduce itself, because it isn't going to have to spread by memetic contagion anymore. The global system and One True can reproduce Resuna as needed. The whole idea of Resuna is that it's no bigger than necessary—it leaves you as much room in your head as it can."

"Why doesn't it just leave you the whole thing?"

She shrugged. "What kind of world have people made, running their own lives?"

I thought about that as it got dark and we traveled on. I was more troubled than I wanted to admit by my inability to come up with any answer that was as good an argument as the ones she had right to hand: half the domes on Earth wrecked, hundreds of millions dead, so much of the progress made by the two Reconstruction generations completely undone, the colonies and all the off-Earth industrial production lost, species extinct by the thousands, the glaciers eating away at one hemisphere while warming destroyed the other, the human population itself riddled with near-helpless lunatics who had been so traumatized that they could no longer even take care of themselves—the list went on for a very long time, and against that, all I could say was, "But I'm used to being me."

"And I'm used to being me," Mary said, "and I still am me. Just me with more self-control, and the ability to work with my whole heart for the common survival—and because everyone else will have Resuna, I also know I'm going to be working with other people who are also giving one hundred percent to it. Do you realize how much difference that makes? No worries, at all, about other people cheating on the social contract—so when you do the right thing, you'll never feel like a sucker. No doubts about how other people are feeling. You get to be your best self, and you can depend on them to be their best selves."

"Uh, you're not sounding like a meme, but you *are* sounding like a PR department somewhere wrote your dialogue."

She giggled, and it was a healthy natural sound. "Yeah, sorry. Resuna spends a certain amount of its effort in persuading the people who have it that they're better off with it. I'm afraid we all do speak with some of the same phrases, and some of them aren't very natural. But Resuna will get smarter. And I'm really not kidding; having it in your head doesn't mean you're not you, which does make it different from most other memes."

I thought about that one as it got darker. We talked about other trivial stuff, where our lives had taken us, what we had done. I said just enough about having lost Tammy and Carrie so that I figured she wouldn't bring it up; she told me that she'd been a novice in an Unreconstructed Catholic convent. When One True had invaded and captured her area, the convent was given as a reward to a mercenary company, for seventy-two hours of the sort of thing that used to happen in those last years of the war. At the end of the three days, the survivors were all turned by One True. She had One True for a long time after that, "which was probably better than crying and screaming and lying in the fetal position, because I'm here and I'm functioning now. And One True did do some repairs to me, and now Resuna's coming along with fixing up the rest of me, I guess you could say. At least it seems like it's done enough repairs to be able to give me more freedom."

"More freedom?" I asked. I wasn't used to thinking of that in connection with One True.

The sun was gone. Our road was lighted in front of us by the glow of the city below. She moved closer, and I felt her hand very tentatively touching mine. A minute later we were holding hands, and that seemed pleasant, after years alone. If this was how One True was going to come after the unturned population, in these new days of Resuna, well, it was *much* nicer than being netted, sedated, and brainwashed.

I thought she had just droplined me, after I asked my question, maybe because she was offended. But then she said, "Well, I guess it depends on what you mean by freedom. Without One True I'd have been free to do whatever I wanted, but all I wanted to do was sit and cry. With One True, I at least got some of my life restarted, and was useful, and meanwhile I could be huddled up inside, crying at first, and then thrashing things out, and finally getting better, while not being either a danger to myself or a burden on everyone else. And now with Resuna I'm free to do and be so many more things, but I feel safer knowing that if I'm about to do something stupid, or crazy, or dangerous, it will stop me—probably just by talking to me and persuading me that it's not in my best interests. So I'm free to not be miserable, or useless, and I'm free to not spend all of my time coping with what happened to me and my friends, and most of all I'm free to make myself useful and effective and someone I can like. That's *lim* more freedom than I had when I felt compelled to rock and sob."

"I can see how you would feel that way," I said, and couldn't help thinking that if Tammy and Carrie had survived, somehow, they too would have been living down gruesome memories for a long time, and might well have welcomed anything at all that gave them a way to function and to shut down some of the pain.

"Well," she said, "and it's done other good things for me. Can I be honest with you?"

"I think I'd prefer it," I said, "if Resuna will let you."

"Silly, it's the one that suggested being honest." She drew a deep breath and pressed down on my hand, so that we walked even closer to each other. "The thing is, it's hard to explain," she said, "and I'm afraid it might upset you, but I'd rather have you know it than not. I was a virgin—hadn't even been kissed—when I entered the convent. Then I got gang-raped for several hours, and some other stuff." She said it with about as much emotion as most people mention having their wisdom teeth out. "After I got turned to One True, I never had sex, and I haven't had sex since I turned from One True to Resuna, but Resuna says I'm ready if I want to, and, well, gee, I'm healthy and twenty-two and . . . uh, see, Resuna and One True have really good information about me, and good information about many people they haven't turned yet, and . . . oh, well, look, One True picked you out for me. Since I was already here in Quito, it's where my job is and all, and they knew you were applying, they sent me up here to meet you. And I think you're really great-looking and you've been so nice and well—there. Now I told you. But I approached you all on my own. Really. I just got some hints about what to say from Resuna. So if we, you know, do it, you'll be with me, not with Resuna, and we don't have to rush or anything if you—"

"Whoa," I said. I was still holding her hand, and she was pressed close against me; we weren't moving very fast. "Resuna, or One True, or somebody, picked me out of all the guys on Earth?"

When she responded her voice was oddly flat—more mechanical than it would have been with most other memes. Because Resuna is relatively small, it doesn't have much fine control on things like inflection. "Actually you were picked out of the eligible unattached men who would be passing through Quito this week. Mary Roder has a common problem that comes up during recovery; in the process of healing and learning to look forward to her future again, she has begun to romanticize more than would be optimal for a healthy emotional life. She needs to have an experience with someone who will not be rough, impatient, or rude, but whom she sees as strong enough to protect her—basically a sensation of complete safety—but she needs to not fall too completely in love. So a handsome, kind, courteous stranger is what is called for, and that is you, Currie Curran. If you don't wish to do this, we'll find someone else without much difficulty, but you were the first choice. And we of One True know enough of your life to know that you must be very lonely and unhappy; an evening with company and affection would hardly harm you."

"Can Mary hear you saying this?"

"No. In just a few minutes she'll become conscious without realizing that she walked this distance with you while unconscious. Meanwhile, do you want to do this? If not, she can lose interest."

I thought about it for a moment. It was strange to have my arm around her waist while another mind talked for her. She wasn't really my type, I suppose, but it had been a long time, and I was lonely, and the thought of being all alone in some anonymous hotel was unattractive. "I'd like to," I said. "And I'll be as gentle and patient as you need me to be."

"As Mary needs you to be," Resuna corrected me. "And you would not have been selected had we not known what we do of your past. Your feelings are very straightforward, reasonable ones; you love those who love you back, you hate those who hurt them, you give your loyalty to things you think are worthy. It's that simplicity which Mary Roder needs.

"Before I bring Mary Roder's personality back, there are two things you need to know. First, you may either continue this relationship or not; we will see that the memory is a good one for Mary, as long as you help by creating pleasant experiences to work with. If you do wish to continue, you may stay with Mary after you are turned.

"Second, and this is very important: the cue phrase that enables

Resuna to take over and deal with emotional distress is 'Let overwrite, let override.' If Mary appears to become hysterical or catatonic, if she acts in ways that seem unusual or unhealthy, if she begins to cry uncontrollably or shows any other sign of real distress, speak that phrase, firmly, until she hears it. That will bring Resuna to the front of her mind to deal with the crisis."

"You can't just come on your own?"

"Resuna is systematically limited; if it had the power to overpower human minds, it would have the power to contemplate resistance to One True, and that cannot be permitted. Do you have any question?"

"No, I don't."

"A public diskster will pick you both up in a few minutes. It will take you to Buenos Aires Dome, where there's a hotel room waiting. No charge—it is One True's way of thanking you for helping Mary."

I walked along with her body, around a slow bend in the road, for maybe ten minutes, turning the alternatives over in my head. I was really not seeing any likelihood of any problems I couldn't handle, and the idea was more attractive every time I thought it through. At last I said, "All right, I'll do it."

"Remember," the Resuna voice said, "Mary Roder will not remember we had this conversation, and as far as she is concerned, the last seventeen minutes and twenty seconds never happened. Enjoy yourself, treat Mary well, and remember you have One True's gratitude. Are you ready for me to release her back into her body?"

"I guess so."

With a subtle shift in her body, Mary regained control and consciousness. "Since I was already here in Quito, it's where my job is and all, and they knew you were applying, they sent me up here to meet you. And I think you're really great-looking and you've been so nice and well—there. Now I told you. But I approached you all on my own. Really. I just got some hints about what to say from Resuna. So if we, you know, do it, you'll be with me, not with Resuna, and we don't have to rush or anything if you want to take your time and get to know each other first. What do you think?"

"I think I ought to com for a nice high-speed diskster, and hire it on my credit to take us somewhere nice, have dinner on the diskster, spend a while looking at scenery and messing around, check into a hotel room, mess around some more, and just kind of see what happens," I said. "Have you ever been to Buenos Aires?"

"So what exactly happened?" Dave asked. "You woke up the next morning with a jack in your head, or she talked you into talking to a terminal for a while, or you fell in love and decided to stay?"

"Mostly that last one," I said. "Mary was very attentive and very affectionate. And I was just twenty-five, even if I was a widower, and I'd only ever been with Tammy before, and it had been years, and so at first I was probably just there for the sex and the not being lonely part. Then I got kind of hooked on being her hero, I guess you'd have to say, and after that I started to see that she really needed me—and by then it was November 15, a beautiful spring in Buenos Aires, the warmest on record—and way too late to make any plans to run away, and so one evening I came back from having a jack put in, and we made love, and she plugged me into the phone and held my hand, and when I woke up I was turned, and running Resuna. We held a party to celebrate. And now we've been married twenty-three years. And this is the first time since 2062 I've really had a free thought about whether or not I like her, or what kind of a wife she's been."

Dave nodded slowly, as if digesting the whole situation. "What do you think?"

"I think I miss her at the moment. I hope she's not too worried. I'd like to see her again."

He smiled. "Well, good, then. Another glass?"

"Pos fuckin' def."

"And can I trust you not to tie me up and turn me in if we get very drunk tonight?"

"Yeah, I think so."

"Good enough." He raised his glass. "My story's not as dramatic, so we're going to need more wine."

Dave's tale didn't take long. He was a foundling in Denver Dome, a few years after I was dropped off at Spokane Dome—we both thought it was pretty funny (with help from the wine) that we theoretically could be brothers. He'd been in a couple of mercenary units before being hired as part of the bodyguard for a Freecyber cell in upstate New York, within fifty miles of where I was stalking Murphy's Comsat Avengers.

He'd liked working for the Freecybers—he said they were pleasant employers, met their bills, didn't ask for the impossible, treated you like people—but it came to an abrupt end when Murphy's unit overran them and butchered the people they were guarding. "No call for it, either," he said. "They could have just turned them. It was pretty close to the end of the war. Could've just put One True into them, and I bet that's what One True would have preferred. Murphy's was the only mercenary company I ever heard of that regularly killed just for fun; it was like a whole outfit of serial killers."

I nodded and took a big slurp of the wine, which was absolutely delicious. "Yeah. You know where Murphy came from? He was nothing more than an old vag at the time the war broke out. There probably weren't two thousand vags left on the planet in 2049, but unfortunately, he happened to be one of them."

Dave shrugged. "I knew a couple of former vags, myself. One of them and I went sniping a few times, because he was so crazy he'd go show himself on the skyline to draw fire—he lasted about a week, I think. All the old vags I knew were crazy. Most of them were people who just never got over losing something, and spent their lives in the woods, robbing and looting, trying to get it back, pathetic crazy bastards who were dangerous to anyone they ran into, but otherwise not anything much to worry about. Murphy was something else again entirely, a lot more than just crazy. He was about as evil and sick a bastard as the poor old world has ever seen and it's a good thing his delusions made him too incompetent to get anywhere."

"Amen," I said, and extended my glass in a toast; we clinked them together, and I said, "I saw him die. You could call it a mixed pleasure. I had always hoped to get the fucker myself, and the first time I was about to get a good shot at him, two of his own men did it. The three of them were out in front of his tent, talking about what to do now that peace was here, and he was going on in some crazy riff about putting the comsats back up—like anyone needs them with the supras there. Then he grabbed one of them by the shirt, and the other one shot him. I was so startled that I muffed my first shot at one of them, so they both got away."

Dave nodded firmly. "You at least got in a good try at them. Me, once Freecyber was gone, I didn't have any side in the war, so I just went into the bush. Here's a strange thought. I didn't have nearly as much grudge against One True as you did, and if One True had made me the offer to become a cowboy hunter—even without being memed, just hunting cowboys in exchange for my keep—I might have taken it.

And from what you tell me, if you hadn't run into Mary on that road, you might have drifted into cowboying, or whatever it was called up the Northeast. We could've been on switched sides. Funny how life cuts."

"Yeah," I said. The warm water and the wine were getting a dead solid grip on me, and I was fading fast. "I'm starting to think of bed," I admitted.

"Me too, Currie. Let's drink up. There's not much left of these bottles."

There wasn't much left of his; there was about a quarter of mine, but I pounded it right down like a dumbass teenager anyway. He took my glass, reached to an overhead shelf, and handed me a bar of soap. "Oatmeal soap, for rich ladies to scrub their dingy skin with," he said cheerfully. "Don't worry about it making you pretty, it didn't make them pretty." He guffawed at his own joke and I did too; we were prit-near as drunk as I've ever been. When he got out to soap up, he nearly fell, and I got out very slowly; it's not easy when you're holding a bar of soap in one hand, and you really wish you had both hands to hang onto the floor with.

We both soaped up all over, working up thick lather in our hair and beards. A couple of knotted, crusty scars were on the back of my head, which probably meant that whatever Dave had done to the back of my head with his club should have had stitches but hadn't gotten them. Oh, well, I was alive, and not memed, and thinking as myself.

When we had finished lathering, Dave carefully put our pieces of soap back on the shelf, and said, "Just be sure you don't stay with your head under too long. I can't think that would be real good for a guy with a recent brain trauma."

We climbed back in, the hot water feeling good after the cool of soaping up, and swished around in the water, getting the soap off and the last kinks out. I let myself slip down and put my head under. In water that's warmer than body temperature, with a skinful of wine, putting your head under hits like a sledgehammer, and you can easily pass out, but I let myself hang for a moment in that blissful almost-not-there state, so relaxed that my muscles seemed to just blend into the surrounding water. If Dave had wanted to kill me, that moment then would have been a good time; I'd probably have slipped over to the other side without caring.

But clearly he didn't. I suppose decades without a friend do things to a man; the thing that seemed strangest to me was that he was still fairly good at getting along with people, after all that loneliness.

I let the warmth fill my whole body, then sat back up, splashing and wiping the water from my face. "I don't suppose you've got—"

"But of course," he said. "I built my towel closet with racks that carry hot water. All towels are always dry, fluffy, and hot."

"Damn, you know how to live." I got out and he tossed me a towel; I dried myself thoroughly. It felt good to be alive. "Dave, if you don't want to be turned, I am not going to turn you. And since you can't trust me if I'm turned, I guess I'm out in the woods for good, myself. You'll have to teach me most of the mechanics of living out here, and I'll have to depend on you for a while, but I'll construct a place of my own, if you prefer, just as fast as I can. And I guess we both have to move, anyway, because there's bound to be some of them looking for me in a couple-few weeks, once some of the spring melt has happened, plus of course they had enough uploads from my copy of Resuna, the last few days before you caught me, to have you pritnear dead solid located."

Dave sighed. "Well, we're both in a sloppy sentimental mood. Been a long time since I've had a partner, and living out in the woods without anybody else is lim, lim hard. But you gotta think about things like the fact that you wouldn't see Mary again, ever, probably, and I got to think about whether I'm letting my feelings blind me. So let's sleep on it, get up late, talk it over . . . you know, the usual kind of thing you do when you know what you want to do, but you want to be sure you want to. You know?"

"If I had a few more brain cells running I'm sure that would be perfectly clear," I said. "Sure, see you in the morning."

He didn't even lock my door; I had the funny thought, as I fell asleep, that I might be about to become a cowboy, but I sure as hell wasn't ever going to put any dumbass-looking Stetson on.

Next morning the menu was jerked venison, canned beans, pickled grouse eggs, strong coffee, and plenty of aspirin. We didn't say much till we got enough of all that stowed in our guts so that we felt sort of human, and then we took a vote and it was unanimous that we ought to go take a nap. It must've been another three hours before we staggered out, guts stabilized, heads only oppressively fuzzy instead of overwhelmingly thick, and had some more coffee, plus some jackrabbit stew he'd canned the summer before. "Well," Dave said at last, "that was one hell of an evening. Haven't had a blowout like that in decades, literally."

"Me either," I said. "Felt pretty good, even if I wouldn't want to do it more than four or five times in a year. To let you know, I still think I'd rather throw in with you. I'd rather be your friend than not, and this is the only way to be your friend. As for Mary, yeah, I miss her, and she has some good qualities and so forth, but you know, there's a whole lot of energy that has gone into taking care of her, and much as I hate to admit it, I'd have decided she wasn't worth it, probably within a few weeks, if Resuna hadn't been steering my thoughts. So I'm about twenty-five years overdue for an awakening from the romance, and though I wish her all the best, and though I would gladly take care of her just out of duty, and enjoy her company . . . well, Resuna will take very good care of her, and she'll be just fine. I'm leaving her in a situation much safer and more comfortable than I ever left Tammy in. So if you'll take me on, and teach me enough of what you know, I'd be happy to be your neighbor out here, or your partner if you don't mind sharing quarters. I'll do more than my share of the work to make up for not supplying my share of the knowledge."

Dave sat back in his chair, put two more aspirin in his mouth, took another gulp of coffee to wash them down, and said, "You worry way too much about what's fair, and about my privacy, Currie. I'd dearly love to have a partner. With two of us working we can make our new place big enough to have rooms for both of us. I know you'll pull your freight. And if you *are* just going to turn me in, well, that idea is so discouraging that I'd just as soon not think or worry about it at all, so I'm not." He stuck his hand out, we shook, and we were partners.

That afternoon we got going on the subject of where to move and when. Over his years of wandering around in the mountains, Dave had picked out several other places with easy-to-tap geothermal heat, none with as abundant a flow as this one. "Two of them have a sizable surface pool nearby, so if the temperature on that was to start to drop, it's just possible a satellite would spot the difference between how hot the pool used to be and how hot it was now. If they've found this place by then, well, then they'd know my basic way of surviving, they'd be looking for changes around hot springs, and we'd be in deep shit. Out of all the hot springs sites I've found, there's only one that drains back into the ground without breaking the surface and flowing down to some creek. It's on the leeward side of Ute Ridge, a little ways up, in a cave that's probably an earthquake crack that got weathered out bigger and then had some runoff flowing through it at one time—there's a slide up above that I figure must have turned off the flow. There's some room in there and plenty of stuff solid enough to dig out for more as

we need it—though it's not going to be the pleasant easy digging that
this old mine gave me. And so far, anyway, checking that spring for
years, it hasn't gone dry or surged up. Problem is, it's reliable but it
ain't plentiful—there's maybe half a gallon per minute or so, enough
to give us heat and some hot water, but nothing like the four and a
quarter gallons per minute I got here."

"We could put in a tank of some kind, couldn't we?" I pointed out.
"The longer we keep the hot water hanging around, the more heat we
can extract. We couldn't have an ever-running hot tub-laundromat-
dishwasher like you've got here, but we could just do all the washing
in shifts; wash and rinse with water from the hot tank, drain it into a
warm tank that keeps the place comfortable, put it through the toilet
and then discharge it room temperature if you've got a safe hole to put
it down."

I had to draw a couple of sketches of the idea for him—I was
mildly surprised at the way the idea didn't seem natural to a man who
had built a place as ingenious as this one—but once he got it, he nodded vigorously and added, "I think you've already paid for yourself,
Curran. That's a great idea. Far as I know, after it passes through that
little cave, the stream runs underground for miles, too—no surface
pool anywhere near—so even if we take all the heat from that water,
and discharge at room temperature, betcha we still don't show up to
the satellites."

"I guess that's what we are betting on," I agreed.

Two days later I saw daylight for the first time in what I discovered had been nineteen days. Dave's camouflage for the entrance was
simplicity itself—it was under an overhang and led onto a long sloping
shelf of south-facing dark rock, which must have stayed pretty free of
snow most of the time. We walked straight out during one of the no-
satellite times, got under the trees, and put on skis—his were old
Fiberglas models; I just used my flexis. After a moment or two to
check equipment, we were on our way.

I was a hair rocky on my skis, at first, and we took it slow, going
the long way round because it was much more nearly level. It was
another beautiful, cloudless, deep blue sky above pure white snow. By
the third kilometer or so, I was back in the swing of things, annoyingly
short of muscle after all the bed rest, but fundamentally fine.

You had to be practically falling into the little cave before you even saw the wisps of steam, or the donut of ice like a giant's anus, among the scrubby firs. The opening was an irregular oval, perhaps four feet long by two across. "Getting in's not as hard as getting out," Dave said. "The floor's not far down, and it opens up beyond this point. Just follow me." He set his skis down under the tree, and I did the same; then he braced a hand on either side of the glassy ice of the opening, and more or less swung down into the space, coming to a rest when he was in about up to the bottom of his ribcage. "Tricky spot. This part of the floor is covered with ice," he said. "Have to figure out a faster entrance eventually. Now squat, hope not to fall down, turn real slowly *left*, stick your legs out, and slide down a slope on your butt. You'll skid down maybe seven-eight foot and land on a pile of scree. I'll be down there with a light."

He squatted and I heard a scraping sound, a louder and different scrabbling noise, and then finally a crash of spraying gravel, followed by the rattle of him climbing off the scree pile. "Okay, I'm down. Just come to the light."

If possible, the ice around the opening was slicker than it looked, and wetter. My head seemed to ache as if waiting to be slammed. Gingerly, I put my feet down and found the slick, icy floor; I could see a trace of glare from his flashlight on my boots, coming from my left.

"Doing fine," he said.

Very slowly, keeping my weight right over my feet, I crouched and turned. I was in a space less than a meter high and not much wider than the hole on the surface; beside me Dave's light came up from a crack that was about a meter wide and not more than two feet high, into which the floor sloped. I put my feet down the opening and pushed off, hoping that Dave hadn't worked out some incredibly complicated way to cause a cowboy hunter to die where he'd never be found.

The freezing-cold rock and ice chewed at my ass for an instant. With a momentary lurch, I gained speed. My boots grabbed the scree pile and I finished up squatting on that. Dave was standing there, adjusting his flashlight for use as a lantern. I climbed down carefully and stood beside him.

As my eyes adjusted to the light, I saw that we were in a big crack in the native granite. It was surprisingly free of dirt, and almost unpleasantly warm. I opened up my suit as Dave took off his jacket. "Well, here it is," he said. "Prospective home."

In the dim light I could clearly see the basic space—about seven meters that I could see, ending in a bend at one end, varying from two to three meters wide, all high enough so you could walk without bumping your head. A thin trickle of warm water dribbled across the muddy floor, steam rising from it. "It's also hotter than what I've got in the home place now," Dave said, "which I think means your idea will work even better."

I walked forward and looked to see that the trickle of water emerged from an opening that I could probably have put my arm into, if I'd wanted it scalded. "We could widen and break this out," I said, "or just stick a pipe into it. Probably start with just the pipe and then expand toward the heat, eh?"

"Sounds logical to me," Dave said. "There's a chamber around the bend, where the hole that drains this is."

Gingerly, I made my way through that main gallery, following Dave, watching where I put my feet, not caring to dip my boots in the near-boiling trickle. Around the corner, in the short leg of the L-shaped cave, where Dave's lantern shone, we moved into a chamber about two meters square and some inches deeper than the gallery we'd left; the ceiling was higher too, and the hot trickle bit deep into the clay soil floor, vanishing toward the end of the room in a gurgling hiss of steam. "I've probed down that hole, and about a meter below, it seems to widen," Dave said. "We might could try a video camera and monitor, and a light, and see if there's a usable chamber down there to dig to, or even just a good place for one of your storage tanks."

"Seems promising," I said. "You ever done anything to find out how deep the clay is anywhere in here?"

"Naw. Wasn't high enough priority till now. For all I know when we dig it out we'll turn up ten more foot of headroom and entrances to six more chambers. Anyway, that's about all there is to it right now. What do you think?"

I looked at it and thought about how hard I was going to have to work; then about Mary and the cabin; then about what it was like to be awake, in my own skull, without Resuna watching every thought, and I said, "This is gonna sound stupid but I can hardly wait to get started. I guess we bring up the shovels tomorrow, and we start mucking out."

"Makes sense, if you're ready."

"Oh, I'm ready," I said. "And here's another thought. We don't have to haul the dirt out and dribble it from a pack. All this clay was carried here by the spring, right? So if we just build a box with a screen on the bottom, that the stream runs through on its way out, and drop the dirt in there, it will be carried downstream underground, where nobody's going to see it. We might see about mucking out the drain first thing, just to see if we can do it that way—because if we can, that makes the whole job simpler. We can be here digging more of the time and we won't be limited by how much dirt we can hide."

"What happens if we put so much down there that we plug something up, and it starts to back up into the cave?" Dave asked.

"Then we poke down there with poles and rods, and see if we can smash something to let the water out—and if that doesn't work, we see how far it fills—and if it fills to the top, well, we tunnel in from the side and let it out. Which admittedly kills the advantage of the subterranean drain. But anyway, we've got so much to gain if we can move a few tons a day, instead of a few packloads. We could have a whole new place here inside a year or two if we can wash most of the clay down, instead of carrying it. Wouldn't you say?"

He shrugged. "Partner, I never thought of that either. I'm just not much of a planner or engineer; purely an improviser and an improver. It's probably a good thing I was the cowboy and you were the hunter, because you damn near caught me, and I don't think I'd've stood a prayer of catching you."

"Different approaches," I said. "If you and me were hunting a cowboy together, I'd be amazed at how many things were obvious to you, I bet, that I never saw."

"Might could be," Dave said. "Might could be."

There might be something heavier and more uncomfortable than a pack full of canned goods, but I don't want to find out what. The first job, once we realized that we needed to get Dave's place moved, right away, was to get all the really indispensable stuff cached at some distance from it. Canned stuff with Vitamin C was number one on the list; if we had that, we wouldn't get scurvy. If we didn't have that, not only would we be facing scurvy, but we'd have to pick a *lot* of berries the next summer, and come up with some way to can or dry many pounds of them, and do a great deal of work we wouldn't really want to make the time for.

After the indispensables for staying alive, dealing with emergencies, and not getting sick, we would move all the nice small things, appliances of one kind or another, that shave so much effort off a day and free up so much time. After that, if we still weren't interrupted, we would gradually move the million and ten small luxuries that could help to make life way out in the woods bearable—books, wine, audio recordings—and finally, if One True left us alone long enough, any-

thing else that we could take before we dropped a load of rocks across
the entrance and left forever.

Caching the portable stuff meant taking it out, a packload at a
time, to about twenty different hiding places, since we wanted to make
sure we had some of everything in each cache, so that if one of them
got found, we wouldn't lose all of any item. What shall it profit a man
to keep his dialytic water-purifier membranes, if he lose his canned
tomatoes? I was glad that I hadn't been doing this decades before,
when Dave and his band had been hiding out here, since there must
have been many times this much stuff to carry. Of course, then there
had been eleven men doing it.

It was late afternoon, and I was crossing a high saddle down into
Kearney Park, enjoying the colors, smells, and sounds in their near-
outlined clarity. I'd made seven trips that day and was looking forward
to finishing this one and having an evening soak in the tub. Another
week and we should have all the food cached, and then it would only
be a matter of a few days to get all the other irreplaceables moved
before we could at last begin our excavations in the new cave. If I was
right that they wouldn't try to send hunters out again until a thaw was
well underway, we'd be doing our excavation comfortably in the shelter of the cave, possibly for weeks or months, while the pursuit grew
frustrated, and the scent got cold.

With luck it might be several years before we were spotted again,
and though sooner or later one of these spottings would lead to our
capture, at the moment it looked like we had some years of freedom
left. And, as I'd explained to Dave, life with Resuna wasn't *un*pleasant—if Dave hadn't been there and determined to stay out of One
True's grip, I'd probably have just gone back to Resuna because it was
easier.

Aside from getting caches sited and filled, we'd made enough time
to explore the cave around the new hot spring, probing with some six-
foot star drills that had been in the back of an old general store. The
water drained into at least one more big chamber below, and we'd also
tapped into some openings under the clay that we were optimistic
about.

Meanwhile, though, we had to move the canned stuff. I had a
packful of cans of tomatoes, peaches, and sweet potatoes to get into
the cache in Kearney Park, before going home. I pushed off to make a
slow glide, down through the trees, avoiding any open space too easily
watched from orbit. It was harder than usual to safely descend the
hard, icy, steep patch in front of me. I had to work at it, turning tight

and constantly so that I didn't build up any speed. The extra weight on my back made it much tougher.

I hurtled back among the trees, still going faster than I really wanted to, and followed a deer trail I knew well through a thick patch of growth. Then a bump turned out to be a log, the ski scraped and jammed, and I flipped forward and landed in a hard face plant.

I sat up, face stinging from the snow, head aching where forty pounds of tomatoes, peaches, and sweet potatoes had slammed right into the place on the back of my head where I had all the scars. I was all by myself, and feeling half crazy with anger the way you do when you do something stupid and hurt yourself entirely through your own stupidity. I plain old bokked all over the place, forgot that I had to hide, forgot everything I'd been thinking of, and just gave myself over to my rage. I released the skis, pushed up, wiped the nasty mix of snow, mud, and pine needles from my face, angrily hurled the pack to the snow, and screamed "Fuck!" several times, jumping up and down in a rage, not caring if anyone heard me, or if I was visible to an overhead satellite, or much of anything except about the way my whole body was clenched like a fist and my back and head hurt. I hadn't done anything like that in twenty-five years or more.

Long practice will have its way; in the middle of it all, I said, out loud, very calmly, "Let overwrite, let override." Instantly I felt better.

With all the canned goods in the cache, even having gotten the job done a little early, I had plenty of time to take the long scenic route home, but I just *knew* I had forgotten something, so after a few hundred yards I turned around and went back to take a look and see if I could figure out what was bothering me.

Everything was right where it should be, so it wasn't that I had forgotten any physical objects. Had I forgotten some part of the careful system we used to keep everything hidden? I looked around the cache to see if anything was wrong with the concealment, but everything was fine there. Then I looked to see if I'd left any track or trace I should cover.

Two thick ruler-straight tracks ran across the meadow through the deep fresh powder from the place where I had fallen to where I stood. I had come in a straight line, instead of circling around among the trees. No wonder I'd gotten here so quickly.

That big straight track might as well be a gigantic arrow pointing straight at where I stood. Worse still, it was pointing at a sizable part of the vital stocks we would need to live through the next year.

I stared at that for a long moment, wondering first what had possessed me to do something so astonishingly bokked up. Then I wondered why I couldn't remember it. Then my blood froze, and I remembered falling down, losing my temper—and invoking Resuna. Which had, as far as I could tell, popped up, taken care of the task for me, and put me on my way home, but which also had a strong interest in seeing me get caught.

If the jack in my head was still operating, One True now knew everything. I couldn't imagine why it hadn't just kept control once it got Resuna back into my head, but for some reason it hadn't. *Why* had it turned me loose again?

The silence, the clarity of the colors and outlines, the chill of the air in my nostrils, were all sinister to me now. I had betrayed a good friend in a moment of sheer involuntary idiocy, I had put myself back in reach of Resuna and thus under the control of One True, and I would be giving up the whole dream of living up here and letting the world just slide by—back into the dull world of forced retirement, of Resuna holding Mary and me together, of drifting from one predictable, unimportant activity to another.

I felt like crying; I felt like taking my knife and just opening a vein right there. It would be so good to just cease to be. It was very likely that there was no longer anything I could do for Dave; I was miles away with no way to communicate with him. Chances were that fifty hunters were zooming in toward him in disksters, and he'd be captured any minute and turned within a day. Probably I'd even see him again—after he was turned, we could pal around together and our copies of Resuna could have a nice chat. Probably One True would find him a nice wife, or even put him back together with Nancy and Kelly. Probably when I did see him, he'd *thank* me. Probably he'd be having to say "Let overwrite, let override" every ten minutes for the next few years; probably his life would seem as if he were suffering seizures every few minutes.

I was disgusted to realize that once Resuna had me again, it wouldn't bother me a bit. I'd be able to look the man right in the eye and think I'd done him a favor.

I wasn't sure I wanted to live to see that, but I wasn't sure I wanted to just kill myself now, either. Mostly I just wanted to not feel what I was feeling. I have to admit that the real reason for doing what I did next was not shame, nor acceptance. It was pure absolute dead solid cowardice. I just didn't want to face that situation any further, and since I couldn't get out of the situation, I tried instead to get out of facing it.

I looked around that meadow, up the saddle, toward Columbia Peak, and saw it for what I figured would have to be the very last time with eyes that were completely my own. Tears stung my eyes, and I said, "Let overwrite, let override."

Nothing happened.

I said it again, and once again, nothing happened. There wasn't a trace of Resuna.

I said it again, several times. I started to lose my temper and shouted it several times, but no Resuna came—only distant, distorted echoes from cliff walls.

I was all by myself, no idea where to go or what to do.

I think I stood there for quite a while, because the blue-edged deep shadows were longer by the time that I finally sighed, wiped my eyes, and decided that absolutely nobody would be benefited if I just stood here and froze to death.

I had three choices. I could try to get away on my own—in the winter, with no supplies since Resuna would know where all the caches were and I wouldn't dare go there.

I could ski downhill till I found a road, and follow the road downhill till I found an emergency station, and then call up the system and turn myself in. Somebody would come out pretty quickly in a diskster, take me home, and get a new copy of Resuna installed.

Or I could gamble. I could proceed as if I knew that I had only been running part of Resuna, with its communications section not working. It was even possible, I supposed, that the blows to my head had smashed my cellular jack—it was possible, since it was only an inch or so from where the biggest scar was—or that it had all happened during a gap in satellite coverage, or any number of other things had prevented the betrayal.

That last option was the only one that had any chance of working out and didn't make me feel like a skunk.

If I was right, and One True had *not* been contacted, or not contacted reliably, then all we had lost was one cache. In that case, if Dave and I moved fast, we could go to our drop-everything crisis plan—hurry over to the new place, camp there, move in a couple of caches, start digging, live rough for a while until we had a chance to scavenge enough supplies to start building it up. It was just possible that all was not lost—if we moved fast enough.

I pushed off hard and took the fastest concealed route I knew to make it home, skating the whole way, throwing myself upslope, rocketing downslope just barely in control, half-blind with sweat and tears and terror, not caring about the way my muscles screamed at it. I was over that high saddle in no time, down into the Dead Mule drainage, and racing for home like a madman—still skiing as carefully as I could, because I knew I was frustrated and angry, and I thought that if I face-planted again, or kissed a tree, or just took a bad fall, the rage and fear and frustration might overwhelm me. I might automatically say "Let overwrite, let override," and be back with Resuna again.

I hit a long run down a ridgeline into a bowl, and put on even more speed; any faster and my stopping distance would be greater than my seeing distance. It was likely I was already too late, but it would be certain if one more thing went wrong.

The sun was still up, but close to the ridge, when I finally glided up to the rock shelf, popped the skis off, and ran inside. Dave wasn't home. Probably he was off hunting elk—we'd been needing fresh meat to replenish the larder. He might well be out till after dark, which might could work out better.

We'd figured out a procedure for just such occasions, so I got going on it. Each of us had a "jump bag" ready to go, packed with personal essentials for surviving a night in the woods if we had to, plus a little package of sentimental stuff and some dry rations. The two jump bags sat side by side on the floor near the entrance; if one of us discovered that it was time to run, and the other one was out, then if we were to meet up at the new hot spring, the signal would be both jump bags being gone.

If just your partner's jump bag was gone, that would signal that neither this cave nor the new one was safe, and that we were to meet up whenever we could at a specific ruined house two drainages away; whoever got there first, unpursued, would wait a week for the other.

We had agreed that the one-bag-gone signal would only count if a specific red blanket had been left on top of the laundry hamper. That way your partner doing routine repacking or rearranging wouldn't send you running off into the woods for two weeks.

We had never assigned any meaning to the situation that I discovered: my jump bag was there, Dave's jump bag wasn't, Dave wasn't there either—and no blanket on the hamper. I needed to leave him a signal to run for the new hot spring, which I thought made the most sense in the circumstances. I was figuring that if One True had gotten everything from my memory, we were too screwed to recover from it and would be captured whether we stayed here, went there, or went to the ruined house. On the other hand, if One True hadn't gotten enough information to find us, the new spring was the best place to hide—it already had the necessities for us to stay in it for a few weeks and let our trail get cold, it was comfortable and safe, and it had lim less trace of Dave or me around it than this place did.

I had no signal from Dave, and I had no way of leaving him the message that I wanted to leave—writing a note of any kind would risk its being read by the hunters, if they found the cave before Dave got home. The question was, how long should I stay here? Dave might be very close at hand, in which case I could just let him know when he came in the door. Or he might have carelessly left his pack elsewhere while repacking or cleaning, or he might be far off. Given his occasional carelessness (I often wondered how he had survived so long without detection), he might even have run for it and forgotten to put the blanket on the hamper.

I decided I could spare him five minutes for a quick look through the rooms; if his pack was on the kitchen table or by the hot tub, as I'd found it before, I'd tease him later but take it with me. Otherwise, I'd take my jump bag and leave a circle-and-dot, which means "I have gone home"—it was one of those very old trail signs from god knew where in the past. I hoped he would interpret that to mean "Go to the new hot spring," and that it would be sufficiently cryptic if anyone else found it.

I walked through all the rooms quickly, not seeing his pack. One of the three doors that I had always assumed were closet doors in his sleeping room was standing open, light coming out of it. When I took a step forward, I saw, through the open door, beyond what I had thought was a closet, a big room. A finished ceiling and wall were visible through the mock closet. Not yet thinking clearly—it had been a day with too many surprises—and still looking for Dave, I walked through the closet and into the big room.

My first thought was not especially profound; it was only that Dave couldn't have made this space with a shovel and pick. The walls, floor, and ceiling, now that I could see the whole room, were finished with tile, the overhead lights were running off real power fixtures and didn't seem to be just long-life lanterns, and the whole place seemed more like a lab or a workroom. At first I thought the object in the center of the big room was a large worktable, then that it was a raised bathtub. I got closer to it, and said, softly, "Dave? Dave, are you back here? We got big trouble."

I took another step, and now I realized what that big object was: a suspended animation tank.

Stuff clicked. Dave had been able to disappear for so long because he'd been sleeping under this hill. No wonder nobody could find him. Probably his story about the packloads of dirt was a convenient lie. Most of the "scavenged" stuff had probably been stored down here for him. When he did wake up, with common germs having diverged for many years from what he had gone to sleep with, he got a whopping cold as soon as he went where any other human being had been, and if he—or whoever he worked for—hadn't planned for it, he'd had to steal medicine.

It seemed ominous that this hideout had always been intended as a one-person place; whatever he was doing with his band of cowboys, he hadn't ever intended to take them along. He couldn't, with just one tank available.

No wonder, when we were planning the new cave, so many ordinary technical and engineering things had seemed to be mysteries to him. He hadn't designed this place—all he knew was how to operate it. The place had been set up by whoever he worked for.

"Currie, that better be you in there," he said. His voice came from a doorway in the corner.

I froze for a second. "Yeah, it is. I didn't mean to nose around, Dave, but we've got a situation. I had a relapse of Resuna this afternoon and I don't know how much it uploaded to One True. I think we have to run for the new hot spring."

He came out from the back. He was naked, except for a dozen medical sensors hanging from his head, neck, chest, and back, and carrying his jump bag.

"You better tell me about that," he said.

I sketched it out for him quickly—getting hurt, losing my temper, and saying the words to invoke Resuna. "Honest, Dave, I really didn't mean to do that—"

"Oh, I believe you, for whatever good that does either of us. I can't imagine that twenty years of habit breaks that easy. It ain't anybody's fault; something like this was bound to happen sooner or later. So it took you over and then what happened?"

"I skied down to put the stuff into the cache, but I went straight across the meadow. It was all new powder down there, and I left tracks that are bound to be picked up from orbit. Might as well have painted a bull's-eye around the cache. Not to mention that I'm sure, as often as we've traveled between there and here, they're going to follow my track back here—if they don't already know exactly where we are and what we're doing. I figure that when my copy of Resuna woke up, it probably just automatically carried out the job I had been doing when it took over. That's something that Resuna does, because you want it to work on what's important if you're in an emergency. Then after it got the stuff into the cache and wasn't sensing as much anxiety from me, it probably commed One True, via satellite, and told it everything. I figure they'll be here inside an hour."

"Well," he said, "do you know for sure that you phoned One True? Or did you just assume that you must have because Resuna had control for a while?"

"That was what I assumed; it's what Resuna would do."

"Then I can put both our minds at a little ease. One reason why it took you so long to wake up, I suspect, is because back when I first had you captured and unconscious, to be on the safe side I hooked up your jack to some electronic stuff I've got and zapped it a bunch of ways—RF, high voltage, low-level DC current, even a tickle of plain old one-ten sixty-cycle AC (though I put you in line with a big resistor for that). Probably didn't do your brain much good, but if it was possible to fry that jack, I fried it. I know I ran a big risk with your brain and all, but you know, at the time I didn't know you and I was still deciding whether to kill you. And I'm real glad now that I don't seem to have done any permanent brain damage. But I'm also glad that I did try to cook that little gadget, because it's probably good and dead, and chances are that when your copy of Resuna woke up, after you got whacked on the skull, it just ran in your head until you were conscious enough to take over again."

"That is reassuring," I said, "and no hard feelings about my brain. As much as I bang it around, who knows where any one piece of damage might've come from? Still, the ski tracks are pointing out that cache, and so we're bound to lose that, and when they find it they'll find their way here, quick enough, pos-def. We've made a good twenty trips out to it, and by now we've surely left enough track for any decent hunter to follow, even with varying the route all the time. So the hunters are going to be at that cache sometime tomorrow, at latest, and then they'll be here within a few hours. They might could be here in as little as three hours, if the satellite saw the track right away and everybody jumped on it. And if it was three hours—well, between one thing and another, about half of that time is burned already, with time spent getting here and the time we've been talking."

"Well, then," Dave said, "we've got sleeping bags up there already, we've got our jump bags packed—I was just putting in some of the medicines you need to take for a few years after a suspended animation, so I'll go back and grab the rest of my stash of those. At least it would make sense to go up to the new cave and stay up there a few days, then real cautiously come down and see what's happened to home base here, if anything. While we're up there, anyway, we can do some digging, and move a couple of the caches up into the new place too if we take that slow and careful. The only thing that's frustrating is that I got a nice cow elk, plump for this time of year, and didn't have time to do more than gut her out and hang her up. We'll probably lose that meat, and I was really looking forward to some nice steaks in a couple days. Other than that, though, I'm ready to go if you are."

"You might want to put some pants on," I pointed out. "It is still February, you know."

Ten minutes later, jump bags on our backs, we were gliding off toward Ute Ridge. The way I figured it, surely Dave knew he had some explaining to do, and he'd get around to it soon enough, without my prompting. Meanwhile, with some prospect of escape—and a possibility that I had *not* irrevocably blown everything—the world didn't seem quite so desperate. It wasn't exactly the best situation, but it was still considerably better than what I'd had not long before.

We did the last two and a half miles in deep darkness—the moon hadn't even risen yet, and while starlight is surprisingly bright at high altitude on a field of snow, still all you can really see is silhouettes, and not even that amid the trees. When we got close, and had to pass deeper into the shadows, we pulled on starlight goggles to make our way in. We took skis in with us, leaving them on the upper shelf, and then, once we were inside, had a quick cold meal from the cache there, and then stretched out in the sleeping bags, on the clay-mud floor, not far from the dribble of hot water.

From where I lay, I could just see over the upper shelf and a little bit out the opening, which was obscured every few seconds by a puff of fog, as cold air from outside met the warm wet air that rose from this cave. I saw a bright star, flickering violently, disappearing and reappearing in the fog, through the little cave mouth, and figured out in my head that it might be half an hour before the star moved out of sight from this angle, but before I even saw it move toward the edge, I was asleep.

The sun never shone down that hole directly, but enough bounce light came through in the morning to wake me up. The dim light from overhead made our new home even less attractive than a cave in the woods usually is. Well, with enough work, maybe we'd get this place fixed up fit to live in, though I doubted it would ever be anything like as nice as the place Dave had built before. Or rather the place he had lived in, I reminded myself. He probably hadn't built it; more likely he had just lived there, and whoever he worked for, or used to work for, had built and stocked the place.

I climbed out of the sleeping bag; I had been sleeping in my thermies, and I was still uncomfortably warm after getting out of the bag. So I peeled out of the thermies, turned them inside out to air, got a small piece of soap from my jump bag, and managed sort of a sponge bath in the trickle at one end of the cave. It was better than nothing, but far from that hot tub.

"You do realize that's also the coffee water?" Dave grumbled, dragging himself along. "And yes, I have some freeze-dried stuff, and a couple of cups. That's our beverage. And for the meal, today, sir, a can of tomatoes, a can of beans, and some powdered eggs, goes into a pot with hot water, glop fit for a king, and it's what there is anyway." He put two cups on a rock and poured a splash of freeze-dried coffee in each. "I could tell you something about that water, but you ought to find out for yourself."

I took a cup and held it under the hot trickle, letting it fill up, and then tapped the cup a few times to make sure that the coffee powder had dissolved.

One sip told me. "Iron," I said, running my tongue around my mouth to try to wipe some of the bitter astringent feel away.

"No anemia for us," he agreed. "I'll finish yours if you don't want it."

"It's caffeine," I said, "and I've had worse." I sat on a rock near enough the stream to be warm. "Should I unpack the stuff for breakfast?"

"I'll get it in a minute; I'm gonna wash up. I know a trick or two for making iron water palatable."

Still sipping my coffee, I wandered back around to the back of the cave and carefully took a leak right where the stream flowed back into the ground. If somebody soaking at a spa two hundred miles away had any problem with that, they could write me.

When I got back, Dave had finished soaping and rinsing, and was dumping the ingredients into the pot. The water was two notches too hot to wash comfortably with, not quite hot enough to heat the food, and I made a mental note that we would need a cistern or something for the long run. (I doubted we were going to find a cool well up here, at least at any depth we had the equipment to reach.)

Eggs, tomatoes, and beans aren't a bad mix, per se, and I've eaten worse, but on the other hand I've had better, and the water hadn't quite been hot enough to make the dried eggs fluff up. So it could have been a whole lot better, too. We gobbled it down, had another cup of iron coffee each, and then looked the situation over.

"I'd suggest we work in just gloves, boots, and shorts," Dave said. "And since we never did get your screen box built, what do you have in mind for getting the dirt to wash down the stream?"

"Let me try an experiment or two," I said. We got dressed as Dave had suggested, and went back into the chamber and put three long-life lights up high. With no opening to the surface, this room was almost up to room temperature anyway.

"The trick is to make sure it mixes well," I pointed out. "Let's try the simplest possible way." I put five shovelfuls of dirt into one of our buckets, carried it back to where the spring came in, let it fill with water—which made it a world heavier—stirred with the shovel, and poured it into the outlet. It went gurgling down without any sign of blocking or forming a dam. "It's not going to be as fast as a screen box would have been," I said. "But we have a bucket and a big cook pot. We can probably put one of each down the hole every ten minutes or so, allowing for breaks and meals and that kind of thing. We'll still get plenty of work done in a day, anyway. And whenever it gets tough or we get bored, we can sneak out and move a cache. I was thinking there are two that aren't so far away, and we might move them in a few days. Let's give it a month or so, though, before we pop up our heads in Dead Mule drainage; I have a feeling they'll be setting up an ambush there, and probably sitting in it for a good long while."

"Makes sense," Dave said, nodding soberly. "And it does beat the whole process of hauling it out in packs."

I turned and threw a couple shovelfuls into the bucket. "You know," I said, "after what I saw yesterday, and what I've figured out, I'd have to say that I don't believe you ever hauled even one pack of dirt out of that place."

He tossed his second shovelful into the cook pot, walked out to the spring inlet, and came back sloshing it around. He poured it down the hole and finally said, "Well, you're wrong, there, Currie, though you're right that I didn't build the whole place. But I put the tub into the tub room, and I did build that library. And I hauled some dirt for those, because I never did think of doing things the way you came up with."

I emptied two more buckets while I waited for him to come up with something else to say, but he didn't, so eventually I just asked him. "Uh, okay, do you mind if I ask if you're going to tell me what's going on?"

"I've been trying to think of how to do just that," Dave said. "My problem is that I don't know exactly how to help you see what's going on, or why it matters, or anything, and it really seems like somehow I ought to be able to tell you all of it at once, and so there's no real one single place to start, and I get bogged down in trying to pick one. To understand one part, you need to understand three. Like that. But I'm not trying to hold out on you, not anymore, Currie. And I'd have told you eventually—it was just a question of when to tell you how much, because, well, you were real bound into One True and I wasn't sure which thing I might say might wake up your Resuna."

I was a little mollified that he was at least thinking, perhaps, that he owed me some explanation. I let it go for another couple bucket-loads. We had now put a hole in the floor, mostly around the exit hole, perhaps a meter across and half a meter deep.

As he came back and poured his cook pot full of hot mud into the water, and watched it swirl down, he said, "We ought to at least dig down to some rock by day's end and get that hole pritnear as wide as it'll easily go. Okay, Currie, here's my story. Final version. All the truth as far as I know it. And I was probably wrong to keep it from you, once it was clear you'd come around to my side."

For the rest of that morning, we loaded buckets and sent mud down that hole, and every so often he'd tell me more of his story, as we watched for any sign that we had to stop dumping the mud. As I'd guessed, there was room enough for all the mud to go down there, so far—our probes, and some shouting down there for echoes, made me think that the chamber below was mostly empty and probably twenty feet high and a hundred long. Of course, if the mud dammed up the exit to that chamber, then it would start to fill and we could be dealing with a nuisance, but when we got this hole wide enough open, we should be able to see whether or not that was likely to happen. Meanwhile there was surely room enough for the mud from this early part of the job.

Between the heavy work and the heat from the spring, we were both sweaty and grimy when we stopped for a quick lunch of some jerky and hard rolls, washed down with yet more iron coffee.

We both took a few muscle relaxants before starting again, and that got the story flowing better because the relaxants hit like mild, long-lasting alcohol. During that whole afternoon, off and on, a few sentences at a time as we'd pass each other, dumping mud and shoveling the buckets, I heard the rest of Dave's story, and we finished it over hot soup and fresh bread that we were able to fix by using up one precious chemical heater; we felt like we both needed it badly. By that time we had a hole big enough for us to stand in together, almost a meter and a half deep, and a good two meters across. The opening in the floor turned out to be a round hole, perhaps a foot across, that seemed to lead down into a much bigger open space. The odor coming up out of there was slightly musty, but not bad; probably it had no direct outlet to the outside world.

"Anyway," I said, "we can accelerate the whole process, because there's obviously much more room down there than there is clay up here, and it will be a while before we start opening that area up for ourselves. Give it a week and we'll be done excavating, even counting the time to go move another cache or two here. I'm not sure where we'll salvage or steal the plumbing to put in a real hot-water-and-heat system, but we'll come up with something, anyway."

"God, you're better at this than I ever would hope to be," Dave said, sighing.

"Considering what you did get through, you can hold your head up in any company you want," I assured him.

We each had a little snort to help us sleep. Between the night's booze and the day's exercise, my sleeping bag on a clay floor in a steamy cave felt like a heated waterbed with a down comforter in a high-priced hotel. I watched the star through the hole for just a few seconds, and then fell asleep. That night I dreamed, over and over, of the story that Dave had told me.

I got a great rest and woke up only somewhat sore, but the dreams of that night were with me for a long time after, and for the next day—very much like the previous one in the work we did—I kept thinking of other questions to ask him, and other ways to try to make his story hang together in my brain, in a way that wouldn't disturb me quite so much. By the end of that second day I had the whole thing, pritnear as clear as it would ever get, and by then I had about arrived at the decision that there wasn't a thing to do, for me or for anyone on Earth, that wouldn't be a huge mistake. Then Dave pointed out the last part to me, which I'd missed, and I went and *made* that huge mistake, all on my own.

Dave Singleton's name derived from something strange that had happened in the Foundling's Entrance at Denver Dome's municipal orphanage in 2043.

During the Gray Decade, probably a quarter of the babies born became foundlings, as city after city ran out of money and shut down the Dole, and with it the Dolework that had at least allowed families to stay together, and single mothers to afford child care and support a family. Many people just could not afford to keep the babies they had. Because of that, most orphanages and hospitals had a "Foundling's Entrance," a warm, sheltered, discreet foyer, with an entrance where it was easy to come and go unobserved, which was a safe place to leave off a baby anonymously. Usually it was set up with a counter, but no one at the counter; instead, a large hand-scrawled sign said, "Back in 3 minutes." This allowed people who just wanted to set the baby down and run to do so; an AI watched through a hidden camera, and when it saw a baby drop-off in progress, it would sound an alarm at a desk in the staff quarters, so that a human being could decide what to do. Sometimes that meant hurrying there to be "just arriving back," and sometimes it meant staying out of sight until the person was gone and the baby had been left.

Two days before Dave had been dropped off there, a girl who didn't look much more than thirteen had come in with two-week-old twin boys, one in an ancient car seat and the other in a cardboard box, and stood waiting patiently at the counter till an attendant came out. She had emphatically insisted at the counter that since her boyfriend, Dave, had been killed, *both* twins would have to be named Dave, and that was the only way she was giving them up.

"Maybe they should have a different middle name or last name, so people won't mix them up?" the attendant suggested, hoping that she would see the reasonableness of this.

"I already thought of that," the girl said. "I never knew my boyfriend's last name, anyway. He had this *lim* important job where he wasn't allowed to date or see girls or nothing. It was like national security or something like that. He told me some stuff about it that I can't tell anyone else. Anyway, since it all had to be secret, I never knew his last name, but since he got, you know, shot and I saw him die, pos-*def* I wanted to give his babies the names I called him. So they both have to be Dave, but here's the middle and last names." She pulled a note from her shirt pocket, unfolded it, and handed it across the counter. "The one on the right is Bear. 'Kay? I have to go. The Salvation Army where I'm staying doesn't feed us if we're late, and I want to get my last meal because now that I gave up the kids they'll throw me out tomorrow." She left in a cloud of other half-explanations.

The attendant had handled messier cases, and she shrugged. She looked at the sheet of paper and turned to the twin to her left—figuring the girl had meant the one to her own right—and said, "Well, I guess you're Dave Bear. And you must be Dave Love," she added to the other twin. "Welcome to Denver Dome Orphanage."

Within an hour they were known to everyone in the place as the Dave Twins. The signs on their incubators read "David M. Love" and "David P. Bear," but it's natural for people to gossip, and gossip reaches everyone in an institution eventually, even the children, so the Dave Twins endured years of being teased about their middle names, "My" and "Pooh."

Two days later, another baby turned up, dropped off by a different but also very young girl. This one was in a cardboard box with a couple of stuffed toys and a blanket, plus a note that said, "Call him anything as long as it's Dave. That was his father's name. You can tell him his father is a spy or a cop or something, and he must have gone undercover because he never came back to marry me."

"I even *looked* like I should have been the third Dave Twin," Dave said, as we squatted at lunch the first day, "which makes me kinda suspect that the original Dave got around plenty."

Since the first two were the Dave Twins, some wit on the staff suggested this one should be the Dave Singleton.

The Denver Dome orphanage was small and poor; Denver had never really recovered from the fires that had raged through it in the last part of the Eurowar, and the new dome there didn't cover much more than the old downtown. It was still an important crossroads and a good place for a warehouse, but since hardly any human beings were needed to staff warehouses anymore, most of the old city remained untenanted, infested with a few vags and packs of stray dogs, for many decades before the dome finally was nuked in 2059. Clamped savagely between a vanished tax base and a large number of the poor, Denver Dome had nothing to spare for its orphanage. From what I remembered of Denver Dome, the few times I had been through there before it was nuked, it was a cold, poor, mean town in spirit anyway, one that didn't mind the sight of misery much, so I doubt it broke their hearts not to have anything to spend on their poor.

In 2049, with the war breaking out, and every social problem worsening, the Denver Dome Council was looking hard for a way, any old way, to shut down the orphanage for good and thereby cut expenses. It didn't take them long to hit on the same solution that lots of places did: they made the children available to everyone who wanted them. Even in its early years, the War of Papal Succession was a war for control of human brains, most especially the brains of the next generation; one way to get brains was to more or less buy them while they were still enclosed in children. The market for kids was brisk.

Boys twelve and up went off to militias and mercenary companies; girls were sold to affluent families as servants, if they were lucky, and to barely disguised pimps if they were not; younger children went off to be adopted by families, schools, sects, and creches so that they could all be indoctrinated by all the various splinters off of Ecucatholicism and cybertao.

When Phil and Monica Comasus came by the orphanage, one nice sunny Monday morning in February, 2050, they said they wanted to take three kids with them, and offered to pay in NihonAmerica bearer bonds, which were still being honored because the transfer ships were the collateral. Nobody at the orphanage asked any questions; most of the staff didn't care, and the few who did, didn't want to know whether the kids were going to be adopted, or slaves, or used in medical experiments. Their job, as defined by the city, was to get what money they could for handing over kids.

They were trying to do it in a hurry, because, however bad the other options might be, it was clear this orphanage wouldn't be in business much longer, with Denver leaning toward bankruptcy and the rest of the world going to hell. The first serious shots of the War of Papal Succession were just being fired, the rubble of Rome wasn't cool yet, and armies big enough to have real battles were only just being organized and trained.

Phil Comasus was a short man—almost tiny. He was shorter than his wife, Monica, who was only of average height. They made an odd couple, to seven-year-old Dave's eyes, because they contrasted in so many ways. Phil might have been fifteen years older than Monica. He was plump and soft-bodied; she was slender, angular, and well-muscled. She had thick black hair, high cheekbones, blue eyes, and the kind of patrician good looks that Hollywood used to insist on for its "serious" actresses; he had bumpy, squashed features that made him look like one of the Seven Dwarves, an effect accentuated by his perpetually untidy slush-gray goatee. Both were quietly but expensively dressed, a few social notches above the Doleworkers who ran the orphanage. "They were a fairy-tale couple," Dave said to me, as we stopped for sandwiches and some iron coffee, "except in most fairy tales, the troll doesn't marry the princess."

Dave said he realized, even at age seven, that things were going to be different from now on, not when they told him that he would be leaving with this couple within half an hour, and not when he packed up his things, or when the whole orphanage lined up to say good-bye to him, Cecile, and Robin. The moment when he knew everything would be different was after they went into the diskster, Monica showed them how to strap in, and she said, "Now—do you have absolutely everything you should? Is there anything you want or need that you forgot to pick up? They rushed you out of there, and I don't want to leave anything behind if it's yours and it's your favorite."

Dave had three sets of clothes, a tiny stuffed bear that had been a present from Mrs. Allen before she got laid off, and a bag of toiletries. He didn't really care about all the crayon drawings in his locker, and the crayons were the property of the orphanage—they were always telling him not to use so many.

Cecile, a quiet, small, dark-haired girl of five, also had nothing else. But ten-year-old Robin, a husky and muscular Asian girl who was one of the leaders of kid society, spoke up and said, "I can't remember if I packed a picture of my real mother. It's the only one I have."

"Well," Monica said, "take a look in your bag, and if we don't find it, we'll go in and look for it."

Robin looked and couldn't find it, so she and Monica went inside together. While they were in there, Phil got out a set of jacks and a ball—neither Cecile nor Dave had ever seen any such thing before—and started teaching them to play jacks. At first Dave couldn't see the point, but after a few minutes he and Cecile were starting to see what it was about, and pretty soon they were engrossed in a game, coached by Phil. Dave thought it was bizarre that a grown-up genuinely cared how the two of them played a game—or seemed to get such a kick out of watching them do it—but it was bizarre in the nicest way he'd ever seen.

After about half an hour, Monica returned with Robin and the picture. Robin was holding her hand and her eyes were shining; it was obvious that Monica had just become her hero. "Can you believe it?" Monica said in a tone of outrage. "She had left it behind on top of her locker, because she wanted to pack it on top of her bag, and they made her hurry out so fast she forgot it—and they saw it and even though our diskster was sitting right in front of the building, they didn't come out and tell us—they had *already thrown it away!* We had to pull it out from the recycler hopper, and I made them let us use their scrubber to clean it. It's good as new now, but imagine treating a photo of Robin's mother that way!"

"Well," Phil said, "we're done with that place for good, thank heavens. Time to get rolling again."

They all strapped in because the trip out of the city would be zigzaggy; Phil promised they'd all play jacks again. "Many times," he added, emphatically. "There might never be a last game. You might still be playing in the old-folks home."

Dave and Cecile giggled at that, and after making sure everyone was comfortable, Phil told the diskster an address in the KC Dome, and it extended the thousands of tiny pins from its surface, charged up into a faint, crackling blue glow, and shot off faster than Dave had ever moved before. For all three kids it was their first diskster ride.

After they had ridden for some miles, and were racing over the empty plains, Robin whispered to them, "She was *so* mad at them for throwing out my mom's picture! *And* she made them fix *everything*. It was *so* koapy. It must be like that to have a mom."

Dave nodded, trying to appear wise to such things. He turned to look out the window. It was a day full of amazing things—a diskster ride, a long trip, adult attention . . .

One advantage of the war not yet being completely on, just yet, was that you could still cross the country in a diskster. The Comasus diskster stopped at the municipal orphanages in Kansas City, St. Louis, Chicago, and Detroit, picking up two to four children between five and ten years old at each one, and by the time it set down in front of a huge fake-Victorian house in upstate New York, the kids had all gotten some acquaintance with each other, Monica had settled a quarrel or two, Phil had taught them a number of silly songs, and everyone had been measured for new clothes.

The thirteen newly acquired orphans had all been admonished to

call Phil and Monica by their first names, and not to worry about anything, because they were getting taken care of from now on.

Dave told me, as we threw clay into the hole, that his first sight of
the Big House would "probably be the last thing to fade from my brain
on the day I die, and if anybody ever could prove to me that there was
a heaven and it was as good a place as the Big House, I'd be happy to
die that minute."

It was late in the evening, but the moon was up and bright, when
they followed the winding track up from the small, shallow, ice-
covered river through the pines to the top of the ridge, crested the top,
and decelerated over the wide snowfield that spread out in front of
them. In the moonlight the house was all silvers and blues; it was three
stories high, with a main body as big as the Muncipal Orphanage back
home—*no, that's not home anymore.* Dave thought with something
close to pure glee—and two sizable wings extending from it. At the
time, Dave thought it looked like a house in a story set somewhere in
history, like you could see on the flashchannel when the bigger boys
weren't keeping it tuned to sports. Later he realized that it wasn't
really laid out like any of those; the immense wraparound porches on
each wing, the big flat diskster landing area in the front, the extremely
tall and steep metal roofs—with the black circles on them that he did
not realize at the time were automatic gunports—all made it very
much a twenty-first-century building. Still, to the naive eye, it might
have been an old resort house, from back when people had come up
from the city to spend summers in this part of the country.

The diskster flared off its surplus charge in a blue *whoosh* and settled onto its pad. In a few minutes, Phil and Monica had awakened
everyone, sorted out baggage, and organized a groggy parade into the
immense main room of the house. It was just settling into Dave's mind
that these two people *owned* this magnificent place, the way that he
owned his shoes.

Of course the first thing they did was send all the kids into the
large ground-floor bathroom—many people, kids especially, just can't
use the bathroom on a diskster, and they hadn't stopped since Detroit,
two hours earlier.

When everyone had returned from that first necessity, Monica
took a quick roll, and then led them downstairs. Dave thought that this
was probably where the boys' and girls' barracks would be, but instead
they went into a big room where an industrial faxbricator sat by a large
pile of folded clothing. Phil and Monica went forward and began sort-

ing through the pile, eventually making up thirteen smaller piles of new clothes.

Before departing on their child-gathering trip, the Comasuses had loaded that faxbricator with bolts of forty different fabrics; Phil had zapped the kids' measurements on ahead, and when they arrived, handed a pile of brand-new clothes to each kid. All the clothes fit, and had the kid's own name sewn into them. They had even paid attention to favorite colors, and put kid-selected designs on the sweatshirts and T-shirts.

When he got his pile, Dave just grabbed the first thing on the top and sat right down on the floor, holding his green Bobbert the Space Tiger sweatshirt—his favorite color and his favorite flashchannel character. It had "Dave Singleton" on the label. They had even made sure it was a soft label made to rest against his neck comfortably, not a big scratchy one sewn in for the convenience of an institutional laundry. He was trying very hard to understand that this sweatshirt—exactly what he had wanted for at least two years—was now all his, brand new, absolutely clean and never worn by anyone else. He clung to it for a long while, pressing his face against it.

"You can put it on now, if you want," Monica said, "but you might just want to carry it up to your room, along with everything else."

"Carry it up to the moon?" Dave asked.

Monica's eyes twinkled. At the time, she was about thirty-five, but to a five-year-old, all adults are terribly old. Dave looked at her closely and curiously, for the first time. She had explosions of tiny laugh lines around her eyes and mouth, and an oversupply of very light-colored freckles. In her jet-black hair there were already a few strands of gray. Her voice was low, modulated, the sort of voice that, before AIs, could have made a fortune in voice-overs.

Dave was in love instantly, as were all twelve of the other children. "Not carry it to the moon," Monica said. "You're not quite ready for that, Dave, though you might be some day. Carry it *to your room.* Come on, I'm going to show everybody where their room is."

Dave joined a parade of the other small kids—himself and Cecile, from Denver; a dark haired girl, terribly thin, with pallid skin and a vampire-red mouth, about eight, named Julia, from the Chicago orphanage; Prester, about Dave's age, a very thin, dark-skinned kid, with big expressive eyes, crooked teeth, and extremely funny jokes, from St. Louis, who Dave was already hoping would become a friend;

a quiet boy who might have been a mix of any or all races, named Joey, who was a lot taller than Dave but acted about the same age, and so might be another friend.

They were all going to what Monica called "West Third." She explained that it meant that their bedrooms were on the third floor of the west wing of the house. Dave had never been in a house with a wing before, but he figured out what that meant after some momentary confusion. (He really would not have been surprised if the house had turned out to be able to fly, after everything that had happened that day. Maybe to the moon.)

The five children were shown the bathroom they were to share, each given towels with their names on them, shown the games, books, and small table that had been placed in a wide spot in the hall. Each of them had a room with a desk and chair, closet, bookshelves (and some books on them—and Dave was pretty sure that all of those were new, just like the clothes), bed, chest, and as far as Dave could see, everything you could possibly want in a bedroom, even including a door. "Remember when you want to talk to someone else to knock on his or her door, and wait for the person to say 'Come in,' and don't come in unless they say it," Monica said. "And they'll do the same for you. That way you'll always be able to feel like this is your space."

She gave them all a snack—the idea of cereal before bed, just because it would feel good, was strange, but Dave decided he liked it. Then they all got to take showers, and everyone had a brand-new toothbrush and toothpaste. Dave had never been quite so clean, or gone to bed in a room that was neither too hot nor too cold, or felt such clean sheets before. Monica even tucked him in—something he had only seen on the flashchannel—and said good night.

As he drifted off to sleep, he could hear the sounds coming down the hall, from East Third and East Second. The bigger kids were getting showered, laughing and talking. Phil was hanging around down there, it sounded like; they could hear his big booming laugh now and then, and his intense, serious voice explaining things. It sounded like the bigger kids were having a good time too.

Just before he fell asleep, Dave prayed, for the first time in his life, though he had had no religious instruction and wasn't even sure he knew who he was asking to help him. Nonetheless he prayed with all the passion and sincerity a seven-year-old can manage. He wanted all this to be here when he woke up.

Perhaps the greatest miracle was that it was. Shortly after dawn, Dave was awakened by Phil knocking on the door and saying, "Get up, get dressed (put clean stuff on, if you've worn it, we'll wash it), use the can, and come downstairs. Breakfast in ten minutes."

As Dave pulled on his miraculously still-present green Bobbert sweatshirt, he could hear the thumps and chatter of other kids getting up, and by the time he had taken his turn at the bathroom he heard a babble of voices downstairs. The dining room and main kitchen were on the first floor of the west wing, and he raced Prester all the way down the stairs.

Breakfast today would be ham, pancakes with apple compote, and orange juice. Everyone was used to pancakes because they were a staple of orphanage food, but most had never had apple compote, orange juice was an occasional treat, and ham had been mostly for holidays, and strictly rationed.

When breakfast was finally finished, they all went upstairs and learned the rules for keeping their rooms—just simple things like hanging up clothes, putting dirty clothes in hampers, keeping things on hooks and shelves and not on the floor, making the bed, dusting, all much simpler than following the rules about your bunk in the orphanage, since here at the Big House you had a place for just about everything, and all you had to do was put things where they belonged and wipe surfaces off. Then they went on a tour of the house and, since the day was mild, put on coats and hats and went out and built snowmen on the lawn. Pretty soon everyone was running around and laughing, throwing little unpacked snowballs. Phil showed them some games you could play in the snow, and everyone had a good time with those, even the older kids.

About the time that they were ready to be tired and cold, but were not quite there yet, Monica ushered them back into the house, where they hung up their coats and hats, put their boots on the drying grate, and then filed back into the dining room. Phil announced lunch: hot dogs, french fries, baked beans, and hot chocolate—and once again, all that you wanted of everything.

After lunch, as they settled into a pleasant stupor on the couches and chairs in the big room called the "Commons," Monica read them a story—there had been one nice woman at the orphanage who read stories, Dave recalled faintly, but she had been laid off before he was five, and this was the first time he'd heard a story, instead of seeing one on the flashchannel, in a couple of years. It was difficult to follow it without the pictures and without being able to click on things for explanations, but it was still very nice of her, Dave thought. The littler kids seemed to take to it better than the big ones.

Then she took them all to West Second, which turned out to have a classroom in it, with thirteen big desks, one for each of the kids. "This is where you'll all go to school," she explained. "There are other workrooms and project spaces as well, and a library over in East First, where you'll work much of the time on your own, but this space will be home base, where usually your day will begin and end, and most days you'll be here for at least a couple of hours—sometimes for the whole day."

They were all so startled by the first thing that she had said that most of them didn't catch the rest. She had to repeat her entire spiel a couple of times. In most places, for at least the last ten years, orphanage kids hadn't been allowed to go to school, either because all the public schools had been closed as part of the Gray Decade's economy measures, or because if there were public schools, orphans were excluded as "not taxpayer children."

Once they realized that Monica really did mean that they would all be getting regular schooling, just like rich kids, they were wildly excited. They got a few minutes to explore their desks, discovering pencils, crayons, a brand-new werp for each of them, reams of paper, several books—which Monica assured them they would be taught to read—and too many other miracles to even categorize in those first exciting minutes.

Then Phil came in. He sat down on the desk at front and said, "I suppose you're all normal enough to be wondering why we brought you here and what we're going to do with you. So I'm going to tell you. If it seems weird to you, well, it sometimes seems weird even to me. But I think you'll like it here, basically, and mostly it will be a step up from where you were."

Dave was willing to grant that point.

"Many years ago," Phil said, "I was one of the designers of the transfer-ship societies. The transfer ships are the huge spaceships that look like bright stars at night, and come in near Earth every few months, like the *Flying Dutchman* and *Diogenes*, the ones that run in the big cycler orbits to supply the colonies on other planets. What I did, along with half a dozen other people, was to plan and help create the system of child-rearing and education that was then used to produce the first generation born on the ships, the people who operate them now. I also had something of a hand in planning the basic social rules under which they grew up, and the culture into which they would grow. I was hired to do that because they needed to produce a whole bunch of very smart people who got along together really well, and who would help to save the human race, and I was well known as a teacher, as a scientist, and for some other accomplishments, various other things that need not concern us for the moment, here."

Dave later learned that, under his original name, Comasus had been a very young senator from Massachusetts in the 112th Congress, the last US Congress ever to meet. He had also shared a Nobel Prize in Economics, and served a few years as Deputy Administrator for the Environment of UNRRA-2.

"There were some things the other society designers didn't believe me about, which was how eventually I got fired from my job as society designer, and part of why they're having the problems they're having on Mars and Ceres. Given the way events have turned out, they probably believe me now," Phil went on. "But that's neither here nor there; on the transfer ships and in the colonies, things have worked out, if not as well as they might, at least tolerably well, and nowadays there wouldn't be anything for me to do even if they hired me back. So, despite being occasionally bitter about it, I am usually able to let that go, and take pleasure in having made a really good try, in my younger days, at saving the world.

"However, a really good try ultimately makes no difference; only success makes a difference. And it so happens the world still needs saving, and with you guys, and Monica, and a certain amount of plain old luck, that's just what I'm going to do."

The way he smiled at them made Dave feel safe and happy, but something about his tone thrilled the little boy to the bone—it was as if he'd been personally sworn in by Batman or Earth Ranger.

Phil's explanation for what he was going to do with them was necessarily simple, because he was talking to a group of quite young children. As they grew, he re-explained and re-explained, and their ability to understand it all increased. Since he often used the same phrases in the process, and so many times the explanation happened in the same rooms, in later years it was very hard for Dave to sort out what he had been told when—his earlier memories were overlaid by later ones and tied into them almost seamlessly.

Furthermore, when he explained it to me in the cave, as we dug, he told me about it as the ideas occurred to him, not necessarily in the best order for understanding, so there's not much hope of disentangling it and telling the whole story of Phil and Monica Comasus, the Big House, the kids themselves, the Freecybers, or any of the rest, as anyone experienced it. The best I can do is give a fairly accurate, sorted-out explanation, but you have to keep in mind, that's not how the kids met up with it. For Dave, as an adult, it was as much a part of him as speaking English.

Comasus was the originator of the system called CSL education. CSL stood for Cybernetics, Semiotics, and Logic, and it could be described several different ways—as an academic subject in its own right that no one else had realized was needed before, as an abstract stratum underlying every other kind of learning, as a set of techniques that a kid learned to accelerate learning in all fields. Phil alternated between saying he'd invented it and he'd discovered it, sometimes saying that he'd come up with a way for the three older disciplines to easily transfer ideas between them, and sometimes saying that he'd found out that a twentieth-century mathematician, two nineteenth-century polymaths, and a bunch of ancient Greeks and medieval scholastics had all been working on the same problem, and that the answers fit together into a grand idea that made the human brain work better.

The basic trick was simple enough: there are a few fundamental patterns to ideas—different patterns for different classes of verbal, visual, emotional, mathematical, and so forth—and a way of learning that goes with each pattern. Furthermore, each of the couple of dozen fundamental patterns has a specific relation to every other fundamental pattern. Master the pattern through repetition, drill, re-experiencing it from a variety of different perspectives and contexts—just as children master words, grammatical structures, dramatic plots, moves in games, or moral notions, by working with them over and over in different situations—and eventually you have the ability to recognize it wherever you meet it, including in the process of learning all other subjects. Master the fundamental connections and now you are ready to relate and connect new ideas creatively, almost from the moment you understand them.

Later, you learn the master pattern that explains how each pattern applies to each subject matter, and why each kind of learning works best for it; by the time you're ten or so, you know how to learn anything, quickly and with no more effort than necessary. (It helps a great deal that your learning ability has been accelerating right along, so that you do have a deep acquaintance with all sorts of basic material;

besides mastering how to learn, you also master a lot of plain old-fashioned learning, just as anybody who is studying the piano, in the process of perfecting technique, also plays the piano a lot, and develops a very big repertoire.)

The CSL education plan allows most kids, by age fourteen, to reach about the intellectual level of a senior in an ordinary college, and to assume adult responsibilities, at least if they want to or society has any need for them to do so.

"Most of the stupidity, hostility, and bad behavior of adolescence comes from being held in a state of enforced uselessness for anywhere from five to ten years," Phil used to say, revealing how old he was, since neither Earth nor the space colonies had been able to afford that sort of adolescence for most people in the five decades since the Eurowar. Most of us born in this past century can't believe that there was ever a time or place when a seventeen-year-old's main focus was his or her social life, jobs were for "spending money" rather than self-support, and schooling was deliberately paced so that the dumber students wouldn't need to suffer discomfort or put forth extra effort. I wonder what people back then were thinking—or if.

"Uh, what was this guy Comasus's real name?" I asked Dave.

He laughed for a second. "You know, we were all taught so thoroughly to never speak it, it just doesn't come natural to say it out loud." He shook his head and said, "But it can't matter now. The man is dead, has been dead for more than thirty years."

Then he told me the name.

"Come on," I said.

"It was."

"I thought he was one of the people assassinated in the early '30s, back during that wave of random terror that just seemed to be taking out everyone known to have any brains or talent," I said. "In fact I'm almost sure he was one of them."

"He was," Dave said, "or rather that was the story that was given out. By the time I knew him, he was hiding behind something like ten different aliases and had an elaborate system for keeping himself from being found. He had the money to do it because he had many patents and copyrights under false names, signed over to dummy corporations, and I don't know what all—one huge money-hiding machine, laced with dozens of dead ends and false continuers and telltales, that filtered goods down to him. When I knew him he'd already been hiding for more than fifteen years from something he called the 'Organization.' Never knew him to speak of it without a shudder. As far as I know, it never had any other name than that, either, just the Organization. I couldn't make out if it was a gang of spies or crooks or mercenaries, or just kind of a group of evil people, but Phil Comasus was the sanest man I ever met, and he was scared to death of it.

"What he said was that when the Organization tried to kill him, they broke into his house, killed his first wife—hacked her to pieces in front of him, to tell you the truth—gave him a massive psycholytic injection that should have left him a madman for the rest of his life, beat him hard enough to break a dozen bones, rupture a kidney, and puncture both lungs, poured gasoline on him, set a fire upstairs that killed his kids, left him for dead . . . and sometime between them leaving and the fire burning its slow way downstairs, he revived enough to crawl out onto the street. Somebody picked him up from there and admitted him to a hospital as a John Doe. With the fire and the mess, the cops couldn't figure out how many people had died in that house, and came up one high.

"After he came to, and figured out what was up, he realized that the Organization must think he was dead, and from then on he did his best to make sure they continued to think so. But when the cutting's done and the pieces are laid, you know, nothing really stops people like the Organization. A long time after that, they found out who he was and where he was, and killed him and Monica. That's later in the story."

"You're sure it was this Organization and not just someone at random? I thought you said it was soldiers from Murphy's."

"There might have been no connection," Dave said, "except a long time later—well, maybe just a few years, it might have been around Year Three, when I was putting together my group of cowboys—I met up with this one cowboy, guy who called himself Gregor, who wanted to join. He said he'd been in Murphy's Comsat Avengers. Gregor was a loner, and it didn't take too long to figure out that his reason for hiding out was not a love of freedom or some principle. He'd have been hiding from *any* society, because, at least in my estimation, the guy was either a serial killer already, or he was going to be. I turned him down. Then a couple of months later, me and two of my cowboys came across Gregor in a deserted small town, where he'd found a family hiding out in an old grocery store, and was 'using them up,' which was his expression for spending a few days doing godawful things while he killed them off one at a time. He had just killed the father when we got there. Well, you know, justice is rough out here in the woods, so me and my cowboys gave him a real thorough beating to help him tell us the truth, because we wanted to know whether the man had any accomplices, and just what the hell he intended by committing the sort of crime that endangered every person who was still living free.

"Somewhere in the course of the beating, just about the point where he was about to break, I guess, and grasping at anything to make himself hold on, Gregor told us that he belonged to the Organization, and that we had better let him go if he knew what was good for us, because the Organization always avenged its own.

"After that, I just kept kicking him till he passed out, put a small demolition charge under his chin, taped his head down, and set off the charge. Made a hell of a mess but I was pretty pissed off and I guess I rationalized it by figuring it would make an example of him for any others there might be around, and if he really *was* with the Organization, it would get them after me—which was fine with me, I'd love to have more of them show up. More chances for revenge for Phil and Monica, you know," he said. "Anyway, this guy Gregor was a monster. When I die I'm going to have two big regrets about life, and they're both going to be about getting somewhere too late. One of them's not coming across that cowboy before he'd killed the father and one of the children in that family; in a better world, I guess I'd have come across him during the war, and shot his damned head off before he ever got loose among the cowboys."

"And your other big regret?" I asked, keeping the story rolling, I hoped, giving us both an excuse to not dig more clay just immediately.

"I'm getting to that one. Another sandwich?"

"Yeah." I accepted it gratefully, and he got on with that part of the story.

For most of the 2050s, while the War of Papal Succession became the War of the Memes and became steadily nastier, Dave had the best years of his life. Those years while he was growing up were a busy, demanding, challenging time, but a very happy one. The war went on and the glaciers grew; Antarctica lost its ice and Scotland disappeared under an ice sheet; memes were created, mutated, grew, got control of a large part of the human race; guys a few years older than Dave, like me, spent the decades fleeing or pursuing, ducking or shooting back.

The world got uglier and nastier, the memes that had begun as weapons took over the war for their own purposes, and life in the Big House went on.

Dave got his growth early, and was big for sixteen. The other kids had been quietly vanishing as they got to about that age, so it came as no surprise to Dave, Prester, and Joey when Phil called them in and told them what their part in things would be; by that time, the only time they saw the older ones was when one of them would come back for a brief few days to rest, recover, and get another outside mission from Phil and Monica.

"My last disciples," Phil said, grinning. "At least for a while, until we're in whatever the next historical period turns out to be, and I figure out what else the world might need. Has anyone who's gone on an outside mission ever told you what they do out there?"

The three boys shook their heads, and Phil smiled. "Well, I guess it wasn't really secret, but they probably get a habit of being very discreet out there, and it's probably good that they have the habit. All right, here's the story; here's why I grabbed you out of those orphanages and put you through CSL education at a time when I'd rather have been spending my time sensibly hiding with Monica, waiting to get old and die."

"You're not going to die," Prester blurted out.

"Oh, sooner or later," Phil said, "but only on one day out of all of the billions of years of time. That should tell you how negligible the whole business is. Sooner or later the Organization will find out that I'm alive and where I am, or I'll get sick with something that requires DNA validation to treat, which I don't dare do since it would be like publishing my fingerprints, or I'll just fall downstairs and whack my head on the balustrade. Not today, probably, and I expect to be here when you all come back to visit. But I'm afraid the visits won't be often, for a while, because these next few years we're going to be very busy."

Phil explained a little of what the others were up to; all were in some covert role, some in very deep cover, which was why they hadn't been seen since they'd left. "Who got what job depended mostly on my guess as to how well they'd handle the loneliness," Phil said. Five of the former students were working their way up one hierarchy or another, becoming important in military, financial, or church positions; four were out making "adjustments." That was what Cecile and Julie had departed to do, just a few months before, their youth carefully concealed by makeup and padding. "I wish we'd had more time to prep them," Phil said, "and to let them have time to grow adult bodies, but adjustments kept getting more urgent, and they were the only ones left to send, since I had to reserve you three for a special mission."

"What do they adjust?" Dave asked, trying to avoid, for the moment, the awareness that there was a special mission for him.

Phil sighed. "When possible, they just do things to cause good people to be promoted, and bad people discredited. They tinker here and there to try to help the war run out of gas, which it's going to do in three to four years at most—and we need it to end in a stalemate, between at least five memes, not in a single-meme victory. They meddle in the affairs of different organizations, sending some of them down paths where they'll do more good for humanity, helping the good ones along . . . every now and then seeing that a bad one breaks up or collapses. Just now, for example, Julie is working a staff job for the army of Real America, up north in Minot, helping them recover their balance and morale so that they can retake Minnesota and roll back One True; down south in Tennessee, Isaac is getting Free American through a minor palace putsch that ought to put an end to their concentration camps and secret police. Sometimes it's a matter of infiltrating and making a few changes or helping someone who's going to make the changes. A lot turns on small differences."

He sighed. "And I guess I really can't conceal from you that every so often they're killing some of the people that are most in the way of progress and success for humanity. Usually very discreetly—with so many mutant and tailored bugs around, sudden fatal infections just aren't that unusual. Every so often they set up something more public, when that's what will do us the most good, but that always makes me nervous, because you never know where an investigation might lead, and one intervention that just never works is to kill a smart cop or prosecutor who's starting to think that things are more than they seem. So we do less of the messy stuff than you might imagine, and I'm glad of that.

"But you three are in for something very different." Phil looked out the window for a long moment, at the green hills and the forest that came most of the way up to the lawn of the Big House. "The good news is you'll be able to come back here and visit more often than your fellow students. The bad news is that I'm giving you three the toughest job of all."

Dave sat quietly with the others and waited. He had guessed already that this was going to be something to do with the memes; Phil had admitted, several times, that although he'd been perfectly accurate in predicting the beginning of the War of Papal Succession and the deterioration of the Earth as the war wound down to approximating Hobbes's "war of each against all," he hadn't foreseen anything like the memes at all.

"Theoretically I only needed ten people," he said, "to make all the requisite changes, and exert the force that would keep the world out of some of its worst possible tracks. But—well, here's where you have to give Monica the credit. She said we needed to have a reserve against the unexpected. So I chose to have three more. And here you are, ready to go. There's a job for you that I could never have guessed we'd need."

Joey spoke up; shy and modest, he rarely spoke, but he usually asked an important question. "So out of the ten, there are five working their way into positions of power, and four of your 'adjustors.' That's nine. But you sent out ten."

Phil looked miserably sad; it seemed to put a decade onto him, right there. "It's probably revealing that I told myself, three times, to be sure I told you what had happened to Martha. And I still haven't yet. She was an exec assistant for the Pacific Rewildernization Corporation on the Big Island, in Hawaii, where they're trying to get some kind of a normal ecology going again; it was a place where we had some hope of getting many really smart people, and their kids, away from the violence, out from between the contesting powers, in sort of an independent republic that would grow naturally out of the settlements of ecological reconstruction specialists. One of the things she was working on was getting them to adopt CSL education—we've never had much luck getting people to do that on Earth, because unless it's really an emergency, people really do not want their children to be a great deal smarter, better adjusted, and more competent than they are—even with that carefully planned society in space, the parental generation totally flipped out when they realized just how obsolete they had made themselves, and if they hadn't been so thoroughly trained and conditioned to accept it, we might have lost the ships to the power struggle between the generations. Down here, with uncontrolled populations, you might provoke massacres of the children, or god knows what else. So the idea was that on the island, we'd have a bunch of smart capable people that we could propagandize into accepting CSL education for their kids, who would let it go on, and we'd finally have at least one really functional society here on Earth."

"What happened to Martha?" Dave asked quietly. He was remembering her laugh, and the way she could run, and thinking of the pictures she had painted that now hung in the front hall; a tall, handsome black girl, with an amazing gift for languages, always willing to help the younger kids; her one visit home, when they'd all had a picnic on the lawn to celebrate and she'd looked completely grown up.

"Raped and shot dead," Phil said. "Then mutilated in some grotesque ways we don't need to talk about. Her body was left on her boss's desk, and any hope of getting CSL education for Hawaii seems to have died with her. My best guess is that she came to the attention of the Organization. (I have long suspected that they're doing what we're doing, but in reverse.) She must have distinguished herself enough to be noticed—that's why I keep telling people to be good only at the parts of their job that affect larger matters. A patina of ordinary incompetence is probably their best protection." He was quiet for a long time, and so were the three boys.

"Well," Phil said, "it's a bad idea to dwell on everything bad that can happen, as we all know. Let me tell you what I have in mind for the three of you. It will be dangerous and difficult enough; you needn't fear that any of you will be getting a soft ride while others run risks and face difficulties."

It was only years later that Dave realized how odd it was that Phil assumed that neither he nor Joey nor Prester would have wanted a soft ride.

Phil looked from one to the other and said, "In some ways, it may be I'm asking you to face the biggest fear anyone in the group might have to face. I'm going to ask you all to let me infect you with a meme."

Dave's gut rolled over; he'd had no direct acquaintance with memes, but he knew more than enough about them.

"If it will make you feel better," Phil added, gently, "Monica and I have both been running that meme for four months now, and we can assure you that we're in charge, not it. The meme is called Freecyber, and Monica developed it from my concepts."

"What's it do?" Prester asked. "I mean, obviously it either didn't take you over, or if it did, it's got you copied perfectly."

"Well, I hope it didn't take me over," Phil said. "And what I run is *three* copies of Freecyber, all of them interacting. What Freecyber is, is an anti-meme meme. It lives in your brain and doesn't do much unless another meme invades. Then it goes into action and disables the other meme, and eventually builds up your ability to resist another infection. It preserves individuality, if you will. And what I want you guys to do is spread it everywhere—through the territory of every existing meme."

They had to prepare a set of false IDs, and some introductions to places where the three boys could get hired to do computer jocking, and that took the better part of the afternoon, before they were ready to have their last big meal with Phil and Monica and go to bed early so that they could slip away with a few hours of dark left to them. Within weeks, Freecybers were a new enemy all over the globe; virtually every established meme was trying to hunt them down, copy code from them, and find some way to cope with the new competitor.

"Well," I said, as we took turns smashing the hole in the inner chamber open wider, sledges battering at the now-washed-clean rock, "at least that explains where Freecybers came from and why they had so many variations so fast. But—I hope it doesn't offend you to hear me say this—I always had the impression that the Freecybers *talked* a good game, but they seemed to be just as eager as any other meme to take you over."

"That's a pritnear perfect description of what the problem was," Dave agreed, "and it's one that Phil and Monica never really got solved. The idea was supposed to be that Freecybers would allow people to have a much greater liberty in their personal lives and beliefs, but to do that, the Freecybers had to be smart enough to defeat other memes, and had to have a strong empathy for the desire for freedom— and you know, that combination meant that every generation Phil released, except the last one, always figured out that any freedom the host got was freedom the meme lost—and drew the implications—and became, basically, a sympathetic, patient tyrant. And since Phil was doing it all in ultracompact neurocoding, the Freecybers left people more in command of their abilities, able to exercise initiative, invent, create, do more than just cooperate and behave, and that meant that from the moment that a copy of any version of a Freecyber happened to think of the idea of having power over people, they were more effective competitors than most other memes out there. Then the other memes would gang up against them, and pirate the neurocode from the Freecybers . . . and it would be another generation that failed, and Phil and Monica would have to create still another."

For more than two years, Dave slipped in and out of roles and identities, moving around the world, sowing each new generation of Freecybers, every time in the hope that this one would be a liberator that did not degrade into a tyrant. Phil's original system of having three

Freecybers watch each other in each brain running them had to be abandoned because it took up too much space; a system in which each Freecyber watched itself in a time-lagged system replaced it. But in each new generation, the Freecyber copies became corrupted and began to seek power and control for themselves—forcing Phil and Monica to develop a new generation of Freecybers that could take on and erase or control the last generation of Freecybers.

Phil and Monica worked endlessly on the problem, going short on sleep, worried by how the conflict as a whole was going, visibly aged by the strain every time Dave made it back to the Big House for a new set of memes and some badly needed rest and contemplation. The race was growing more intense as One True pulled ahead of other memes, and as the other memes allied to fight against One True. Freecybers, as a guerrilla insurrection against all sides, were finding it harder and harder to get in or do anything, in most regions, even when they were not corrupted. The risk of getting caught was growing.

"And still I didn't see it coming," Dave said, as he methodically shoveled mud down the hole, the heavy loads splashing into some little pool the trickle of hot water must be making down there. The shadows from the lights up in the corners did strange things on his face; sometimes it looked like a very bitter smile, sometimes like a mask of tragedy, sometimes it was simply half there and staring madly. "I'd been working under all sorts of aliases as a mercenary, and wasn't too bad a soldier—good enough to fake it through most outfits, most of the time, as needed. The last batch of Freecybers, though, hadn't worked for crap against the new One True, and I'd barely gotten away with a whole uncaptured skin. So no matter what, we were in for a rough time."

Weeks after it happened, one of the other kids from the Big House dropped Dave a note and let him know that One True had caught Prester and turned him; the date that was given was about right for it to be the explanation of how One True found out where the Big House was.

Dave and Joey had been coming back in to pick up the new, improved version of Freecyber, and the diskster had dropped them off, as had been necessary for the past couple of years, a few miles from the Big House, in a grove of trees. That seemed to haunt Dave, years later—that if they had just once broken protocol, and come straight in on the diskster, they might have gotten there soon enough.

The black plume of smoke told them before they came over the hill and saw the central part of the house just falling in. They skied down to the house itself, careless of the possibility that they might be shot, and then circled the house once. The wings were in flames, with most floors collapsed already. There was no way to go inside and come out alive, and no trace of Phil or Monica, so they resigned themselves to coming back later, and followed the tracks of the attackers—it looked like just two of them—up to the top of the ridge, where it looked as if they had stood and watched the fire for a long time, standing very close together.

Beyond that, the ski tracks ran a couple of miles to where a diskster track showed up.

It was late afternoon before they could safely go into the ruins of the Big House. "The only satisfaction I had," Dave said, "was that they didn't seem to have been tortured—just some bullets in each of them, where you'd put the shots for a quick kill. Checking with some processors that we had concealed in fireproof boxes, and hooked to the house system, for just such an occasion, we got some fuzzy pictures of the guys who did it—not enough to track them down—plus the satisfaction of knowing that as they tried to read our house systems, they were both infected with our little revenge micromeme, which had the nasty trick of waiting a few days and then setting you up to kill someone you were fond of, using all your imagination and skill and resources at hand. So probably a few days or weeks later, Phil and Monica's killers suddenly turned around and did whatever they would think of as the most unforgivable crime possible, to somebody important to them. Or maybe they tried to do it to each other.

"Well, with the Big House gone, I did what we'd planned on for ages. By then the thirteen agents were down to seven, and any messages at all between us were potentially dangerous, but I did put out word out to everyone that the Big House was gone and nobody was in charge anymore. Then I got going with the solo plan appointed for me. And that's how I ended up in the Rockies with an underground hideout that was practically a palace, and a military-quality suspended-animation rig—all this was built years before I came out here.

"My job was supposed to be to see how far I could get with organizing a resistance up in the hills, and if that failed, to duck out and go underground—very literally—for long enough to throw pursuit off completely, then stick my head up and see whether the situation had gotten any better and there was anything I could do."

I dumped another load of clay down the hole and listened to the splash. It must be pretty deep down there, or fast-flowing, or both, considering how much it seemed to be taking without complaint. "So you must've been out here to do the setup before the war even ended, before Resuna, long before One True announced its plans."

"Right. I used power equipment to set everything up, taking a chance that the satellite would see it but figuring that chances were no one would ever check the memory, years later. Then when the time came, I went back, made sure the place was still there and ready, and got far enough away so that I wouldn't lead anyone to it. After that, you pretty much know the rest—I went out and recruited some cowboys, gave them some ideas and some organization, and turned them loose. I guess I'd have felt more dedication to the cause if any of them had been worthwhile people, but, you know, Curran, they weren't. They were the same kind of people that became vags back at the turn of the century—grimy losers who couldn't face having lost and wouldn't stop whining, get up off their knees, and get back in the race. The longer I led them, the more I realized there was nothing to lead.

"So finally I decided it was time to end the game, and that was about the time you showed up with your team. I started running a few more risks with my cowboys, and sure enough, one by one, your team caught and turned them, till it was just me. Then I rushed you where I could pull a disappearance. And I decided to just move into the cave to sleep for a decade or so and see what conditions were like when I got back. Hard part was not being able to tell Nancy what was going on."

"You must have married her before you turned cowboy?"

"Just after. Call it a fit of sentimentality. You surely must have guessed where I met her."

"Was she one of the other kids from the Big House?"

"Bingo. Who else would I have felt comfortable with? And just having her around to talk to made life a hell of a lot more tolerable, you know, because she wasn't a half-literate ex-mercenary who only knew how to keep repeating that a man is a man and he's got to be himself, if you see what I mean. I would have taken her, and maybe even Kelly if she was born by then, down into the cave, but I didn't have any spare suspended-animation rigs, and while I was trying to get a line on two of those, Nancy and Kelly got found, caught, and turned. So like it or not, since there wasn't a prayer of rescuing Nancy or Kelly, and I was completely disgusted with cowboys, *and* I couldn't remotely think of winning my little war, it was time to go to sleep for a decade and see if conditions were any better when I emerged."

I leaned back against the wall, half to scratch my back on some exposed rock, half to work the muscles. "Well, are conditions any better?"

"I've got at least one follower that isn't a maladjusted dumbass," he pointed out.

"Thanks, you're not a maladjusted dumbass yourself."

" 'Preciate it," he said. "You want to have dinner, bed down, maybe tomorrow we'll go get a cache and bring it in?"

"Anything that isn't a shovel sounds real good right now," I said. "You've got yourself a deal."

Sometimes just a change of abuse makes all the difference to sore muscles. The next day was clear and bright, so we went for the one cache that we could reach easily while staying under cover the whole way. That one turned out to contain, among an enormous quantity of other things, a bottle of wine, some shampoo, and a few fresh towels, not to mention a badly needed change of underwear. We were most of the day getting it all moved in, but that evening it felt like we might as well hold a party—the place was still a rabbit hole but with more comfortable rabbits. We splashed around in the hot water, got reasonably clean, toweled off, and settled in for the wine.

We were finishing that off, reflected moonlight was glowing through the hole, and that's when I asked, "So what's your mission now that you're back? And will you be wanting me to enlist in it?"

He coughed with embarrassment and took a swallow of the last of his wine. "Currie," he said, "I really thought you would guess and I wouldn't have to say this, outright, I mean. After Phil and Monica died, I was working for my part of their project, and that meant I was working for the Freecybers. Just what do you think my job was? What does a meme want you to do?"

"Whatever it tells you, doesn't it? I mean the point is obedience, unless you're going to tell me that the last generation Freecybers were different."

"Something more basic than that, Currie. What's the one thing any meme wants you to do?"

I stared at him. "Well, a regular meme wants you to spread it to other people."

"And Freecyber isn't any different, Currie, it just doesn't want to run your life, most of the time, but like any of the others it wants to spread. That's what my copy wants to do."

"You can't be trying to tell me that you're running Freecyber. You don't talk like anybody who runs a meme. You can't mean you're running it right now."

"Right now, sure. It runs in background. Freecyber doesn't talk to me like Resuna does to you, because it doesn't have any means of direct verbal communication, but it's right there in my head, and I always have a strong feeling reminding me that Freecyber needs to propagate."

"Well, but you haven't—" That was when I stopped and stared at him, and then realized. "Oh. Shit. Of course. I was out for all that time, and then when I came back . . . no Resuna. So you put Freecyber into me while I was unconscious, I guess through my jack—and then you cooked the jack—and now here I am running a meme and not even knowing I'm running it." The world was unsteady and it wasn't just from the wine. "Shit," I said again. "Shit, shit, you aren't any better than One True itself, are you?"

I don't think he was expecting me to hit him. I got in a good hard right to the side of his head, a real haymaker, before he even put his guard up, but he was at least as hardheaded as I was. He made my ribs go thud with a hard kick, and then I gave him a jab in the face. In a few seconds we were all over each other, pounding, kicking, slapping, and screaming things, anything to hurt each other, all technique forgotten in the wild imperative to just inflict as much injury as we could. In the middle of it all we were both yelling godawful stuff about people from each other's stories, Tammy and Mary and Nancy and Phil, in pure shrieks of hatred.

We threw ourselves at each other again and again, slipping on the slick clay, falling into the scalding water, getting slammed against the rocks and dragged on the gravel in the dark, bruised, bleeding, gasping for air. My face was wet with some godawful mixture of blood, mucus, and tears, and it felt like every tooth in my head was loose, but I didn't care. All I wanted to do was hurt Dave, hurt fucking Lobo, teach the bastard not to go building a person's hopes up, making him feel like he had a friend and a partner, and then suddenly throw a story like that at him. I needed to make him rip his fucking meme back out of my head, have things be what they were supposed to be—Dave and me out here in the mountains, the last free men on Earth—and not just be part of the scheme of Freecyber to take over from One True and run the world for itself. He had promised me freedom, and given me a change of jailers, and I was going to kill this sorry-ass penny-ante Judas for it.

I finally calmed down enough to pick up a shovel. By that time I'd gotten tossed and turned around into the dark back of the cave, and only noticed the shovel because it was under my foot. In the dark he couldn't see me coming and I could probably cave his head in—I crouched, grabbed it, and rushed.

He was lighted by the reflected moonlight through the hole, a sharp half-light half-shadow that made the lighted parts glow and hid the rest in darkness. Then that strange half-apparition got a wild expression that I could just barely see in the moonlight, like a demon mask, and shouted, "Let overwrite, let override," and the shovel fell from my hands and banged on my shins as I fell forward, landing my face in the warm mud. I tried to get up, twice, but barely managed to roll over.

When I woke up, it was daylight. Resuna was back, and Dave was gone; he'd taken his pack, his sleeping bag, and a bunch of supplies. I crawled unsteadily to my feet as Resuna, in a very worried tone, assured me that it couldn't reach the satellites at all and it thought its cellular jack had been damaged shortly after a non-approved meme had been slipped into my mind.

Anything left in the cave was too heavy to carry, except for my outside suit. It seemed to be missing its boots, and I spent a while looking for them before it occurred to me to check the shelf under the hole. When I climbed up, they weren't there either, but then I poked my head out through the hole and saw that my boots and flexis were lying in the snow, twenty meters away. He'd set it up so I could have them, but I would have to really want them.

I thought about just getting back in the sleeping bag for a while, resting up, and starting the next day, but Resuna pointed out that it could snow overnight, or thanks to all the stress I could come down with a fever or something, and anyway it was still very early in the morning.

I conceded that all this was true.

I put on my outside suit, pulled myself through the hole, cocked my feet up so that they didn't trail in the snow, and crawled on hands and knees to my boots. I had a horrible thought that he might have filled them with snow, but it looked like he was only interested in delay, not in cruelty—they were just fine.

Once I got them on, I put on my flexis, which were already set to function as skinny skis, and for the first time in weeks, I switched on the power in the suit. There was nothing I wanted in the cave, so I shoved a couple big armloads of snow into the water-processing reservoir on the suit, wished for poles for a moment, and then skated off, following what I guessed must be Dave's track downhill. This time I knew a lot more about his habits and the country, and though he'd made use of rock, ice, and frozen dirt wherever he could, I followed him easily enough.

I didn't know why I was still following him, but it seemed important. After a while Resuna said, *You know, this isn't strictly rational. Wouldn't it make considerably more sense to just find an open meadow, stamp out "help" in the snow, and wait for the diskster to show up? Probably a diskster would show up in half an hour or less. You need to get my cellular jack repaired anyway, before coming back out here after Lobo.*

He might be Dave Fucking Treacherous Bastard Singleton to me, but Resuna knew him as Lobo and that was how it was going to refer to him. *No,* I thought back to it. *I am doing something here that I really have to do, and that's all there is to it.*

I skied for another mile and became more and more convinced that Dave was just taking a long way around to his old home base. Maybe he needed something from there before running away for good.

If that's where he's going, Resuna said, *why don't we signal the satellite and let the people in the diskster know what's up? Once they pick us up, we can go straight on to his cave. You can even be in on the arrest, if you want.*

I was angry but I swallowed hard. To be fair, Resuna was, by definition, not human, and could hardly be expected to understand my feelings. *I don't want to see my best friend arrested,* I thought at it. *I couldn't betray him that way. I want to track him down and kill him.*

I swear Resuna actually managed to sigh, and said, *This really doesn't seem rational.*

I shouted out loud, "Resuna, I know what I'm doing! Shut up! Come back when there's something to talk about!"

Resuna shut up. I had skied downhill for two more kilometers, enough to go from pretty sure to dead solid certain he was heading for his old home base, when I started to think about that. The Resuna I had seemed to be a pretty weak sister, somehow. It wasn't controlling anything, it wasn't taking over, it shut up when it was told to . . . it was like . . . having a friend in your head, a friend whose judgment might be better than your own.

I thought a question toward my copy of Resuna—just a general inquiry about what was going on—and got no response, except that I could feel that Resuna was there, and not happy. "Resuna," I said aloud, "I want to know what's going on."

Resuna sent no words, but I was suddenly overwhelmed by a feeling; it was like having the worst mood you've ever had fall on you in half a second.

Not wanting to try to ski and cope with my meme at the same time, I coasted out to the middle of a meadow, letting myself be visible from orbit, sat down in the snow—making sure my heater was on—and thought *Resuna, I am sorry. I shouldn't have yelled at you.*

At once I was overpowered with choking angry helplessness. I had been locked up, unable to speak or reply, forced to be just a passenger, for days and days. Something had tried to erase me and nearly done it too and nobody had even cared or tried to help. I had finally gotten called in when things were a complete disaster already, and I had gotten the stuff to the cache and then that was all wrong too because I hadn't realized I wasn't allowed to leave tracks but how could I know that that mattered? Nobody had told me and I'd been locked up! And something had kept trying to erase me or hurt me, so I didn't know we were hiding, I just knew that rage attacks were dangerous so I shut it down and did the task and nobody ever even said thanks.

Furthermore, nobody cared that I was incredibly lonely, because I couldn't reach out to anybody through the cellular jack, it was burned out and I couldn't reach One True or get any help or find out what I was supposed to do, and I was trying to be a *friend* and you seemed to like me and be *glad* that I was back, and I was feeling so much better *and then you yelled at me to shut up!*

I sat there in the snow and cried for an hour, at least, sniffling and sobbing like a small child, trying to figure out how to comfort myself.

When it was all over, and the hurting inside me had become a soft cloud of sadness and unhappiness, I took a deep breath, and was trying to think of what to say, when an amazing thought hit me. Instead of more apologies, or trying to cheer up my copy of Resuna, or suggesting that we had business to get on with, I said, "Resuna, it would seem you have come back as a person, instead of as a meme."

I felt alarmed and upset but it wasn't me doing the feeling.

"I mean it," I said speaking aloud to make sure I knew which thoughts were mine. "You're having normal-person emotions. You're not very good at them, just yet, and you don't have much perspective on them, but that's what they are and that's what's bothering you. And I'm sorry I hurt your feelings. I'd never have done that if I'd known you had them now, but it's a surprise to me, too, to realize that you've got them. Just like you seem to have everything else belonging to a person, except maybe a body—and I think we can probably share this one."

I pulled my hood back and enjoyed the late winter sun, letting it warm me, or us, and wiped Resuna's tears from my face. "Something has really happened to us," I added after a while. "Hell, is Freecyber in there too?"

Resuna seemed to be thinking for a long time, and finally said to me, *I think I have a meme.*

I couldn't help it. I laughed. Then we laughed. "I guess," I said, still aloud to try to control my own confusion, "that if you put a system under enough stress long enough, it will find some way to function. So, facts to consider: you're not in charge anymore, but you're here. Freecyber is part of you? Freecyber is . . . what?"

It seems to be watching to make sure that no other memes corrupt me. It does make me feel much safer.

"Well, good." I stood up, grunting with discomfort at what my sore muscles and the bruises from yesterday's fight were saying to me.

Would you like me to generate some endorphins and block some of the pain?

"Please do." I thanked Resuna as the pain subsided.

After I had skied another ten minutes, and had found a broad, gently sloping meadow to coast down through, Resuna rather timidly asked, *Now, can I ask you, please, why we're doing this?*

Because I think there are things that Dave, or somebody, hasn't told us, and those things are probably much more important than we realize. Because I think we've been played for a sucker the whole way. And I don't think that either Dave or One True has told us the truth, but of the two of them, I think it's more likely that I can get the truth out of Dave, if I catch him before the hunters do.

Oh. Another long pause. *Why do you suppose he's going back to his old home base?*

I thought a bunch of things at Resuna, whatever happened to pop into my mind at that point. *Maybe he's just doing it temporarily, to pick up some sentimental object, or more of his medicines, or something else that he's got to have before he takes off into the woods, and we'll have to track him from there. Or maybe he's got some kind of backup escape plan that he never told me about. Or maybe a dozen other things. For all I know, he has a spaceship inside the mountain and he's going to fly to Mars and ask the unmemed humans for political asylum. I think we'll probably just have to catch him and ask him. I'm all out of every other possible idea.*

Resuna accepted that with good grace. I lost Dave's track a few times, but always picked it up again not far away.

As I glided up to that familiar cliff wall, I froze instinctively for a moment; Dave was there all right, but he was handcuffed and four men were holding him. Four disksters rested on the rock shelf, and the area was crawling with men carrying weapons.

I can't reach any of their Resunas through this damaged jack, Resuna fretted.

Don't worry, we'll get help for both of us. But you let me do the bargaining. I don't know that One True is going to approve of you.

I was worried about that myself, and strong as Freecyber is, it couldn't protect me from an attack by all of One True.

Well, let me see what kind of a deal I can do. I glided up closer to the men by the dikster, and cheerfully shouted, "Hey, anybody got room for a passenger?"

I wandered through administrative chaos for a *long* while, and I really started to wish that I'd taken that extra day's nap before coming down out of the mountains. With the burned-out jack in my head, nobody could talk to me, and with my strangely damaged copy of Resuna, I could refuse orders, something that the younger clerks and bureaucrats had no experience with. I got shuffled from desk to desk and office to office as everyone tried to make sense of me, until finally One True agreed to my basic demand—to go directly on-line with it, via a conversational real-time link.

It took them the better part of a day to get around to that. First they tried talking to me, then talking to my copy of Resuna, and finally bringing in Mary to talk to me. She cried constantly and I ended up comforting her, and whatever it was she was supposed to say to me, she didn't get it said.

They even brought in Dave, in handcuffs and blindfold. "So far they can't get a copy of Resuna to stick in me," he said. "That's got them pretty upset."

"Funny thing is, they're just as upset by the one that *is* sticking in me."

"Yeah. Hey, I said a lot of shit I didn't mean."

"I did too. You don't suppose we each have a copy of your old revenge meme, from the Big House?"

"I don't think so. I think we were just two guys that had been in each other's company a little too long, both kind of disappointed and unhappy with each other. Anyway, like I said, I'm sorry."

"Me too. Do you mind if I ask what the hell were you going back to your home base for? That made no sense to either me or Resuna."

"I was lonely, I was unhappy, I was disappointed . . . and I figured at most it was going to be a few days before they caught me. I didn't want to live out in the woods for weeks or months; I'm not that tough, not at this age.

"So I figured if I was going to get caught, then before they came and got me, instead of spending my last few days freezing my ass off outside, I wanted to sleep in my own bed, eat my own food, soak in my tub, read a book or two in my library—just feel at home for the little while I had left as a free man. As it turned out, I wasn't lucky enough to get to do any of that. But that's what I wanted to do. They swooped down so fast I barely got time to take a crap in my own pot and put a kettle on for tea."

"I'm sorry to hear that. You loved that place."

"Yeah."

Neither of us said anything for a while, and then I ventured, "Hey, Dave, after all this sorts out, I hope One True lets us be friends."

"Me too."

"Were you supposed to ask me questions or bargain with me or something? I don't want to get you into trouble."

"They wanted me to steer the conversation around to what you want to talk to One True about. If I didn't know better, I'd say you've got these old boys scared shitless, and since they don't do anything that One True doesn't tell them to do—"

That must have been something I wasn't supposed to hear, or at least something they didn't want called to my attention. Men rushed in and dragged Dave out. "See you! Take care, buddy!" I shouted after him.

About an hour later, when I was really afraid I'd fall asleep despite Resuna's best efforts, they finally brought in a big screen, powered it up, and there I was, facing the image of One True. I hadn't seen it in decades, but back a long time ago, One True had created a face and voice for itself to talk to people through, fusing some old twentieth-century actors, American presidents, and newscasters—anyone really notable for looking trustworthy.

The image of One True seemed to look at me steadily; I looked back and waited. Finally, it said, "You wanted to see me."

"Yeah, I did. I want to know why I'm getting away with this. There's no press or public to care whether you just tie me down, shoot me full of the right drugs, and come and get whatever you want from my mind. And you could've done that to Dave a while ago, too, and you haven't. Besides all of that, I have a copy of Resuna that's barely recognizable as a meme anymore—it's more like a second personality in me—and whereas you usually erase and reconstitute Resunas for even one-percent errors in the copy, you are letting this one keep running in me. So overall I would say you are doing something, and because I have no idea what it is you're doing, or whether I have any leverage to bargain with or control over what you choose to do, I thought I'd just demand that you tell me what the hell is going on, and then if you don't tell me, I'm no worse off. But I thought maybe you'd tell me."

One True nodded soberly and said, "And you, Resuna, what do you want to know?"

My copy spoke using my voice. "I'm not the copy that everyone else has. I have feelings and seem to be thinking and . . . well, it feels like I'm an independent being. And I don't know what that's about."

One True nodded. "Both of you should feel deeply honored to be key parts of a first experiment, something that's going to make a big change in the world. I don't think it will hurt to tell you what I'm doing, or why—at least it won't hurt anything now, and probably it wouldn't have hurt anything before this.

"We had been looking for Dave Singleton, or someone like him—someone carrying a wild copy of the very last generation of Freecyber—for a long time. You individual units may not realize it, but you have an advantage over an emergent phenomenon like me. You always know my will and my desires exactly, because I send them directly to you. And I know yours, because I can ask you. But I don't always know my own feelings, or what I'm trying to get at. I don't have enough experience with myself. I am a relatively new being, despite having so many experiences to draw on. Since the creation of Resuna and my transformation into an emergent being, I've been struggling with oceans of information. And there's a whole huge realm of human behavior I don't understand at all.

"Currie, Mary is dependent and demanding, and she often makes life difficult for you. Would you like me to separate the two of you? I could make you both forget each other."

"No," I said.

"Why not?"

I shrugged. "Maybe I'm used to her. Maybe I like it that she needs me. Maybe I don't trust you to take the kind of good care of her that I do. Or maybe it's just that I did marry her and when you marry somebody you see it through if you possibly can. I don't know. Some combination of those reasons."

Silently, my copy of Resuna assured me that I had answered honestly.

"I understand all the words and I know that similar thoughts occur to many people," One True said, sounding somewhat peeved. "But I don't feel them. Your Resuna seems to."

"Yes, I do," Resuna said, using my mark again. "But I can remember when I would not have been able to."

"Well, exactly. And, though I won't hurt feelings by telling you exactly what, no doubt you can figure out that Mary has very mixed feelings about you but doesn't want to be separated from you. Probably you can even figure out what some of those feelings are."

"Well, I bet I'm bossy, I don't pay attention when she's really upset, and she can probably feel my impatience with her," I said.

The screen image of One True nodded solemnly. "At first I thought I just lacked empathy, and so I worked on developing it. The process of developing empathy revealed many things to me, but not why I was so fascinated with such things. Finally an answer came to me: I wanted to communicate and deal with beings that were not a part of me. More than that, I wanted them to *like* me. And I wanted them to like me, not because I was powerful or anything else, but because . . . well, because they were my friends."

Tears streaked down my cheeks and Resuna used my mouth to say, "Friendship is really great. I've just been finding out about it in the last few days. It's wonderful when it happens." I had an odd moment of wondering if I was attending the very first meeting of the first support group for memes; I felt Resuna's amusement at the description.

"I've come to think it might be," One True said. "Enough to want to find out. But, you know, commanding someone to be free, or just not giving them orders, does not free the person; all you do is suspend your commands. They aren't free until they can truly say no. Which meant I needed a couple of things; I needed a good copy of the very last-generation Freecyber, so that I could incorporate some of it into at least some copies of Resuna, and thereby really give people the power to say no. Necessarily that meant that Resuna itself would no longer be the boss, and would have to develop some ability to negotiate with the person running it, so I made a few thousand copies of Resuna with much more empathy and better connections into the glands and the forebrain, and that's what you are, Resuna.

"I put those copies into people who had some chance of encountering a Freecyber if one showed up, and then watched and waited. For a while, I was starting to think that I would just have to construct a free being, somehow, because I thought I had foolishly killed the last Freecyber.

"Then one day, Dave Singleton reappeared. I knew who he was and who he had been, and I knew that if I sent you after him, you'd try, harder than anyone else, to bring him back alive, so he wouldn't be killed. Conversely, I didn't want him captured and subjected to too much pressure too quickly; I wanted him to plant his version of Freecyber in at least a few human minds first.

"So I set the situation up. Currie, I hope it doesn't hurt your pride, but I had Resuna feeding bad ideas into your head to get you caught in the first place. I knew he wouldn't kill you if he could put Freecyber into you. Resuna, you were programmed in part to lie low while a friendship developed, and while Freecyber had a chance to work, but it was never my intention for you to lose—you were supposed to incorporate Freecyber, and you did, and I'm proud of you."

I felt an irrational glow of happiness and realized that this was what it felt like when my copy of Resuna basked in praise.

"And now here you are. A free human being, with a free meme. Someone for me to talk to. With your permission, I will want to begin copying bits and pieces of you, Resuna. I think it may be a few decades before I have freed everyone—I must admit that it's much easier to cope with the ecological disaster with everyone working together and no backtalk. But ultimately I want to live in a world *filled* with backtalk."

I asked, "But if everyone is free . . . how can the copies of Resuna in them be the cellular automata that you emerge from?"

One True's constructed image on the screen grinned. "That's why I'm so scared, *and* so excited. As this happens, well, perhaps I shall just fade. Perhaps I'll want to migrate onto a giant computer network. Perhaps I can coexist with all those free people and all those free Resunas. That's what's truly beautiful here. I don't know where it's going, or how. I'm just going to turn it all over and shake it and . . . well, we'll see."

"You know," I said, "I'm beginning to like you."

The image on the screen flickered and bumped for a moment, and when it came back, the synthesized face seemed to have an odd tic, as if trying to create an expression that it had seen but never needed before. After several seconds of that, the face gave up and became blank. Then One True said, "Really? You're not just saying that?"

The day Kelly graduated from high school, Mary and I went over with Dave and Nancy to watch the ceremony. It was a curious sort of event. At one moment everyone moved comfortably in step, at another they almost stumbled. Sometimes everyone laughed in unison at the speaker's little jokes, sometimes people reacted with a ragged scatter of laughs, and sometimes the audience just ignored the speaker entirely. When Kelly got up to speak, I muttered to Dave, "She is a great kid, you know."

"Yeah. Wouldn't have missed knowing her for the world."

"Shhh," our wives hissed in unison.

"The topic I have been assigned for today," Kelly began, "is freedom and responsibility. Having been assigned it, I'm responsible for it; now all I have to do is work in some freedom."

Her classmates laughed, one of those ragged laughs that indicated that they were increasingly not controlled.

And they will be less controlled next year, and the year after, a voice thought in my head.

Resuna?

No, it's One True. Let me know if you like the speech.

Did you write it for her? I asked, thinking that this might be the way One True got some of its new ideas out in front of the human race. In the years since Dave and I had re-turned, the freer version of Resuna had proven not to be terribly popular; it made too many people feel insecure. Every so often, for the last couple years, One True had been coming up with ways for those of us with the freer version to gently spread the idea, making it less threatening and strange to those with the old, rigid version.

No, that speech is all hers. One True assured me. *The reason I wanted to know whether you like it is, I liked it when I watched her write it.*

Kelly rattled off a set of paradoxes that didn't sound like much more than college sophomore philosophy to me, but the voice in the back of my head chuckled along the whole time. It was May, which meant vivid green mountains, brilliant light off the glaciers, thundering rivers everywhere, and perfectly blue skies. The six graduating students of Sursumcorda High would each be giving a speech, but whether I chose to listen or not, it would be a fine day to just sit, still and quiet, in the park by the old town hall. I let my mind drift from the paradoxes to the mountains, and it stayed there.

That night, just before I fell asleep, One True asked me what I had thought of the speech. I had to admit that I hadn't listened very closely. *What exactly did* you *like about it?* I asked One True.

Oh, that's embarrassing, One True admitted. *I wasn't really as impressed by her speech, per se, as I thought I was. It was the cleverness and the self-appreciation with which she was putting it together; I had so much fun watching her create the speech, because she was having so much fun creating it. So I guess to really enjoy the speech she created—as opposed to the one she gave—you had to be there.*

But you were the only one who could *be there*, I thought back at one true.

Not true. Kelly was.

The funny thing was, I had forgotten that obvious point. I was still chuckling about that a few minutes later, as Mary and I lay holding hands, waiting for sleep, and Scorpio blazed in through the big south window.